Grace Livingston Hill Collection #5

Grace Livingston Hill (1865–1947) remains popular more than fifty years after her death. She wrote dozens of books that carry her unique style of combining Christian faith with tasteful and exciting romance.

Isabella Alden (1841–1930), an aunt of Grace Livingston Hill, was a gifted storyteller and prolific author as well, often using her writing to teach lessons espoused by her husband, Gustavus R. Alden, a minister. She also helped her niece Grace get started in her career as a best-selling inspirational novelist.

The Enchanted Barn, Grace Livingston Hill
Shirley Hollister and her family must vacate their dark little house in the city. She sets out to find a suitable place to live. What she discovers is an old stone barn in an idyllic setting—with a tiny stream, an elm tree, fresh air, and sunshine. But she must convince the handsome owner to rent it to her—at a price she can afford.

The Love Gift, Grace Livingston Hill
Young minister John MacFarlane proudly escorts his mother into church—amid hushed laughter from some of his congregation. Then he notices his mother's outdated hat and determines to buy her a new one. After visiting the uptown shops, he stumbles into a small millinery and finds what he needs—and through his gift helps a young woman find faith in the loving God.

Miranda, Grace Livingston Hill
In part 3 of the *Miranda* trilogy, Grace Livingston Hill brings to the forefront one of her most delightful characters, Miranda Griscom. For many years Miranda has kept a secret in her heart. She once helped a murder suspect escape from jail. Now she must prove his innocence and expose the real criminal. Will justice be served, and will her true secret ever be revealed?

Agatha's Unknown Way, Isabella Alden
Growing up in India, Agatha Hunter returns to America because of failing health. She moves in with her aunt and uncle where she regains her strength but encounters opposition to her views. One day she ventures into the city, expecting to meet others who share her zeal for missions, only to discover apathy. But a chance conversation and a mistaken identity revolutionize Agatha's life and the lives she touches.

Grace Livingston Hill

COLLECTION NO. 5

FOUR COMPLETE NOVELS
Updated for today's reader

BARBOUR
PUBLISHING, INC.
Uhrichsville, Ohio

Edited and updated for today's reader by Deborah Cole.

© 2000 by R. L. Munce Publishing Co., Inc.

ISBN 1-57748-725-7

Published by Barbour Publishing, Inc., P.O. Box 719, Uhrichsville, Ohio 44683
http://www.barbourbooks.com

Member of the
Evangelical Christian
Publishers Association

Printed in the United States of America.

The Enchanted Barn

Chapter 1

Shirley Hollister pushed back the hair from her hot forehead, pressed her hands over her tired eyes, then dropped her fingers again to the typewriter keys and flew on with the letter she was writing.

No one else was in the inner office where she sat. Mr. Barnard, the firm's senior member, whose stenographer she was, had stepped into the outer office for a moment with a telegram he'd just received. His absence gave Shirley a moment's respite from feeling she must keep strained up to meet his gaze and not let trouble show in her eyes. A great lump was choking in her throat, though, and the tears stung her hot eyelids and blurred her vision now and then. But she gave way only for an instant. Her fingers flew on with their work, for this was an important letter, and Mr. Barnard wanted it to go in the next mail.

As she wrote, a vision of her mother's pale face appeared with tears on her cheeks and that despairing look in her eyes. Mother hadn't been able to get up for a week. It seemed as if life's cares were almost too much for her, and the warm spring days made the little brick house in the narrow street stifling. Mother's room had only one small window, opening against a brick wall, for they'd had to rent the front room with its two windows.

But, poor as it was, the brick house had been home, and now they weren't to have that long. They'd received notice they must vacate in four weeks; the house, in fact the whole row of houses in which it was situated, had been sold and was to be pulled down to make way for a big apartment house to be built.

Where they were going and what they would do throbbed on Shirley's brain night and day, kept her from sleeping and eating, choked in her throat when she tried to speak to Mr. Barnard and stared from her feverish eyes as she looked at the sunshine on the street or tried to work in the busy office monotony.

They had lived in the house nearly a year, ever since her father died. It took all they could scrape together to pay the funeral expenses, and now with her salary, the roomer's rent and what George got as cash-boy in a department store, they barely managed. Not a cent was left over for sickness or trouble, and nothing to move with, even if they had anywhere to move or anytime to hunt for a place. Shirley knew from her experience in hunting for the present house that it would be nearly impossible for them to find a habitable place for as little as they were paying, and how could they pay more? She was only a beginner, and her salary was small. There were three others in the family, not yet wage-earners.

Must Carol, only fourteen years old, stop school and go to work somewhere to earn a pittance also? She was slender and pale and needed fresh air and nourishing food. She was too young to bear burdens yet; besides, who would be housekeeper and take care of Mother if Carol had to go to work? It was different with George. He was a strong, sturdy boy; he had his school in the department store and was getting on well with his studies. George would be all right. He belonged to a baseball team, too, and got plenty of exercise. But Carol was frail; there was no denying it.

Harley was a boisterous nine-year-old, always on the street these days when he wasn't in school. Who could blame him? The narrow, dark brick house was no place for a lively boy. But the burden and anxiety for him were heavy on the heart of his sister, who had taken over her mother's worries. Then there was the baby Doris, with her big, pathetic eyes and her round cheeks and loving ways. Doris, too, had to be shut in the dark house with the summer heat coming on and no one with time or strength to take her to the park. Doris was only four.

Oh, it was terrible! And Shirley could only sit there, click those keys and earn her poor salary. Someday, of course, she'd get more—but someday might be too late!

She shuddered as the terrible thought flashed through her mind, then went on with her work again. She must shake off this state of mind and attend to her duty, or she would lose even this opportunity to help her dear ones.

The door of the outer office opened, and Mr. Barnard entered.

"Miss Hollister," he said hurriedly, "if you have those letters ready, I'll sign them at once. We've just had word that Mr. Baker of the firm died last night in Chicago, and I must go at once. The office will be closed for the rest of the day. You can let those other matters I spoke of go until tomorrow, and you may have the day off. I won't be at the office at the usual hour tomorrow morning, but you can come in and look after the mail. I'll leave further directions with Mr. Clegg. You can mail these letters as you go down."

Ten minutes later Shirley stood on the street below in the warm spring sunshine and gazed about her half dazed. It seemed a travesty on her poor life to have a holiday and no way to make it count for the dear ones at home. How should she use it? Should she go home and help Carol? Or should she see whether she could find a house somewhere that they could move to? That, of course, was the sensible thing to do; yet she had no idea where to go. But they didn't expect her home at this time of day. Perhaps it was as well to use this time and find out something without worrying her mother. At least she'd have time to think undisturbed.

She grasped the lunch she brought from home and looked about her helplessly. In her thin purse was the dime she always carried with her to pay her carfare in case something happened that she had to ride either way—though she seldom rode, even in a storm. But her mother insisted on the dime. She said it wasn't safe to go without any money at all. This dime was her capital for hunting a house. Perhaps the day had been given her by a kind heavenly Father to search. She lifted her bewildered heart to ask for light and help, and then she went and stood on the street corner. Which trolley should she take, and where should she go? The ten cents must cover all her riding, and she must save half of it for her return.

She studied the names on the cars. "Glenside Road," one read. What had she heard about that? Ah! It was the longest ride someone could take within city limits for five cents! Her heart leaped at the word. It sounded restful anyway and would give her time to think. It wasn't likely, if it went near any glens, that any houses within her means would be along its way. But it might pass some as it went through the city, and she could notice the streets and numbers and get out on her return trip to investigate if anything proved promising. Or, if it were too far away from home for her to walk back, she could come another time in the evening with George, when he didn't have school. Her resolve taken, she stepped out and signalled it.

Not many people rode out to the suburbs at that hour, so only a woman, a little girl and two workmen with rolls of wallpaper slung in burlap bags were in the car.

Shirley settled back in her seat and leaned her head against the window sash. She felt so tired she'd have been glad to sleep and forget for a while, but she needed to be up and doing. Her room had been oppressively warm the night before, and Doris, who slept with her, had rolled from one side of the bed to the other, making sleep nearly impossible for the elder sister. She felt bruised and bleeding in her soul and longed for rest.

The car was passing through the thickest of the city's business thoroughfares, and the noise and confusion whirled about her ears like some fiendish monotonous music that set the time for the mad dance of the world.

They passed around city hall and up Market Street. A waft of air from a fruit store entered the open windows bearing the scent of overripe bananas, late oranges and lemons; a moment later that blended into a deadly smell of gas from a yawning hole in the pavement and mingled with the sweat of the swarthy laborers grouped about it, picks in hand. It seemed as though all the smells in creation were met in that street within four or five blocks, and one by one they tortured her: leather, paint, metal and soap; rank cheese in a fellow traveler's basket; thick smoke from a street engine chomping up the gravel they fed it to make a new patch of paving; the stench from the cattle sheds as they passed the railroad and stockyards; the dank odor of the river as they crossed the bridge and then an oilcloth factory just beyond. The faint, sweet breath of early daffodils and violets from an occasional street vendor stood no chance at all with these, and the air sickened the girl as she rested against the window with closed eyes and tried to think.

They slipped at last into the subway, where the cool, clean smell of the cement seemed to rise and drown the memory of the upper world and came refreshingly in at the windows. Shirley wondered whether it would be like that in the grave, restful and quiet and clean, with the noisy, heartless world roaring overhead. Then they emerged suddenly from the subway, with a kind of triumphant leap and shout of brakes and wheels, into the light and sunshine above and a new world. Here were broad streets, clean pavements, ample houses, well-trimmed lawns, quiet people walking and flower boxes on the windowsills filled with pansies and hyacinths; and the air was sweet and clean. The difference made Shirley sit up and look about her, and the contrast reminded her of the heaven that lay beyond the grave. Her thoughts took this solemn form because she was so tired and disheartened.

But now her heart sank again, for this was far beyond her means. In neither direction could she see any side streets with tiny houses that would rent for fifteen dollars a month. They were in the city, she knew; but they were scarce and leased as soon as vacant.

But here was spaciousness, and even the side streets had three stories and smug porches with tidy rockers and bay windows.

She looked at the great plate-glass windows with their lace draperies and thought how it would be if she could take her mother and the children to such a home. Why, if she could afford that, George could go to college and Doris wear a velvet coat with rosebuds in her bonnet, like the child on the sidewalk with her nurse and doll carriage.

But she had no rich old uncles to leave them a fortune; she wasn't bright and gifted to invent some wonderful toy or write a book or paint a picture that would bring the fortune; and no one would ever come her way with a fortune to marry her. Those things happened only in story-books, and she wasn't a storybook girl; she was just a practical, every-day, hard-working girl with a good complexion, good blue eyes and a firm chin. She could work hard and was willing, but she couldn't bear anxiety. It was eating into her soul, and she could feel a mental paralysis stealing over her, benumbing her faculties.

The car glided on, and the houses grew less stately and farther apart. They weren't pretentious now but were still substantial and comfortable, with more ground and an air of having been there always, with no room for newcomers. Now and then came a nucleus of shops and an old tavern with a group of new groceries and crying competition of green, blue and yellow stamps posted in their windows. Here busy people swarmed, and children ran and shouted; but every house they passed seemed full to overflowing.

Now the car left the paved, built-up streets and wandered out between the open fields, where trees arched lavishly overhead and new green grass grew in the sunshine. A new smell, the smell of rich earth and growing things, of skunk cabbage in bloom in the swamps, of budding willows and sassafras, roused her senses. She heard the hum of a bee, sweet and restful, with the distant call of a wild bird. Ah! This was a new world! What a contrast to the office and the stifling brick house where Mother lay, while Doris cut strings of paper dolls from an old newspaper and sighed to go out in the park! This was heaven! If she could only stay and the dear ones come!

She had spent summers in the country, of course, and knew and loved nature, but for five years she hadn't been free to get outside the city limits for more than a day, and then not far. She'd never sensed the beauty of the country as today—perhaps because she never needed it as now.

The road continued smoothly straight ahead, then curved into another long stretch. Men were plowing in the fields on one side, and on the other lay an emerald field of spring wheat. More people had come into the car as it left the city. Plain, substantial men; nice, pleasant women—but Shirley didn't notice them for the changing landscape and her dismal thoughts. Thinking, too, she was spending her money with nothing to show for it, her conscience condemned her.

They were coming now to a wide, old-fashioned stone barn, with ample grassy stone-coped entrance rising like a carpeted stairway from the barnyard. It was resting on the top of a green knoll, and a great elm tree arched over it. A tiny stream purled below at one side, and the ground sloped off at the other. Shirley wasn't noticing the place much except as part of the landscape until she heard the conductor talking about it to the man across the aisle.

"Good barn," he was saying. "Pity to have it standing idle so long. But they'll never rent it without a house, and they won't build. It belongs to the old man's estate and can't be divided until the youngest boy's of age, four or five years yet. The house burned down two years ago. Some tramps set it on fire. No, nobody was living in it at the time. The last renter didn't make the farm pay—too far from the railroad, I guess—and there ain't nobody near enough round to use the barn since Halyer built his new barn." He indicated a great red structure down the road on the other side. "Halyer use t' use this—rented it fer less'n nothing—but he got too lazy to come this far, so he sold off half his farm fer a dairy and built the barn. So now I s'pose that barn'll stand idle and run to waste till that kid comes of age and there's a boom up this way and it's sold. Pity about it, though. It's a good barn. Wisht I had it up to my place—I could fill it."

"Make a good location for a house," said the other man, looking intently at the big stone pile. "Been a fine barn in its time. Old man must uv had a pile of chink when he built it. Who'd y' say owned it?"

"Graham, Walter Graham, big firm down near the city hall—guess you know 'em. Got all kinds of money. This ain't one, two, three with the other places they own. Got a regular palace out Arden way fer summer and a town house in the swellest neighborhood and own land all over. Old man inherited it from his father and three uncles. They don't even scarcely know they got this barn, I reckon. It ain't stylish out this way yet."

"Be a big boom here someday—nice location," said the passenger.

"Not yet awhile," said the conductor. "Railroad station's too far. Wait till they get a station out Allister Avenue. Then you can talk. Till then it'll stay as it is, I reckon. There's a spring down behind the barn, the best water in the county. I use t' get a drink every day when the switch was up here. I missed it a lot when they moved the switch to the top o' the hill. Water's cold as ice and clear as crystal—can't be beat this side the soda fountain. I sometimes stop the car on a hot summer day now and run and get a drink."

The men talked on, but Shirley heard no more. Her eyes were intent on the barn as they passed it. What a wonderful house it would make! She almost longed to be a cow to enter that peaceful shelter and feel at home for a while.

The car went on and left the barn in the distance. But Shirley kept going over almost unconsciously what the men said about it. Walter Graham! Where had she seen that name? Oh, of course, in the Ward Trust Building, the whole fourth floor. Leather goods of some sort, she thought.

The man said the barn rented for almost nothing. What could that mean in dollars? Would the fifteen dollars a month they were paying for the brick house cover it? But she and George would need carfare. Walking that distance twice a day, or even once, would be impossible. Ten cents a day, sixty cents a week—twice sixty cents! If they lived out of the city, they could afford only twelve dollars a month. They never would rent that barn for that, of course; it was so grand-looking. And yet—it was a barn!

Could they even live in a barn? Did barns have floors inside, or only stalls and mud? Only two tiny windows were visible in front—how did they get light inside? It couldn't be much darker than the brick house, though, no matter what it was. Perhaps there was a skylight, with pleasant hay to rest on. If they could only get out there for the summer, they could bear some discomforts just to sit under that tree and look up at the sky. To think of Doris playing under that tree and Mother sewing under it! Mother could get well out there in that fresh air, and Doris would get rosy cheeks again. There wouldn't likely be a school around for Carol.

But that wouldn't hurt her for the summer, and maybe by fall they could find a little house. If they could only go somewhere now!

What would Mother say? Would she feel it was a disgrace? Would she call it one of Shirley's wild schemes? But what were they going to do? They must live somewhere, unless they were destined to die homeless.

The car droned on through the open country, coming now and then to settlements of prosperous houses. Some of them were small, but no empty ones beckoned her. Indeed, they appeared too high-priced for a second look; besides, she'd left her heart behind with that beautiful barn with the brook beside it and the arching tree and gentle green slope.

At last the car stopped in a commonplace town in front of a red brick church, and everybody got out. The conductor disappeared, too, and the motorman leaned back on his brake and looked at her.

"End of the line, lady," he said with a grin, as if she were dreaming and hadn't noticed her surroundings.

"Oh," said Shirley, rousing and looking about her. "Well, you go back, don't you?"

"Yes, in fifteen minutes," said the motorman. Something in the girl's sad eyes made him think of his young daughter at home.

"The same way?" she asked with sudden alarm. She wanted to see that barn again and get its exact location so she could come back to it someday, if possible.

"Yes, we go back the same way," said the motorman.

Shirley sighed and sat back in her seat. The motorman took up his dinner pail, sat down on a high stool with his back to her and ate. It was a good time for her to eat her lunch, but she wasn't hungry. She knew she would be if she didn't eat, and there would be no other time when people wouldn't be around. She put her hand in her coat pocket for her handkerchief, and her fingers touched something small and hard. It was a five-cent piece! Yes, she remembered now. She had put the nickel in her pocket last night when she went for the extra loaf of bread and found the store closed. She'd made johnnycake instead, and supper was late; but the nickel stayed in her pocket forgotten.

Suddenly she felt tempted to spend that nickel in carfare, riding to the barn, getting out for a closer look at it and then taking the next car into the city. Was it foolish and perhaps wrong to spend the nickel that way when they needed so much at home? A wild idea—for how could a barn ever be their shelter?

She thought so hard about it that she forgot to eat her lunch until the motorman slammed the cover down on his tin pail and put the high stool away. The conductor, too, was stepping out of a tiny frame house, wiping his mouth with the back of his hand and calling to his wife, who stood in the doorway and told him about an errand she wanted him to do for her in the city.

Shirley's cheeks grew red with excitement, for the nickel was burning in her hand, and she knew she'd spend it getting off that car near the barn. She would eat her lunch under the tree by the brook. At least it would be something to tell the children about at night. But they'd think her silly and selfish to waste a whole day and fifteen cents on herself. Still, it was for them. If they could only see that beautiful spot!

When she handed her nickel to the conductor, she felt almost guilty, and it seemed as if he could see her intention in her eyes. But she told herself she wasn't sure she'd get off; she could decide as she came near the place. She'd have to get off either before she got there or after she passed and walk back. The conductor would think it strange if a young girl got off the car in the country in front of an empty barn. But what was that avenue where they said the railroad would come someday with a station? Allister Avenue! She'd ask the conductor to let her off at Allister Avenue.

She watched intently, and, as they neared the place where Allister Avenue should be, her heart pounded as if she were going to steal a barn and carry it home in her pocket.

She quietly signalled the car to stop, however, and stepped down to the pavement as if it were her regular stopping place. She was aware of the curious gaze of both motorman and conductor, but she held her head up and walked a few steps up Allister Avenue until the car had whirred on out of sight. Then she turned anxiously, looked down the road and to her joy saw the stone gable of the barn high on its knoll in the distance.

Chapter 2

Shirley walked excitedly down the dusty road by the side of the track. To be alone in this unfamiliar, beautiful spring country, and nobody to interfere! It was her Father's beautiful outdoors, and she'd paid her extra nickel to have a right to it for a little while. Perhaps her mother would have worried at her being alone in the country, but Shirley wasn't afraid. Young people seldom have fears. A bright light shone in her eyes. She had to see that barn!

She was almost breathless when she reached the bottom of the hill and stood in front of the barn. The up car passed her as she got there, and the people looked out at her apathetically as they would at any country girl. She stood still a minute and watched the car go up the hill and out of sight, then picked her way across the track. Entering the field where the fence was broken, she walked up the grassy slope to the front of the barn and stood still at the top in front of the double doors, grim and forbidding.

The barn was larger than it appeared in the distance. She felt very small; yet her soul rejoiced in its bigness and the space it would give.

She tried to find a crack in the doors to look through, but they were tight and fitted well. She turned and ran down the grassy slope, then around the side to the back of the barn. There she found a door ajar, opening into what must have been the stables, and slipped in. An angel must have been protecting her, for that dark basement could hide a regiment of tramps. But she found only a field mouse to dispute her entrance, and it scurried under the foundation and disappeared.

The stables evidently hadn't been occupied for a number of years, for the place was clean and littered with dry straw, as if it had fallen and sifted from the floor above. The stalls were empty now, and old farm implements, several plows and a rickety wagon occupied the dusty, cobwebby spaces beyond the stalls. Crude doorways and windows provided openings, and the place wasn't unpleasant. The back opened directly onto a sloping hill which dropped away to the brook below and a stone springhouse, with its mossy roof half hidden by willows.

This lower place wouldn't do for human habitation, she realized; it was too low and damp, and the floor was only mud.

Presently she found a rough ladder, with cleats nailed to uprights against the wall. She crept up this to the opening above and emerged onto the floor of the real barn.

Several small windows had been left open, and the spring air swept in with patches of pale sunshine in the recesses of the dim room. Another ladder rose to the loft above, and ancient hay and cobwebs hung down from the opening. After investigating the corners of the room, Shirley imagined how grand it would be to set the table at one end and put her mother's bed behind a screen at the other end, with the old piano somewhere in the center. The parlor chair, once mended, would stand nearby, with the old couch covered with a portière on the other side. Then she turned her attention to the loft and climbed up.

Two large openings let in light, but they seemed like mouse holes in the great place. The hay lay sweet and dim, thinly scattered over the floor. In one corner was a thick pile of it, and Shirley lay down on it for a minute and looked up at the dark rafters lit with beams of sunlight creeping through cracks here and there. She wondered how the boys would enjoy sleeping up here, though plenty of room was downstairs for a dozen sleeping rooms.

It was foolish and impossible, as all daydreams were. But it seemed so real she could scarcely abandon it. The investigation had made her hungry, however, so she decided to go outside in the sunshine and eat her lunch under the tree. It was dark and stuffy inside, though one could realize how beautiful it would be with those two doors flung open and the light and fresh air streaming in.

The day was perfect, and Shirley found a place to sit, high and sheltered, where she wouldn't be noticed when the trolley sped by. As she ate her sandwiches, she imagined a piazza where the grassy slope rose to the front of the barn and pictured her mother sitting with the children at the door. How grand it would be to live in a home like this, even if it were a barn! It would put new heart into her mother for the winter's hard work, and perhaps by fall she'd be well enough to keep boarders as she longed to and help out with the finances more.

Well, of course, this was just one of her wild schemes, and she mustn't think anymore about it, much less even speak of it at home, for they'd never stop laughing and teasing her for it.

She finished the last bit of one-egg cake Carol had made the day before and ran down to the spring to see if she could get a drink.

An old tin can was lying on the stones in the springhouse, doubtless used by the last tramp or conductor who came that way. Shirley scrubbed it carefully in the sand, drank a delicious draught and washed her hands and face in the clear cold water. Then she returned to the barn with a new thought. Even if they could rent that place for the summer at a reasonable price, how could they cook and keep warm? Of course they could use candles and oil lamps for lighting, but cooking? Would they have to build a fire outdoors and play at camping? Or must they use oil stoves? Oil stoves had sticky, oily outsides and mysterious moods of smoke and sulkiness, out of which only an expert could coax them.

But, though she stood on all sides of the barn, gazed up at the roof and searched each floor diligently, she found no sign of a chimney, nor did she know if barns had chimneys. Two wooden, chimney-like structures decorated the roof, but they were solely for ornaments. Her heart sank. A grand fireplace might have occupied the middle of the wall opposite the door. She could imagine Mother sitting in front of it, with Harley and Doris on the floor playing with a kitten. But there was no fireplace. She wondered vaguely whether a stovepipe could be put out the window and make possible a fire in a small cookstove. She was sure she'd seen stovepipes coming out of all sorts of odd places in the cities. But would the owners allow it? And would any fire make it dangerous and affect the fire insurance? But it was all impossible, of course.

She turned with a heavy heart and climbed down the ladder. It was time to go home, for the afternoon was well on its way. She could hear the whir of the trolley car going up. She must be down the road a little to get the next one when it came back. With a wistful glance about she went down to the ground floor and out into the afternoon sunshine.

As she crossed the knoll and stepped over the broken fence, she saw a clump of clover and among the tiny stems one bearing four leaves. She wasn't superstitious, and the clover didn't mean anything special to her, but she stooped, and plucked it, tucking it into the buttonhole of her coat. Then she hurried down the road, for she could hear the returning trolley and wished to be farther from the barn before it overtook her. She shrank from having people in the car know where she'd been; it seemed like exposing her audacious wish to the world.

Finally seated, she took a last glimpse of the stone gables and the sweeping branches of the budding tree as the car sped down the hill and curved away behind another slope.

It was only half past four when the car reached city hall. Its route lay half a mile nearer the brick house, and she could stay in it and have a shorter walk if she chose. It wasn't likely anyone with authority would be in an office at this hour, but Shirley felt she must get out, long walk or not. A strong desire seized her to put her fate to the test and either crush out this dream or find out whether it had a foundation to live.

She walked straight to the Ward Trust Building and searched the bulletin board in the hallway carefully. Yes, there it was: "Graham, Walter—fourth floor front."

She entered the elevator and tried to steady her trembling voice as she said, "Fourth." What would she say when they asked her in the office what she wanted?

But Shirley's lips were set, and her head had that tilt that her mother knew meant business. She would see the matter to the finish, even if it was ridiculous. Now that she was actually on the elevator and almost to the fourth floor it seemed extraordinary for a girl to enter a large business office and demand that its head should rent her an old barn out in the country for the tiny sum she could offer. He'd probably have her put out.

But she stepped out of the elevator calmly and walked down the hall to a ground-glass door that proclaimed in gold letters the name she was hunting. Turning the knob quietly, she entered a spacious room with a high ceiling, Turkish rugs on the inlaid floor, leather chairs and mahogany desks.

No one was present but an office boy leaning on the table, reading the comics of the afternoon paper. She looked about her. It was almost a quarter to five by the clock on the wall. No head of a business firm would likely stay in his office that late in the day, she thought. Yet she could hear the steady click of typewriter keys in an inner office. Perhaps he remained to dictate a letter.

The office boy glanced up.

"Is Mr. Graham in?" asked Shirley.

"Which Mr. Graham?"

"Why—Mr. Walter Graham," she said, catching the name on the door.

"No, he isn't here. Never here after four o'clock." The boy dropped on his elbow again and resumed his reading.

"Oh!" said Shirley, dismayed. "Well, is there another—I mean, is the other—Mr. Graham in?"

Someone stirred in the inner office. In a moment a man with an overcoat and hat on stood in the doorway.

"Edward!" he said sharply to the boy. "See what the lady wants."

"Yes, sir!" said Edward, standing up straight like a shot.

Shirley caught her breath and plunged in.

"I would like to see some Mr. Graham, if possible, for just a moment." Something self-possessed and businesslike in her voice commanded the boy's attention. Her brief business training was rallying.

The man in the doorway stepped forward, removing his hat. He was young and strikingly handsome, with heavy dark hair that waved over his forehead and clear, strong features. His eyes were both keen and kind. Something luminous in them made Shirley think of Doris's eyes when she asked a question. Doris had wonderfully wise eyes.

"I'm Mr. Sidney Graham," he said. "What may I do for you?"

"Oh, I wanted to ask you about a barn," began Shirley eagerly, then stopped. How could she ask this immaculate son of luxury if he'd rent a young girl his barn to live in during the summer? She could feel the color mounting in her cheeks and would have fled but for her determined purpose. She was aware of the man's kind eyes upon her—and of the gaping boy taking it all in—and could say no more.

But the young man saw how it was and smiled pleasantly, as if he was used to young women coming into his office and inquiring about barns.

"Oh, certainly," he said. "Won't you step in here and sit down? We can talk better. Edward, you may go. I won't need you any longer now."

"But I'm detaining you. You were just going out!" exclaimed Shirley. "I'll come another time—perhaps." She'd do anything to get away without telling her errand.

"Not at all!" said young Mr. Graham. "I'm in no hurry whatever. Just step this way and sit down."

His kind tone reassured her so much that she followed him. Crimson spread over her face, and she felt ready to cry. What a predicament she'd gotten herself into! What would her mother say? How could she tell this strange young man why she'd come? But he was seated in the chair opposite her, watching her and taking in her little attempts at neatness, style and beauty. She was conscious of a loose fluff of gold-glinted hair that had come down over one hot cheek and ear. How dusty and dishevelled she must look, after climbing through that dirty barn!

Then she plunged into her subject.

Chapter 3

I don't know what you'll think of my asking," said Shirley, "but I want very much to know whether there's any possibility you would rent a beautiful stone barn you own out on the old Glenside Road, near Allister Avenue. You do own it, don't you? I was told you did, or at least that Mr. Walter Graham did. They said it belonged to 'the estate.' "

"Well, now you've got one on me," said the young man with a smile. "I don't know whether I own it or not. I'm sorry. But if it belongs to Grandfather's estate—his name was Walter, too—I suppose I do own part of it. I'm sorry Father isn't here. He knows all about it—or the attorney would, of course. But I think he's left the office. That doesn't matter, though. What was it you wanted? To rent it, you say?"

"Yes," said Shirley, "that is, if I can afford it. I suppose it will be way beyond my means, but I thought it wouldn't do any harm to ask." Her eyes were almost filled with tears.

"Not at all," he said quickly. "I'm just sorry I don't know about it. Where did you say it was? Out on Glenside Road? A barn? Come to think of it, I remember one of my uncles lived out that way once, and I know there's a lot of land somewhere out there belonging to the estate. You say there's a barn on it?"

"Yes, a beautiful barn," said Shirley. Her eyes took on a faraway look, and her cheeks glowed. "It's stone and sits high up from the road on a small hill. A wide grassy road leads up to it, and there's a tall tree standing over it, with a brook just below."

"Oh, yes!" he said, nodding eagerly. "I see! I can almost remember it. And you wanted to rent it for the summer, you say? You're—ah—in the agricultural business, I suppose?" He looked at her respectfully, as if he understood modern women and honored them. He didn't seem at all startled that she wanted to rent a barn for the summer.

But Shirley didn't understand and looked bewildered.

"Oh, no! I'm only a stenographer myself—but my mother—that is—" She paused in confusion.

"Oh, I see. Your mother is the farmer, I suppose. Your home is near the barn you want to rent?"

Then she understood. "Oh, no! We don't want to use the barn for a barn at all. I want to use it for a house!"

The horrible truth was out at last!

"Use it for a house!" he exclaimed. "Why, how could you? To live in, do you mean? Or just to take a tent and camp out there for a few days?"

"To live in," said Shirley. She lifted her eyes in one swift defiant look and then dropped them to her worn gloves and thin pocketbook, empty now even of the last nickel. If he said anything else, she was sure she'd cry. If he patronized her the least bit or grew haughty, now that he saw how low she was reduced, she would turn and flee from the office.

But he did neither. Instead, he just talked in a natural tone, as if it were the most common thing in the world for a girl to live in a barn and nothing to be surprised over.

"Oh, I see," he said pleasantly. "Well, now, that might be arranged. Of course I don't know much about things, but I could find out. I don't suppose we often have calls to rent the property that way—"

"No, of course not," said Shirley, gathering up her scattered confidence. "I know it's odd for me to ask, but we have to move—they're going to build an apartment house where we're renting now, and Mother is sick. I'd like to get her out into the country—our house is so little and dark. I thought if she could be all summer where she could see the sky and hear the birds, she might get well. I want to get my little sisters and brothers out of the city, too. But we couldn't likely pay enough rent. I suppose it was silly of me to ask."

"Not at all!" said the young man. "I don't see why we couldn't get together on some kind of proposition—that is, unless Father has other plans I don't know about. A barn shouldn't be worth such a big price. How much would you feel like paying?"

He was studying the girl before him with interest, noting the well-set head on the pretty shoulders; the delicate features; a glint of gold in the brown hair; the tilt of the firm chin; and a wistfulness in the big blue eyes. This was a new kind of girl, and he felt like giving her what she wanted if he could. And he could. He knew that anything he strongly willed wouldn't be denied him.

The color flushed the delicate cheeks again.

"We're paying only fifteen a month now," she said, "and I couldn't pay any more because we don't have it. In fact I couldn't pay as much, because George and I would each have to pay sixty cents a week to come in to our work from there. I couldn't pay more than twelve! And

I know that's ridiculous for such a beautiful place, but—I had to ask."

She glanced up as if to apologize, then looked at the floor again. The young man felt sympathy for her and a deep desire to help her.

"Why, certainly," he said. "Of course you did. And it's not ridiculous at all for you to make a business proposition of any kind. You say what you can do, and we accept it or not as we like. That's our lookout. Now of course I can't answer about this until I've consulted Father. Not knowing the place well, I haven't the least idea what it's worth. It may not be worth even twelve dollars." (He made a mental note that it should not be if he could help it.) "Suppose I consult with Father and let you know. Could I write or phone you, or will you be this way anytime tomorrow?"

Shirley's breath was almost gone as she realized he was actually considering her proposal in earnest. He hadn't laughed at her for wanting to live in a barn, and he hadn't turned down the price she offered. He was looking at her in a kind way as if he liked her for being frank.

"Why, yes," she said, "I can come in tomorrow at my noon hour—if that wouldn't be too soon. I always have a little time to myself then, and it isn't far from the office."

"That will be all right for me," smiled young Graham. "I'll be here till half past one, and you can ask the boy to show you to my office. I'll consult with Father the first thing in the morning and be ready to give you an answer. But I'm wondering if you've seen this barn. I suppose you have, or you wouldn't want to rent it. But I suppose a barn would be an awfully unpleasant place to live, kind of almost impossible. Are you sure you realize what the proposition would be?"

"Yes, I think so," said Shirley, looking troubled. "It's a beautiful place, and the view is wonderful. I was there today and found a door open at the back and went in to look around. The upstairs middle floor is so big we could make several rooms out of it with screens and curtains. It would be lovely. We could live in picnic style. Yes, I'm sure Mother would like it. I haven't told her about it yet, because if I couldn't afford it I didn't want to disappoint her. So I thought I'd wait till I found out. But I'm almost certain she'd be delighted. Besides, we've got to go somewhere."

"I see," said the young man. He tried not to show his amazement at this girl who so coolly discussed living in a barn with curtains and screens for partitions. He thought of his own luxurious home and his comfortable life, where every need was supplied even before he realized it. He found this glimpse into the girl's heart refreshing.

"Then I'll expect you," he said. Opening the door, he escorted her to the elevator, tipping his hat as he left her.

Shirley wouldn't have been a normal girl if she hadn't felt a flutter in her heart at his attention to her and the pleasant tones in his voice. It was as if she were dressed in broadcloth and fur. She looked down at her serge suit—it had done duty all winter with an old gray sweater under it— half in shame and half in pride in the man who hadn't let it hinder him from showing respect. He was a man. He must be. She had bared her poverty-stricken life, and he hadn't taken advantage of it. He acted as if she were just like other people with the same needs and as good as anyone with whom he did business.

Well, it was probably only a habit of refinement he'd cultivated. But she was going to enjoy the bit of it that had fallen at her feet.

Shirley walked the ten blocks to her narrow little home feeling she'd had a good day overall. She was weary, but it was a healthy weariness. The problem pressing on her for days and nights didn't seem so impossible now, and for the first time she felt hopeful of finding a way out. It was good to get away from the office and the busy monotony and be outside. It was also good to meet a real gentleman, even if it were only in passing and on business.

She decided not to tell her mother and the children of her outing yet—not until she was sure there would be results. Besides, it might only worry her mother more and give her a sleepless night if she let out the secret about the barn.

One more touch made this day stand out from others as lovely. When she turned into Chapel Street and was hurrying to get home at her usual time and not alarm her mother, a car rolled past to the middle of the block and stopped under a streetlight. In a moment a lady came out of the door of a house, entered the car and was driven away. As she closed the car door, something fell from her hand. When Shirley reached the place she found two pink rosebuds that must have slipped from the lady's corsage onto the pavement. She picked them up almost reverently, inhaling their perfume and taking in their delicate curves and texture.

She looked up quickly and saw the limousine turning into a street three blocks away. It would be impossible for her to overtake it, and the lady wouldn't likely return for two roses. She'd probably never miss them. Shirley turned toward the house, thinking she should take them in, but discovered it bore the name of a fashionable dressmaker, who wouldn't, of course, have any right to the roses. Shirley's conscience decided Providence intended them for her. So she hurried on to the brick house, bearing the wonderful flowers to her mother.

She hurried so much that she reached home ten minutes earlier than usual, and they all gathered around her as if it were some great event, while her mother called from her bedroom upstairs to know if something had happened. She was always expecting some new calamity like sickness or one or more of her children to lose their positions.

"Nothing at all the matter, Mother dear!" called Shirley as she hung up her coat and hat and hugged Doris. "I got off earlier than usual because Mr. Barnard had to go away. But see what I've brought you—found them on the street—a lady dropped them. You don't need to be afraid of them—she and her limousine looked perfectly hygienic—and it wasn't stealing, because I couldn't have caught her. Aren't they lovely?"

By this time she was up in her mother's room, with Doris and Carol following close behind exclaiming over the roses.

She kissed her mother and put the flowers into a glass beside the bed.

"You're looking better tonight, I believe, dear," said the mother. "I've been worried about you all day. You were so pale and tired this morning."

"Oh, I'm feeling fine, Mother!" said Shirley. "And I'm going down to make your toast and poach you an egg while Carol finishes getting supper. George will be here in ten minutes, and Harley should be in any minute. He always comes when he gets hungry. My! I'm hungry myself! Let's hurry, Carol. Doris, darling, you get Mother's table ready for her tray. Put on the white cloth, take away the books and set the glass with the roses in the middle very carefully. You won't spill it, will you, dear?"

Beaming with the responsibility accorded her, Doris promised, "No, I yun't spill it. I'll move it tarefully."

Shirley's buoyant air that night lifted them all above the cares that had oppressed them for weeks and gave them new hope. She flew around, getting the supper things together, making her mother's tray pretty and taking extra pains for each one as she hadn't felt able to do before. Carol even mashed the potatoes more carefully, so they didn't have a single lump in them.

"Goodness! But it's been hot in this kitchen all day, Shirley," said Carol. "I had the back door open, but it seemed stifling. I finished the ironing, except a tablecloth, and I guess I can do that this evening. I don't have much studying to do for tomorrow. Nellie Waite stopped and left me my books. I don't believe I'll have to stay at home another day this week. Mother says she can get along. I can leave her lunch all ready, and Doris can manage."

Shirley's conscience gave a sudden twinge. There she was sitting under a lovely tree by a brook, eating her lunch and daydreaming about living in a barn, while Carol stayed home from school and worked in the kitchen! Perhaps she should have come home and sent Carol back to school. And yet that nice young Mr. Graham might be able to do something. She wouldn't condemn herself until tomorrow. She'd tried to do her best. She hadn't gone off selfishly to have a good time by herself when her dear ones were suffering. It was for their sake.

Then George came in whistling, and Harley banged in a minute later, calling to know whether supper was ready.

" 'Cause I gotta date with the fellas this evening, and I gotta beat it," he declared impatiently.

A shadow of anxiety passed over Shirley's face, but she quieted her heart with her hopes for tomorrow. If her plan succeeded, Harley would be away from "the fellas" and wouldn't have so many questionable "dates" to worry them all.

George was in a hurry, too.

"I gotta be at the store for class all evening," he said, bolting his food. "I wouldn't 'a' come home at all, but I knew you'd worry, and Mother gets so upset. What we gonta do about a house? It's getting almost time to move. I went to all those places you suggested at noon today, but there wasn't a vacant spot anywhere. There's some rooms on Louden Street, but there's all sorts in the house. Mother wouldn't like it. It's dirty besides. I suppose if we look long enough we could find rooms. But we'd have to get along with only two or three, for they come awful high. We'd have to have three anyway—you girls and Mother in one, us boys in the other, and one for parlor and kitchen together. Say! Wouldn't that be fierce? I oughtta get a better job. We can't live that way."

"Don't worry, George. I think we'll find something better," said Shirley with a ring in her voice. "I've been thinking out a plan. I haven't got it all arranged in my mind yet, but I'll tell you about it soon. You don't have school tomorrow night, do you? Maybe we can talk it over then. We may have to go out together and look up a place." She gave him an encouraging smile and sent him off to his work.

She extracted a promise from Harley that he'd be in by nine o'clock; discovered he was only going to a movie show around the corner with one of the fellows who was going to "stand treat" because of a ball game they won; found out where his lessons were for the next day; promised to help him when he returned; and sent him away with a feeling of comfort and responsibility to return early. She washed the dishes and ironed the tablecloth so Carol could go to her lessons. Then she went up and put Doris to bed with a story about a little bird who built a nest in a tall tree that grew beside the place where a little girl lived; the bird drank from a brook, took a bath on its pebbly shore, ate the crumbs and berries the little girl gave it, and sat all day on five blue eggs.

Harley came in at five minutes after nine and did his lessons with her help. George came home just as they finished. He was whistling, though he looked tired. He said "the prof" had been "the limit" all the evening. Shirley fixed her mother comfortably for the night and went at last to her own bed, more tired than she'd been for weeks and yet happier. Through it all she was sustained by a hope and inspired by a cultured, pleasant voice and eyes that seemed to understand and wanted to help.

As she drifted off to sleep, that pleasant voice and those kind eyes mingled with her dreams and seemed to promise relief from her anxieties.

With excitement and anticipation she dressed the next morning and dashed off to work. Something was coming, she felt sure—some help for their trying situation. She felt it when she knelt for her usual prayer that morning, and it throbbed in her heart as she hurried through the streets to the office. It almost frightened her to feel so sure, for she knew how disappointed she'd be if she got her hopes too high.

At the office she had plenty of letters to answer and a telegram with directions from Mr. Barnard. But she worked more easily than she had for some time and was finished by half past eleven. When she took the letters out to Mr. Clegg to be signed, he told her she wouldn't be needed the rest of the day and might leave then if she chose.

She ate her lunch quickly and freshened up as much as possible in the office. Then she went to the fourth floor of the Ward Trust Building. With throbbing heart and glowing cheeks she entered Walter Graham's office and asked for Mr. Sidney Graham.

The office boy had evidently received instructions, for he bowed respectfully this time and led her at once to the inner office.

Chapter 4

The afternoon before, when Sidney Graham returned to his office from seeing Shirley to the elevator, he had stood several minutes gazing thoughtfully at the chair where she'd sat, while he drew on his gloves.

The girl's spirited face, with its delicate features and wistful eyes, held something interesting and appealing. He couldn't seem to get away from it. It left an impression of character and a struggle with forces he'd had only a vague conception of in his sheltered life. It left him feeling she was stronger in some ways than he was, and he didn't like that sensation.

He'd always aimed to be a strong character, and for a young man who inherited $250,000 on coming of age and double that amount two years later, with the prospect of another goodly sum when his paternal grandfather's estate was divided, he'd done very well indeed. He had stuck to business ever since leaving college, where he was by no means a nonentity either in studies or athletics, and he wasn't spoiled by the adulation a young man of his good looks, wealth and position receives in society. He took society as a sort of duty but never gave it an undue proportion of his time and thoughts. Notably he was a young man of fine balance and self-control and not given to impulsive or erratic likes and dislikes. So he couldn't understand why a person with a wisp of gold over one crimson cheek and tired, discouraged eyes had made such a strong impression on him.

He had intended, before Shirley's arrival, to leave the office and drop in on Miss Harriet Hale. If the hour seemed propitious, he would take her for a spin in his new racing car that waited even now in the street below. But after Shirley's visit his plan no longer appealed to him. He felt the need of being alone. After pacing his office floor briefly he rode the elevator down to the street floor, dismissed his chauffeur and set off in his car, taking the opposite direction from the Hale residence.

Harriet Hale was an attractive young woman with a brilliant mind and a royal fortune. She could entertain him and stir him up, and sometimes he almost thought the attraction was strong enough to last him through life. But she couldn't appreciate his present mood or explain to him why fifteen minutes in his office with a nervy little stenographer who was willing to live in a barn would make him so dissatisfied with himself. If he tried to tell her about it, he felt sure he'd meet with taunts and sarcasm.

He took little notice of where he was going, threading his way through the congested portion of the city and out onto the less-traveled highways, until at last he found himself in the suburbs. The street name as he slowed up at a grade crossing gave him an idea. Why shouldn't he take a run out and hunt up that barn for himself? Where did she say it was? He consulted the memo he'd written for his father: "Glenside Road, near Allister Avenue." He further searched his memory. "Big stone barn, wide approach, tall tree hanging over, brook." This should be enough to help him identify it. Surely there weren't many stone barns in that neighborhood that would answer that description.

He turned onto Glenside Road with satisfaction and watched for the names of the cross-avenues with a view to finding Allister Avenue. Once he stopped and asked a man in an empty milk wagon where Allister Avenue was and was informed that it was "on a piece, about five miles."

There was something interesting in hunting up his own barn, and he began to look about him and try to see things through the girl's eyes.

Most of the fields were green with spring and alive with an air of activity, as if growing were a business one could watch, like housecleaning and paperhanging and painting. Graham had never noticed before that outdoors in spring seemed to have a character all its own and even an attraction. Later when the trees were out, the orchards in bloom and the wildflowers blowing in the fields, he could rave over spring. But he'd never seen the charm of its beginnings. He wondered why he did now.

The sky was opalescent with pastel colors along the horizon, and a few tall trees were clothed in soft green fuzz, discernible only to a close observer. The air had a chill with evening coming on, and the bees were no longer proclaiming the way to the skunk cabbages. Graham drew in long breaths of the sweet perfume, not knowing where it came from, and let out his car over the smooth road.

Behind a copse of old willows, tall with age and hoary with weather and standing knee-deep in the brook on its way to a larger stream, he caught sight of the old barn.

He knew it at once. Its stone spaciousness, mossy roof, arching tree and brook that backed away from the wading willows, up the hillside, under the rail fence and around its side—all were unmistakable. He could see it just as the girl had seen it, and something in him responded to her longing to live there and make it into a home. Perhaps he was a dreamer, as she, although he passed in the world of business for a practical young man.

He slowed his car and looked at the place intently as he passed by. He was convinced this was it. He didn't need to find Allister Avenue—though he did and then turned back again, stopping by the roadside. He got out of the car, looking all the time at the barn and seeing it through the girl's eyes. As he walked up the grassy slope to the front doors, he had some conception of what it must be to live so that this would seem grand as a home. Unspoiled by his life of luxury, he could glimpse the grandeur of the spot and the dignity of the building with its long simple lines and rough old stones.

The sun was just going down as he stood there. It touched the stones and turned them into jewelled settings, glorifying the old structure into a palace. The evening was sweet with the songs of birds nearby. One above the rest, a wood thrush, high in the elm tree over the barn, spilled its silver notes down to the brook.

The young man removed his hat and stood in the evening air, listening and looking. He could see the poetry of it, and somehow he could see the girl's face as if she stood beside him, her eyes as bright as when she described it. She was right. It was beautiful, and it was a lovely soul that could see it and feel what a home this would make in spite of the ignominy of its being a barn.

Some dim memory of a stable long ago and its glory hovered on the horizon of his mind. But his education wasn't along religious lines, so he didn't form the memory into a definite thought. It was just the sense of a great fact of the universe he might have understood at some other, distant time.

Then he turned to the building itself. He was practical, after all, even if he was a dreamer. He tried the padlock. How did the girl get in? Dare he break into his own barn?

He walked down the slope around to the back and found the entrance close to the ladder. But the place was dark within the great stone walls, and he peered into the gloomy basement with disgust at the dirt and murk. Only here and there, where a crack looked toward the setting sun, a bright needle of light sent a shaft through to let one see the inky shadows. He was about to turn back when he remembered the girl had said she climbed up a ladder to the middle floor. If she had, surely he could. Again that sense that she was stronger than he rebuked him. He got out his pocket flashlight and stepped inside the gloom. Holding the flashlight above his head, he surveyed his property disapprovingly. Then with the light in his hand he climbed gingerly up the dusty rounds to the middle floor.

As he stood alone in the shadows, with the darkness of the hayloft overhead pierced only by the flashlight's sharp rays and a few feebler darts from the sinking sun, the poetry suddenly left the old barn, and a shudder passed through him. To think of living here! How horrible!

Yet still that same feeling that the girl had more nerve than he had forced him to walk the length and breadth of the floor, peering carefully into the dark corners and acquainting himself fully with the place. And it led him to climb partway up the ladder to the loft and send his flashlight searching through its dusty hay-covered recesses.

With a feeling at variance with the place he turned away in disgust and made his way down the ladders again, out into the sunset.

In that short time evening had arrived. The sky had flung out banners, fringed by fine saplings like slender brown threads against the sky. The earth was sinking into dusk, and as he gazed about him a single star burned into being in the clear atmosphere above him. The birds were still now, and the frogs with the brook for accompaniment held the stage. Once more the charm of the place stole over him, and he stood with hat removed, wondering no longer that the girl was willing to live here. A conviction grew within him that somehow he must make it possible for her to do so, that things wouldn't be right unless he did. In fact, he was curious for her to do it and see whether it could be done.

He walked slowly to his car at last, glancing back often. The beauty of the location was unquestioning and evoked admiration. It was too bad only a barn occupied it. He'd like to see a fine house built there. But then in his heart he was glad a fine house wasn't standing there against the evening sky and he could let the girl try living there.

Could he have made a mistake, though? Could he have found the right barn? He must make sure, of course.

But he turned his car toward home, feeling reasonably sure he'd found the right spot. And his thoughts, as he drove, were woven with the softness of the spring evening and permeated with its sounds. He seemed to be in touch with nature as never before.

At dinner that night he asked his father, "Did Grandfather Graham ever live out on the old Glenside Road?"

A pleasant twinkle came into the elder Graham's eyes.

"Sure!" he said. "Lived there myself when I was five years old, before the old man got to speculating and made his pile, and we got too grand to stay in a farmhouse. I remember rolling down a hill under a big tree and your uncle Billy pushing me into the brook that ran at the foot. We boys used to wade in that brook, build dams and catch minnows—and sail boats. It was great sport. I used to go back holidays now and then after I got old enough to go away to school. We were living in town then, but I used to like to go out and stay at the farmhouse. It was rented to a strange old man, but his wife was a good sort and made the bulliest apple turnovers for us boys—and doughnuts! The old farmhouse burned down a year or so ago. But the barn is still standing. I can remember how proud your grandfather was of that barn. It was finer than any barn around. We boys used to go up in the loft and tumble about in the hay. Once when I was little I got lost in the hay, and Billy had to dig me out. I can remember how scared I was when I thought I might have to stay there forever and have nothing to eat."

"Say, Father," said the son, leaning forward eagerly, "I think I'd like to have that old place in my share. Do you think it could be arranged? The boys won't care, I'm sure. They're always more for the town than the country."

"Why, yes, I guess that could be fixed up. You just see Mr. Dalrymple about it. He'll fix it up. Billy's boy got that place up river, you know. Just see the lawyer, and he'll fix it up. No reason in the world why you shouldn't have the old place if you care for it. Not much in it for money, though, I guess. They tell me property's way down out that direction now."

The talk passed to other matters, and Sidney Graham said nothing about his afternoon caller or of the trip he'd taken out to see the old barn. Instead, he took his father's advice and saw the family lawyer, Mr. Dalrymple, the first thing in the morning.

It was all arranged in a few minutes. Mr. Dalrymple called up the other heirs and the children's guardians. An office boy hurried out with some papers and came back with the signatures of heirs and guardians, who all happened to be within reach. Presently the control of the old farm was formally put into the hands of Mr. Sidney Graham, after he signed certain papers agreeing to take this as such-and-such portion of his right in the whole estate.

It was a simple matter. Yet, at half past eleven o'clock, when Mr. Dalrymple's stenographer laid a folded paper on Sidney Graham's desk and left the room, he reached out and touched it with more satisfaction than he'd felt in any acquisition in a long time, not even his last racing car. It wasn't the value the paper represented, however, that pleased him, but the fact that he could now do as he pleased concerning the prospective tenant for the place and conduct an experiment. He wanted to study the girl and see whether she had the nerve to live in a barn—a girl with a face like that to live in a barn!

The morning light might present her in a different aspect from that in which she appeared the evening before, and he mentally reserved the right to turn her down completely if she showed the least sign of not being all he'd thought her. At the same time, he intended to be entirely sure. He wouldn't turn her away without a thorough investigation.

Graham was greatly interested in the study of social science when in college, and human nature interested him at all times. He had to admit to himself that this girl had taken a most unusual hold upon his thoughts.

Chapter 5

As the noon hour approached, Sidney Graham found himself almost excited over the prospect of the girl's coming. He struggled to keep his mind on the day's business. What if she'd given up the idea and wouldn't come at all, or if she did come what would he say to her? When at last she was announced, he pushed his chair back from his desk and stood up trembling slightly. It annoyed him and brought a frown to his otherwise kind features. It seemed out of keeping with his position as junior member of his father's firm that he should be so childish over a simple matter like this. He began to wonder if he wasn't doing an unwise, irregular thing by having anything at all to do with this girl's preposterous proposition.

Then Shirley entered the office and looked eagerly into his eyes, and he forgot his doubts. He met her with a reassuring smile.

She drew in her breath half relieved and smiled shyly back.

She was wearing an old crêpe de chine waist she'd dyed apple-blossom pink in the washbowl with a bit of pink crêpe-paper and a kettle of boiling water. The collar showed neatly over the worn dark-blue coat and seemed to reflect apple-blossom tints in her pale cheeks. Something skylike in the tint of her eyes gave the young man a sense of spring as he looked at her. He was glad she looked as good to him in bright daylight as she had in the dusk of evening. She still had that spirited lift of her chin and firm set of her lips that conveyed strength. He reflected that he'd seldom seen it in the girls he knew. Had poverty and privation and responsibility caused it, or was it innate?

"You—you found out?" she asked as she sat down on the edge of the chair.

"Sure! It's all right," he said. "You can rent it if you wish."

"And the price?"

"Why, the price will be all right, I'm sure. It really isn't worth what you mentioned at all. It's only a barn, you know. We couldn't think of taking more than ten dollars a month, if we took that. I must look it over again. But it won't be more than ten dollars, and it may be less."

Young Graham used his most businesslike tone to say this, while his eyes were on the paper-knife he was digging into his clean blotter pad on the desk.

"Oh!" breathed Shirley, the color almost leaving her face entirely with the relief of his words. "Oh, really?"

"And you haven't lost your nerve about living out there in the country in a big old empty barn?" he asked quickly to cover her embarrassment—and his own, perhaps.

"Oh, no!" said Shirley with a smile. "It's a lovely barn, and it won't be empty when we all get into it."

"Are there many of you?" he asked.

The conversation was taking on a slightly personal tinge, but neither of them was aware of it.

"Two brothers and two sisters and our mother," she said, so delighted over finding she could rent the barn that she hardly knew what she was answering. She was unaware that she'd taken the young man into her confidence by her sweet tone and manner.

"Your mother approves of your plan?" he asked. "She doesn't object to the country?"

"Oh, I haven't told her yet," said Shirley. "I don't know that I shall. She's been quite sick, and she trusts me entirely. She loves the country, and it will be wonderful to her to get out there. She might not like the idea of a barn beforehand. But she's never seen the barn, and besides it won't look like a barn inside when I get it fixed up. I must talk it over with George and Carol, but I don't think I'll tell her at all till we take her out there and surprise her. I'll tell her I've found a place I think she'll like and ask her if I may keep it a surprise. She'll be willing, and she'll be pleased, I know!" She was smiling dreamily as she spoke. Then suddenly the strong look returned to her face.

"But anyhow," she finished after a pause, "we have to go there for the summer—we have nowhere else to go that we can afford. And anywhere out of the city will be good, even if Mother doesn't choose it. I think it will be easier for her if she doesn't know about it until she's there. It won't seem so much like not going to live in a house."

"I see," said the young man. "I shouldn't wonder if you're right. And anyhow I think we can manage between us to make it pretty habitable for her."

He was speaking eagerly and forgetting he had no right. But a flush came into the girl's cheek.

"Oh, I wouldn't want you to go to any trouble," she said. "You've been very kind already, and you've made the rent so reasonable! I'm afraid it isn't right and fair—it's such a lovely barn!"

"Perfectly fair," said Graham. "It will do the barn good to be lived in and taken care of again."

If he'd been called upon to tell just what good it would do the barn to be lived in, he might have floundered; but he took care not to make that necessary. He went on talking.

"I'll see that everything is in good order, the doors made all right, and the windows—I—that is, if I remember right a few little things should be attended to before you go in. How soon did you want to take possession? I'll try to have it ready for you."

"Oh, why, that's very kind," said Shirley. "I don't think it needs anything—that is, I didn't notice anything, but perhaps you know best. Why, we have to leave our house the last of this month. Do you suppose you could begin the rent a few days before that, so we could get things moved gradually? I haven't much time, only at night."

"We'll date the lease the first of next month," said the young man. "And then you can put your things in anytime you like from now on. I'll see that the locks are made safe and a simple partition put in at one end of the upstairs room, where you could lock up things. Then you could take them up there when you like. I'll attend to that partition at once. The barn needs it. This is as good a time as any to put it in. You wouldn't object to a partition? That wouldn't upset any of your plans?"

He spoke as if it would be a great detriment to the barn not to have a partition, but of course he wouldn't insist if she disliked it.

"Oh, why, no, of course not," said Shirley bewildered. "It would be lovely. Mother could use that for her room, but I wouldn't want you to do anything on our account that you don't have to do anyway."

"Oh, no, certainly not, but it might as well be done now as anytime, and then you get the benefit of it. I wouldn't want to rent the place without putting it in good order, and a partition is always needed in a barn, you know, if it's to be a really good barn."

It was good that no wise people were listening to that conversation; they might have laughed aloud at this point and betrayed the young man's strategy. But Shirley was unschooled in farm lore and knew less about barns and their needs than she did of Sanskrit; so the remark passed without exciting her suspicion.

"Oh, it's going to be lovely!" said Shirley suddenly, like an eager child. "I can't thank you enough for being so kind about it."

"Not at all," said the young man. "And now you'll want to go out and look around again to make your plans. Were you planning to soon? I'd like to have you look the place over again and see if anything else should be done."

"Oh, why," said Shirley, "I don't think there could be anything else. But I'd like to have a key to that big front door, for we couldn't carry things up the ladder very well. I was thinking I'd go out this afternoon, if I could get George a leave of absence for a little while. There's been a death in our firm, and the office is working only half a day, and I'm off again. I thought I'd like for George to see it if possible; he's very wise in his judgments, and Mother trusts him a lot next to me. But I don't know whether they'll let him off on such short notice."

"Where does he work?"

"Farwell and Story's department store. They're very particular, but George is allowed a day off every three months if he takes it out of his vacation—so I thought I'd try."

"Here, let me fix that. Harry Farwell's a friend of mine." He picked up the telephone.

"Oh, thank you!" murmured Shirley, overcome at the blessings falling at her feet.

Graham already had the number and was calling for Mr. Farwell, Junior.

"That you, Hal? Oh, good morning! Have a good time last night? Sorry I couldn't have been there, but I had three other engagements and couldn't get around. Say, I want to ask a favor of you. You have a boy there in the store I want to borrow for the afternoon if you don't mind. His name is George Hollister. Could you look him up and send him over to my office pretty soon? It will be a personal favor to me if you'll let him off and not dock his pay. Thank you! I was sure you would. Return the favor sometime myself if opportunity comes my way. Yes, I'll hold the phone till you hunt him up. Thank you."

Graham looked up from the phone into the astonished girl's eyes and caught her look of admiration, which quite confused Shirley for a moment and set her to thanking him again.

"Oh, that's all right. Farwell and I went to prep school together. It's nothing for him to arrange matters. He says it will be all right. Now what are your plans? I wonder if I can help in any way. How were you planning to go out?"

"Oh, by the trolley, of course," said Shirley. How strange it must be to have other ways of traveling at one's command!

"I was thinking," she added hesitantly, "that perhaps I'd stop at the schoolhouse and get my sister. It might be better to get her judgment about things. She's a rather wise girl."

She looked up suddenly and, seeing the young man's eyes on her, grew ashamed that she'd brought her private affairs to his notice; yet it had seemed necessary to say something to fill in the embarrassing pause. But Sidney Graham didn't let her continue to be embarrassed. He entered into her plans as if they concerned him, too.

"Why, I think that's a good plan," he said. "It'll be much better to have a family council before you decide about moving. Now I've thought of something. Why couldn't you all go out in the car with me and my kid sister? I've been promising to take her for a spin in the country, and my chauffeur is to drive her down this afternoon for me. It's almost time for her to be here now. Your brother will be here by the time she comes. Why couldn't we just go around by the schoolhouse and pick up your sister and all go out together? I want to go out and look things over, and it seems to me that would save time all around. Then, if there's anything you want done—"

"Oh, there's nothing I want done," gasped Shirley. "You've been so kind. I couldn't think of asking for anything at the price we'll be paying. And we mustn't impose on you. We can go out in the trolley perfectly well and not trouble you."

"It's no trouble when I'm going anyway." Then into the telephone he said, "Hello! He's coming, you say? He's on his way? Good. Thank you very much, Hal. Good-bye!"

"That's all right!" he said, smiling. "Your brother is on his way, and now excuse me just a moment while I phone my sister."

Shirley felt apprehensive while the young man called up a girl he addressed as "kid" and told her to hurry the car right down and bring some extra wraps along for some friends he was taking with him.

He left Shirley no opportunity to express her thanks but gave her some magazines and hurried from the room to attend to some business matters before he left.

Chapter 6

Shirley sat with shining eyes and glowing cheeks, turning over the pages of a magazine with trembling fingers, unable to read a word, for the joy of what was before her. A real automobile ride! Her first! And it was to include George and Carol! How wonderful! And how thoughtful of him to take his own sister and hers and so make the trip perfectly conventional and proper! What a nice face he had and what fine eyes! He didn't seem in the least like the society man she knew he must be from the frequent mention of his name in the papers. He was a real gentleman! It was nice to know of them now and then, even though they moved in a different orbit from the one where she'd been placed. She felt better about the universe to have seen how nice a man could be to a nobody when he didn't have to.

It couldn't be anything to him to rent that barn—at ten dollars a month! That was ridiculous! Was he thinking of her as an object of charity and feeling sorry for her? Was that why he set the price so low? She couldn't have that. It wasn't right or honest, and—it wasn't respectable! That was the way unprincipled men did when they wanted to humor foolish girls. Did he think of her that way?

Her cheeks flamed, and her eyes flashed. She sat up straight and began to tremble. Why hadn't she thought of it before? Her mother had warned her to be careful about having anything to do with strange men, except in the most distant business way. And here she was telling him the family's private affairs and letting him make plans for her. How did it happen? What must he think of her? This came from trying to keep a secret from Mother. She might have known it was wrong. Yet the case was so desperate and Mother so likely to worry about any new and unconventional suggestion. It had seemed right.

But of course it wasn't right for her to allow him to take them all in his car. She must go in the trolley if she went at all. In fact she thought she'd better call the whole thing off and tell him they couldn't live in a barn, that she'd changed her mind. It would be dreadful if he took her for one of those girls who wanted to attract a young man's attention!

In the midst of her thoughts the door opened, and Sidney Graham walked in again. His clean-cut face and clear eyes dispelled her fears again. His bearing was dignified and respectful, and something in his voice as he spoke to her restored her confidence in him and in his impression of her. Her decision to decline the ride with him fled, and she sat quietly looking at the pictures in the magazine with unseeing eyes.

"I hope you'll find something to interest you for a few minutes," young Graham said pleasantly. "It won't be long, but I promised Father I'd attend to one or two matters before I left this afternoon. There's an article in that other magazine under your hand about decorating country homes, bungalows and the like. It may give you some ideas about the old barn. I think a few flowers and vines might do a whole lot."

He found the place in the magazine and left her again. Strangely enough she became absorbed in the article because she was imagining how glorious it would be to have a few flowers growing where Doris could water and pick them. She grew so interested in the remarks about what flowers would grow best in the open and which were easiest to care for that she got a pencil and paper from her coat pocket and began copying some of the lists. Then suddenly the door opened again, and Graham returned with George.

The boy stopped short on the threshold, startled, a white wave of apprehension passing over his face. He didn't speak. The boy-habit of silence and self-control in a crisis was upon him. He looked from one to the other.

Shirley jumped to her feet.

"Oh, George, I'm so glad you could come! This is Mr. Graham. He's been kind enough to offer to take us in his car to see a place we can rent for the summer, and it was through his suggestion that Mr. Farwell let you off for the afternoon."

The tension in the young face relaxed, and the boy sighed with relief.

"That's great! Thanks awfully for the holiday. They don't come my way often. It'll be great to have a ride in a car, too. Some lark, eh, Shirley?"

The boy warmed to the situation with the friendly grasp the young man gave him, and Shirley could see her brother had made a good impression. Graham was smiling, as if he enjoyed the boy's offhanded way of talking.

"I'm going to leave you here for ten minutes more until I talk with a man out here in the office. Then we'll go," he said and hurried away again.

"Aw, Shirley!" said the boy, flinging himself down in a leather chair. "Say! You certainly gave me some start! I thought Mother was worse, or you got arrested or lost your job or something, finding you here in a strange office. Some class to this, isn't there? Look at that rug!" He kicked the thick Turkish carpet happily. "Say, he must have some coin! Who is the guy anyway? How'd ya get onto the tip? You don't think he's handing out Vanderbilt residences at fifteen a month, do you?"

"Listen, George. I must talk fast because he may come back any minute. Yesterday I got a half holiday, and instead of going home I thought I'd go out and hunt a house. I took the Glenside trolley, and when we got out past the city I heard two men talking about a place we were passing. It was a big, beautiful stone barn. They told who owned it and said a lot about its having such a splendid spring of water beside it. It was a beautiful place, George. I couldn't help thinking what it would be for Mother to be out in the country this summer and what a wonderful house that would make—"

"We couldn't live in a barn, Shirl!" said the boy, aghast.

"Wait, George. Listen. Don't say that till you see it. It's the biggest barn you ever saw, and I guess it hasn't been used for a barn in a long time. I got out of the trolley on the way back and went in. It's just enormous, and we could screen off rooms and live like royalty. It has a huge front door, and we could have a hammock under the tree, and there's a brook to fish in and a big third story with hay in it. I guess it's what they call in books a hayloft. It's great."

"Say!" was all the electrified George could utter. "Oh, say!"

"It's on a little hill with the loveliest tree in front of it and right on the trolley line. We'd have to start a little earlier in the morning. But I wouldn't mind, would you?"

"Naw!" said George. "But could we walk that far?"

"No, we'd have to ride, but the rent is so much lower it would pay our carfare."

"Say!" said George again. "Isn't that great? And is this the guy that owns it?"

"Yes, or at least he and his father do. He's been very kind. He's taking all this trouble to drive us out in his car today to see if anything needs to be done for our comfort there. He certainly is an unusual man for a landlord."

"He sure is, Shirley. I guess maybe he has a case on you the way he looks at you."

"George!" said Shirley severely, the red flushing her cheeks and her eyes flashing angrily. "George! That was a dreadful thing for you to say. If you ever even think a thing like that again, I won't have anything to do with him or the place. We'll just stay in the city all summer. I suppose that would be better anyway."

Shirley got up and began to button her coat, as if she were leaving that minute.

"Aw, Shirley! I was just kidding. Can't you take a joke? This thing must be getting on your nerves. I never saw you so touchy."

"It certainly is getting on my nerves to have you say a thing like that, George."

Shirley's tone was still severe.

"Aw, cut the grouch, Shirley. I tell you I was just kidding. 'Course he's a good guy. He probably thinks you're crossed-eyed, knock-kneed—"

"George!" Shirley started for the door.

But the irrepressible George saw it was time to stop, and he put out an arm with muscles that were like iron from wrestling and ball games with his fellow laborers at the store.

"Now, Shirley, cut the comedy. That guy'll be coming back next, and you don't want to have him ask what's the matter, do you? He certainly is some fine guy. I wouldn't like to embarrass him, would you? He's a peach of a looker. Say, Shirley, what do you figure Mother's going to say about this?"

Shirley turned, half mollified.

"That's just what I want to ask you, George. I don't want to tell Mother until it's all fixed up and we can show it to her. You know it will sound much worse to talk about living in a barn than it will to go in and see it fixed up with rugs and curtains and screens. And the piano will be there and a couch and the supper table set, with the sun setting outside the open door and a bird singing in the tree."

"Wouldn't that be some class? Say, Shirley, let's not tell her! Let's just make her say she'll trust the moving to us to surprise her. Can't you kid her along and make her all right with that?"

"Why, that was what I was thinking. If you think there's no danger she'll be disappointed and think we should have done something else."

"What else could we do? Say, it would be great to sleep in the hayloft!"

"We could just tell her we were coming out in the country for the summer to camp in a nice place where it was safe and comfortable, and then we'd have plenty of time to look around for the right kind of house for next winter."

"That's the dope, Shirley! You give her that. She'll fall for that, sure thing. She'll like the country. At least, if it's like what you say it is."

"Well, wait till you see it."

"Have you told Carol?" asked George, suddenly sobering. Carol was his twin sister, inseparable chum and companion when he was at home.

"No," said Shirley, "I haven't had a chance. But Mr. Graham suggested we drive around by the school and get her. Then she can see how she likes it, too. And if Carol thinks so, we'll get Mother not to ask any questions but just trust us."

"That guy's great. He's got a head on him. Some lark, what?"

"Yes, he's been very kind," said Shirley. "At first I told him I couldn't let him go to so much trouble for us, but he said he was going to take his sister out for a ride—"

"A girl! Aw! I'm going to beat it!" George stopped in his eager walk back and forth across the office and seized his old faded cap.

"George, stop! You mustn't be impolite. Besides, I think she's only a little girl, probably like Doris. He called her his 'kid sister.' "

"H'm! You can't tell. I ain't going to run any risks. I better beat it."

But George's further intentions were suddenly halted by Sidney Graham's entrance.

"Well, Miss Hollister," he said with a smile, "we're ready at last. I'm sorry to have kept you waiting so long. Something was wrong with one of my tires, and the chauffeur had to run around to the garage. Come on, George," he said to the boy, who hung shyly behind now, wary of any female who might be haunting the path. "Guess you'll have to sit in the front seat with me and help me drive. The chauffeur has to go back and drive for Mother. She has to go to some tea or other."

George suddenly forgot the possible girl and followed his new hero to the elevator with a swelling soul. What would the other fellows at the store think of him? A whole half holiday, an automobile ride and a chance to sit in the front and learn to drive!

But all he said was, "Sure thing!"

The strange girl suddenly loomed on his consciousness again as they emerged from the elevator and came out on the street. She was sitting in the back seat alone, arrayed in a blue velvet coat the color of her eyes, and George felt at once all hands and feet. She was a slender wisp of a thing about Carol's age, with a lily complexion and wealth of gold hair caught in a blue veil. She smiled when her brother introduced her as "Elizabeth." There was nothing snobbish or disagreeable about her, but that blue velvet coat suddenly made George conscious of his common clothes and gave Shirley a pang of dismay at her worn suit.

But Sidney Graham soon covered all differences in his guests' clothing when he insisted they don the two long blanket coats he handed them. Then when George was seated in the leather front seat, with that handsome coat around his shoulders, he didn't much mind the blue velvet girl behind him. He resolved to earn enough to get Carol a coat like it someday, but Carol's should be pink or red to go with her black eyes and pink cheeks.

After all, it was Shirley, not George, who felt embarrassed over the strange girl and wished she hadn't come. She was vexed with herself for it, too. It was foolish to let a child no older than Carol fluster her so, but the thought of a long ride alone on that back seat with the dainty young girl frightened her.

But Elizabeth wasn't frightened. She'd been brought up in the society atmosphere and was at home with people everywhere. She tucked the robes about her guest and helped Shirley button the dark-blue coat about her, remarking that it got awfully chilly when they were going. Before Shirley could think of a single word to say in response, the conversation seemed to be moving along easily without her aid.

"Sid says we're going to pick up your sister from her school. I'm so glad! How old is she? About my age? Won't that be fun? I'm rather lonesome this spring because all my friends are in school. I've been away at boarding school and got the measles. Wasn't that silly for someone my age? And the doctor said I couldn't study anymore this spring because of my eyes. I've been home six weeks now, and I don't know what to do with myself. What's your sister's name? Carol? Carol Hollister? That's pretty! Is she the only sister you have? A baby sister? How sweet! What's her name? Oh, I think Doris is the cutest name ever. Doris Hollister. Why don't we go and get Doris? Wouldn't she like to ride, too? Oh, it's too bad your mother is ill. But of course she wouldn't want to stay all alone in the house without some of her family."

Elizabeth was tactful. She knew at a glance that trained nurses and servants could not be plentiful in a family where the young people wore such plain, old-style garments. She gave no hint of such a thought, however.

"That's your brother," she went on, nodding toward George. "I've got another brother, but he's seventeen and away at college, so I don't see much of him. Sid's very good to me when he has time, and often he takes me to ride. We're chums, Sid and I. Is this the school where your sister goes? She's in high school then. The third year? My! She must be bright. I've only finished my second. Does she know she's going with us? What fun to be called out of school by a surprise! Oh, I just know I'm going to like her."

Shirley sat still with amazement and listened to the girl's eager gush, wondered what shy Carol would say and tried to rouse herself to answer the young questioner in the same spirit in which she asked questions.

George soon came out with Carol, who was struggling into her coat and trying to straighten her hat, while George mumbled in her ear as he helped her clumsily.

"Some baby doll out there, kid! You better preen your feathers. She's been gassing with Shirley to beat the band. I couldn't hear all they said, but she asked a lot about you. You should worry! Hold up your head, and don't flicker an eyelash. You're as good as she is any day, if you don't look all dolled up like a new saloon. But she's some looker! Pretty as a red wagon! Her brother's a peach of a fellow. He's going to let me run the car when we get out of the city limit. And say! Shirley says for me to tell you we're going out to look at a barn where we're going to move this summer, and you're not to say a word about its being a barn. See? Get onto that sky-blue-pink satin scarf she's got around her head? Ain't she some chicken, though?"

"Hush, George! She'll hear you!" murmured Carol in dismay. "What do you mean about a barn? How could we live in a barn?"

"You just shut up and saw wood, kid, and you'll see. Shirley thinks she's got onto something good."

Then Carol was introduced to the beautiful blue-velvet girl and sat down beside her, wrapped in a soft furry cloak of garnet, to be whirled away into a wonderland.

Chapter 7

Carol and Elizabeth got along well together. Shirley was amazed to see the ease with which her sister entered into this new relationship, unawed by the garments of her hostess. Carol had more of the modern young America in her than Shirley, perhaps, whose early life had been more conventionally guarded. Carol was democratic and, strange to say, felt slightly superior to Elizabeth because of going to public school. The high school girls were in the habit of referring to a neighboring boarding school as "Dummy's Retreat." Therefore Carol wasn't at all awed by the other girl, who declared in a friendly manner that she'd always been crazy to go to public school and asked rapid intelligent questions about the events there. Before they were out of the city limits the two girls were talking a steady stream, and one could see from their eyes that they liked each other. Shirley, relieved, settled back on the comfortable cushions. She tried to think how it would feel to own a car like this and be able to ride around when she wanted to.

On the front seat George and Graham were already friends, and George was gaining valuable information about running a car, which he had opportunity to practice as soon as they got outside the crowded thoroughfares.

They were perhaps halfway to the old barn and running smoothly on an open road, with no one in sight a long way ahead, when Graham turned back to Shirley, leaving George to run the car for a moment himself. The boy's heart swelled with gratitude and utmost devotion to be thus trusted. Of course he only had to keep things as he'd been told, but this man realized he'd do it and not show off. George set himself to be worthy of this trust. To be sure, young Graham had a watchful eye on things and was taking no chances. But he let the boy feel free and didn't make him aware of his espionage, which will win any boy to give his best to any responsibility, if he has any best at all.

The conversation between the girl and the man in brief sentences now and then wasn't the kind one would expect between landlord and tenant. He called her attention to the green spreading over the treetops more distinctly than the day before; to the clouds floating overhead; to the fields taking on new colors. So at last they arrived at the old barn.

Like eager children they tumbled out of the car and hurried up to the barn, talking at once and forgetting any difference in station.

Graham had brought a key for the padlock, and with George's help, though both were unused to such maneuvers, he unlocked and shoved back the two great doors.

"These doors are too heavy. They should have ball bearings," remarked Graham. "I'll attend to that at once. They should move with a light touch. It doesn't pay to let property lie idle without a tenant; so many things get neglected."

He walked around with a wise air as if he'd been an active landowner for years, though indeed he was looking at everything with ignorant eyes. His standard was a home where every detail was perfect and where necessities came and vanished with the need. This was his first view into "being up against it," as he phrased it in his mind.

Elizabeth in her blue velvet cloak and blue cloudy veil stood in the wide doorway and looked around with delight.

"Oh, Sid, wouldn't this be perfect for a party?" she exclaimed. "You could put the orchestra over in that corner behind a screen of palms and decorate with Florida moss and asparagus vine with daffodils wired on in showers from the beams and palms all around the walls, with colored electrics hidden everywhere. You could run a wire in from the street, couldn't you? The way they did at Uncle Andy's. And serve the supper out on the lawn with individual rustic tables. Brower has them and brings them out with rustic chairs to match. You could have the tree wired, too, and have colored electrics all over the place. Oh! Wouldn't it be heavenly? Say, Sid, Carol says they're coming out here to live maybe. Why couldn't we give them a party like that for a housewarming?"

Sidney Graham looked at his excited, impractical young sister and then at the faces of the three Hollisters and tried not to laugh as the tremendous contrast of circumstances was presented to him. But his rare tact served him in good stead.

"Why, Elizabeth, that would probably be fun. But Miss Hollister tells me her mother's been quite ill. I'm sure, while that might be the happiest thing imaginable for you young folks, it would be rather trying on an invalid. I guess you'll have to have your parties somewhere else for the present."

"Oh!" said Elizabeth with quick recollection. "Of course! They told me about their mother. How thoughtless of me! But it would be lovely, wouldn't it, Miss Hollister? Can't you see it?"

She turned in wistful appeal to Shirley, and that young woman, being a dreamer herself, at once responded with a radiant smile.

"Indeed I can, and it would be lovely. But I've also been thinking what a lovely home it could be made into."

"Yes?" said Elizabeth, looking around with a dubious frown. "It would need a lot of changing, I'd think. You'd want hardwood floors and lots of rugs and some partitions and windows—"

"Oh, no," said Shirley, laughing. "We're not hardwood people, dear. We're just plain hard-working people, and all we need is a quiet, sweet place to rest in. It'll be heavenly here, with that tree outside to shade the doorway and all this wide space to walk around in. We live in a narrow little city house now and never have any place to get out except the street. We'll have the birds and the brook for orchestra, and we won't need palms, because the trees and vines will soon be in leaf and make a lovely screen for our orchestra. I imagine at night the stars will have almost as many colors as electrics."

Elizabeth looked at her somewhat puzzled.

"Well, yes, perhaps they would," she said and smiled. "I've never thought of them that way, but it sounds very pretty, quite like some of Browning's poetry that I don't understand—or was it Mrs. Browning? I can't quite remember."

Sidney Graham, investigating the loft, watched the scene and listened to the conversation, though they couldn't see him. He realized it might not be a bad thing for his sister, with her boarding-school rearing, to be near these true-hearted young people, who were still dreamers and poets, and get her standards somewhat modified by theirs. He took special note of the gentle way in which Shirley answered the girl now when she thought herself alone with her.

George and Carol had grasped hands and run wildly down the slope to the brook after a casual glance at the barn's interior. Elizabeth now turned her high-heeled boots in the brook's direction, and Shirley was left alone to walk the length and breadth of her new abode and make real plans.

Graham observed her as she looked from one wall to the other, measuring distances with her eye, then walking to the window and rubbing a clear space on the dusty pane with her handkerchief so she might look out. He couldn't help comparing her with the girls he knew, though their garments would have far outshone hers. But even in the serge suit she seemed lovely.

The young people returned, and both Carol and George of their own accord joined Shirley in a brief council. Graham called his sister away, ostensibly to watch a squirrel in the elm tree, but really to admonish her not to propose any more parties, since the young people he'd introduced her to weren't well off and had no money or time for elaborate entertainments.

"But they're lovely, Sid, aren't they? Don't you like them just awfully? I know you do, or you wouldn't have taken the trouble to bring them out here in the car with us. Say, you'll bring me to see them often after they live here, won't you?"

"Perhaps," said her brother, smiling. "But shouldn't you wait until they ask you?"

"Oh, they'll ask me," said Elizabeth with a charming smile and confident toss of her head. "I'll make them ask me."

"Be careful, kid," he said, still smiling. "Remember that they won't have much money to entertain you with, and probably their things are very plain and simple. You may embarrass them if you invite yourself out."

Elizabeth raised her azure eyes to her brother's face thoughtfully for a moment, then smiled back confidently once more.

"Don't worry, Sid, dear—there's more than one way. I won't hurt their feelings, but they'll ask me, and they'll want me, and I'm going to come. Yes, and you're going to bring me!"

She turned with a laughing pirouette and danced down the length of the barn to Carol, catching her hand and twirling her after her.

"Well, do you think we should take it? Do you think I dare give my final word without consulting Mother?" Shirley asked her brother when they were left alone for a minute.

"Sure thing! No mistake! It's great. You couldn't get a place like this if you went the length and breadth of the city and had a whole lot more than you have to spend."

"But remember it's a barn!" said Shirley. "Mother may mind that very much."

"Not when she sees it," said Carol, whirling back to the consultation. "She'll think it's the most sensible thing we ever did. She isn't foolish like that. We'll tell her we've found a place to camp with a shanty attached, and she can't be disappointed. I think it'll be great. Just think how Doris can run in the grass!"

"Yes," put in George. "I was telling Carol down by the spring— before that girl came and stopped us—I think we might have some chickens and raise eggs. Harley could do that, and Carol and I could raise flowers, and I could take 'em to town in the morning. I could work evenings."

Shirley smiled. She almost felt like shouting that they agreed with her. The place seemed almost like heaven to her when she thought of the close, dark quarters at home and the summer heat coming on.

"We couldn't keep a lodger, and we'd have that much less," said Shirley thoughtfully.

"But we wouldn't have their laundry or their room-cleaning to do," said Carol, "and I could have that much more time for the garden and chickens."

"You mustn't count on being able to make much that way," said Shirley. "You know nothing about gardening and would probably make a lot of mistakes at first."

"I can make fudge and sandwiches and take them to school to sell," declared Carol stoutly. "And I'll find out how to raise flowers and parsley and little things people have to have. Besides, there's watercress down by that brook, and people like that. We could sell that."

"Well, we'll see," said Shirley, "but you mustn't get up too many ideas yet. If we can only get moved and Mother is satisfied, I guess we can get along. The rent is only ten dollars."

"Good night! That's cheap enough!" George said and drew a long whistle. Then, seeing Elizabeth approaching, he put on an indifferent air and sauntered to the dusty window at the other end of the barn.

Sidney Graham appeared now and took Shirley over to the east end to ask her where she thought a good place would be to put the partition, and did she think it would be good to have another one at the other end just like it? And so they stood and planned, quite as if Shirley were ordering a ten-thousand-dollar alteration put into her ten-dollar barn.

Then suddenly the girl remembered her fears. Looking straight up into the young man's face, she asked, "You're sure you were going to put in these partitions? You're not making any change on my account? Because I couldn't think of letting you go to any trouble or expense."

Her straightforward look embarrassed him.

"Why, I—" he began, growing a little flushed. "Why, you see, I hadn't been out to look things over before. I didn't realize how much better it would be to have those partitions in. But now I intend to do it right away. Father put the whole thing in my hands to do as I pleased. In fact, the place is mine now, and I want to put it in good shape to rent. So don't worry yourself in the least. Things won't go to wrack and ruin so quickly, if someone is on the place."

He finished his sentence briskly. It seemed quite plausible even to him now, and he searched about for a change of topic.

"You think you can get on here with the rough floor? You might put padding or something under your carpets, but it will take pretty large carpets—" He looked at her dubiously. To his conventional mind every step of the way was blocked by some impassable barrier. He didn't honestly see how she was going to do it at all.

"Oh, we don't need carpets!" exclaimed Shirley, laughing. "We'll spread down a rug in front of Mother's bed and another one by the piano, and the rest will be just right. We're not expecting to give receptions here," she added mischievously. "We're only campers, and very grateful campers at that, too, to find a nice, clean, empty floor where we can live. The only thing that troubles me is the cooking. I've been wondering if it will affect the insurance if we use an oil stove to cook with, or would you rather we get a woodstove and put the pipe out one of the windows? I've seen people do that sometimes. Of course we could cook outdoors on a campfire if it was necessary, but it might be a little inconvenient when it rains."

Graham gasped at the girl's coolness as she discussed hardships as if they were necessities to be accepted pleasantly and without a murmur. She actually wouldn't be daunted by cooking her meals on a fire outside! Cooking indeed! That was of course a question people had to consider. The question had never crossed his mind. People cooked—how did they cook? By electricity, gas, coal and wood fires, of course. But now he perceived it was one of the first main things to be looked out for in a home. He looked at the waiting girl with a curious mixture of admiration and dismay in his face.

"Why, of course you'll need a fire and a kitchen," he said as if those things usually grew in houses without any help, and it hadn't occurred to him before that they weren't indigenous to barns. "Well, now, I hadn't thought of that. There's no chimney here, is there? H'm! Every barn needs a chimney. It would be better for the—ah—for the hay, I'd think —keep it dry, you know, and all that sort of thing. And then I'd think it might be better for the animals. I must look into that matter."

"No, Mr. Graham," said Shirley firmly. "There's no need for a chimney. We can have the pipe go through a piece of tin set in the back window if you won't object, and we can use the little oil stove when it's very hot if that doesn't affect the insurance. We could bring our gas stove, but there isn't any gas in a barn."

Graham looked around blankly at the walls covered with cobwebs as if expecting gas jets to break forth simultaneously with his wish.

"No, I suppose not," he said, "though I think there should be. In a barn, you know. But I'm sure there'll be no objection to your using any kind of stove that will work here. This is a stone barn, you know, and I'm sure it won't affect the insurance. I'll find out and let you know."

Shirley still felt a bit uneasy about those partitions and the low rent, but somehow the young man had impressed her with the fact that he was under no unpleasant delusions regarding her and had the utmost respect for her.

He looked at her for a moment without saying a word, and then he began hesitantly, "I wish you'd let me tell you how brave you are about all this, planning to come out here in this lonely place and not being afraid of hard work, rough floors, a barn and even a fire outdoors."

Shirley's laugh rang out, and her eyes sparkled.

"Why, it's the nicest thing that's happened to me in ages," she said. "I can hardly believe we can come here—can really afford to come to a great country place like this. Of course there'll be hard things. There always are, and some of them have been just about unbearable, but even the hard things can be fun if you try. This will be wonderful!" She looked around on the dusty rafters and rough stone walls with a little air of possession.

"You are rather"—he paused—"unusual!" he finished thoughtfully as they walked toward the doorway and stood looking off at the distance.

But now Shirley had almost forgotten him.

"Just think of waking up to that every morning," she declared with a sweep of her arm. "Those purply hills, the fringe of brown and green against the horizon, that white spire nestling among those evergreens! Is that a church? Is it near enough for us to go to? Mother wouldn't want us to be too far from church."

"We'll go home that way and see," said Graham. "You'll want to get acquainted with your new neighborhood. You'll need to know where the nearest store is and where your neighbors live. We'll reconnoiter a little. Are you ready to go?"

"Oh, yes. I'm afraid we've kept you too long already, and we must get home about the time Carol usually comes from school, or Mother will be terribly worried. Carol is never later than half past four."

"We have plenty of time," Graham said, glancing at his watch. "Call the children, and we'll drive around the neighborhood before we go back."

And so the little company was reluctantly persuaded to climb into the car again and start on the way.

Chapter 8

The car surged ahead up the smooth white road, and the barn seemed to smile at them in farewell as they looked back. Shirley tried to think how it would be to come home every night and see Doris standing at the top of the grassy incline waiting to welcome her. She tried to picture her mother in a hammock under the elm tree when summer arrived and the boys working in their garden. It seemed too wonderful to be true.

The car swept around the corner of Allister Avenue and curved down between tall trees. The white spire in the distance drew nearer now, and the purplish hills stood off at one side. The way was fresh with smells of spring, droning bees and croaking frogs. The spirit of the day seemed to enter into the young people and make them glad. All at once they seemed to have known each other a long time and be intimately acquainted with their tastes and interests. They exclaimed together over the distant view of the misty city with the river winding away and shouted simultaneously over a frightened rabbit that scurried across the road and hid in the brushwood. Then the car wound around a curve, and they saw the small white church below them.

The little white church in the valley
  Is bright with the blossom of May,
And true is the heart of your lover
  Who waits for your coming today!

George quoted that from a favorite selection of the department store victrola, and all the rest looked interested. It was a pretty church, nestled under the hills as if it were part of the landscape and making a center for the town.

"We can go to church and Sunday school there," said Shirley. "That will please Mother!"

Elizabeth looked at her curiously and then toward the church.

"It looks awfully small and cheap," said Elizabeth.

"All the more chance for us to help!" said Shirley. "It will be good for us."

"What could you do to help a church?" asked Elizabeth. "Give money to paint it? The paint is scaling off."

"We couldn't give much money," said Carol, "because we don't have it. But there are lots of things to do in a church besides give. You teach in Sunday school, and you wait on tables at suppers when they have Ladies' Aid."

"Maybe they'll ask you to play the organ, Shirley," suggested George.

"Oh, George!" reproved Shirley. "They'll have plenty who can play better than I can. Remember I haven't had time to practice for ages."

"She's a crackerjack at the piano!" confided George to Graham in a low growl. "She hasn't had a lesson since Father died, but before that she used to be at it all the time. She c'n sing, too. You oughtta hear her."

"I'm sure I'd like to," agreed Graham. "I wonder if you'll help me get her to sing sometime if I come out to call after you're settled."

"Sure!" said George. "But she mebbe won't do it. She's awful nutty about singing sometimes. She's not stuck on herself or nothing."

But the church was left far behind, and the city swept into view. They were nearing home now, and Graham insisted on knowing where they lived, so he could put them at their door. Shirley would have pleaded an errand and had them let off in the business part of town. But George airily gave the street and number, and Shirley couldn't prevail upon Graham to stop at his office and let them go their way.

And so the last few minutes of the drive were silent for Shirley, and her cheeks flushed with humiliation over the dark, narrow street where they would presently arrive. Perhaps when he saw it this cultured young man would think they were too poor and common to be good tenants even for a barn. But when they stopped before the two-story brick house, you would have thought from the young man's face as he glanced at the number that the house was a marble front on the most exclusive avenue in the city. He helped Shirley and Carol out with grace, as if they were millionaire's daughters, and spoke to George as if he were an old chum.

"I want you to come and see me next Saturday," called Elizabeth to Carol as the car glided away from the curb. "And I'm coming out to help you get settled—remember!"

The brother and two sisters stood in front of their house and watched the car move away. Were they dreaming? They rubbed their eyes as the car disappeared around the corner, then turned to look up at the familiar windows and make sure where they were. For a moment they discussed how they should explain to the waiting mother why they happened to be home so early.

It was finally decided George should hunt up a drayman and find out what he would charge to move their things to the country, and Shirley should go to a neighbor's to inquire about a stove she heard they wanted to sell. Then Carol could go in alone, and there would be nothing to explain. There was no telling when either George or Shirley would have a holiday again, and it was as well to get these things arranged as soon as possible.

Meanwhile, Elizabeth Graham was questioning her brother, having taken the vacant front seat.

"Sid, where did you find those dear people? I think they're just great! And are they really going to live in that barn? Won't that be fun? I wish Mother'd let me go out and spend a month with them. I mean to ask her. That Carol is the nicest girl ever. She's just a dear!"

"Now look here, kid," said Graham, turning to his sister. "I want you to understand a thing or two. I took you on this expedition because I thought I could trust you. See?"

Elizabeth nodded.

"Well, I don't want a lot of talk at home about this. Do you understand? I want you to wait and go slow. If things seem to be all right later, you can ask Carol to come and see you. But you'll have to look out. She may not have fine clothes to go visiting in, and they seem fairly proud. I guess they've lost their money. Their father died a couple of years ago, and they've been up against it. They do seem like awfully nice people, I'll admit. And if it's all right later on, you can get to be friends, but you'll have to go slow. Mother wouldn't understand it, and she mustn't be annoyed, you know. I'll take you out to see them sometime when they get settled if it seems all right. But until then can you keep your tongue still?"

Elizabeth's face fell, but she gave her word to her brother immediately.

"But can't I have her out for a weekend, Sid? Can't I tell Mother anything about her? I could lend her some dresses."

"You go slow, kid, and leave the matter to me. I'll tell Mother about them when I've had a chance to see a little more of them and am sure Mother wouldn't mind. But don't fret. I'll take you out when I go on business, and you'll see her soon."

Elizabeth had to be content with that. She perceived that for some reason her brother didn't care to have the matter talked over in the family. She knew they'd tease him about his interest in a girl who wanted to rent his barn, and she felt herself that Shirley was too fine to be talked about in that way. The family wouldn't understand unless they saw her.

"I know what you mean, Sid," she said after a thoughtful pause. "You want the folks to see them before they judge what they are, don't you?"

"Exactly," said Sidney. "That's what makes you such a good pal, kid. You always understand."

Elizabeth smiled again and patted her brother's sleeve.

"Good old Sid," she murmured. "You're all right. And I know you're going to take me out to that barn soon. Aren't you going to fix it up for them a little? They can't live there that way. It would be a fine place to live if the windows were bigger and it had doors like a house, and a porch and some fireplaces. A stone fireplace in the middle there opposite that door! Wouldn't that be perfect? And they'll need electric lights and some bathrooms, of course."

Her brother leaned back and laughed.

"You wouldn't make much of a hand to live in a barn," he said. "You're too much of an aristocrat. How much do you want for your money? My dear, they don't expect tiled bathrooms and electric lights and inlaid floors when they rent a barn for the summer."

"But aren't you going to do anything, Sid?"

"Well, I can't do much, for Miss Hollister would suspect right away. She's very businesslike, and she has suspicions already because I said I was going to put in partitions. She isn't an object of charity, you know. I imagine they're all fairly proud."

Elizabeth sat quietly. It was the first time she'd ever contemplated what it would be like to be poor.

Her brother watched her with interest. He had a feeling it would be very good for Elizabeth to know these Hollisters.

Suddenly he brought the car to a stop before the office of a lumberyard they were passing.

"I'm going in here for a minute to see if I can get a man to put in those partitions."

Elizabeth studied the office window through whose large dusty panes could be seen tall strips of molding, unpainted window frames and a fluted column or two, evidently ready to fill an order. The sign over the door indicated that window sashes, doors and blinds were to be had. Suddenly Elizabeth sat up straight and read the sign again, strained her eyes to see through the window, and then opened the car door and sprang out. In a moment more she stood beside her brother, pointing to a large window frame that stood against the wall.

"What is it, kid?" he asked kindly.

"Sid, why can't you put on great big windows like that? They'd never notice the windows, you know. It would be so nice to have plenty of light and air."

"That's so," he murmured. "I might change the windows some without being noticed."

Then he inquired of the man at the desk, "What's the price of that window? Got any more?"

"Yes," said the man, looking up interested, "got half a dozen, made especially for a party, and then he wasn't pleased. Claimed he ordered sash-winders 'stead of casement. If you can use these six, we'll make you a special price."

"Oh, take them, Sid! They're perfectly lovely," said Elizabeth. "They're casement windows with diamond panes. They'll be so quaint and artistic in that stone!"

"Well, I don't know how they'll fit," said the young man. "I don't want to make it seem as if I was trying to put on too much style."

"No, Sid, it won't seem that way. They'll never notice the windows are bigger, and casement windows aren't like a regular house. See, they'll open wide like doors. I think it would be just perfect!"

"All right, we'll see! We'll take the man out with us. If he says it can be done, I'll take them."

"That's just what it needed!" she declared. "They couldn't live in the dark on rainy days. You must put two in the front on each side of the door and one on each end. The back windows will do well enough."

"Well, come on. Mr. Jones is going out with me at once. Do you want to go with us, or shall I call a taxi and send you home?" asked her brother.

"I'm going with you, of course," said Elizabeth, hurrying out to the car as if she thought the thing would be done all wrong without her.

So Elizabeth sat in the back seat alone, while her brother and the contractor discussed the price of lumber and the relative values of wood and stone for building purposes, and the car retraced its earlier path.

They stopped on the way out and picked up one of Mr. Jones's carpenters who was just leaving a job with his toolbox. He climbed into the back seat and sat as far away from the blue-velvet miss as possible, while taking furtive notes to tell his own little girl about her when he went home.

Elizabeth stepped out and walked about the barn with them, listening to what they said.

The two men took out pencils and foot rules and measured and figured. Elizabeth watched them with bright, attentive eyes, whispering a suggestion now and then to her brother.

"They can't go up and down a ladder all the time," she offered. "There should be some rough stairs with a railing, at least as good as our back stairs at home."

"How about it?" said Graham aloud to the contractor. "Can you put in some steps, just rough ones, to the left? I'm going to have a party out here camping for a while this summer, and I want it to be safe. Need a railing, you know, so nobody will fall."

The man measured the space with his eye.

"Just want plain steps framed up with a handrail?" he said, squinting up again. "Guess we better start 'em up this way to the back wall and then turn back from a landing. That'll suit the overhead space best. Just pine, you want 'em, I s'pose?"

Elizabeth stood like a blue bird alight on the doorsill, watching and listening. She was a woman and saw great possibilities in the building. She would have enjoyed ordering parquet flooring and carved posts and making a palace.

The sun was setting behind the purply hill and sending a glint from the weather vane on the church spire when they started back to the city. Elizabeth gazed at it and wondered about the rapt expression on Shirley's face when she spoke of "working" in the church. How could one get pleasure out of that? She meant to find out. At present her life was monotonous, and she longed to have some new interests.

That night after she'd gone to bed she lay in her luxurious, downy nest and tried to think how it would be to live in that barn and fall asleep in the hayloft. Suddenly life's mysteries were upon her. Why, for instance, was she born into the Graham family with money and culture and opportunity, and that sweet, bright Carol was born into the Hollister family where they had a hard time living at all?

Chapter 9

Early the next morning Sidney Graham was in his office at the telephone. He conferred with the carpenter, agreeing to meet him out at the barn and make final arrangements about the windows in a short time. Then he called up the trolley company and the electric company and made arrangements with them to have a wire run from the road to his barn, with a satisfactory agreement whereby he could pay them a certain sum for the use of as much light as he needed. This done, he called up an electrician and arranged for him to send some men out that morning to wire the barn.

He hurried through his morning mail, giving his stenographer a free hand with answering some of the letters, and then rushed out to Glenside.

Three men were already there, two of them stonemasons, working away under the contractor's direction. They had already begun working at the massive stone around the windows, striking musical blows from a light scaffolding that made the old barn look as if it had suddenly awakened and gone to housecleaning. Sidney Graham stopped his car by the road and got out. He liked for things to be done on time. If this contractor did well on the job he'd see that he got bigger projects to do. He liked it that his work had been begun at once.

The next car brought a quartette of carpenters, and before young Graham went back to the city a truck arrived with lumber and window frames. This new toy barn that had suddenly come into his possession fascinated him, and he could hardly tear himself away from it and go back to business. One wouldn't have supposed he needed to do so, either, since he was so well off that he could have managed comfortably the rest of his life without any more money. But he was conscientious and believed that no living being had a right to exist in idleness. Further, he had gone into business to do his best and keep up the honorable name of his father's firm. So after he'd given careful directions for the electricians when they came he rushed back to his office.

The next two days were filled with adventure. He raced from office to barn and back to the office again, and before evening of the second day he decided a telephone was a necessity in the barn, at least while the work was proceeding. So he called up the telephone company and arranged for connection to be installed at once. That evening he wrote a short note to Miss Shirley Hollister, telling her the partitions were under way and would soon be completed, and in a few days he'd send her the key so she might begin to transport her belongings to the new home.

The next morning, when Graham drove out to the stone barn, he found that the front windows were in and gave an inviting appearance to the edifice, both outside and in. As Elizabeth had surmised, the big latticed windows opening inward like casement doors seemed quite in keeping with the rough stone structure. Graham began to wonder why all barns didn't adopt this style of window; they were so attractive. He was thoroughly convinced the new tenants wouldn't likely remember or notice the difference in the windows; he was sure he wouldn't have unless his attention had been called to them in some way. Of course the sills and sashes looked new, but he gave orders for them to be painted an unobtrusive dark green which would match the mossy roof, and he trusted his particular young tenant wouldn't think he'd done anything to change the windows. If she did, he'd have to think up some excuse.

But as he stood at the top of the grassy slope and gazed about, he noticed the great pile of stones under each window from the masonry that had been torn away to make room for the larger sashes, and an idea came to him.

"Mr. Jones!" he called to the contractor, who had just come over on the car to see how the work was progressing. "Wouldn't there be stones enough all together from all the windows to build some kind of a crude chimney and fireplace?" he asked.

Mr. Jones thought there would, and there were stones enough down in the meadow to piece out with in case they needed more anyway. Where would Mr. Graham want the fireplace? Directly opposite the front doors? He'd thought of suggesting that himself but didn't know if Mr. Graham wanted to go to any more expense.

"By all means make that fireplace!" exclaimed the owner. "This is going to be a fine place when it's finished, isn't it? I declare I might even like to come out here and live."

"It would make a fine old house, sir," said the contractor respectfully, looking up almost reverently at the barn. "I'd like to see it with verandys and more winders and a few such. You don't see many of these here old stone buildings around now. They knew how to build 'em substantial in those old times, so they did."

"H'm! Yes. It would make a fine site for a house, wouldn't it?" said the young man, surveying the improvements. "We'll have to think about that sometime perhaps. But I think it looks very nice for the present."

At each end of the barn a good room, long and narrow, had been partitioned off, each of which by use of a curtain would make two very large rooms; yet the main section of the floor looked as large as ever. A simple stairway of plain boards had been constructed a little to one side of the middle toward the back, going up to the loft, which had been made safe for the children by a plain railing consisting of a few uprights with strips across. The darkening slats at the small windows in the loft had been torn away and shutters substituted that would open wide and let in air and light. Rough spots in the floor had been mended, and around the place both upstairs and down, and even in the basement below, electric wires ran with simple lights and switches conveniently arranged, so the whole place could be made a blaze of light.

Graham didn't like to think of this family of unprotected women and children coming out into the country without arrangements to make them feel safe. For this reason also he installed the telephone. He talked it over with the agent, paying a certain sum for its installation, and had a telephone put in that they could pay for whenever they used it. This would make the young householder feel more comfortable about leaving her mother out in the country all day and prevent her pride from being hurt. The telephone was there. She didn't have to use it unless needed. He felt he could explain that to her. If she didn't like it, of course she could have it taken away.

He wanted to do more things to make the place habitable, but he didn't dare. Sometimes even now his conscience troubled him. What did he know about these people, and what kind of flighty youth was he becoming that he let a strange girl's appealing face drive him to such lengths? Telephone, electric lights, stairs, and a fireplace in a barn! It was preposterous, and, if his family found out, he'd never hear the last of it—of that he was certain.

At such times he would hunt up his young sister and carry her off for a long drive in the car, always ending up at Glenside Road, where she exclaimed and praised to his heart's satisfaction and renewed her promise not to tell anyone until he was ready.

Indeed, Elizabeth was wild with delight. She wanted to find some of her mother's old Turkish rugs stowed away in dark closets, decorate the walls with pictures and bric-à-brac from her own room, and smother the place in flowering shrubs for the tenants' arrival. But her brother forbade more being done. He waited with fear and trembling for when the clear-eyed young tenant would look upon the changes he'd already made. Something told him she wouldn't stand charity, and he mustn't go beyond a certain point if he wished to see her again.

At last one morning he called her on the telephone at her office.

"My sister and I were thinking of going out to see how things are progressing at the Glenside place," he said. "I was wondering if you'd care to come along and look things over. What time do you get through at your office this afternoon?"

"That's very kind of you, Mr. Graham," said Shirley, "but I'm afraid that won't be possible. I'm not usually finished until half past five. I might get through by five, but not much sooner, and that would be too late for you."

"Not at all, Miss Hollister. That would be very agreeable. Some matters will keep me here late tonight, so that will be just right for me. Shall I call for you at five? Or is that too soon?"

"Oh, no, I can be ready by then, I'm sure," said Shirley. "You're very kind—"

"Not at all. It will be a pleasure," came the answer. "Then I'll call at your office at five." The receiver clicked at the other end, leaving Shirley in a whirl of doubt and joy.

How wonderful! And yet should she go? Would Mother think it was all right? His sister was going, but was it right for her to accept this much attention even in a business way? It wasn't customary or necessary, and both he and she knew it. He was just doing it to be nice.

And then there was Mother. She must send a message somehow, or Mother would be frightened when she didn't come home at her usual time.

She finally reached Carol at her school and told her to tell Mother she might not be home till after seven. Then she rushed to complete her work before five o'clock.

But when she came down at the appointed time, she found Carol sitting excitedly in the back seat with Elizabeth, almost bursting with the double pleasure of the ride and of surprising her sister.

"They came to school for me and took me home, and I explained to

Mother I was going with you to look at a place we were going to move to. I started the potatoes and put the meat in the oven, and Mother's going to tell George how to finish supper when he gets home. And, oh, isn't it lovely?"

"Indeed it is lovely," said Shirley. Her face flushed with pleasure, and her eyes spoke gratitude to the young man who was opening the door for her to sit beside him.

The spring had made tremendous advances in her work during the ten days since they'd driven that way before. The flush of green the willows had worn had become a bright feather of foliage, and the maples had sent out crimson tassels to offset them. Down in the meadows and along the roadside the grass was thick and green, and the bare brown fields had disappeared. Brooks sang as they glided under bridges, and the birds darted here and there in noisy pairs. Frail wavering blossoms starred the swampy places, and the air was perfumed with scents of living things.

But when they came in sight of the barn, Elizabeth and her brother grew silent from sheer desire to talk and not act as if anything was different about it. Now that they had actually brought Shirley here, the new windows seemed to flaunt themselves in their shining mossy paint and diamond panes, so that the two conspirators were deeply embarrassed and dared not face what they'd done.

Carol broke the silence that had come upon them all.

"Oh! Oh! Oh!" she exclaimed. "Shirley, just look! New, big windows! Isn't that great? Now you needn't worry whether it will be dark for Mother on days when she can't go out! Isn't that the best ever?"

Shirley looked, while her cheeks grew pink and her eyes shone. She opened her lips to speak and then closed them again, for words wouldn't come, and tears came instead. But she drove them back and then managed to say, "Oh, Mr. Graham! You've gone to so much trouble!"

"No, no trouble at all," he said almost crossly. He hadn't wanted her to notice those windows, at least not yet.

"You see, it was this way. The windows were left over from another order, and I had a chance to get them at a bargain. I thought they might as well be put in now as any time, and you get the benefit of them. The barn really needed more light. It was a very dark barn. Hadn't you noticed it? I can't see how my grandfather thought it would do to have so little light and air. But you know in the old times they didn't use to have such advanced ideas about ventilation and germs and things—"

He felt he was getting on well until he looked down at the girl's clear eyes and knew she was seeing through his talk. She hadn't the nerve to tell him, though, so he boldly continued, making up fine stories about things barns needed until he almost believed them himself. When he got through, he needed only to finish with "And if it isn't so, it should be" to have a regular Water-Baby argument out of it. He managed to talk on in this vein until he could stop the car and help Shirley out, and together they all went up the velvety green incline to the door.

"It's beautiful, just beautiful!" murmured Shirley. She couldn't yet realize she was to come to this charmed spot to live in a few days.

Graham unlocked the doors and sent them rolling back with a touch, showing what ball bearings and careful workmanship can do. The group stepped inside and looked again.

The setting sun was casting a red glow through the diamond panes and over the wide floor. The new partitions, unpainted, for Graham hadn't dared go further, were mellowed into ruby hangings. The stone fireplace rose at the opposite side of the room, and the new staircase was just at the side, all in the ruddy evening glow that carried rich dusky shadows into the corners and hung a curtain of vagueness over blemishes.

Then, before they'd taken in the changes, beyond the partitions they expected, Graham stepped to the side of the door and touched a button. Behold, a myriad of lights burst forth about the place, making it bright as midday.

"Oh! Oh! Oh!" breathed Carol in awe and wonder, and "Oh!" again, as if she could say nothing else.

But Shirley only looked and caught her breath. It seemed a palace too fine for their means, and a sudden fear gripped her.

"Oh, Mr. Graham! You've done too much!" she choked. "You shouldn't have done it! We can never afford to pay for all this!"

"Not at all!" said young Graham quickly. "This isn't anything. The electric people gave permission for this, and I thought it would be safer than lamps and candles. It cost hardly anything for the wiring. Our regular man who attends to the wiring and lights at the office did it. It was simple and will make things a lot more convenient for you. It's nothing to the company. They just gave permission for a wire to be run from the pole there. Of course they might not do it for everyone. But I have some good friends in the company, so it's all right."

"But the fireplace!" said Shirley, walking over to look at it. "It's beautiful! It's like what you see in magazine pictures of beautiful houses."

"Why, it was just the stones left from cutting the windows larger. I thought they might as well be used. It wasn't much more work to pile them up that way while the men were here than if we'd had them carted away."

Here Carol interrupted.

"Shirley! There's a telephone! A real telephone!"

Shirley's accusing eyes were on her landlord.

"It was put in for our convenience while the workmen were here," he explained defensively. "It's a pay phone, you see, and is no expense except when used. It can be taken out if you don't care to have it, of course. But it occurred to me since it was here your mother might feel more comfortable out here all day if she could call you when she needed to."

Shirley's face was a picture of varying emotions as she listened, but relief and gratitude conquered as she turned to him.

"I believe you've thought of everything," she said at last. "I've worried about that all week. I wondered if Mother would be afraid out in the country with only the children and the neighbors not quite near enough to call. But this solves the difficulty. You're sure it hasn't cost you a lot to have this put in?"

"Why, don't you know the telephone company is glad to have their phones wherever they can get them?" he evaded. "Now don't worry about anything more. You'll find hardships enough living in a barn without fretting about the few conveniences we could manage."

"But this is real luxury!" she said, sitting down on the steps and looking up where the lights blazed from the loft. "You've put lights up there, too, and a railing. I was so afraid Doris would fall down sometime!"

"I'm glad to find you're human, after all, and have a few fears!" declared the owner, laughing. "I'd begun to think you were Spartan through and through and weren't afraid of anything. Yes, I had the men put what lumber they had left into that railing. I thought it wasn't safe to have it open like that, and I didn't want you to sue me for life or limb, you know. There's one thing I haven't managed yet, and that's piping water up from the spring. I haven't gotten hold of the right man yet. But he's coming out tomorrow, and I hope it can be done. There's a spring on the hill back of us, and I believe it's high enough to get the water to this floor. If it is it'll make your work much easier and involve only a few rods of pipe."

"Oh, but, indeed, you mustn't do anything more!" pleaded Shirley. "I'll feel so ashamed paying such little rent."

"But," said Graham in his most dignified business manner, "you don't at all realize how much lower rents are in the country, isolated like this, than they are in the city, and you haven't realized how many inconveniences you have to contend with. When you return to the city in the winter, you'll be glad to get away from here."

"Never!" Shirley said and shuddered. "Oh, never! You don't know how dreadful it seems that we'll have to go back. But of course I suppose we shall. One couldn't live in a barn in the winter, even though it's a palace for the summer." She looked about wistfully.

Then she said in a low tone, for the young man's benefit alone: "I think God must have made you do all this for us!" She turned and walked swiftly over to one of the new casement windows, looking out at the red glow the sinking sun had left in the sky. And against the fringes of willows and maples shone out the bright weather vane on the spire of the little white church in the valley.

"I think God must have sent you to teach me and my little sister a few things," said a low voice just behind Shirley as she struggled with tired, happy tears that blurred her eyes. But when she turned to smile at the owner of the voice, he was walking over by the door and talking to Carol. Soon they tumbled into the car and returned to the city.

That night the Hollister children told their mother they'd found a place in which to live.

Chapter 10

The crisis was precipitated by Shirley's finding her mother crying when she came up to see her.

"Now, Mother dear! What's the matter?" she cried, sitting down on the bed and drawing her mother's head into her lap.

But it was sometime before Mrs. Hollister recovered her calmness, and Shirley began to be frightened. At last, when she'd kissed and comforted her, she called to the others to come upstairs quickly.

George and Harley got there first with dish towels over their shoulders, then Carol with her arithmetic and pencil, and finally little Doris trudging up breathless, one step at a time. And all were asking at once, "What's the matter?"

"Why, here's our mother lying here all by herself, crying because she doesn't know where in the world we can find a house!" explained Shirley. "So I think it's time we told our beautiful secret, don't you?"

"Yes," chorused the children, although Harley and Doris had no idea until then that there was a beautiful secret.

"Well, I think we better tell it," said Shirley, looking at George and Carol. "We don't want Mother worrying." So they all clustered around her on the bed and the floor and sat expectantly while Shirley told.

"You see, Mother, it's this way. George and I've been looking around a good deal lately, and we hadn't found a thing in the city that would do. So one day I took a trolley ride out of the city and found something I think will do nicely for the summer anyway, and that will give us time to look around and decide. Mother, would you mind camping if we made you a nice, comfortable place?"

"Camping!" said Mrs. Hollister in dismay. "Dear child! In a tent?"

"No, Mother, not in a tent. There's a–sort of a house—that is, there's a building where we could sleep and put our furniture. But there's a lovely outdoors. Wouldn't you like that for Doris and yourself?"

"Oh, yes," sighed the mother. "I'd like it. But, child, you haven't any idea what you're talking about. Any place in the country costs terribly, even a shanty—"

"That's it, Mother—call it a shanty!" put in Carol. "Mother, would you object to living in a shanty all summer if it was good and clean, and you had plenty of outdoors around it?"

"No, of course not, Carol, if it was respectable. I wouldn't want to take my children among a lot of low-down people—"

"Of course not, Mother!" put in Shirley. "And there's nothing of that sort. It's all respectable, and the few neighbors are nice, respectable people. Now, Mother, if you're willing to trust us, we'd like to leave it at that and not tell you more about it till we take you there. George and Carol and I have seen the place, and we think it'll be just the thing. There's plenty of room and sky and a big elm tree and birds, and it only costs ten dollars a month. Now, Mother, will you trust us for the rest and not ask any questions?"

The mother looked from one to another and, seeing their eager faces, broke into a weary smile.

"Well, I suppose I'll have to," she said with a doubtful sigh. "But I can't understand how any place you could get would be only that price, and I'm afraid you haven't thought of a lot of things."

"Yes, Mother, we've thought of everything—and then some," said Shirley, stooping to kiss the thin cheek. "We're sure you're going to like this when you see it. It isn't a palace, of course. You don't expect plate-glass windows, you know."

"Well, hardly," said Mrs. Hollister dryly, struggling to be cheerful. She could see that her children were trying to make a cheerful occasion out of their necessity. She was never one to hang back, so she assented.

"You're sure," she began, looking at Shirley with troubled eyes. "There are so many things to think of, and you're so young."

"Trust me, Mother," said Shirley, remembering the fireplace and the electric lights. "It really isn't so bad. And there's a beautiful hill for Doris to run down and a place to hang a hammock for you right under a big tree where a bird has built its nest."

"Oh–h?" echoed Doris. "And could I see de birdie?"

"Yes, darling, you can watch him every day and see him fly through the blue sky."

"It's all right, Mother," said George in a businesslike tone. "You'll think it's great after you get used to it. Carol and I are crazy over it."

"But can both of you get to your work? I wouldn't want you to take long, lonely walks, you know," said the troubled mother.

"Right on the trolley line, Mother, and the difference in rent will more than pay our fare."

"Besides, I'm thinking of buying a bicycle from one of the fellows. He says he'll sell it for five dollars, and I can pay fifty cents a month. Then I could go in on my bike in good weather and save that much," offered George.

"Oh, say!" said Harley breathlessly. "Then I could ride it sometimes, too."

"Sure!" said George.

"Now, Mother," said Shirley in her "brigadier-general" manner, as the children called it, "put your worries out of your head this minute and go to sleep. Your business is to get strong enough to be moved out there. When you get there, you'll get well so quick you won't know yourself. But you've got to rest from now on, or you won't be able to go when the time comes. Then what will happen? Will you promise?"

Amid the laughing and pleading of her children the mother promised, half smiling, half tearful, and succumbed to being prepared for the night. Then they tiptoed to the dining room for a council.

It was still two weeks before they must vacate the brick house—plenty of time to get comfortably settled before they took their mother out there.

It was decided that George and Shirley would go out the next evening from their work, not returning for supper but eating downtown. Now that the place was lighted and they'd been told to use the light as freely as they chose, with no charge, the question of getting settled was no longer a problem. They could do it evenings after work. First they'd need to clean house, and for that they needed pails, pans, brooms, mops, and the like. It would be good to take a load of things out the next day if possible.

So George went out to interview the man with the moving wagon, while Shirley and Carol listed the things to go in that first load. George came back and reported that the man could come at half past four in the afternoon. If they had the things ready, his son could help load them, and they'd get out to Glenside by six o'clock or seven at the latest. Harley might go along if he liked and help unload at the other end.

Harley was excited at the responsibility placed on him and at the prospect of seeing the new home. It almost made up for leaving "the fellows" and living in a strange place.

The young people were late getting to bed that night, for they had to get things together so Carol wouldn't have her hands full the next day when she got home from school. Then they hunted up soap, scrubbing pails, rags, brushes and brooms. When they finally went to bed, they were too excited to sleep.

Of course they encountered many hindrances to their plans and delays waiting for the cartman, who didn't always keep his word. But the days passed, and everyone saw some progress toward making a home out of the barn. Shirley wouldn't let them stay past ten o'clock, for they must be ready for work the next morning; so cleaning the barn progressed slowly. After the first night a neighbor sat with their mother and Doris, enabling Carol and Harley to come out on the car to help. So with four willing workers the barn took on a nice smell of soap and water.

The old furniture arrived gradually and was put in place, until by the end of the first week the middle room and the dining room and kitchen looked livable.

On Saturday evening of that first week, Shirley was sitting on the old couch beside the fireplace, resting, watching George, who was reeling out a stormy version of chopsticks on the piano, and gazing about on her growing home. Suddenly they heard a gentle tapping at the barn door, and George as the man of the house went to the door with his gruffest air on. But it melted at once when he saw the landlord and his sister standing in the moonlight.

"Are you ready for callers?" asked Graham, taking off his hat in greeting. "Elizabeth and I took a spin out this way, and we saw the light and thought we'd stop and see if we could help any. My, how much like home you've made it! This is great!"

Sidney Graham stood in the center of the big room and looked about him.

The young people had put things in order as far as they'd gone. A fire was laid in the big stone fireplace, ready for lighting, and gave a homey, cleared-up look to the whole place. On each side of the chimney stood a simple set of bookshelves filled with volumes that had the appearance of being beloved and in intimate association with the family. On top of the shelves Carol had placed some bric-à-brac and in the center of each a tall vase. Beside them were a few photographs in simple frames: a strong-faced man with eyes reminding one of Shirley and a brow like George's; a delicate-featured, refined woman with a sweet, sensitive mouth and eyes like Carol's; and a lovely child with fair curls.

The old couch stood at one side of the fireplace, at a convenient angle for watching the firelight, without hiding the bookshelves. On the other side, with its back toward the first landing of the crude staircase, stood an old upright piano with a pile of music on the top and a book of songs open on the rack. On the floor in the space between was spread a faded ingrain rug, its original colors and pattern long since blended into neutral grays and browns, which strangely harmonized with the rustic surroundings. A few comfortable but worn chairs were scattered about in a homelike way, and a few pictures in plain frames were hung on the clean new partitions. Under one stood a small oak desk and a few writing materials. A little farther a plain library table held a few magazines and papers and a cherished book or two. No attempt was made to cover the bare floor, except by a small dingy rug or two or a strip of carpet carefully brushed and flung here and there in front of a chair. There was no pretension and therefore no incongruity. The only luxurious thing in the place was the bright electric light, and yet it all looked pleasant and inviting.

"Say, now, this is great!" repeated the young landlord, sinking into the nearest chair. "Who would ever have imagined you could make a barn look like this? Why, you're a genius, Miss Hollister. You're a real artist."

Shirley, in an old gingham dress, with her sleeves rolled up and her hair straying about her flushed cheeks, stood before him in dismay. She'd been working hard and was conscious of the brief time before they must be finished. To have company now—and such company— confused her. But the honest admiration in his voice did much to restore her equilibrium. She rolled down her sleeves and sat down to receive her callers properly. He at once insisted she shouldn't delay on his account and immediately plunged into some question about the water pipes, which created a more businesslike footing and relieved her embarrassment. He walked over to the partitioned corner which was to be the kitchen, telling Shirley it would be no trouble to run a pipe from the spring and have a faucet put in and that it would be done the next day. Then he called to Elizabeth.

"Kid, what did you do with those eats you brought along? I think it would be a good time to hand them out. I'm hungry. Suppose you take George out to the car to help you bring them in, and let's have a picnic!"

Turning to Shirley, he explained: "Elizabeth and I are great ones to have something along to eat. It makes a person hungry to ride."

The children needed no second word but hurried out to the car and returned with a bag of oranges and boxes of cakes and crackers. Then they ate, laughing and chattering, not at all like landlord and tenants.

"Now what needs to be done next?" demanded the landlord as soon as they'd finished. "I'm going to help. We're not here to hinder, and we must make up for the time we've stopped you. What were you and George doing, Carol, when we arrived?"

"Unpacking dishes," giggled Carol, looking at the frowning Shirley, who was shaking her head at Carol behind Graham's back. Shirley had no desire for the landlord to see the dismal state of the Hollister crockery.

But the young man wasn't easily put off and to Carol's secret delight insisted on helping, despite Shirley's protests that they didn't need to do anything more that evening. He and Elizabeth crossed to the dining room end of the barn and helped unpack dishes, pans, kettles, knives and forks and arrange them on the shelves George had improvised from a large old bookcase that used to be his father's.

After all, there was something in good breeding, thought Shirley, for from the way Mr. Graham handled the old cracked dishes and set them up, you'd have thought they were Haviland china. He never seemed to see the cracks. One might have thought he'd been a family member for years; he made things seem so comfortable and sociable.

They accomplished wonders that night, for Shirley let them stay until nearly eleven o'clock "just this once." Then Shirley, Carol, and Elizabeth piled in the backseat, with George and the happy Harley beside Graham in the front. The young Hollisters were having the time of their lives, and as for the Grahams, they may have been, too. Certainly society had never seen on Sidney Graham's face that contented expression the moon shone down on that night. And, after all, they arrived home almost as soon as if they'd taken the ten-o'clock trolley.

After that on one pretext or another those Grahams were always dropping in on the Hollisters at their work and managing to "help," and presently even Shirley ceased to be annoyed or apologize.

The east end of the barn had been selected for bedrooms. A pair of cretonne curtains was stretched across the long, narrow room from wall to partition, leaving the front room for their mother's bed and Doris's crib, and the back room for Shirley and Carol. The boys took possession of the loft with shouts and elaborate plans and spread out their treasures, with enough room to display them.

Little by little the Hollisters were getting settled. It wasn't so hard, after all, because they had that glorious "attic" in which to store things not needed below, and they had the whole basement for tubs and things and a lovely faucet down there, too, so a lot of work could be done below the living floor. It seemed ideal to the girls, who were accustomed to the cramped quarters of a tiny city house.

At last even the beds were made, and everything was moved but the bed and a few necessities in their mother's room, which were to come the next day while they were moving their mother.

Moving Mother was a problem to Shirley until Graham anticipated her need and said in a matter-of-fact way he hoped Mrs. Hollister would let him take her to her new home in his car. Then Shirley's eyes filled with tears of gratitude. She knew her mother couldn't travel comfortably in a trolley yet, and the price of a taxicab was more than they could afford. She'd intended to get one anyway, but she didn't need to now.

Shirley's words of gratitude were few and simple, but something in her eyes as she lifted them to Graham's face set his heart glowing and fully repaid him for his trouble.

Before they left the barn that night they set the table; it looked cozy and inviting with a white cloth and the dishes on it to look their best. Shirley glanced back at the whole scene: the comfortable living room, the open door into the dining room on one hand and the view of a white bed on the other side through the bedroom door. She smiled, switched off the electric light and stepped out into the spring night. Graham, who had watched her as one might watch the opening of a rare flower, closed and locked the door behind them and followed her down the grassy slope to the car.

"Do you know," he said, "that it's been great to watch you make a real home out of this bare barn? It's wonderful! It's like a miracle. I wouldn't have believed it could be done. But you've done it! It's going to be a delightful home."

Something in his tone made Shirley forget he was rich and a stranger and her landlord. She lifted her face to the night.

"You can't know how much like heaven it's going to be for us after coming from that awful little house," she said. "But if it hadn't been for you I never could have done it."

"Oh, nonsense, Miss Hollister! You mustn't think of it. I haven't done anything at all, just the simplest things that were absolutely necessary."

"Oh, I understand," said Shirley. "And I can't ever repay you, but I think God will. That's the kind of thing the kingdom of heaven is made of."

"Oh, really, now," said Graham, embarrassed. He wasn't used to being connected with the kingdom of heaven. "You—you overestimate it. As for pay, I don't ask any better than the fun my sister and I have had helping you get settled. We never really moved, you see. We've always gone off and had someone do it for us. I've learned a lot since I've known you."

That night as she prepared to lie down on the mattress and blanket that had been left behind for her and Carol to camp out on, Shirley remembered her first worries about Mr. Graham. She wondered whether he thought she'd been forward in any way and what her mother would think when she heard the whole story of the new landlord. Up to this time the secret had been kept from her, with the children clapping their hands over wayward mouths that started to utter telltale sentences. The mystery grew and became almost like Christmas-time for little Doris and her mother.

Mrs. Hollister, however, as she lay awake that last night on her bed in the bare room in the brick house, had many misgivings and wondered whether she mightn't be sighing to be back even here twenty-four hours later. She held her peace since she could do nothing about it, even if she was stepping out of the frying pan into the fire. But the tumult in her heart was by no means bliss. So midnight approached, and the weary family slept for the last night in the cramped old house where they'd lived since trouble and poverty had come upon them.

Chapter 11

Shirley was awake early that morning, too excited to sleep through the night. Now that they were actually moved into a barn she had fears and doubts about it. She imagined her delicate mother shrinking as if struck when she first learned they'd come to this. Try as she would to recall the sensible philosophy that led her to this, she felt only trouble. She longed to rush into her mother's room, tell her all about it and get the dreaded episode over. But it was inevitable now. They were moved. They had barely enough money to pay the cartage and get things started before next payday. She must take her mother there, even if she shrank from the idea.

Of course her mother had always been sensible, but responsibility for decision making rested so heavily on her young shoulders that morning that it seemed as if she could no longer bear the strain.

They still had a good fire in the kitchen range. Shirley hurried to the kitchen, prepared toast, a poached egg and tea, and took it to her mother's room, tiptoeing lightly lest she still slept.

But her mother was awake and glad to see her. She'd been awake since the first streak of dawn had crept into the back window. She looked like someone prepared for the worst. But when she saw her daughter's face, the mother in her triumphed over the woman.

"What's the trouble, little girl? Has something happened?"

The tenderness in her voice was the last straw that broke Shirley's self-control. The tears suddenly sprang into her eyes, and her lip trembled.

"Oh, Mother!" she cried, setting the tray down on a box and fumbling for her handkerchief. "I'm so worried! I'm so afraid you won't like what we've done, and then what shall we do?"

"I shall like it!" said the mother with instant determination. "Don't for a minute think of anything else. After doing something irrevocably, never look back and think you might have done something better. You did the best you could—or you thought you did anyway—and there didn't seem to be anything else at the time. So now just consider it was the very best thing in the world, and don't fret about it. There'll be something nice about it, I'm sure, and goodness knows we've had enough unpleasant things here. We're just going to make it nice, little girl. Remember that! We're going to like it. There's a tree, you say. Well, when we find things we don't like, we'll just go out and look up at our tree and say, 'We've got you, anyway, and we're glad of it!' "

"You blessed little mother!" laughed Shirley, wiping her tears away. "Maybe you'll like it after all, though I've doubted it all night. I wondered if perhaps I shouldn't have told you all about it. But I knew you couldn't judge until you saw it yourself, and we wanted to surprise you."

"Well, I'm determined to be surprised," said the brave woman. "So don't worry. We're going to have a grand time today. Now run along. It's almost time for your car, and you haven't eaten breakfast yet."

Shirley kissed her mother and went smiling down to breakfast, then hurried to the office.

Work at the office was rushed, or Shirley would have asked for a half holiday. But she didn't dare endanger her position by asking at such a busy season. She was glad the next day was Sunday and they'd have a whole day to themselves in the new home before she'd have to hurry to the office again. It would make it seem less lonely for her mother, having them home that first day. She meant to work fast today and get all the letters written before five if possible. Then she'd have time to get home a few minutes before Mr. Graham arrived with his car and see that her mother was comfortably ready. It was too much for Carol to look after everything. Nor did they have neighbors to help out a little, for they were the last tenants in the doomed block to leave. All the others had gone two or three weeks before.

She was so thankful Mother wouldn't have to sleep in those breathless rooms after the heat began. The doctor said she needed rest and air and plenty of sunshine. She'd have those at the barn, and what else mattered? Mother was game. Mother wouldn't let herself feel bad over such a silly thing. They would be more comfortable than they'd been for several years. Think of that wonderful electric light. And clear cold water from the spring! A thrill of ecstasy passed over her, the first she'd let herself feel since she'd taken the responsibility of transplanting her family to a barn.

After all, the day passed quickly. At half past four the telephone rang, and Mr. Graham's voice announced he'd be down at the street door waiting for her in half an hour; she needn't hurry—he'd wait till she was ready. Her heart gave a little start of joy. It was as if school was out and she was going on a picnic like other girls. How nice of him! Yet she heard only friendliness in his voice, such as any kindly disposed land-lord might use if he chose—nothing to feel uncomfortable about. She was relieved that after tonight Mother would know all about it. And if she didn't approve, Shirley could decline any further kindness. Now she'd take Mother's advice and forget everything but the pleasant part.

Meanwhile Carol and Harley bustled about in the empty house like two bumblebees, washing up the dishes, packing everything left for their last night's sleeping in an open box and getting lunch. Doris, running between her mother's room and downstairs, kept singing: "We goin' to tuntry! We goin' to tuntry! See budies an' twees and walk on gween gwass!"

After lunch was over and the dishes packed carefully into the big box between comforters and blankets, Carol had her mother take a nap, with Doris sleeping by her side. After that Carol and Harley tiptoed down to the bare kitchen and sat on a box side by side to talk.

"Say! Ain't you tired, Carol?" said the boy, pushing his hair back from his hot face. "Don't it seem funny we aren't coming back here anymore? It kind of gets my goat I won't see the fellows so often, but it'll be great to ask 'em to see us sometime. Say, do you suppose we really can keep chickens?"

"Sure!" said Carol. "I asked Mr. Graham if we might. George said we should—he was such a good scout we'd want to be sure he'd like it. And he said, 'Sure, it would be great.' He'd like to come out and see them sometime. He said he used to keep chickens himself when he was a kid, and he thought they might have a few too many at their place they could spare to start with. He told me he'd look it up and see soon's we got settled."

"He's a peach, ain't he? Say, has he got a case on Shirl?"

"I don't know," said the girl. "Maybe he has, but he doesn't know it yet, I guess. But anyhow you must promise you'll never breathe such a word. Why, Shirley would just bust right up if you did. I said a lit-tle something to her like that. It wasn't much—just he was awfully nice, and I guess he liked her by the way he looked at her—and she fairly froze. You know the way her eyes get when she's sore at us? She said I must never even think anything like that, or she'd give the place right up, get a few rooms down on South Street and stay in the city all summer! She said Mr. Graham was a gentleman, and she was only a working girl, and it would be a disgrace for her to accept any favors from him except what she could pay for. And it would be an insult for him to offer them, because she was only a working girl and he was a gentleman."

"H'm!" growled Harley. "I guess our sister's as good as he is any day."

"Of course!" snapped Carol. "But he mightn't think so."

"Well, if he don't, he can go to thunder!" bristled Harley. "I'm not going to have him looking down on Shirley. She's as good as his baby-doll sister with her pink cheeks and little white hands and high heels and airs any day! She's a nut."

"Harley! Stop!" declared Carol. "Elizabeth's a dear, and you're not going to talk about her that way. Just because she's pretty and doesn't have to work."

"Well, you said her brother looked down on our sister," declared Harley.

"I did not! I only said he might! I only meant that was the way some gentlemen would. I only said people kind of expect gentlemen to do that."

"Not if they're real gentlemen, they won't. And anyhow he won't. If I find him looking down on Shirley, I'll punch his face for him. Yes, I will! I'm not afraid. George and I could beat the stuffing out of him, and we will if he pulls any looking-down stunts, and don't you forget it!"

"Well, I'm sure he won't," said Carol, putting a soothing sound in her voice as elder sisters learn to do. "If he did look down on her, Shirley would know it—right away she'd know it. Nobody would have to tell her! She'd see it in his voice and smile and everything. If he had, she wouldn't have gone out there to live in the place he owns. So I guess you can trust Shirley. I think he's been great, fixing up that fireplace and stairs and lights and water and everything."

"Well, mebbe!" said Harley grudgingly. "Say, this is slow. I'm going out to meet the fellows when they come from school and see what the game score is. I wish I could play today!"

"You'll be sure to come back in time?" asked Carol.

"Sure! You don't suppose I'd miss going out in that car, do you?" said the brother. "Not on your tintype!"

"Well, maybe there won't be room for you. Maybe Elizabeth'll come along, and you'll have to go in the trolley with George."

"No chance!" declared the boy. "Mr. Graham said I'd ride with him in the front seat, and he looks like a man who keeps his word."

"You see! You know he's a gentleman!" exclaimed Carol. "Well, I think you'd better stay here with me. You'll forget and be late and make a mess waiting for you."

"No, I won't!" said the restless boy. "I can't be bothered sticking 'round this dump all afternoon." Harley seized his cap and disappeared with a whoop around the corner.

After he was gone Carol found she was tired, too, and, curling up on a mattress that was ready for the cartman, was soon asleep. Harley found her that way when he hurried back an hour later, anxious, it must be confessed, lest he'd stayed too long. He stirred up the small household and in no time had Carol in a panic brewing the cup of tea that was to give her mother strength to take the journey, dressing Doris, smoothing her own hair, putting the last things into bags and boxes, and directing the cartman, who arrived half an hour sooner than he promised. Carol was quite a little woman, going from one thing to another and taking everybody's place.

Meanwhile Elizabeth Graham and her brother had been spending the afternoon in business of their own. Elizabeth suggested it, and her brother saw no reason why she shouldn't carry out her plan and why he shouldn't help her.

She came down in the car after lunch, the chauffeur driving her, with a great basket of cut and potted flowers from the home conservatory in the tonneau beside her, carefully wrapped in wax paper. She stopped at the office for her brother, and together they went about to several shops giving orders and making purchases. When they finished they drove out to Glenside to unpack their bundles and baskets. Graham left Elizabeth with the old servant to help her and rushed back to his office, where he telephoned Shirley.

Elizabeth had never had such fun in her life. She scarcely knew what to do first and had only about two hours before the family arrived.

She decided to decorate first. The great hamper of flowers was brought into the barn, and the chauffeur set to work twining ropes and sprays of smilax and asparagus fern over doorways and pictures and training it like a vine about the stone chimney. Then came the flowers— pots of tall starry lilies; exquisite roses of pink, white, yellow and crimson; and daffodils and sweet peas, with quantities of sweet violets in the bottom of the basket. With deft fingers Elizabeth selected the flowers, putting pots of lilies on the windowsills. She massed pink roses in a dull gray jar she found among the kitchen things, that looked to the initiated as though it might once have been part of a water filter, but it suited the pink roses. The tall vases on the bookcases on each side of the fireplace held daffodils. Sweet peas were glowing in small vases and glasses and bowls, and violets in saucers filled the air with fragrance. White and yellow roses were on the dining table, and three tall crimson rosebuds glowed in a slender glass vase Elizabeth had brought with her. This she placed in Mrs. Hollister's room on the little stand she guessed would be placed beside the bed when the bed arrived. The flowers gave an atmosphere to the place in more senses than one. She was delighted and fluttered from one spot to another, changing the position of a vase or bowl and then standing off to get the effect.

"Now bring me the big bundle, Jenkins, please," she said at length when she was satisfied with the effect. "Oh, and the long box. Be careful. It's broken at one end, and the screws may fall out."

He was soon back with the things.

"Now you put up the rods at the windows, while I get out the curtains." She untied the bundle eagerly.

Jenkins was adaptable, and the rods were simple affairs. He was soon at work, and Elizabeth ran the rods into the curtains.

They weren't elegant curtains. Graham had insisted she get nothing out of keeping with the simplicity. They were soft and straight and creamy, with a frost-like pattern in same-color threads, illuminated here and there with a single rose and a leaf in color. There was something cheerful and springlike to them; yet they looked plain and suitable, with no ruffles or trim, just hems. To Elizabeth's mind they were very cheap. Shirley would have exclaimed over their beauty and turned from them with a gasp when she heard their price. They were one of those quiet fitting things that cost without flaunting it. They transformed the room into a dream.

"Oh, isn't it beautiful!" exclaimed Elizabeth, standing back to look as the first curtain went up.

"Yes, miss, it's very stunning," said the man, with good will in his face.

When the curtains were up, Elizabeth pinned one of her cards to the curtain nearest the front door, inscribed, "With love from Elizabeth."

Then in a panic she looked at her watch.

"Oh, Jenkins! It's almost six o'clock," she cried in dismay. "They might get here by half-past. We must hurry! Bring the other things in quick now, please."

So Jenkins brought in bundles and boxes, an ice cream freezer and the cooking outfit belonging to their touring car.

"Now you get the hot things ready, Jenkins, while I fix the table," directed the girl.

Trained in such things, he opened cans and started his chafing-dish fire, while Elizabeth opened her parcels—a platter of chicken sandwiches, a dish of fruit and nut salad surrounded by crisp lettuce leaves, a plate of delicate rolls, cream puffs, chocolate éclairs, macaroons, a coconut pie—all things she liked herself. Then because she knew no feast without them, there were olives, salted almonds and bonbons.

Delicious odors from the kitchen end filled the air. Jenkins was heating a pail of rich soup—chicken with rice gumbo—from one of the best caterers in the city. He made cocoa to be drunk with whipped cream that Elizabeth was pouring into a glass pitcher—if she'd only known the pitcher came from the ten-cent store. Then Jenkins heated canned peas and brown potato croquettes. The ice cream freezer was out in full sight, where they couldn't miss it. Everything was ready now.

"Jenkins, you better light up their odd stove now if you're sure you know how—she said it works like a lamp—and put those things in the oven to keep warm. Then we'll pack up our things, hide them out in the grass where they can't see and get them in the car when they get out. Hurry, for they'll be here soon, I think."

Elizabeth stuck a card in the middle of the rose bowl that said in pretty letters, "Welcome Home," stood back a minute to see how everything looked and then scurried to the door to watch for the car.

Chapter 12

When Shirley came down to the street at five o'clock, Graham was waiting for her as he promised and swung the car door open for her with as much eagerness as if he were taking a special girl on a picnic instead of doing a poor stenographer a kindness.

"I telephoned to the store and sent a message to George. We're going to pick him up on our way," he said as the car made its way through the traffic.

She was sitting beside him, and he looked over at her as if they were partners in a pleasant scheme. A strange sense of companionship with him thrilled through her and was properly rebuked and fled at once, without rippling the surface of her joy much. She'd determined to enjoy this one evening ride at least and wouldn't let her thoughts suggest what sweeter realms might be for other girls. She was having this good time. It was for her and no one else, and she would enjoy it as much as she could and keep it the sweet, sane, innocent pleasure it was. If she wasn't a fool, everything would be all right.

George was waiting for them as they swept up to the employees' entrance, and a line of admiring fellow laborers stood gaping on the sidewalk to watch his departure.

"Oh, say! Isn't this great?" shouted George, climbing into the back seat. "Got a whole omnibus of a car this time, haven't you?"

"Yes, I thought we'd have plenty of room for your mother, so she could lie down if she liked."

"That was very kind of you," murmured Shirley. "You think of everything, don't you? I'm sure I don't see how we ever could have managed without your help. I'd have been frightened a dozen times and ready to give up."

"Not you!" said Graham. "You're the kind that never gives up. You've taught me several valuable lessons."

As they turned the corner onto the street where the brick house stood, Shirley suddenly realized she'd told her mother nothing about Mr. Graham. What would she think, and how could she explain his presence? She'd expected to get there before Graham arrived and have time enough to make her mother understand. But now she realized her real reason for leaving the matter unexplained was that she didn't know what to say without telling the whole story from beginning to end.

"I'll hurry in and see if Mother's ready," she said, as the car stopped in front of the house and the children rushed out eagerly, Doris behind the others, to see the "booful tar."

"Mother," said Shirley, slipping into the house and going over to the bed where she lay with hat and coat on, ready. "Mother, I won't have time to explain all about it, but it's all right—so don't think anything. Mr. Graham, the man who owns the place where we're going, has been kind enough to offer to take you in his car. He thinks it'll be easier for you than the trolley, and he's out at the door now waiting. It's perfectly all right. He's been very kind about it—"

"Oh, daughter, I couldn't think of troubling anyone like that!" said the mother, shrinking from the thought of a stranger.

But, looking up, she saw him standing, hat in hand, in the doorway. The children had led him to the door when he offered to help their mother out to the car.

"Mother, this is Mr. Graham," said Shirley.

Mrs. Hollister, a pink spot on each cheek, tried to rise, but the young man came forward instantly and leaned over her.

"Don't try to get up, Mrs. Hollister. Your daughter tells me you haven't been walking about for several weeks. You must reserve your strength for the journey. Just trust me. I'm strong and can lift you and put you into the car almost without your knowing it. I often carry my own mother upstairs for fun, and she's larger and heavier than you. Just let me put my hand under your back like this and this hand here. Now if you'll put your arms around my neck—yes, that way—no, don't be a bit afraid. I'm strong, and I won't drop you."

Mrs. Hollister cast a frightened look at her daughter and another at the face bent above her. Then she felt herself lifted like thistledown before she had time to protest and found herself putting her arms around his neck and resting her head against his shoulder. A minute more, and the young man was piling pillows about her and tucking her up with soft, furry robes.

"Are you comfortable?" he asked. "I didn't strain your back or tire you, did I?"

"Oh, no, indeed!" said the bewildered woman. "You're very kind, and I hardly knew what you were doing till I was here. I never dreamed of anything like this. Shirley didn't tell me about it."

"No," said the young man, smiling, "she said she wanted to surprise you. She thought you might worry if you heard the details of the journey. Now, kitten, are you ready to get in?" He turned a smiling face to Doris, who stood solemnly waiting her turn, with an expression of one who sees the gates of the kingdom opening before her.

"Soor!" said Doris in a tone as like Harley's as possible.

She lifted one shoe and tried to reach the step but failed. Then she surrendered her trusting hands to the young man, and he lifted her in beside her mother.

"Sit there, kitten, till your sister comes out," he said, admiring her flower face.

Doris giggled.

"I ain't a kitty," she declared. "I'm a 'ittle gurrul!"

"Well, little girl, do you like to ride?"

"Soor! I do 'ike to wide! Oh! There goes muvver's bed!" she said as the drayman carried out the headboard.

Shirley was putting the last things from her mother's bed into the box, tossing items into the empty clothes basket left for this purpose and directing the man who was taking down the bed and carrying out the boxes and baskets. At last everything was out of the house, and she was free to go. She turned for one swift moment and caught a sob in her throat. There hadn't been time for it before. It had come when she saw the young man stoop and lift her mother tenderly and bear her out to the car.

But the children were calling for her to come. She dabbed at her eyes with her handkerchief to make sure no tears had escaped and walked out of the brick house forever.

A middle seat had been turned down for Carol, and Doris was in her lap. Graham turned the other middle seat down for Shirley; the boys piled into the front seat with him; and they were off.

In her amazement Mrs. Hollister forgot to look back at what she called in the stifling summer days her "frying pan" or wonder whether she were about to jump into the fire. She just lay back on the cushions, softer than any she'd rested on before, and felt herself glide away from the hated dark house forever! It seemed as if a chariot of fire had swooped down and gathered her little flock with her and was carrying them to some gracious heaven where comfort would be found at last. A bit of hope sprang up, unpremeditated and unreasonable, and persisted so that she couldn't help feeling happy. As yet she hadn't wondered who this handsome young man was that presumed to carry her like a baby and move her on downy beds to unknown regions. She was too taken up with it all. If Doris hadn't been prattling and asking questions of her, and the light breeze hadn't flapped a lock of hair into her eyes, she might have thought she was dreaming.

And now they left the narrow streets, through crowded thoroughfares for a brief space, then out beyond and free. Fair houses and glimpses of green were appearing. The car was gliding smoothly, for the invalid's sake not at high speed, and she could see on every side. The trees were in leaf; the sky was vast and blue; the air was fresh. She sighed and closed her eyes to pray, "Oh, my Father!" and then opened them again to see whether it was all true.

Shirley, sensitive to her mother's slightest breath, turned and drew the robes closer about her and asked if she was warm enough or wanted another pillow under her head.

Graham didn't intrude on the family behind him. He was absorbed in the two boys, who were entirely willing to be monopolized. He told them all about the car and discussed the mysteries of the different makes with a freedom that gave George the impression he himself was almost a man to be honored by such talk.

It was nearly seven o'clock when they reached Glenside and the big stone barn came in sight, for they traveled slowly to make it easier for the invalid.

Elizabeth sighted the car far down the road below the curve. Switching on every electric light, she fled down the ladder to the basement, dragging the willing Jenkins after her. Here they waited until the family had gone inside, when they could slip out the east end, across the brook, under the fence and down the road, to be picked up by the car according to previous arrangement.

As the car came in sight of the barn a deep silence fell on the company. Even Doris felt it and ceased prattling to look from one to another. "Whatzie mattah?" she asked Shirley, putting out her hand to pat Shirley's face in a way she had when she was uneasy or troubled. "Whatzie mattah, Surly?"

But Shirley only squeezed her hand and smiled.

As they drew near, the young people noticed that the bars of the fence in front of the barn had been taken down and the ditch filled in smoothly. Then they saw that the car was turning in and going straight up the grassy incline to the door.

Mrs. Hollister, lying among her cushions, was looking at the evening sky, hearing a bird that reminded her of long ago, and scarcely noticed they'd turned until the car stopped. The children swarmed out of the car and with one consent stood back and watched their mother, as the young man came to the open door and gathered her in his arms.

"Now we're almost home, Mrs. Hollister," he said. "Just put your arms around my neck again, and we'll soon have you beside your own fire." He lifted her and bore her in to the wide couch before the crackling fire Elizabeth had started before she looked out the door the last time.

Then into the blazing light of the transformed barn they all stepped, and everyone stood back and stared, blinking. What was this? What wondrous perfume met their senses? What luxury! What flowers! What hangings!

They stared and couldn't understand. And between them they forgot to wonder what their mother was thinking or do anything but say, "Why!" and "Oh!" and "Ah!" half under their breath.

"Just phone me if you need anything, Miss Hollister, please. I'll be glad to serve you," said Graham, stepping quickly over to the door. "Mrs. Hollister, I hope you'll be none the worse for your ride." He slipped out the door and was gone.

The sound of the car backing softly down the slope brought Shirley out of her daze. But when she turned and understood he was gone, the car was backing into the road, turning with a quick whirl, and was away before she could make him hear.

"Oh! He's gone!" she cried out, turning in dismay to the children. "He's gone, and we never thanked him!"

George was out and down the road like a shot, and the rest, forgetful for the moment of the invalid who was the anxiety all day, crowded at the door to watch him. They could hear the throbbing machine; they heard it stop down the road and start over again almost immediately, growing fainter with every whir as it moved farther from them. In a moment more George came running back.

"He's gone. He meant to, I guess, so we could have it to ourselves right at first. Elizabeth and the man were down the road waiting for him. They've been dolling the place up to surprise us."

"Oh!" said Shirley, turning to look around, her cheeks growing rosy. "Oh! Isn't it beautiful?" Then, kneeling quickly by the couch, she said, "Oh, Mother!"

"What does it mean, daughter?" asked the bewildered mother, looking about on the room that seemed like a palace to her.

But they all began to clamor at once, and she could make nothing of it.

"Oh, Shirley, look at the curtains! Aren't they dear?" cried Carol.

"Deah!" echoed Doris, dancing up and down.

"And here's a card, 'With love from Elizabeth'! Isn't it sweet of her? Isn't she a darling?"

"Who is Elizabeth?" asked Mrs. Hollister, rising to her elbow and looking around.

"Say! Look at the flowers!" broke in George. "It's like our store at Easter! I say! Those lilies are something, aren't they, Shirl?"

"Wait'll you see the dining room!" called Harley, who was investigating with the help of his nose. "*Some* supper table! Come on quick—I'm starved. Hello! Here's another signboard!"

They went to the dining room. Harley, still following his nose, discovered the source of the savory odors in the kitchen and raised another cry so appreciative that the entire family, except the invalid, followed him and found the supper steaming hot and crying to be eaten.

After the excitement was somewhat quieted Shirley took command.

"Now, children, you're getting Mother excited, and this won't do. And, besides, we must eat this supper right away before it spoils. Quiet down and bring the hot things to the table while I get Mother's things off. Then we'll tell her all about it. There's plenty of time. We're going to stay right here all summer."

"Aw! Can't we bring Mother out to the table?" pleaded George. "Harley and I could lift that couch just as easy."

"Why, I don't know," said Shirley, hesitating. "You know she isn't strong, and she'll worry about your lifting her."

"Oh, Shirley, let her come," pleaded Carol. "We could all take hold and wheel the couch out here. The floor is real smooth since those new boards were put in, and the couch has good casters."

"Mother! You're coming out to supper!" they chorused, rushing back to the living room.

Before the mother realized what was happening, her couch was being wheeled into the brilliantly lighted dining room, with Doris dancing attendance and shouting, "Mudder's tumin' to suppy! Mudder's tumin' to suppy!"

The mother gazed at the table, so smothered in flowers that she didn't recognize the old cracked blue dishes.

"Children, I insist," she raised her voice above the happy din. "I insist on knowing immediately what all this means. Where are we, and what is this? A hotel? And who was the person who brought us here? I can't eat anything or stay here another minute until I know. People can't rent houses like this for ten dollars a month anywhere, and I didn't suppose we'd come to charity, even if I am laid up for a few days."

Shirley could see the hurt in her mother's eyes and hear the alarm in her voice and came around to her couch, smiling.

"Now, Mother, we'll tell you the whole thing. It isn't a hotel we're in, and it isn't a house at all. It's only an old barn!"

"A barn!" Mrs. Hollister sat up on her couch and looked at the rose bowl in the middle of the table, at the soft curtains at the window and the Easter lilies on the stand in front, and exclaimed, "Impossible!"

"But it is, Mother, just an old stone barn! Look at the walls. See, those two are rough stones, and this one behind you is a partition made of common boards. That's only an old brown denim curtain over there to hide the kitchen, and we've got the old red chenille curtains up to partition off the bedrooms. The boys are going to sleep up in the hayloft, and it's going to be great!"

Mrs. Hollister glanced at the stone walls and back at the new partition, recognizing one by one the ancient chairs, the old bookcase now converted into a china closet, the brown denim curtain that once covered the dining room floor in the brick house. Now it was washed and mended and was doing its faded part to look like a wall and fit into the scheme of things. She darted questioning glances at the flowers and the table, then settled back on her pillow only half satisfied.

"They don't have curtains in a barn!" she remarked dryly.

"Those are a present from Elizabeth, the little sister of the landlord. She was out here with him when he came to see about things, and she got acquainted with Carol. She hung those curtains and brought the flowers and fixed the table for a surprise. See, Mother!" Shirley brought the card on which Elizabeth had printed her crude welcome.

Mrs. Hollister took the card as if it were a life preserver and smiled with relief.

"But this is a great deal to do for strangers," she said, and tears glittered in her eyes. "They must be wealthy people."

"Yes, Mother, I think they are," said Shirley, "and they've been very kind."

"But, daughter, wealthy people don't usually do things like that for nothing. And ten dollars a month for a barn could be nothing to them."

"I know, Mother, but he seems satisfied with the price," said Shirley with a troubled brow. "I—"

"Something's burning!" yelled Harley from the kitchen, and immediately they rushed out to rescue the supper, which took that moment to assert itself.

"Now, Mother," said Shirley, coming in with a big soup tureen, "we've got to eat this supper or it'll spoil. You're not to ask another question till we're through."

They settled down at the table, with Doris climbing into her high chair, calling, "Suppy! Suppy! Oh, goody!"

Such a clatter and a clamor, such shouts over the sandwiches and such jumps up and down to carry something to Mother! Such lingering over the delicious ice cream and fresh strawberries found in the freezer! Think of it! Real strawberries for them at that time of year!

Then, when they'd eaten all they could and realized it was time to get Mother to bed, they pushed the chairs back and cleared the table and put things away. Then Carol discovered the roasted fowl and bowl of salad set away in the tiny icebox ready for tomorrow. How did Elizabeth, who never kept house in her life, know what would be nice for a family tired out with moving and needing to rest before starting on with living?

The dishes were almost washed when the cart arrived with the last load of things, and the drayman helped George put up Mother's bed.

They wheeled the couch into the living room after the doors were closed and safely fastened for the night. Before the fire Shirley helped her mother put on her gown, then rolled her couch into the bedroom and got her to bed.

"Do you mind very much that it's only a barn, Mother?" asked Shirley, after she was settled.

"I can't make it seem like a barn, dear. It seems like a palace! I'm glad it's a barn, because we could never afford a house with space like this—and air!"

She threw out her hands as if to express her delight in the rooms and breathed in the country air, so different from the air in the dusty brick house in the city.

"Daughter!" she drew Shirley down where she could whisper to her. "You're sure he's not looking on us as objects of charity, and you're sure he understands you're a self-respecting girl earning her honorable living and paying her way? You know this is a wicked, deceitful world we live in, and there are all sorts of people in it."

"Mother! I'm sure. Sure as anybody could be. He's been a perfect gentleman. You didn't think he looked like one of those—those people—that go around misunderstanding girls, did you, Mother?"

The mother remembered the gentle, manly way in which the young man lifted her and carried her to and from the car, and her heart warmed to him. Yet her fears lingered as she watched her sweet-eyed girl.

"No–o–o," she answered slowly. "But then you can't always judge. He certainly was a gentleman, and he was very nice-looking." Then she looked sharply at Shirley.

"You won't get any notions in your head, child?" Her eyes were wistful and sad as she searched her daughter's face. "You know rich young men follow whims sometimes for a few days. They don't mean anything. I wouldn't want your heart broken. I wish he was an old man with white hair."

"Oh, Mother!" exclaimed Shirley with a ring to her voice. "Do you think you have a young fool for a daughter? He was only being nice because he's a gentleman. But I know he's not in the same universe as I am, as far as anything more than kindness is concerned. We'll probably never see him again now that we're settled. But don't you think I should telephone thanks to his little sister? They'll be home by now, and it seems as if we should acknowledge her great kindness."

"By all means, dear—but how can you? Is there a pay station near here? I thought you said this was out in the country."

"Why, we have a telephone of our own! Just think of the luxury of it! Us with a telephone! Mr. Graham had it put in the barn when he was making some repairs, so he could communicate with his workmen. He said we might keep it if we'd like it. It's one of those 'pay-as-you-go' phones, with a place to drop nickels and dimes in. So we're perfectly independent. Mr. Graham thought it would be a comfort to you when

George or I had to stay late in town."

"How thoughtful of him! He must be a wonderful rich man! By all means telephone at once, and tell the little girl to say to her brother from me that I'll consider it a privilege to thank him personally for all he's done for my children—sometime when he's out this way. Think. A real rose by my bed!" She reached out a frail hand and touched the petals lovingly. "It's wonderful!"

So Shirley went into the living room to telephone, while the children stood about to watch and comment and tell her what to say.

Doris sat on a cushion at her feet in awe and listened, asking Carol with large eyes: "Is Shirley tautin to Dod? Vy doesn't see sut her yeyes?"

Shirley's conversation over the telephone sounded to the little sister much like a prayer of thanksgiving, except she wasn't accustomed to hearing laughter in a voice when people prayed.

Then Doris was put to bed in her own little crib, and the light in Mother's room was switched off amid Doris's flood of questions.

"Vat makes it light? Vy did it do avay? Will it tum adin?"

At last she was asleep, and the other children tiptoed about preparing for bed, treading up and downstairs softly, whispering back and forth for this or that they couldn't find, till quiet settled down upon the tired, happy household, and the bullfrogs in the distance droned out the nightly chorus.

Chapter 13

It was beautiful to wake the next morning with the birds singing a matin in the trees, with a wonderful Sabbath quiet over everything. Tired as she was, Shirley was the first to awaken. She lay there beside Carol for a while with her eyes closed, listening and saying a prayer of thanksgiving for the peace of the place and the wonder of its coming into her life. Then suddenly a strange luminousness about her forced her to open her eyes.

The eastern window was across the room from her bed, and the sky was rosy with the dawn and flooding the room. It was the first time in years she'd watched the sun rise. She had almost forgotten in the dark city house that a sun rose and made things glorious. The sun had seemed an enemy to burn and wilt and stifle.

But here was a radiant new friend, to be waited for and enjoyed, to give glory to their lives. She raised herself on one elbow and watched until the red ball rose and burst into the brightness of day. Then she lay down again and listened to the birds. They seemed wild with joy over the new day. Presently the chorus grew less. The birds had gone about their morning tasks, and only a single bright song now and then from a soloist in the tree overhead marked the morning's silence.

In the quiet Shirley recalled events since she'd first seen this spot and thought about living in the barn. She gave thanks that her mother hadn't disliked it as she feared. It had no sense of being a stable, no odor of living creatures having occupied it before—only dusty clover like a lingering of past things packed away carefully. It was like a camping expedition. And then all those flowers! The scent of the lilies was on the air. How lovely of the young girl out of her luxury to pass on some of the sweet things of life! And the gracious man, her brother! She mustn't let him think she'd presume on his kindness. She mustn't let even her thoughts cross the line and dwell on the ground of social equality. She knew where he belonged, and there he'd stay. She was free in her heart and happy and only too glad to have such a kind landlord.

She drifted off to sleep again, and it was late when she awoke the next time. A silvery bell from the church in the valley was ringing. Sabbath, real Sabbath, seemed hovering happily in the air. Shirley dressed quickly. She felt as if she'd already lost too much of this first wonderful day in the country.

A thrush was filling the tree overhead with his music when she tiptoed into her mother's room.

Doris opened her eyes in wonder, then whispered, "Vat is dat, Surly? Vat is dat pitty sound?"

"A birdie in the tree, dear!" whispered Shirley.

"A weel budie! I yantta see it! Take Doris up, Surly!"

So Shirley wrapped a shawl about her and carried her to the window, where she looked up in wonder and joy.

The boys tumbled down from their loft in a few minutes, and no more sleep was to be had. Carol was up and out, and one after another they shouted with triumph over some new delight.

"I saw a fish in the brook!" Harley called out under his mother's window. "It was only a little fellow, but maybe it'll grow bigger someday, and then we can fish!"

"You silly!" cried George. "It was a minnow. Minnows don't grow to be big. They're only good for bait!"

"Hush, George. There's a nest in the tree. I've been watching, and the mother bird is sitting on it. That was the father bird singing a while ago." This came from Carol.

George, Harley and Carol decided they'd go to church. That was likely the first bell that rang, their mother told them, and they could get there if they hurried. It was only half past nine. Country churches rang a bell then, another at ten and the final bell at half past ten, probably. Maybe Sunday school was at ten. They could go and find out. Besides, it wouldn't matter if they were a little late the first time.

So they ate a quick breakfast, took sandwiches from the night before, crossed the road, climbed the fence and hurried over the green fields to church, thinking how much nicer it was than walking down a brick-paved street, past the same old grimy houses to a dim church.

Shirley surveyed the pantry and decided that roast chicken, potato croquettes and peas would warm up quickly. Since some ice cream and cakes were left, they would fare royally without any work. So she sat beside her mother and told the whole story of her ride, finding the barn, her visit to the Graham office and all that transpired until the present.

The mother listened, watching her, but said nothing of her inner thoughts. If it occurred to her that her oldest daughter was fair to look upon and that her winning ways, unspoiled face and wistful eyes had something to do with the price of their summer abode, it would be no wonder. But she didn't mean to trouble her child further. She would investigate for herself when opportunity offered. So she quieted anxieties Shirley might have had about her approval of their home, kissed her and told her she felt in her bones she was going to get well right away.

And, indeed, lifting the burden of where they should live helped much to brighten her eyes and strengthen her heart.

When George, Harley and Carol came home from church, Shirley was putting dinner on the table, and her mother was arrayed in a pretty kimono, a relic of their better days, and ready to be helped to the couch and wheeled out to the dining room. Shirley enjoyed seeing her brothers and sister come across the green meadow and getting things ready for them when they rushed in hungry. She was so happy she felt like crying.

After the dishes were washed they shoved the couch into the living room among the flowers, where George had built up a beautiful fire, for it was still chilly. They gathered around their mother and talked, making plans for the summer and chattering about the church service. The mother watched them and was content. Sometimes her eyes searched the dim rafters overhead and glanced along the stone walls, and she'd say to herself: "This is a barn! I'm living in a barn! My husband's children have come to this, that they have no place to live but a barn!" She was testing herself to see if the thought hurt her. But, looking on their happy faces, she couldn't feel sad.

"Children," she said suddenly in a quiet moment, "do you realize Christ was born in a stable? It isn't so bad to live in a barn. We should be very thankful for this splendid one!"

"Oh, Mother! It's so wonderful for you to take it that way!" cried Shirley, with tears in her eyes.

"Doris, sing your little song about Jesus in the stable," said Carol. "I'll play it for you."

Doris, nothing loath, got a little stool, stood up beside her mother's couch, folded her small hands and began to sing without waiting for accompaniment.

Away in a manger,
No trib for His bed,
The litta Lord Jesus
Lay down His sveet head.
The tars in the h'aven
Look down vhere 'e lay—
The litta Lord Jesus
As'eep in the hay.

The catta are lowing,
The poor baby wates;
But the litta Lord Jesus
No cwyin' He mates.
I love Thee, Lord Jesus;
Look down fum the sky,
An' stay by my trib,
Watching my lul-la-by!

Shirley kissed Doris, and then they sang other things, standing around the piano. By and by that distant bell from the valley called again.

"There's a vesper service at five o'clock. Why don't you go, Shirley? You and George and Harley," said Carol.

"Me 'ant do, too!" declared Doris.

They finally decided the walk wouldn't be too long. So the boys, Shirley and the baby started off across the fields, while Carol stayed with her mother. And this time Mrs. Hollister heard all about Elizabeth and how she wanted Carol to come and see her sometime. Heard, too, about the proposed party and its quiet squelching by the brother. Heard, looked thoughtful and wondered more.

"I'm afraid they're not quite our kind of people, dear!" she said gently. "You mustn't get your heart bound up in that girl. She may be very nice, but she's a society girl, and you're not, you know. She'll have other interests pretty soon, and then you'll be disappointed when she forgets about you."

"She won't forget, Mother. I know she won't!" declared Carol. "She's not that kind. She loves me; she told me so. She wanted to give me one of her necklaces to 'bind our friendship.' But I wouldn't let her till I asked you, because I didn't have any but Grandmother's to give her, and

I couldn't give her that."

"That was right, dear. You can't begin things like that. You'd find a great many of them, and we haven't the money to keep up with a little girl who's used to everything."

Carol's face dropped, and tears entered her eyes.

"Can't we have even friends?" she said, turning her face away to hide the tremble in her lip and the tears rolling down her cheeks.

"Yes, dear," said the mother, "but don't choose them from among another people. People who can't have much in common with us. It's sure to hurt hard with differences in station like that."

"But I didn't choose them. They chose us!" declared Carol. "Elizabeth went wild over us the first time she saw us, and her brother told Shirley he was glad, that it would do Elizabeth a lot of good to know us. He said, 'We've learned a lot of things from you already'— just like that, he said it! I was coming down the stairs behind them when they stood here talking one day, and I couldn't help hearing them."

"Yes?" said Mrs. Hollister thoughtfully. "Well, perhaps, but, dear, go slow and don't pin your heart to a friendship like that, for it will most likely be disappointing. Just be happy in what she's done for us already and don't expect anything more. She may never come again. It may just have been a passing whim. And I don't want you to be always looking for her and always disappointed."

"I won't be disappointed, Mamma," said Carol. "You'll see!" And her face brightened.

Then as if to make good her words a car whirred up the road and stopped in front of the barn, and almost before she could get to the window to look out Carol heard Elizabeth's voice.

"Carol! Car–rol! Are you there?" And she flung the door open and rushed into her new friend's arms.

Graham came more slowly up the incline, smiling apologetically and hoping he didn't intrude, coming so soon.

Carol led them over to her mother and introduced Elizabeth.

"I'm afraid this is rather soon to obey your summons, Mrs. Hollister," he said. "Elizabeth couldn't stand it without coming over to see if you really found the ice cream freezer, so I thought we'd drop in for a minute and see if you're comfortable."

Suddenly Mrs. Hollister's fears and conclusions concerning these two young people vanished, and she felt as Shirley had, that they were genuine in their kindness and friendship. Carol, watching her, was satisfied, and her eyes shone. Nevertheless, Mrs. Hollister gathered her caution about her as a garment and in dignified, pleasant phrases thanked the two in a way that they must see that neither she nor her children would ever presume upon what had been done for them or take it for more than a passing kindness.

But to her surprise the young man was scarcely listening to her words. He seemed to be studying her face with deep intention that was almost embarrassing. Pink stole into her thin cheeks, and she stopped speaking and looked at him in dismay.

"I beg your pardon," he said, seeing her bewilderment, "but you can't understand how interested I am in you. I'm afraid I've been guilty of staring. You see, it amazes me to find a woman of your refinement and evident culture and education who is content—I might even say joyful—to live in a barn! I don't know another woman who would be satisfied. And you seem to have brought up your children with the same happy, adaptable natures, that it's a great puzzle to me. I–I—why, I feel rebuked! You and your children are among the great ones of the earth. Don't thank Elizabeth and me for the little we could do toward making this barn habitable. It was a sort of—I might say honor due you, that we were rendering. And now please don't think anything more about it. Let's just talk as if we were friends—that is, if you're willing to accept a couple of humble strangers among your friends."

"Why, surely, if you put it that way!" smiled the woman. "Although I'm sure I don't know what else we could do but be glad we had a barn like this to come to under such a lovely blue sky, with a bird and a tree thrown in, when we literally didn't know where we could afford to lay our heads. You know beggars shouldn't be choosers, but I'm sure one would choose a spacious place like this any day to most of the ordinary city houses with their tiny dark rooms and breathless windows."

"Even if it was called a barn?"

"Even if it was called a barn!" said the woman with a flitting dance in her eyes that reminded him of the girl Shirley.

"Well, I'm learning a lot, I tell you!" said the young man. "The more I see of you all, the more I learn. It's opened my eyes to a number of things in my life that I'm going to set right. By the way, is Miss Hollister here? I brought over a book I was telling her about the other day. I thought she might like to see it."

"She went to the vesper service at the little church across the fields. They'll be coming home soon, I think. It must be nearly over."

He looked at his watch. "Suppose I take the car and bring them back. You stay here, Elizabeth. I'll be back soon. I think I can catch them around by the road if I hurry."

He was off, and the mother lay on the couch watching the two girls and wishing her children might indeed have these two fine young people for friends. But of course such things couldn't very well be in this world of stern realities and conventionalities. What, for instance, would be said in the Grahams' social set if it were known that some of their intimate friends lived in a barn? No, such things didn't happen even in books, and the mother sighed and listened to the two girls chattering.

"You're coming home with me to stay over Sunday pretty soon. Sid said he'd fix it up with your mother. We'll sleep together and have the grandest times. Mother likes me to have friends stay with me, but most of the girls I know are off at boarding school now, and I'm dreadfully lonesome. We have tennis courts and golf links and a bowling alley. Do you play tennis? And we can go out in the car whenever we like. I'll show you my dog and my pony I used to ride. He's getting old now, and I'm too big for him, but I love him just the same. I have a saddle horse, but I don't ride much. I'd rather go motoring with Sid—"

And so she rattled on, and the mother sighed for her little girl who was being tempted by a new world and hadn't the wherewithal to enter it, even if she could.

Out in the sunset the car was speeding back again with the seats full, Doris gleeful at the ride, for her little legs had grown weary with the long walk through the meadow, and Shirley was almost sorry she'd taken her along.

The boys were shouting questions about dogs and chickens and cars and a garden, and Graham was answering them all good-humoredly. Now and then he turned around to throw back a pleasant sentence and a smile at the quiet girl with the happy eyes sitting in the back seat with her arm around her little sister.

There was nothing notable about the ride—just one of those pleasant bits of color that fit into the mosaic of any growing friendship, without which the whole isn't perfect. Shirley's part in it was small. She said little and listened happily to the boys' conversation with Graham. She had settled it with her heart that morning that she and the young man on the front seat had nothing in the future with each other, but it was pleasant to see him talking with her brothers. There was no reason why she shouldn't be glad for that and glad he wasn't a snob. For every time she looked at him and saw his kind gray eyes on her, she was surer he wasn't a snob.

The guests stayed a while after they all got back and accepted quite naturally the lunch Carol and Elizabeth, slipping away unobserved, prepared and brought in on trays—salad left from dinner, a few round rolls Shirley had brought out with her Saturday, cut in two and crisply toasted, cups of delicious cocoa and little cakes. The two self-invited guests enjoyed it immensely. Then they all stood around the piano and sang hymns, and it's safe to say the guests at least hadn't spent as "Sabbathy" a Sabbath in all their lives.

Elizabeth was quite astonished when she suggested they sing a popular song and Carol answered in a polite tone, "Oh, not today, you know."

"Why not? Doesn't your mother like it?" whispered Elizabeth.

"Why, we don't any of us usually sing things like that on Sunday. It doesn't seem like Sunday. It doesn't seem quite respectful to God." Carol was terribly embarrassed and struggling to make her idea plain.

"Oh!" Elizabeth said, looking wistful. She wondered at her friend and finally slipped her hand into Carol's and squeezed it, as if to let her know she understood. Then they lifted up their voices again over the same hymnbook.

> Thine earthly Sabbaths, Lord, we love,
>   But there's a nobler rest above;
> To that our longing souls aspire
>   With cheerful hope and strong desire.

Graham looked about on the group singing and joined his tenor in the words, with his eyes lingering on his sister's face as she stood arm in arm with Carol. He was suddenly thrilled with what a Sabbath might be, kept in this way. It had never appealed to him before. Sabbath-keeping had seemed like a dry, thankless task for a few fanatics; now a new possibility took vague shape in his mind. He could see that people like this could make the Sabbath something to love, not just a day to pass the time away.

When they finally left, only a streak of dull red remained in the western horizon where the day had disappeared.

"Sidney," said Elizabeth after a long time, "did you ever feel as if God were real?"

"Why, how do you mean, kid?" asked the brother, embarrassed. These subjects weren't discussed in the Graham household.

"Did you ever feel as if there really was a God somewhere, like a person, that could see and hear you and know what you did and how you felt? Because they do. Carol said they didn't sing 'Tipperary' on Sunday because it didn't seem quite respectful to God, and I could see she meant it. It wasn't because her mother said she had to or anything like that. She thought so herself."

"H'm!" said Graham thoughtfully. "Well, they're rather remarkable people, I think."

"Well, I think so, too, and I think it's about time you fixed it up with Mamma to let Carol come and visit me."

"I'm going to get Mother to go out there and call this week if I can," said Graham after another longer pause. "I think she'll go, and I think she'll like them," he added. "After that we'll see, kid. Don't you worry. They're nice, all right." He was thinking of the look on Shirley's face as she sat at the piano playing for them to sing.

Chapter 14

The first few days in the new home were filled with wonder and delight. They couldn't get used to having plenty of room indoors, with all outdoors for a playground. Doris's cheeks took on a lovely pink, and her eyes began to sparkle. She and Harley spent all day outdoors. They were digging a garden. Not that they had any experience or tools. They found an old hoe and a broken spade in the basement of the barn, and with these Harley managed to remove a few square feet of young turf and mellow up an inch or two of soil depth. In this they planted violet roots and buttercups and daisies they found in the meadows.

Doris had her own corner, with neat rows of tiny stones from the brook laid in baby patterns around the edge, and in this she stuck twigs and weeds of all descriptions and was never daunted, only pained and surprised, when they drooped and died in a day or two and had to be supplanted by others.

Harley stopped school to stay at home with Mother and Doris, which indeed he was willing to do under the glamour of the new life. The school itself never had much attraction for him, and "the fellows" were almost forgotten in searching for angleworms and building dams in the creek.

Carol went to high school every morning with Shirley and George on the trolley. Only six weeks remained till the term was over, and it was better for Carol to finish out her year and get her credits. Shirley thought they could afford the extra carfare for that little while, and so all day Mother and Doris and Harley stayed at the old barn, and the meadows rang with Doris's shouts and Harley's answers.

One day the doctor came out in his machine to see Mrs. Hollister as he'd promised to do and found her so much better that he told her she might get up and go around a little every day if she didn't get too tired. He prophesied a speedy return to health if she kept on looking happy and breathing such good air. He praised the good sense that brought her to the country to live, instead of in a closed-up house in town, and said if she could only get well enough to work outdoors in the ground and have a flower bed it would be the making of her. Her eyes brightened at that, for she loved flowers; when she was young she was quite success-ful at making things grow.

The doctor was deeply interested in the barn. He walked about with his hands in his pockets, looking the rooms over, as delighted as a child at seeing a new toy.

"Well, now, this is great!" he said. "I admire you people for having the nerve to go against conventionality and come out here. If I had more patients who'd go out to the country and fix up some of the unused old barns to live in, I'd have to change my occupation. It's a great idea, and I mean to recommend it to others if you don't mind. Only I doubt I find two others who have the nerve to follow your example."

Mrs. Hollister laughed.

"Why, doctor, I can't see the nerve. We really had no choice. We couldn't find a decent place we could afford, and this was big and healthful and cost less than the worst tenement that would have done in town. Anyone would be a fool not to have come here."

"Mrs. Hollister, do you know that most people would rather starve and swelter, yes, and die in a conventional house, than to live in a barn, no matter how delightful that barn might be? You're a fine woman, Mrs. Hollister, and you deserve to get well and see your children prosper. And they will. They have the right spirit."

After his visit Mrs. Hollister got up a little every day, and her health improved rapidly. She even ventured out to see Doris's garden and watch the "budie" in his nest in the tree.

One day a drayman stopped at the place and left several large rolls of chicken wire and a couple of big crates. One crate was bigger than the other and contained half a dozen yellow hens and a rooster. The small crate held two white rabbits.

The children hovered over the crates.

"Mine wabbits!" declared Doris solemnly. "Nice Mistah Dwaham give Doris wabbits."

"Did Mr. Graham say he was going to send you some rabbits?" questioned her mother.

" 'Es. He say he was goin' to sen' me some wabbits. On 'e way fum chutch in big oughtymobeel. He say he would give me wabbits. Oh, mine wabbits!" Doris was in ecstasy.

Mrs. Hollister looked at the rolls of wire.

"George and I told him we wanted some chickens. I guess that's why he sent 'em," announced Harley.

"I hope you boys didn't hint. That's very bad manners. You know I can't have Mr. Graham giving you such expensive presents. It won't do, dear."

"No, Mother, we didn't hint. George just asked him if he minded if we kept chickens here, and he said no, indeed, he'd like to go into the business himself. He said he used to have a lot of his own when he was a boy, and he guessed a lot of wire from the old chicken run was still at his place. If there was, he said he couldn't think of any reason why it shouldn't be in use, and he'd look it up. And if it was, he said he'd go into business with us. He'd furnish the tools and we could do the work, and maybe someday we could sell eggs and make it pay."

"That's very kind of him, I'm sure. But, Harley, that looks like new wire. It isn't the least bit rusted."

"It's galvanized, Mother. Galvanized wire doesn't rust—don't you know that?" said Harley in a superior, man's voice.

Harley and Doris were wild over their pets and could do nothing all day but hover about them. The minute George arrived, the boys went out and put up some of the wire to make a temporary abode for the creatures until they could plan an elaborate chicken run.

Before dark Graham arrived. He brought a book on chicken raising and offered a good many suggestions. A golden-brown dog with a white-starred face, affectionate eyes and a plumy white tail rode with him in the front seat of the car. He bounded floppily out after Graham and up to the door as if he understood everything. Seeing him, the children went wild.

"I brought this fellow along, thinking you might like him to help look after things here. He's only a puppy, but he's a good breed, and I think you'll find him a splendid watchdog. You don't need to keep him, of course, if you don't want him, Mrs. Hollister. But I thought out in the country this way it might be as well for you to have him on guard, at night especially. He'll be good company for the children. We've got so many of them that we want to give this one away."

And what was there to do but accept him with thanks, a dog like that begging for a home and a home like that needing a dog?

So the dog was promptly accepted as a family member, was named Star and accepted overtures of affection with amiable tail-waggings and a puppy laugh on his face. He stayed behind contentedly when Graham departed after conferring with George and Harley over the "chicken" book and discussing in the backyard the best place for the chicken run. He seemed to know from the start that he'd come to stay; this was his "job," and he was on it for life.

Mrs. Hollister fell asleep that night more contented, knowing that big dog was lying across the door out in the living room. The hillside had seemed a bit lonely at night, though she hadn't admitted it even to herself, and she was glad the dog had come. That evening in the nightly prayer she said with her children gathered about her couch in front of the fire, she added, "We thank You, Lord, for sending us such good kind friends to make the world happier for us."

A few days later Mrs. Graham came to call.

Her son didn't explain to her anything about the Hollisters or the place where they were living. He merely remarked casually, "Mother, there are some people I'd like you to call on if you don't mind. They live out Glenside way, and I'll take you any afternoon you have time."

"I really haven't much time now before we go to the shore, Sidney," she said. "Couldn't they wait till the fall when we return?"

"No, Mother, I'd like you to call now. It needn't take you long, and I think you'll like them—her—Mrs. Hollister, I mean. Can't you go this afternoon? I'll call for you with the car anywhere you say, about half past four or five o'clock. It will be a pleasant little drive and rest you."

"Shall I have to be much dressed?" asked the mother thoughtfully. "I wouldn't have time for elaborate preparations. I have to go to Madame's for a fitting, meet with the Red Cross committee, drop in at the hospital for a few minutes and see Mrs. Sheppard and Mrs. Follette about our alumni anniversary banquet."

"Just wear something simple, Mother. They're not society people. It's you I want to show them, not your clothes."

"You ridiculous boy! You're as unsophisticated as your father. Well, I'll be ready at half past four. You may call for me then at the Century Building."

Elizabeth had been loyal to her brother's commands and said nothing about her newfound friend, awaiting his permission. Graham discussed the pros and cons of woman's suffrage with his mother during the drive, so that she was unprejudiced by any former ideas concerning the Hollisters, which was exactly what her son desired her to be. He knew his mother was a woman of the world and hedged about by conventions of all sorts, but he also knew her to judge fairly when she saw a thing right and to read character well. He wanted her to see the Hollisters without any chance to judge them beforehand.

So when the car drew up in front of the old barn Mrs. Graham was quite unprepared to have her son get out and open the car door and say, "Mother, this is the place. May I help you out?" She was talking earnestly and thought he was getting out to look after something wrong about the car. Now she looked up startled.

"Why, Sidney! You must have made a mistake! This isn't a house— it's a barn!"

"This is the place, Mother. Just come right up this way."

Mrs. Graham picked her way over the short green turf up to the door and stood astonished while her son knocked. What in the world did he mean? Did he bring her out to see a new horse? That must be it, of course. He was always taking a fancy to a horse or a dog. She really hadn't the time to spare for nonsense this afternoon, but one must humor one's son once in a while. She stepped back absentmindedly, her eyes resting on the soft greens and purples of the foliage across the meadows, her thoughts on the next paper she intended to write for the club. This would soon be over, and then she might pursue the even tenor of her busy way.

Then the door slid back, and she became aware of something unusual in the tension of the moment. Looking up quickly she saw a beautiful girl of about Elizabeth's age, with a wealth of dark wavy hair, lovely dark eyes and vivid coloring, and by her side one of the loveliest golden-haired, blue-eyed babies she'd ever seen. In the wonder of the moment she forgot that the outside of the building had been a barn, for the curtain had risen on a new setting, and here on the threshold opened before her amazed eyes a charming, homelike room.

At first she didn't take in the details of furnishings. Everything was tastefully arranged, and the dull tones of wall, floor and ceiling in the late afternoon light mellowed the old furniture into its background so perfectly that the imperfections and make-shifts didn't appear. It was just a place of comfort and beauty, even though the details might show poverty.

But her son was speaking.

"Mother, this is Miss Carol Hollister, and this little girl is her sister Doris—"

Doris put out a fat hand and gravely laid it in the lady's kid glove, saying carefully, with lashes drooped sideways and blue eyes furtively searching the stranger's face, "How oo do?"

Then, as if she'd performed her duty, she flashed her smile and dimples and, grasping Graham's hand, said, "Now, Mistah Dwa'm, oo tum out an' see my wabbits!"

It was evident to the mother that her son had been here before. She looked at him for an explanation, but he only said to Carol, "Is your mother able to see callers for a few minutes?"

"Oh, yes," said Carol with a ring in her voice. "Mother is up in a chair this afternoon. See! The doctor says she may get up now—she's so much better!" She turned and flung out her arm toward the easy chair where her mother sat.

Mrs. Hollister arose and came forward to meet them.

She was dressed in a plain gown of cheap gray challis, much washed and mended, but looking very nice. Carol had just fastened one of Shirley's sheer white collars around her neck, with a bit of pink ribbon looped in a knot. Her hair was tastefully arranged, and she looked every inch a lady as she stood to receive her unexpected guests.

Graham had seen her only in invalid's garb before, and he stood amazed for a moment at the likeness between her and Shirley. He introduced his mother with a few words and then yielded to Doris's eager, pulling hand and went out to see the rabbits.

The situation was a trifle trying for both ladies, but to the woman of the world perhaps more embarrassing. She hadn't a clue as to who this was she'd been brought to see. She was used to dominating any situation, but for a moment she was almost confused.

Mrs. Hollister, however, tactfully relieved the situation with a gentle "Won't you sit here by the fire? It's getting a little cool this evening, don't you think?" and put her at ease at once. Only her family would have guessed from the pink spots in her cheeks that she was excited over her guest.

She took the initiative at once, leading the talk into natural channels, about the spring and its wonderful unfolding in the country; exhibited a vase with jack-in-the-pulpits and a glass bowl of hepaticas blushing blue and pink; told of the thrush that had built a nest in the elm over the door and pointed out the view over the valley where the sinking sun was flashing crimson from the weather vane on the church spire. She said how much they'd enjoyed the sunsets since coming out here to live, taking it for granted that her visitor knew all about their circumstances and making no apologies or comments.

And the visitor, being what her son called "a good sport," showed no hint she'd never heard of the Hollisters before but smiled and said the right thing at the right moment. And somehow, neither knew just how, they got to the subject of Browning and Ibsen and from there to woman's suffrage.

When Graham returned with Carol and Harley, and Doris chattering beside him and the dog bounding in ahead, they were deep in future politics. Graham sat and listened for a while, interested to note that the quiet woman who'd spent the last few years of her life working in a narrow dark city kitchen could talk as thoughtfully and sensibly as his cultured, versatile mother.

The next trolley brought Shirley and George, and again the mother was amazed to find how free and easy the relationship seemed to be between all these young people.

She looked sharply at Shirley and then at her son but saw nothing that gave her uneasiness. The girl was unconscious as a rose and gracious to the guests as if she'd been in society all her life. She slipped away at once to remove her hat; when she returned her hair was brushed, and she looked as fresh as a flower in her clean white ruffled blouse. The older woman couldn't take her eyes from her face. What a charming girl to be set among all this shabbiness! For by this time her discriminating eyes had discovered that everything—literally everything—was shabby. Who were these people, and how did they happen to get put here? The baby was ravishingly beautiful, the girls were charming, and the boys looked like splendid, manly fellows. The mother was a product of culture and refinement. Not one word or action revealed she knew her surroundings were shabby. She might have been mistress of a palace for all she showed of awareness of the poverty about her. It was as if she were just dropped down for the day in a stray barn and making a palace out of it while she stayed.

Unconsciously the woman of the world lingered longer than was her wont in making calls. She liked the atmosphere and was strangely interested by them all.

"I wish you'd come and see me," she said as she rose at last to go. She said it as if she meant it—as if she lived right around the corner and not twenty-two miles away—as if she really wanted her to come and not as if this other woman lived in a barn at all.

"Good old sport!" commented her son in his heart as he listened. He knew she must see their worth, and yet he was strangely afraid.

Mrs. Hollister received the invitation with a flush of pleasure.

"Thank you," she answered graciously. "I'm afraid not. I seldom go anywhere anymore. But I've been very glad to have had this call from you. It will be a pleasure to think about. Come sometime again when you're out this way. Your son has been most kind. I cannot find words to express my thanks."

"Has he?" Mrs. Graham looked questioningly at her son. "Well, I'm very glad—"

"Yes, and Elizabeth! She's a dear sweet girl, and we all love her!"

Revelations!

"Oh, has Elizabeth been here, too? Well, I'm glad. I hope she hasn't been a nuisance. She's such an impulsive, erratic child. Elizabeth is quite a problem just now. She's out of school because of her eyes, and since most of her girlfriends are away at school, she's perfectly forlorn. I'm delighted to have her with your children. I'm sure they're charming associates for her."

Her eyes rested approvingly on the sparkling Carol in her simple school dress of brown linen with its white collar and cuffs. There was nothing countrified about Carol. She looked dainty in the commonest raiment, and she smiled radiantly at Elizabeth's mother and won her heart.

"Would you let Elizabeth stay overnight with us here sometime?" she asked shyly.

"Why, surely! I presume she'd be delighted. She does about as she pleases these days. I really don't see much of her—I'm so busy this time of year, at the end of the season, you know, with committee meetings and teas and things."

They stopped at the doorway to look up into the tree, in response to the earnest solicitations of Doris, who tugged at the lady's gloved hand, murmuring, "Budie! Budie! See mine budie in the twee!"

The Hollisters stood grouped at the doorway when at last the visitors got into their car and went away. Mrs. Graham looked back at them wistfully.

"What a lovely group they make!" she murmured. "Now, Sidney, tell me at once who they are, why they live in a barn and why you brought me out here. I know you had some special object. I knew the minute I saw that charming woman."

"Mother, you certainly are great! I thought you'd have the good sense to see what they are."

"Why, I haven't spent a more delightful hour in a long time than I spent talking with her. She has very original ideas and expresses herself well. As for the children, they're lovely. That oldest girl has a great deal of character in her face. But what are they doing in a barn, Sidney, and how did you come to know them?"

As they speeded out the smooth turnpike to their home Sidney Graham told his mother as much of the story of Shirley Hollister and the old barn as he thought she'd care to know, and his mother watched his handsome, enthusiastic face while he talked.

One comment she made as they swept up the beautiful drive to their luxurious country home. "Sidney, dear, they're delightful and all that, and I'm sure I'm glad to have that little girl come to see Elizabeth, but if I were you I wouldn't go out there too often when that handsome oldest girl is at home. She's not exactly in your set, charming as she is, and you wouldn't want to give her any ideas. A gentleman looks out for things like that, you know."

"What does being in our set have to do with it, Mother? Do you know any girl in our set who's better looking or has nicer manners or a finer appreciation of nature and books? You should hear her talk!"

"Yes, but, Sidney, that isn't everything! She isn't exactly—"

"Mother, were you and Father, when you used to have good times together? Now, Mother, you know you're just talking twaddle when you let that idea about 'our set' rule your mind. Be a good sport and look the facts in the face. That girl is as good as any other girl I know, and you know it. She's better than most. Please admit the facts. Yet you never warned me to be careful about calling on any of the girls in 'our set.' Please be consistent. But don't worry about me. I have no idea at present of paying any special attention to anybody." And he swung the car door open and jumped down to help her out.

Chapter 15

A man arrived one morning with a horse and plow and other farm implements of which Harley didn't know the name. He announced that Mr. Graham had sent him to plow the garden. Would Mrs. Hollister please tell him where she wanted the ground broken and how much? He volunteered the information that he was her next neighbor and if he was in her place he'd plow the south slope of the meadow, and if she wanted flower beds a strip along the front near the road; the soil was best in those spots, so she wouldn't need much fertilizer.

Mrs. Hollister asked him how much he'd charge to do it, and he said a little job like that wasn't worth talking about; he used to rent the barn himself and did a little turn for Mr. Graham whenever he needed it. He did it for Mr. Graham, and it wouldn't cost her "nothin'."

When she came in a few minutes later and dropped down on the couch to rest from her unusual fatigue a new thought was racing through her mind. They could have a garden, a real garden, with lettuce and green peas and lima beans and corn! She knew all about making them grow. She'd been brought up in a village home, where a garden was necessary equipment for everyone. She used to help her father every spring and all summer. Her own patch always took the family prize. But for years she'd been in the city without an inch of space.

Now, however, the old gardening fever took possession. If she could get out and work in the ground, as the doctor suggested, she'd get well right away. And with Harley to help, and George and Carol to work a little every evening, couldn't they raise enough on all that ground to sell some?

George could take things into town early in the morning, or they could find some private families who would buy all they had to sell. It was worth thinking about, anyway. She could raise flowers for sale, too. She'd always wanted a hothouse and a chance to experiment. She heard the children say there were some old window sashes down under the barn. She would get George to bring them out and see what she could do with a cold frame or two. Violets and a lot of other things would grow under a cold frame.

Oh, if they could always live here and not have to go back to the city in the fall! But of course there was no way to heat the barn in winter so that was out of the question. Nevertheless, she liked the idea of making money with growing things. She thought of it often and talked of it now and then to Shirley and the other children.

Shirley bought some seed packages at the ten-cent store, and they planted them eagerly. Then Mr. Graham sent over vegetable and flower seeds with shrubs, cuttings and bulbs he said were "leftovers" at their country house that he thought the children could use. So before the Hollisters knew it they possessed a garden, which almost in a breath lifted up its green head and began to grow.

Life was full for the Hollisters in those days, and those who went to the city for the day could hardly bear to tear themselves away from the country pleasures. The puppy was getting bigger and wiser every day, tagging along with Doris and Harley wherever they went or sitting adoringly at Mrs. Hollister's feet, and always attending the others to the trolley in the morning.

Out behind the barn a tiny coop held a white hen and her seven downy balls of chicks. Another hen was ensconced in a barrel of hay with ten blue duck eggs under her wings, and farther down toward the creek a chicken run ended in a poultry roost. George had manufactured it out of a packing box and some boards. The feathered family had been increased by two white leghorns and three bantams. George and Harley spent their evenings watching them and discussing the price of eggs and chickens per pound. They were all very happy.

Elizabeth came out to spend Sunday as she promised. She got up early to see the sunrise and watch the birds. She helped fix breakfast and wash the dishes. Then she went with the others across the fields to Sunday school and church. She was as hungry and enthusiastic as any of them when she came home, helping with the work and taking pride in the potatoes she warmed up under careful tutelage. In the afternoon she listened closely to the Bible story Shirley told Doris and the book she read aloud to them all afterward; her clear, sweet voice rang out in the hymns they sang together; and she was eager to go with Shirley to the Christian Endeavor.

"I shouldn't wonder if Sidney wishes he was here, too," she remarked dreamily that evening, as she sat before the fire on a cushion, her chin in her hands, her eyes on the shadows in the ashes.

She went to school with Carol the next morning and returned home with her in the afternoon. When her brother came for her in the evening she was reluctant to go home to the elegant, lonely house and begged that Carol might come soon and see her.

Friday afternoon Elizabeth called up Mrs. Hollister.

"Please, Mrs. Hollister, let Carol come and stay with me till Monday. I'm so lonesome, and Mamma says she'll be glad if you'll let her come."

"Oh, my dear, that would be impossible. Carol isn't suitably dressed to visit," answered the mother quickly, glad she had such a good excuse for keeping her child from this venture into an alien world about which she had many grave doubts.

But the young voice at the other end of the telephone was insistent.

"Dear Mrs. Hollister, please! She doesn't need any other clothes. I've got lots of things that would fit her. She loaned me her gingham dress to work in the garden, so why shouldn't I loan her a dress to wear on Sunday? I've got plenty of clean middy blouses and skirts and can fix her all out fresh for school, too, Monday morning. If you'll let her stay, Sidney will take us both down to her school when he goes to the office. You have all those children there at home, and I have only myself. Sidney doesn't count, you know, for he's grown up."

So, with a sigh, the mother consented, and Carol found the Graham car waiting for her when she came out of school. Thus she started on her first venture into the world.

That wonderful weekend was like fairyland to the young girl whose memories were full of burdens and sacrifices: the palatial home of many rooms and rich furnishings; servants and the anticipation of every want; the vast grounds with all a heart could wish in beauty and amusement; the music room with grand piano, harp, and violin lying mute most of the time; the library with its walls lined with rare books, mostly unread. Everything to satisfy any whim, reasonable or unreasonable, and nobody using it much.

"Not a room in the whole place as cozy and homey as this!" sighed Carol, sinking into the old denim-covered couch before the fireplace in the barn living room Monday night after she got home. "I declare, Mother—I don't see how Elizabeth stands it. Her mother is nice, but she's hardly ever there, unless she has a swarm of people dinnering or teaing or lunching. She hardly ever has time to speak to Elizabeth, and Elizabeth doesn't seem to care much either. She almost seems to think more of that old nurse Susan, who cared for her when she was a baby, than she does of her mother. I'm so glad I was sent to you instead of to her!"

Carol suddenly slipped across the room and buried her face in her mother's neck, hugging and kissing her, leaving a few bright tears on her mother's face.

Mrs. Hollister was greatly relieved to find her child unspoiled by her first experience of the world and glad to get back to her home, after the anxiety her mother-heart had felt. Carol presently sat up and told them in detail about her visit: the concert Sidney took them to Friday evening in the Academy of Music, where a world-renowned pianist was the soloist with the symphony orchestra; the tennis and riding Saturday morning; the luncheon at a neighboring estate, with three girls and a brother who were "snobs" and had bad manners; the evening party that lasted so late they didn't get to bed till long after midnight; the beautiful room they slept in, with every imaginable toiletry article in sterling silver with monograms; the strange Sabbath, with no service in the morning because they woke up too late, and no suggestion of anything but a holiday—except the vesper service in a cold, formal chapel Carol begged to go to; just a lot of worldly music and entertaining, with a multitude of visitors for the end of it.

She told of the beautiful dresses Elizabeth loaned her: coral crêpe de chine accordion-plaited for the concert; white with an orange sash for the luncheon; pale yellow with a black velvet belt for the party; a blue-silk affair and another lovely white organdie for Sunday; and all with their accompanying silk stockings and slippers and gloves, and necklaces and bands for her hair. It was quite wonderful to her.

As they listened they marveled that their Carol had returned to them so gladly and rejoiced to see her nestling in her brown linen skirt and middy blouse close beside her mother's chair. She declared herself satisfied with her flight into the world. She might like to go again for a glimpse now and then, but she thought she'd rather have Elizabeth out to Glenside. She hated to lose any of the time out here; it was so pretty. Besides, it was lonesome without them.

About that time Shirley picked up the morning paper in her office one day to look up a matter for Mr. Barnard. Her eye happened to fall on the society column and catch the name of Sidney Graham. She glanced down the column. It was an account of a wedding in high circles in which he served as best man, with Miss Harriet Hale—in blue tulle and white orchids as maid of honor—for his partner down the aisle. She read the column hurriedly, hungrily, gleaning every detail, white spats, gardenia and all, until in those few printed sentences a picture was printed indelibly on her vision, of Sidney Graham walking down the lily-garlanded aisle with the maid in blue tulle and white orchids on his arm. To make it more vivid the lady's picture was in the paper along with Graham's, just under those of the bride and groom, and her face was both handsome and haughty. One could tell by her tilted chin, the short upper lip, the cynical curve of mouth and sweep of long eye-lashes, her dress and the arrangement of her hair. Only a beauty could have stood that hair and not been positively ugly.

Shirley suddenly realized what she was doing and turned the page with a jerk that tore the sheet from top to bottom, continuing her search for the real estate column and the item she was after. All that morning her typewriter keys clicked rapidly; yet her work was strangely correct and perfect. She was working under a tense strain.

By noon she had herself in hand, realized what she was doing with her vagrant thoughts and could laugh at Miss Harriet Hale—whoever or whatever she was. What did it matter, Miss Harriet Hale or somebody else? What was that to Shirley Hollister? Mr. Graham was her landlord and a kind gentleman. He'd probably continue being that to her to the end of her tenancy, without regard to Miss Hale or any other intruding miss, and what else mattered? She wanted Mr. Graham only to be a kind gentleman whenever she must come in his way.

But although her philosophy was on hand and her pride aroused, she realized where her heart might have been tending if it weren't for this little jolt. She resolved to keep out of the gentleman's way whenever possible and, as far as she could, to think no more about him.

Keeping out of Sidney Graham's way was one thing, but keeping him out of her way was quite another, and Shirley realized it every time he came out to Glenside, which he did frequently. She couldn't tell him she wished he wouldn't come. She couldn't be rude to him when he came. There was no way of showing him she wasn't thinking of him in any way but as her landlord, because he never showed in any way he was expecting her to. He just happened in evening after evening in his frank, jolly manner on one pretext or other, never staying long, never showing her any more attention than he did her mother or Carol or the boys, and not even as much as he showed Doris. How was she to do anything but sit quietly and take the whole thing as a matter of course? She must deal with it in her own heart alone. And there the battle must be fought if ever battle there was to be.

Meanwhile, she could only admit that this cheerful young man brought a lot of life and pleasure to their lives, dropping in that way, and why shouldn't she enjoy it when it came, seeing it in no wise interfered with Miss Harriet Hale's rights and prerogatives? Nevertheless, Shirley withdrew more and more into quietness when he came and often slipped into the kitchen on some household pretext. But one day he boldly walked out into the kitchen after her with a book he wanted her to read and was so frank and companionable that she led the way back to the living room and concluded it would be better in the future to stay with the rest of the family.

Shirley had no intention of letting her heart stray after any impossible society man. She had her work in the world, and to it she meant to stick. If she had dreams she kept them under lock and key and only took them out now and then at night when she was tired and discouraged and life looked long and lonely. Shirley had no intention that Sidney Graham should ever think, when he married Miss Harriet Hale or someone equivalent to her, that any poor stenographer living in a barn had at one time imagined him fond of her. No, indeed! Shirley tilted her firm chin at the thought and declined to ride with Graham and Elizabeth the next time they called at the office for her, on the plea that she promised to go home in the trolley with one of the office girls. And yet the next time she saw him he was just as pleasant and showed no sign that she'd declined his invitation. In fact, the whole basis of their acquaintance was such that she felt free to go her own way and yet know he'd be as pleasant a friend whenever she needed one.

Matters stood in this way when Graham was suddenly obliged to go west on a trip for his office, to be gone three or four weeks. Mrs. Graham and Elizabeth took a short trip to the Adirondacks, and the people at Glenside settled down to quiet country life, broken only by a few visits from their farm neighbors and a call from the cheery pastor of the valley church.

Chapter 16

Sidney Graham didn't forget his friends while he was gone. The boys received a number of postcards from time to time, with fine views of California, Yellowstone Park, the Grand Canyon and other spots of interest. A wonderful picture book came for Doris, with Chinese pictures and rhymes printed on crêpe paper. The next morning a tiny sandalwood fan arrived for Carol with Graham's compliments and a few days later a box of oranges for Mrs. Hollister with no clue as to their sender. Shirley began to wonder what her part would be and what she should do about it and presently received—a letter! Then, after all, it was only a pleasant request that she not pay the rent, about which she was always so punctual, until his return, as no one else understood his affairs. He added a few words about his pleasant trip and a wish that they were all prospering—and that was all.

Shirley was disappointed, of course, and yet, if he'd said more or ventured to send her even the least gift, it would have made her uncomfortable and set her questioning how she should treat him and it. In the perfection of his behavior he hadn't overstepped a single bound the most particular might set for a landlord and his respected tenant. She drew a deep sigh and put the letter back into the envelope; as she did so she spied a small card, smaller than the envelope, on which was an exquisite bit of scenery, a colored photograph apparently, and underneath had been pencilled, "One of the many beautiful spots in California I'm sure you'd appreciate."

Her heart gave an unforbidden leap and was promptly taken to task for it. Yet when Shirley returned to her typewriter the bit of a picture was pinned to the wall back of her desk, and her eyes rested on it many times that day when she lifted them from her work. It is questionable whether Shirley remembered Miss Harriet Hale at all that day.

The garden was growing beautifully now. Soon lettuce and radishes would be ready to eat. George had secured a number of customers through people at the store and, when his produce was ripe, planned to take early trips to town to deliver it. They watched every night and looked again every morning for signs of the first pea blossoms and the green spires of onion tops, like sparse hairs, sprouting up. Every day brought some new wonder.

They almost forgot they ever lived in the brick house, until George rode by there on his bicycle one noon and reported it had been half pulled down, and he could see the outline of where the stairs and closets had been, in plaster, on the side of the next house. They were silent for a minute thinking after he told that, and Mrs. Hollister looked around the great airy place in which they were sitting and then out the open door where the faint stain of sunset was still lingering against the horizon.

"We should be very thankful, children. George, get the Bible and read the thirty-fourth psalm." Wonderingly George obeyed, and they listened as the words sank into their souls.

When the psalm was finished and the last words read—"The Lord redeemeth the soul of his servants, and none of them that trust in him shall be desolate"—the mother said, "Now let's kneel down and thank Him."

And they knelt while she prayed a few words of thanksgiving and commended them to God's keeping.

By this time Mrs. Hollister was so well she worked every day for a little while in the garden and could do a great deal in the house. The children were overjoyed and lived in a continual state of delight over the wild, free life they were living. Carol's school had closed, and she was home all day. This made one more to help in the garden. George was talking about building a pigeon house and raising squabs for sale. The man who did the plowing had given him a couple to start with and told him there was money in squabs if one only went about it right. George and Harley pored over a book that told all about it and talked much on the subject.

The weather was growing warm, and Shirley was wishing her vacation came in July or August instead of the first two weeks in September. Somehow she felt used up these hot days, and the hours dragged by slowly. At night the trolleys were crowded until they were halfway out to Glenside. She often had to stand, and her head ached. Yet she was very happy and thankful—only there was so much to be done in this world, and she seemed to have so little strength to do it all. The burden of next fall came occasionally to mar the summer's beauty and rested heavily on her young shoulders. If only there wouldn't be any winter for just one year, and they could stay in the barn and get rested and get a little money ahead somehow for moving. It was going to be so hard to leave that beautiful abode, barn though it was.

One morning, nearly four weeks after Graham left for California, Shirley was called from her desk to the outer office to take some dictation for Mr. Clegg. While she was there two men entered the outer office and asked for Mr. Barnard. One of them was a short, thickset man with a pretentious gray mustache parted in the middle and combed out on his cheeks. He had a red face, cunning eyes and a cruel set to his jaw, which somehow seemed ridiculously at variance with his loud, checkered suit, sporty necktie of bright blue satin, set with a scarfpin of two magnificent stones, a diamond and a sapphire, and with the three showy jewelled rings he wore on his pudgy hand. The other man was sly, gray and unobtrusive, obviously the first one's henchman.

Mr. Clegg told the men they might wait in the inner office for Mr. Barnard, who would probably be in shortly. Shirley watched them go, wondering idly why those exquisite stones had to be wasted in such an out-of-place spot on that coarse-looking man's necktie and if a man like that really cared for beautiful things. It was only a passing thought, and then she picked up her pencil and took down the closing sentences of the letter Mr. Clegg was dictating.

In a moment more she was free to go back to her alcove just behind Mr. Barnard's office that connected with it. It had an entrance from the cloak room, which she always used when Mr. Barnard had visitors in his office, and through this she now went, having a strange repugnance toward being seen by the two men. She had an innate sense that the man with the gaudy garments wouldn't treat a young girl in her position with any respect, and she didn't care to come under his gaze. She slipped quietly through the cloak room and passed the open door like a shadow into Mr. Barnard's office, where they sat with their backs toward her, having evidently just settled down and begun to talk.

She could hear a low-breathed comment on the office furnishings, indicating the owner's good bank account, and a coarse jest about a photograph of Mr. Barnard's wife which stood on his desk. It made her wish the door between the rooms was closed; yet she didn't care to rise and close it lest she called attention to herself, and of course it might be only a minute or two before Mr. Barnard returned. A pile of envelopes to be addressed lay on her desk, and this work she could do without any noise, so she slipped into her seat and began to work.

"Well, we got them Grahams good and fast now!" a voice, which she knew belonged to the man with the loud clothing, said. "The young feller bit all right! I thought he would. He's that kind."

He stopped for a contemptuous laugh, and Shirley's heart stood still. What could it mean? Was it something about her Grahams? Some danger threatening them? Some game being played on them? He looked like a man who lived on others' blindnesses. What were they called? Parasites? Instinctively she was on the alert and automatically reached for the pad on which she took dictation and began to write down in shorthand what she'd just heard. The voice in the other room continued, and her fountain pen kept eager pace, her breath coming quickly now and her face white with excitement.

"He went out to see the place, examine the mines and all that. Oh, he's awful cautious! Thought he took a government expert with him to test the ore. We fixed that up all right—had the man on tap at the right minute, government papers all OK—you couldn't have told 'em from the real thing. It was Casey—you know him; he's a crackerjack on a job like that—could fool the devil himself. Well, he swore it was the finest kind of ore and all that kind of dope and led that Graham kid around as sweetly as a blue-eyed baby. We had a gang out there all bribed, you know, to swear to things and took particular pains so Graham would go around and ask the right ones questions—Casey tended to that. Now he's come home with the biggest tale and ready to boost the thing to the skies.

"I've got his word for it, and his daddy's to sign the papers this morning. When he wakes up one of these fine days he'll find himself minus a hundred thousand or so and nobody to blame for it, because how could anyone know those are only pockets? He'll recommend it right and left, too, and we'll clean out a lot of other fellers before we get done. Teddy, my boy, pat yourself on the back! We'll have a tidy sum between us out of this deal and take a foreign trip for our health till the fracas blows over. Now, mind you, not a word of this to Barnard when he comes in. We're only going to pave the way this morning. The real tip comes from Graham himself. See?"

Shirley was faint with excitement as she finished writing, and her brain was in a whirl. She felt as if she'd scream in a minute if this strain kept up. The papers were to be signed that morning! Even now the deed might be done, and it might be too late to stop it. Yet she must make no sign, mustn't let the men know she was there and that they'd been heard. She must sit here breathless until they were gone, or they might manage to prevent her getting word to Graham. How long would they stay? Would they talk on and reveal more? The other man had only grunted something unintelligible in reply, and then before more could be said an office boy opened the outer door and told them Mr. Barnard had just phoned that he wouldn't be back before two o'clock.

The men swore and went out grumbling. Suddenly Shirley knew her time had come to do something. Stepping quickly to the door she scanned the room carefully to make sure they were gone; then closing her door she picked up the telephone on her desk and called the Graham number. She didn't know what she meant to say or what she'd do if Sidney Graham weren't in the office—and he'd hardly be there yet if he had only arrived home the day before. He'd likely take a day off before getting back to work. Her throbbing heart beat out these questions to her brain while she waited for the number.

Would she dare ask for Mr. Walter Graham? And if she did, what would she say to him? He didn't know her and probably never heard of her. He might think her crazy. Then there was always the possibility there was some mistake—and yet it seemed a coincidence that two men of the same name should both be going west at that time. It must be these Grahams the plot was against. But how to explain enough over the phone to do any good? Of course she must give them a copy of what she'd taken down in shorthand, but first she must stop the signing of those papers, whatever they were, at all costs.

Then all at once, in the midst of her whirling thoughts, came a voice at the other end of the phone: "Hello!" And her frantic senses realized it was a familiar one.

"Oh, is this—this is Mr. Sidney Graham, isn't it? This is Shirley Hollister."

A catch in her voice sounded almost like a sob as she drew in her breath with relief to know he was there, and his answer came in swift alarm.

"Yes? Is anything the matter, Shirley? You're not ill, are you?"

The young man's voice held a sharp note of anxiety, and even in her excitement it made Shirley's heart leap to hear it.

"No, there's nothing the matter with me," she said, trying to steady her voice, "but something has happened that I think you should know at once. I don't know whether I should tell it over the phone. I may be overheard."

"I'll come to you immediately. Where can I find you?"

Her heart leaped again at his willingness to trust her and obey her call.

"In Mr. Barnard's private office. If you ask for me they'll let you come right in. One thing more: If your father was to decide anything important this morning, could you get him to wait till you return or till you phone him?"

There was a second's hesitation, and the reply was puzzled but courteous: "He's not in the office at present and won't be for an hour."

"Oh, I'm so glad! Then please hurry!"

"I'll get there as soon as I can." The phone clicked into place.

Shirley sat back in her chair and pressed her hands over her eyes to concentrate all her powers. Then she turned to her typewriter and copied off the shorthand, her fingers flying over the keys with more than their usual swiftness. As she wrote she prayed, prayed that nothing might have been signed and that her warning might not come too late; prayed, too, that Mr. Barnard might not return until Mr. Graham had been and gone, and that Mr. Graham might not think her an utter fool in case this proved to have nothing to do with his affairs.

Chapter 17

When Graham entered the office Shirley came to meet him quietly, without a word of greeting other than to put her cold hand into his that he held out to her. She spoke in a low voice full of suppressed excitement. She had a vague fear the two men might be lingering about the outer office waiting for Mr. Barnard and a momentary dread lest Mr. Barnard might enter the room at any minute. She must get the telling over before he came.

"Mr. Graham, two men were sitting in this room waiting for Mr. Barnard a few minutes ago, and I was in my room just back there. I couldn't help hearing what they said, and when I caught the name of Graham in connection with what sounded like an evil plot I took down their words in shorthand. It may not have anything to do with your firm, but I thought I should let you know. I called you on the phone as soon as they left the office and wouldn't hear me, and I made this copy of their conversation. Read it quickly, please, because if it has anything to do with you, you'll want to phone your father at once, before those men get there."

Her tone was cool, and her hand was steady as she handed him the typewritten paper, but her heart was beating wildly. For his eyes held a look as he greeted her that made her feel he was glad to see her, and it touched an answering gladness in her heart and filled her with both delight and apprehension. What a fool she was!

She turned sharply away and busied herself with arranging some papers on Mr. Barnard's desk while he read. She must still this excitement and get control of herself before he was through. She must be the cool, impersonal stenographer and not let him suspect for a moment she was excited about seeing him again.

The young man stood still, reading rapidly, his face growing graver as he read. The girl snatched a furtive glance at him and felt convinced the matter was a serious one and had to do with him.

Suddenly he looked up.

"Do you know who those men were?" he asked, and she saw his eyes were full of anxiety.

"No," said Shirley. "But I saw them as they passed through the outer office and stopped to speak to Mr. Clegg. I was taking dictation from Mr. Clegg at the time. I came back to my desk through the cloak room, so they didn't know I was within hearing."

"What did they look like? Do you remember?"

She described them.

Certainty grew in his face as she talked, with grave concern.

"May I use your phone a minute?" he asked after an instant's thought.

She led him to her desk and handed him the receiver, then stepped back into the office and waited.

"Hello! Is that you, Edward?" she heard him say. "Has Father come yet? Give me his phone, please. Hello, Father; this is Sidney. Father, has Kremnitz come in yet? He has? He's waiting in the office to see you? Well, don't see him, Father, till I get there. Something has turned up that I'm afraid is going to alter matters entirely. Yes, pretty serious, I'm afraid. Don't see him. Keep him waiting. I'll be there in five minutes and come in the back way directly to your office. Don't talk with him on any account till I can get there. Good-bye."

He hung up the receiver and turned to Shirley.

"You were just in time to save us. I don't have time now to tell you how grateful I am for this. I must hurry right over. Do you suppose if we need you, you could come over and identify those men? Thank you. I'll speak to Mr. Clegg about it as I go out, and if we find it necessary we'll phone you. In case you have to come I'll have an office boy in the hall take your hat, and you can come right into the office as if you were one of our employees—just walk over to the bookcase as if you were looking for a book—any book. Select one and look through it, while glancing around the room, and see if you find those men. Then walk through into my office. I'll be waiting there. Good-bye, and thank you so much!"

He gave her hand one quick clasp and was gone, and Shirley found she was trembling from head to foot. She walked quickly into her room and sat down, burying her face in her hands and trying to get control of herself, but the tears came to her eyes in spite of all she could do. It wasn't the excitement of getting the men and stopping their evil plans before they could do any damage, although that had something to do with her nervous state, of course. And it wasn't that she'd been able to do a little thing in return for all he'd done for her. Nor was it even his gratitude. It was—she couldn't deny it—it was a certain quality in his voice, something in the look he gave her, that made her whole soul glow and seemed to fill the hungry longing in her heart.

It frightened her and made her ashamed, and as she sat with bowed head she prayed for strength to act like a sensible girl and crush out such foolish thoughts before they dared lift their heads and be recognized even by her own heart. Thus strengthened, she resolved to think no more about the matter but get her work done and be ready to enter into that other business if it became necessary. Mr. Barnard would be coming soon, and she must have his work finished. She'd lost almost an hour by this matter.

She went at her typewriter pell-mell and soon finished Mr. Clegg's letters. She was nearly through with the addressing Mr. Barnard left for her to do when the telephone called her to Graham's office.

She slipped on her hat and hurried out.

"Will it be all right for me to take my noontime now, Mr. Clegg?" she said, stopping by his desk. "Mr. Graham said he spoke to you."

"Yes, he wants you to help him identify someone. That's all right. I'll explain to Mr. Barnard when he comes. There's nothing important you have to finish, is there? All done but those envelopes? Well, you needn't return until one o'clock anyway. The envelopes can wait till the four o'clock mail, and if Mr. Barnard needs anything in a hurry Miss Dwight can attend to it this time. Just take your time, Miss Hollister."

Shirley went out bewildered by the unusual generosity of Mr. Clegg, who was usually abrupt. She realized, however, that his warmth must be due to Mr. Graham's visit and not to any desire to give her a holiday. She smiled to think what a difference wealth and position made in the eyes of the world.

The same office boy she met on her first visit to Mr. Graham's office was waiting for her now in the hall when she stepped out of the elevator. She gave him her hat and walked into the office according to plan, going straight to the glass bookcase full of calf-bound volumes and selecting one after running her finger over two rows of them. She was as cool as though her part had been rehearsed many times, although her heart was pounding unmercifully, and it seemed as though the people in the next room must hear it. She stood and opened her book, glancing casually about the room.

There, sure enough, quite near her sat the two men, fairly bursting with impatience. The once immaculate hair of the loudly dressed one was rumpled as if he'd run his fingers through it many times, and he played nervously with his heavy rings and caressed half viciously his mustache, working his thick lips all the while. Shirley took a good look at him, necktie, scarfpin and all; looked into the face of the gray one also; then coolly closed the bookcase door and carried the book she selected into Sidney Graham's office.

Graham was there, standing to receive her, and just back of him stood a kind-faced elderly man with merry blue eyes, gray hair and a stylishly cut beard. By their attitude and manner Shirley sensed they'd both been watching her. Then Graham introduced her.

"This is my father, Miss Hollister."

The elder man took her hand and shook it heartily, speaking in a gruff, hearty way that won her from the first.

"I'm glad to know you, Miss Hollister. I certainly am! My son has been telling me what you've done for us, and I think you're a great girl! That was bully work you did, and I appreciate it. I was watching you out there in the office. You were as cool as a cucumber. You should be a detective. You found your men all right, did you?"

"Yes, sir," said Shirley, much abashed and feeling the return of that foolish trembling in her limbs. "Yes, they're both out there, and the short one with the rings and the blue necktie is the one who did the talking."

"Exactly what I thought," drawled the father, with a twinkle in his eyes. "I couldn't somehow trust that chap from the start. That's why I sent my son out to investigate. Well, now, will you just step into my private office, Miss Hollister, and take your seat by the typewriter as if you were my stenographer? You'll find paper in the drawer, and you can just be writing—write anything you choose, so it looks natural when the men come in. When we get to talking I'd like you to take down in shorthand all that's said by all of us. You're pretty good at that, I judge. Sid, will you phone for those officers now? I think it's about time for the curtain to rise." And he led the way into his own office.

Shirley sat down at the typewriter as directed and began to write mechanically. Mr. Graham touched the bell on his desk and told the office boy who answered to send in Mr. Kremnitz and his companion.

Shirley was seated so she could glimpse the men without being noticed, and she was especially interested in the twinkle that shone in the bright blue eyes of the elder Graham as he surveyed the men who thought he was their dupe. Her heart warmed to him. His kind, merry face, his hearty, unconventional speech, all showed him to be a warm-hearted man without a bit of snobbishness.

The son came in, and talk began as if the matter of the mine were going on. Mr. Kremnitz produced some papers he evidently expected to be signed at once and answered questions complacently—keen questions Shirley saw they were afterward, and in the light of the revelation she overheard in Mr. Barnard's office Kremnitz perjured himself hopelessly by his answers. Presently the office boy announced someone's arrival in the next room. Shirley had taken down in detail a great deal of valuable information the Grahams had together drawn from their victim. She was surprised at the list of wealthy businessmen who were to have been involved in the scheme.

Then suddenly the quiet scene changed. The elder Graham signalled his office boy, which looked merely like waving him away, and the door was flung open, revealing four law officers, who stepped into the room without further word. Graham arose and faced his two startled callers, with his hand firmly planted on the papers on his desk which he was supposed to sign.

"Mr. Kremnitz," he said—and even in the midst of this serious business Shirley imagined she heard a half-comic drawl to his words; he simply couldn't help letting his sense of humor come on top—"it won't be possible for me to sign these papers this morning, as you expected. I don't feel satisfied that all things are as you've represented. In fact, I have the best evidence to the contrary. Officer, these are the gentlemen you've come to arrest."

And he stepped back and waved his hand toward the two conspirators, who sat with startled eyes and blanched faces, appalled at the sudden developments where they'd thought all was moving smoothly toward their desired end.

"Arrest! Who? On what charge?" flashed the gaudy Kremnitz, springing to his feet and dashing toward the door, while his companion slid furtively toward the other end of the room, evidently hoping to gain young Graham's office before he was noticed. But two officers blocked their way, and the handcuffs clanked in the hands of the other two policemen.

"Why, arrest you, my friend," said Graham senior, as if he rather enjoyed the little man's discomfiture. "And for trying to perpetrate the biggest swindle attempted for ten years. I must say you've worked hard and done the trick neatly, but you made one unfortunate slip that saved all us poor rich men. It seems a pity that so much elaborate lying should have brought you two nothing but those bracelets you're wearing—they don't seem to match your other jewels—but that's the way things go in this world. Now take them away, officer. I've no more time to waste on them this morning!" He turned and walked over by Shirley's desk, while the curtain fell over the brief drama.

"Do you know how much money you've saved us, little girl—just plain saved? I'll tell you. A clean hundred thousand! That's what I was going to put into this affair! And I expected to influence a lot of other men to put in a good deal also. Now, little girl, I don't know what you think about it, but I want to shake hands."

He put out his hand, and Shirley laid her own in it, smiling and blushing and saying with what excited breath she had, "Oh, I'm so glad I got you in time!" Then she became aware the man had continued talking.

"I don't know what you think about it," he repeated, "but I feel that you saved me a clean hundred thousand dollars, and I say that a good percentage of that belongs to you as a reward of your quickness and keenness."

But Shirley drew her hand away and stepped back, her face white, her head up, her chin tilted, her eyes dark. She spoke clearly and earnestly.

"No, Mr. Graham, nothing whatever belongs to me. I don't want any reward. I couldn't think of taking it. It's out of the question!"

"Well, well, well!" said the elder Graham, sitting down on the edge of his desk and watching her in undisguised admiration. "Now that's a new kind of girl that won't take what she's earned—what rightly belongs to her."

"Mr. Graham, it was a very little thing I did—anybody would have done it—and it was just in the way of simple duty. Please don't say anything more about it. I'm only too glad to have an opportunity to give a little help to people who've helped me so much. I feel that I'm under deep obligation to your son for making it possible for us to live in the country, where my mother is getting well."

"Well, now, I'll have to inquire into this business. I haven't heard anything about obligations, and for my part I feel a big one just now. Perhaps you think it was a very little thing you did, but suppose you hadn't done it. Suppose you'd been too busy, or it hadn't occurred to you to take down that conversation until it was too late; or suppose you hadn't had the brains to see what it would mean to us. Why, then it would have become a very big thing indeed, and we'd have been willing, if we'd known, to pay a mighty big sum to get that evidence. You see, a hundred thousand dollars isn't a little thing when you're swindled out of it. It's the swindling that hurts more than the loss of money. And you saved us from that.

"Now, young lady, I consider myself under obligation to you, and I intend to discharge it somehow. If I can't do it one way I shall another, but in the meantime I'm deeply grateful, and please accept our thanks. If you're willing to add one more to your kindness, I shall be glad if you'll make a carbon copy of those shorthand notes you took. I may need them for evidence. And, by the way, you'll probably be called upon to testify in court. I'm sorry. That may be unpleasant, but I guess it can't be helped. So before you get through you may not think you did such a very small thing after all.

"Sid, I think you better escort this young lady back to her office and explain to Barnard. He's probably been on the verge of being buncoed also. You said Kremnitz was waiting for him when the conversation took place? I guess you better go with Miss Hollister and clear the whole thing up. Say, child, have you had your lunch yet? No, of course not. Sidney, you take her to get some lunch before she goes back to the office. She's had an exciting morning. Now, good-bye, little girl. I won't forget what you've done for us, and I'm coming to see you pretty soon and get things squared up."

So in spite of her protests, Mr. Sidney Graham escorted Shirley Hollister into one of the city's most exclusive tearooms and seated her at a little round table set for two, while off at a short distance Miss Harriet Hale sat with her mother, eating her lunch and trying in vain to "place" the pretty girl she didn't recognize.

It never occurred to her for a moment that Sidney Graham's companion might be a stenographer, for Shirley had a knack about her clothes that made her seem well dressed. That hat she wore had seen service for three summers and was a different shape and color from when it began life. A scrub in hot water had removed the dust of toil, some judiciously applied dye had settled the matter of color, and a trifling manipulation on her head while the hat was still wet had made the shape not only exceedingly stylish but becoming. The chic rosette and strictly tailored band, its sole trimming, were made from a much-soiled waist ribbon, washed and stretched around a bottle of hot water to dry it and teased into the latest thing in rosettes by Shirley's adept fingers. The simple linen dress she wore fitted well and at a distance couldn't have been told from something better, and neither were gloves and shoes near enough to be inspected critically. So Miss Hale was puzzled and jealously watched the pretty color come and go in Shirley's cheek and the simple grace of her movements.

Fortunately, Shirley didn't see Miss Hale and wouldn't have recognized her anyway from her one brief glimpse of the newspaper picture. So she ate her delectable lunch, ordered by Graham. And she enjoyed herself so intensely that it seemed to her she could never make the rest of her life measure up to this hour's privileges.

For Shirley was a normal girl. She couldn't help being pleased to be doing for once as other more favored girls did constantly. To be lunching at Blanco's with one of the most-sought-after men in the upper set, to be treated like a queen and to be talking about travels and pictures and books—it was all too wonderful to be real. Shirley began to feel that if it didn't end soon with her back in the office addressing the rest of those envelopes she'd think she'd died in the midst of a dream and gone to heaven.

Something else brought an undertone of beauty, which she wasn't acknowledging even to her inmost self. That was the way Graham looked at her, as if she were some fine beautiful angel from above that he loved to look at; as if he really cared what she thought and did; as if a soul-harmony were between them, setting them apart this day and others and putting them into tune with one another; as if he were glad to see her once more after the absence! All through her being it thrilled like a song that brings tears to the throat and gladness to the eyes and makes one feel strong and pure. That was how it seemed when she thought about it afterward. At the time she was just living it in wonder and thanksgiving.

At another time her pride might have risen and swelled over the number of people who eyed her enviously as they walked out together; over the many bows and salutations he received from people of evident consequence, for she had the normal human pride in her nature as we all have. But her heart was too humble then with a new, strange happiness to feel it or take it in, and she walked with unconscious grace beside him, feeling only the joy of being there.

Later, in the quiet of her chamber, her mother's warning came to her, and her cheeks burned with shame that her heart had made so much of a common little luncheon, a mere courtesy after she did a favor. Yet through it all Shirley knew something fine and true belonged just to her, and presently she would rise above everything and grasp it and keep it hers forever.

She felt the distinction of her escort anew when she entered Barnard and Clegg's in his company and saw Mr. Clegg spring to open the door and set a chair for his young guest, saw even Mr. Barnard rise and greet him with almost reverence. And this honor she knew was being paid to money, the great demagogue. It wasn't the man she admired to whom they were paying deference; it was to his money! She smiled to herself. It was the man she admired, not his money.

All afternoon she worked with flying fingers, turning out the work at marvelous speed, amused when she heard the new note of respect in Mr. Barnard's voice as he gave her a direction. Mr. Barnard was impressed with the story Graham told him and was also deeply grateful on his own account that Shirley had acted as she had, for he was on the verge of investing a large trust fund in his keeping in the new mining operation, and it would have meant absolute failure for him.

When Shirley left the office that night she was almost too tired to see which trolley was coming. But someone touched her on the arm, and there stood Sidney Graham waiting for her beside his car—a little two-passenger affair she'd never seen and that went like the wind. They took a road they hadn't traveled together before, and Shirley sat there, her heart in a tumult of doubts and joys and questions.

Chapter 18

W hat that ride was to Shirley she hardly let herself think afterward. Sitting cozily beside Graham in the racing car, gliding through the better part of town, where the tall, imposing houses slept with drawn blinds and dust-covered shutters proclaimed their owners were far away from heat and toil. Out through wide roads and green-hedged lanes, where stately mansions set in flowers and mimic landscapes loomed far back from the road in dignified seclusion. Passing now and then a car of people who recognized Graham and nodded in the same deferential way as in the tearoom. And all the time his eyes were on her, admiring, delighting, and his care about her was solicitous for her comfort.

Once he halted the car and pointed off against the sunset, where wide gables and battlemented towers stood gray amidst a setting of green shrubbery and trees, and velvety lawns reached far, to high, trim hedges arched in places for an entrance to the beautiful estate.

"That's my home over there," he said and watched her widening eyes. "I wish I had time to take you over tonight, but I know you're tired and should get home and rest. Another time we'll go around that way." And her heart leaped up as the car went forward again. There was to be another time! Ah! But she mustn't allow it. Her heart was far too foolish already. Yet she'd enjoy this ride, now that she was started.

They talked about the sunset and a poem he'd read lately. He told her bits about his journey, referring to his experience at the mines, touching on some amusing incidents, sketching some of the odd characters he met. Once he asked her quite abruptly if she thought her mother would be disturbed if he had a cement floor put in the basement of the barn sometime soon. He wanted to have it done before cold weather set in, and it would dry better now in the hot days. Of course, if it would disturb any of them in the least it could wait, but he wanted to store a few things there that were being taken out of the office buildings, and he thought they'd keep drier if there was a cement floor. When she said it wouldn't disturb anyone in the least, would on the contrary be interesting for the children to watch, he returned easily to California scenery and never referred to it again.

All through the ride, which was across country she'd never seen and ended at Glenside approaching from a new direction, a subtle something lay between them, a sympathy and quick understanding as if they were comrades, almost partners in a lot of common interests. Shirley chided herself for it every time she looked up and caught his glance and felt the thrill of pleasure in this close companionship. Of course it was wholly in her imagination and due entirely to the nervous strain she'd experienced that day, she told herself. Of course, he had nothing in his mind but the most ordinary kind desire to give her a good time out of gratitude for what she did for him. But nevertheless it was sweet, and Shirley was loath to surrender the joy of it while it lasted, dream though it might be.

It lasted all the way, even up to the front of the barn when he took her hand to help her out, and his fingers lingered on hers with just an instant's pressure, sending a thrill to her heart again and almost bringing tears to her eyes. Foolishness! She was overwrought. It was a shame human beings were so made that they had to become weak like that in a time of pleasant rejoicing.

The family came out noisily to meet them, rejoicing openly at Graham's return. George and Harley vied with each other to shout the news about the garden and the chickens and the dovecote, while Carol demanded to know where Elizabeth was.

And Doris earnestly looked in his face and repeated, "Ickle budie fy away, Mistah Gwaham. All gone! All ickle budies fy away!"

Even Mrs. Hollister came smiling to the door to meet him, and the young man had a hearty greeting and a handshake for each one. It was as if he'd just come home to a place where he loved to be, and he couldn't show his joy enough. Shirley stood back for a moment watching him, admiring the way his hair waved away from his temples, thinking how handsome he looked when he smiled, wondering that he could so easily fit himself into this group, which must in the nature of things be utterly different from his native element, rejoicing over the deference he paid to her plain, quiet mother and thrilling over the kiss he gave her sweet little sister.

Then Mrs. Hollister did something unexpected and dreadful—she invited him to stay to dinner! Shirley stood back and gasped. Of course he'd decline, but think of inviting the wealthy and cultured Mr. Graham to take dinner in his own barn!

Oh! But he wasn't declining at all. He was accepting as if it were a great pleasure Mrs. Hollister was conferring upon him. Sure, he'd stay! He was wishing all the way out they'd ask him. He wondered whether he dared invite himself.

Shirley with red cheeks hurried in to see that the tablecloth was on straight and look after one or two little things. But, behold, he followed her out and, gently insisting and assisting, literally compelled her to come and lie down on the couch while he told the family what she went through that day. Shirley was so happy she almost cried before them all. It was so wonderful to have someone take care of her that way. Of course it was only gratitude—but she'd been taking care of other people so long that it completely broke her down to have someone take care of her.

The dinner went much more easily than she'd supposed it could with those cracked plates and the forks from which the silver was worn off. Doris insisted the guest sit next to her and butter her bread for her, and she occasionally caressed his coat sleeve with a sticky little hand, but he didn't seem to mind it in the least and smiled down on her in quite a brotherly way, arranging her bib when it got tangled in her curls and seeing that she had plenty of jelly on her bread.

It was a wonderful dinner. Mother Hollister had known what she was about when she selected that particular night to invite unexpected company. They had stewed chicken on little round biscuits, with plenty of gravy and currant jelly, mashed potatoes, green peas, little new beets, and a delicious custard pie for dessert, velvety yellow with a golden-brown top. The guest ate as if he enjoyed it and asked for a second piece of pie, as if he were one of them. It was unbelievable!

He helped clear off the table, too, and insisted on Carol's giving him a towel to help with the dishes. It was like a dream.

The young man tore himself reluctantly away about nine o'clock and went home, but before he left he took Shirley's hand and looked into her eyes with another of those deep understanding glances. Shirley watched him riding away in the moonlight and wondered if there would ever be another day as exciting and wonderful as this had been and whether she could come down to sensible, everyday living again by morning.

Then the day's story had to be told again after he was gone, with the family touches that were left out when the guest was there and with the comments of "Oh, did you notice how admiring he looked when he told Mother that Shirley had a remarkably sharp mind?" and "He said his father thought Shirley was the most unspoiled-looking girl he'd ever seen!" and a lot of other things Shirley hadn't heard before.

Shirley told her mother what the senior Mr. Graham had said about giving her a reward, and her mother agreed she did right in declining anything for such a simple service. But she looked after Shirley with a sigh as she went to put Doris to bed and wondered if for this service the poor child was to get a broken heart. A girl couldn't be given attention such as Shirley received that day, from as attractive a young man as Graham, without feeling it keenly not to have it continue. And of course it was out of the question that it should continue. Mrs. Hollister decided she was wrong to invite the young man to stay to supper and resolved never to offend in that way again. It was a wrong to Shirley to put him on such intimate footing in the household, and it could only bring her sadness. He was a most unusual young man to have even wanted to stay, but one mustn't take that for more than a passing whim, and Shirley must be protected at all hazards.

"Now," said the elder Graham the next morning, when the day's business was well under way and he had time to send for his son, "I want you to tell me all about the little girl and what you think we should give her. What did she mean by 'obligations' yesterday? Have you been doing anything for her, son? I meant to ask you last night, but you came home so late I couldn't sit up."

And then Sidney Graham told his father the whole story. It was different from telling his mother. He knew no barn would have the power to prejudice his father.

"And you say that girl lives in the old barn!" exclaimed the father when the story was finished. "Why, the nervy little kid! And she looks as if she came out of a bandbox! Well, she's a bully little girl and no mistake! Well, now, son, what can we do for her? We should do something nice. It wasn't just the money we might have lost. That would have been a trifle beside getting those other folks balled up in the mess. Why, I'd have given every cent I own before I'd have Fuller and Browning and Barnard and Wilts get entangled. I tell you, son—it was a great escape!"

"Yes, Father, and it was a great lesson for me. I'll never be buncoed as easily again. But about Miss Hollister, I don't know what to say. She's very proud and sensitive. I had an awful time doing the little things I just had to do to that barn without her suspecting I was doing it especially for her. Father, you should go out there and meet the family—then you'd understand. They're not ordinary people. Their father was a college professor and wrote things. They're cultured people."

"Well, I want to meet them. Why don't we go out there and call today? I think they must be worth knowing."

So late that afternoon the father and son rode out to Glenside. When Shirley and George reached home they found the car standing in front of their place and the Grahams seated comfortably in the open doorway, enjoying the late afternoon breeze and seemingly at home in their own barn.

"I'm not going to swarm here every day," said the son, rising and coming out to meet her. "Father hadn't heard about the old barn's transformation, and the minute I told him about it he had to come right out and see it."

"Yes," said the father, smiling, "I had to come and see what you'd done out here. I've played in the hay up in that loft many a day in my time, and I love the old barn. It's great to see it fixed up so cozy. But we're going home now and let you have your dinner. We just wanted to say howdy to you before we left."

They stayed a few minutes longer, however, and the senior Graham talked with Shirley while he held Doris on his knee and stroked her silky hair, as she nestled in his arms.

Then, although young Graham was quite loath to leave so soon, they went, for he couldn't, in conscience, expect an invitation to dinner two days in succession.

They rode into the sunset, going across the country to their home without returning to town, and Doris, as she stood with the others watching them, murmured softly: "Nice favver-man! Nice Gwaham favver-man!"

The "nice-Graham-father-man" was at that moment remarking to his son in decided tones, as he turned to glimpse the old barn: "That old barn door should come down right away, Sid, and an old-fashioned door with glass around the sides be made to fill the space. That door is an eyesore on the place, and they need a porch. They can't live with a heavy door like that to open and shut every day."

"Yes, Father, I've thought of that, but I don't know how to manage it. They're not objects of charity. I've been thinking about some way to fix up a heating arrangement without hurting their feelings, so they could stay there all winter. I know they hate to go back to the city, and they're only paying ten dollars a month. It's all they can afford. What could they get in the city for that?"

"Great Scott! A girl like that living in a house she could get for ten dollars, when some of these feather-brained baby dolls we know can't get on with less than three or four houses that cost from fifty to a hundred thousand dollars apiece! Say, son, that's a peach of a girl—do you know it? I've been talking with her, and she has a superior mind."

"I know she has, Father," answered the son humbly.

"I say, Sid—why don't you marry her? That would solve the whole problem. Then you could fix up the barn into a regular house for her folks."

"Well, Father, that's just what I've made up my mind to do—if she'll have me," said the son with a glow of triumph in his eyes.

"Bully for you, Sid! Bully for you!" And the father gave his son's broad shoulder a resounding slap. "Why, Sid, I didn't think you had that much sense. Your mother led me to understand you were philandering around with that dolly-faced Harriet Hale, and I couldn't see what you saw in her. But if you mean it, son, I'm with you every time. That girl's a peach, and you couldn't get one finer if you searched the world over."

"Yes, I'm afraid Mother's got her heart set on Harriet Hale," said the son, "but I can't see it that way."

"H'm! Your mother likes show," sighed the father, "but she's got a good heart, and she'll bowl over all right and make the best of it. You know your mother and I weren't such high and mighties when we were young, and we married for love. But now, if you really mean business, I don't see why we can't do something right away. When does that girl have her vacation? Of course she gets one sometime. Why couldn't your mother just invite the whole family to occupy the shore cottage for a little while—get up some excuse or other—ask 'em to take care of it? You know it's lying idle all this summer, and two servants are down there growing fat with nothing to do. We might ship Elizabeth down there and let 'em be company for her. They seem like a fine set of children. It would do Elizabeth good to know them."

"Oh, she's crazy about them. She's been out a number of times with me, and don't you remember she had Carol out to stay with her?"

"Was that the black-eyed, sensible girl? Well, I declare! I didn't recognize her. She was all dolled up out at our house. I suppose Elizabeth loaned 'em to her, eh? Well, I'm glad. She's got sense, too. That's the kind of people I like my children to know. Now if that vacation could only be arranged to come when your mother and I take that Western trip, why, it would be just the thing for Elizabeth and, work right all around. Now the thing for you to do is to find out about that vacation. Then you could have everything planned and rush the work so it would be done when they came back."

So the two conspirators plotted, while unconscious of their interest Shirley was trying to get herself in hand and not think how Graham's eyes had looked when he said good night to her.

Chapter 19

Since the pastor from the village had called on them, the young people of the stone barn had been identified with the church in the valley. Shirley took a class of boys in the Sunday school and was playing the organ, as George predicted. Carol was helping the primary teacher, George was assistant librarian and secretary, Harley was in Shirley's class, and Doris was one of the primaries.

Shirley identified herself at once with the struggling Christian Endeavor society and was putting new life into it, with her enthusiasm, her ideas about getting hold of the young people in the community and her knack of getting the silent ones to take part in the meetings. She suggested new committees, invited the music committee to meet at her home some evening to plan out special music and even cooperated with the social committee in planning for music at the socials. She carried a few appropriate clippings or verses or other quotations to slip into the hands of some who hadn't prepared to speak, and she saw to it that her brothers and sisters were ready to say something. In fact she did her part so unobtrusively that none of the old members could think she was trying to usurp power or make herself prominent. She became a quiet power behind the powers, to whom the president and other officers came for advice, and who seemed always ready to help in any work or find a way out of any difficulty.

Christian Endeavor took great strides after the Hollisters' advent, and even the idlers on the street corners were moved with curiosity to drop in on the young people's twilight service and see what went on and why everybody seemed so interested. But the secret, Shirley thought, was the five-minute prayer service the prayer meeting committee held in the primary room just before the regular meeting. Shirley, as leader of the prayer meeting committee, had started this little meeting, and she always came into the larger room with a radiance on her face and a feeling of strength in her heart from this brief speaking with her Master.

Shirley was somewhat dismayed the next Sabbath when Sidney Graham arrived and asked her to take a ride with him.

"Why, I was just going to church," she said, hesitating and then smiling up at him. "Besides, I have a Sunday school class. I couldn't very well leave them, you know."

He looked at her for a moment thoughtfully, trying to bridge in his thoughts this difference between them.

Then he said quite humbly, "Will you take me with you?"

"To church?" she asked, with a glad ring in her voice. Would he really go to church with her?

"Yes, and to Sunday school if I may. I haven't been to Sunday school in years. I'd like to go if you'll let me."

Her cheeks grew rosy. She had a quick mental picture of putting him in Deacon Pettigrew's Bible class.

"I'm afraid there's no class you'd enjoy," she began with a troubled look. "It's only a little country church, you know. They don't have the modern system and very few teachers."

"I'd enjoy going into your class very much if I might."

"Oh, mine are just boys, just little boys like Harley!" said Shirley, aghast.

"I was a little boy once, you know. I'd enjoy it very much," said the applicant with satisfaction.

"Oh, but—I couldn't teach you!"

"Couldn't you, though? You've taught me more in the few months I've known you than I've learned in that many years from others. Try me. I'll be very good. I'll be a boy with the rest of them, and you can just forget I'm there and go ahead. I really am serious about it. I want to hear what you have to say to them."

"Oh, I couldn't teach with you there!" exclaimed Shirley, putting her hands on her hot cheeks and looking like a frightened child. "Indeed I couldn't really. I'm not much of a teacher. I'm only a beginner. I wouldn't know how to talk before anyone but children."

He watched her for a minute, his face wistful.

"Why do you teach them?" he asked rather irrelevantly.

"Because—why, because I want to help them live right lives; I want to teach them how to know God."

"Why?"

"So they'll be saved. Because Christ commanded His disciples to give the message. I'm His disciple, so I want to tell the message."

"Was there any special stipulation as to whom that message should be given?" asked the young man. "Did He say you were just to give it to those boys?"

"Why, no, it was to be given to—all the world, every creature." Shirley spoke the words hesitatingly, a dimple showing in her cheek.

"And I don't come in on that?" asked Graham, with a twinkle that reminded Shirley of his father.

Shirley had to laugh then.

"But I couldn't!" said Shirley. "I'd be so scared I couldn't think of a thing to say."

"You're not afraid of me, are you? You wouldn't be scared if you thought I needed to know the message, would you? Well, I do, as much as any of those kids."

Shirley looked steadily into his earnest eyes and saw something there that steadied her nerve. The laughter died out of her own eyes, and a beautiful light of longing entered them.

"All right," she said, lifting her chin a little as if girding up her strength to the task. "You may come, and I'll do the best I can, but I'm afraid it will be a poor best. I have only a little story to tell them this morning."

"Please give them what you'd intended. I want the real thing, just as a boy would get it from you. Will the rest of them come in the car with us?"

Shirley was quiet during the ride to church. She let the rest talk, while she sat looking off at the woods and praying for help, trying to calm the flutter of her frightened heart, to steady her nerves and brace herself to teach the lesson just as she'd intended to teach it.

She watched him furtively during the opening exercises, with the untrained singing, the monotonous prayer of an old farmer-elder, the dry platitudes of the illiterate superintendent. But he listened respectfully, taking it for what it was worth, the best service these people knew how to render to their Maker.

Her heart had gained the strength she needed from the prayers she breathed continually, and when the time for teaching the lesson arrived she came to her class with quietness.

A little awe fell upon the boys because of the stranger in their midst. They didn't fling the hymnbooks down with a noisy thud or send the lesson pages flying like winged darts across the room as much as they were wont to do. They looked askance at Harley, who sat proudly by the visitor, supplying him with Bibles, hymnbooks and lesson pages, and finding the place for him officiously. But Graham sat among the boys without ostentation and made as little of his own presence as possible. He smiled at them now and then, put a handful of silver into the collection envelope when they would have passed him by and promised a ride to one fellow who ventured to ask him hoarsely if that was his car outside the church.

Shirley determined to forget as far as she could the visitor's presence in the class, and to this end she fixed her eyes on the worst little boy present, the boy who created all the disturbances, made all the noises and was the most adorable, homely, sturdy young imp the valley church could produce. He sat straight across from her, while Graham was at the side, and she could see in Jack's eye that he meant mischief if he could overcome his awe of the stranger.

So before Jack could get started she began her story and told it straight to him, never taking her eyes from his face from start to finish, and before she was halfway through she had her little audience enthralled. It was a Bible story told in modern setting and told straight to the heart of a boy who was the counterpart in his own soul of the man Christ cured and forgave.

What Graham was thinking or how he was looking Shirley didn't know. She had literally forgotten his existence after the first few minutes. She'd seen the gleam of interest in Jack's eyes; she knew her message was going home to a convicted young soul and that he saw himself and his own childish sins in the hero of the tale. Her whole soul was bent on helping him see the Savior who could make that young life over.

Not until the story was almost finished did any of the listeners, unless perhaps Harley, who was used to such story recitals, suspect it was just an ordinary chapter out of the Bible.

Then suddenly one of the elder boys broke out, "Aw! That's just the man in the Bible let down through the roof!"

The class stirred slightly at the discovery as it dawned upon them that the teacher had "put one over on us" again. But interest for the most part was sustained breathlessly until the superintendent's bell rang, and the heads drew together in an absorbed group around her for the last few sentences, spoken lower because the general hum of teaching in the room had ceased.

Graham's face was grave and thoughtful as she finished and slipped away from them to take her place at the organ. One could see it wasn't in the teacher alone, but in her message as well, that he was interested. The boys all had that subdued, half-ashamed, half-defiant look boys have when caught looking serious. Each boy frowned and studied his toes or hunted assiduously in his hymnbook to hide his confusion, and the class in various keys lifted up young voices vigorously in the last hymn.

Graham sat beside Shirley in the crowded church during the rather monotonous service. The regular pastor, who was a good, spiritual man if not a brilliant one and gave his congregation solid, practical sermons, was on vacation. The pulpit was supplied by a young theologue who was so new to his work that his sermon was an involved effort. But so strong was the power of the Sunday school lesson he'd just listened to that Graham felt as if he were sitting in some hallowed atmosphere. He didn't see the red-faced young preacher or notice his struggles to bring forth his message bravely. He saw only the earnest young teacher as she spoke the words of life to her boys; saw the young imp-faces of her boys softened and touched by the story she spoke; and knew there was something in it he wanted.

The seat was crowded and the day was warm, but the two who looked over the same hymnbook didn't notice it. The soft air came in from the open window beside them, breathing sweet clover and wild honeysuckle, and the meadowlarks sang their songs and made it seem like a bit of heaven.

Shirley's muslin frills trembled against Graham's hand as she reached to catch a fluttering hymnbook page the wind had caught. Once her hand brushed the coat sleeve beside her as they turned the page, and she felt the soft texture of the fine dark-blue goods with a pleasant sense of fitting. It thrilled her to think he was standing beside her in her own church, yielding himself to the same worship with her in the common country congregation. It was wonderful! And to have come to her!

She glanced shyly up at him, so handsome, standing there singing, his hand almost touching hers holding the book. He felt her glance and answered it with a look and smile. Their eyes held each other for the fraction of a second in which some inner thought was interchanged, some question asked and answered by the invisible flash of heartbeats, a mutual joining in the spiritual service. Then half-frightened Shirley dropped her eyes to the page, and the soft roses stole into her cheeks again. She felt as if she'd seen something in his eyes and acknowledged it in her own, as if she'd inadvertently shown him her heart in that glance, and that heart of hers was leaping and bounding with an uncontrollable joy, while her conscience sought by every effort to get it in control. What nonsense, it said, what folly, to make so much of his coming to church with her once! To allow her soul to get into such a flutter over a man who had no more idea of noticing her or caring for her than for a bird on the tree.

And with all the tumult in her heart she didn't see the envious glances of the village girls who stared with all their might at the handsome man who came to church in an expensive car and brought the girl who lived in a barn! Shirley's social position jumped several notches, and she never even knew it. In fact, she was becoming a great puzzle to Glenside residents.

And for once the little church's collection box was borne back to the altar laden with a goodly bill, put in with so little ostentation one might have judged it only a penny, though even a penny would have made more noise in the unlined wooden box.

After the service was over Graham went out with the children, while Shirley lingered to play over an accompaniment for a girl who was going to sing at the vesper service that afternoon. He piled all the children in the back seat of the car, put the boy he'd promised a ride in the seat beside him, took a spin around the streets and was back in front of the church by the time Shirley came out. Then her foolish heart leaped again at the thought that he'd saved the front seat for her. The boy descended as if he'd been caught up into heaven for a brief space and wouldn't forget it the rest of his life.

Graham's eyes held that same steady look of trust and understanding whenever he looked at her on the way home, and once while the children were talking together in the back seat he leaned toward her and said in a low tone, "I wonder if you'll let me take you away for a little while this afternoon to a quiet place I know with a beautiful view, and let's sit and talk. I want to ask you some things about what you said this morning. I was very much interested in it all, and I'm deeply grateful you let me go. Will you go with me? I'll bring you back in time for the Christian Endeavor service, and, you see, in the meantime I'm inviting myself to dinner. Do you think your mother will object?"

What could Shirley do but accept this alluring invitation? She didn't go off on pleasure excursions on the Sabbath, but this request that she ride to a quiet place outdoors for a religious talk couldn't offend her strongest sense of what was right on the Sabbath day. And surely, if the Lord had a message for her to bear, she must bear it to whomever He sent. This, then, was this man's interest in her, that she could make him think of God. A glad elation filled her heart; something deep and true stirred within her and lifted her above thought of self, like a blessing from on high. To be asked to bring light to a soul like this one was honor indeed. This was an answer to her morning prayer, that she might fulfill God's pleasure with the day's lesson. The message then had reached his soul. It was enough. She would think no more of self.

Yet whenever she looked at him and met that smile again she was thrilled with joy in spite of herself. At least they had a friendliness here beyond the common acquaintance, something true, deep, lasting, even though worlds should separate them in the future; something built on a deep understanding, sympathy and common interests. Well, so be it. She would rejoice it was given her to know one man of the world in this beautiful way; and her foolish human heart should understand what a high, true thing this was that mustn't be misunderstood.

So she reasoned with herself and watched him during dinner, among the children, out in the yard among the flowers and animals; everywhere he seemed so fine and splendid, so far above all other men she'd met. And her mother, watching, trembled for her when she saw her happy face.

"Do you think you should go with him, daughter?" she asked with troubled eyes, when they were left alone for a moment after dinner. "You know it's the Sabbath, and his life is very different from ours."

"Mother, he wants to talk about the Sunday school lesson this morning," said Shirley shyly. "I guess he's troubled, perhaps, and wants me to help him. I guess he's never thought much about religious things."

"Well, daughter, be careful. Do all you can for him, of course, but remember—don't let your heart stray out of your keeping. He's very attractive, dear, and very unconventional for a wealthy man. I think he's true and wouldn't mean to trifle, but he wouldn't realize."

"I know, Mother. Don't be afraid for me!" said Shirley with a lofty look, half of exultation, half of proud self-command.

He took her to a mossy place beside a stream, where the light filtered down through the lacy leaves flecking the bank and braided golden currents in the water; with green and purple hazy hills in the distance and just enough seclusion for a talk without being too far from the world.

"My sister says you people have a 'real' God," he said, when she was comfortably fixed with cushions from the car at her back against a tree trunk. "She says you seem to realize His presence—I don't know just how to say it, but I'd like to know if this is so. I'd like to know what makes you different from other girls and your home different from most homes I know. I'd like to know if I may have it, too."

That was the beginning.

Shirley, shy at first, having never spoken on such subjects except to children, yet being well versed in the Scriptures and feeling her faith with every atom of her being, drew out the little Bible she'd slipped into her pocket when they started and then plunged into the great subject.

Never had preacher more earnest listener or more lovely temple in which to preach. And if sometimes the young man's thoughts strayed from the subject to rest his eyes in tenderness upon the young teacher's lovely face and long to draw her into his arms and claim her for his own, he might well have been forgiven. For Shirley was fair, with the light of other worlds in her face, her eyes sparkling with her eagerness, her lips aglow with words that seemed to be given her for the occasion. She taught him simply, not trying to go into deep arguments, but urging the only way she knew, the way of taking Christ's promise at its face value, being willing to do His will, trusting Him to reveal Himself and the truth of the doctrine and make the believer sure.

They talked until the sun sank low and the calling of the wood birds warned them the Endeavor hour was near. Before they left the place he asked her for the little Bible, and she laid it in his hand with joy that he wanted it, that she was chosen to give him a gift so precious.

"It's all marked up," she said apologetically. "I always mark the verses I love or have had some special experience with."

"It will be that much more precious to me," he said gently, fingering the pages reverently.

Then he looked up and gave her one of those deep looks that seemed to say so much to her heart. And all at once she realized she was on earth again and that his presence and his look were precious to her. Her cheeks grew pink with the joy of it, and she looked down in confusion and couldn't answer, so she rose to her feet.

But he, springing up at once to help her, kept her hand for just an instant with earnest pressure and said in deeply moved tones, "You don't know what you've done for me this afternoon, my—*friend!*" He waited with her hand in his a moment as if he were going to say more but decided not to. The silence was so compelling she looked up into his eyes, meeting his smile, and that said so many things her heart went into a tumult again and couldn't quite come to itself throughout the Christian Endeavor service.

On the way home from the church he talked a little about her vacation: when it came, how long it lasted, what she'd do with it.

Just as they reached home he said, "I hope you'll pray for me, my friend!"

There was something wonderful in the way he said that word "friend." It thrilled her through and through as she stood beside the road and watched him speed away into the evening.

"My friend! I hope you'll pray for me, my friend!" It sang a glory song down in her heart as she turned to go in with the sunset's vivid glory on her face.

Chapter 20

The cement floor was down a week and was hard as a rock, when one day two or three wagon loads of things arrived with a note from Graham to Mrs. Hollister to say he'd be glad if these might be stored in one corner of the basement floor, where they'd be out of her way and not take up too much room.

Harley and George went down to look them over that evening.

"He said something about some things being taken from the office building," said Harley, kicking a pile of iron pipes with his toe.

"These don't look like any old things that've been used," said George. "They look new." Then he studied them a few minutes more from another angle and shut his lips judiciously. He belonged to the boy species that has learned to "shut up and saw wood," whatever that expression may mean. If anything was to come out of that pile of iron in the future, he didn't mean to break confidence with anybody's secrets. He walked away whistling and said nothing further about them.

The next day Mrs. Graham came down to the Hollisters in her limousine and an exquisite outfit of organdie and ribbons. She was attended by Elizabeth, wild with delight over getting home again. She begged Mrs. Hollister charmingly and sincerely to take care of Elizabeth for three or four weeks, while she and her husband were away, and to take the entire family down to the shore and occupy their cottage, which had been closed all summer and needed opening and airing. She said nothing would please Elizabeth so much as to have them all her guests during September. The maids were there, with nothing to do, and would love to serve them; it really would be a great favor to her if she could know Elizabeth was getting a little salt air under such favorable conditions.

She was so genuine in her request and suggested so earnestly that Shirley and George needed the change during their vacation and could just as well come down every night and go up every morning for a week or two more after the vacations were over, that Mrs. Hollister actually promised to consider it and talk it over with Shirley when she came home. Elizabeth and Carol nearly went into spasms of joy over the thought of all they could do at the shore together.

When Shirley came home she found the whole family quite upset discussing the matter. Carol had brought out the family wardrobe and was showing how she could wash this and dye that and turn this skirt upside down and put a piece from the old waist in there to make the lower part flare. And Harley was telling how he could get the man next door to look after the hens and pigeons, and nothing needed much attention in the garden now, for the corn was about over except the last picking, which wasn't ripe yet.

Mrs. Hollister was saying they should really stay at home and look up another place to live during the winter, and Carol was pleading that another place would be easier found when the weather was cooler anyway and that Shirley was awfully tired and needed a change.

When she heard of the invitation Shirley's cheeks grew pink in spite of the headache she'd been fighting all day, and she sat down to think it out. Was this, then, another of the kind schemes of her kind friend to make the way easier for her? What right did she have to take all this? Why was he doing it? Why was the rest of the family? Did they really need someone to take care of Elizabeth? But of course it was a wonderful opportunity and one her mother at least shouldn't let slip by. And Doris! Think of Doris playing in the sand at the seaside!

Supper was flung onto the table that night anyway it happened, for they were all too excited to know what they were about. Carol got butter twice and forgot to cut the bread, and Harley poured milk into the already filled water pitcher. They were even too excited to eat.

Graham arrived with Elizabeth early in the evening to add his pleading to his mother's, and before he left he about succeeded in getting Mrs. Hollister's promise to go.

Shirley's vacation began the first of September, and George had asked for his at the same time so they could enjoy it together. Each had two weeks. Graham said the cost of going back and forth to the city for the two would be very little. By the next morning they were saying what they'd take along and planning what they'd do with the dog. It was very exciting. They had only a week to get ready, and Carol wanted to make bathing suits for everybody.

Graham came again that night with more suggestions. There were plenty of bathing suits down at the cottage, all sizes and kinds. No need to make bathing suits. The dog, of course, was to go along. He needed the change as much as anybody, and they needed him there. That breed of dog was a great swimmer. He'd take care of the children when they went in bathing. How would Mrs. Hollister like to have one of the old Graham servants come over to sleep at the barn and look after things while they were gone? The man had nothing to do at home while everybody was away, since the whole corps of servants would be there, and this one would enjoy coming out to the country. He had a brother living on a place about a mile away. As for the trip there, Graham would love to take them all in the big touring car with Elizabeth. He'd intended to take her that way, and there was no reason in the world why they shouldn't all go along. They'd start Saturday afternoon as soon as Shirley and George were free, and they'd be down before bedtime. It would be cool and delightful journeying at that hour and a great deal pleasanter than the train.

So one by one the obstructions and hindrances were removed from their path, and it was decided the Hollisters were to go to the seashore.

At last the day came.

Shirley and George went off in the morning shouting last directions about things. They were always having to go to their work no matter what was happening. It was sometimes hard on them, particularly this day when everything was so exciting.

The old Graham servant arrived about three o'clock and proved himself invaluable in doing the last little things without being told. Mrs. Hollister had her first glimmer of what it must be to have trained servants about to anticipate one's needs. He entered the barn as if barns were his native heath and moved about with the ease and unobtrusiveness that mark a perfect servant, but with none of the hauteur and disdain many of those individuals entertain toward all they consider poor or beneath them. He had a kind face and seemed to understand what was to be done. Things moved more smoothly after he arrived.

At four o'clock Graham arrived with the car and a load of long linen dust cloaks and veils. The Hollisters donned them and bestowed themselves where they were told. The servant stowed away the wraps and suitcases; Star mounted the seat beside Harley, and they were ready.

They turned to look back at the barn as the car started. The old servant was having trouble with the big door, trying to shut it. "That door is a nuisance," said Graham as they swept away from the curb. "It must be fixed. It's no fit door for a barn, anyway." Then they curved up around Allister Avenue and left the barn far out of sight.

They were going across country to the Graham home to pick up

Elizabeth. That beautiful ride in the late afternoon was a wonderful experience for them. When they swept into the great gates and up the broad drive to the Graham mansion and stopped under the porte cochère, Mrs. Hollister was overcome with the idea of being beholden to people who lived in such grandeur as this. To think she actually invited their son to dine in a barn with her!

Elizabeth came rushing out and climbed in beside Carol. Even George, usually silent when she was about, gave her a grin of welcome. The father and mother came out to say good-bye, gave them good wishes and declared they were happy to leave their daughter in such good hands. Then the car curved about the great house, among tennis courts, greenhouses, garage and, stable, and back to the pike again, leaping out onto the perfect road as if it were as excited as the children.

Two more stops they made to pick up George, who was getting off early, and Shirley, who was through at five o'clock, and then they threaded their way out of the city, across the ferry, through another city and out into the open country, dotted all along with clean, pretty towns.

They reached a lovely grove at sundown and stopped to have supper. Graham stepped down and had George help him get out the big hamper.

They ate a delectable lunch: sandwiches of delicate and unknown condiments; salad as bewildering; soup kept hot in a thermos bottle, served in tiny white cups; iced tea and ice cream meringues from another thermos compartment; and plenty of delicious little cakes, olives, nuts, bonbons, and fruit. It seemed a wonderful supper to them all, eaten out there under the trees, with the birds beginning their vesper songs and the stars peeping out. Then they packed up their dishes and hurried on, a silver thread of a moon coming out to make the scene more lovely.

Doris was almost asleep when they began to hear the sea booming and smell the salt breeze as it swept inland. But she roused up and opened wide, mysterious eyes, peering into the darkness and murmuring softly, "I yant to see ze osun! I yant to see the gate bid watter!"

Stiff and filled with ecstasy, they finally unloaded in front of a big white building that looked like a hotel. They tried to see into the deep, mysterious darkness across the road, where a great voice boomed and dashing spray loomed high like a waving phantom hand to beckon them now and again, and far-moving lights told of ships and a world beyond the one they knew—limitless like eternity, the universe, chaos.

With reluctance they turned away from the mysterious unseen lure and crossed a wide veranda into the bright light of a hall, where every-thing was clean and shining, and a fireplace with friendly flames wel-comed them. The children stood bewildered in the brightness while two maids unfastened their wraps and dust cloaks and helped them take off their hats. Then they all sat around the fire, for Graham had come in by this time, and the maids brought trays of some delicious drink, with lit-tle cakes and crackers and tinkling ice and straws. Doris almost fell asleep again and was carried upstairs by Shirley and put to bed in a white crib she was too sleepy to look at. Meanwhile, Carol, Elizabeth, George and Harley went with Graham across the road to look at the black, yawning cavern they called ocean and see the shore lighthouses.

They were all asleep at last, a little before midnight, in spite of the excitement over the spacious rooms and who should have which. Think of it! Thirty rooms in the house and each one as pretty as the other! What luxury! And nobody else to occupy them! Carol could hardly get to sleep. She felt as if she'd dropped into a novel and was living it.

When Graham came out of his room the next morning, the salt breeze swept invitingly through the hall and showed him the front door of the upper piazza open and someone standing in the sunlight, with light, glowing garments, gazing at the sea in rapt enjoyment. Coming out softly, he saw Shirley dressed in white, with a ribbon of blue at her waist and a soft pink color in her cheeks, looking off to sea.

He stood for a moment to enjoy the picture and said in his heart that sometime, if he got his wish, he would have her painted so by some great artist, with that simple white dress and blue ribbon, her round white arm lifted, her small hand shading her eyes and the sunlight bur-nishing her brown hair into gold. He could scarcely refrain from going to her and telling her how beautiful she was. But when he stepped qui-etly up beside her only his eyes spoke and brought the color deeper into her cheeks; and so they stood for some minutes, looking together and drawing in the wonder of God's sea.

"This is the first time I've ever seen it," spoke Shirley at last, "and I'm so glad it was on Sunday morning. It will always make the day seem more holy and the sea more wonderful to think about. I like best things to happen on Sunday, don't you, because that's the best day of all."

Graham looked at the sparkling sea in azure and pearls, realized the Sabbath quiet and marveled at the beauty of the girl's soul, even as her feeling about it seemed to enter into and become part of him.

"Yes, I do," he said. "I never did before, but I do now—and always shall," he added under his breath.

That was almost as wonderful a Sabbath as the one they'd spent in the woods a couple of weeks before. They walked and talked by the sea and visited an Episcopal chapel, where the windows stood open for the chanting of the waves and the salt of the breeze to enter freely, and then they walked by the sea again. Wherever they went, whether resting in the many big rockers on the broad verandas or walking on the hard smooth sand or sitting in some cozy nook by the waves, they felt the same deep sympathy, the same conviction that their thoughts were one, the same wonderful thrill of the day and each other's nearness.

Somehow in the new environment Shirley forgot this young man wasn't of her world, that he was probably returning soon to the city to join in the winter's season in society, that other girls would claim his smiles and attentions, and she would likely be forgotten. She lost the sense of it entirely and companioned with him as if there had never been anything to separate them. Her mother, looking on, sighed, feared, smiled and sighed again.

They walked together in the sweet darkness beside the waves that evening. He told her how when he was a little boy he wanted to climb up to the stars and find God. Later he thought the stars and God were myths like Santa Claus and that the stars were only electric lights put up by men and lighted from a great switch every night, and when they didn't shine somebody had forgotten to light them. He told her many things about himself that he'd never told anyone, and she opened her shy heart to him, too.

Then they planned what they'd do next week when he returned. He told her he must go back to the city in the morning to see his father and mother off and attend to a few matters of business at the office. It might be two or three days before he could return, but after that he was coming down to take a vacation himself if she didn't mind, and they would do a lot of delightful things together—row, fish, go crabbing—and he'd teach her to swim and show her all the walks and favorite places where he used to go as a boy. Reluctantly they went in, his fingers lingering about hers for a second at the door, vibrating her mysterious heartstrings again, sweeping dearest music from them and frightening her with joy that took her half the night to put down.

Chapter 21

S idney Graham drove back to the city the next morning. They all stood out on the veranda to watch the car glide away.

Doris stood on the railing with Shirley's arm securely about her and waved a fat hand. Then puckering her lips she demanded: "Fy does mine Mister Dwaham do way? I don't yant him to do way. I yant him to stay wif me aw-ways, don't oo, Sirley?"

Shirley with glowing cheeks turned from watching the retreating car and put her little sister down on the floor suddenly.

"Run get your hat, Doris, and we'll take a walk on the sand!" she said, smiling at the child, till Doris forgot her grievance and beamed out with answering smiles.

That was a wonderful day.

They all took a walk on the sand first, George pushing his mother in a big wheeled chair belonging to the cottage. Elizabeth was guide and pointed out the beauties of the place, telling bits of reminiscence from her childhood memories to which even George listened attentively. From only tolerating her, George now considered Elizabeth "a good scout."

When Mrs. Hollister grew tired they took her back to the cottage and established her in a big chair with a book. Then they rushed off to the bathhouses and presently emerged in bathing suits, Doris looking like a little sprite in her scarlet flannel scrap of a suit, her bright hair streaming and her beautiful baby arms and legs flashing white like a cherub's in the sunlight.

They came back from their dip in the waves, hungry and excited, to the wonderful dinner that was served so exquisitely in the cool dining room, from the windows of which they could watch the lazy ships sailing in the distance.

Doris fell asleep over her dessert and was tumbled into the hammock to finish her nap. Carol and Elizabeth and the boys started off crabbing, and Shirley settled herself in another hammock with a pile of new magazines and prepared to enjoy a whole lazy afternoon. It was so wonderful to lie still, at leisure, with all those lovely magazines to read and nothing to disturb her. She leaned her head back and closed her eyes for a minute to listen to the sea and realize how good it was to be here. Back in her mind was a pleasant consciousness of the beautiful yesterday and the beautiful tomorrows that might come when Sidney Graham returned, but she wouldn't let her heart dwell on them; that would be humoring herself too much and perhaps give her a false idea of things. She simply wouldn't let this wonderful holiday be spoiled by thinking it would have to end someday and she'd be back at the old routine of care and worry again.

She was roused from her reverie by the postman's step bringing a single letter—for her!

It was in a long envelope addressed in an unknown hand. Wonderingly she opened it and found inside a bankbook and a blank checkbook with a note.

Dear Little Girl:
    This is just a trifle of that present we were talking about the other day that belongs to you. It isn't all by any means, but we'll see to the rest later. Spend this on chocolates or chewing gum or frills or whatever you like and have a good time down at the shore. You're a bully little girl and deserve everything nice. Don't be too serious, Miss Shirley. Play a little more.

Your elderly friend,
Walter K. Graham

In the bankbook was an entry of five thousand dollars, on a check account. Shirley held her breath and stared at the figures with wide eyes, then slipped away and locked herself in her big white room. Kneeling down by the bed she cried and prayed and smiled all in one and thanked the Lord for making people so kind to her. After that she went to find her mother.

Mrs. Hollister was sitting on the wide upper veranda in a steamer chair looking off to sea and drawing in new life at every breath. Her book was open on her lap, but she'd forgotten to read in the joy of all that was about her. To tell the truth she was wondering if the dear father who was gone from them knew of their happy estate and was thinking how glad he'd be for them if he did.

She read the letter twice before she looked at the bankbook with its astonishing figures and heard again Shirley's tale of what happened the morning of the arrest. Then she read the letter again.

"I'm not sure, daughter," she said at last with smile, "what we should do about this. Are you?"

"No," said Shirley, smiling. "I suppose I'll give it back, but wasn't it wonderful of him to do it? Isn't it great there are such men in the world?"

"It certainly is, dear, and I'm glad my little girl could help him and that she's won his good graces so simply and sweetly. But I'm not so sure what you should do. Hadn't we better pray about it before you decide? How soon should you write him? It's too late to reach him before he leaves for California, isn't it?"

"Oh, yes, he's just about starting now," said the girl. "Don't you suppose he planned it so I couldn't answer right away? I don't know his address. I can't do a thing till I find out where to write. I wouldn't like to send it to the office because they'd probably think it was business and his secretary might open it."

"Of course. Then we'll just pray about it, shall we, dear? I'm not sure whether it's a well-meant bit of charity we should hand back with sincere thanks, or whether it's God's way of rewarding my little girl for her faithfulness and quick action. Our Father knows we've been—and still are—in a hard place. He knows we need the things money has to buy. You really did a good thing and saved Mr. Graham from great loss, and perhaps he's the kind of man who would feel much happier if he shared a little of it with you and could make some return for what you did for him. But five thousand dollars is a great deal of money for a brief service. What do you think, dear?"

"I don't know, Mother. I'm muddled as you say, but I guess it will come right if we pray about it. Anyhow, I'm going to be happy over his thinking of me, whether I keep it or not."

Shirley went thoughtfully back to her hammock and her magazines, a smile on her lips, a dream in her eyes. She found herself wondering whether Sidney Graham knew about this money and what he'd wish her to do about it. Then suddenly she cast the whole question from her and plunged into her magazine, wondering why almost any question that entered her mind promptly entangled itself with Mr. Sidney Graham. What did he have to do with it anyway?

The magazine story was interesting, and Shirley soon forgot everything else in the pleasure of surrendering herself to the printed page. An hour went by, another passed, and Shirley was still oblivious to all about her. Suddenly she became aware of a boy on a bicycle, riding almost up to the very steps and whistling vigorously.

"Miss Shirley Hollister here?" he demanded as he alighted on one foot on the lower step, the other foot posed for flight as soon as his errand was performed.

"Why, yes," said Shirley, startled, struggling to her feet and letting a shower of magazines fall about her.

"Long distance wants yer," he announced, looking her over apathetically. "Mr. Barnard, of Philadelphia, wants to talk to yer!" With the final word chanted nasally he alighted upon his obedient steed and spun away down the walk again.

"But wait! Where shall I go? Where's the telephone?"

"Pay station!" he shouted, turning his head over his shoulder. "Drugstore! Two blocks from the post office!"

Without waiting to go upstairs Shirley, trained to answer the telephone at once, caught up Elizabeth's parasol that lay on a settee by the door, rumpled her fingers through her hair and hurried down the steps in the direction the boy had disappeared, wondering what in the world Mr. Barnard could want of her? Was he going to call her back from vacation? Were these the only days she'd have, this and yesterday? She would always have yesterday! With a sigh she looked wistfully at the sea. If she'd only known a summons was to come so soon she wouldn't have wasted a second on magazines. She would have sat and gazed all afternoon at the sea.

If Mr. Barnard wanted her, of course she'd have to go. Business was business, and she couldn't afford to lose her job even with that fantasy dream of five thousand to her credit in the bank. She knew, of course, she meant to give that back. It was hers for the day, but it couldn't become tangible. It was wonderful, but it must go back. And if her employer felt he must cut short her vacation, why, of course, she must acquiesce and be glad she'd had this much. Perhaps it was just as well, anyway, for if Sidney Graham came down and spent a few days there was no knowing what foolish notions her heart would take, jumping and careening the way it had lately when he just looked at her. Yes, she'd go back if Mr. Barnard wanted her. It was the best thing she could do. But perhaps he was only calling her to ask where she left something they were searching for. That silly Ashton girl who took her place might not have remembered all her directions.

Breathless, with possibilities crowding her mind, she hurried into the drugstore and sought the telephone booth. It seemed ages before the connection was made and she heard Mr. Barnard's dry familiar tones over the phone.

"That you, Miss Hollister? This is Mr. Barnard. I'm sorry to disturb you right in the midst of your holiday, but a rather serious matter has come up, and I'm wondering if you could help us out for a day or two. If you would we'd be glad to give you fifty dollars for the extra time and let you extend your vacation to a month instead of two weeks. Do you think you could spare a day or two to help us right away?"

"Oh! Why, yes, of course!" faltered Shirley, her eyes dancing at the thought of the extra vacation and money.

"Thank you! I was sure you would," said Mr. Barnard, with relief in his voice. "You see, we have that government contract. The news just came in the afternoon mail. It's rather particular business because it concerns matters the government wishes to keep secret. I'm to go down tomorrow morning to Washington to receive instructions, and I have permission to bring a trusted private secretary with me. Now you know, of course, that I couldn't take Miss Ashton. She couldn't do what I want even if I could trust her not to say a word about the matter. I'd take Jim Thorpe, but his father just died and I can't very well ask him to leave. And I can't delay longer than tomorrow.

"Now the question is, would you be willing to go to Washington in the morning? I looked up the trains, and you can leave the shore at 8:10 and meet me in Baltimore at ten o'clock. I'll wait for you at the train gate, but in case we miss each other wait in the station, close to the telephone booths, till I find you. We'll take the next train for Washington and be there a little before noon. If all goes well we should be through our business in plenty of time to make a four o'clock train home. Of course there may be delays, and you might have to remain in Washington overnight, though I hardly think so. But in case you do I'll see that you're safe and comfortable in a quiet hotel near the station where my wife's sister is staying this summer.

"Of course your expenses will be paid. I'll telegraph and have a mileage book at your disposal that you can call for there in your station in the morning. Are you willing to undertake this for us? I assure you we won't forget the service."

When Shirley finally hung up the receiver and looked about the country drugstore, the bottles on the shelves seemed to be dancing about before her eyes. What strange exciting things were happening to her in such breathless haste! Only one day at the shore and a piece of another, and here she was with a trip to Washington on her hands! It certainly was bewildering to have things come in such rapid succession. She wished it had come at another time and not now when she wasn't used to the sea yet and the beautiful place where they were staying. She didn't want to be interrupted just yet. It wouldn't be quite the same when she got back to it, she was afraid.

Of course she couldn't refuse. It never entered her head to refuse. She knew enough about the office to realize Mr. Barnard must have her. Jimmie Thorpe would have been the one to go if he were available, because he was a man and had been with Barnard and Clegg for ten years and knew their most confidential business. But of course he couldn't go with his father lying dead and his mother and invalid sister needing him. So there was no one else but her.

She thought it out on the way back to the cottage, with a little pang at the thought of losing the next day and perhaps staying over in Washington a day and missing Sidney Graham's arrival, if he came in a day or two, as he promised. He might even come and go back before she could return, and perhaps he'd think her ungrateful to leave when he was so kind to plan this lovely vacation for her pleasure. Then she brought herself up firmly and told herself it was nothing to him whether she was there or not, and it certainly had no right to be anything to her. It was good she was going and would probably be good for all concerned if she stayed until he went back to the city again.

With this firm determination she hurried up to the veranda where her mother sat with Doris and told her story.

Mrs. Hollister looked troubled.

"I'm sorry you gave him an answer, Shirley, without talking it over with me. I don't like the idea of your going to a strange city, alone that way. Of course Mr. Barnard will look after you in a way, but still he's a good deal of a stranger. I wish he'd let you alone for your vacation. It seems as if he might have found somebody else to go. I wish Mr. Graham was here. I shouldn't wonder if he'd suggest some way out of it for you."

But Shirley stiffened into dignity at once.

"Really, Mother, I'm sure I don't see what Mr. Graham would have to say about it if he were here. I shouldn't ask his advice. You see, Mother, there's nobody else who could do this but Jimmie Thorpe, and he's out of the question. It would be unthinkable for me to refuse in this emergency. And you know Mr. Barnard has been very kind. Besides, think of the fine vacation I'll have afterward—a whole month! And all that extra money for renting a better house for winter! Don't worry, Mother! Not a thing in the world could happen to me. I'll be the most cautious person you ever heard of. I'll even glance shyly at the White House and Capitol! Come on—let's go up and get dolled up for supper! Won't the children be surprised when they hear I'm going to Washington? I'm so excited I don't know what to do!"

Mrs. Hollister said no more and entered pleasantly into the merry talk at the table, telling her daughter what she must be sure to see at the nation's capital. But the next morning as Shirley was leaving for the station, escorted by all the children, Mrs. Hollister came with a package of addressed postal cards she'd asked George to get for her the night before and put them in Shirley's bag.

"Just drop us a line as you go along, dear," she said. "I'll feel happier about it to be hearing from you. Mail one whenever you have a chance."

Shirley laughed as she looked at the fat package.

"All those, Mother? You must expect me to stay a month! You know I won't have much time for writing, and I fully expect to be back tonight or tomorrow at the latest."

"Well, that's all right," said her mother. "You can use them another time. But you can just put a line on one whenever it's convenient. I'll enjoy getting them even after you get back. You know this is your first journey out into the world alone."

Shirley stooped to kiss the little mother.

"All right, dear! I'll write you a serial story—each one continued in our next. Good-bye! Don't take too long a walk today. I want you rested to hear all I'll have to tell when I get back tonight!"

Shirley wrote the first postal card as soon as she was settled in the train, describing the car's other occupants and painting a vivid picture of the landscape slipping by her windows. She wrote the second in the Baltimore station, after she met Mr. Barnard, while he went to get seats in the parlor car, and she mailed them both at Baltimore.

The third was written as they neared Washington, with the dim vision of the great monument dawning on her sight in the distance. Her last sentence gave her first impression of the nation's capital.

They ate lunch in the dining car, and she promised herself another postal devoted to that, but she had no time to write more after they reached Washington. She was put into a taxi and whirled away to an office. She caught glimpses of great buildings on the way and gazed with awe at the dome of the Capitol building. Mr. Barnard was kind and pointed out this and that, but his mind was plainly on the coming interview. When Shirley sat at last in a quiet corner of a big dark office, with her pen poised and her notebook ready for work, and looked at the serious faces of the men in the room, she felt as if she'd been rushed through a treasure vault of glorious jewels and thrust into a dark tomb.

Presently the talk about her interested her. Things were being said about the country's vital affairs, scraps of sentences reminding her of talk in the daily papers and headings of front columns. She looked about her and noted the familiarity with which these men quoted the words of those high up in the government. With awe she began her work, taking down whatever Mr. Barnard dictated, her fingers flying over the notebook's tiny pages, in small neat characters, and keeping pace with the voices going on about her. The detail work she was setting down wasn't of especial interest to her, except that it was concerned with government work, for its phraseology was familiar and part of her daily routine office work at home. But she alerted every sense to catch the tiniest detail and not make the smallest mistake, understanding from the men's voices about her that it was of vital interest to the country that this order should be filled quickly and accurately.

As she capped her fountain pen and slipped the rubber band on her notebook when it was over, she heard one of the men just behind her say in a low tone to Mr. Barnard: "You're sure of your secretary, of course? I want you to know this thing is being very closely watched. We have reason to believe spying is planned. Keep your notes carefully and don't let too many in on this. We know pretty well what's going on, but it isn't desirable to make any arrests until we can watch a little longer and round up the whole party. So keep your eyes open, and don't talk."

"Oh, certainly! I understand," said Mr. Barnard, "and I have a most discreet secretary." He glanced with a significant smile toward Shirley as she rose.

"Of course!" said the other. "She looks it." He bowed to Shirley as she passed.

She didn't think of it at the time, but afterward she recalled how in acknowledging his courtesy she stepped back and almost stumbled over a page, a boy about George's age, who was standing withdrawn into the shadow of the deep window. She remembered he had a keen intelligent look and apologized and vanished immediately. A moment later it seemed to be the same boy in blue clothes and gilt buttons who held the outer door open for them to pass—or was this a taller one? She glanced again at his side face with a lingering thought of George as she paused to fasten her glove and slip her notebook into her handbag.

"I think I'll put you in the taxi and let you go right back to the station while I attend to another errand over at the War Department. It won't take me long. We can easily catch that four-o'clock train back. I suppose you're anxious to get back tonight?"

"Oh, yes," said Shirley, "I must, if possible. Mother isn't well, and she worries so easily."

"Well, I don't know why we can't. Then perhaps you can come up to town tomorrow and type those notes for us. By the way, I guess it would be better for me to take them and lock them in the safe tonight. No, don't stop to get them out now," he said as Shirley began to unfasten her bag and get the notebook. "We don't have much time if we want to catch that train. Just look after them carefully, and I'll get them when we're on the train."

He helped her into the taxi, gave the order "To the station" and, touching his hat, went rapidly over to the War Department building. No one saw a boy with a blue cap and brass buttons steal forth on a bicycle from the court just below the office and, circling about the asphalt uncertainly for a moment, shoot off across the park.

Shirley sat up very straight and kept her eyes about her. She was glad they were taking another way to the station so she might see more. When she got there she'd write another postal, and perhaps it would go on the same train with her.

It was all too short, that ride up Pennsylvania Avenue and around by the Capitol. Shirley gathered up her bag and prepared to get out. She wished she might have just one more hour to go about, but of course that would be impossible if she wished to reach home tonight.

But before the driver could get down and open the door for her to get out, a boy on a bicycle slid up to the curb and, touching his gilt-buttoned cap respectfully, said: "Excuse me, Miss, but Mr. Barnard sent me after you. He says there's been some mistake and you'll have to come back and get it corrected."

"Oh!" said Shirley, too surprised to think for a minute. "Oh! Then please hurry, for Mr. Barnard wants to get back in time to catch that four-o'clock train."

The driver frowned, but the boy stepped up and handed him something, saying, "That's all right, Joe. He sent you this." The driver's face cleared, and he started his machine again. The boy vanished into the throng. It was another of Shirley's after-memories that she glimpsed a scrap of paper along with the money the boy handed the driver and that he stuffed it in his pocket after looking intently at it. But at the time she thought nothing of it. She was only glad they were skimming along rapidly.

Chapter 22

Shirley's sense of direction had always been keen. Even as a child she could tell her way home when others were lost. It was some minutes, however, before she realized the car was being driven in an entirely different direction from where she'd just left Mr. Barnard. For a moment she looked around puzzled, thinking the man was merely taking another way around, but a glance back where the white dome of the Capitol loomed, palace-like, above the city made her sure something was wrong. She looked at the buildings they were passing, at the names of the streets—F Street—they hadn't been on that before! These stores and tall buildings were new to her eyes. Down there at the end of the vista was a great building all columns. Was that the Treasury, and were they merely seeing it from another angle? It was confusing. But the time was short—why hadn't the man taken the quicker way?

She looked at her small wristwatch anxiously and watched for the end of the street. But before the great building was reached the car suddenly curved around a corner to the right—one block—a turn to the left—another turn—a confusion of new names and streets! New York Avenue! Connecticut Avenue! Thomas Circle! The names spun by so fast she could read only a few of them, and those she saw she wanted to remember so she might weave them into her next postal. She opened her bag, fumbled for the silver pencil in her coat pocket and scribbled down the names she could read as she passed, on the back of the bundle of postal cards, without looking at her writing. She didn't wish to miss a single sight. Here were rows of homes, pleasant and palatial, some of them even cozy. The broad avenues were enchanting, the park spaces, the lavish scattering of noble statues. But the time was hastening by, and they were going farther and farther from the station and from the direction of the offices where she'd been. She twisted her neck once more, and the Capitol dome loomed soft and blended in the distance. A thought of alarm leaped into her mind.

She leaned forward and spoke to the driver: "You understood, didn't you? I'm returning to the office where you took me with the gentleman?"

The man nodded.

"All right, lady. Yes, lady!"

The car rushed on, leaping out onto a beautiful way and disclosing new sights ahead. For a few minutes more Shirley was distracted from her anxiety in wondering whether the buildings on her right belonged to any of the embassies or not. And then as the car swerved and plunged into another street and darted into a less thickly populated district, with trees and vacant lots almost like the country, alarm arose once more, and she looked wildly back and tried to see the signs. But they were going faster still on a wide empty road past stretches of park, with winding drives and charming views and a stone bridge to the right, arching over a deep ravine below, with a railroad crossing it. There were deer parks fenced with high wire and filled with the pretty creatures. Everything went by so fast that Shirley hardly realized something must be wrong, before she seemed to be in a strange world.

"I'm sure you've made a mistake!" The girl's clear voice cut through the driving wind as they rushed along. "I must go back right away to that office you brought me from. I must go at once, or I'll be too late for my train! The gentleman will be very angry!" She spoke in the tone that always brought instant obedience from the employees around the office at home.

But the driver was stolid. He scarcely stirred in his seat to turn toward her. His thick voice was brought back to her on the breeze.

"No, lady, it's all right, lady! I had my orders, lady! You needn't worry. I get you there plenty time."

A wild fear seized Shirley, and her heart lifted itself, as was its habit, to God. "Oh, my Father! Take care of me! Help me! Show me what to do!" she cried.

Thoughts rushed through her brain as fast as the car rushed over the ground. What was she up against? Was this man crazy or bad? Was he trying to kidnap her? Why? She shuddered to look the thought in the face. Or was it the notes? She remembered the men in the office and what they said about keeping still and "spying enemies." But perhaps she was mistaken. Maybe this man was only stupid, and it would come out right in a few minutes. No, she mustn't wait for anything like that. She must take no chance. The notes were in her keeping. She must put them where they'd be safe. No telling how soon she would be over-powered and searched if that was what they were after. She must hide them, and she must think of some way to send word to Mr. Barnard before it was too late. No telling what moment they would turn from the main road and she'd be hidden far from human habitation. She must work fast.

What could she do? Scream to the next passerby? No, for the car was going too fast for that to do any good, and the houses up this way seemed to be isolated with few people about. There were houses on ahead beyond the park. She must have something ready to throw out when they came to them. "Oh, God! Help me think what to do!" she prayed again, and then looking down at her bag she saw the postal cards. Just the thing! Quickly she scribbled, still holding her hand within the bag so her movements weren't noticeable.

"Help! Quick! Being carried off! Auto! Connecticut Ave.! Park. Deer. Stone bridge. Phone Mr. Clegg. Don't tell Mother! Shirley."

She turned the card over, drew a line though her mother's name and wrote Carol's in its place. Stealthily she slipped the card up her sleeve, dropped her hand carelessly over the side of the car for a moment, let the card flutter from her fingers and wrote another.

She had written three cards and dropped them in front of houses before it suddenly occurred to her that even if these cards should be picked up and mailed it would be sometime before they reached their destination and far too late for help to reach her in time. Her heart suddenly dropped, and her breath almost left her. Her head was reeling, and all the time she was trying to tell herself she was exaggerating this thing, that probably the man would slow up or something and it would all be explained. Yes, he was slowing up, but for what? It was in another lonely spot, and out from the bushes there appeared, as if by magic, an odd-looking man with a heavy mustache that looked as if it didn't belong to him. He stood alertly waiting for the car and sprang into the front seat without waiting for it to stop or even glancing back at her, and the car shot forward again with great leaps.

Shirley dropped out the two cards together that she'd just written and leaned forward, touching the newcomer on the arm.

"Won't you please make this driver understand he's taking me to the wrong place?" she said with a pleasant smile. "I must get back to an office two or three blocks away from the Treasury Building. I must turn back at once, or I'll miss my appointment and be late for my train. It's important. Tell him, please, I'll pay him well if he'll get me back at once."

The stranger turned with an oily smile.

"That's all right, miss. He isn't making any mistake. We're taking you right to Secretary Baker's country home. He sent for your man, Mr.— What's his name? I forget. Barnard? Oh, yes. He sent for Mr. Barnard to come out there, sent his private car down for him. And Mr. Barnard, he left orders we should go after you and bring you along. It's something they want to change in those notes you was taking. There was a mistake, and the secretary wanted to look after the matter himself."

Shirley sat back with a sudden feeling of weakness and a fear she might faint, although she'd never done such a thing in her life. She wasn't deceived for an instant now, although she saw at once she mustn't let the man know it. That Secretary Baker would pause in the midst of his many duties to look into the details of a small article was ridiculous! It was equally impossible Mr. Barnard would have sent strangers after her and let her be carried off in this odd way. He was most particular that she should be looked after carefully.

She was horribly to blame for allowing herself to be carried back at all until Mr. Barnard himself appeared. Yet was she? That surely had been the page from the office who came with the message. Well, never mind, she was in for it now, and she must do her best while she had any chance to do anything. She must drop all those postals somehow, and she must hide those notes somewhere and perhaps write some others— fake ones. What should she do first?

"Father, help me! Show me! Oh, don't let me lose the notes! Please take care of me!" Again and again her heart prayed as her hand worked stealthily in her bag, while she tried to put a pleasant smile on her face and pretend she was still deceived.

Leaning forward she spoke to the strange man again. "Is Secretary Baker's home much farther from here?" she asked, feeling her lips draw stiffly in the frozen smile she forced. "Will it take long?"

" 'Bout ten minutes!" the man answered, with a peculiar look toward the driver. "Nice view 'round here!" he added with a leering look of admiration toward her.

Shirley's heart stood still with new fear, but she managed to make her white lips smile again and murmur, "Charming!"

Then she leaned back again and fussed around in her bag, bringing out a clean handkerchief, though she really had been detaching the pages containing the notes from her loose-leaf notebook. There weren't many, for she always wrote in small characters. But where should she hide them? Pull the lining away from the edge of her bag and slip them inside? No, for the bag would be the first place they'd likely search, and she couldn't poke the lining back smoothly so it wouldn't show. If she dropped the tiny pages down her neck inside her blouse, the men would likely see her. Dared she slip the pages under the linen robe that lay over her lap and put them inside her shoe? She was wearing plain black pumps, and the pages would easily fit in the soles, three or four in each. Once in they'd be well hidden and wouldn't rattle and give notice of their presence. But, oh, what a terrible risk if anything knocked off her shoe or if they searched her! Still she must take some risk, and this was the safest risk at hand. She must try it and then write out some fake notes, giving false numbers and sizes and other phraseology.

Or stay! Wasn't something already written in that book that would suffice? Some specifications she'd written for the Tillman-Brooks Company. Yes, she was sure. It wasn't at all for the same articles or the same measurements, but only an expert would know that. She leaned down quite naturally to pick up her handkerchief and deftly slipped five small pages into her right shoe.

It occurred to her she must keep her keepers deceived, so she asked again in gracious tones, "Would it trouble you to mail a card for me as soon as possible after we arrive? I'm afraid my mother will be worried about my delay, and she isn't well. I suppose they have a post office out this way."

"Sure, miss!" said the man again, with another leering smile that made her resolved to have no further conversation than was necessary.

She took out her fountain pen and hurriedly wrote, "Detained longer than I expected. May not get back tonight. S. H.," and handed the card to the man. He took it and turned it over, reading it, and put it in his pocket. Shirley felt she'd given an impression of innocence by the move which so far was good. She put away her fountain pen deliberately and managed in so doing to manipulate the rest of the pages of notes into her left shoe. Somehow that gave her a little confidence, and she sat back and wondered if she could do more. Those dropped postals were worse than useless, of course. Why hadn't she written an appeal to whoever picked them up? Suiting the action to the thought she wrote another postal card—her stock was getting low; she had only two left.

"For the sake of Christ send the police to help me! I'm being carried off by two strange men! Shirley Hollister."

She marked out the address on the other side and wrote: "To whoever picks this up." She fluttered it to the breeze cautiously, but her heart sank as she realized how little likelihood there was of its being picked up for days. For who would stop in a car to notice a bit of paper on the road? And there seemed to be few pedestrians. If she only had something larger, more attractive. She glanced at her belongings and suddenly remembered the book she'd brought with her to read, one of the new novels from the cottage, a good-sized volume in a bright red cover. The very thing!

With a cautious glance at her keepers she took up the book as if to read and opening it at the flyleaf wrote surreptitiously much the same message as on her last postal, signing her name and home address and giving her employers' address. Her heart was beating wildly when she finished. She was trying to think how to use this last bit of ammunition to the best advantage. Should she drop it in the road quietly? If only she could fasten the pages open so her message would be read! Her handkerchief! Of course! She folded it cornerwise and slipped it in across the pages so the book would fall open at the flyleaf, knotting the ends on the back of the cover. Every moment had to be cautious, and she must remember to keep her attitude of reading with the printed pages covering the handkerchief. It seemed to take hours—her fingers trembled so. If it hadn't been for the rushing noise of wind and car she wouldn't have dared so much undiscovered, but apparently her captors were satisfied she still believed their story about going to Secretary Baker's country house. They seemed mainly occupied in watching to see if they were pursued, casting anxious glances back now and then, but scarcely noticing her at all.

Shirley had observed two or three times when a car passed that the men both leaned down to do something at their feet to the car's machinery. Were they afraid of being recognized? Would this give her a chance to fling her book out where it would be seen by people in an oncoming car? Oh, if she only had the strength and skill to fling it into a car. But of course that was impossible without attracting the two men's attention. She must try what she could, though.

She lifted her eyes to the road ahead, and, lo, a large car was bearing down upon them! She'd almost despaired of meeting any more, for the road was growing lonelier and they must have come many miles. As soon as the two men in front of her sighted the car, they seemed to settle in their seats and draw their hats down further over their eyes. The same trouble seemed to develop with the machinery at their feet that Shirley had noticed before, and they bobbed and ducked and seemed wholly engrossed with their own affairs.

Shirley's heart was beating so fast it seemed as though it would suffocate her, and her hand seemed powerless as it lay innocently holding the closed book with the knotted handkerchief turned down out of sight. But she was nerving herself for one last effort and praying to be guided.

The car came on swiftly and was about to pass, when Shirley half rose and hurled her book straight at it and then sank back in her seat with a fearful terror upon her, closing her eyes for one brief second, not daring to watch the results of her act—if there were to be any results.

The men in the front seat suddenly straightened up and looked around.

"What's the matter?" growled the second man in a different tone from any he'd used before. "What you tryin' to put over on us?"

Shirley gasped and caught at her self-control.

"I've dropped my book," she stammered out wildly. "Could you stop long enough to pick it up? It was borrowed," she ended sweetly as if by inspiration and wondered at her steady tone when blood was pounding in her throat and ears, and everything was black before her. Oh, perhaps they'd stop, and she could cry out to the people for help.

The man rose up in his seat and looked back. Shirley cast one frightened glance back, too, and saw in that brief second that the other car had stopped and someone was standing up and looking back.

"No!" said her captor briefly, ducking down in his seat. "Push it!" he howled to the driver, and the car broke into a galloping streak, the wheels hardly seeming to touch the ground, the tonneau bounding and swaying this way and that.

Shirley had all she could do to keep in her seat. At one moment she thought how easy it would be to spring from the car and lie in a heap at the roadside. But there were the notes! She mustn't abandon her trust even for such a fearful escape from her captors. Suddenly, without warning, they turned a sharp curve and struck into a rough, almost unbroken road into the woods, and the thick growth seemed to close in behind them and shut them out from the world.

Shirley shut her eyes and prayed.

Chapter 23

The next trolley that passed the old barn after the Hollisters left brought a maid and a man from the Graham place. The other old servant met them, and together the three went to work. They'd brought with them large dustcovers and floor spreads like those used by housemaids in cleaning a room, and with these they now proceeded to cover all the large pieces of furniture in the place. In a short time the rugs and bits of carpet were carefully rolled up, the furniture piled in the middle of the rooms and everything enveloped in thick coverings. The curtains, bric-à-brac, and even the dishes were put away carefully, and the whole inviting home was suddenly denuded. The clothes from the calico-curtained clothespresses were folded and laid in drawers, and everything was made safe for workmen to come into the house. Even the hayloft bedrooms shared in this process.

Only a cot was left for the old servant and a few things for him to use, and most of these he transported to the basement out of the way. When the work was done the man and maid took the trolley back home again, and the other old servant arranged to make his Sabbath as pleasant as possible with his brother from the nearby farm.

Monday morning promptly at eight o'clock the trolley landed a bevy of workmen—carpenters, plasterers, plumbers, and furnace men—with a foreman who set them all at work as if it were a puzzle he'd studied out and memorized the solution. In a short time the quiet spot was full of sound, the symphony of industry, the rhythm of toil. Some men were working away with the furnace that had been stored in the cellar; others were measuring, fitting, cutting holes for lead pipes; still others were sawing away at the roof, making great gashes in its mossy extent; and two men were taking down the old barn door. Out in front more men were building a vat for mortar and opening bags of lime and sand that began arriving. Three men with curious aprons made of ticking, filled with thin wire nails, were frantically putting laths on the uprights the carpenters had set up and were stabbing them with nails from a seemingly inexhaustible supply in their mouths. It was as if they'd all engaged to build the tower of Babel in a day and meant to win a prize at it. Such sounds! Such shouts, such bangs, thumps and harsh, raucous noises! The bird in the tall tree looked and shivered, thankful her young ones were well away on their wings before this cataclysm came to pass.

Presently a load of sashes, doors and wooden frames and another load of lumber arrived. Things can be done in a hurry if you have money and influence and the will to insist on what you want. Before night they'd made a good start toward big changes in the old barn.

Plumbers and gas fitters and men installing the hot-water heat chased one another around the place, each man seeking to get his pipes in place before the lathers got to that spot. And the contractor was everywhere, proving his right to be selected for this rush job. As soon as the lathers had finished with a room the plasterers took possession, and the old door was rapidly being replaced with a great glazed door set in a frame of more sashes, so the old darkness was gone entirely.

In the roof big dormer windows were supplanting the two or three little eyebrow affairs that had given air to the hay before this, and the loft was fast becoming more pleasant than the floor below.

Outside laborers were busy building up a terrace, where a wide cement-floor veranda with stone foundations and low stone walls was to run across the entire front. Another chimney was rising from the region of the kitchen. A white enamel sink with a wide drain shelf attached appeared next, with signs of a butler's pantry between the kitchen and dining room. A delightful set of china-closet doors with diamond panes that matched the windows was put in one corner of the dining room, and some bookcases with sliding doors developed along the living-room walls. Down in the basement a man was fitting stationary tubs for a laundry, and on both the first and second floors bathrooms were being made. If the place weren't so big, the workmen would have been in one another's way. Closets big and little were being put in, and parts of a handsome staircase were lying about, until you wouldn't know the place at all.

Every evening the old servant and the neighbor next door, who used to rent the old barn before he built his new one, came together to look over what had been accomplished during the day and to discourse upon this changing world and its wonders. The farmer, in fact, learned a great deal about modern improvements and at once brought some of them to bear on his own modest farmhouse. He had money in the bank, and why shouldn't he "have things convenient for Sally?"

When Sidney Graham reached the city on Monday morning he

scarcely took time to read his mail in the office and attend to the day's work before he was up and off again, flying along Glenside Road as fast as his car would carry him. His mind certainly wasn't on business that morning. He was as eager as a child to see how work at the old barn was progressing, and the workmen stood small chance of lying down on their job that week, for he meant to make every minute count, no matter how much it cost. He spent a large part of Monday hovering about the old barn, gloating over each sign of progress, using his imagination on more things than the barn. But when Tuesday arrived an accumulation of work at the office concerning a large order that had just come in kept him close to his desk. He'd hoped to get away in time to reach Glenside before the workmen left in the afternoon. But four o'clock arrived with a pile of letters still for him to sign, before his work would be done for the day.

He had just signed his name for the forty-ninth time and laid his pen down with an impatient sigh of relief when the telephone on his desk rang. He hesitated. Should he answer it and be hindered again, or call his secretary and let her attend to it while he slipped away to his well-earned respite? A second insistent ring, however, brought him back to duty, and he reached out and picked up the receiver.

"Is this Mr. Sidney Graham? Long distance calling!"

The young man frowned impatiently and wished he'd sent for his secretary. It was probably another tiresome confab on that Chicago matter, and it really wasn't worth the trouble anyway. Then a small scared voice at the other end of the wire spoke.

"Is that you, Mr. Graham? Well, this is Carol. Say, Mr. Graham, I'm afraid something awful has happened to Shirley! I don't know what to do, and I thought I'd better ask you." Her voice broke off in a gasp like a sob.

A cold chill struck the young man's heart, and a vision of Shirley battling with the ocean waves was instantly conjured up.

"Shirley! Where is she? Tell me quick!" he managed to say, though the words seemed to stick in his throat.

"She's down at Washington," answered Carol. "Mr. Barnard phoned her last night. There was something special nobody else could take notes about, because it was for a government contract and has to be secret. Mr. Barnard asked her to go, and she went this morning. Mother didn't like her to go, but she addressed a lot of postal cards for her to write back, and one came postmarked Baltimore in this afternoon's mail, saying she was having a nice time. But just now a call came for Mother to go to the telephone. She was asleep, and George was crabbing so I had to come. It was a strange man in Washington. He said he just found three postal cards on the road addressed to Mother—that all said 'Help! Quick! Two men are carrying me off! Please phone the police.' He took the postals to the police station, but he thought he should phone us. And, oh, Mr. Graham, what shall I do? I can't tell Mother. It will kill her, but how can we help Shirley?"

"Don't tell your mother," said Graham quickly, trying to speak calmly out of his horror. "Be a brave girl, Carol. A great deal depends on you just now. Have you phoned Mr. Barnard? He's in Washington? He was to meet your sister in Baltimore? He did meet her, you say? The postal card said she met him? Well, the next thing is to phone Mr. Clegg and find out if he knows anything. I'll do that at once, and unless he's heard she's all right I'll start for Washington on the next train. Suppose you stay right where you are till half-past five. I may want to call you up again and need you in a hurry.

"Then you go back to the cottage as fast as you can and talk cheerfully. Say you went for a walk. Isn't Elizabeth with you? Well, tell her to help keep your mother from suspecting anything. Above all don't cry! It won't do any good, and it may do lots of harm. Get George off by himself and tell him everything, and tell him I said he was to make some excuse to go downtown after supper and stay at the telephone office till ten o'clock. I may want to call him up from Washington. Now be a brave girl. I suspect your sister Shirley would tell you to pray. Good-bye."

"I will!" gasped Carol. "Good-bye!"

Graham pressed his foot on the bell under his desk, slammed his desk drawers shut and put away his papers. His secretary appeared at the door.

"Get me Barnard and Clegg on the phone! Ask for Mr. Barnard or, if he isn't in, Mr. Clegg. Then go out to the other phone and call up the station. Find out when's the next express to Washington. Tell Bromwell to be ready to drive me to the station and bring my car back to the garage."

He was working as he talked: putting papers in the safe, jotting down a few notes for the next day's work, trying to think of everything at once. The secretary handed him the phone, quietly saying, "Mr. Clegg on the phone," and left the room.

Excited conference with Mr. Clegg brought out the fact that he was just in receipt of a telegram from police headquarters in Washington. It said that a book with Barnard and Clegg's address and an appeal from a young woman named Shirley Hollister, who was apparently being kidnapped by two strange men in an auto, had been flung into a passing car and brought to them. They'd sent forces in search of the girl at once and would do all in their power to find her. Meanwhile they'd like any information helpful in the search.

Mr. Clegg was very excited. He seemed glad to have another cooler mind working on the case. He spluttered a good deal about its importance and the need for secrecy. He said he hoped it wouldn't get into the papers and that it would be Barnard and Clegg's undoing if it did. He seemed more concerned about that and the notes Shirley probably had than the girl's situation. When Graham brought him up rather sharply he admitted a message had come from Barnard that he'd be detained overnight probably, but he'd attached no significance to that. He knew Barnard's usual hotel address in Washington but hadn't thought to phone him about the telegram from police headquarters. Graham hung up at last in a panic of fury and dismay, ringing violently for his secretary again.

"The next train leaves at five o'clock," she said, as she entered. "Bromwell has gone after the car. I told him to buy you a mileage book and save your time at this end. You have forty minutes, and he'll be back in plenty of time."

"Good!" said Graham. "Now call up long distance and get me police headquarters in Washington. No! Use the phone in Father's office, please. I'll have to use this while you're getting them."

As soon as she left the room he called up the shore again and was fortunate in getting Carol almost immediately, the poor child being close at hand and trembling, with Elizabeth in no less a state of nervousness, bravely waiting for orders.

"Can you give me an exact description of your sister's dress and everything she had with her when she started this morning?" asked Graham, prepared with pen and paper to write it down.

Carol summoned her wits and described Shirley's simple outfit exactly, even down to the black pumps on her feet, and went mentally through the small handbag she'd carried.

"Oh, yes!" she added. "She had a book to read! One she found here in the cottage. It had a red cover and was called From the Car Behind.

Graham wrote them all down carefully, asked a few more details of Shirley's plans and bade Carol again be brave and go home with a message to George to be at the phone from half-past eight to ten.

He was ready to go to his train when the Washington call came in, and as he hurried to his father's office to answer it he found his heart crying out to an Unseen Power to help in this trying hour and protect the sweet girl in awful peril.

"Oh, God, I love her!" he found his heart saying over and over again, as if it had started out to be an individual by itself without his will or volition.

There was no comfort from Washington police headquarters. Nothing more had been discovered except another crumpled postal lying along the roadside. They received with alacrity, however, Mr. Barnard's Washington hotel address and the description of the young woman and her belongings.

When Graham finished the hasty conversation he had to fly to make his train, and when at last he lay back in his seat in the parlor car and let the waves of his anxiety and trouble roll over him he was almost overwhelmed. He'd led a comparatively tranquil life for a young man who had never tried to steer clear of trouble, and this was the first great calamity to come his way. Calamity? No, he wouldn't own it was a calamity yet. He was hurrying to her! He would find her! He wouldn't allow himself to think anything had befallen her.

But wherever she was, if she was still alive, no matter how great her peril, he was sure she was praying now, and he would pray too! Yes, pray as she taught him. Oh, God! If he only knew how to pray better! What was it she'd said so often? "Whatsoever ye ask in my name"— yes, that was it—"I will do it." What was that name? Ah! Christ! "Oh, God, in the name of Christ—" But when he came to the thought of her she was too exquisite and dear to be put into words, so his petition went up in spirit form, with no words to weigh it down, wafted up by the pain of a tortured soul.

At Baltimore it occurred to Graham to send a telegram to Barnard to meet him at the train. When he got out at Union Station the first person he saw was Barnard, white and haggard, looking for him through the bars of the train gate. He grasped the young man's hand as if it were a last straw for a drowning man to cling to and demanded in a shaking voice to know if he'd heard anything from Miss Hollister.

One of Graham's first questions was whether Barnard had returned to the office where Miss Hollister had taken the dictation, to report her disappearance.

"Well, no, I hadn't thought of that," Barnard said blankly. "What would they know about it? The fact is, I was rather anxious to keep the facts from getting to them. They warned me certain parties were anxious to get hold of those specifications. It's government work, you know."

"They should know at once," said Graham sternly. "They may have inside information which would give us a clue to follow. The secret service men are onto a lot of things we common mortals don't suspect."

Mr. Barnard looked mortified and convinced.

"Well, what have you done so far? We'd better understand each other thoroughly so as to save time and not go over old ground. You've been in communication with police headquarters, of course?" asked Graham.

"Why, no," said the older man apologetically. "I got here just in time for the train. Since I didn't find the young lady in the station where we agreed to meet, I took it for granted she used the extra time driving about to see a few sights in the city, as I suggested, and failed to get back in time. I couldn't understand it because she was anxious to get home tonight. I could have caught the train myself but didn't like leaving her alone in a strange city—though, of course, it's perfectly safe for a steady girl like that.

"Afterward it occurred to me she might have gotten on the train and perhaps I should have done so too, but there was very little time to decide, for the train pulled out two minutes after I reached the station. I waited about here for a while and then went over to the Continental, where my sister is stopping, thinking I'd ask her to stay in the station and watch for the young lady and I'd go home. But my sister had run down to the shore for a few days. So I ate something, and while I was in the dining room your telegram came. I was hoping you'd seen Miss Hollister or had word from her, and it was all right."

One could see the poor man had no conception of what was due a lady in his care, and Graham looked at him for a moment with rage, wishing he could take him by the throat and shake some sense into him.

"Then you don't know she's been kidnapped and the police are out on track for her?" said Graham dryly.

"No!" exclaimed Barnard, turning white and showing he had some real feeling after all. "Kidnapped! Why—why—how could she? And she's got those notes! Why, Graham! You're fooling! Why, how do you know?"

Graham told the man tersely as he walked him over to the telephone booths, finishing with: "Now you go in that booth and phone your government man, and I'll call up police headquarters and see what's going on. We've got to work fast, for there's no telling what may have happened in the last three hours. It's up to us to find that girl before anything worse happens to her."

White and trembling Barnard tottered into the booth. When he came out again the Secret Service sleuthhounds were on the trail of Shirley Hollister's captors.

Chapter 24

The car bearing Shirley Hollister through the lonely wooded road at a breathless speed suddenly halted in the rear of an old house whose front faced on another road equally lonely. During the brief time they were in the woods, the sky seemed to have perceptibly darkened with the coming evening.

Shirley looked about her with increased fright. It was almost night, and here was her prison, far from town or human dwelling place. Even the road was at some distance in front of the house, and more woods were on either side.

"This is Secretary Baker's summer home," announced the man who had done the talking, as he climbed out of the car and opened the door for her. "You can just step in the back door and go through to the parlor; the help's all out this afternoon. The secretary'll be down presently. He always takes a nap afternoons about this time. I'll tell him you've come."

There seemed to be nothing to do but obey, and Shirley chose to let the farce continue. Surely the man must know she wasn't an idiot, but it was better than open hostility. There was nothing to be gained by informing him she knew he was fooling her.

"Oh, Jesus Christ, I trust myself to You!" she breathed in her heart as she stepped across the leaf-strewn grass and looked about her, wondering whether she'd ever walk the earth again after she entered the dim tree-shrouded house. But why go in?

"I think I'll remain out here," she said calmly, albeit her heart was pounding away like a trip-hammer. "Please tell Mr. Baker to come to me here. It's much pleasanter than in the house on a day like this."

"Aw, no! You won't neither! The secretary don't receive in the open air even in summer," drawled the man.

She noticed that he and the driver straightened up and stepped closer to her, one on either side. She gave one wild glance toward the open space. There was simply no chance at all to run away even if she succeeded in eluding them at the start by a quick, unexpected dash. They were alert athletic men, and no telling how many more were hidden in the house.

"Oh, very well, of course, if it's a matter of etiquette!" said Shirley pleasantly, determined to keep up the farce as long as possible.

A cold, dark air met the girl as she stepped within the creaking door and looked about her. At her left was an old-fashioned kitchen, dusty and cobwebby. A long, narrow hall led to the front of the house, and her guide pointed her toward a room on the right. There was something hollow and eerie in the sound of their footsteps on the old oaken floor. The room into which she was ushered was musty and dusty as the rest. The floor was covered with an ancient ingrain carpet. The table was covered with magenta felt stamped with a vine of black leaves and riddled with moth holes. The walls were hung with old prints and steel engravings suspended by woolen cords and tassels. The furniture was dilapidated. Everything was covered with dust, but she noticed fingerprints in the dust here and there that showed the place had been recently visited. Through an open doorway an old square piano was visible in what must be the parlor.

The place seemed to Shirley fairly teeming with memories of some family now departed. She leaped to the quick conclusion that the house was long deserted and only recently entered and used as a rendezvous for illegal conferences. It occurred to her she might have an opportunity to hide her precious papers safely if she must be searched. How about that piano? Could she slip some of them between the keys? But she'd hardly have an opportunity for anything like that.

She felt strangely calm as she looked about on her prison.

"H'm! He ain't come yet!" remarked her guide as he glanced into the front room. "Well, you can set down. He won't be long now. Joe, you jest look about a bit and see if you can find the secretary and tell him the young lady is here." The man flung himself full length on the carpet-covered couch and looked at her with satisfaction.

"What train did you say you must make? I'm afraid you might be late if he don't get a hustle on. But you can't hurry a great man like that, you know."

"Oh, it doesn't matter!" said Shirley, looking around her innocently. "What a quaint old house! Has it been in the family a long time?"

The man looked at her with amusement.

"You're a cute one!" he remarked. "I believe you're a good sport! You know you're in my power and can't help yourself. Yet you sail around here as calm as a queen! You're some looker, too! Blamed if I'm not enjoying myself. I wouldn't mind a kiss or two from those pretty lips—"

But Shirley had melted through the doorway into the other room, and her voice floated back with charming indifference as if she hadn't heard, though she was ready to scream with loathing and fear of the man.

"Why, isn't this a delightful old piano? The keys are actually mother-of-pearl. Isn't it odd? Would Mr. Baker mind if I played it?"

And before her astonished captor could get himself to the doorway she'd sat down on the rickety old haircloth stool and swept the keys lightly. The old chords trembled and shivered as if awaking from a tomb and uttered a quavering, sweet sound like ancient memories.

The man was too much astonished to stop her, amused too, perhaps, and interested. Her white fingers over the dusty pearls in the growing dusk charmed the hardened reprobate strangely, like the wonder of a flower dropped into the foulness of a prison. Before he could recover, he was startled again by her voice soaring out in the empty echoing house.

Rock of ages, cleft for me,
  Let me hide myself in Thee;
Let the water and the blood
  From Thy riven side which flowed,
Be of sin the double cure;
  Save me, Lord, and make me pure!

Perhaps those gloomy walls had echoed before to the grand old tune, but never could it have been sung in direr strait or with more earnest cry from a soul in distress. She chose the first words that seemed to fit the chords she struck, but every syllable was a prayer to the God in whom she trusted. The man may have felt the power of her appeal as he stood rooted in the doorway and listened while she sang through all the verses she could remember. But the last trembling note was broken harshly by Joe's voice at the kitchen door in sharp, rasping orders.

"Hist there! Can that noise! Do you want to raise the dead here? Wake up, Sam! Get onto your job. Hennie's comin'."

"That's all right, Joe! Dry up! This is good Sunday school dope! This won't rouse no suspicions. Go to the devil and mind your business! I know what I'm about!"

Shirley was almost ready to cry, but she drew a deep breath and started on another song.

Jesus, Lover of my soul,
  Let me to Thy bosom fly,
While the nearer waters roll,
  While the tempest still is high!
Hide me, oh, my Savior hide,
  Till the storm of life is past.

On through the time-worn words she sang, while the sin-hardened man stood silently and listened. His eyes had gradually lost their leer and grown soft and tender, as if childhood memories of home and mother and a time when he was innocent and good were looking out his eyes, reminding him of what he once intended to be before he ate the apple of wisdom and became as the gods and devils. Shirley gradually became aware that she was holding her strange audience, and a power beyond herself steadied her voice and kept her fingers from trembling on the old pearl keys. She wandered from song to song, perhaps happening on the very ones—who knows?—that this man, standing in the dying twilight of the old gloomy house, had sung beside his mother's hearth or in church during his childhood? He stood there silent and listened for at least half an hour without interruption, while the light in the room grew dimmer and all about the house seemed still as death in the intervals between her voice.

She was just beginning,

Abide with me,
  Fast falls the eventide,
The darkness deepens,
  Lord, with me abide!

when the man put his hand in his pocket and brought out a candle. Scratching a match on his trousers, he lit the candle and set it carefully on the piano, where its light fell flickering, wavering over her tired young face. And who shall say she wasn't a messenger from another world to this man who had long trod the downward path?

They were interrupted, however, before this song was finished by a newcomer who entered like a shadow and stood at the end of the piano looking from Shirley to the man. She glanced up. Then she stopped, startled, for although he wore no brass buttons or blue clothes she was sure those were the same gray eyes that had looked at her from the recess of the window in the government office that afternoon, perhaps the same boy who had come after her car and sent her off on this long way into the wilderness.

The man Sam straightened up suddenly and looked about him with an apologetic grin.

"Oh, you've come, have you, Hennie? Well, you been a long time about it! But now I guess we'll get to work. Where's Joe? Out on the watch? All right then, miss, if you've no objection, we'll just take a little vacation on the psalm singin' and turn our attention to worldly things. I calculate you're sharp enough to know what we brought you out here for. I acknowledge you can sing real well, and you sorta got my goat for a while with that mourning bench tra-la, for you certainly have that holy dope down fine. But the time's come for business, and you needn't think that because I can enjoy a little sentiment now and then in a leisure moment that you can put anything over on me, for it can't be did! I mean business, and I've got you in my power!

"We're ten miles from any settlement, and no neighbors anywhere's about. Everybody moved away. So it won't do any good to work any funny business on us. You can't get away. We're all armed, and no one knows where you are! If you behave yourself and do as you're told there won't be any trouble. We'll just transact our business, and then we'll have a bit of supper and mebbe a few more tunes—got any ragtime in your repitwar? Then sometime after midnight, when the moon's dark, we'll get you back to civilization where you won't have no trouble gettin' home. But if you act up and get funny, why, you know what to expect. A young girl was murdered once in this house and buried in the cellar, and ever since folks say it's haunted, and they won't come near it. That's the kind of place we're in! So now are you ready?"

Shirley sat cold and still. It seemed as if her life blood had suddenly congealed in her veins, and for a second she felt as if her senses would desert her. Then the echo of her own song, "Hide me, oh, my Savior, hide!" seemed to cry out silently from her soul, and she rallied once more and gained her self-control.

"Well, miss," continued the man impressively, "I see you're ready for the question, and you've got your nerve with you, too—I'll hand you that! But I warn you it won't do no good! We brung you out here to get hold of that notebook you wrote in this morning, and we're goin' to have it. We know Barnard left it in your care. Hennie here heard him say for you to keep it. So it won't be of any use for you to lie about it."

"Of course!" said Shirley, standing up and reaching for her handbag, which she'd laid on the piano beside her while she played. "I understand perfectly. But I'd like to ask you a question, Mr.—?"

"Smith, or Jones, whichever you like to call it. Spit it out!"

"I suppose you're paid to bring me out here, Mr. Smith, and get my property away from me?" she asked gravely.

"Well, yes, we don't calculate to do it just for sweet charity."

"And I am paid to look after my notebook, you see. It's a trust that's been given me! I just have to look after it. It's out of the question for me to desert it!" Shirley spoke coolly and held her bag firmly with her two hands.

The man stared at her and laughed. The boy Hennie fairly gaped in his astonishment.

"A girl with all that nerve!"

"Of course, I understand perfectly that you can murder me and bury me down in the cellar beside that other girl who was murdered, and perhaps no one will find it out for a while, and you can have a good time on the money you'll get for it. But the day will come when you'll have to answer for it! You know I didn't come here alone today—!"

Both men looked startled and glanced uneasily into the shadows, as if there might be someone lurking there.

"God came with me, and He knows! He'll make you remember someday!"

The boy laughed out a nervous ha! of relief, but the man seemed held, fascinated by her look and words. Silence ruled for a second while the girl held off the ruffian in the man by sheer force of her strong personality. Then the boy laughed again, with a sneer in the end of it, and the spell was broken. The leer came into the man's eyes again. The boy's sneer had brought him to himself—to the self he had come to be.

"Nix on the sob stuff, girlie!" he said gruffly. "It won't go down with me! We're here for business, and we've been delayed too long already. Come now, will you hand out that notebook, or will we have to search you?"

He took one stride across to where she stood and wrenched the handbag from her grasp before she was aware of his intention. She hadn't meant to give it up without a struggle, much as she loathed the thought of one. She must make the matter last as long as possible, if perchance God was sending help to her, and must contest every inch of the way as far as lay in her power. Oh, did anyone pick up her cards? Did the book with its message reach any friendly eye?

Pale and stern she stood with folded arms while they turned out the bag's contents and scattered it over the piano, searching with clumsy fingers among her dainty things.

She had rolled the notebook within her handkerchiefs and made it hard to find. She feared lest her ruse would be discovered when they looked it over. The boy was the one who clutched for the book, recognizing it as the one he'd seen in the office that morning. The man hung over his shoulder and peered in the candlelight, watching the boy anxiously. It meant a good deal of money if they put this thing through.

"Here it is!" said the boy, fluttering through the pages and carefully scrutinizing the shorthand characters. "Yes, that's the dope!"

He ran his eye down the pages, caught a word here and there, technicalities of manufacture, the very items he wanted, if this had been the specifications for the government order. Shirley remembered with relief that none of the details was identical, however, with the notes she carried in her shoes. The book notes were in fact descriptive of an entirely different article from that demanded by the government. The question was, would these people be wise enough to discover that fact before she was out of their power?

Furtively she studied the boy. There was something keen and cunning about his youthful face. He was thickset, with blond hair and blue eyes. He might be of German origin, though his speech had no accent. He had the bulldog chin, retreating forehead and eagle nose of the Kaiser in embryo. Shirley saw all this as she studied him. That he was an expert in shorthand was proved by the way he read some of her obscure sentences, translating rapidly here and there as he examined the book. Was he well enough informed about the government contract to realize these weren't the notes she'd taken in the office that morning? And if he failed to recognize it, would they be shown to someone higher in authority before she was released? She shivered and set her weary toes tight with determination over the crinkling papers in her shoes. Somehow she would protect those notes from being taken, even if she had to swallow them. There surely would be a way to hide them if the need came.

Suddenly the tense strain under which she was holding herself was broken by the man. He looked up with a grin, rubbing his hands with evident self-gratulation and relief.

"That's all right, girlie! That's the dope we want. Now we won't trouble you any longer. We'll have supper. Hennie, you go and get some of that wood out in the shed, and we'll have a fire on the hearth and make some coffee!"

But Shirley, standing pale and tense in the dim shadow of the room, suddenly felt the place whirling about her and the candle dancing afar off. Her knees gave way beneath her, and she dropped back to the piano stool weakly and covered her face with her hands, pressing hard on her eyeballs. She tried to keep her senses and stop this black dizziness that threatened to submerge her consciousness. She mustn't faint—if this was fainting. She must keep her senses and guard her precious shoes. If one of those should fall off while she was unconscious all would be undone.

Chapter 25

The man looked up from the paper he was twisting for a fire and saw Shirley's despairing manner.

"Say, kid," he said, with a kind of gruff tenderness, "you don't need to take it that a-way. I know it's tough luck to lose out when you been so nervy and all, but you knew we had it over you from the start. You hadn't a show. And say! Girlie! I tell you what! I'll make Hennie sit down right now and copy 'em off for you, and you can put 'em in your book again when you get back and nobody be the wiser. We'll just take out the pages. We gotta keep the original, o' course, but that won't make any beans for you. It won't take you no time to write 'em over again if he gives you a copy."

Somehow it penetrated through Shirley's tired consciousness that the man was trying to be kind to her. He was pitying her and offering her a way out of her supposed dilemma, offering to assist her in some of his own kind of deception. The girl was touched even through all her other crowding emotions and weariness. She lifted up her head with a faint smile.

"Thank you," she said wearily, "but that wouldn't do me any good."

"Why not?" asked the man sharply. "Your boss would never know it got out through you."

"But I would know I failed!" she said sadly. "If you had my notes I'd know I failed in my trust."

"It wouldn't be your fault. You couldn't have helped it!"

"Oh, yes, I could and should have. I shouldn't have let the driver turn around. I should have gotten out of that car and waited at the station as Mr. Barnard told me to do till he came. I was warned, and I should have been on my guard. So you see, it was my fault."

She dropped her head forward and rested her chin on the palm of her hand, her elbow on her knee. The man stood looking at her for a second in half-indignant astonishment.

"My!" he said at last. "You certainly are some nut! Well, anyhow, buck up, and let's have some tea. Sorry I can't see my way clear to help you out any further, being as we're sort of partners in this job and you certainly have some nerve for a girl. But you know how it is. I guess I can't do no more'n I said. I got my honor to think about, too. See? Hennie! Get a move on you. We ain't waitin' all night fer eats. Bring in them things from the cupboard, and let's get to work."

Shirley declined to come to the table when at last the repast was ready. She said she wasn't hungry. In fact, the smell of the crackers and cheese and pickles and dried beef sickened her. She felt too hysterical to try to eat, and besides she had a lingering feeling that she must keep near that piano. If anything happened, she had a vague idea she might somehow hide the precious notes inside the old instrument.

The man frowned when she declined to come to supper, but a moment later he stumbled awkwardly across the room with a slopping cup of coffee and set it down beside her.

"Buck up, girlie!" he growled. "Drink that and you'll feel better."

Shirley thanked him and tried to drink a few mouthfuls. Then it occurred to her that it might be drugged, and she swallowed no more. But she tried to look a bit brighter. If she must pass this strange evening with these rough men, it wouldn't help matters for her to give way to despair.

So after toying with the teaspoon a moment, she put the cup down and began to play soft airs on the old piano again while the men ate and took a stealthy taste now and then from a black bottle. She watched them furtively as she played, marveling at their softened expressions, remembering the old line, "Music hath charms to soothe the savage beast," and wondering if perhaps there wasn't really something to it. If she hadn't been in such a terrifying situation she would have enjoyed the character study this view of those two faces afforded her, as she sat in the shadow playing softly while they ate with the flaring candle between them.

"I like music with my meals!" the boy suddenly declared in an interval.

But the man growled in a low tone, "Shut up! Ain't you got no manners?"

Shirley prolonged that meal as much as music could, for she had no relish for a more intimate tête-à-tête with her companions. When she saw them grow restless she began to sing again, light little airs this time with catchy words or old tender melodies of home and mother and childhood. They were songs she'd sung that last night in the dear old barn when Sidney and Elizabeth Graham were with them, and unconsciously her voice took on the wail of her heart for all that dear past so far away from her now.

Suddenly, as the last tender note of a song died away Joe stumbled breathlessly into the room. The boy Hennie slithered out of the room like a serpent at his first word.

"Beat it!" he cried in a hoarse whisper. "Get a move on! They're after us! I bet they heard her singin'! Take her an' beat it! I'll douse the fire an' out the candle."

He seized a full bucket of water and dashed it over the dying fire. Shirley felt the other man grasp her arm in a fierce grip. Then Joe snuffed out the candle with his broad thumb and finger, and all was pitch dark. She felt herself dragged across the floor regardless of furniture in the way, stumbling, choking with fear—her one thought that whatever happened she mustn't let her shoes get knocked off. She held her feet in a tense strain with every muscle extended to keep the shoes fastened on like a vise. She was haunted with a wild thought of how she might have slipped under the piano and eluded her captor if only the light had gone out one second sooner before he reached her side. But it was too late to think of that now, and she was being dragged along breathlessly, out the front door, perhaps, and down a walk. No, it was among trees, for she almost ran into one. The man swore at her, grasped her arm till he hurt her and she cried out.

"You shut up, or I'll shoot you!" he said with an oath. He'd lost all his suaveness, and there was desperation in his voice. He kept turning his head to look back, urging her on.

She tripped on a root and stumbled to her knees, bruising them painfully, but her only thought was one of joy that her shoes hadn't come off.

The man swore a fearful oath under his breath, then snatched her up and began to run with her in his arms. It was then she heard Graham's voice.

"Shirley! Where are you? I'm coming!"

She thought she was swooning or dreaming and that it wasn't really he, for how could he be here? But she cried out with a voice as clear as a bell: "I'm here, Sidney! Come quick!"

In his efforts to hush her, the man stumbled and fell with her in his arms. Other voices and forms came through the night. She was gathered up in strong, kind arms and held. The last thought she had before she sank into unconsciousness was that God didn't forget. He was remembering all the time and sent His help before it was too late—just as she knew all along He must do, because He had promised to care for His own, and she was one of His little ones.

When she came to herself again she was lying in Sidney Graham's arms with her head against his shoulder feeling so comfortable and tired. Two automobiles with powerful headlights stood between the trees, with a lot of policemen in the shadowy background. Her captor stood sullen against a tree with his hands and feet shackled. Joe stood between two policemen with a rope bound about his body spirally, and the boy Hennie, also bound, beside his fallen bicycle, turned his ferret eyes from side to side as if he hoped even yet to escape. Two other men with hawklike faces that she hadn't seen before were there also, manacled, and with eyes of smoldering fire.

Mr. Barnard was climbing out of one of the big cars, his usually clean pink face smutty and weary, his sparse white hair rumpled giddily and a worried pucker creasing his kind face.

"Oh, my dear Miss Hollister! How unfortunate!" he exclaimed. "I do hope you haven't suffered too much inconvenience!"

Shirley smiled up at him from her shoulder of refuge as from a dream. It was all so amusing and impossible after what she'd been through. It couldn't be real.

"I assure you I'm very much distressed on your account," continued Mr. Barnard, politely and hurriedly, "and I hate to mention it at such a time, but could you tell me whether the notes are safe? Did those horrid men get anything away from you?"

A sudden flicker of triumph passed over the faces of the fettered man and the boy, like a ripple over still water dying away into unintelligence.

But Shirley's voice broke forth in a glad, clear laugh. "Yes, Mr. Barnard, they got my notebook, but not the notes! They thought the Tillman-Brooks notes were what they were after, but the real notes are in my shoes. Won't you please get them out, for I'm afraid I can't hold them on any longer—my feet ache so!"

It's a pity Shirley wasn't in a position to see the look of astonishment, followed by a twinkle of actual appreciation that crossed the face of the shackled man beside the tree as he listened. One could almost imagine he was saying to himself: "The nervy little nut! She put one over on me after all!"

It was also a pity Shirley couldn't have the full view of the altogether precise and conventional Mr. Barnard kneeling before her on the ground, removing carefully, with deep embarrassment and concern, first one, then the other, of her black pumps, extracting the precious notes, counting over the pages and putting them ecstatically into his pocket. No one of that group but Shirley could fully appreciate the ludicrous picture he made.

"You're entirely sure no one but you has seen these notes?" he asked anxiously as if he hardly dared believe the blessed truth.

"Entirely sure, Mr. Barnard!" Shirley said happily. "And now if you wouldn't mind putting on my shoes again I can relieve Mr. Graham of carrying me any farther."

"Oh, surely, surely!" said Mr. Barnard, quite fussed and kneeling down laboriously again, his white hair all tossed and his forehead perplexed over the unusual task. How did women get into such a little item as a shoe anyway?

"I assure you, Miss Hollister, our firm appreciates what you've done! We shall not forget it. You'll see—we shall not forget it!" he puffed as he rose with beads of perspiration on his brow. "You've done a great thing for Barnard and Clegg today!"

"She's done more than that!" said a burly policeman glancing around the group of sullen prisoners, as Graham put her on her feet beside him. "She's rounded up the whole gang for us, and that's more than anybody else has done! She oughtta get a medal of some kind fer that!"

Then, with a daredevil lift of his head and a gleam of something like fun in his sullen eyes, the manacled man by the tree spoke out, looking straight at Shirley, with real admiration in his voice: "I say, pard! I guess you're the winner! I'll hand you what's comin' to you if I do lose. You certainly had your nerve!"

Shirley looked at him with compassion in her eyes.

"I'm sorry you have to be—there," she finished. "You were—as fine as you could be to me under the circumstances, I suppose! I thank you for that."

The man met her gaze for an instant, a flippant reply on his lips, but checked it and, dropping his eyes, was silent. The whole company under the trees was hushed into silence before the miracle of a girl's pure spirit, leaving its impress on a blackened soul.

Then Graham led her quietly away to his car with Mr. Barnard and the detectives following. The prisoners were loaded into the other cars and hurried on the way to judgment.

Chapter 26

The ride back to the city was like a dream to Shirley afterward. To see the staid Mr. Barnard so excited, babbling away about her bravery and exulting like a child over the recovery of the precious notes, was wonder enough. But to feel Sidney Graham's quiet protection and tender interest filled her with ecstasy. Of course it was only kind interest and friendly anxiety, and by tomorrow she'd have put it into order with all his other kindnesses. But tonight, weary and excited as she was, with the sense of horror over her recent experience still upon her, it was sweet to feel his attention and let his voice thrill through her tired heart, without analyzing it and being sure she wasn't too glad over it. What if he would be merely a friend tomorrow! Tonight he was her rescuer, and she would rest on that and be happy.

"I was much to blame for leaving you alone to go to the station with a bait like these notes in your possession," said Mr. Barnard humbly. "Though of course I didn't dream you could be in danger."

"It's just as well not to run any risks these days when the country is so unsettled," said the detective dryly.

"Especially where a lady is concerned!" remarked Graham significantly.

"I suppose I should have taken Miss Hollister with me and left her in the cab while I transacted my business at the War Department!" said Barnard with self-reproach in his tones.

"They would only have done the same thing in front of the War Department," said the detective. "They had it all planned to get those notes somehow. You only made it easier for them by letting the lady go alone. If they hadn't succeeded here, they would have followed you to your home and gotten into your office or your safe. They were determined, desperate men. We've been watching them for some time, letting them work till we could find out who was behind them. Tonight we caught the whole bunch red-handed, thanks to the lady's cleverness. But you'd better not risk her alone again when there's anything like this on hand. She might not come out so easy next time!"

Graham muttered a fervent applause in a low tone to this advice, tucking the lap robes closer about the girl.

Barnard gave little shudders of apology as he humbly shouldered the blame. "Oh, no, of course not! I certainly am so sorry!"

But Shirley suddenly roused herself. "You mustn't blame Mr. Barnard. He did the perfectly right and natural thing. He always trusts me to look after my notes, even in the most important cases, and I heard the warning as much as he did. It was my business to be on the lookout! I'm old enough and have read enough in the papers about spies and ruffians. I should have known something was wrong when that boy ordered me back and said Mr. Barnard had sent me word. I should have known Mr. Barnard would never do that. I knew as soon as I stopped to think. But I was giving half my attention to looking at the strange sights out the window and thinking what I'd tell the folks at home about Washington, or I wouldn't have ended up in such a position. I insist that you not blame yourself, Mr. Barnard. It's a secretary's business to be on her job and not be out having a good time when she's on a business trip. I wasn't beyond the city limits before I knew exactly what I should have done. I should have asked the boy more questions, and I should have gotten out of that car and told him to tell you I'd wait in the station till you came for me. It troubled me from the start that you sent for me that way. It wasn't like you."

Then they turned their questions on her, and she had to tell the whole story of her capture, with Graham and Barnard exclaiming indignantly and the detective sitting grim and serious, nodding his approval now and then.

Graham's attitude toward her grew more tender and protective. Once or twice as she told of her situation in the old house or spoke of how the man dragged her along in the dark, he set his teeth and drew his breath hard, saying in an undertone, "The villain!" And something in the way he looked at her made Shirley hasten through the story, because of the wild, joyous clamor of her heart.

As soon as they reached the city limits, Graham stopped the car to telephone. It was after eleven o'clock, and there was little chance George would have stayed at the phone so long. But he'd leave a message for the early morning at least. George, however, had stuck to his post.

"Sure! I'm here yet. What'd ya think? Couldn't sleep, could I, with my sister off alone with a fella somewhere being kidnapped? What'd ya say? Found her? She's all right? Oh, say! That's good! I told Carol you would! I told her not to worry! What'd ya say? Oh, Shirley's going to talk? Oh, hello, Shirley! How's Washington? Some speed, eh? Say, when ya coming home? Tomorrow? That's good. No, Mother doesn't know a thing. She thinks I went to bed early 'cause I planned to go fishing at sunrise. She went to bed early herself. Say, Mister Graham's a prince, isn't he? Well, I guess I'll go to bed now. I might make the fishing in the morning yet, if I don't sleep too late. I sure am glad you're all right! Well, so long, Shirley!"

Shirley turned from the phone with tears in her eyes. It wasn't what George said that made her smile tenderly through them, but the gruff tenderness in his boy tones that touched her so. She hadn't realized before what she meant to him.

They drove straight to the station, got something to eat and took the midnight train back to their home city. Graham had protested that Shirley should go to a hotel and get a good rest before attempting the journey, but she laughingly told him she could rest anywhere and would sleep like a top in the train. When Graham found it was possible to secure berths in the sleeper for them all and that they wouldn't have to get out until seven in the morning he withdrew his protests. His further activities took the form of supplementing her supper with fruit and bonbons. His lingering handclasp as he bade her good night told her how glad he was she was safe—as if his eyes hadn't told her the same story every time there was light enough for them to be seen.

Locked at last in her safe little stateroom, with a soft bed to lie on and no bothersome notes to be guarded, one would have thought she might have slept, but her brain kept time to the wheels and her heart with her brain. She was going over the scenes of the eventful day and living through each experience again, until she came to the moment when she looked up to find herself in Sidney Graham's arms, with her face against his shoulder. Her face glowed in the dark at remembering, and her heart thrilled with the memory of his look and tone and his carefulness for her. How wonderful he came so many miles to find her! That he found her first, with all those other men on the hunt. He forged ahead and picked her up before any of the others reached her. He wasn't afraid to rush up to an armed villain and snatch her from her perilous position. He was a man among men! Never mind if he wasn't her own personal property! Never mind if others in his own world might claim him later. He was hers for tonight! She would never forget it!

She slept at last, profoundly, with a smile on her lips. No dream of villains or wild automobile rides troubled her thoughts. And when she woke in the home station with familiar sounds outside and realized a new day was before her, her heart was flooded with a happiness that her common sense found hard to justify. She tried to steady herself while she freshened up, but the face that was reflected rosily from the mirror in her dressing room smiled contagiously back at her.

"Well, then, have it your own way for just one more day!" she said aloud to her face in the glass. "But tomorrow you must get back to common sense again!" Then she turned, fresh as a rose, and went out to meet her fellow travelers.

She went to breakfast with Sidney Graham, in a wonderful place with fountains and palms and quiet, perfect service. Mr. Barnard had excused himself and hurried away to his home, promising to meet Shirley at the office at half-past nine. And so these two sat at a table by themselves and held sweet conversation over their coffee. Shirley forgot for the time that she was only a poor stenographer working for her bread and living in a barn. Sidney Graham's eyes were upon her, in deep and unveiled admiration, his spirit speaking to hers through the quiet commonplaces to which he must confine himself in this public place.

Not until the meal was over and he was settling his bill did Shirley suddenly come to herself and the color flood her face. How was she better than any other poor foolish girl who let a rich man amuse himself for a few hours in her company and then let him carry her heart away with him to toss with his collection? She drew her dignity about her and tried to be distant as they went out to the street, but he didn't recognize it. He just kept his tender manner and smiled at her with that wonderful look that made her dignity seem cheap. So she could only look up as a flower would to the sun and be true to the best that was in her heart.

She was surprised to find his own car at the door when they came out on the street. He must have phoned for it before they left the station. He was so kind and thoughtful. It was wonderful to be cared for in this way. "Just as if I were a rich girl in his social set," she thought.

He gave his chauffeur the orders and sat beside her in the back seat, continuing his role of admirer and protector.

"It certainly is great to know you're here beside me," he said in a low tone as they threaded their way in and out of the crowded thoroughfare toward the office. "I didn't have a very pleasant afternoon and evening yesterday, I can tell you! I don't think we'll let you go off on any more such errands. You're too precious to risk like that, you know!"

Shirley's cheeks were beautiful to behold as she tried to lift her eyes to his glance and take his words as if they were ordinary. But something in the tone of his voice and something intent and personal in his glance made her drop her eyes and covered her with confusion.

They were at the office almost immediately, and Graham was helping her out.

"Now when will you be through here?" he asked, glancing at his watch. "What train were you planning to take down to the shore? I suppose you'll want to get back as soon as possible?"

"Yes," said Shirley, "I do. But I don't know whether to run out home first and get Mother's big old shawl and two or three other little things we should have brought along."

"No," said Graham quickly, with a flash of anxiety in his face, "I wouldn't if I were you. They'll be anxious to see you, and if it's necessary you can run up again sometime. I think you'll find lots of shawls at the cottage. I'm anxious to have you safely landed with your family. I promised Carol you'd be down the first train after you finished your work. How long will it take you to fix Mr. Barnard up so he can run things without you?"

"Oh, not more than two hours, I'd think, unless he wants something more than I know."

"Well, it's half-past nine now. We'll say two hours and a half. That should give you time. I think there's a train about then. I'll phone to the station and find out and let you know the exact time. The car will be here waiting for you."

"Oh, Mr. Graham, that's not a bit necessary! You've taken trouble enough for me already!" protested Shirley.

"No trouble at all!" declared Graham. "My chauffeur has nothing to do but hang around with the car this morning, and you might as well ride as walk. I'll phone you in plenty of time."

He lifted his hat and gave her a last look that kept the glow in her cheeks. She turned and hurried in to her elevator.

Sidney Graham dropped his chauffeur at the station to inquire about trains and get tickets, with orders to report at his office within an hour, and then he himself took the wheel. Working his way out of the city's traffic he put on all possible speed toward Glenside. He must see that all was going well before he went to the office. What would Shirley say if she carried out her plan of coming out for her mother's shawl? He must stop that at all costs. She simply mustn't see the old barn till the work was done, or the whole thing would be spoiled. Strange it hadn't occurred to him she might want to come back after something! Well, he'd just have to be on the continual lookout. For one thing he'd stop at a store on the way back and purchase a couple of big steamer rugs and a long warm cloak. He could smuggle them out for common use as if they belonged to the house.

He was as eager as a child over everything that was started during his absence and walked about with the head carpenter, settling two or three questions that had come up the day before. In ten minutes he was back in his car, speeding toward the city again, planning how he could get the rugs and cloak into the housekeeper's hands at the shore without anybody suspecting they were new. Then it occurred to him to take them down to Elizabeth and let her engineer the matter. There must be two cloaks, one for Shirley, for he wanted to take her out in the car sometimes and her little scrap of a coat was entirely too thin even for summer breezes at the shore.

Shirley met with a great ovation when she entered the office. Her fame had evidently gone before her. Mr. Barnard was already there, smiling benevolently, and Mr. Clegg, nodding his head approvingly at her. The other office clerks came to shake hands or called congratulations, till Shirley was quite overwhelmed at her reception. Clegg and Barnard both followed her into the inner office and continued to congratulate her on her bravery and to express their appreciation for her loyalty and courage on the firm's behalf. Mr. Barnard handed her a check for a hundred dollars as a slight token of their appreciation of her work, telling her that beginning with the first of the month her salary was to be raised.

When at last she sat down to her typewriter, clicking out the notes that had made so much trouble and putting them in shape for practical use, her head was in a whirl, and her heart was beating with a childish ecstasy. She felt as if she were living a real fairytale and could never get back to everyday life again.

At half-past eleven Graham called her to tell her there was a train a little after twelve if she could be ready, and the car would be waiting for her in fifteen minutes.

When she finally tore herself away from the smiles and effusive thanks of Barnard and Clegg and took the elevator down to the street she found Sidney Graham himself awaiting her eagerly. This was a delightful surprise, for he hadn't said anything about coming himself or mentioned when he'd be coming back to the shore, so she thought it might be sometime before she'd see him again.

He had just slammed the car door and taken his seat beside her when a large gray limousine slowed down next to them and a well-groomed young woman leaned out of the car and smiled at Graham. She passed over Shirley with one of those unseeing stares with which some girls know how to erase other girls.

"Oh, Sidney! I'm so glad I saw you!" she cried. "Mother's been phoning everywhere to find you. We're at our country place for a couple of weeks, and she wants to ask you to come over this afternoon for a little tennis tournament we're having, with a dance on the lawn afterward."

"That's very kind of you, Harriet," said Graham pleasantly, "but I can't possibly be there. I have an engagement out of town for this afternoon and evening. Give my regards to your mother, please, and thank her for the invitation. I know you'll have a lovely time—you always do at your house."

"Oh, that's too bad, Sidney!" pouted the girl. "Why must you be so busy—and in the summertime, too! You should take a vacation! Well, if you can't come tonight, you'll run down over the weekend, won't you? We're having the Foresters and the Harveys. You like them, and we simply can't do without you."

"Sorry," said Graham, smiling, "but I've got all my weekends filled up just now. Harriet, let me introduce you to Miss Hollister! Miss Hale, Miss Hollister!"

Then Harriet Hale had to take over her unseeing stare and acknowledge the introduction—somewhat stiffly, it must be acknowledged, for Harriet Hale didn't enjoy having her invitations declined, and she couldn't quite place this girl with the lovely face and the half-shabby garments, that somehow had an air of being made by a French artist.

"I'm sorry, Harriet, but we'll have to hurry. We're catching a train at twelve-fifteen. Hope you have a beautiful time this afternoon. Remember me to Tom Harvey and the Foresters. Sorry to disappoint you, Harriet, but you see I've got my time full up at present. Hope to see you again soon."

They were off, Shirley with the impression of Harriet Hale's smile of vinegar and roses—the roses for Graham, the vinegar for her. Shirley's heart was beating wildly underneath her quiet demeanor. She'd at last met Harriet Hale, and Graham wasn't ashamed to introduce her! Protection and esteem were in his tone as he spoke her name. Miss Hale couldn't patronize her after that. Shirley was still in a daze of happiness. She didn't think ahead. She had all she could do to register new occurrences and emotions and realize her joy wasn't merely momentary. It hadn't occurred to her to wonder where Graham was going out of town. It was enough that he was here now.

When they reached the station Graham took two large packages out of the car and gave some directions to the chauffeur.

"Sorry we can't go down in the car again," he said as they walked into the station. "But it needs some repairs, and I don't want to take a long run until it's thoroughly overhauled."

Then he was going down too! He declined Harriet Hale's invitation to go back to the cottage with her! Shirley's breath came in happy little gasps as she walked beside her companion down the platform to the train.

She was soon seated in a green velvet chair in the parlor car while the porter stowed away the two packages in the rack overhead.

Chapter 27

Only one other passenger occupied the car, an old man nodding behind a newspaper, with his chair facing in the other direction. Graham surveyed him swiftly and turned back with a smile to Shirley.

"At last I have you to myself!" he said with a sigh of satisfaction that made Shirley's cheeks bloom out rosily again.

He whirled her chair and his away from the old man's vision, so they were at the nearest possible angle to each other and facing the windows. Then he sat down and leaned toward her.

"Shirley," he said in a tone of proprietorship that was tender and beautiful, "I've waited as long as I'm going to wait to tell you something. I know it's lunchtime, and I'm going to take you into the dining car soon and get you some lunch. But I must have a chance to talk with you first, please."

Shirley's eyes gave glad permission, and he hurried on.

"Shirley, I love you. I guess you've seen that for sometime. I knew I should hide it till you knew me better, but I simply couldn't do it. I've never seen a girl like you, and I knew the minute I looked at you that you were of finer clay than other girls. I knew that if I couldn't win you and marry you I would never love anybody else. But yesterday when I heard you were in danger away off in Washington and I was up here helpless to save you, and not even having the right to organize a search for you, I nearly went wild! All the way down on the train I kept shutting my eyes and trying to pray the way you told your Sunday school boys to pray. But all I could get out was, 'Oh, God, I love her! Save her! I love her!' Shirley, I know I'm not one-half worthy enough for you, but I love you with all my heart and I want you for my wife. Will you marry me, Shirley?"

When she recovered a little from her astonishment and realized he'd asked her to marry him and was waiting for an answer, she lifted her eyes to his face and tried to speak as her conscience and reason bade her.

"But I'm not like the other girls you know," she said bravely.

Then he broke in on her. "No, you're not like any other girl I know in the whole world. Thank God for that! You're one among a thousand! No, you're one among the whole earthful of women! You're the only one I could ever love!"

"But listen, please—you haven't thought. I'm not a society girl. I don't belong in your circle. I couldn't grace your position the way your wife should do. Remember—we're nobodies. We're poor! We live in a barn!"

"What do you suppose I care about that?" he answered eagerly. "You may live in a barn all your days if you like, and I'll love you just the same. I'll come and live in the barn with you if you want me to. My position! My circle! What's that? You'll grace my home and my life as no other girl could do. You heart of my heart! You strong, sweet spirit! The only question I'm going to ask of you is, Can you love me? If you can, I know you'll be happy, for I love you better than my life. Answer, please. Do you love me?"

She lifted her eyes, and their spirits broke through their glances. If the old man at the other end of the car was looking they didn't know it.

They came back to the shore cottage with a manner so blissful and unmistakable that even the children noticed. Elizabeth whispered to Carol at the table: "My brother likes your sister a lot, doesn't he? I hope she likes him, too."

"I guess she does," responded Carol philosophically. "She should. He's been awfully good to her and to all of us."

"People don't like people just for that," said wise Elizabeth.

Harley, out on the veranda after dinner, stepped near Carol.

"Say, kid, I guess he has got a case on her all right now. Say! Wouldn't that be great? Think of all those cars!"

But Carol giggled.

"Good night! Harley! How could we ever have a wedding in a barn? And they're such particular people, too!"

"Aw!" said Harley, disgusted. "You girls always think of things like that! As if that mattered. You can get married in a chicken run if you really have a case on each other! You make me tired!" And he stalked away in offended male dignity.

Meanwhile the unconscious subjects of this discussion had gone to Mrs. Hollister, and the sea was forgotten by all three for that one evening at least, even though the moon was bright and made a golden pathway across the dark water. For a great burden had rolled from Mrs.

Hollister's shoulders when she found her beloved eldest daughter was loved by this young man, and he wasn't just amusing himself for a while at her expense.

The next days were like one blissful dream to Shirley. She couldn't get used to the fact that she was engaged to such a prince among men! She felt as if she were dreaming, and that presently she'd wake up and find herself in the office with a pile of letters to write and the perplexing problem before her of where they were going to live next winter. She broached that subject once to Graham shyly, saying she must look around as soon as she got back to town. He put her aside, asking her to leave that question till they all went back, as he had a plan she might think well of, but he couldn't tell her about it yet. He also urged her to write at once to Mr. Barnard and resign her position, but that she wouldn't hear of.

"No," she said decidedly. "We couldn't live without my salary, and there are a lot of things to be thought out and planned before I can be married. Besides, we need to get to know each other and grow into each other's lives a little. You have no idea even now how far I am from being suited to be the wife of a man in your position. You may be sorry yet. If you're ever going to find it out, I want you to do it beforehand."

He looked into her eyes.

"I know perfectly now, dear heart!" he said. "And I'm not going to be satisfied to wait a long time for you to find out that you don't really care for me. If you've got to find that out, I'd rather have you close and fast so you'll have to like me anyway."

And then the wonder of it would roll over her again, and she would look into his eyes and be satisfied.

Still she continued quite decided that nothing could be done about prolonging her vacation, for she meant to go back to Barnard and Clegg's on the day set.

"You know I'm the man of the house," she said archly. "I can't see it at all—how I'm ever going to give up."

"But I thought I was going to be the man of the house," pleaded Sidney. "I'm sure I'm quite capable and eager to look out for the interests of my wife's family."

"But you see I'm not the kind of girl who's been looking around for a man to support my family."

"No, you surely are not!" said the young man, laughing. "If you were, young lady, you'd still be looking as far as I'm concerned. It's because you are what you are that I love you. Now that's all right about being independent, but it's time to fight this thing to a finish. I don't see why we all have to be miserable just because there are a lot of unpleasant precedents and conventions in the world. Why may I not help take care of your family if I want to? It's one of the greatest pleasures I'm looking forward to, to try and make them as happy as I can, so you'll be the happier. I've got plenty to do it with. God has been very good to me in that way, and why should you try to hinder me?"

And then the discussion would end in a bewildering look of worshipful admiration on Shirley's part and a joyous taking possession of her and carrying her off on some ride or walk or other on Graham's part.

He didn't care now that she was slow to make plans. He was enjoying each day to the full. He wanted to keep her from thinking about the future, especially the winter, till she got home, and so he humored her and led her to other topics.

One night, as they sat on the dark veranda alone, Graham said to George, "If you were going to college, where would you want to prepare?"

He wondered what the boy would say, for the subject of college had never been mentioned concerning George. He didn't know whether the boy had ever thought of it. But the answer came promptly in a ringing voice.

"Central High! They've got the best football team in the city."

"Then you wouldn't want to go away to some preparatory school?"

"No, sir!" was the decided answer. "I believe in the public school every time! When I was a kid I remember my father taking me for a walk and pointing out the Central High School and telling me that someday I'd go there to school. I used to call that 'my school.' I used to think I'd get there yet, someday, but I guess that's out of the question."

"Well, George, if that's your choice you can get ready to enter as soon as you go back to the city."

"What?" George's feet came down from the veranda railing with a thud, and he sat upright in the darkness and stared at his prospective brother-in-law. Then he relaxed, and his young face grew grim and stern.

"No chance!" he said.

"Why not?"

"Because I've got my mother and the children to support. I can't waste time going to school. I've got to be a man."

Something sudden like a choke came in the young man's throat, with a great love for the brave boy who was so courageous in his self-denial.

"George, you're not a man yet, and you'll shoulder the burden twice as well when you're equipped with a college education. I mean for you to have it. Do you suppose I'll let my new brother slave away before his time? No, sir. You're going to get ready to make the best man that's in you. And as for your mother and the family, isn't she going to be my mother, and aren't they to be my family? We'll just shoulder the job together, George, till you're older—and then we'll see."

"But I couldn't take charity from anybody."

"Not even from a brother?"

"Not even from a brother."

"Well, suppose we put it another way. Suppose you borrow the money from me to keep things going, and when you're ready to pay it back we'll talk about it then. Or, better still, suppose you agree to pass it on to some other brother when you're able."

They talked a long time in the dark, and Graham had quite a hard time breaking down the boy's reserve and independence and gaining a brotherly confidence.

But at last George yielded, saw the common sense and right of the thing, and laid an awkward hand in the man's, growling out, "You're a pippin and no mistake, Mr. Graham. I can't ever thank you enough! I never thought anything like this would happen to me!"

"Don't try thanks, George. We're brothers now. Just do your best at school, and it's all I ask. Shirley and I will be wonderfully proud of you. But please don't call me Mr. Graham anymore. Sid, or Sidney, or anything you like, but no more mistering."

He flung a brotherly arm across the boy's shoulders, and together they walked into the house.

Meanwhile the days passed by in one long, golden dream. The children were having the time of their lives, and Elizabeth had never been so happy. Shirley sat on the wide verandas and read the wealth of books and magazines the house contained, roamed the beach with the children and Star, or played in the waves with Doris and wondered if it was really Shirley Hollister having this good time.

Chapter 28

The morning they started back to the city was memorable. Graham had insisted that Shirley ask for a holiday until Tuesday morning so she might go up with them in the car and have the whole day to be at home and help her mother get settled. She consented and found to her surprise that Mr. Barnard was most kind about it. He even added he intended to raise her salary, and she might consider that hereafter she was to have ten dollars more per month for her services, which they valued very highly.

George sent his resignation to the store and wasn't to go back at all. Graham had arranged that, for school began the day after his return and he'd need to be free at once.

Elizabeth, to her great delight, was to go with the Hollisters and remain a few days until her parents returned. Mrs. Graham had written from the West proposing to Mrs. Hollister that Carol be allowed to go to school with Elizabeth the next winter; Mrs. Graham felt it would be good for Elizabeth to have a friend like that.

Mrs. Hollister, however, answered that she felt it better for her little girl to remain with her mother longer and that she didn't feel it would be a good thing for her child, who would otherwise have a simple life before her with few luxuries, to go to a fashionable finishing school where the standards would be so different from those of her own station in life. Kind as the offer was, she must decline it. She didn't say that Carol had fairly bristled at the idea of leaving her beloved high school now when she was a senior and only one year before her graduation. That bit of horror and hysterics on Carol's part was carefully suppressed within the four walls of her mother's room.

But Elizabeth, deeply disappointed, wept her heart out over the matter and finally was comforted by Mrs. Hollister's promise to write and ask Mrs. Graham to allow Elizabeth to go to school with Carol the coming winter. That proposition was now on its way West, together with an announcement of Sidney's engagement to Shirley.

Sidney was confidently expecting congratulatory telegrams that morning when he reached the city. He'd written his father in detail about their plans for returning and how the work at the old barn was progressing, and Mr. Walter Graham was too good a manager not to greet the occasion properly. Therefore Graham stopped at his office for a few minutes before taking the family out to Glenside and, sure enough, came down with his hands full of letters and telegrams and one long white envelope he tucked in his breast pocket. They had a great time reading the telegrams and letters.

The way out to Glenside seemed short now, watching as they did for each landmark. The children were as eager to get back as they'd been to leave, and Star snuggled in between Harley's feet, held his head high and smiled on everybody, as if he knew he was going home and was glad. They began to wonder about the chickens and if the garden was dried up and whether the doves were all right. There was an undertone of sadness and suppressed excitement, for it was in the minds of all the Hollisters that the time in the old barn must be growing brief. The fall would soon be upon them and a need for warmth. They must go house-hunting at once. And yet they all wanted this one delightful day before they faced that question.

At last they reached the final curve and could see the tall old tree in the distance and the clump of willows knee-deep in the brook. By common consent they all grew silent, watching for the first glimpse of the dear old barn.

Then they came around the curve, and there it was! But what was the matter?

Nobody spoke. It seemed as if they couldn't get their breath.

Shirley rubbed her eyes and looked again. Mrs. Hollister gave a star-tled look from her daughter to Graham and back to the barn again. Elizabeth and Carol were silent, grasping each other's hands in ecstasy.

The boys murmured inarticulately, of which the only audible words were, "Good night! Some class!"

Doris looked for a long second, puckered her lips as if she were going to cry and inquired pitifully: "I yant my dear barn house home! I yant to doh home!"

And Star uttered a sharp, bewildered bark and bounded from the car as if this were something he should attend to.

But before anybody could say anything more, Graham brought out the long white envelope and handed it to Shirley.

"Before you get out and go in I just want to say a word," he began. "Father and I both want Shirley to have the old barn for her very own, to do with as she pleases. This envelope contains the deed for the property made out in her name. We've tried to put it in thorough repair before handing it over to her, and if she can think of anything more it needs we'll do that too. And now welcome home to the old barn! Mother, may I help you out?"

"But there isn't any barn anymore," burst forth the irrepressible Elizabeth. "The barn's gone! It's just a house!"

And, sure enough, a stately stone mansion stood there on a wide green terrace, where shrubs and small trees were grouped about, erasing all signs of the old pastureland. The old grassy incline to the door now rolled away in velvety lawn on either side of a smooth cement walk bordered with vivid scarlet geraniums. Trailing vines and autumn flowers blossomed in jars on the wide stone railing. The old barn door had been replaced by glass which gave a glimpse of strange new rooms beyond, and the roof had broken forth in charming colonial dormer windows like a new French hat on a head that had worn the same old poke bonnet for years.

No wonder Doris didn't recognize the dear old barn. It was transformed. How was one to know that only a brief half-hour earlier the old gardener from the Graham estate set the last geranium in the row along the walk and trailed the last vine over the stone wall? Or how could one guess that even now the men who had been hastily laying and patting the turf in place over the terrace were hiding in the basement, with their wheelbarrows and picks and spades, after beating a hasty retreat at the sound of the car coming, and were only waiting till they could get away unobserved? For orders were orders, and the orders were that the work was to be done and every man out of sight by the time they arrived. A bonus to every man if the orders were obeyed. That's what money and influence can do in a month!

In due time they got out of the car in a bewildered daze and walked up the new cement path, feeling like intruders as they met the bright stare of geraniums.

They walked the length of the new veranda in delight. They exclaimed and started and smiled and almost wept in one another's arms. Graham stood and watched Shirley's happy face and was satisfied.

When Doris got inside the lovely glass door she started to run for her little willow chair and her old rag doll that had been left behind, and down she went on the slippery floor. And there, behold, the old barn floors too had disappeared under a coating of simple matched hardwood flooring, oiled and polished smoothly, and Doris wasn't expecting it. She got up quickly, half ashamed, and looked around laughing.

"I vas skating!" she declared with a ringing laugh. "I skated yite down on mine nose."

Then she hurried more cautiously to the haven of her own chair, and with her old doll hugged to her breast she reiterated over and over as if to reassure herself: "Mine! Doris! Mine! Doris!"

Words would fail to describe all they said about the wonderful rooms, the walls shining in a soft rough-finish plaster, tinted creamy on the upper half and gray below and finished in dark chestnut trimmings; the beautiful staircase and the wide bay window opening from the first landing like a little halfway room, with seats to rest on.

Standing in this bay window Graham called Mrs. Hollister's attention to something strange and new outside behind the house. It was a long, low glass building with green things gleaming through its shining roof.

"There, Mother," he said, coming up softly behind her. "There's your plaything. You said you always wanted a hothouse, so we made you one. It's heated from a coil in the furnace, and you can try all the experiments with flowers you want to. We put in a few things to start with, and you can get more at your leisure."

Mrs. Hollister gave one look and then turned and put her arms around the tall young man, reaching up on her tiptoes to do so, brought his handsome face down to hers and kissed him.

"My dear son!" she said.

That was all, but he knew she had accepted him and given him a loving place with her own children in her heart.

The children shouted and ran, first one and then another, upstairs and down, discovering the bathrooms one by one. Then they rushed down into the basement by the new stairs to see the new laundry, the new furnace and the entrance to the hothouse, and the hothouse itself, with its wealth of bloom transplanted from the Graham greenhouses.

They almost forgot the chickens and the doves, and the garden was a past Eden not to be remembered till long hours afterward.

The sunset was fading in the sky, and the stars were large and piercing in the twilight night when Shirley and Sidney came walking up the terrace arm in arm. They found Doris sitting in the doorway cuddling her old rag doll and a new gray kitten the farmer next door had brought her, singing an evening song to herself.

Shirley and Sidney turned and looked off at the sky where a rosy stain was blending into the evening gray.

"Do you remember the first night we stood here together?" Sidney said in a low tone, as he drew her fingers within his own. "I loved you then, Shirley, that first night—"

And then Doris's voice chimed above their murmurings: "Oh, mine nice dear home! Mine kitty an' mine dolly! And mine porch! And mine bafroom wif a place to swim boats! An' mine f'owers an' pitty house! No more barn! Barn all dawn! Never tum bat anymoh! Oh, mine nice, pitty dear home!"

The
Love Gift

Chapter 1

S hells are fine on a seashore, on white sand with a fresh breeze blowing. But in this stuffy room on the mantelpiece, in a wooden butter dish and considered an ornament—that is too much. Oh! Ugh!"

The new occupant, who was small and slight, was apparently exclaiming at a cockroach standing in the middle of the room watching her. She had looked at the room in the morning, rented it and left. And now, as the gray, drizzly day was closing, she'd returned, taken off her hat and jacket, and thrown them on the bed.

The fixed gaze of the cockroach must have attracted her attention, for as soon as she uttered that last word she gathered up her dress and started toward him. He rose up on his hind legs and scurried off toward the bed. She stooped to strike him under the edge of the bed. But by the time her eyes reached floor level, he'd disappeared from view, and she could see only a stretch of faded ingrain carpet.

Too weary to keep searching, she came back to contemplate the mantelpiece with its dish of dusty shells. Over the mantel hung an old engraving of a wooden-faced baby and a prim little girl with one foot under her, sewing. The engraving was framed in black walnut with a carved leaf at each corner and the words *Watching Baby* inscribed underneath.

On the walls were its companions in similar frames. One called *Meditation* showed a chalk-faced woman with a low-necked dress and a sheet over the top of her head, gazing up into the sky with a sad expression. The touching scene, *The Soldier's Farewell,* was also there, in which a stiff man and woman were clasped in each other's arms, with other stiff family members about them.

The girl turned from them in disgust and, with a curling lip that expressed more weariness than contempt, surveyed the rest of the room. The bedstead, bureau and washstand were imitation cherry and looked brisk and new, as if they could do cheap honors gracefully. But the fireplace was covered with a thick coat of dull, black paint, while the grate was one-sided and imparted to the tongs and coal scuttle a dismal appearance. The table was old and rickety and spread with a moth-eaten red cloth with dirty cretonne storks sewed on for decoration. A cheese box covered with dark green felt stood in front of the window. That was all besides the two chairs and the occupant.

Her face showed despair as she finished the inventory. The room was cheap and had a good-sized clothespress, and that was all that could be said in its favor. She tried to remember how much better this was than many rooms she'd looked at and to be thankful for finding it. But visions of a dainty white room luxuriously furnished, with her precious belongings scattered about, would come and contrast themselves with her present surroundings. How would her handsome jewel case look standing on that miserable stork tablecloth? But then she remembered it was sold with everything else and wouldn't need to associate with low-bred storks. Tears filled her eyes, and she walked to the small-paned window to occupy her thoughts elsewhere.

In a moment she heard a knock at the door. "Your trunk has come, miss. Where should I put it?"

With the trunk unstrapped and the man paid and gone, she returned to the window. The street was dark now, and lights glinted everywhere. She could see the tops of people's heads as they passed the street lamp in front of the house. The city's hum and buzz sent a shiver over her. It was far worse to hear it through the dark.

Perhaps the past few weeks were a dreadful dream, and she'd wake up tomorrow morning and find it past—and herself back in her pretty room, with the door open into her mother's and all her bright hopes hers again. But that could never be, and she must go on and bear her sorrow. She turned and went searching for the Irish girl to petition for a lamp since her room seemed to have no gas.

Her story was like many she'd read. But she thought it couldn't happen to her—the sudden death of her mother and shortly after that her father; then discovering the money they thought almost unlimited was swept away and even the home must be given up. A familiar story, yet new and terrible to each one who experiences it. When she found she must earn her living, she wouldn't choose the ways other girls in her position and with her accomplishments would have chosen.

"No," she said to a friend who tried to reason with her, "I can't do those things well enough, and I don't like to do them. Besides, places like that are overflowing already. If I knew how to cook I'd find a housekeeper position somewhere. But I don't. I only know how to trim hats!"

And trim hats she would, despite all that could be said. She'd done it for herself and her friends for years and was always said to have good taste. No one could place a feather or a bit of lace more gracefully.

Neither would she stay among her acquaintances and do her work; for in losing her home and money she also lost some friends she'd considered her nearest and dearest. She longed to get away from the pain and everything familiar. She came to this strange city and rented a small store on an unpretentious street. With a little money saved from the wreck she would buy a small stock and try her hand at millinery. A "cheap milliner," she told herself. Of course she couldn't hope to get the patronage of wealthy people immediately.

This was her first night in her new home. She had hunted all day for a store and a room and still had much work and worry before she could feel she'd started. Life looked hard that night.

"I hope yez won't be troubled wid the roaches," said the woman who presided over the lamps, handing her a dripping one.

That must be the reason for the cheapness, thought the weary girl as she dragged herself and her lamp up the two flights of stairs.

She opened the door, and, lo, they'd come to meet her—a whole army of them, great and small! They vanished from her in all directions, leaving her standing there. She was so disgusted and weary she didn't even attempt to catch one. She eyed the closet door. Who knew how many generations of those horrid, shiny things were hiding behind its grim boards? Would they, could they, come out and crawl over her when she was asleep? This thought was too much. She put the lamp on the rickety table, closed the door, threw herself on the not-too-clean bed and cried.

No roach came near her that night.

A bright Sunday morning sun woke her a few hours later. She went drearily to church because she couldn't bear to spend the morning alone in that room. But she sat in a back seat and let the minister's sermon float over her head while she entertained bitter thoughts. She was glad when the long service ended.

The people in the boardinghouse where she took her meals were dull and so different from those she usually associated with. She rushed back to her room from dinner, refusing the invitation to remain in the parlor and sing with the other boarders so haughtily that Miss Branson, who invited her, walked back to the piano with a face the color of her rose dress. There she slept some, unpacked some and thought a great deal, until at last the day was over. She was relieved she could go to work in the morning.

She enjoyed buying her stock, though it was tiring as she visited one wholesale store after another. She bought only what was pretty or tasteful, though many clerks assured her certain articles were "just the thing" and would sell better than those she chose. But she preferred good taste to having the "correct" thing and remained firm in her selections.

"If I'm going to make hats for poor Irish girls, I'll see if I can't elevate their tastes. I just cannot put such ugly things together," she told herself as she passed boxes of artificial green roses and nameless imitations of what never grew on the earth. She had to buy inexpensive things, for her purse was limited. But she expected to serve people who would require them, and many inexpensive things were also pretty.

So she spent much time and nerve and at last had her store ready for work. She was guilty of only one extravagance. She found a spray of white, starry blossoms, set among fine, fernlike leaves. The whole thing was so delicate and unobtrusive and yet so natural and in such perfect taste that it rested her tired eyes, which had been filled all day with gaudy colors and hideous straw shapes. They were fine French flowers and very expensive.

Her conscience and her judgment both rose up in horror. But she firmly put them down and said to the clerk, "I'll take them." Neither would she listen to these aggrieved advisors when she reached her room and they tried to reason with her.

"There's no telling—I may have some aristocratic customer, and she'll demand such flowers. Anyway, they'll help me do my work; it'll be pleasant just to know they're there. Those wall-eyed daisies I felt obliged to buy won't hurt my feelings so much if these dainty, lovely things are in front of them." Thus she spoke to her conscience and her judgment, and they gave up in despair.

At last she was established. A neat sign over the door said "Millinery" in large letters; underneath a smaller sign read "Miss M. L. Hathaway." She disliked the sign. It sounded stiff and far away, as if someone else were being talked about and not her, Marion Hathaway. But of course she didn't want to put that name out in the street for everyone to see.

The spring season was starting, and customers began coming in. The hats Marion had trimmed and placed in the window attracted attention; they were tasteful and unique. The orders came in so fast she couldn't do everything herself and needed someone to wait on customers.

The "Girl Wanted" sign she put in the window brought a procession of various girls, but not one was satisfactory to the fastidious milliner. At last, growing desperate, she resolved to hire the next girl who entered, good, bad or indifferent.

Not more than five minutes later Lilly Bates walked in. She wore big sleeves, arranged her hair in a yellow knob at the back of her head, with two stiff curls sticking out in the center and a frizzle of bangs in front, and chewed gum.

Marion's heart sank. But she remembered her resolve and hired her. She gave the new clerk careful instructions regarding her duties, with Lilly chewing between smiles the whole time. Marion later wondered if she chewed gum all night; she never seemed to stop in the daytime. The young milliner sat behind a calico curtain and trimmed, establishing her new apprentice behind the counter. Whenever a customer entered the store, Lilly stood up, laid her hands on the counter and, chewing, awaited a word from the person.

~

On that same first Sunday of Marion's stay in the strange city, the young minister of Bethany Mission led up the aisle for the first time a woman who was the most beautiful woman in the world to him. It was her first Sunday in this city, and he took great joy in having her there and escorting her to church. It was his mother.

You wouldn't have thought her beautiful. Her face was wrinkled, her hair thin and her hat odd-looking. But her son didn't think so. He'd been in the city for years and seen scores of fashionable women, but it never occurred to him his mother's attire wasn't all it should be. He hadn't noticed it was unlike others. If he had, he'd have thought it belonged distinctively to his mother and suited her.

She knew better herself, even though she'd spent most of her life in the country. She might have sighed over the faded shawl and wrinkled hat strings that had done duty for many years and perhaps wished in her heart she could have some new things for coming to the city. But she knew it was impossible; even the money for her ticket had been hard to spare, and the salary from that struggling mission church was small.

She wasn't well versed in the fashions, though, and didn't know that besides being old and faded, her hat had a shape that looked, even to the members of that rough mission, odd. They were city heathen and knew the fashions, whatever else they didn't know. Plainly they expected better things of the minister's mother.

The young man seated his mother and walked to the platform. He bowed his head in prayer, thankful that at last his dear mother was with him. When he raised his head he glanced again at the sweet, peaceful face sitting in front of him. He saw no wrinkles or faded hat strings—only the happy light in the eyes he loved so well.

But he heard a titter—low, but unmistakably a titter. Just behind his mother sat two young women dressed in some bright patterned stuff, with large hats covered with gaudy flowers. They were looking through their frizzed bangs at the large old hat in front of them and nudging each other. The young minister saw it and wondered why. He looked at his mother's hat and at her. The ugly titter brought a frown to his brow. But a glance at his mother's peaceful face, looking up at him, cleared it away, and he turned to the service with a thankful heart.

When the sermon ended and the last hymn was being sung, a shadow stole over his heart. Some unpleasant memory seemed to be stirring. He glanced about the church, and his eye lighted on those two girls. Ah! He knew what caused the shadow. A foolish thing, indeed, and not worth troubling over. Yet disappointment lingered in his heart that his mother hadn't inspired in others the admiration he felt for her. How could one look at that dear beautiful face and laugh?

These reflections tinged the benediction with a little severity. He surveyed his mother critically on the way home, trying to decide what the girls had been laughing at. As they met and passed two or three women, he saw them smile and glance at his mother, and he heard one say in a loud whisper, "Just look at that ridiculous hat!"

Then he studied that hat! He compared it with the hats he passed and realized there was a difference.

"John MacFarlane!" his mother said just then. They were nearing the house with the small rooms they called home. "That was a good sermon. You preach like your father, dear. I pray the Lord's blessing will be upon your work!" The mother beamed at her tall son.

And his happy heart forgot her hat for a little while.

Chapter 2

The mother and son spent a pleasant Sunday together. She'd arrived the day before, and they'd had no time until now for one of those long talks that made his boyhood a tender, beautiful memory. There were old friends to be asked about in the country home, and many questions to be answered about his new parish work. Then they read a chapter in the Bible together as they did when he was a boy. As the twilight drew on, the mother spoke of his sermon again and told him things about his father she'd never told him before.

John felt as if a benediction had fallen upon him and hastened to his evening service with renewed zeal. Nevertheless, as the working days of a new week dawned, he found himself oppressed with that hat. It troubled him through Monday, and he studied more ladies who passed by. He haunted the windows of fashionable millinery establishments and tried to discover with his untrained eye the problem with his mother's hat.

He told her once that if she needed any new things she must let him know, and he'd give her money. She thanked him and thought of her old faded shawl and worn hat strings and said she guessed she could get along without anything a while longer. She even took out her hat after dinner, smoothed out the crumpled strings and sighed. But she soon put it back in the box. The old hat had done its best. In its day it was neat and pretty, but it had seen hard service.

What would the dear lady have thought if she'd seen her son standing before Madame LeFoy's aristocratic millinery establishment? He was looking with a troubled expression at a large black tulle hat, rolled up at one side and bearing in its gauzy arms pink roses and buds, their thorny stems hanging gracefully over the edge of the brim. How would his mother look in that? He wondered dimly how they kept those flowers so fresh; they certainly must be real. He turned to a smaller headdress of violets, set close together and bordered with dark leaves, with only a strap of purple velvet for strings. In the other window was a silver gray hat with a sparkling tinsel cord for border and spears of steel oats gleaming among the waving gray plumes that towered aloft. Everything else was pink, blue and scarlet.

He turned from the window in despair. None would do for his mother.

He looked in other windows with similar results, until it grew near Sunday, and he feared for his sermon. He threw himself into his work and tried to forget the fashions. But he felt nervous every time he thought of that hat going to church. He wasn't ashamed of his mother. He'd have hated himself for such a feeling. But he was so proud of her he couldn't bear for her to appear in something that would hide the loveliness of her dear face to others.

When Sunday came, Mrs. MacFarlane stayed at home from the service with a heavy cold. Coming home alone that noon, John was startled to feel relieved he hadn't had to preach facing that hat. He called himself all sorts of names for caring so much about it. But he knew it was true and resolved to do something about it Monday morning. What or how, he didn't know. This was the Lord's day, though; he wouldn't think about it now.

Monday morning bright and early he consulted with himself and resolved to buy a new hat and present it to his mother, cost what it might. Some milliner could help him surely. He was certain he could tell what would not do, although he didn't know what would. He took from his wallet a slender roll of bank notes, selected a two-dollar bill and laid it on the table. He gazed at it a minute or two. After some hesitation he opened the wallet again and took out another two-dollar bill, adding it to the first. There was no telling what a hat might cost. Yes, he could spare that if necessary and counted the few remaining bills. Then he started on his perplexing mission.

He entered the first millinery establishment he came to, which proved to be Madame LeFoy's. A tall, smiling girl asked what she could do for him. He'd never been inside a millinery, and the hats swaying on the wire frames about the room seemed to whirl around him wildly. He felt as if he might be surrounded and wafted away somewhere in spite of himself.

But he looked into the cold, steel eyes above the smiling mouth and said, as though he were accustomed to shopping like this: "Could you show me something suitable for an old lady?"

She led him to a glass case and took from it hats of various sizes, shapes and colors, until the young man felt as if she'd captured the rainbow and was offering it for sale in patches.

"Here's just the thing for an old lady. Does she wear blue?" She held up a small plat of gold-brown straw, faced with delicate blue and trimmed with rich brown ribbon and aigrettes of the same blue.

John looked at it and said he didn't think she wore blue.

"Not wear blue? Ah! Then how would a dash of red do? It's being worn now by old ladies—dull reds, you know."

She produced an arrangement of various shades of dull reds, which John thought was quite a large "dash." He frowned at it and glanced up at the rows of other hats for relief. But they gleamed at him out of their brilliancy. He put his hands in his pockets and looked down at the red dash thoughtfully.

"Haven't you something—ah, something not quite so—so—bright?"

"Something more subdued? Oh, certainly! Though I assure you these dull reds are quite the correct thing now. A great many old ladies are buying them. It gives the face a youthful look."

John raised his eyes to the ceiling and waited during this speech, until the more subdued hat was brought out.

"How would she like black? Here's something sober, though it's quite stylish, too."

Black sounded hopeful. He turned to see. It looked like a small coal scuttle with something stuck on top. But as it came nearer, it winked and blinked at him from every speck of its small space. The things on top jumped and danced, and lights shot out unexpectedly from their blackness. He didn't like it. But what could he do? How did women get out of hat stores when they didn't like the hats?

Then he remembered he'd come to buy a hat, and a hat he must have, whether he liked it or not. A dim thought crossed his mind that this thing was worse than the one it was supposed to supplant. He decided to vary the monotony by asking the price.

"Twenty-five dollars," said the woman, twirling it on her fingers and admiring it through the fringes above her eyes, "and cheap at that. It's real cut jet."

He was appalled. He kept his face passive, however, and to the woman seemed to be considering the hat.

"Haven't you something cheaper?" he murmured, half under his breath. He felt as if those hats were stylish ladies listening and laughing.

At that moment the door opened, and Madame LeFoy's steely eyes were turned in another direction. He blessed the woman in the green hat who entered.

"Bella!" called Madame. "Come and show the gentleman those hats in the last case on the left-hand side!" She moved toward the newcomer, with the jet hat still twinkling in her hand.

Bella came slowly out from the maze of hats with an indifferent air about her. She led him to the back of the room, opened some glass doors and took out a hat, holding it on her hand and gazing out the opposite window at a pile of packing boxes in the backyard. She half sat on the little shelf running below the glass, while he stood looking at the specimen she placed before him. It was black, with feathers and a few of those impish, jumping jet things for trim.

"How much is that?"

He asked the question grimly. What did people do for hats anyway?

The girl brought her eyes back from the boxes and studied a ticket pinned to one of the strings. "Seven dollars and a half," she drawled.

He looked at it in dismay, as if to say, "If you cost that, how can I find one I can afford?" The hat seemed to lift its feathers with importance at him, but he turned away.

"Is that the cheapest you have?"

"Mis' LeFoy!" called the girl with a nasal twang. "D'you have anything cheaper'n this black hat here?"

"The one with feathers and jet? No!" said Madame.

"It's the cheapest we have," echoed the girl without moving from her seat on the shelf.

He turned and walked out of the store with as much dignity as he could command, feeling all the time that the hats were jeering at him. What should he do? He could breathe better now that he was out of the place and felt thankful for that. But he was no nearer the desired hat than he was the week before.

He paused before several other windows on Fourth Street. The ribbons and feathers seemed to laugh at him, and he couldn't bring himself to go into those places. He walked on, scarcely knowing where he went, turning any corner he came to, until he halted before Marion's modest store. It was quiet here, and he could look into the windows without feeling that the passersby were watching him. These hats didn't look as flaunting and foolish as those at Madame LeFoy's. There was a small gray gauze hat with tiny moss rosebuds nestled on it. They looked like the buds that grew on the bush before the dear old farmhouse. He gazed at them, enjoying their similarity. Then his eyes rested on the white flowers Marion had wrestled with her conscience to buy. They were lying against some black net lace and looked dainty and quiet. He felt immediately that they would fit his mother's face—so small and meek amid their fine moss setting. The young man opened the door without more hesitation and walked in.

Lilly Bates stood up, chewing vigorously. A young man was always an interesting object to her. Young gentlemen customers were rare. This young man was fine looking with a dignified bearing about him that penetrated even the brains under Lilly Bates's yellow bangs. But her practiced eye noted the shiny black coat he wore, and she decided he was of no account. She put her hands on the counter and waited for him to open the conversation.

He hardly knew where to begin. He cleared his throat. The chewer on the other side of the counter didn't intend to help. He took another step toward her and cleared his throat again.

"I want to get—"

Lilly Bates held her jaws midway and waited for the rest of the sentence. He cleared his throat desperately and began again, trying to make his voice sound natural.

"I want to get a hat!"

His voice sounded ghastly. He realized he was in a trying position. But he said it, and surely he had a right to buy a hat if he paid for it. He looked at Lilly in defiance.

She slowly started her jaws again before asking, "For yourself?"

Marion, behind her shielding curtain, was sewing an obstinate feather in place and listening. Suddenly she drove her needle into her thumb. With a jump that threw Sallie Hogan's new hat under the table, she stood up quickly.

"Lilly!" she called.

Lilly stopped chewing. "Ma'am?" she asked meekly.

"I want you to take this ribbon up to Barnes and Brainard's and match it immediately!"

"Can't just now! I've got a customer!" she answered.

"I'll attend to the customer! I want the ribbon right away. Go, please, as fast as you can!" Marion laid down her thimble and came out from behind the curtain.

Lilly reluctantly took her jacket and hat from the nail in the corner, received her directions and departed, still chewing.

Chapter 3

Marion turned to the young man. "Do you wish something trimmed or untrimmed?"

Ah! Here was a new question. How many were connected with hats! He knit his brows over it, picturing himself sitting at his study table trying to trim a hat. He smiled.

"Trimmed, I guess," he answered. "I wouldn't make much of a job trimming it myself." Then he added more soberly, "I want to give it to her all ready to put on. It's for my mother. She's an old lady—not so very old, either, but she has white hair. I don't know what would be suitable. It seems to me she'd like something"—he hesitated, searching for the new word he'd learned at Madame LeFoy's—"subdued," he added triumphantly.

No glitter of steel appeared in Marion's eyes. They were brown and seemed to take in what he said and appreciate it. She thought a moment.

"I don't think I have anything already trimmed that would suit," she answered, "but I think I could get up a hat that would please you. Would you like black or gray?"

He remembered the jet coal scuttle and was doubtful.

"I don't know!" he said desperately.

"Either would be quiet and suitable," she said.

Stooping to a box under the counter, she selected two hats of fine straw, one of gray and one of black. He took one in either hand. Was that how they looked untrimmed? What remarkably innocent things they were, he thought.

She could have laughed at the funny expression on his face. But she stood quietly waiting and studying him. She wondered what the mother was like. There was something touching in this serious-looking young man's buying a hat for his mother.

"How would you trim them?" he asked after a moment.

She took some ribbon and lace and a bit of velvet and laid them on the hats. He was amazed to see what a difference that made in the hideous shapes.

"Then you might have some small flowers besides," she said.

"Flowers? Yes, I saw some flowers in the window that I liked very much."

He took two strides forward and peered through the muslin curtain that separated the show window from the room. She drew the curtain aside, curious to see his taste in flowers. To her pleased surprise he pointed to the spray of delicate blossoms. With a strange feeling she took them up and placed them first on one hat and then on the other. He surveyed them with satisfaction.

"Yes, I like those," he said. "I think they would please Mother. They're like some flowers that used to grow in the garden at home."

"Which color do you prefer?" she asked.

"Which do you think would be most suitable?"

"How old is your mother?" she asked again, smiling. "If you'd tell me how she looks I could judge better."

"She's about sixty. Her hair is white—but her face doesn't look old. She isn't very large—I never thought about how she looks exactly—but she has a sweet, dear face." He hesitated, as if trying to paint her portrait.

Marion was touched with his description.

"That's not old!" she said brightly. "I think she'd like the gray better. It's quiet enough for anyone. If she were very old I'd choose the black, but for someone only sixty I think the gray would be prettier."

He blessed her in his heart for saying his mother wasn't old and mentally compared her to Madame LeFoy. But those thoughts recalled another troublesome question.

"How much are such hats? They seem more expensive than I thought. Do you ever have anything as low as four dollars?"

He tried to ask these questions in a dignified manner but realized it might be unheard of. He wouldn't have dared ask Madame LeFoy. But this milliner was different and had taken an interest in his mother. He kept his eyes on the gray hat until she answered.

She picked up a pencil and started figuring, while John looked at the hats and thought how much better they looked than those on Fourth Street.

"If you had it without flowers," said Marion at last, resting her elbow on the counter and her head on her hand, "I could make it for four dollars."

John never knew he could feel so disappointed about a hat. He glanced down at the starry blossoms. Marion saw his disappointment, without his realizing it.

"Very well," he finally answered. "When can I get it?"

"I can have it ready by tomorrow morning. You may come in any-time after nine o'clock and see if it's what you wish. What's the name, please?"

"MacFarlane," he said, bringing out one of the Bethany Mission invitation cards.

He sighed as he went out the door. What work to buy a hat! How did women stand it two or three times a year? And then, as a woman would, he worried because he couldn't afford the flowers. At the first corner he almost turned to go back and ask their price. But his better sense reminded him he couldn't afford another dollar; it would take away from the necessary comforts he hoped to give his mother now that she'd come to live with him.

Marion watched him as he went out the door, and then her eyes returned to the hat and flowers. She felt strangely sorry about those flowers. She picked them up and laid them against the soft gray lace. They were very pretty. She figured a little more, shook her head and then remembered Barnes & Brainard's wasn't far away. Lilly, with her inquisitive eyes, would soon be back. As she leaned over to place them in the right position, they seemed to look up wistfully at her. She studied her figures again, until she heard Lilly's step outside. Gathering up the gray hat and trimmings, she hastened to her work room.

But Sallie Hogan's green chip hat remained under the table, while she wrought out a sweet gray hat. She wondered to herself why she took such pleasure in this special order and tried to picture the face that would smile beneath the hat. Still the flowers troubled her, and she thought how much prettier and more perfect that hat would be with them. And the young man's face haunted her with its disappointment. It was strange for a young man to care about flowers on a hat. He must have a good deal of taste himself, or he never would have noticed the difference.

She glanced at his card on the table beside her, as she fashioned the gray ribbon into shining loops above the soft, white ruching border. Pastor of a mission chapel! His salary must be small. She could afford to be liberal with a poor minister, and the flowers pleaded again. But she told herself she'd already given much. She'd promised to make the hat much cheaper than she would for others or could afford. She jerked her thread through and fastened it. Her judgment and conscience fought her impulses again. The gray hat was finished. But its maker wasn't pleased and placed it in a dark bandbox, dropping John MacFarlane's card after it and shutting the cover tight.

Then she brought out the green chip and sewed fast. White flowers hovered in her thoughts, though. She was disappointed in that gray hat. She took it out in the afternoon and worked a whole hour on it; then she tried it on to persuade herself it was better as it was. But all the time it lacked something. It looked bare on one side. She put two more loops of ribbon in, but that did no good.

After Lilly had gone home that night she went to the window and took out the white flowers. She laid them on the hat in the vain hope they would be too much and detract, rather than enhance, its beauty. But the sweet things seemed to nestle among the loops of ribbon as if they were meant for that place, and she imagined they even smiled approval at her. She put them quickly back in the window, shut the hat in its box, turned out the lights, locked the door and went home.

The cockroaches met her at the door of her room, escorted her in and then vanished. It tired her strained nerves to see them, but she was growing used to them. It had become a standing rule with her to shake every dress she took out of the closet until two dropped out, and then she felt sure no more were there. There were always two in each dress.

She'd tried everything to get rid of them, even making pills of borax and Indian meal and daubing them around, but they only seemed to thrive on that. She dusted everything with powder and spread pieces of bread with ill-smelling compounds. But most of them remained unscathed, and only a few languid ones crawled out for water or medical assistance.

She was very tired tonight, and it annoyed her that such a small thing had tired her. She sat down in the hard rocking chair, and conscience and judgment confronted her.

"We told you not to buy those flowers," they said. "You knew you couldn't afford them. You were weak. When we upbraided you, you silenced us on the ground that some rich customer would want them, and now you want to give them away to someone you don't know at all— just because a young man looked disappointed and a hat you made doesn't suit your extravagant taste!"

In vain Marion brought up the picture of the mother and her pleasure in the hat and how much better the hat would look with those flowers. Judgment was inexorable. She gave up at last and went to bed.

She was in the little room back of the store early the next morning, trying again to make the gray hat look as she thought it should. She was holding it at arm's length to discover the problem when she heard Lilly's voice. It was raised from the pleasant drawl she usually used in talking with customers.

"Miss Hath'way, how much d'you say these little white flowers was?"

She lifted the curtain slightly and peered out. An elegant young lady stood there with the flowers in one hand, waiting for her answer, while Lilly was taking a leisurely survey of the customer's wardrobe and getting pointers for her next shoddy suit. Marion made a sudden resolution and dropped the curtain.

"They're not for sale," she said. "They're going on a hat that goes out this morning."

Judgment stood appalled, while the young lady put the flowers down in disgust and walked out of the store.

"Now see what you've done!" said judgment. "You've lost a patron. She was a rich lady, too. When you had a good chance to sell those miserable little flowers, you threw it away and will lose the money you paid for them."

For answer she glanced at the small clock on the table. It was almost the time she'd set for the gray hat to be inspected, so she sent Lilly on an errand that would likely keep her some time. She had no notion of having those eyes watching when the young minister came for the hat or of her overhearing talk about the price.

With Lilly out of the way, she took the hat out again and went for the flowers. Her fingers trembled slightly as she fastened them, but she felt triumphant. Perhaps it was foolish, but it was nice. She was tired of having judgment lord it over her. She liked to follow her sweet will once in a while, and it was nobody's business but her own what she did with those flowers. Since she'd bought them against her judgment, why shouldn't she dispose of them without consulting that autocrat? The knob of the store door turned as she fastened the last stitch. Her eyes glowed with excitement, and her cheeks flushed. She stepped out to wait on the young minister with the same grace that had made her charming in society.

Chapter 4

Before she opened the box she explained to him she found she could make the hat and put the flowers on for the price he mentioned. Then she brought it forth.

John MacFarlane's eyes expressed unmistakable delight on seeing that hat. The soft white ruche looked to him like his mother, and the dainty flowers, settled among the rich folds of gray ribbon, seemed like small Quakeresses. It was quietness itself, and yet he felt it could hold up its head with any aristocratic hat at Madame LeFoy's.

"I like it," he said simply. "I'm so glad for the flowers."

It seemed as if he were thanking her for a favor done to a personal friend, not at all in a businesslike way.

She put the hat carefully in its wrappings in the box. As she did, the flowers seemed to nod and say, "You did right. You won't be sorry."

As he paid for the hat, John thanked her for her help. He felt almost as happy this morning as he did when he was little and had a holiday in which to go fishing. That hat had troubled him all night, appearing in dreams in various forms, until he feared his mother never could wear it. He'd gone after it now with misgivings. He wished he'd never thought of a hat and almost dreaded seeing it. And, lo, here it was, flowers and all, and prettier than any hat he'd seen for twenty-five dollars! How could he help expressing some of his delight?

"I'll tell my mother you helped about this, and she'll be very grateful. I never could have found one if someone hadn't helped me," he said as he was going out.

It was a strange thing to say to a milliner perhaps, but he said it. She smiled and said she was glad to have helped and hoped his mother would like the hat. Then he was gone, and she returned to her work.

It was lonely with the flowers gone. Perhaps she was foolish to have put them on. But she was glad she had and wished she could peep in at the window when the hat was presented and see the mother and hear what was said. She thought of her own mother, and tears gathered in her eyes. She brushed them away. The flowers had somehow started painful thoughts.

Soon Lilly came back and chewed and waited on a few customers.

The day wore away until Marion could go back to her room and her cockroaches.

John MacFarlane carried his white box proudly through the streets. He already felt he could give more heart to his next sermon. He looked in at Madame LeFoy's as he passed. As he neared home he wondered how to present his gift and wished it were Christmas or a birthday for an excuse. He felt awkward about it and finally decided to put it away until Saturday evening, when he and his mother were having their after-tea talk.

He had trouble getting it out of sight and changed its hiding place often, lest his mother, in cleaning up, should stumble on it and spoil his surprise. Then he waited for Saturday evening to arrive with as much impatience as a boy waits for Christmas morning. Two or three times he took the box out and lifted the tissue-paper wrappings, and the flowers always reassured him. Over his study, his work and even his pastoral visits during that week the gray hat hovered like a pleasant thought.

The hour arrived at last. Her work finished for the week, his mother sat down by the bright student lamp with her knitting. Now was the time. He went to his study and brought the box from its hiding place.

"Mother, I have a present for you," he tried to say calmly. But in spite of himself some of his old boyish eagerness stole into his tone.

"Why, bless you, boy! What is it?" she said, looking over her glasses at the box and holding her knitting with both hands.

He untied the cord, pulled aside the wrappings, drew out the hat and held it on his hand. Triumph shone in his eyes and pleased surprise in his mother's. Neither of them spoke for a full minute.

John stood with his head a little to one side, taking a back view of the hat and seeing how it would appear to the two gigglers if they should come to church tomorrow.

And the mother looked at it and at her handsome son and then beyond the hat into her past. Tears gathered in her eyes.

"John, dear boy!" she said, her voice trembling. "Your father did that for me once. You're like your father, John."

The tender tones touched the young man's heart. It pleased him beyond anything to know he was like his father. He walked over to his mother and kissed her forehead. Then he gave her the hat. She held it off admiringly, then drew it nearer and smoothed the shining folds of rich new ribbon. She liked hat strings that weren't crumpled.

"It's a beautiful hat, John. I'm afraid you've been extravagant. I'm nothing but an old woman now, and anything would do for me." She touched the flowers. "The dear things! They look like the flowers that bloomed in our front yard at home. You don't remember them, I suppose. I feel as if I must smell them." She bent her head toward the flowers.

John still stood beside her, watching, pleased by the praise she gave it.

"Mother, tell me about the other hat, the one Father brought you," he said gently.

The tears came to her eyes again, and that faraway, longing look settled over her face.

"It was before we were married, dear," she said. "He'd heard me say I must have a new hat. So one day when he went to the city he remembered it and brought me one when he came back."

She smiled to herself as she said it, gazing off into the shadowy corner of the room. She could almost see her tall young lover standing with the hat in his hand and waiting for her admiration, even as her son had stood. How it all came back to her—the pleasure they had in her trying it on and their walk in the moonlight afterward! It seemed only a few days ago. And now here was her son, as old as his father had been, doing the same thing—except this hat wasn't as youthful as the other.

"It was white," she said, turning back to face him. "You think your old mother would look odd in a white hat now, don't you? Well, so she would, but she looked nice then. It was white straw, trimmed with white ribbon and tied with white strings, and it had a soft white ruching inside, just like this one," she said, touching the lace tenderly, "with a fine, green vine mixed in with it."

They talked about that other hat but soon returned to the present and admired the new one again.

"I never would have known what to get if it hadn't been for that young lady."

"What young lady?" asked his mother with keen interest. Her son had up to now, in her judgment, been almost too indifferent to all womankind except her.

"Oh, the milliner, though she didn't seem like one. Try it on, Mother. Let's see how it looks."

Mrs. MacFarlane nervously smoothed down her shining, unrumpled white hair and, taking hold of the hat where the strings were fastened on, raised it to her head, settled it and looked at her son, still holding the strings with one hand under her chin.

"Why, Mother, it makes you look younger! She said sixty wasn't old. Don't let me hear you calling yourself an old woman. You won't be an old woman these ten years yet. It actually takes some of the tired look out of your eyes. You're the prettiest woman I know of!" he said, kissing her again. He brought a faint pink to her wrinkled cheek.

She smiled at her son, as she raised her face to return the kiss.

"You're like your father, John," she said again.

Then they talked more about the hat and the milliner, and Mrs. MacFarlane said she'd like to meet her and thank her.

That same evening Marion was sitting in her room, too weary to read or work, letting her idle thoughts wander. They settled presently on the gray hat and white flowers. She wondered where they were tonight and if they would go to church tomorrow. Suddenly a strange idea seized her. She'd go to that mission chapel and see what sort of face appeared under the hat. She'd like to see the flowers doing their appointed work and know if they fit their surroundings and whether, after all, judgment had been right and she had been wrong. She liked the idea. It might be interesting to see what sort of sermon that young man would preach. At any rate it would do no harm, and she meant to go. It would relieve the day's monotony and keep the painful thoughts away.

So the next morning when John MacFarlane escorted the gray hat down the aisle and seated it in front of the two gaudy gigglers, the hat maker sat in a back seat and watched them.

She couldn't glimpse the face beneath its soft gray framing. But she noticed with relief that the hat was set on the head as it should be and the woman's bearing was dignified and refined, though her black shawl was a bit threadbare. The instant she saw it she thought of her mother's beautiful India shawl packed away in one of her unused trunks. But that was only a passing thought. She turned her eyes to the young man and noted the pride with which he seated his mother. His face was serious and without any tinge of conceit.

She examined the audience. A few were well-to-do, but many were poorly dressed. Some children were even ragged. It was the strangest audience she'd ever seen gathered in a church. She watched the young minister during the opening exercises and tried to remember that this dignified man, who seemed to feel so thoroughly at home in the pulpit, was the same one who'd been ill at ease and almost embarrassed over a hat a few days before.

Then he read his text: " 'Their Redeemer is strong; the Lord of hosts is his name: he shall thoroughly plead their cause, that he may give rest to the land, and disquiet the inhabitants of Babylon.' "

Marion listened carefully; she didn't recall ever reading those words. She watched the children's faces as the preacher described the Redeemer and fastened the explanation to their wandering minds by telling a simple story. She was interested in the story herself. It was restful to think of something strong. She was tired and lonely and felt as if she were a captive in a strange land. This was simple preaching. Marion realized as never before what it would be to have the Lord of hosts for her Redeemer. What rest it would bring to her heart to know He was pleading her cause! The young minister's hearers could only ask themselves, "Am I a captive of sin, as those people were captives in Babylon? Is the Lord of hosts my Redeemer? Can I rest in the belief that He's pleading my cause?"

Chapter 5

Marion was surprised when the sermon was over. It seemed only a few moments. As she bowed her head for the closing prayer, the first words of the text kept ringing in her ears: "Their Redeemer is strong."

She'd unconsciously expected to find many things to criticize in the young minister. But as she thought it over during the closing hymn, she could scarcely recall anything he said. She only knew she felt in her heart what Jesus Christ wanted to do for her if she would let Him. He seemed a real person to her, and she sensed a great invisible Presence about her.

During the general rush that followed the benediction, Marion stood still at her seat to let others by and avoid getting into the press. Then she turned, hoping to glimpse the face under that hat; after all, that was her purpose in coming. The white flowers seemed to greet her across the people's heads.

The minister stepped quickly down from the pulpit, leaned across two seats and whispered to his mother. Then they walked toward her.

She didn't realize they were coming to speak to her until they were near. Her eyes were on the peaceful face of the minister's mother. She noted that the hat was becoming and fit the kind of woman she was. Then she forgot to look at the hat in admiring the happy face beneath.

John MacFarlane stood before her, bowing respectfully.

"My mother has wanted very much to see you," he said and turned toward the gray hat at his shoulder.

Mrs. MacFarlane took both of Marion's hands. "I've wanted to meet you, dear, and thank you for your help to my son. He told me, and I like the hat very much."

It was so sweet to Marion to be called "dear" again that she lost her milliner's dignity and said with her old girlishness that she was so glad Mrs. MacFarlane liked it. She glanced up again at those flowers that actually seemed to be winking at her. And then they walked out together into the spring sunshine.

"Isn't this a beautiful Sunday? God must take delight in making such days for us!" said Mrs. MacFarlane as they came down the steps. "You must be glad when this day comes, and you can get away for a little while from your store."

Marion's face clouded over. "Sunday's a dreary day for me. I'm alone in the city. There isn't anything pleasant about a boardinghouse Sunday, Mrs. MacFarlane!" Then she suddenly realized she wasn't this woman's friend, as she almost felt a moment before, only her milliner.

"All alone!" said the sympathetic voice. "But God is here. You can enjoy Him! A boardinghouse must be a dreary place, though. Is your home far from here?"

"I have no home now," said Marion. "My father and mother are gone, and I'm the only one left. I'm trying to make this my home, but it's hard work."

"Now, dear, is that so? It must be lonely for you then. I know what it is to have dear ones leave me, but I never was left entirely alone." She smiled up at her tall son.

"I'll tell you what you must do," she said suddenly, turning back to Marion. "Come home with us to dinner. We've nothing very nice. But I'd like to have you, and you can pretend you're at home for a little while. I'll try to cheer you up a bit. We haven't known each other very long, but I think we could be friends. The King's children should always be able to get acquainted quickly."

Marion paused at the corner where she turned off toward her boardinghouse. She was about to decline politely, but a great desire seized her to accept the invitation. She longed to be inside a real home again. Glancing at the motherly face, she wavered.

"Do come!" said the minister. "We'd be very glad to have you."

And so, after a little demurring, instead of declining, she turned and walked on with her new friends, horrified judgment berating her meanwhile.

They talked of the beautiful day and other matters people speak of when they're getting acquainted. After her first surprise at finding herself in this unexpected situation, Marion began to enjoy it. It was so pleasant to have some friends to talk with again. They came presently to the sleepy-looking house where the MacFarlanes lived. It wasn't any less dreary looking than the one where Marion had her room. But white curtains hung by the windows and gave such a feeling of hominess that it seemed a palace in comparison.

Seated in the little parlor alone a few minutes later, with the soft wind blowing in at the open window, swaying the ruffles on the dimity curtains and fanning her cheeks, she admitted to herself that she'd done a strange thing in accepting this invitation. Nevertheless, she didn't feel at all sorry. This room was so cozy, with its plain furnishings and air of neat contentment.

Mrs. MacFarlane had emerged from her bedroom a few moments before, her black dress enveloped in a large clean apron. While she pinned it around her ample waist, she told Marion to rest and make herself at home for a few minutes. Then she went to the kitchen, and her son followed her. She could hear their voices now through the unlatched door. By the sound she judged the young man was bringing wood, making a fire and then drawing water and helping his mother. She shut her eyes and let the breeze cool her lids.

Presently the minister returned. The talk drifted to books, and she found they'd read many in common. It was a treat to her, discussing favorite books again with someone who knew and loved them.

As she sat down to the small white table, Marion wondered when she'd ever been so hungry. There wasn't such a great variety for dinner, nothing so elaborate as at her boardinghouse. But everything looked nice. The cold meat, cut into thin, pink slices, and the warmed-up potatoes had a homelike taste. Homemade bread, too, was a rare treat to her now, and the coffee was just right.

She asked about the mission chapel and its work and gained a new idea of city missions. After dinner she offered to help clear the table, but Mrs. MacFarlane said she could do it alone and Marion was to rest. But she persisted, and then they talked. Marion found that the mother was as intelligent as the son. After the work was finished, and they returned to the parlor to talk, the most helpful time for Marion came. She remembered that talk her whole life afterward with thankfulness.

The minister had gone to his mission chapel, and they were alone. His mother coaxed from Marion the story of her sorrows, and she told it with trembling lips. The elder woman listened sympathetically.

"But, Mrs. MacFarlane," Marion said, looking up as she finished, "you're mistaken in me about one thing. I don't want to wear a false character. You said I was one of the King's children, but I'm not."

Her head dropped at the last words, and the tears gathered in her eyes while she waited for a reply. It came in a loving but disappointed tone.

"Not one of the King's children, dear? Whose child are you then?"

"Whose am I?" asked Marion, puzzled.

"Yes, dear," said the mother. "You must belong to someone. Whose child are you, if you aren't the King's?"

"Oh, don't!" said the girl shuddering and hiding her face in her hands. "That's dreadful! I never thought of it so before."

Then she felt a loving arm around her. "Dear child, you're His, even though you haven't been serving Him. Don't you know He bought you with a price? You're His, but you've been serving someone else and haven't acknowledged your true Father."

They had a long talk. Marion's tears flowed, but gradually she saw the light. She knelt with Mrs. MacFarlane and gave herself to Christ and arose with a new peace in her heart. Her soul had been reaching out for help for a long time, but she didn't know where to go to satisfy her great longings. Now she felt that Jesus Christ was going to fill her heart and all would be different.

The afternoon passed swiftly, and she suddenly realized it was growing dark and the walk home wasn't short. She hurried away then but not until they'd made her promise to come again.

Chapter 6

S he thought it over when she sat alone in her room that evening. How strange it had been—the hat, the flowers, her resolve to go to the chapel, the invitation, and now the wonderful Presence that seemed to fill her heart and overflow into the room! She glanced about. She didn't mind the dusty shells with their mockery of the sea or the forlorn engravings or even the cockroaches. She had something now to be happy about. She hummed a tune as she prepared for bed.

As the week progressed, a determination grew stronger in her mind. She would go to that little chapel every Sunday. It was quite a walk, but so what? It would do her good. Besides, her only friends in the city were there, and she'd found more good there than in any other church she'd attended. She knew, of course, she hadn't been in the right frame of mind to benefit from the other churches, but she felt drawn to the chapel and meant to go. She decided her judgment would have to be re-educated.

Soon her new pastor called on her and then called again and brought his mother, who took her in her arms and kissed her and called her "My dear," quite as if she were an old friend. It brought a warm glow to Marion's lonely heart to feel she had such friends, and life looked less dreary to her after that call.

The following Wednesday evening she was called down to the dingy parlor of her boardinghouse. There stood John MacFarlane, hat in hand. Would she like to go the chapel prayer meeting? If so, he'd be pleased to have her company. The young minister was so entertaining that it thoroughly rested her after her day's confining work. Then the prayer meeting was homelike and helped her as she hadn't been helped in years. She found herself wondering why she hadn't gone to prayer meetings before. After that he often stopped for her on his way to the meeting. And it made a bright spot in the long, busy week for the milliner.

One afternoon John stepped into the store to bring a note from his mother, begging Marion to take tea with them that evening. On this occasion Lilly was out, and he looked about him at the hats and wondered why he'd ever been afraid of one. He felt himself a connoisseur of hats now.

Marion had many pleasant times in the MacFarlanes' cheery parlor. She found a restfulness and peace she'd never found in the homes of her fashionable friends. The young minister dropped into the store often to bring these delightful invitations. Now and then he brought a book he thought she'd enjoy. Once or twice he asked her to a fine lecture or concert; little by little they grew better acquainted.

The busy summer flew by more pleasantly than Marion had imagined it could, and the autumn came on. When the wind began to blow chilling messages from the approaching winter, Marion thought of her mother's shawl and for several Sundays contemplated the thin black one Mrs. MacFarlane wore to church.

One day she unpacked hers from the camphor wrappings and shook it out in soft folds on her bed. Then she sat for a long time with tears in her eyes. Would she, could she, give up her mother's shawl? She didn't expect to use it herself; it would hardly suit her. Besides, she had other warm wraps and didn't need it. But would Mrs. MacFarlane accept it? Could she bear to give up the shawl and see someone else wearing it, when it reminded her of her dear mother?

"But Mother would be pleased if she knew it—she always gave away her beautiful things. Mrs. MacFarlane has been so good to me, and I love her dearly," she said to herself.

A few days afterward, the shawl, wrapped in heavy paper and bearing Mrs. MacFarlane's address, was sent to her by Lilly's little brother, who was playing marbles outside the store. A note accompanied it, touching the lady even more than the gift of the shawl, which was saying a good deal. She read it through twice, with tears in her eyes. "Dear child!" Wiping the moisture from her glasses with her handkerchief, she handed it to her son.

Dear Mrs. MacFarlane,

You've been so good to me, and I love you so much that I want to send you this shawl. It was my dear mother's, and I'd like to see you wearing it. I think, too, that it would please her. She must love you for having brightened her child's lonely life. Please accept it as a small token of the gratitude and love I have for one who has helped bring peace to my heart.

Yours lovingly,
Marion Hathaway

The shawl was a welcome surprise to Mrs. MacFarlane. She'd planned to make her black one do all winter by folding a smaller thick red one inside. But even then it would have been thin. Her son was more pleased than he expressed even to his mother. He enjoyed seeing her with the heavy, beautiful shawl around her. Beautiful things seemed to belong to his mother, though she appeared queenly to him in her most common attire.

Toward spring again, almost a year from when Marion and Mrs. Mac-Farlane moved to the city, the postman rang the doorbell at the MacFarlane home and handed John a letter. He glanced at the postmark hastily, then went to his study and closed the door, tearing open the letter. As he read, the anxious look on his face changed to one of gladness. He almost turned to open the door and read it to his mother; but thinking better of it he reached up to the hook behind his study door for his hat and overcoat.

"I'm going out for a little while, Mother," he said, passing through the sitting room.

He walked rapidly down the street, never looking up at the bright-eyed spring hats that nodded to him from Madame LeFoy's window. On he walked, straight to the side street where his milliner lived.

"May I come into your work room for a few minutes?" he asked Marion, as she came forward, smiling, to meet him. "I want to talk a little, and I don't want to hinder you. Lilly is safe," he said, when he saw Marion hesitate and glance uneasily out the window. "She's reached only the next corner with the hat you sent her out with, and she's talking with a young man. She's likely to stand there sometime yet. How far does she have to go?"

"Over to East Fletcher Street. Come in. I wouldn't let you, but I'm very busy this morning."

He sat down. She took up her work, and they talked for a minute or two.

Suddenly he said, "I've received a call to Springdale!" He handed her the letter.

She started slightly but took the letter and read it. The color mounted into her face, but her lips wore their firm little curve, with perhaps more dignity than usual.

"It's a very good salary and a pleasant field for work, I'd think," she said, trying to speak with composure. "But I—"

She hesitated, and a flush spread over her face. She began again. "We shall—"

She caught herself again, the red in her cheeks deepening. She realized there was no one, besides Lilly Bates, with whom she might use that pronoun "we."

She resolved this time to gain control of herself and, straightening a ribbon loop, began the sentence again. "Your congregation will miss you very much," she said, this time in a clear, unnatural voice. And then realizing she'd muddled things and feeling vexed over it, she thrust her needle through ribbon, hat and finger with a force that set every nerve tingling in sympathy with the poor abused finger. When she looked up it was only to find the minister's eyes on her and an amused expression on his face.

"Finish your first sentence, won't you, please?" he asked in a tone that demanded an answer.

She looked down a moment.

"It began with 'I,' " he said, as she still hesitated.

"I shall miss your mother very much indeed," she finished quickly and went on with her work, though her cheeks were glowing.

Then they both laughed. He recovered his seriousness first. Perhaps he realized Lilly Bates's continued absence was uncertain, and his time might be short. He put the letter in his pocket and drew his chair close to hers.

"Marion," he said, taking both her trembling, cold hands into one of his and the other landing the hat she was sewing, with its trimmings, in the middle of a box of crushed roses, "will you go to Springdale with me and help me begin the new work?"

If Lilly Bates had known what was going on behind the calico curtain in the little store that morning, she wouldn't have stood smiling and simpering so long on the corner of Second Street with the young man who wore an elegant paste-diamond scarfpin. But the world moves on and waits for no one. Even Lilly Bates and young Mosely were called, by what they used for a conscience, to move on. And in course of time Lilly had finished her errand and was returning.

Marion finally succeeded in impressing this fact on John Mac-Farlane. He discreetly took himself away in time to escape Lilly's scrutinizing gaze, promising to return at six o'clock and take her home to his mother.

"Mother," he said a little after six, as he threw open the parlor door and stood filling the doorway, "I have a present for you."

"Bless the boy! What is it? Another hat?" she asked with a twinkle in her eyes.

"No, it isn't a hat this time; it's the milliner herself." And he stood aside and gently pushed the blushing Marion in front of him.

Now the cockroaches are looking for a lodger, and the store windows where the white blossoms once smiled are full of candy canes and dogs and cats, with a box of apples and a few wilted bananas for variety. And many ladies who had just discovered Marion's dainty taste wonder what's become of that elegant milliner who made such "lovely hats at such ridiculous prices!"

But there's a small white parsonage with green blinds, set in a wide green lawn that slopes away to a stone church. On the porch in pleasant weather sits a kind old lady, whose hair is crowned by beautiful soft white caps. She knows what has become of the milliner, and so does the minister. And the people who live in the village streets and out on the green hills love her with all their hearts.

Miranda

Chapter 1

Miranda Griscom opened the long wooden shutters of the Spafford parlor and threw them back with a triumphant clang, announcing the opening of a new day. She arranged the slat shades at just the right angle, glanced around the immaculate room and whisked out on the front stoop with her broom.

No cobweb reared in the night remained for any early morning visitor to view with a condemning eye—not if he arrived before breakfast —for Miranda always sprang upon the unsightly gossamer and swept it out of existence the first thing in the morning.

She swept the steps clean, the seats on either side of the stoop, even the ceiling and rails. Then she descended to the brick pavement and plied her broom like a whirlwind till every fallen leaf and stray bit of dust hurried away before her onslaught. With an air of duty for the moment done, Miranda returned to the stoop and, leaning on her broom, gazed diagonally across the street to the great house set back a little from the road and surrounded by a row of stately stiff gray poplars.

Just so she'd stood and gazed every morning, briefly, for the past five years—ever since the stately mansion's owner had offered her his heart and hand and the opportunity to bring up his family of seven.

The first time he came to see her was a dark rainy night in the middle of November. All day long it drizzled and by evening settled into a dismal downpour. Miranda was upstairs when he knocked, hovering over the baby Rose, tucking the soft blankets, stooping low over the cradle to catch the soft music of her rose-leaf breath. David Spafford had gone to the door to let his neighbor in.

Nathan Whitney, tall, gaunt, gray and embarrassed, stood under his streaming umbrella on the front stoop with a background of rain and gravely asked if he might see Miss Griscom.

David, surprised but courteous, asked him in, took his dripping umbrella and overcoat from him, and escorted him into the parlor. But his face was a study of mingled emotions when he came softly into the library and shut the door before he told his young wife, Marcia, that Nathan Whitney was in the parlor and wanted to see Miranda.

Marcia's face expressed surprise and wonder, but without a word, only a moment's questioning with her eyes, she went to call Miranda.

"Goodness me!" said the dazed individual, shading the candle from her eyes and looking at her mistress—and friend—with eyes that were almost frightened. "Goodness me! Mrs. Marcia, you don't mean to tell me Nathan Whitney wants to see me?"

"He asked for you, Miranda."

"Why, Mrs. Marcia, you must be mistooken. What would he want of me? He must uv ast fer Mr. David."

"No, David went to the door," said Marcia, smiling, "and he distinctly asked for Miss Griscom."

"Griscom! Did he say that name? Didn't he say Mirandy? Then that settles it. It's sompin' 'bout that rascally father uv mine. I've ben expectin' it all along since I was old 'nough to think. But why didn't he go to Grandma? I couldn't do nothin'. Ur—d'you 'spose, Mrs. Marcia, it could be he's a lawin' fer Grandma, tryin' to fix it so's I hev to go back to her? He's a lawyer, y'know. But Grandma wouldn't go do a thing like that 'thout sayin' a thing to Mr. David, would she?"

Miranda's eyes were dilated, and her breath came fast. It seemed strange to Marcia to see the invincible Miranda upset this way.

"Why, of course not, Miranda," she said soothingly. "It's likely nothing much. Maybe he's just come to ask you to look after his baby or something. He's seen how well you cared for Rose, and his baby isn't well. I heard today that his sister has to go home next week. Her daughter is going away to teach school this fall."

"Well, I ain't a reg'lar servant, I'll tell him that," said Miranda with a toss of her head, "an' ef I was, I wouldn't work fer him. He's got a pack of the meanest young'uns ever walked this earth. They ought to be spanked, every one o' them. I'll jes' go down an' let him know he's wastin' his time comin' after me. Say, Mrs. Marcia, you don't want me to go, do you? You ain' tired of me, be you? 'Cause I kin go away, back to Gran'ma's ef you be, but I won't be shunted off ont' Nathan Whitney."

Marcia assured her the one dread of her life was that Miranda would leave her. Comforted, the girl descended to the parlor.

Nathan Whitney, tall, pale, thin, blue-eyed, scant of straw-colored hair and eyebrow, angular of lip and cheekbone, unemotional of manner, came to his point at once in a tone so cold it seemed part of the November night sighing around the house.

Miranda, her freckled face pale with excitement, her piquant, tip-tilted nose alert, her blue eyes under their red lashes keen as steel blades and even her red hair waving back rampantly, sat and listened with growing animosity. She was like an angry lioness guarding her young, expecting momentarily to be torn away yet intending to rend the hunter before he could accomplish his intention. Her love in this case was the little sleeping Rose upstairs in the cradle.

Miranda didn't tell him so, but she hated him for even suggesting anything that would separate her from that beloved baby. That this attempt came in the form of an offer of marriage didn't blind her eyes to the real facts in the case. Therefore she listened coldly, drawing herself up with a new dignity as the brief and chilly declaration drew to its close, and her eyes flashed sparks at the calmly confident suitor.

Suddenly, before her gaze, had come the vision of his second wife not dead a year. Her brown eyes with their golden glints and twinkles were filled with sadness as if the life in them were slowly being crushed out. Her thin cheeks held a dash of crimson in their whiteness that looked as if at one time they might have dimpled in charming curves. And her drooping lips had yet a hint of cupid's bow in their bending. Her oldest boy with all his mischief looked like her, but he was bold and wicked in place of her sadness and submission. Miranda, bursting with romance herself, had always felt for the ghost of young Mrs. Whitney's beauty and wondered how such a girl came to be tied as second wife to a dried-up creature like Nathan Whitney.

Miranda, therefore, held him with her gaze until his well-prepared speech was ended. Then she asked dryly, "Mr. Whitney, did Mis' Whitney know you wuz calc'latin' to git married right away agin fer a third time?"

A flush slowly rose from Nathan Whitney's stubbly upper lip and mounted to his high bare forehead, where it mingled into his scant straw-colored locks. His hands, thin and bony with big veins like cords to tie the bones together, worked nervously on his knees.

"Just why would you ask that, Miss Griscom?" he demanded, his cold voice a trifle shaken.

"Wal, I thought 't might be," said Miranda nonchalantly. "I couldn't see no other reason why you'd come fer me, ner why you'd come so soon. 'Tain't skurcely decent, 'nless she 'ranged matters 'n made you promus. I've heard o' wives doin' thet frum jealousy, bein' so fond o' their lovin' husband thet they couldn't bear to hev him selec' 'nuther. I thought she might a-picked me out ez bein' the onlikelist she knowed to be fell in love with. Folks don't gen'lly pick out red hair an' freckles when they want to fall in love. I never knowed your fust wife, but you showed sech good taste pickin' out the second, Mr. Whitney, thet I couldn't ever think you didn't know I was homebley, n'less your eyesight's begun failin'."

Nathan Whitney had flushed and paled angrily during this speech but maintained his cold self-control.

"Miss Griscom, we won't discuss my wife. She was as she was, and she's now departed. Time goes slowly with the bereaved heart, and I've been driven to look around for a mother to my children. If it seems sudden to you, remember that I have a family to consider and must put my own feelings aside. Suffice it to say that I've been looking about for some time, and I've noticed your devotion to the child in this household. I felt you would be thoroughly trustworthy to put in charge of my motherless children and have therefore come to put the matter before you."

"Wal, you kin gather it right up agin and take it home with you," said Miranda with a toss. "I wa'n't thinkin' of takin' no famblies to raise. I'm a free an' independent young woman who can earn her own livin', an' when I want to take a fambly to raise I'll go to the poor farm an' selec' one fer myself. At present I'm perfickly comfort'ble a-livin' with people 'at wants me fer *myself.* I don't hev to git married to someone thet would allus be thinkin' uv my red hair an' freckles and my father thet ran away—"

"Miss Griscom," said Nathan Whitney severely, "I thoroughly respect you, else I wouldn't have offered you my hand in marriage. You're certainly not responsible for the sins your father has committed, and as for your personal appearance, a meek and quiet spirit is often a better adorning—"

But Miranda's spirit could bear no more.

"Well, I guess you needn't go on any further, Mr. Whitney. I ain't considerin' any sech offers at present, so I guess that ends it. Do you want I should git your ombrell? It's a rainy evenin', ain't it? That your coat? Want I should hep you on with it? Good even'n', Mr. Whitney. Mind thet bottom step. It gits slipp'ry now an' agin."

Miranda closed and bolted the front door hard and stood with her back leaning against it in relief. Then suddenly she broke into clear merry laughter and laughed so hard that Marcia came to the library door to see what was the matter.

"Goodness! Mrs. Marcia, wha' d'ye think? I got a perposal. Me, with my red hair'n all—I got a perposal! I never 'spected it in the world, but I got it. My, ain't it funny?"

"Miranda!" said Marcia, coming out into the hall and watching her serving maid in dismay. "Miranda, what in the world do you mean?"

"Jest what I say," said Miranda. "He wanted to marry me so's I could look after his children." She bent double in another convulsion of laughter.

"He wanted you to marry him? And what did you tell him?" asked Marcia, scarcely knowing what to think as she eyed the strange girl in her mirth.

"I tol' him I hed a job I liked better, 'r words to that effect," said Miranda, suddenly sobering and wiping her eyes with her white apron. "Mrs. Marcia, you don't think I'd marry thet slab-sided tombstone of a man ennyhow he'd fix it, do you? An' you ain't a-supposin' I'd leave you to tend that blessed baby upstairs all alone. Not while I got my senses, Mrs. Marcia. You jest go back in there to your readin' with Mr. David, an' I'll go set the buckwheats fer breakfast. But, my! Ain't it funny? Nathan Whitney perposin' to me! I'll be swithered!" And she vanished into the kitchen laughing.

The next morning, when she opened the shutters to the new fresh day with its bright cold air and business-like attitude of having begun the winter, Miranda began those brief maternal surveys of the house across the way. She took it all in, from the gable ends with their little oriole windows, to the dreary flags that paved the way to the steps with the lofty pillared porch suggesting aristocracy.

It was immensely satisfying to Miranda's red-haired, freckle-faced soul to reflect that she might have been mistress of that mansion. It wasn't like thinking all her life nobody wanted her and nobody would have her and she could never marry because she would never be asked. She had been asked. She'd had her chance and refused, and her bosom swelled with pride. She was here because she wanted to be here on this side of the street, but she might have been there in that other house if she'd chosen.

She might have been stepmother to that horde of scared straw-colored girls and naughty handsome boys who scuttled out of the gate now and then with fearful backward glances toward the house as if they were afraid of their lives and never meant to do what they should if they could help it. The girls looked like their drab, straw-colored father, but the boys were handsome little fellows with eyes like their mother's and a hunted look about their faces. Miranda in her reflections always called them brats!

"The idea uv him thinkin' I'd swap my little Rose fer his spunky little brats!" she always exclaimed before she went in and shut the door.

Five separate times during the intervening five years, Nathan Whitney had taken his precise way across the street and proffered his request. In varied forms and with ever-increasing fervor he'd pressed his suit, until Miranda came to believe in his sincere desire for her as a housekeeper, if not as a companion. She held her head higher with pride, as the proposals increased and the years passed.

Day after day she swept the front stoop and day after day looked over toward the big house with the question in her soul. "You might uv. Ain't you sorry you didn't?"

Always her soul responded, "No, I ain't!"

The last time he came Miranda had her final triumph, for he professed he'd conceived a sort of affection for her, in spite of her red hair and questionable parentage. The girl had sense enough to see that the highest this man had to give he'd laid at her feet. She was gracious in her quaint manner, but she sent him on his way with such a decided refusal that no man in his senses would ever ask her to marry him again.

After the deed was done she surveyed her wholesome features in the mirror with entire satisfaction. Not a heartstring of her well-packed outfit had been stirred during the five years' courting; only her pride had been rippled pleasantly. But now she knew it was over; she could no longer look at the neglected home and feel that any day she might step in and take possession. She cut the cold man to his heart, what little chilly heart he had, and he wouldn't look her way again, for she dared to humble him to confessing affection and then refused him after all. He'd keep his well-trained affections in their place after this and look about in genuine earnest now to get a housekeeper and a mother for his wild flock which had been making rapid strides downward while he was meandering through the toilsome paths of courtship.

Nathan Whitney looked about to such purpose that he could soon have his banns published in the church. Everybody at once said how altogether suitable and proper it was for Nathan Whitney to take another wife after all these five long years of waiting and mourning his sweet Eliza. And who in all that country around was as fit as Maria Bent to deal with the seven wild unruly Whitneys, young and old. Wasn't she mistress of the district school for nearly twelve years past, and hadn't she dealt with the Whitneys time and again to her own glory and the undoing of their best-laid schemes? Maria Bent was just the one, and Nathan Whitney was a fool not to ask her before. Maybe she might have saved the oldest boy, Allan, from disgrace.

Strange to say, as soon as Miranda felt safe from becoming related to them, her heart softened toward the little Whitneys. Day after day as she swept the front stoop, after the banns were published, and gazed toward the great house that might have been hers but by her own act was put out of her life forever, she sighed and thought of the little Whitneys and questioned her soul: "Could I? Should I uv?" But always her soul responded loyally, "No, you couldn't uv. No, you shouldn't uv. Think o' him! You never could uv stood him. Bah!"

And now on this morning of Maria Bent's wedding day Miranda came down with a whisk and a jerk and flung the blinds open triumphantly. The deed was almost done; the time was nearly over. In a few more hours Maria Bent would walk that flagging up to the grand pillared porch and enter that mansion across the way to become its mistress. And she, Miranda Griscom, would be Miranda Griscom still, plain, red-haired, freckled—and unmarried. No one would ever know, except her dear Mrs. Marcia and her adored Mr. David, that she had "hed the chancet an' never tuk it." Yet Miranda, on her rival's wedding day, looked across at the great house and sang her joy of freedom.

"I might uv endured them brats, poor little hanted-lookin' creatoors, but I never could a-stood that slab-sided, washed-out, fish-eyed man around, nohow you fixed it. Goodness! Think o' them all 'long side o' my little Rose!"

And Miranda went into the house, slamming the door joyfully and singing.

David, upstairs shaving, remarked to Marcia, "Well, Miranda doesn't seem to regret her single blessedness as yet, dear."

Marcia, tying a bright ribbon on little Rose's curls, answered happily, "And it's a good thing for us she doesn't. I wonder if she'll go to the wedding."

Miranda, later, after the breakfast was cleared away, announced her intention.

"Yes, I'm goin' jest to show I ain't got no feelin's about it. 'Course she don't know. I don't s'pose he'd ever tell her; 'tain't like him. He's one o' them close, sly men thet think it's cost him something ef he tells a woman ennythin', but I'm goin' jest fer my own satisfaction. Then 'course I'll own I'd kinder like to watch her an' think thet might o' ben me ef I ben *willin'* to leave little Rose, an' you an'—well, ef I'd a' ben willin'—which I never was. Yes, 'course I'm goin'."

Chapter 2

T he afternoon ceremony was held in the schoolhouse. Maria Bent lived with her old mother in two small rooms behind the post office, not a suitable place for the wedding of Nathan Whitney's bride. So Maria, because of her years of service as teacher, was granted permission to use the schoolhouse.

The joyful scholars, radiant at the thought of a new teacher—any teacher so it wouldn't be Maria Bent—and excited beyond measure over a holiday and festivity all theirs, joyously trimmed the schoolhouse with roses, hollyhocks and long trailing vines from the woods. For once the smoky walls and much-hacked desks blossomed as the rose smothered in the wealth of nature.

The only children who didn't participate in the noisy decorations were the young Whitneys. Like scared yellow leaves in a hurricane they scurried away from the path of the storm and hid from the scene, peering from safe coverts with jealous eyes and swelling hearts at the enemy who was scouring the woods and gardens in behalf of her who was about to invade the sacredness of their home. Not that they'd cared much about that home before this; but it was all they had, and the world looked blank and unlivable to them now with the terror of their school days installed for incessant duty.

The little girls, with drooped yellow lashes and peaked, sallow faces strangely like their father's, hurried home to hide away their treasures in secret places in the attic, known only to them, and to whisper awesomely about how it would be when "she" came.

"She smiled at me in school yesterday," whispered Helena, the sharp fourteen-year-old. "It was like a gnarled spot on a sour apple that falls before it's ripe."

"Oh, be careful," hushed Prudence, lifting her thin little hands in dismay. "What if Aunt Jane should hear you and tell her. You know she's going to be our mother, and she can do what she likes then."

"Mother nothing!" flouted Helena. "She'll not mother me, I can tell you that. If she lets me alone I'll stay, but if she tries to boss me I'll run away."

Nevertheless Helena took the precaution to tiptoe lightly to the head of the stairs, to be sure the attic door was closed so no one could hear her.

"Helena!" gasped Prudence, crying softly. "You wouldn't dare! You wouldn't leave me alone?"

"Well, no," said Helena, relenting. "I'd take you with me p'raps. Only you'd be so particular we'd get caught, like the time I stole the pie and had it all fixed so Aunt Jane would think the cat got it, and you had to explain because you thought the cat might get whipped!"

"Well, you know Aunt Jane hates the cat, and she'd have whipped her worse'n she did us. Besides—"

"Aw, well, you needn't cry. We've got enough to do now to keep quiet and keep out of the way. Where's Nate?"

"I saw him going down toward the sawmill after school—"

"Nate won't stay here long," stated Helena sagely. "He just despises Maria Bent."

"Where would he go?" said Prudence, drying her tears as her little world broke up bit by bit. "Helena Whitney, he's only ten years old!"

"He's a man!" snapped Helena. "Men are diffrunt. Come on—let's go hide in the bushes and see what they get. The idea of Julia Fargo and Harriet Wells making all that fuss getting flowers for her wedding when they've talked about her so. And only last week she took that lovely book away from Harriet just because she read it in geography class."

Hand in hand, with swelling throats and smarting eyes filled with tears they wouldn't shed, the motherless children hurried away to the woods to watch in bitterness the wedding preparations, which was almost like watching the building of their own funeral pyres.

Nevertheless the time of hiding couldn't be forever, and the little brood of Whitneys still came under stern discipline. Aunt Jane held them with no easy hand. Promptly at half past two they issued from the big white house clothed in wedding garments, with their respective heads dressed in plait or net or glossy ringlet, or plastered down. Young Nathan's rebellious brown curls were smooth as satin, with the water from their late anointing trickling down his clammy back. With dogged tread and downcast, insurgent look he marched beside his frightened, meek little sisters to the ceremony which was to them all like a death knell.

The familiar old red schoolhouse appeared in the distance down the familiar old street. Yet the choking sensation in their throats and the strange beating and blurring of their eyes gave it an odd appearance of disaster. That surely couldn't be the old hickory tree Nate had climbed so often and hidden behind to watch Maria Bent as she came forth from the schoolhouse door searching for him. How often he'd encircled its shielding trunk to keep out of sight when he saw her looking for him! Now, alas, there'd be no sheltering hickory for sanctuary from her strong hand, for Maria Bent wouldn't be merely the schoolmarm. She'd be at close range in their only home; she would be mother! The name had suddenly taken on a gruesome sound, for Aunt Jane told them that morning as she combed and scrubbed and dressed them that such address would be required of them from now on. Call Maria Bent "Mother"! Never!

Nate, as he trudged on, thought over the long list of disrespectful appellations it had been their custom among themselves to call their teacher, beginning with "Bent Maria" and ending with "M'wry-faced-straighten-er-out." He resolved to call her nothing at all, or anything he pleased, knowing he'd never dare.

Miranda, on the other side of the street, watched the disconsolate little procession, with their aunt Jane bringing up the rear, and thanked her stars she wasn't going forth to bind herself to their upbringing.

She purposely lingered behind the Spaffords as they started to the wedding, saying she'd follow with little Rose. She came out of the front door and locked it carefully, just as the Whitneys emerged from Aunt Jane's grooming. Rose jumped daintily down the steps, one at a time, watching the toes of her new pink slippers and tilting the ruffled pink silk parasol her father had brought her from New York. She looked like a sweet pink human rose, and the prim Whitneys, sleek and scared though they were, turned envious eyes to watch her. They almost forgot the lumps in their throats and the hot, angry feeling in their hearts, while they took in the beauty of the parasol, the grace of the small light feet and the bobbing golden curls as Rose skipped along by Miranda's side.

Miranda herself was wearing a new green and brown plaid silk, the pride and glory of her heart, bought with her own money and selected by her beloved Mrs. Marcia on her last trip to New York. Her bonnet was green shirred silk with a tiny green feather, and her red hair looked like burnished copper glinting out beneath. Miranda didn't know it and never would, but she was growing to be a most attractive woman. And the twinkle of mischief in her eyes made a person look a second time at her cheerful freckled face.

Proudly she looked down at the dainty Rose and compared her with the unhappy Whitneys doing the funeral march to their father's wedding. Not for any money would she be in Maria Bent's place today, but she walked the prouder and more contented that she'd had the chance.

There was a pleasant bustle about the schoolhouse door when they arrived. But the little Whitneys, their feuds laid aside at this time of their common sorrow, huddled together just inside the schoolroom door, as far from the action as possible, with dropped eyes and furtive sidewise glances, never daring even to whisper.

Adorning each desk were wreaths of flowers—zinnias, peonies, asters, roses, pansies, larkspurs, and columbine. Some of the smaller flowers were wreathed around a plateau of velvety moss on which the letters MB and NW were tastefully entwined in white pebbles and designs. Each scholar had taken pride in getting up an original design for his or her own desk, and the result was unique and startling.

"How touching of them to want to please the teacher!" exclaimed Ann Bloodgood, who lived in the next township and therefore didn't know the current feeling.

But, however touching, the decorations only reminded the three older Whitneys of their own mother's funeral. Nate hung his head and frowned hard behind the goldenrod-embowered stove, trying not to see or think of that other day five years ago when odors of flowers filled the air and he'd had that same lump in his throat and gasp in his chest. That was bad enough, but this day was worse. He had half a mind even now to bolt through that schoolhouse door and never come back. But when he looked out to calculate how likely he was to get off without being seen, his father came walking up the schoolhouse path.

Maria Bent was hanging on his arm, in bright blue silk with a white lace bonnet, white kid gloves, and a lace parasol. She was smirking and smiling to this side and that and bestowing unwontedly loving greetings on the festive row of schoolgirls lined up on either side of the path, stiff and straight in their best dresses.

"Walking pride," Miranda called it and secretly exulted she might have been there if she would; yet she didn't regret her choice.

Miranda had taken up her position where she could stand Rose on a desk to get a good view of the ceremony. From her vantage point she also got a vision of handsome little Nathan Whitney, his well-brushed Sunday suit squeezed between the stove and the wall, his soapy curls rumpled by the goldenrod, his stiff collar holding up a trembling chin surmounted by hard little lips and an angry frown.

Plainly young Nathan wasn't happy at his father's wedding. Something in the whole slouch of his sturdy little figure touched Miranda, and she watched him with a hitherto unsuspected sympathy. It wasn't to be expected, of course, that a bad boy like Nate Whitney would like to have a stern schoolteacher for his new mother. A gleam of something like pity shone in her eyes as she reflected how often Maria Bent would probably get her "comeuppance" for marrying Nathan Whitney and how often little Nate Whitney would probably get his "comeuppance" for his pranks. Of the two Miranda was just the least bit inclined to side with the boy for the sake of his half brother Allan with whom she'd gone to school.

Miranda looked up to find him again after the prayer was over, but though her eyes searched quite carefully behind the stove and under the goldenrod bowers, he was gone. High in the branches of the friendly hickory, with his Sunday clothes bearing a jagged tear in the seat of the trousers, his collar awry and his shiny Sunday shoes hopelessly marred and scratched, Nathan Whitney the second surveyed the scene. The prayer had been long enough for him to reach his old shelter in safety. Only the Whitney twins, Julia and Julius, and the five-year-old brother Samuel had seen his escape, and they were too frightened to tell.

Miranda's searching gaze finally caught the uplifted look of the twins and Sammy and, following it, saw the old hickory tremble. She quickly lowered her eyes, knowing instinctively what had happened. But before she lowered them she caught the gleam of a pair of sorrowful brown eyes so like another pair of brown eyes she knew, looking between the leaves, and they haunted her all through the day.

The ceremony was over, and all the guests had gone home to discuss at length how "he looked" and how "she looked" and the prospect of happiness for the two who were united in marriage.

Miranda had changed her green and brown plaid silk for a brown calico and a white apron and was stirring up muffins for tea when she thought she saw a stealthy little figure stealing through the yard close by the hedge. But the early dusk was falling, and it was easy to imagine it was only the shadows on the grass. Miranda was about to light a candle and set the table, but it was early yet. Mr. David would be late coming home from the office today because of the time he'd taken off for the wedding. Instead she took a bowl and went out to see if she could find some late yellow raspberries on the vines, though she knew there wouldn't likely be any.

Humming a lively tune, she approached the berry vines, while her sharp eyes studied the great leaves of pieplant growing next to the hedge. They were stirring now, almost imperceptibly, one minute, and the next, bobbing vigorously back and forth as if they'd suddenly become animate. Miranda watched them, walking deliberately past them and humming her tune. The leaves became absolutely still as she passed them, though she didn't turn her eyes down to them noticeably but went on a little farther and knelt down by the berry bushes voicing her tune in words now.

> Thur wuz a man in our town,
> > an' he wuz wondrus wise.
> He jumped into a bramble bush
> > an' scratched out both his ey-i-es;
> An' when he saw his eyes were out,
> > 'ith all his might an' main,
> He jumped into another bush
> > an' scratched 'em in again.

"Land sakes!" she exclaimed suddenly. "Wisht I hed a boy t' hep hunt berries. Guess I'm gettin' nearsighted in the dark. Here's three whole ras'berries right clost together, an' I come real nigh missin' 'em."

She cast an eye toward the pieplant leaves, but they remained motionless. Perhaps she'd made a mistake after all. Perhaps no dark little figure had been stealing along by the hedge.

She kept on feeling after berries that weren't there. Finally, after securing no more than a handful, she crept softly back by the pieplant bed, for she thought she'd heard a soft gasp like the catching of breath, and something stirred within her. She must find out what was moving the leaves.

She set her bowl down on the grass and made a soft, quick dive with her hands, lifting up two or three broad leaves and peering under.

It was almost dark now, and the forlorn little figure under the hedge could scarcely be seen. But Miranda's eyes were keen and kind, and she made out the outline of Nate Whitney's curly head, so sleek in the morning, now tousled and rough. He shrank back with his face in the grass as she lifted the leaves, hoping to escape her notice. But she reached out her two strong hands and pulled him forth, resisting furiously.

"Lemme alone. I ain't doin' you any harm!" he declared sulkily as she pulled his head and shoulders out from the entangling stalks.

She had light enough in the garden to see his face, tear-stained and smeared with mud streaks. His collar was crushed and twisted awry, and his jacket had a great jagged tear in one elbow.

"You poor little motherless sinner!" exclaimed Miranda in a tone she'd never used in her life except for little Rose.

She sat down on the garden walk and took the forlorn little fellow into her arms, at least as much as she could get hold of, for he was still wiggling and twisting away from her strong hand with all his discomfited young might.

She leaned over his dirty face and laid her lips on his forehead.

"You poor little soul, I know how you feel, and I don't blame you one mite," she whispered, her young arms encircling him gently.

Then quite suddenly the struggling ceased, the fierce wiry body relaxed, and the dirty face and curly head buried themselves quite childishly in her arms. The boy sobbed as if his heart would break and clung to her as if his life depended on it.

Something wonderfully sweet and new stirred in Miranda's soul— motherhood. The clinging hands, the warm wet face, the pitiful sight of this sorrowful child in place of the saucy, impudent, self-possessed boy, who dared any mischief his bright restless mind suggested, touched her heart. A fierce desire seized her to protect and love this boy who needed someone sorely, and for the first time a regret stole into her heart that she wasn't his new mother. What a thing it would be to have those clinging arms belong to her!

Then a wicked exultant thrill passed through her. She hadn't "walked pride" with Nathan Whitney. But his son had turned to her for comfort, and she loved the boy for it with all her heart. Maria Bent might hold her head high and reign severely in his home, but she, Miranda Griscom, would love the little son and help him out of his scrapes from this time forward.

"There, there," she soothed, passing her rough, work-worn hand over the tumbled curls and exulting in their tendency to wrap about her fingers. How soft they were, like a baby's, and yet they belonged to that hard, bad little boy she'd always called a "brat"!

"There, there! Just cry it out," she murmured. "I know. I jest guess I know how you feel. I kin see you ain't overly pleased at the change over to your house. You jest cry good an' hard oncet, an' it'll make you feel better. Ef you can't do it hard 'nough by yerself I'll hep you." And Miranda laid her freckled face on the muddy little cheek of the boy and let her tears mingle with his.

Perhaps those hot tears falling on his face, tears that weren't his own, called him back to his boy senses and ended the first crying spell he remembered since he was six years old. Then Aunt Jane sneered at him and called him a crybaby when he cut his foot on a scythe. He'd been a self-contained, hard, bad little man ever since till now, when all the foundations of his being seemed shaken with this unexpected sympathy from one he'd ranked among his enemies.

His sobs stopped as suddenly as they'd begun, and for some time he lay still in her arms, with his head pressed against her shoulder where she'd drawn it and his breath coming hot and quick against her face.

"Can't you tell me what's the matter? Is't anythin' special?" asked the girl gently. One would scarcely have known Miranda's voice. All the hardness, sharpness and mirth were gone. Only gentleness, tenderness and deep understanding remained. " 'Course I know 'tain't altogether pleasant hevin' a stranger—especially ef she's one you've known afore an' ain't fond of—"

"I *hate* her!" came with sudden vehemence from the boy's lips. His throat had a catch in it, but his lips were set, and no more tears were allowed to come.

"Well, 'course, that ain't the way you're expected t' feel, but I onderstand, and I guess they wouldn't enny of 'em do much better in your place. I never did admire her much myself, so I ken see how you look at it."

"I hate her!" reiterated the boy, but this time not so fiercely. "I hate her, and I won't let her be my mother ever! Say, why didn't *you* be it?"

The question was balm and pride to Miranda's heart. She put her arms closer around the lonely boy, rocked him gently back and forth, and then smoothed his hair back from his hot dirty forehead. The marvel was he let her do it and didn't squirm away.

"Why didn't I? Bless him! Well, I didn't think I'd like it enny better'n you do her. B'sides, ef I had, you'd a hated me then."

The boy looked at her steadily through the twilight as though he were turning it over in his mind and then suddenly broke into a shy smile.

"Mebbe I would," he said, with honest eyes searching her face. Then half shamefaced, he added shyly, "But anyhow I like you now."

A wild sweet rush of emotion flooded Miranda's soul. Not since she left her unloved, unloving grandmother Heath who lived next door and came to live with David and Marcia Spafford receiving wages, doing honest work in return and finding a real home, had such sweet surprise and joy come to her. Sweeter even than the little cherished Rose's kisses was this shy, veiled admiration of the man-child whose lonely life she seemed strangely to understand. All at once she seemed to know how and why he earned the name of being a bad boy, and her heart went out to him as to a kindred spirit. She'd seen his soul looking out of his beautiful brown eyes in the dusk at her, and she knew he wasn't all bad and that it was mostly other people's fault when he really did wrong.

Miranda's arms in their warm pressure answered the boy's words, and she stooped again and laid her lips on his forehead lingeringly, though as shyly as a boy might have. Miranda wasn't one to show deep emotion, and she was more stirred than ever before.

"Well, I guess we sort o' b'long to each other somehow. Ennyhow we'll be friends. Say, didn't you tear your cloes when you went up that hick'ry?"

The child in her arms suddenly straightened up and became the boy with mischief in his eyes and a knowing tilt to his handsome head.

"Say, did you see me go up that tree?"

"No, but I saw you gone. And I saw Sammy's eyes lookin' up, an' I saw the hick'ry movin' some, so I calc'lated you was up there, all right."

"An' you won't tell?"

" 'Course I won't tell. It's none o' my business, an' b'sides I could see you wasn't enjoyin' yerse'f to the weddin'. What's more, I'll mend them cloes. There ain't no reason fer M'ria Bent, as was, to come inspectin' you yet a whiles. You kin shin up the kitchen roof, can't yeh, to my winder an' take off them rips an' tears an' hop into my bed? I'll come up an' mend yeh so's she won't know. Then you ken shin up a tree to yer own winder t' hum an' go to bed, an' like's not she'll never notice them cloes till yer aunt Jane's gone. An' she'll think they been tore an' mended sometime back, an' she ain't got no call to throw 'em up to yeh. Hed yer supper?"

"Naw. Don't want any."

"That's all right. I'll bring you up some caraway cookies. You like 'em, don't yeh? Er hev yeh et too much weddin' cake?"

"Didn't touch their old wedding cake," said the boy sulkily.

"Boy, didn't you go home 'tall since you was in the hick'ry? Wal, I declare! To think you missed the reception with all them good things to eat! You must a felt pretty bad. Never mind you, honey. You do's I tell yeh. Just shin right up that roof. Here, eat them raspberries first; they ain't many, but they'll stay yeh. I got some fried chicken left over. Don't you worry. Now let's see you get up there."

Miranda helped Nate from the back kitchen window mount to the roof and saw him climb lightly and gleefully in at her window. Then she bustled in to put supper on the table. Mr. David wasn't home yet when everything was ready, so with a glass of milk, a plate of bread, jelly and chicken and another of cookies she slipped up the back stairs to her small boy. She found him contentedly awaiting her coming, his eyes shining a welcome to her through the room's gathering darkness, as he might have done to any pal in a youthful conspiracy.

"I've got a boarder," she explained grimly a few minutes afterward to the astonished Marcia, as she came downstairs with her lighted candle, a small pair of trousers and a jacket over her arm.

"A boarder!" Marcia had learned to expect the unusual from Miranda, but this was out of the ordinary even for Miranda, at least without permission.

"Yes, you ken take it off my wages. I don't guess he'll remain more'n an hour or so; leastways I'll try to get him off soon fer his own sake. It's that poor little peaked Nate Whitney, Mrs. Marcia. He's all broke up over hevin' that broomstick of a M'ria Bent fer his mother, an' seein' as I sorta shirked the job myself I thought 'twas only decent I should chirk him up a bit. He was out behind the pieplant cryin' like his heart would break, an' he ast me, why didn't *I* be his mother, 'at he *hated* her, an' he was all tore up with climbin' trees to get out of sight, so I laid out to mend him up a little 'fore he goes home. I know M'ria Bent. I went to school to her one year 'fore I quit, an' she's a tartar! It ain't reasonable fer him to start in with her the first day all tore up. She'd get him at a disadvantage. Ain't you got a patch would do to put under this tear, Mrs. Marcia?

"I took him up some supper. I knowed you wouldn't care, an' I want you should take it off my wages. Yes, that's right. I'll feel better about it ef you do. Then I could do it agin ef the notion should take me. I owe a little sumpin' to that boy fer my present state of freedom, an' I kinda take a likin' to him when he's cryin', you know. After all, I do' no's 'e was ever so awful bad."

Marcia laid an understanding touch on Miranda's arm and, with a smile in the off-corner of her mouth and an unseen tear in the eye, went to get the patch.

Inside two hours young Nathan departed by way of the roof, washed and combed, mended and pressed, as well as Aunt Jane could have done—but with more than he had for years, a heart that was almost comforted. He felt now he had at least one friend in the world who understood him, and he wondered, sliding down the kitchen-shed roof, whether it mightn't be practicable for him to grow up fast and marry Miranda so no one else would carry her off. By the time he scaled his own kitchen roof and cautiously removed his clothing, hung it up and crept to his own little bed, he'd quite forgotten this vague idea. But the comfort remained in his heart and enabled him to waken cheerfully the next morning to his new world without that sinking feeling that had been in his heart and stomach ever since he knew Maria Bent was to be his father's wife.

So that was how it all came about that Miranda Griscom became mother-confessor and chief-comforter to Nathan Whitney's second son, and Nathan became the slave and adorer of little Rose Schuyler Spafford when she was five-years-old-going-on-six. And it all began in the year 1838.

Chapter 3

One chapter in Miranda's life she'd never told to a living soul, and only on rare occasions did she take it out of her heart and look it over. Just when the wellsprings of her very being were deeply touched, as in the quiet dark of her starlit window or on her knees at her odd devotions, did she let her mind dwell upon it.

Miranda was twenty-two years old and entirely whole of heart; yet a romance had been and still was in her life as sweet and precious as any more favored girls had experienced. That it was sad and brief, and the hope of its ever coming to anything had long since departed from her heart, made it no less precious to her. Because of her strength and sweetness of character, her bubbling good nature and interest in others, and her keen sense of humor, her experience hadn't hardened or sharpened her. She was one of those strong souls who, through not having, has learned to forget self and be content in others' joy. She didn't have a fiber of selfishness in her quaint, intense, delightful makeup.

She lived her somewhat lonely life and picked up what crumbs of pleasure she could find; fought her merry, sometimes questionable, warfare for those she loved; served them worshipfully; would give her life for theirs any day. Yet she kept in her heart one secret shrine for the love of her young heart, furnished royally with all the hopes and yearnings any girl knows.

Years ago, it seemed centuries now, before David brought his girl-bride to the old house next door to Grandmother Heath's, where Miranda was a schoolgirl, eleven, twelve, thirteen years old, she'd had a hero in her life. No one knew it, not even the hero. But no knight of old was ever beloved or watched or exalted by fair lady more than Allan Whitney, half brother of young Nathan.

Allan Whitney was tall and strong, with straight dark hair that fell over his forehead till he was continually tossing it back; a mouth that drooped pathetically above a strong purposeful chin; eyes that held depths of fierceness and sadness that only a passionate temperament knows how to combine; and a reputation altogether worse than any boy ever brought up in the town.

Allan was kind to his stepmother when his father was cold and hard and in some way cheered her last days. But she never had time or fortitude to do much in the way of bringing him up. In fact he never was brought up, unless he did it himself. If one might judge by his strong will, if he'd inherited it from his own mother, she alone might have been able to do something toward molding him. Certainly his father never held the slightest influence with the boy. Nathan Whitney could make money and keep it, but he couldn't make boys into good men.

Allan Whitney was quick and bright, but he wouldn't study at school, and he wouldn't go to work. He was very much in his time as young Nathan wasn't, only more so, Miranda thought as she placed the facts honestly before her in the starlight, while she watched to see if a light would appear in the boy's window across the way.

Allan was in continual rebellion against the universe. In school he was whipped whenever the teacher felt out of sorts with anybody, and he took it with the careless jocular air of one who knows he could "lick the teacher into the middle of next week" if he undertook the job. As it was he generally allowed chastisement for the sake of relief from monotony for the other scholars.

He'd wink slyly at Miranda who sat down in a front seat demurely studying her spelling, as he lounged forward and held out his hand. By a sort of natural feeling he knew her to be of his same temper and that she both understood and sympathized with him. Five desks back Rowena Higginson was in tears because of his sufferings, and gentle Annetta Bloodgood turned pale with the sound of each blow from the ferrule, half shuddering in time to the chastisement.

But Allan Whitney hugely enjoyed their sentimental sufferings. He knew every boy in the room admired him for the way he took his whippings, and sought provocations for like martyrdom, that they might emulate his easy air of indifference. When his punishment was over Allan would seek his seat lazily, with a happy grimace on his face, another wink for Miranda, sometimes a lollipop or some barley sugar laid surreptitiously on her desk as he passed by, and a knowing tweak of her red pigtails. And she waited for those endearments with a trembling eagerness he never suspected. She was only a smart child who knew almost as much as a boy about a boy's code of life and took his good-natured tormentings as well as a boy could have; therefore he enjoyed tormenting her.

Nevertheless, though Miranda witnessed his punishments with outward serenity and gloried in his indifference to them, her young soul was filled with bitterness against the teachers for their treatment of her hero. Many hard knocks of discipline she laid up in store for those same teachers in the future if ever she had opportunity to give them, and she generally managed sometime, somehow to give them.

"Miss Menchant, is this your hankercher'?" she asked sweetly one day.

Allan had just retired indifferently from a whipping Miranda knew must have hurt, which was given merely because Miss Menchant found a large drawing of herself in lifelike lines on the blackboard near Allan's desk and couldn't locate the artist.

Miss Menchant said severely that it was—as if Miranda were in some way to blame for its being on the floor—as indeed she was. She'd filched it from her teacher's pocket in the coatroom and brought it into the schoolroom ready, bated for her prey.

A moment later Miss Menchant picked up the handkerchief from where Miranda had laid it on the desk at her hand and wiped her face. Immediately she dropped it with loud exclamations and put her hand to her nose with pain, while a large honeybee flew away through the open door of the schoolhouse.

"Miranda!" called the suffering teacher. "Miranda Griscom!"

But Miranda, like a good child, had taken her dinner pail and gone home. Her bright brown eye might have been seen peeking through a knothole at the end of the schoolhouse, but Miss Menchant didn't happen to be looking that way.

The next morning when the teacher asked the little girl if she noticed anything on the handkerchief when she picked it up, Miranda's eyes were sweetly unconscious of the large red knob on the teacher's nose as she answered serenely, "I didn't take notice to nothin'."

The next time Allan Whitney was called up for discipline, the ruler, usually playing a prominent part in the affair, was strangely missing and might have been found in Miranda Griscom's desk if anyone knew where to look for it. It met a watery grave that night in the old mill stream down behind the mill wheel, along with several of its successors of later years.

Time cures all things, and they usually had women teachers in that school. Allan presently grew so large that few women teachers could whip him. It then became a vital question, when engaging a new teacher, as to whether or not she'd be able to "lick" Allan Whitney. One winter they tried a man, a little, knotty shrimp of a man, with a high reputation as to intellect, but no more appreciation of a boy than if he were a boiled owl. Those days delighted the souls of the scholars of that school, for it was soon noised abroad that every day was a delight because every day a new drama was flung on the stage for their pleasure.

Now behind the platform, where the teacher's desk and chair were placed, stood a long dark room where coats and dinner pails were kept. It had a single small, narrow window at one end, and the other end came up to a partition that cut off the teacher's private closet from it. This was the girls' cloakroom and was part of the improvements to the old red schoolhouse about the time Miranda began to go to school. The boys had a small closet at the back of the room, so they never went to this. But as the school grew, this cloakroom was well filled, especially in winter when everybody had plenty of wraps.

To make more light, an opening was made from it into the schoolroom, window-like with a wide shelf or ledge behind the teacher's desk. This was frequently adorned with a row of dinner pails. A door to the right of the platform opened into the teacher's closet and was usually kept closed, while that to the left opened into the girls' cloakroom and was usually standing open. Miranda's desk was directly in front of this door, since the teacher found it handy to have Miranda where he could keep a weather eye out for plots under a serene and innocent exterior.

The man teacher, Mr. Applethorn by name, had been in the school about three weeks and tried every conceivable plan for conquering Allan Whitney except the timeworn one of "licking" him. It became apparent, then, that the issue was to be brought to a climax.

Miranda had heard low words by Allan to his friend Bud Hendrake about what he meant to do if "old Appleseed tried it." While the little girl had great faith in Allan's strong body and quick mind against the teacher's little flabby body and quickly aroused temper, she nevertheless reflected that behind him were all the selectmen, and authority was always at war with poor Allan. It would go hard with him this time, she knew, if the matter were put in the selectmen's hands.

She'd heard Grandfather Heath talking about it. "One more outrage and we're done with him."

That sentence sent terror to Miranda's heart, for the long stretches of school days unenlivened by Allan Whitney's careless smile and merry sayings were unbearable for her to think about. Something must be done to save him, and she must do it, for no one else cared.

So Miranda lay awake for a long time trying to devise a plan by which the teacher's injustice to Allan could not only be avenged, but the immediate danger of a fight between Allan and the teacher averted, at least for a time. If Allan fought with the teacher and "licked" him, everybody would feel sorry for the teacher, for nobody liked Allan—that is, nobody with any authority. There it was, always authority against Allan! Poor little Miranda tossed on her small bed and thought and finally fell asleep with her problem unsolved. But she started for school the next morning with firmly set lips and a determined frown. She'd do something, see if she wouldn't!

And then Grandmother Heath called her back to carry a pail of sour cream to Granny MacVane's on her way to school.

Now ordinarily Miranda wouldn't have welcomed the errand around by Granny MacVane's before school—and Grandmother was very particular she should go before school. Miranda liked to get to school early and play hide-and-seek in the yard, and Grandmother Heath knew it and disapproved. School wasn't established for amusement but for education, she frequently remarked when remonstrating with Miranda for starting so early. But this particular morning the girl's face brightened, and she took the shining tin pail with alacrity and responded modestly, "Yes, ma'am," when her grandmother repeated the command to be sure and go before school. She was so nice and obedient about it that the old woman looked after her suspiciously, having learned Miranda's ways were devious and when her exterior was calm, then was the time to be on the alert.

Miranda had suddenly seen light in the darkness with the advent of this pail of sour cream. Sour cream would keep. That is, it would only grow sourer, which was desirable in a thing like sour cream. There was no reason in the world why that cream had to go to Granny MacVane's before school, especially when it might come in handy for something else besides making gingerbread for the old woman. Besides, Granny MacVane lived beyond the schoolhouse, and Grandmother Heath would never know whether she went before or after. Sour cream was a delicacy often sent to old Mrs. MacVane, and if she brought the message, "Granny says she's much obliged, Gran'ma," there'd be no question and likely nothing further ever thought about it.

Besides, Miranda was willing to risk it if the stakes were high enough, so she hurried happily off to school with her head held high and the sour cream pail clattering against her dinner pail with reckless hilarity, while she laid her neat little plans.

At the schoolhouse she deposited the pail of sour cream with its mate the dinner pail inconspicuously on the inner ledge of the window over the teacher's chair. The ledge was wide and the pails almost out of sight from the schoolroom. At noon, however, Miranda, after eating her lunch, replaced her empty dinner pail and carefully rearranged all the pails on the ledge, her own and others, so they were grouped quite innocently closer to the front edge. Miranda herself was seated early at her desk studying quietly when the others came in.

The atmosphere that afternoon seemed electric. Even the very little scholars seemed to understand something was going to happen before school "let out." Just as the master was about to send the school out for afternoon recess, he paused and announced solemnly, "Allan Whitney, you may remain in your seat!" And they knew it was almost at hand.

Chapter 4

Miranda had played her cards well. She sat studiously in her seat until everybody was out of the schoolroom except Mr. Applethorn, Allan and her, and then she raised her hand demurely for permission to speak.

"Teacher, please may I go's soon 'z I finish my 'gzamples? Grandma wants me to go to Granny MacVane's on a errand, an' she don't want me to stay out after dark."

The teacher gave a curt permission. He had no time just then to fathom Miranda Griscom's deeps and had always felt that she belonged to the enemy. She was as well out of the room when he gave Allan Whitney his dues.

Miranda worked away vigorously. The examples were already finished, but she had no mind to leave until the right moment. Such studious ways in Miranda were astonishing, and if Mr. Applethorn hadn't been otherwise occupied he'd certainly have suspected something, seeing Miranda, the usually alert one, bending over her slate, with a stubby pencil in her hand, her brows wrinkled hard over a supposedly perplexing question, her two red plaits sticking out at each side, and no eyes or ears for what was going on in the playground.

Allan Whitney sat whittling a small stick into a very tiny sword and half whistling under his breath until the master, in a voice that was meant to be stentorian, uttered a solemn "Silence, sir! I say, silence!"

Allan looked up pleasantly. "All right, sir. Just as you say, sir."

The master was growing angry. Miranda saw it out of the corner of her eye. He glowered at the boy a minute.

"I said silence!" he roared. "You've no need to answer further. Just keep silence!"

"Very well, sir. I heard you, sir, and I said all right, sir. Just as you say, sir," answered Allan sunnily again, with the most aggravating smile on his face, but not a shade of impudence in his voice. Allan knew how to be impudent in a perfectly respectful way.

"Hold your tongue, sir!" fairly howled the master.

"Oh, thank you, I will, sir," said Allan.

But it was the teacher who, red and angry, found he had to hold his, while Allan had the last word. Just then the boy appointed to ring the bell for recess to end appeared in the doorway and gave it three taps, and the eager scholars who were hovering in excited groups hurried back to their seats wondering what was about to happen.

They settled into quiet sooner than usual and sat in breathless attention, with their eyes apparently riveted on their books, awaiting the call to the last class of the afternoon. But in reality they were watching alternately the angry visage of the teacher and the calm, pale one of Allan Whitney who now drew himself to his full height and sat with folded arms.

The master reached into his desk, pulled out the ferrule and threw it with skillful twirl straight into the boy's face. Then Allan, accepting the challenge, arose and came forward to the platform, but he didn't stoop to pick up the ruler and bring it with him according to custom. Instead he came as a man might have come who'd just been insulted, with his head held high and his eyes glowing darkly in his white set face, for the ruler struck him across the mouth, and its sting sank into his soul. In that blow all the injustices of all the years of being misjudged by his teachers and fellow townsmen seemed concentrated. It wasn't that he hadn't been a mischievous, bad boy often, but not always. And he resented the fact that when he tried to do right nobody gave him credit for it.

Just at this crucial moment Miranda arose with her completed arithmetic paper and fluttered conspicuously up to the desk.

"May I go now, teacher?" she asked sweetly. "I've got 'em all done, every one."

The master waved her away without ceremony. She was to him like an annoying gadfly when he needed all his senses to master the trouble at hand.

Miranda slipped joyously into the cloakroom, apparently as unconscious of Allan Whitney standing close beside her as if he were miles away. A moment later those who sat in the extreme back of the room might have seen the dim flutter of a brown calico sunbonnet landing on top of the dinner pails just over the master's head, if they hadn't been too occupied with the master's changing visage and Allan's quiet form standing in defiant attitude before him.

Mr. Applethorn was a great believer in deliberation and never afraid of a pause. He thought it impressive. At this moment, while he gathered his courage for the encounter he knew was before him, he paused and expected to quell Allan Whitney by the glance of his two angry eyes.

The schoolmaster was still seated, though drawn up to his full height with folded arms, looking dignified as he knew how to look and far more impressive than if he were standing in front of his tall pupil. Suddenly, before a word was spoken, and very quietly for a metal thing, the tin pail on the ledge over his chair began to move forward, as if pushed by a phalanx of its fellows from behind. It came to the edge— it toppled—and a broad avalanche of thick white substance gushed forth. It was preceded by a giddy tin cover, which reeled and pirouetted for a moment on the master's astonished head, took a step down his nose and waltzed off to the platform and under the stove. A concluding white deluge followed as the pail descended and settled down over the noble brows of Mr. Applethorn, who arose in haste and horror, dripping sour cream, spluttering and snorting like a porpoise, amid a howling, screaming, shouting mob of irreverent scholars who were laughing until the tears streamed down their cheeks.

Miranda appeared penitently at the cloakroom door, with her brown sunbonnet in her hand and tears ready to be shed if need be at the loss of her precious sour cream—accidentally knocked over when she went to get her sunbonnet which some malicious girl must have put up high out of her reach. But she found no need for any further efforts on her part. Obviously the fight was over. The schoolmaster was in no condition to administer either justice or injustice to anybody.

Allan Whitney at this crisis rose magnificently to the occasion. With admirable solicitude he relieved the schoolmaster of his unwelcome helmet and with his own soiled and crumpled handkerchief wiped the lumps of sour cream from his erstwhile adversary's features.

For one blessed hilarious moment the schoolmaster had stood helpless and enraged, blinded and speechless, choking and gasping, and dripping sour cream from every point of his hair, nose, collar, chin, and fingertips. And the wild mob of hysterical pupils stood on the desks and viewed him, bending double with their mirth or jumping up and down in their ecstasy. The next moment Allan Whitney took command and with one raised hand silenced the hilarity and with a second motion cleared the room, and a low word to one of his devoted slaves brought a pail of water to his side. Then in the seclusion of the empty schoolroom he applied himself to rescuing Mr. Applethorn.

Miranda, in the shelter of the cloakroom door, secure for the moment from the teacher's cream-filled eyes, watched her hero in awe as he mopped away at his enemy, as tenderly and kindly as if he'd been a little child in trouble. She was too filled with mixed emotions to play the guileless, saucy part she'd prepared for herself in this comedy. She was filled with dread lest after all Allan didn't approve of what she'd done or like it. That he'd be in the least deceived by her sunbonnet trick she never for a moment expected. That he'd be angry because she stopped the fight hadn't crossed her mind before.

Now she stood in an agony of fear, forgetting the comical sight of the schoolmaster in sour cream, and trembled lest she'd hopelessly offended her hero. Perhaps, after all, it wasn't fair to interfere with the game. Perhaps she'd transgressed the code's rules and lost her high place in his estimation. If she had, no punishment would be too great, no penance suffice, to cover her transgression. The sun would be blotted out of her little world and her heart broken forever.

At that instant of dejection Allan turned from wiping out the victim's left eye and gave the cringing Miranda a large, kind, appreciative wink. Suddenly her sun rose high once more, and her heart sprang lightly up again. She responded with her tongue in her cheek and a knowing grimace, departing, warmed and satisfied, safely through the cloakroom window. Down behind the alders by the creek, however, her natural being asserted itself, and she sat down to laugh till she cried over the spectacle of her teacher in a tin pail enveloped in sour cream.

The next morning she found a large piece of spruce gum in her desk with a bit of paper wrapped around it on which was written in Allan's familiar scrawl: *"You are a little brick."*

The strange thing about it all was that Allan and Mr. Applethorn became excellent friends after that. But the selectmen, though they offered every inducement in their power, couldn't prevail upon the teacher to remain longer than month's end. Poor little Mr. Applethorn couldn't get over his humiliation before his scholars, and he never quite understood how that sour cream got located over his head, though Allan gave a very plausible explanation and kept him in some mysterious way from making too close an investigation.

After that Allan Whitney always had a glance and a wink and, on rare occasions, a smile for Miranda. But the boy didn't come back to school again after Mr. Applethorn left, and the little girl seldom saw him except on the street. Her worship of him relaxed not a bit, however, and her young heart resented the things said about him. She was always on the watch to do him a good turn, but it didn't come for a long time. And then it came with a vengeance, a short, sharp trial of her loyalty.

Chapter 5

I t was a bitter cold night in November. Miranda had crept up close to the fireplace with her spelling book—not that she cared in the least for her spelling lesson, though there was to be a spelling-down contest the next day in school. But her spelling book always provided a good excuse to Grandma Heath for not knitting or spinning during an evening.

Grandpa Heath came in presently, stamping away the snow and shutting the outside door noisily. One could see he was excited. He strode across the room and hung up the big key that locked the old smokehouse door. Mr. Heath was constable, and the old smokehouse was being used for a lockup. Plainly something had happened.

Miranda glanced up alertly but looked down at once to her book and was apparently a diligent scholar, even conning her words half aloud. She knew by experience that if she appeared to be listening, all the news would be saved till she was sent off to bed. Then she'd have to lie on the floor in the cold with her ear to the pipe hole that was supposed to warm her room, to get necessary information. If she kept still and was absorbed in her work, chances were her grandfather would forget she was there.

He hung up his coat, muffler and cap, and sat down heavily in his chair across the table from his wife, who was diligently knitting a long gray stocking. The light of the one candle, frugally burning high on the shelf over the fireplace, flickered fitfully over the whole room and made the old man's face look ashen gray with shadows as he began to talk, fingering his scraggly gray beard nervously.

"Well, I guess we've had a murder!" he spoke shakily, as if he couldn't quite believe it himself.

"You guess!" said his wife sharply. "Don't you know? There ain't any halfway about a murder usually."

"Well, he ain't dead yet, but there ain't much chance fer his life. I guess he'll pass away 'fore the mornin'."

"Who? Why don't you ever tell the whole story?" snapped Grandmother Heath excitedly.

"Why, it's old Enoch Taylor. Didn't I say in the first place?"

"No, you didn't. Who done it?"

"Allan Whitney—leastways he was comin' away with a gun when we found him, an' we've got him arrested. He's down in the smoke-house now."

"H'm!" commented his wife. "Just what I expected he'd come to. Well, the town'll be well rid of him. Ain't he kinda young, though, to be hung?"

"Well, I guess he's about seventeen, but he's large fer his age. I don't know whether they ken hang him er not. He ain't ben tried yet, of course, but it'll go against him, no question o' that. He's ben a pest to the neighborhood fer a long time—"

At this point Miranda's spelling book fell clattering to the hearth, where it knocked off the cover from the bowl of yeast set to rise by the warmth. But when her startled grandparents turned to look at her she was apparently sound asleep, sitting on her little cushion on the hearth with her head against the fire jamb.

Her grandmother arose and gave her a vigorous shaking.

"M'randy, git right up off'n that hearth and go to bed. It beats all how a great girl like you can't keep awake to get her lessons. You might a' fell in the fire. Wake up, I tell you, an' go to bed this minute!"

Miranda awoke with studied leisure, yawning and dazed, and ad-mirably unconscious of her surroundings. Slowly she picked up her book, rubbing her drowsy eyes, lit her candle and dragged herself yawning up the stairs to her room. But when she arrived there she didn't prepare for bed. Instead she wrapped herself in a quilt and lay down with her ear to the stovepipe hole, her whole body tense and quivering with agony.

The old couple waited until the stair door was latched and the girl's footsteps unmistakably toward the top of the stair. Then the grand-mother spoke.

"I'm real glad he's got caught now 'fore he growed up any bigger. I always was afraid M'randy'd take a notion to him an' run off like her mother did. He's good-lookin'—the kind like her father was, and such things run in the blood. She was real fond of him a couple of years back—used to fly up like a scratch cat every time anybody mentioned his cuttin's up, but she ain't mentioned him lately."

"Aw—you didn't need to worry 'bout that, I guess," said her husband meditatively. "He wouldn't ever have took to her. Red hair and a little turned-up nose like hers don't go down with these young fellers. Besides, she ain't nothin' but a child, an' he's 'most a grown man."

"She ain't so bad looking," bristled her grandmother with asperity.

And it's a pity that poor, plain Miranda, who imagined herself a blot on the face of the earth for homeliness, couldn't have overheard her; it would have softened her heart toward her hard, unloving grandmother to an astonishing degree. Miranda knew she was a trial to her relatives and never supposed they cared for her in the least.

But though Miranda lay on the floor until her grandparents came upstairs for the night, she heard no more about the murder or Allan. Wrapped in her quilt she crept to the window and looked out through the snowy night. There was no wind, and the snow came down like fine powder, small and still, but invincible and steady. Out through the white veil she could dimly see the dark walls of the old smoke-house, white-capped and still.

Out there in the cold and dark and snow was Allan—her fine, strong, merry Allan! It seemed incredible! He was there charged with murder! And awaiting tomorrow! As happened before, she, Miranda, was the only one in the whole wide world who seemed to have a mind to save him.

When she first heard her grandfather's words downstairs, her heart almost froze within her, and for once her natural cunning almost deserted her. When her book fell, with difficulty she kept herself from crying out. But she had sense enough left to put her head against the fireplace and pretend to be asleep. As she closed her eyes the vision of the great black key hanging on the wall beside the clock seemed burned into her brain. It was the symbol of Allan's imprisonment and seemed to mock her from its nail and challenge her to save her hero now if she could.

She knew from the first instant she would save him, or at least she'd do all in her power to do so. The key threw her the challenge, and her plan was forming even as she listened to the story. Now she went over it carefully in every detail.

Out there in the smokehouse Allan was stiff and cold. She knew the smooth, chilly floor of hard clay and the rough, unfriendly brick walls with mortar hanging in great blotches over their surface. On the dim raftered ceiling a ham or two still hung, because it was nearer the house than the new smokehouse, where most of the winter stores were kept.

The lockup was seldom used—in fact, only twice in the three years Mr. Heath had been constable. And it was handy to run to the old smokehouse door when they needed a slice of ham.

Ah, that was an idea. Allan would need food. He could take one of those hams. Her busy brain thought it all out as an older girl might have done, and as soon as she heard the distant rumble of her grandfather's snore, she crept about with her preparations. It was too early to make any decided moves, for her grandmother, though quite deaf, wasn't always a ready sleeper and had a way of "sensing" things she couldn't hear.

Under the eaves, opening through her tiny closet, stood a trunk containing some of her mother's clothes. She remembered an old overcoat of her father's among them. It wasn't fine or handsome, but it was warm. From all she knew of Allan's habits he probably wore no overcoat when he was out that afternoon, for it wasn't as cold then, and the snow wasn't falling. He'd need something warm this minute.

How she yearned to make him a good, hot cup of coffee and take it out to him, but she dared not attempt it. If her grandmother's ears were growing dim, at least her nostrils weren't failing, and she'd smell the coffee in the middle of her night's sleep. But the overcoat he could wear away, and no one would be any wiser. Grandmother wouldn't overhaul that trunk for any vagrant moths until next spring now, and what did it matter then what she thought about its absence? She'd probably be glad to have it gone because it belonged to the hated man who ran away from their daughter and left her and her little red-haired child to be a burden.

She hesitated about lighting a candle, finally deciding not to risk it, and crept into the eaves closet on her hands and knees in the dark, going by her sense of feeling straight to the little hair trunk and finding the overcoat at the bottom. She put the other things carefully away and got back quietly to her room again with the coat, hugging it like a treasure. She laid her cheek for an instant against the worn collar and had a fleeting thrill of affection for the wanderer who'd deserted his family, just because the coat was his and was helping her help Allan.

People were "early to bed and early to rise" in those days. Mr. and Mrs. Heath had retired at nine o'clock that night. It was ten before Miranda left her window to stir about the room. The old clock in the kitchen struck eleven before she found the overcoat and put everything back in the trunk.

She waited until she'd counted out the slow strokes of twelve from the clock before she dared steal downstairs and take the key from its nail by the clock. The cold iron of the key bit into her trembling fingers as if it had been alive, and she almost dropped it. She stood shaking with cold and fright, for it seemed as if every floorboard she stepped on creaked. Once she fell over her grandmother's rocking chair, and the rockers dug into her ankles as if they had a grudge against her. Her nerves were so keyed up that the hurt brought tears to her Spartan eyes, and she had to sit down for a minute to bear the pain.

She carefully canvassed the idea of going out the door downstairs and gave it up. The door opened noisily, and the bar put across it at night fit tightly. It was liable to make a loud, grating sound when it was moved. Also, the snow was deep enough that footprints by the door would be noticeable in the morning unless it snowed harder than it was now and the wind blew to cover them up. Besides, it would be terrible if anyone saw her coming out the door and told her grandfather. He'd never forgive her, and she'd have to run away. But, worst of all, she dreaded being seen and stopped before she accomplished her purpose, for the downstairs door was just under her grandmother's window. So with the key secure she slipped into the pantry, found half a loaf of bread, two turnovers and some cookies, and with her loot crept back upstairs again.

When she was at last safely back in her room she sighed with relief and sat down for a moment to listen and be sure she hadn't disturbed the sleepers. Then she tied the key on a strong string and hung it around her neck. Next, she wrapped the bread, turnovers and cookies in some clean pieces of white cloth that were given her for the quilt she was piecing, stuffed them carefully into the old overcoat's pockets and put on the coat.

It was dark in her room, and she dared not light her candle lest some neighbor see the light in the window and ask her grandmother the next morning who was sick.

Cautiously, with one of her strange upliftings of soul that she called prayer, Miranda opened her window and crept out upon the sill. The roof below was covered with snow, three or four inches deep; but the window and roof were at the back of the house, and no one could see her from there. It wouldn't be easy getting back with all that snow on the roof, but Miranda wasn't thinking about getting back.

Clinging close to the house, she stepped slowly along the shed roof to the edge, trying not to disturb the snow. She'd slipped on a pair of stockings over her shoes so their dampness in the morning might not call forth comments from her grandmother. At last she reached the cherry tree close to the woodshed roof and could take hold of its branches and swing herself into it. Then she breathed more freely. The rest was relatively easy.

Carefully she balanced in the tree, making her way nimbly down with her strong young body swinging lithely from limb to limb, and dropped to the snowy ground. She took a few cautious steps as far apart as she could spring. But once out from under the tree she saw that if it continued snowing thick and fast and fine as it was now there'd be little danger her footsteps would be discovered in the morning. She reached the smokehouse, however, by a detour through the corn patch where tracks in the snow wouldn't be so noticeable.

Then, suddenly, she faced a new difficulty. The old rusty padlock was reinforced by a heavy beam firmly fixed across the door, and it was all the girl could do, snow-covered as it was, to move it from the great iron clamp that held it in place. But a big will and a loving heart can work miracles, and the great beam moved at last, with a creak that set Miranda's heart thumping wildly. The still night was deadened with its blanket of snow, and the sound seemed shut in with her in a small area. She held her breath for a minute to listen and then thankfully fitted the key into the padlock, her trembling fingers stiff with cold and fright.

With her hand on her heart and her eyes straining through the darkness, Miranda stepped inside, her pulses throbbing wildly now and her breath coming short and quick. There was something awfully gruesome about this dark silent place; it was like a tomb.

Chapter 6

She heard no sound or movement inside and started thinking her quest had been in vain or perhaps the prisoner had already escaped. If there was a way of escape she made sure Allan would find it. But after a second her senses cleared, and she heard soft breathing over in the corner. She crept toward it and made out a dark form lying in the shadow. She knelt beside it, put her hand out and touched the heavy beautiful hair she'd admired so many times in school when the head was bent over his book and the light from the window showed purple shadows in its dark depths. It thrilled her now strangely with a sense of privilege and almost awe to feel how soft it was. Then her hand touched his smooth boy face, and she bent her head so close she felt his breath on her cheek.

"Allan!" she whispered. "Allan!"

But it was some minutes before she could get him awake with her quiet efforts. She dared not make a noise, and he was dead with fatigue and anxiety, besides being almost numb with the cold. His head was pillowed on his arm, and he'd wrapped around him some old sacking given him for his bed. As constable, Grandfather Heath didn't believe in making the transgressor's way easy; while he went contented to his warm, comfortable bed, he left only a few yards of old sacking and a hard clay floor for the supposed criminal to lie upon. To Grandfather Heath this wasn't cruelty. He called it justice.

At last Miranda's whispered cries in his ear and her gentle shakings roused the boy to his surroundings. Her arms were around his neck, trying tenderly to bring him to a sitting posture, and her cheek was against his as though her soul could catch his attention by drawing nearer.

Her little freckled saucy face, all grave and sorrowful now in the darkness, gave him a conviction of sympathy he hadn't known in all his lonely boyhood days, and with his first waking sense her comforting presence touched him warmly. He held himself still just to be sure she was there holding him and it wasn't a dream, that somebody was caring and calling to him with almost a sob in her breath. For an instant he thought of his own mother he never knew, and then almost immediately he knew it was Miranda. All the hideous truth of his situation came back to him, as life's tragedies will on sudden waking; yet the strong, warm arms and the soft breath and cheek were there.

"Yes," he said softly but distinctly in her ear, not moving yet, however. "I'm awake. What is it?"

"Oh, I'm so glad," she caught her breath with a sob and instantly was her alert businesslike self again, all sentiment laid aside.

"Get up quick and put on this overcoat," she whispered, unbuttoning it with hurried fingers. "There's some things to eat in the pockets. Hurry! You ain't got any time to waste. Grandma wakes up awful easy, and she might find out I had my door buttoned and get Grandpa up. Or somebody might a' heard the door creak. It made a turrible noise. Ain't you 'most froze? Your hands is like ice—" She touched them softly and then drew them up to her face and blew on them to warm them with her breath. "There's some old mittens of mine in the pocket here; they ain't your size, but mebbe you ken git into 'em, and ennyhow they're better'n nothin'. Hurry, 'cause it'd be no use ef Grandpa woke—"

Allan sprang up suddenly.

"Where's your grandfather?" he asked anxiously. "Does he know you're here?"

"He's abed and asleep this three hours," said the girl, holding up the coat and catching one of his hands to put it in the sleeve. "I heard him tell about you bein' out here, and I jest kep' still and let 'em think I was asleep, so Grandma sent me up t' bed, and I waited till they went upstairs and got quiet. Then I slipped down an' got the key and some vittles and went back and clumb out my window to the cherry tree so's I wouldn't make a noise with the door.

"You better walk the fence rails till you get out the back pasture and up by the sugar maples. Then you could go through the woods, and they couldn't track you even ef it did stop snowin' soon and leave any kind of tracks. But I don't guess it'll stop yet awhile. It's awful fine and still like it was goin' on to snow fer hours. Hev you got any money with you? I put three shillin's in the inside coat pocket. It was all I hed. I thought you might need it. Reach up and git that half a ham over your head. You'll need it. Is there anythin' else you want?"

While she talked she hurried him into the coat, buttoning it around him as if he were a child and she his mother. And the tall fellow stooped and let her fasten him in, tucking the collar around his neck.

He shook his head and whispered a hoarse no to her question, but it caught in his throat with something like a sob. The memory of that sound sent the sobs of his young brother Nathan piercing to her soul, years later, down beside the pieplant bed.

"Don't you let 'em catch you, Allan," she said anxiously, her hand lingering on his arm, her eyes searching in the dark for his beloved face.

"No, I won't let 'em catch me," he murmured menacingly. "I'll get away all right, but, Randa"—he always called her Randa though no one else in the village ever called her that—"Randa, I want you to know I didn't do it. I didn't kill Enoch Taylor; indeed I didn't. I wasn't even there. I didn't have a thing to do with it."

"O' course you didn't!" said Miranda indignantly.

Her whole slender body stiffened in the dark. He could feel it as he reached out to put a hand on either of her shoulders.

"Did you 'spose I'd think you could? But ef you told 'em, couldn't you make 'em prove it? Ain't there any way? Do you hev to go away?" Her voice was wistful, pleading, and revealed her heart.

"Nobody would believe me, Randa. You know how folks are here about me."

"I know," she said sorrowfully, her voice trailing almost into tears.

"And anyhow," he added, "I couldn't because—well, Randa—I know who did it, and I wouldn't tell!"

His voice was deep and earnest. She understood. It was the rules of the game. He knew she'd understand.

"Oh!" she said in a breath of surrender. "Oh! O' course you couldn't tell!" Suddenly rousing, she added anxiously, "But you mustn't wait. Somebody might come by, and you ain't got a minute to lose. You'll take care o' yourself, Allan, won't you?"

" 'Course," he answered almost roughly. "And say, Randa—you're just a great little woman to help me out this way. I don't know's I ought to let you. It'll mebbe get you into trouble."

"Don't you worry 'bout me," said Miranda. "They ain't going to know anything about me helpin' you, and ef they did they can't do nothin' to a girl. I'd just like t' see 'em tryin' t' take it out o' me. Ef they dare I'll tell 'em how everybody has treated you all these years. You ain't had it fair, Allan. Now go quick—"

But the boy turned suddenly and took her in his arms, holding her close in his great rough overcoated clasp and putting his face down to hers as they stood in the deepest shadow of the old smokehouse.

"There wasn't ever anybody but you understood, Randa," he whispered, "and I ain't going to forget what you've done this time—" The boy's lips searched for hers and met them in a shy embarrassed kiss that sought to pay homage of his soul to her. "Good-bye, Randa. I ain't going to forget, and mebbe—mebbe someday I can come back and get you—that is, ef you're still here waiting."

He kissed her again impetuously, and then as if half ashamed of what he'd done he left her standing there in the darkness and slipped out through the blackness into the still, thick whiteness of the snow. He stepped from the door to the rail fence as she'd suggested and disappeared into the silence of the storm in the direction of the sugar maples.

Miranda stood still for several minutes unconscious of the cold, the night and her loneliness—despite the fact she'd taken off a warm overcoat and had no wrap over her flimsy little school dress. She wasn't cold now. A fine glow enveloped her in its beautiful arms. Her cheeks were warm with the touch of Allan's face, and her lips glowed with his parting kiss. But most of all his parting words had filled her with joy. He'd kissed her and told her he would come back and get her someday if she were still there waiting. What wonder! What joy!

The memory of those words hovered about her like some bright defending angel when Allan's father came six years later to ask her to marry him and taught her that fine scorn of him. It kept her there waiting all the years and drew her to the younger brother, who was like and yet so unlike Allan.

When Miranda realized where she was standing and that she must finish her work and get back to her room before she was discovered, she raised both hands to her face and laid them gently on her lips, one over the other, crossed, as if she'd touch and hold the sacred kiss that lay there the moment before. Then she lifted her face slightly, and with her eyes open looking up at the dark rafters and her fingers still lightly on her lips she murmured solemnly, "Thanks be!"

Gravely she reached and fastened the padlock with her warm fingers melting the snow that already again lay thick upon it. Then she made sure the key was safe about her neck and dropped inside her dress against her warm, throbbing breast to keep it from getting wet and telling tales. She struggled putting the beam back into place, forcing it into its fastening with all her might until it rested evenly against the door as before. With her hands and feet she smoothed and kicked the snow into levelness in front of the door.

She mounted the fence rail for an instant and glanced off toward the sugar maples but saw no sign of a dark figure creeping in the blanketed air of the storm and heard no sound but the steady falling of the snow, grain by grain, the little, mighty snow! In a few minutes all possible marks of the escape would be obliterated.

With a sigh of relief Miranda stole quickly back to the cherry tree. She'd intended to smooth her tracks in retreat one at a time so the snow would have less to do, but it wasn't necessary except around the smoke-house door. The snow was doing it all and well. Ten minutes would cover everything; half an hour would make it one white level plain.

Climbing the cherry tree was difficult with a chilled body and numb hands, but she accomplished it and crept back over the roof and into her window. Fortunately the snow was dry and brushed off easily. Her dress wasn't wet so she didn't need to invent an excuse for that. With deep thanksgiving she dropped on her knees beside her bed and sobbed her heart out into her pillow. Miranda didn't often cry. In a crisis she was ready for action. She could bear hardships with a jolly twinkle and meet snubbing with a merry grimace, but that kiss had broken her down. She cried as never before and prayed her odd heartfelt prayers.

"Oh, God, I never expected no such thing as his being good t' me. It was turrible good of You t' let him. An' I'm so glad he's safe! You won't let him get caught, will You? He didn't do it, You know—say, did You know?—'thout his tellin' You? I 'spose You did, but I like t' think You would a' let me save him anyway, even ef he had. But he didn't do it. He said he didn't, and You know he never told what wasn't so—he never minded even when it made out against him. But who did it?

"God—are You going to let Enoch Taylor die? Allan can't never come back ef You do. He said mebbe—but then I don't suppose there could ever be anythin' like that fer me. But, please, I thank You fer makin' him so kind. I can't never remember anybody to huv kissed me before. Of course it was dark, an' he couldn't see my red hair—but then he knowed it was there—he couldn't forget a thing like that—an' it was 'most as if I was real folks like any other girl.

"An', please, You'll take good care of him, won't You? Not let him get lost er froze er hungry, an' find him a nice place with a warm bed an' work to do so's he can earn money, 'cause it ain't in conscience people'll find out how folks felt about him here. He ain't bad, You know, and anyhow You made him, and You must uv had some trust in him. I guess You like him pretty well, don't You, or You wouldn't uv let me get him away 'thout bein' found out. So, please, I thank You, and ef You've got ennythin' coming to me anytime that's real good, jest give it to him instead. Amen."

The prayer ended, she crept into her bed, her heart warm and happy. Though the hour was well on to morning she couldn't sleep, for she kept going over the wonderful experience in the smokehouse. Allan's tired, regular breathing, the soft feel of his hair when she touched it, his cheek against hers, his lips when they kissed her and his whispered words—all stirred something in her heart. What it meant to her for him to take her in his arms and thank her that way and be so kind and glad for what she did, only a lonely, loveless girl like her could understand. She felt she'd have laid down her life to save him.

That was twelve long years ago, and not a word had been heard from Allan since. Yet on starlit nights Miranda looked out, remembered and waited. Long ago she'd given up all hope of his return. He was dead or married, or he'd forgotten, she told herself in her practical daytime thoughts. But when night came and the stars looked down upon her she thought of him, that perhaps he was somewhere looking at those same stars, and she prayed he might not be in want or trouble —so she waited.

She found it hard to believe Allan could die easily; he was so young and strong and vivid—so adequate to all situations. It was easy to find excuses for his not coming back. The world was large and far apart in those days of few railroads, expensive travel and no telegraph. Even letters were expensive and not unduly indulged in. It would still be dangerous for him to return, for old Enoch Taylor's sudden and tragic death, when he was shot in the back near the edge of town at early candlelight, was still remembered. And the shadow of young Allan's supposed crime and mysterious disappearance had fallen over his younger brother's reputation and made it what it was. Even his father spoke of him just to warn his younger sons now and then not to follow in his footsteps. Only in Miranda's heart did he really live. That was why his younger brother, slender and dark and in many ways much like him, found a warm place in her heart and love, for he seemed somehow like Allan come back to her again.

Love wasn't in just getting it back again to yourself. It was great just to love, just to know a beloved one existed.

Not that Miranda ever reasoned things out in so many words. She was keen and practical in daily life. But in her dreams strange notions floated half formed amid her practicalities, and great truths loomed large upon her otherwise limited horizon. Thus she often caught life's meaning where wiser souls have failed.

The world is not so large and disconnected after all. One evening, soon after Miranda went next door to live with David and Marcia, she heard David reading the *New York Tribune* aloud to his wife while she sewed—little news items, what the politicians were doing and how work was progressing on the canal locks.

"Listen to this," he said half amusedly. "A boy has traveled through England, Ireland, and Wales with only fifty-five dollars when he started and has returned safely. He says he's only five dollars in debt and gives as his reason for going that he *wished to see the country!*"

Miranda didn't understand the sympathetic glance of amusement that passed between husband and wife. Her attention was caught by the facts. A boy! Traveled through all those countries! How like Allan to do that and on just a little money! It was like him, too, to want to see things. It was one thing that had always made good practical people misunderstand him—that wanting to do things just because it was pleasant to do them and not for any gain or necessity. Miranda smiled to herself as she set the heel of the stocking she was knitting. But she never saw how strange it was that she, the most practical of human beings, should heartily understand and sympathize with the boy idealist. Perhaps she had the same thing in her own nature but never knew it.

Nevertheless, it became a pleasant pastime for Miranda to look up at the stars at night and share with them her belief it was Allan who journeyed all that way and her pleasure in feeling he was back in his own land again, nearer her. All these years she'd dreamed out things he might have done. As the years passed, however, and he didn't come, her dreaming became almost without foundation, a foolish amusement of which she was fond, but ashamed, and only to be indulged in when the world was asleep and no one could know.

Thus Miranda watched for the light in the gable window across the way, and when it didn't come she knew Nathan had crept to his bed without a candle. Soon she went to her bed and dreamed Allan came and kissed her as he did so long ago when she was only a little girl.

Chapter 7

For the next few years after his father's marriage to Maria Bent young Nathan Whitney lived two distinct lives. One he lived in the village and the red schoolhouse, where he was rated the very worst boy in town and all the more despised and hunted by everyone in authority because he was bright enough to be better. The other he lived in the company of Miranda and little Rose, out in the woods and fields, down by the trout brook fishing or roaming through the hills watching birds and creeping things. Sometimes he'd sit at little mother Marcia's feet as she told beautiful stories to Nate and Rose and held in her arms little Rose's sleeping baby brother.

Here he was a different being. Every hard handsome feature of his face softened into gentleness and set with purpose. All the stubbornness and native error melted away, and his great brown eyes seemed to be seeing things too high for an ordinary boy to comprehend. One could be sure he almost worshipped Marcia, the girl-wife of David Spafford, and looked into her face as she talked or sang softly to her baby, with a foreshadowing of the look the man he was to be would have someday for the mother of his children.

As for little Rose, she was his comrade and pet. With her, always accompanied by Miranda carrying a generous lunch basket, he roamed all the region round about on pleasant holidays. He taught her to fish in the brook, jump and climb like any boy, and race over the hills with him. Miranda, pleased, would stray behind and catch up with them now and then or sit and wait till they chose to race back to her.

Rose thought Nathan the strongest and best boy in town, or in the world, for that matter. He was her devoted slave when she demanded flowers or a high branch of red leaves from the tall maple. For her sake he applied himself to his lessons as never before, because the first day of her advent in school he found her with red eyes from weeping her heart out at the reprimand he'd received for not knowing his spelling lesson. Spelling was his weakest point, but after that he scarcely ever missed a word. His school life became decidedly better as far as knowing his lessons was concerned, though his pranks continued.

Rose, in truly feminine fashion, rather admired his pranks, and he knew it. He always tried to keep them under control, however, after the day the teacher started to whip him and Rose walked up the aisle with flashing eyes and cheeks like two flames and said in a brave little voice: "Teacher, Nate didn't throw that apple core at all. It was Wallie Eggleston. I saw him myself!" Then her lip trembled, and she broke down in tears.

Nate's face crimsoned, and he hung his head, ashamed. He hadn't thrown the apple core, but he'd done enough to deserve the whipping and knew it. From that day he refrained from over torment of the teacher and kept his daring feats for out of school. Also he taught Rose, by that unspoken art of a boy, never to "tell on" another boy again.

Marcia watched the intimacy of the little girl and big boy favorably. She felt it was good for Rose and good for the boy, also. Always Miranda or she was at hand, and never had either of them doubted the wisdom of the comradeship that had grown between the two children.

But matters wouldn't likely continue this way without someone's interference. Nathan Whitney got into too many scrapes and slid out of their consequences with a too exasperating skill to have many friends in town. His impudence was unrivalled, and his daring was equalled only by his indifference to public opinion. Such a state of things naturally didn't make him liked or understood.

No one but the three—Rose, her mother, and Miranda—ever saw the gentle look of holy reverence on his handsome face or heard the occasional brief utterances which showed his thoughts were tending toward higher ambitions and finer principles. No others saw the rare smile that glorified his face by a gleam of the boy's real soul. In after years Marcia often recalled the beautiful youth seated on a low stool holding her baby boy carefully. His face was filled with deep pleasure at the privilege, his whole spirit in his eyes in wonder, awe and gentleness as he looked at the little living creature in his arms or handled it shyly, with rarely tender touch, while Rose sat close beside him content. At such times the boy seemed almost transfigured.

Neither Marcia nor Miranda knew the Nathan who broke windows, threw stones or tied old Mr. Smiles's office door shut while he was dozing over his desk one afternoon. Nor did they know the one who filed a bolt, letting out a young scapegrace from the village lockup and helping him escape from justice and an unappreciative neighborhood into the world. They saw only Nathan's angelic side that nobody else in the world dreamed he possessed.

Nathan spent little time in his home. Shelter during his sleep and food enough to keep him alive were all he needed from it, and more and more the home and the presiding genius there learned to require less of him. She knew she didn't possess the power to make him do what she required. Nathan wouldn't perform any duties about the house or yard unless someone stood over him and kept him at it. If his stepmother attempted to make him rake the leaves in the yard and took her eyes from him a minute, he was gone and wouldn't return until sometime the next day.

An appeal to his father brought only a cold response. Nathan Whitney senior wasn't calculated by nature to deal with his alert temperamental son, and he knew it. He informed his wife concisely that that was why he married her, or words to that effect, and she appealed no more.

Gradually Nathan Whitney junior had his way and was left alone, for what could she do? When she attempted to discipline him he wasn't there. He wouldn't return for hours, sometimes even days, until she became alarmed lest he'd run away like his older brother and she might be blamed for it. She found her husband wasn't as easily ruled as she'd supposed, and her famous discipline from school-day times must be limited to the little girls and baby Samuel.

Nathan seemed to know by instinct just when it was safe to return and drop into family life as if nothing had happened and be left alone. One word or look and he was off again, staying in the woods for days and knowing wild things, trees and brooks as some men know books. He could always earn a few pennies doing odd jobs for men in the village, for he was smart and handy and with what he earned kept himself comfortably during his temporary absences from the family board. As for sleeping, he well knew and loved the luxury of a bed on the pine needles under the singing, sighing boughs or tucked under the sheltering ledge of a rock on a stormy night. His brooding young soul watched storm and lightning with wide eyes and thought much about the world and its ways. Now and again the result of these thoughts would come out in a single wise sentence to Miranda or little Rose and rarely, but sometimes, to Mrs. Marcia, always shyly and as if he'd been surprised out of his natural reserve.

Nathan made no display of his intimacy at the Spaffords'. When he went there it was usually just at dusk, unobtrusively slipping around to

Miranda at the back door. When they went roaming on the hills or fishing, he never started out with them. He always appeared in the woods just as they were beginning to think he'd forgotten. He usually dropped off their path on the way home by going across lots before they reached the village, having a fine instinct it might bring criticism upon them if they were seen with him.

And thus, because of his carefulness, the beautiful friendship between Rose and the boy went on for some years, and no one thought anything about it. Nathan never attempted to walk home from school with Rose as other boys did with the girls they admired. Once or twice when an unexpected rain came on before school closed he slid out of his last class and whirled away through the rain to get her cloak and umbrella, returning just as school "let out," drenched and shamefaced. But he let the little girl think her father had brought them and asked him to give them to her.

One unlucky day, toward evening, Nathan slipped in at the side gate and brought a great bag of chestnuts for Rose, while David's two prim maiden aunts, Miss Amelia and Miss Hortense Spafford, were tying on their bonnets before going home after an afternoon call.

When Nathan perceived the guests, his face grew dark, and he backed away toward the door, holding out the bag of nuts toward Rose and murmuring that he must go at once. By some slip the bag fell between the two, and the nuts rolled out in a brown rustling shower over the floor. The boy and girl stooped in quick unison to pick them up, and their golden and brown curly heads struck together in a sounding crack. They forgot their elders' presence and broke into laughter, as they ruefully rubbed their heads and gathered up the nuts.

Nathan was his gentle best self for three or four whole minutes while he picked up nuts and made comical remarks in a low tone to Rose, unconscious of the grim visages of the two aunts in the background. They, meanwhile, had paused with horrified astonishment in tying their bonnet strings, to observe the evident intimacy between their grandniece and a dreadful boy they recognized as that rascal son of Nathan Whitney.

Marcia didn't notice their expressions at first. She was standing close by with her eyes on the graceful girl and alert boy as they struggled playfully for the nuts. She liked to see the two together in the entire unconsciousness of youth playing like children.

But Nathan, sensitive almost to a fault, was quick to feel the antagonistic atmosphere and suddenly looked up to meet those two keen old pairs of eyes focused on him in disapproval. He colored all over his handsome face, then grew white and sullen as he rose suddenly to his feet and flashed his defiant habitual attitude, never before worn in the Spafford house.

He stood there for an instant, white with anger, with his brows drawn low over his fine dark eyes, his chin raised slightly in defiance (or was it only haughtiness and pride?), his shoulders thrown back and his hands unconsciously clenched down at his sides, and looked straight back into those two pairs of condemning, disapproving eyes. In doing so he seemed to embody the modern poem "Invictus." And if he'd been a picture it would have borne the inscription "Every man's hand is against me."

There was utter silence in the room, while four eyes condemned and two eyes defied—offending anew by their defiance. The atmosphere of the room seemed charged with lightning, and oppression sat suddenly on the hearts of the mother and daughter who stood by, with growing indignation. What right had the aunts to look that way at Nathan in his friends' house?

In vain Rose summoned a merry laugh, and Marcia tried to say something pleasant to Nathan about the nuts. It was as if they hadn't spoken. They weren't even heard. The contest was between the aunts and the boy, and, in the eyes of the two watching, the boy came off victor.

"What right have you to look at me like that? What right have you to condemn me unheard and wish me off the face of the earth? What right have you to resent my friendship with your relatives?" That was what the boy's eyes said.

And the two narrow-minded little old ladies, red with indignation, cold with pride and prejudice, declined to look honestly at the question but let their eyes condemn merely for the joy of condemning him whom they'd always condemned.

The boy's haughty undaunted look held them at bay for several seconds, before he turned coolly away and, with a bow of real grace to Marcia and Rose, went out of the room and closed the door quietly behind him.

Silence filled the room. The tenseness in all faces remained until they heard him walk across the kitchen entry and close the outside door, heard his quick, clean step on the flagstones that led around the house and then heard the side gate click. He was gone out of hearing, and Rose drew a quick involuntary sigh. He was safe, and the storm hadn't broken in time for him to hear. But it broke now in low threats of look and tone. Rose was shriveled to misery by her aunts' contemptuous glances, coming as they did in unison and meaning only one thing, that she was to be blamed in some way for this terrible disgrace to the family. Having disposed of Rose to their satisfaction, they turned to her mother.

"Well, I must say I'm surprised, Marcia." It was Aunt Amelia as usual who opened up the first gun. "In fact, to be plain, I'm deeply shocked! Living as you have in this town for thirteen and a half years now [Aunt Amelia always aimed to be exact], you must know what a reputation that boy has. It's the worst in the county, I believe. And you, the mother of a sweet daughter just budding into womanhood [Rose was nearly eleven], should be so unwise, even wicked and thoughtless, as to allow a person of Nathan Whitney's character to enter your house intimately —through the back door unannounced—and to present your daughter with a gift! I'm shocked beyond words to express—"

Aunt Amelia paused impressively and stood looking steadily at the indignant Marcia, shaking her head slightly as if the offense were too great to be quite comprehended in a breath.

Then Aunt Hortense took up the condemnation. "Yes, Marcia, I'm deeply grieved," she spoke weepily, "to think our beloved nephew's wife, who's become one of our own family, should forget herself and her position, and her family's rights, and allow that scoundrel to enter her doors and speak to her child. It's beyond belief! You can't be ignorant of his character, my dear! You must know he's the one who's committed all the outrages in this town, or he's instigated them. And in my mind that's even worse, because it shows cowardice in not being willing to bear the penalty himself—"

At this point Rose, with flashing blue eyes and cheeks as red as the flowers she was named after, stepped forward.

"Aunt Amelia, Nathan isn't a coward! He isn't afraid of anything in the whole world! He's brave and splendid!"

Aunt Amelia turned shocked eyes upon her grandniece, and Aunt Hortense, chin up, fairly snuffed the air.

"In my days little girls didn't speak until they were spoken to and were never allowed to put in when their elders were speaking!"

"Yes, Marcia," agreed Aunt Hortense, getting out her handkerchief and wiping her eyes, "you see what your headstrong ideas have brought upon you already. You can't expect to have a well-behaved child if you allow her to associate with rough boys, especially when you pick out the lowest in the village, the vilest of the vile!"

Aunt Hortense had the fire of eloquence in her eyes, and plainly more would follow. The village bad boys were her especial hobby, and for ten years she'd held a grudge against Nathan because of her pet cat.

Marcia, cool and controlled, tried to interrupt. She was feeling angry both for her sake and the boy's, but she knew she could do nothing to pour oil on the troubled waters if she lost her temper.

"I think you've made a mistake, Aunt Hortense," she said gently. "Nathan isn't a bad boy. I've known him a good many years, and he has some beautiful qualities. He's been over here playing with Rose a great deal, and I've never seen him do a mean or selfish thing. In fact, I'm very fond of him, and he's made a good playmate for Rose. He's a little mischievous, of course—most boys are—but there's no real badness in him, I'm sure."

Rose looked at her mother with shining gratitude, but the two old ladies stiffened visibly in their wrath.

"I'm mistaken, am I?" sniffed Aunt Hortense. "Yes, I suppose young folks always think they know more than their experienced elders. I have to expect that, but I must do my duty. I'll feel obliged to report this to my nephew, and he must deal with it as he sees fit. But whether you think I'm mistaken or not, I know you are, and you'll sadly rue the day when you let that young emissary of Satan darken your door."

Aunt Hortense retired into the folds of her handkerchief, but Aunt Amelia at this juncture swelled forth in denunciation.

"You're quite wrong, Marcia, in thinking my sister mistaken," she said severely. "You forget yourself when you attempt to tell your elders they're mistaken. But you're excited—you're young [as if that were the worst offense in the category]. My sister and I have had serious reason to know what we're talking about. Our pet cat, Matthew—you may remember him as still being with us when you came to live here; he died about five years ago, you know—was as inoffensive and kind an animal as one could have about a house. He was tortured terribly before our very eyes by this same paragon of a boy you're attempting to uphold.

"My dear [here she lowered her voice and hissed out the words with her thin lips], that dreadful boy tied a tin can filled with pebbles to our poor dear Matthew's tail. Think of it! His tail—that he always kept so beautifully clean and tucked around him so neatly! We always had a silk patchwork cushion for him to lie on by the fire, and he never presumed upon his privileges. Then for him to be so outraged! My dear, it was more than human nature could bear. Poor Matthew was frantic with fear. He was a dignified cat and had always been treated with consideration, and of course he didn't know what to make of it. He tried to break away from his tormentors but couldn't, and the tin can came after him, hitting his poor little heels.

"Oh, I can't describe to you the awful scene! Poor Hortense and I stood on the stoop and fairly implored that little imp to release poor Matthew, but he went after him all the harder—the vile little wretch—and poor Matthew didn't return to the house until after dark. For days he sat licking his poor disfigured tail, from which the beautiful fur had all been rubbed, and looking reproachfully at us—his best friends. He lived four years after that, but he never was the same cat! Poor Matthew! And I always thought that caused his death! Now do you understand, Marcia?"

"But, Aunt Amelia," broke in Marcia gently, trying not to smile, "that was nine years ago, and Nathan has grown up now. He was only five or six years old then and had run wild since his mother's death. He's almost sixteen now and very much changed in a great many ways—"

The two old ladies frowned upon her at once in differing magnitudes.

" 'If they do these things in a green tree, what shall be done in the dry?' " quoted Aunt Amelia solemnly. "No, Marcia, you're mistaken. The boy was bad from his birth. We aren't the only ones who've suffered. He's tied strings across the sidewalk many dark nights to trip people. I've heard of hundreds of his pranks, and now he's older he doubtless carries his accomplishments into deeper crime. I've heard he does nothing but hang around the stores and post office. He's a loafer, nothing short of it. As for honesty, there isn't a safe orchard in the neighborhood. If he'll steal apples, he'll do worse when he gets the chance—and he'll make the chance, you may depend upon it. Boys like that always do.

"You've taken a great risk in letting him into your house. You have fine old silver that's been in the family for years and many other valuable things. He may take advantage of his knowledge of the place to rob you some dark night. And as for your child, you can't tell what awful things he may have taught her. I've often watched his face in church and thought how utterly bad and without moral principle he looks. I wouldn't be at all surprised if he turned out one day to be a murderer!"

Aunt Amelia's tones had been rising as she reached this climax. As she spoke the word "murderer" she threw the whole fervor of her intense and narrow nature into her speech, pausing dramatically to impress her audience.

Suddenly, like a flash of a glittering sword in the air, a piercing scream arose. As she might have screamed if someone had struck her, Rose uttered her furious young protest against injustice. Her beautiful little face, flushed with outraged innocence and glorious in its righteous wrath, shone through the gathering dusk in the room and fairly blazed at her startled aunts. They jumped as if she were some wild animal let loose upon them. The scream cut through the space of the little room, seeming to pierce everyone in it, and quickly upon it came another.

"Stop! Stop!" she cried as if they were continuing. "You'll not say those things! You're bad, wicked women! You'll not say my Nathan is a murderer. You're a murderer yourself if you say so. The Bible says he that hateth his brother is a murderer, and you hate him or you wouldn't say such wicked things that aren't true. You'll not speak them anymore. My Nathan is a good boy, and I love him. Don't you dare talk like that again."

Another scream pointed the sentence, and Rose burst into a furious fit of tears and flew across the room, fairly flinging herself into her mother's arms and sobbing as if her heart would break.

Into this tumultuous scene came a calm, strong voice: "Why, what does all this mean?"

Chapter 8

The aunts looked up from their fascinated, horrified stare at their grandniece to see two doors on opposite sides of the room open and a figure standing in each. In the front hall doorway stood David, perplexed, seeking an answer in his wife's face. In the pantry doorway stood Miranda, arms akimbo, nostrils spread, eyes blazing like the warhorse she was, snuffing the bale from afar and only waiting to be sure how the land lay.

For a moment nobody could say anything, for Rose's sobs drowned out everything else. Marcia had all she could do to soothe the excited child who'd been so restrained for a few minutes that she was now like a runaway team going downhill, unable to stop.

David had sense enough to keep still until the air cleared. Meanwhile he studied the faces of each one in the room, not forgetting Miranda, and could get a pretty clear idea of how matters stood before anybody explained.

Presently, however, Rose subsided into low convulsive sobs smothered in her mother's arms.

Marcia drew the little girl down into her lap in the big armchair and, laying her lips against the hot wet cheek, said softly, "There, there, Mother's dear child—get calm, little girl—get calm. Get control of yourself."

The sudden lull gave an opportunity for speech, and Aunt Amelia, shaken in body if not in mind, hurried to avail herself of it.

"You may well ask what this means, David," she began, gathering her forces for the combat and reaching out to steady her trembling hand on the back of a chair.

"Sit down, Aunt Amelia," said David, bringing forward two chairs, one for each of the old ladies. "Sit down and don't excite yourself. There's plenty of time to explain."

"Thank you," said Aunt Amelia, drawing herself up to her full height. "I prefer to stand until I've explained my part in this disgraceful scene. I want you to understand that what I've said has been wholly unbiased. I've been merely trying to protect you and your child from the thoughtless folly of one whose youth must excuse her for her conduct. Your wife, David, has been letting your innocent daughter associate with a person wholly unfit to mingle in respectable society. He came in tonight while we were here, a rough, ill-bred, lubberly fellow, whose familiarity was an insult to your home.

"I was merely informing Marcia what kind of boy he was when Rose broke out into the most shocking screams and used the most disrespectful language toward me, showing plainly the result of her companionship with evil. Not only that, but she expressed herself in terms that were unseemly for a girl, almost a woman, to use. Your mother would never have allowed herself to forget herself and say she loved—actually loved, David—a boy. And that, too, a boy who only needs a few more years to become a hardened criminal. I refer to that scoundrel, Nathan Whitney's son. And she dared to call him hers—my Nathan, she said—and was most impudent in her address to me. I think she should be punished severely and never allowed to see that young wretch again. I'm sure you'll bear me out in feeling I've been outraged—"

But now Rose's sobs dominated everything again, heartbroken and indignant, and Marcia had much to do to keep the child from breaking away from her and rushing from the room. David looked from one to another of his excited relatives and prepared to pour oil on the troubled waters.

"Just a minute, Aunt Amelia," he said coolly, as soon as he could be heard. "I think there's been a little misunderstanding here—"

"No misunderstanding at all, David," said the old lady severely, drawing herself up with dignity again. "I assure you there's no possible chance for misunderstanding. Your wife actually professes fondness for the scoundrel, calls his wickedness mischief and tries to condone his faults, when everybody knows he's been the worst boy in town for years. I told her I'd inform you of all this and demand for the sake of the family honor that you never allow that fellow!—that loafer!—that low-down scoundrel!!—to enter this house again or speak to our grandniece on the street."

Miss Amelia was trembling with rage and insulted pride and was purple in the face. At this juncture Miranda beat a hasty retreat to the pantry window.

"Goodness!" she exclaimed softly to herself. "Wouldn't that old lady make a master hand at cussin' ef she jest didn't hev so much fambly pride! She couldn't think of words 'nough to call 'im."

Miranda stood for a full minute chuckling and thinking and staring at the sky that was just reddening with the sunset. Words from the other room hurried her thinking. Then with cool deliberation she approached the door again to reconnoiter and take a hand in the battle.

David was just speaking. "Aunt Amelia, suppose we lay this subject aside for a time? I feel I'm fully capable of dealing with it. I have entire confidence in anything Marcia has done, and I'm sure you will also when you hear her side of the matter. Rose doubtless is overwrought. She's very fond of this boy, for he's been her playmate for a long time and has been very gallant and loyal to her in many ways—"

But Aunt Amelia wasn't to be appeased. Two red flames of wrath stood on her thin cheekbones, declaring war, and two swords glanced from her sharp black eyes. Her bony old hands grasped the back of the chair shakily, and her whole body trembled. Her thin lips shook nervously and caught on her teeth in an agitated way as she tried to enunciate her words with extreme dignity and care.

"No, David, we will not lay the subject aside," she said, "and I shall never feel confidence in Marcia's judgment after what she has said to me about that young villain. I must insist on telling you the whole story. I cannot compromise with sin!"

And then Miranda discreetly approached with a smile of sweetness on her freckled face.

"Miss 'Meelia, 'scuse me fer interruptin', but it wasn't your spare bedroom winders I see open when I went by this afternoon, was it? You don't happen t' r'member ef you left 'em open when you come away, do yeh? 'Cause I thought I sensed a thunderstorm in the air, an' I thought mebbe you'd like me to run down the street an' close 'em fer you, ef you did. Miss Clarissa's all alone, ain't she?"

"A thunderstorm!" said Miss Amelia, stiffening into attention at once, alarm bristling from every loop of ribbon on her best black bonnet. "We must go home at once! I never like to be away from home in a thunderstorm. One can never tell what may happen. Come—let's hurry."

"A thunderstorm!" said David incredulously.

Then, catching the innocent look on Miranda's face, he stopped suddenly. The sky was as clear as an evening bell, and a single star glinted out at that moment as the two old ladies hurried out of their nephew's door. But they didn't see it. And David, thinking there was more than one kind of thunderstorm, said nothing. It might be as well to let the atmosphere clear before he took a hand in affairs.

"Shall I walk down with you, Aunt Amelia?" he asked half doubt-fully, glancing back toward the stairs up which Marcia had just taken the sobbing Rose.

"No, indeed, David," said Miss Amelia decidedly. "Your duty is to your family at a time like this. One can never tell what may happen, as I said before, and my sister and I can look out for ourselves."

They closed the door and hastened down the walk.

Miranda stood at the side gate with bland benevolence on her features.

"You got plenty o' time," she said smilingly. "You ain't got any call to hurry. It'll be quite a spell 'fore the storm gets here. I'm a pretty good weather profit."

"It isn't best to take chances," said Aunt Hortense, looking up ner-vously at the rosy sky. "Appearances are often deceitful, and a great many windows must be closed for the night."

They swept on down the street, and Miranda watched them a moment with satisfaction. Then she looked over at the white-pillared house across the way and frowned. The mother in her trembled at the injustice done the boy she'd grown to love.

"There's some folks has a good comeuppance comin' to 'em some-wheres, or I miss my guess," she murmured, turning slowly toward the kitchen door and wondering what Mr. David would think of her. Mr. David was too sharp to be deceived long about a thunderstorm, and she wouldn't like to incur his disfavor, for she worshipped him from afar.

Miranda went into the house and made herself scarce for a while, moving conspicuously among her pots and pans and voicing her hilar-ity in a hymn the church choir had sung the day before.

But David was for the present quite occupied upstairs. The trembling Rose was fully subdued and quite horrified at what she'd said to her aunts, for she'd always been taught to show them the utmost respect. She lay now on her little bed with a pale, tear-stained face, her body now and then convulsed with a shivering sob. She confessed her sins freely after her aunts departed and agreed the only thing possible was an abject apology the next day. But her sweet drooping mouth and long fluttering lashes indicated her trouble wasn't gone, and at last she brought it out in a sobbing breath.

"Nathan won't come here anymore. I know he won't. I saw it in his face. He'll think you don't want him, and he'll never come round again. He's always that way. He thinks people don't like him." She began to cry softly again.

David sat down beside his little girl and questioned her. Sometimes Marcia added a gentle word, and the eyes of the father and mother met over the child in sweet confidence, with utmost sympathy for her in her childish grief. But they hadn't at all condoned the words she'd spoken in her quick wrath to her aunts.

"Well, little daughter, close up the tears now," said the father. "Tomorrow you'll go down to see your aunts and make it all right with them by telling them how sorry and ashamed you are for losing your temper and speaking disrespectfully to them. But you leave Nathan to me. I want to get acquainted with him. He must be worth knowing from all you've said."

"Oh, Father, you dear father!" exclaimed Rose ecstatically, springing up to throw her arms around his neck. "Will you truly get acquainted with him? Oh, you're such a good dear father!"

"I surely will," said David, stooping to kiss her. "Now get up and wash your face for supper, and we'll see what can be done."

A whispered conference in the hall for a moment with Marcia sent David downstairs as eagerly as a boy might have gone. Miranda's heart was in her mouth for a full minute when she looked up from the johnny-cake she was making for supper and saw him standing in the kitchen door. She thought a reprimand must surely be forthcoming.

"Miranda, do you have a good supper cooking, and do you think there'd be enough for a guest if I brought one in?"

"Loads!" said Miranda, drawing a deep breath of relief and beating her eggs with vigor. "How many of 'em?"

"Only one, and I'm not sure of him yet, but you might put another plate on the table," David said and, taking his hat from the hall table, went out the front door.

Miranda put her dish of eggs down on the kitchen table and tiptoed softly into the dining room where the window commanded a view of the street. The candles weren't yet lighted so she couldn't be seen from without, and curiosity was too much for her. She saw David walk across the street to the big pillared Whitney house. Just as he reached the gate she saw a dark figure that walked like young Nate come down the street and meet him. The two shadowy figures stood at the gate a minute or two talking. Then David turned and walked back to the house, and the boy scurried around to his own back door. Miranda hurried back to her eggs with a happy heart and was beating away serenely when David opened the kitchen door.

"Well, he'll be here in half an hour. Be sure to have plenty of jam and cake."

Then David went into the library, took out the New York evening paper, and was soon deeply engrossed in the latest reports of Professor Morse's new electromagnetic telegraph and a bill before Congress for appropriating thirty thousand dollars for its testing. It was one of the absorbing topics of the day, and David immediately forgot not only his guest but the unpleasant events that caused him to give the invitation.

In the kitchen Miranda dashed about stirring some tea cakes and setting out an assortment of preserves and jams boys are supposed to like. She no longer feared any reference to thunderstorms, as she sang her hymns loud and clear:

> *My willing soul would stay*
> *In such a frame as this,*
> *And wait to hail the brighter day*
> *Of everlasting bliss.*

Rose presently came down to the kitchen, chastened and sweet, with her eyes like forget-me-nots after the rain and her cheeks rosy. Miranda gave her a little hotcake from the pan and patted the soft cheek tenderly. She dared not speak openly against the prim aunts who'd brought all this trouble on her darling. But her looks pitied and petted Rose and assured her she didn't blame her for anything hateful she might have said to those old spitfires. Rose took the sympathy but didn't presume upon it, and her lashes drooped humbly over her cheeks. She knew now she was wrong to speak so to poor Aunt Amelia, no matter how excited she was. Aunt Amelia, of course, didn't know Nathan as she did and therefore couldn't get the right point of view. Aunt Amelia did it for what she thought was her good. That was what her mother wanted her to feel.

After eating her cake, Rose walked around the pleasant dining table and noted the festive air of jams and preserves, the sprigged china and the extra place opposite her own.

"Oh, is there going to be company?" questioned Rose, half dismayed.

"Your pa said there might be," said Miranda, trying not to show how glad she was.

"Who?"

"Your pa didn't say who," answered Miranda, as if she hadn't seen those two shadowy figures conversing outside the Whitney gate.

Rose slid into the library and sat down on the arm of her father's chair, putting a soft arm around his neck and laying her cheek against his.

"Father, Miranda says we're having company tonight?" She laid the matter before him seriously.

"Yes," said David, rousing out of his perusal of the various methods of insulating wires. "Yes, Rosy posy, Nathan Whitney's coming to supper. I thought I'd like to get acquainted with him at once."

"Oh, Father dear! You dear father!" cried Rose, hugging him with all her might.

Marcia came smiling downstairs. And just as Miranda was taking up the golden brown loaves of johnnycake, Nathan presented himself, shy and awkward but with eyes that danced with pleasure and anticipation. He'd done his best to put himself in festive array and was good to look on as he stood waiting beside his chair at the table with the candlelight from the sconces above the mantel shining on his short chestnut curls. He seemed to Rose suddenly to have grown old and tall, dressed up in his Sunday clothes, with his hair brushed and his high collar and neck cloth like a man. She gazed at him half in awe as she slipped into her chair and folded her hands for the blessing.

It was a strange sensation for Nathan, sitting there with his bowed head before that table loaded with tempting good things and listening to the simple strong words of the grace. The firelight and the candlelight played together over the room's hush. Opposite him was the little girl who'd been his pet and playmate in her pretty blue and white dress with her golden curls bowed—he could just see the sheen of gold in her hair as he raised his eyes in one swift glance. Miranda stood at the kitchen door with a steaming dish in her hand and her head bowed decorously, its waves of shining hair like burnished copper. And the gracious sweet lady mother he adored was seated there by his side. Strange thrills of hot and cold crept over his body, and his breath came slowly lest it sound too loud. This was actually the first time Nathan Whitney had ever taken a meal at any home other than his own!

Many meals he'd eaten out of a tin pail on his old scarred desk in school or down by the brook in summer. More meals he went without or took on the road, cold pieces hastily purloined in his aunt's or stepmother's absence. But never before had he been invited to supper and sat at a beautiful table with snowy linen, silver, china and all the good things people give company. All this in his honor! He was almost frightened at himself. Not that he was unaccustomed to nice things, for the great house across the way had plenty of fine linen, rare china and silver. But it hadn't been used familiarly since his mother's death and was mostly brought out for company occasions. And on those occasions it was young Nathan's habit to be absent, because the company always seemed to look at him as if he had no right in his father's house.

Chapter 9

He looked about the cheery table after grace was concluded. Nathan Whitney could hardly believe he was really here and by invitation. He rubbed his eyes and almost thought he must be dreaming. So he answered only briefly the opening remarks directed to him and mainly by "Yes, ma'am" and "No, ma'am," "Yes, sir" and "No, sir."

But David with rare tact told a story with a point so humorous Nathan forgot his new surroundings and laughed. After that the ice was broken, and he talked more freely; gradually his awe melted so he could do a boy's full justice to the good things Miranda had prepared.

The talk drifted to the telegraph, for David felt a deep interest in the great invention and couldn't keep away from the subject for long. Marcia, too, was just as interested and ready with intelligent questions to which the boy listened appreciatively. He had a boy's natural keenness for mechanical appliances, but no one had ever taken the trouble to explain the telegraph to him. David saw the boy's bright eyes watching him as he attempted to describe to Marcia the principle on which the wonderful new instrument was supposed to work. Then he went into more detail than needed for Marcia, who was following each account in the papers as eagerly as if she were a man and who, understanding, helped by asking questions. Finally the boy himself ventured one or two.

David was pleased to see understanding and insight in his questions, and his heart warmed quickly toward the young fellow. He forgot he was examining the guest at his maiden aunts' instigation and to protect his young daughter. He may never have thought of "getting acquainted" with Nathan, but he certainly didn't expect it to be so interesting and gratifying. He understood at once why Marcia said he was "unusual if you could only get at his real soul." As they talked, the boy's face brightened with pleasure in his surroundings, forgetting his usual feeling of being considered an outlaw.

David had studied the telegraph extensively and been present several times by special invitation when Professor Morse exhibited his instrument at work to a few scientific friends. He could therefore speak from an intimate knowledge of his subject.

The boy listened in charmed silence and at last broke forth: "Why doesn't he make a telegraph himself and start it working so everybody can use it?"

David explained how expensive it was to prepare the wire, insulate it and make the necessary parts of the instrument. Then he told him about the bill of appropriation for testing it that was before Congress at the time. The boy's eyes shone.

"It'll be great if Congress lets him have all that money to try it, I think—don't you? It'll be sure to succeed, won't it?"

"I think so," said David with conviction. "I'm firmly convinced the telegraph has come to stay. But it isn't strange that people doubt it. It's even a more wonderful invention than the railroad. Why, it's been only about fifteen years since people were hooting and crying out against the idea of the steam railway, and now look how many we have and how indispensable to travel it's become."

The boy looked at the man admiringly. "Say, you go on the railroad a lot, don't you?"

"Why, yes," said David, "my business makes it necessary for me to run up to New York frequently. You've been on it, of course?"

"Me? Oh, no! I've never been and never expect to have the chance, but it must be a great experience. I've tried to think how it would feel going along like that without anything really pulling you. I've dreamed lots of times about riding on the railroad, but I guess that's as near as I'll ever get."

"Well, I don't see why," said David. "Suppose you go up with me the next time I go. I'd like the company and can explain to you all about it. I know the engineer well, and he'll show us all about the engine's workings. Will you go?"

"Will I go?" exclaimed Nathan, excited. "Well, I guess I will if I get the chance. Do you mean it, Mr. Spafford?"

"Certainly," said David, smiling. "I'll be delighted to have your company. I'll probably go a week from today. Can you get away from school?"

Nathan's face darkened.

"I guess there isn't any school going to keep me out of that chance," he said.

"Would you like me to speak to your father about it?"

"Father won't care," said the boy looking up in surprise. "He never knows where I am—just so I don't bother him."

A fleeting wave of pity swept over Marcia's face as she took in what this must mean to the boy.

But David, seeing this was a sore point, said pleasantly, "I'll make that all right for you," and passed on to discuss the difference the steam railway had made in the length of time it took to go from one city to another and the consequent ease with which business could be transacted between places at a distance from one another. From that they went on to speculate about the changes that might come with the telegraph.

"Wouldn't it be wonderful to be able to get a message from Washington in half an hour, for instance?" said David. "Professor Morse claims it's possible. Many doubt it, but I'm inclined to believe he knows what he's doing and to think it's only a question of time before we have telegraphs all over the United States, at least in the larger cities and towns."

Nathan's eyes were large. "Say, it's a big time to be living in, isn't it?"

"It is indeed," said David, his eyes sparkling. "But, after all, have you ever thought that almost any time is a big time to be living in for a boy or a man who has a work to do in the world?"

It was beautiful to see the waves of feeling spread over the boy's face in rich coloring, and David could only admire him as he watched. How could people let this boy remain with the mark of evil on his reputation? Why had no one tried to pull him out of his lawless ways before? Why had he never tried? How could Mr. Whitney let a boy like this go to ruin as everybody said he was going? David resolved he'd never go if he could help save him.

While they talked, the johnnycake, biscuits, cold ham, fried potatoes, tea cakes, jam, preserves and cake were disappearing in large quantities, and at last it seemed the boy could eat no more. Marcia made a little movement to rise.

"We'll go in the other room for worship," she said and led the way to the parlor where Miranda had quietly preceded them and lit the candles.

An open fire was burning in the fireplace here, too, and the room was bright and cheery with stately reflections in polished mahogany furniture and long mirrors. Nathan hung back at the door and looked around almost in awe. He hadn't been in this room when he came to the house other times, and it seemed like entering a new world. Almost instantly his attention was held by the pianoforte that stood at one side of the room. And for the moment he forgot his shyness over the idea of "worship," which had brought a sudden tightness around his heart when Marcia mentioned it.

Worship in the Whitney home was dull, formal and wearisome. Nathan had escaped it in recent years, and neither his father's nor his stepmother's reprimands had made him even an occasional attendant. So when David Spafford invited him to supper it didn't occur to him family worship would be part of the evening's program. If he'd stopped to think he might have known, though, for David was a church elder, and it was strange for any respectable church family to be without family worship in that day. It was a mark of respectability if nothing else.

Miranda was waiting primly in her chair by the door with her hands folded in her lap and her most seraphic look on her merry face. One might almost say she seemed glorified tonight; her satisfaction beamed from every golden freckle and every gleaming copper wave of her hair.

Nathan dropped suddenly into the chair on the other side of the door, feeling awkward and out of place for the first time since his host had welcomed him and made him feel at home. Here in this "company" room, with a religious service before him, he was again keenly aware of his own shortcomings in the community. He didn't belong here, and he was a fool to come. The sullen scowl involuntarily darkened his brow as Rose slipped about the room giving each one a hymnbook— like church. Nathan took the book because she gave it, but his self-consciousness was so great he dropped it awkwardly, and, stooping to pick it up, his face reddened with embarrassment.

Marcia, noticing, tried to put him at ease. "What hymn do you like best, Nathan?"

The boy turned redder and mumbled he didn't know.

"Then we'll sing the shepherd psalm. Rose is fond of that," she said, seating herself at the pianoforte.

Nathan fumbled the pages until he found the place and then was suddenly entranced with the first notes of the tune as Marcia began to play it over.

Now young Nathan could remember hearing his mother sing the shepherd psalm to him when he was little and to the twins and Samuel when they were babies. He associated it with her gentle voice, her smiling eyes and her arms around him as she tucked him in at night. So when the song burst forth from the family's lips the young guest struggled to keep back a lump in his throat and a strange moisture in his eyes.

The Lord's my shepherd, I'll not want;
He makes me down to lie
In pastures green, He leadeth me
The quiet waters by—

Miranda's voice was high and clear while little Rose, sitting in the shelter of her father's arm, joined her bird-like treble to his bass, and Marcia sang alto, blending the whole most exquisitely. Nathan stole a covert glance about, saw they weren't noticing him at all and soon forgot his own situation and began to grumble out the air.

My table thou hast furnished
In presence of my foes—

(How he wished those Spafford aunts were there to see him sitting thus!)

My head thou dost with oil anoint
And my cup overflows.

He had a faint idea it was overflowing now.

Goodness and mercy all my life
Shall surely follow me;
And in God's house forevermore
My dwelling place shall be.

Would it? Wouldn't that be strange? Would his enemies be surprised someday if they found him dwelling in heaven?

They were only fleeting thoughts passing through his mind, but the psalm David read when the hymn was over kept up the thought: " 'Who shall ascend into the hill of the Lord? or who shall stand in his holy place? He that hath clean hands, and a pure heart; who hath not lifted up his soul unto vanity, nor sworn deceitfully. He shall receive the blessing from the Lord and righteousness from the God of his salvation.' "

Nathan looked down at his rough boy hands, scrubbed till they showed the lines of walnut stain from his afternoon's climbing after nuts. Clean hands and a pure heart? The hands could be made cleaner by continued washings—but the heart?

The boy was still thinking about it when they knelt to pray, and he heard himself prayed for as "our dear young friend who is with us tonight" and a blessing asked on his "promising young life." It was almost too much for Nathan. But the prayer just then branched off into matters of national importance in thanksgiving for "all the wonders wrought in this generation" and with a petition for the president and his cabinet that they might have light and wisdom to decide the vital questions placed in their keeping. Otherwise Nathan mightn't have made it through without shedding a tear in his excitement.

He rose from his knees with an uplifted expression on his face and looked about on the room and the dear people as if he'd suddenly found himself among angels.

Miranda bustled out to clear the table. Marcia called Nathan and Rose to the piano, and they all sang for a few minutes. Then she played one or two lively melodies for them. After that they all went into the library and, gathering around the big carved table, played jackstraws until it was Rose's bedtime. When Miranda finished the dishes she, too, came and took a hand in the game and kept them all laughing with her remarks about the jackstraws as if they were people.

When the hall clock struck the half hour after eight, Rose looked regretfully at her mother and, meeting her nod and smile, stood up and said good night. Nathan, taking her hand awkwardly for good night, arose also to make his adieus, but David told him to sit down for a few minutes; he wanted to talk to him. So while Marcia and Rose slipped away upstairs, and Miranda went to set the buckwheat cake for breakfast, Nathan settled back half scared and faced his host's pleasant smile. He wondered if he was to be called to account for some of his numerous pranks and if, after all, the happy time had only been a ruse to get him in a corner.

But David didn't leave him in uncertainty long.

"What are you going to do with your life, Nathan?" he asked kindly.

"Do with it?" asked the surprised Nathan. "*Do* with it?" Then his brow darkened. "Nothing, I s'pose."

"Oh, no, you don't mean that, I'm sure. You're too bright a boy for that, and this is a great age in which to be living, you know. You've got a man's work to do somewhere in the world. Are you getting ready for it, or are you just drifting yet?"

"Just drifting, I guess," said Nathan softly after considering.

"Don't see any chance for anything else," he added. "Nobody cares what I do anyway."

"Oh, that's nonsense. Why—Nathan—I care. I like you, and I want to see you succeed."

The boy's face and neck reddened, and his eyes flashed a wondering glance at David. He wanted to say something but couldn't. Words would choke him.

"You're going to college, of course?" asked David.

Nathan shook his head.

"How could I?" he asked. "Father'd never send me. He says any money spent on me is thrown away. He was going to send my half brother, Allan, to college, but he ran away, and he says he'll never send any of the rest of us—"

"Well, send yourself," said David as if it were expected for a loving parent to talk like that. "It'll really be the best thing for you in the end anyway. A boy who has to pay his own way makes twice as much of college as the fellow who has everything made easy for him, and I guess you have grit enough to do it. Get a job right away and begin to lay up money."

"Get a job! Me get a job!" laughed Nathan. "Why, nobody'd give me a regular job I could earn anything much with. They don't like me well enough. They wouldn't trust me. I can get errands and little things to do, but nobody would give me anything worthwhile."

"Why is that?" David asked, with an alert but kind look at him.

The boy blushed and dropped his eyes. At last he answered, "My own fault, I guess," and smiled as if he were sorry.

"Oh, well, you can soon make that right by showing them you're trustworthy now, you know."

"No," said the boy decidedly. "It's too late. Nobody in this town will give me the chance."

"I will," said David. "I'll give you a job in the printing office if you'd like it."

"Wouldn't I though!" said the boy, springing to his feet in his excitement. "You just try me. Do you really mean it?"

"Yes, I mean it," said David with a smile. "But how about the school?"

"Hang the school," said Nathan, frowning. "I want to go to work."

"No, it won't do to hang the school, because then you'll never be able to hold your own working or reach up to the bigger things when you've learned the smaller ones. How far are you in school? What are you studying?"

Nathan told him gloomily. It was plain the boy had little interest for his school.

"I been through it all before anyway," he added. "This teacher doesn't know as much as my—as—that is—as Miss Bent did."

His face was very red, for he couldn't bring himself to speak of his father's wife as mother.

David was quick to catch the idea. "I see. You're merely going over the old ground, and it isn't very interesting. How thoroughly did you know it before?"

Nathan shook his head. "Don't know. Guess I didn't study very hard, but what's the use? They never gave me credit anyway for what I did."

"Had any Latin?" David thought it better to ignore a discussion of teachers. He didn't think much of the present incumbent himself.

"No."

"Are you in the highest class?"

"Yes."

"What would you think of leaving school and working in the printing office days and studying Latin and mathematics with me evenings?"

The boy looked at David for a moment and then dropped his eyes and swallowed hard several times. When he finally raised his eyes again they were full of tears, and this time the boy wasn't ashamed of them.

"What would you do it for?" he asked when he could speak, with his voice utterly broken with feeling.

"Well, just because I like you and I want to see you get on. And, besides, I think I'd enjoy it. I'm glad you like the idea. We'll see what can be done. I think in two years at most you might be ready for college if you put in your time well, and by that time you should have saved at least enough to start you. There'll be ways to earn your board when you get to college. Lots of fellows do it. Shall I see your father about it, or would you rather do it yourself?"

"Father?" asked Nathan. "Why, you don't need to see Father. I never ask him about anything. He'd rather not be bothered."

Subsequent experience led David to believe Nathan was right. When he went to see Mr. Whitney the next day, that grim, unnatural parent strongly advised David to have nothing whatever to do with his scapegrace son. He declared himself unwilling to be responsible for any failure that might ensue if he went against this advice. He said Nathan was like his mother, not practical in any way, and that he'd been nothing but a source of anxiety since he was born. He'd kept him at school because he didn't know what else to do with him. He never expected him to amount to a row of pins.

With this encouragement David Spafford undertook the higher education of young Nathan Whitney, suspecting the father's lack of interest in the son's welfare had its source in an inherent miserliness. Mr. Whitney, however, gave a reluctant permission for his son to leave school and learn the printing business at the *Clarion Call*. But he vowed he wouldn't help him fool his time away and spend money pretending he was getting a college education. If he left school now he needn't expect to get a penny from him for any such nonsense, for he wouldn't give it.

David was wise enough that night, however, to say nothing further to the boy about consulting his father, merely telling him, as he said good night, that he'd expect him to be ready to go to New York with him a week from that day on the early morning train. They would then look into purchasing some Latin books and perhaps run over to the university and find out about entrance requirements so their work might be suitable.

In the meantime Nathan should finish out the week at school, since it was now Wednesday. That would allow time to arrange matters at the office and with his father; then if all was satisfactory he might come to the office Monday morning. He could do things both to prepare for the journey and, while they were away, to help with business, and his salary would begin Monday morning. It wouldn't be much at first, but he might consider that his work began Monday and that the trip to New York was all in the way of business.

With a heart almost bursting with wonder and joy, Nathan walked across the street to his home, climbed a tree to his bedroom window, for he couldn't bear to see anyone just yet, and crept to his bed. There kneeling with his face in the pillow, he tried to express in an odd little lonely prayer his thanks for this great thing. It was mingled with a wistful desire for the "pure heart and clean hands" of those who may have the Lord's blessing. With all his heart he meant to do his part toward making good.

Across the street, high in the side gable, Miranda's candle twinkled for a few minutes and then went out while its owner sat at the window, gazing out at the stars above her, thinking.

Now Miranda was the soul of honor on most occasions. But if it was to the advantage of those she loved for her to do a little quiet eavesdropping or stretch the truth to fit a particularly trying circumstance, she generally could convince her conscience to let her do it. Therefore, while David was talking with Nathan in the library, Miranda had a sudden call to hunt for something in the hall closet. It was located so close to the library door that one standing in the crack of one door might easily hear whole sentences of what was spoken behind the crack of the other door.

Miranda would never have listened if the visitor were an older person on business and only did it if she felt the inner call to help or protect someone. Tonight it was her great anxiety for Nathan that caused her to look so diligently for her overshoes, which she knew were standing in their appointed place in her own closet upstairs. But she heard a great deal of what David proposed to do for Nathan, and her heart swelled with pride and joy: pride in David and his wonderful little wife whom she knew was at the bottom of the whole scheme, and joy for Nathan of whom she was so fond and for whose reputation and encouragement she was intensely jealous.

So with a light heart and feet that almost danced she made her candlelit way to her little gable room and, after a few simple preparations for the night, put out the light and sat down under the stars to think.

Chapter 10

Nathan was on hand bright and early Monday morning at the office, with a look of suppressed excitement in his dark eyes and a dawning dignity and self-respect in his whole manner.

He'd never been expected anywhere and greeted as if he had a right to a businesslike welcome. Even in school he'd always felt the teacher's covert protest against him and maintained an attitude of having to fight for his rights.

"You're to use this desk for the present," said Morton Howe, the office manager, "and Mr. Spafford wants you to copy those names on that list into that ledger. He'll be down in about an hour. You'll find enough to keep you busy till then, I guess." The gracious old man pointed to a stool by a high desk and showed Nathan where to hang his cap.

"It's a real pleasant morning," he added by way of showing the new assistant a little courtesy. "I guess you'll like it here. We all do."

Nathan's face beamed unexpectedly. "I should say I would!"

"Mr. Spafford's a real kind man to work for." Morton Howe was in his employer's confidence and was also devoted to David.

"I should say he is!" responded Nathan.

Then a new life began for Nathan. The two days preceding the journey to New York were one long dream of wonder and delight to the boy. He had hard work, to be sure, but Nathan didn't have a lazy streak in him. Every word he copied, every errand he ran and every duty he performed gave him intense pleasure. To be needed and be able to please were so new to him that he looked on each moment of his day with awe lest it might prove a dream and slip away from him.

Never had one of David's workers been more attentive, more punctilious in performing a task or more respectful—and all his employees loved him.

"I see you got that young nimshi, Nate Whitney, in your office, Dave," said old Mr. Heath the second day of Nathan's service. "You better look out fer yer money. Keep yer safe well locked. He belongs to a bad lot. He's no good himself. I don't see what you took him for."

"I've never had a better office helper in my experience," said David crisply, with a smile. "He seems to have ability."

"H'mph!" said Grandfather Heath. "Ability to be a scamp, I'd say. You're a dreamer, David, like your father was before you, and there don't no good come of dreamin' in my opinion. You gen'ally wake up to find your nose bit off, er your goods stolen afore yer eyes."

"Well, I haven't found it that way yet," answered David good-naturedly, "and I shouldn't wonder if my boy Nathan will surprise you all someday. If I know anything at all he's going to amount to something."

"Surprise us all, will he? Wal, his brother did that a number of years ago when he made out to murder Enoch Taylor an' then git out o' the smokehouse 'ithout unlockin' the door, an' a beam acrost it, too. An' me with the key all safe in its usual place and no way of explainin' it, 'cept thet he must a carried some kind o' tools 'long with him and then fixed the lock all right so's we wouldn't suspect very early in the mornin'. Oh, he surprised us all right, an' your fine little man'll likely turn out to s'prise you in jest some sech way."

"By the way, Mr. Heath," said David, more to change the subject than because he had much interest in the matter, "how was it they suspected Allan Whitney of that murder? He never owned up to it, did he?"

"Oh, no, he lied about it, o' course."

"But just how did you ever get an idea Allan Whitney had anything to do with it? He didn't bring the news, did he? I've forgotten how it was—it happened so long ago."

"Not he, he didn't bring no news. He hed too much sense to bring news. No, it was Lawrence Billings brought word about findin' Enoch Taylor a moanin' by the roadside."

"Lawrence Billings!" said David. "Then where did Whitney come in? Billings didn't charge him with it, did he?"

"No, we caught Allan Whitney with a gun not a quarter of a mile away from the spot, tryin' to sneak around to git home 'thout bein' seen."

"But that wasn't exactly proof positive," said David, who had now reached his own gate and was in a hurry to get in the house.

"It was to anybody that knowed Allan," said the hard, positive old man. "An' ef it wa's't, what more'd you want thun his runnin' away?"

"That told against him, of course," said David quietly. "Well, Mr. Heath, I'm going to New York in the morning—anything I can do for you?"

"No, I gen'ally make out to do with what I ken get in our hum stores. You take a big resk when you travel on railroads. I saw in the New York paper the other day where a train of cars was runnin' west from Bawstun last Sat'day and come in contact with a yoke of oxen near Worcester, throwing the engine off the track and renderin' it completely unfit fer use—*and killin' the oxen!* It seems turrible to encourage a thing that's such a resk to life and property. And here just a few days back there was another accident down below Wilmington. They was runnin' the train *twenty miles an hour!* An they run down a hand car and overturned their engine and jest ruined it! A thing like that ain't safe ner reasonable. Too much resk fer me!"

"Yes, there has to be risk in all progress, I suppose. Well, good night, Mr. Heath," David said and went smiling into the house to tell Marcia how far behind the times their neighbor was.

Miranda was singing and hovering back and forth between the kitchen and dining room, trying to catch any news items. She was happy about the pleasure coming to Nathan the next day, and she heard the whole account of David's talk with Mr. Heath, though David thought she was absorbed in preparing supper. Miranda had a way like that, leaving an ear and an eye on watch behind her while she did duty somewhere else, and nobody suspected. It was always, however, a kind ear and eye for those she loved.

The reference to Allan Whitney and the murder brought a serious look to her face, and she managed to get behind the door and hear all of it. But when Lawrence Billings was mentioned, her face blazed with sudden illumination. Lawrence Billings! He committed the crime, of course! Strange she never thought of him before! Strange she never overheard he brought the news!

Lawrence Billings, as a little boy, had followed Allan Whitney like a devoted dog. His sleek head, pasty countenance and furtive blue eyes were always just behind wherever Allan went. No one ever understood why Allan protected him and tolerated him, for he wasn't Allan's type, and his native cowardliness was a byword among the other boys. His devotion may have touched the older boy, or else he felt sorry for his widowed mother, whose graying hair, tired eyes and drooping mouth looked pitifully like her son's.

However it was, it was understood from the first day little Lawrence Billings, carrying his slate under his arm and clinging to his mother's hand, was brought to the schoolhouse that Allan Whitney had constituted himself a defender. Miranda knew, for she'd stood by the school gate when they entered. And she saw the appeal of the widow's eyes toward the tall boy in the schoolyard as the rabble of hoodlums around her son set up a yell: "Here comes Mother's pet!"

Something manly in Allan's eyes had flashed forth and answered that mother's appeal in true knightly fashion, and never again did Lawrence Billings want for a champion while Allan was around. Of course Allan had protected Lawrence Billings! It was just like Allan, even though it meant his own reputation—yes, and life!

For a moment tears of pride welled into Miranda's eyes, and behind the kitchen door she lifted her face and muttered softly, "Thanks be!" as a recognition of the boy's nobility. Then she moved thoughtfully back to her cooking, though with an exalted look on her face, as if she'd seen the angel of renunciation and been blessed by it.

When she thought of Lawrence Billings, however, her face darkened. What of the fellow who would allow such sacrifice of one he professed to love? Did Lawrence know he'd exiled Allan from his home all these years? Did he realize what it had meant? Had he consented that Allan should take his crime, or was he in any way a party to the arrest?

Lawrence Billings still lived on the edge of the village in his mother's old rundown house and allowed his mother to take in sewing for her living and part of his, for his inefficiency had made it hard for him to get or keep any position. But Lawrence always managed to stay neatly dressed and go out with the girls whenever they'd have him. His unlimited leisure and habit of tagging made him a frequent sight at social gatherings, whether at church or in town.

But the thorough-going Miranda had always despised his weak mouth and expressionless eyes, though she'd tolerated him because of Allan. Now, however, her mind stirred fiercely against him. Could something be done to clear Allan Whitney's name even if he never came back to take advantage of it? It was terrible to have a man like Lawrence Billings walking around smirking when Allan was exiled and despised.

Of course, Miranda grudgingly admitted to herself she might be mistaken about Lawrence Billings being the criminal—but she knew she wasn't. Now that she'd thought of it, Allan's every word, his behavior toward Lawrence in the past, even the meaningful tone of his voice when he said, *"But I know who did it,"* pointed to the weaker man.

Miranda felt she had a clue, but she saw nothing she could do with it.

The conditions were the same as when Allan left. Mrs. Billings, just as faded and wistful, a bit more withered, was sewing away and coughing her little hacking apologetic cough on Sundays—a trifle more hollow perhaps, but just as sad and unobtrusive. Who could do anything against such a puny adversary? The girl had an instant's revelation of why Allan had run away instead of defending himself. It brooded with her through the night and while she was preparing the early breakfast Nathan was invited to share with David.

Fried mush, sausage and potatoes, topped off with doughnuts, coffee and applesauce—how good it tasted to Nathan, eaten in the early candlelit room, with the pink dawn just flushing the sky. Rose, her eyes still cloudy with sleep, sat opposite smiling. The boy felt as if he were transformed into another being and entering a new life where all was heaven.

Afterward they had a brief sweet worship. Then Miranda stuffed Nathan's pockets with seed cakes. Rose walked beside her father, holding his hand silently, while Nathan proudly carried the valise which held his own insignificant bundle with David's things. The early morning light was over everything, and summer had glanced back and waved a fleeting hand at the day with soft airs and a lingering warmth of sunshine. The boy's heart was fairly bursting with happiness.

Oh, the glories and wonders of that journey! At Schenectady the train stopped several minutes. David took Nathan forward and introduced him to the engineer, who kindly showed him the engine, taking apparent pride and pleasure in explaining every detail of its working. The engineer had become a hero to the boys and knew his admirers when he saw them. He invited Nathan to ride to Albany in the engine with him. With shining eyes the boy let David accept the invitation for him and climbed on board feeling as if he were about to mount up on wings and fly to the moon. David returned to his coach and his discussion of Whig versus Loco-Foco.

At Albany a new engineer came on duty, and Nathan went back to his place beside David in the carriage. But there he watched the new world with delight, and David was ready to explain everything and introduced him to two men nearby. One, a Mr. Burleigh, was going down to New York to give a lecture, "In Opposition to the Punishment of Death," as the notices in the *Tribune* stated. Nathan listened with tense interest to the discussion for and against capital punishment, the more because the subject had come so near the elder brother who'd been his youthful paragon and idol. David, turning once, caught the look in the boy's eyes and wondered again at the intellectual appreciation he seemed to have, no matter what the subject.

The other gentleman was a Mr. Vail, an intimate friend and close associate of Professor Samuel Morse, the inventor of the electromagnetic telegraph. He'd recently set up a private telegraph of his own at his home and was making interesting experiments in connection with Professor Morse. This man noticed the boy's deep interest when the subject was mentioned and the eager questions in his eyes that dared not come to his lips. He took out a pencil and paper, making numerous diagrams to explain the different parts of the instrument and the theory on which they worked. As the coach's occupants bent over the paper and listened to his story, the boy traveler almost forgot the beauties of the strange new way, and his eyes glowed over the fairy tale of science.

Then as they neared the great city of New York he'd dreamed so many dreams about, the boy's heart beat high with excitement. His face paled with suppressed emotion. He was a boy of few words and not used to letting anyone know how he felt, but the three men in the coach couldn't help seeing he was stirred.

"A fine fellow that," murmured Mr. Vail to Mr. Burleigh as the train drew in at the station and Nathan seemed engrossed in the various things David was pointing out to him.

"Yes," agreed Mr. Burleigh. "He asked some bright questions. He'll do something in the world himself one day, or I'm mistaken. Has a good face."

"Yes, a very good face. I've been thinking as I watched him this morning if more boys were like that we needn't be afraid for the future of our country."

Nathan turned then, lifting his eyes to the two men opposite him, and perceived in a flash, by their close talk, that the words he overheard were spoken about him. A look of wonder and then of deep shame crossed his face.

He dropped his gaze, and his dark lashes swept like a gloomy veil over the bright eager eyes that had glowed, while crimson spread over his face.

These gentlemen thought that of him seeing him once! But if they knew how people regarded him at home! Ah, if they knew! He could hear even now the echo of old Squire Heath's exclamations concerning him: "That young Whitney's a rascal an' a scoundrel. He should have his hide tanned."

Nathan's confusion was so great that it was unmistakable, and David turning toward him suddenly saw that something was wrong.

"I've just been caught in expressing my opinion of your young friend here," acknowledged Mr. Vail, smiling. "I hope he'll pardon my being so personal, but I've taken a great liking to him. I hope he'll find it possible to come to Philadelphia sometime soon and visit me. I can show him my instrument then. If you come down next month, perhaps you'll bring him with you."

The color flooding the boy's face was illumined by wonder as he looked from one gentleman to the other. Truly he'd been lifted out of his old life and set in a sphere where no one knew he was a worthless scoundrel not to be trusted. He heard David promising to bring him with him if possible the next time he went to Philadelphia, and he managed to stumble out a few broken words of thanks to both gentlemen, feeling all the time how inadequate they were. But words were unnecessary, for his eloquent eyes spoke volumes of gratitude.

The train came to a standstill then, and the fellow travelers exchanged pleasant good-byes. Afterward David and Nathan made their way through the city to the hotel where David usually stayed, while Nathan felt suddenly shy, young and countrified.

Chapter 11

The New York visit stretched into nearly two weeks, for the business on which David had come was important and proved more difficult to settle than he expected. Meanwhile life was a happy dream for Nathan. He was with David all day long, except when that busy man was closeted with some great men talking over private business matters. Even then David often took Nathan with him as his secretary, asking him to take notes of things that were said or occasionally to copy papers. The boy was acquiring great skill in such matters and could write a neat, creditable letter quite to his employer's satisfaction. He possessed a good, natural handwriting as well as a keen mind and willing heart, great assets in any work.

Everywhere they went, David explained who and what people, places and things were. Their trip was a liberal education for the boy. He met great men and saw the sights of the whole city.

Every evening when business allowed, they visited some gathering or entertainment. He heard a lecture of phrenology and magnetism which interested him and resolved to try some of the experiments with the boys when he got home. He attended the New York opera house for the thirty-eighth anniversary of the Peithologian Society of Columbia College, of which David Spafford was a member, and met Mr. J. Babcock Arden, the secretary, whose name was signed to the notice of the meeting in the *Tribune*. It seemed wonderful to meet a man whose name was printed out like that in a New York paper. Mr. Arden greeted him as if he were already a man and told him he hoped he'd be one of their number someday when he came to college. And Nathan's heart swelled with the determination to fulfill that hope.

They attended several concerts, and Nathan discovered he enjoyed music immensely. The Philharmonic Society gave its first concert during their stay in the city, and it was the boy's first experience in hearing fine singing. He sat as one entranced. Another night they heard Rainer and Dempster, two popular singers who were making a great impression, especially with their rendering of "The Lament of the Irish Emigrant," "Locked in the Cradle of the Deep" and "The Free Country." The melodies caught in the boy's brain and kept singing themselves over and over. He also came to know "Auld Robin Gray," a new and popular ballad, "The Death of Warren," "Saw Ye Johnnie Coming," and "The Blind Boy."

When he was alone he sang them over bit by bit until he felt they were his own. Thus, coming upon him unaware one day, David discovered the boy possessed a wonderfully clear, flute-like voice and resolved he must go to singing school during the winter and sing in the choir, for such a voice would be an acquisition to the church. He decided to talk with the minister about it as soon as he got home.

Two days after their arrival in New York the completion of the Croton Water Works was celebrated. Heralded for days beforehand both by friends and enemies, the day dawned bright and clear, and Nathan awoke as excited as if he were a little boy on General Training Day.

A six-mile pageant formed on Broadway and Bowling Green, marching through Broadway to Union Square and down Bowery to Grand Street. Twenty thousand were numbered in the procession, and so great was the enthusiasm, according to the papers, that "there might have been two hundred thousand if there had been room for them."

First came the New York firemen, whose interest in the new water system was natural, and in full uniform the Philadelphia firemen followed, with their helmets and bright buttons gleaming in the sun. Then came the Irish and the Germans, with banners and streamers flying in a brilliant display.

A float bore the identical printing press on which Franklin worked, and Colonel Stone sat in Franklin's chair printing leaflets all about the Croton Water Works, which were distributed along the way as the procession moved. Another float bore two miniature steamboats, and next followed the gold and silver artisans. After them came the cars with models of the pipes and pieces of machinery used in the water works and maps of the construction and then the artisans whose labor had brought about the great system. After them came the College, Mechanical and Mercantile Library Society, and last of all the temperance societies, whose beautiful banners bearing noble sentiments the people greeted with loud cheers.

Speeches and singing were heard, and Samuel Stevens gave the history of New York water, telling about the old tea-water pump that supplied the only drinkable water until 1825. After that, cisterns were placed in front of the churches, and later the city appropriated fifteen hundred dollars for a tank on Thirteenth Street.

It was a great day, with bells ringing from morning to night, and the Croton Water Works sent out beautiful jets of water from the hydrants while the procession was moving. At night the Astor House and the Park Theatre were illuminated. Nathan felt he'd been present at the greatest event in the world's history, and he wondered as he dropped off to sleep that night what the boys at home would say if they could know all that was happening to him.

A few days later David and Nathan were walking on the Battery, talking earnestly. At least David was talking, and Nathan was listening and responding eagerly now and then. They were talking about the wonderful new telegraph and its inventor, whom they'd met that day and who had invited them to watch an experiment that was to be tried publicly the next day. It was a beautiful moonlit night.

As they walked and talked, looking out across the way they saw a little boat proceeding slowly along, one man at the oars and one at the stern. Other idlers on the Battery that night might have wondered what kind of fishing the two men were engaged in that took so long a line. But David and Nathan watched with deep interest for they were in the secret of the little boat. In its stern sat Professor Morse with two miles of copper wire wound on a reel, paying it out slowly. It took two hours to lay that first cable between Castle Garden and Governor's Island, and the two who watched didn't remain until it was completed for they were invited to be present early the next morning when the first test was to be made. So they hurried back to the Astor House to get some sleep before the wonderful event should take place. Nathan was almost too excited to sleep.

The *New York Herald* came out the next morning with this statement:

Morse's Electromagnetic Telegraph

This important invention is to be exhibited in operation at Castle Garden between the hours of twelve and one o'clock today. One telegraph will be erected on Governor's Island and one at the castle, and messages will be interchanged and others transmitted during the day. Many have been incredulous as to the power of this wonderful triumph of science and art. All such may now have an opportunity of fairly testing it. It is destined to work a complete revolution in the mode of transmitting intelligence throughout the civilized world.

At daybreak Professor Morse was on the Battery and was joined almost immediately by David and Nathan and two or three other interested friends. Preparations for the great test began. At last everything was ready, and the eager watchers actually witnessed the transmission of three or four characters between the termini of the line.

Suddenly communication was interrupted, and it was found impossible to send any more messages through the conductor. The excitement and anxiety were high for a few minutes, while the professor worked with his instrument. Then looking up he pointed out on the water, and light broke on his face. There lying along the line of the submerged cable were no fewer than seven vessels!

A few minutes' investigation revealed that one of these vessels in getting under way had raised the line on its anchor. The sailors didn't understand what it meant and hauled in about two hundred feet of the line on deck. Finding no end, they cut off what they had and carried it away with them. Thus ended ignominiously the first attempt at submarine telegraphing.

A crowd had assembled on the Battery, but when they discovered there was to be no exhibition they dispersed with jeers. Most of them believed they were the victims of a hoax. Nathan watched the strong patient lines of the inventor's face and found angry, pitying tears crowding to his own eyes as he felt the disappointment for the man who seemed to him such a great hero. How he wished in his heart he were a man and rich, that he might furnish the wherewithal for a thorough public test immediately. But he turned away with his heart full of admiration for the man who was bearing so patiently this new disappointment in his great work for the world. Nathan believed in him and in his invention. Didn't he hear the click, click of the instrument and see with his own eyes the strange characters produced? Others might disbelieve and jeer, but he knew, for he saw and heard.

Nathan met and heard other great men, whom in later years he was to know more about and feel pride at having met. Because David knew a great many, Nathan saw them also. One was Ralph Waldo Emerson, who wrote for the *New York Tribune.* That was all Nathan knew about him at the time and thought that was enough because, being with a journalist, he thought journalism the very highest thing in literature. In after years he learned better, of course, and was proud of his brief meeting with such a great man in the world of letters. Then he met the Honorable

Millard Fillmore, Henry Clay, a kind-faced man, and William Lloyd Garrison, all special friends of David's and honored accordingly by the boy.

He heard talk about such things as the Indian Treaty; a man named Dickens from England who had traveled in America awhile and written some bitter criticisms of American journalists (Nathan didn't like him!); and a wonderful flying machine that was being invented by a man named McDermott. The machine was a giant kite 110 feet long and 20 feet broad, tapering like a bird's wings. The owner stood under the center—the frame was 18 feet high—and operated four wings horizontally like the oars of a boat. The wings were made of a series of valves like Venetian blinds which opened when moving forward and closed when the stroke was made; each blade had 20 square feet of surface and was moved by the muscles of the legs. The wood was made of canes, the braces of wire, and the kite and tail of cotton cloth. And the kite had an angle of ten degrees to the horizon. Nathan wrote it all down in his neat hand and entertained secret hopes of making one for himself someday when he had time.

Another flying machine being talked about was made by a man in New Orleans. It had a hollow machine like a bird's body and wings like a bird's with a man inside and light machinery to work the wings. But this didn't seem as easy to carry out, so Nathan was inclined to the first one.

Then he heard talk about postage and the failure to have the rates cut down. Many thought it should be cut to five and ten cents with fifteen for long distances, so Nathan found a great deal to think about.

But most of all he heard talk of politics, Whigs and Loco-Focos, and began to take a deep interest in it all. Almost at the close of their stay David announced he meant to take in the Whig Convention on the way home, and the boy's heart rose to great heights. The convention was to be held in Goshen, Orange County, twenty-two miles by steamboat and forty-four miles by railroad, and the journey would take five hours. A hundred passengers made up the party, including notable men, and the experience meant much to the boy in later years.

Chapter 12

Nathan came home from New York a new creature. He walked the old familiar streets and met the neighbors he'd known ever since he could remember, as if he were in a dream. It was as though years had passed and given him a new point of view. Behold the former things had passed away, and all things had become new. He knew he was new. He knew his life's aspirations and desires had changed, and he bore himself accordingly.

The neighbors looked at him with a puzzled, troubled expression, paused and turned again to look as he passed, and then said reflectively, "Well, I'll be gormed! Ain't that young Whitney?"

At least that was what Squire Heath said, as he braced himself against his own gatepost and chewed a straw while Nathan walked erectly down the street away from him. It reminded one of those in centuries past who asked: "Is not this he that sat and begged?"

In former times nobody had been wont even to look at Nathan as he passed.

The boys, his companions in wicked pranks, fell upon him uproariously on his return, inclined to treat his vacation as a joke, and then fell back from him bewildered. He seemed no longer one of them. Already he gave them the impression he looked down on them, although he had no such notion in his mind and was heartily glad to see them. But he was confused and hardly knew how to reconcile the new emotions striving for precedence in his breast. These foolish, loud-voiced children, once part and parcel of him, didn't appeal to him in his new mood. In his heart of hearts he was still loyal to them, but he wondered just a little why they seemed so different to him.

It wasn't altogether the more grown-up suit of clothes David encouraged him to buy in New York with his advance wages. This of course made him look older. But he'd seen a great deal in his short stay and carried more than a few responsibilities, besides coming in contact with the great questions and some of the great people of the day. He'd had a vision of what it meant to be a man, and his ideals were reaching forth to higher things.

He came and went among them gravely with a new, upright bearing, and gradually they left him to himself. They planned escapades, and he agreed readily enough to them; but when the time arrived he didn't turn up. He always had some good excuse—extra work, the office or a lesson with Mr. Spafford. At first they regarded these interruptions sympathetically and put off their plans. But they waited in vain, for when he happened to come he didn't take the old hold on things; his thoughts seemed far away at times, and they gradually regarded his disaffection with disgust and finally left him out of their calculations altogether.

When this happened, Nathan walked the world singularly alone, except for his friends the Spaffords. It was an inevitable circumstance of the new order of things, of course. But it puzzled and darkened the boy's outlook on life. Yet he would not, could not, go back.

The town's attitude toward him had indeed slightly, even imperceptibly, changed. Instead of ignoring him altogether or being combative toward him, they assumed a righteous tolerance of his existence which to the proud young nature was perhaps just as hard to bear. Their eyes held a certain sinister quality of grimness, too, as they watched him; he couldn't help but feel it, for he was sensitive as a flower in spite of his courage and strength of character. Some were actually disappointed he was seeming to turn out so differently from their prophecies. Had they really wanted him to be bad so they could gloat over him?

Nevertheless, great new joys opened up to the boy that fully outweighed these other things. His work was an intense satisfaction to him. He took pleasure in doing everything as well as it could be done and often stayed late to finish some writing that could have waited until the next day, just to see the pleased surprise in David's eyes when he found out. Also he was actually getting interested in Latin. Not that he was a great student by nature. He'd always acquired knowledge too easily to have to work very hard for it until now, and he'd also always had too much mischief to give him time to study. But now he desired above all this to please his teacher and stand well in his eyes.

A man couldn't do as much for Nathan as David had done and not win everlasting gratitude and adoration from him. So Nathan studied.

David was a good teacher, enjoying his task. Great progress was made, and the winter sped by on fleet wings.

Miranda, hovering in the background with cookies and hot gingerbread when the evening tasks were over, enjoyed her part in the boy's education and transformation. He was going to college, and she would have at least a cookie's worth of credit in the matter.

As she cooked and swept and made comfortable those in her care, she was turning over in her mind a plan and biding her time. She longed to do something but didn't yet see her way clear to it. The more she thought, the more impossible it seemed, yet the more determined she became to do it one day.

Chapter 13

In the midst of the bitterest cold weather poor Mrs. Billings slipped out of life as inconspicuously as she'd stayed in it. Lawrence Billings inherited the property, a forlorn house needing repair, one cow, several neglected chickens and an income of sixty dollars per year from property his father had left. Lawrence couldn't sew as his mother had. To work at anything he could do he was ashamed, and he couldn't get anything he would do. Obviously all he could do for himself was marry a girl with a tidy income and a thrifty hand. This Lawrence Billings set about doing with a will.

He was good looking in a washed-out sort of way and could drape himself elegantly about a chair in a nice parlor. The girls rather liked him around; he was handy. But marrying was another thing! He tried several hearty farmers' daughters in vain. They flouted him openly.

But just after Christmas a young cousin of the postmistress came to town. She was an orphan with, rumor said, a fine house and farm in her own right. The farm was rented out, and she was living on the income. She was pretty and liked to go about, so she accepted the attentions of Lawrence Billings eagerly. They were seen together everywhere, and it was commonly spoken of as "quite a match after all for poor Lawrence! What a pity his poor mother couldn't have known!"

Miranda, alert and attentive, bristled like a fine red thistle. Lawrence Billings marry a pink-cheeked girl and live on her farm comfortably, when all the time Allan Whitney was, goodness knew where, exiled from home to keep Lawrence comfortable! Not if she could help it.

She came home from church in high dudgeon with a bright spot on either cheek and her eyes snapping. She had sat behind Lawrence Billings and the pink-cheeked Julia Thatcher and seen their soft looks. Between their heads—his sleek one and her bonneted one—young Allan's shadowy face seemed to look down, fine and exalted, his sacrifice on him as he went forth into the storm's whiteness those long years ago. Miranda felt it was time for action.

It was late winter, 1842. The heavy snows were yet on the ground and had no notion of thawing. Miranda went up to her room, carefully laid aside her heavy pelisse, her muff and silk-corded bonnet, and changed her dress. Then she went quietly down to the kitchen to place the Sunday dinner, already cooked the day before, on the table. It was a delicious dinner, with one of the best mince pies ever eaten, but Miranda forgot for once to watch for David's praise and Marcia's quiet satisfaction in the fruit of her labors. She was absorbed beyond any mere immediate interests to rouse her.

"Don't you feel well, Miranda?" asked Marcia.

"Well'z ever!" she responded briefly and slammed off to the kitchen where she could have quiet.

Never since Phoebe Deane's trouble, when Miranda had put more than one finger in the pie before Phoebe was free from a tyrannical sister-in-law and an undesired suitor, had Marcia seen Miranda so distracted. But she knew that to find out the problem, she must not let on she thought anything, and then perhaps she might have a chance. So Marcia held her peace and made things as easy for Miranda as possible.

All that day, the next and the next Miranda moped, rushed and absented herself from the family as much as was consistent with her duties. Her lips were pursed till their merry red disappeared. Even to Rose she was almost short. Nathan was the only one who brought a fleeting smile, and that was followed by a look of pain. Miranda was always intense, and during this time she was more so.

The third day David came into the dining room with the evening papers, just as Miranda was putting on the supper. He was tired and cold, and the firelight looked inviting. Instead of going to the library as usual until Miranda called him for supper, he settled down in his place at the table and began to read.

When his wife came into the room he looked up exultantly. "Hurrah for John P. Kennedy! Listen to this, Marcia!

The Hon. John P. Kennedy submitted a resolution that the bill appropriating thirty thousand dollars, to be expended under the direction of the Secretary of Treasury, in a series of experiments to test the expediency of the telegraph projected by Professor Morse, should be passed.

"Isn't that great? Sit down, dear, and I'll read it to you while Miranda is putting on the supper."

Marcia settled herself in her sewing chair and took up the knitting that lay on the small stand between the dining room windows. Miranda, her ears alert, tiptoed about so as not to interrupt the reading or lose a single word. Throughout her years in the household she had acquired a creditable education this way. David realized her eagerness to hear and raised his voice pleasantly so it might reach the kitchen.

On motion of Mr. Kennedy, of Maryland, the committee took up the bill to authorize a series of experiments to be made in order to test the merits of Morse's electromagnetic telegraph. The bill appropriates thirty thousand dollars, to be expended under the direction of the Postmaster General.

On motion of Mr. Kennedy, the words "Postmaster General" were stricken out and "Secretary of the Treasury" inserted.

Mr. Cave Johnson wished to have a word to say upon the bill. As the present had done much to encourage science, he did not wish to see the science of mesmerism neglected or overlooked. He therefore proposed that one-half of the appropriation be given to Mr. Fisk to enable him to carry on experiments, as well as Professor Morse.

Mr. Houston thought that Millerism should also be included in the benefits of the appropriation—

A snort from the kitchen door brought the reading to a sudden stop, and David looked up to see Miranda, hands on her hips, arms akimbo, standing indignant in the doorway.

"Who be they?" she asked, her eyes snapping.

David loved to see her in this mood and often wished some of the people who incited her to it could meet her at such a time.

"Who are who, Miranda?"

"Why them two, Mr. Millerism and the other feller. Who be they and what rights hev they got to butt in to thet there money thet was meant fer the telegraphy?"

Marcia suppressed a smile, and David looked down quickly at his paper.

"They're not men, Miranda; they're 'isms.' Millerism is a belief, and mesmerism is a power."

Miranda looked puzzled.

"Millerism is the belief a religious sect called the Millerites hold. They're followers of a man named William Miller. They believe the end of the world is near, that the day in fact is already set. They have a paper called *The Signs of the Times*. Do you know, Marcia—I read in the *New York Tribune* the other day that they've now set May twenty-third of this coming year as the time of the second coming of Christ. They make it a point to be already dressed in white robes awaiting the end when it comes."

"Gumps!" interpolated Miranda with scorn. " 'Z if them things made any diffrunce! When it comes to a matter o' robes I'd prefer a heavenly one, and I calc'late on its being furnished me free o' charge. What's the other 'ism'? Messyism? Ain't it got no more sense to 't than Millerism?"

"Mesmerism? Well, yes, it has. There's perhaps some science behind it, though it's at present little understood. A man named Franz Mesmer started the idea. He has a theory that one person can produce in another an abnormal condition resembling sleep, during which the mind of the person sleeping is subject to the operator's will. Mesmer says it's due to animal magnetism. A good many experiments have been made on this theory, but to my mind it's dangerous. Evil-minded people could use it for great harm to others. It's also claimed that under this power the one who's mesmerized can talk with departed spirits."

"Humph!" commented Miranda. "More gumps! Say, what'r they thinking about to put sech fool men into the governm'nt t' Washin'ton? Can't they see the diffrunce atween things like thet and the telegraphy?"

Miranda, proud of her scientific knowledge, sailed back to her kitchen and took up the muffins for tea. But she also had food for thought, and the rest of the evening was quieter than usual. If she had only been in the habit of keeping a diary and setting down her quaint philosophies— but most of them were buried in her heart, and only 'Z fortunate intimate friend was favored with them now and then.

About a week later Marcia returned home from the monthly missionary meeting, which Miranda resolutely refused to attend. She declared she had missionary work enough in her own kitchen without wasting time hearing a lot of stories about people who lived in the geography and likely weren't much worse than most folks if the truth were told.

"Miranda," said Marcia, coming into the kitchen to untie her bonnet, "you're going to have an opportunity to find out what mesmerism is. Your cousin Hannah is having a man visit at her house—he understands it and is going to mesmerize some of the young people. It's Thursday evening, and we're invited. Hannah wanted me to ask if you'd help serve and clean up afterward. She's having coffee and doughnuts."

Miranda tossed her chin high and sniffed, albeit a bit of interest glittered in her eyes. She wasn't fond of her cousin, blonde and proud and selfish, who had been Hannah Heath before she married Lemuel Skinner and who usually looked down on her cousin Miranda. Ordinarily Miranda would have refused such a request, and Marcia knew it, but the mesmerist was too great a bait.

"I s'pose I kin go ef she wants me so bad," she reluctantly consented.

Hannah Skinner hit the latest fad when she secured the mesmerist to come to her party. Everyone had read about the things purported to be done by mesmerism, and those who were invited to the party could talk of little else. Miranda heard it every time she went to the post office or the store. She heard it when a neighbor ran in to borrow a cup of molasses for a belated gingerbread and when she visited her grandmother Heath on an errand for Marcia. And the more she heard, the more thoughtful she became.

"Who's Hannah hevin' to her tea party, Grandma?" she'd asked.

Mrs. Heath paused in her knitting, looked over her spectacles and enumerated them: "The Spaffords, the Waites, Aaron Petrie's folks, the Van Storms, Lawrence Billings, o' course, and Julia Thatcher'n her aunt, Abe Fonda, Lyman Brown and Elkanah Wilworth's nieces up from New York—"

But Miranda heard no more after Lawrence Billings, and her mind was off in a tumult of plans. She could hardly wait until David came home that evening to question him.

"Say, Mr. David, wisht you'd tell me more 'bout that mesmerism thing you was readin' 'bout. D'ye say they put 'em to sleep, an' they walked around an' didn't know what they was doin' an' did what the man told 'em to?"

"Well, Miranda, I think you've got the idea."

"Say, d'yu reely b'leeve it, Mr. David? 'Cause I don't b'leeve nobody could make me do all them fool things 'thout I'd let 'em."

"No, of course not without your consent, Miranda. I believe they make that point. You've got to surrender your will to theirs before they can do anything. If you resist, they have no power. It's a good deal like a temptation. If you stand right up to it and say no, it has no chance with you. But if you let yourself play with it, why, it soon gets control."

"But d'you reely b'leeve ther is such a thin' anyway? Could anybody make you do things you didn't think out fer yerself?"

"Why, I'm not sure, but I think it could be so. There is in us a power called animal magnetism which if exercised has a very strong influence over other people. You know yourself how some people can persuade others to do almost anything. The power of the eye in looking does a great deal; the touch of the hand in persuasion does more sometimes. Some people, too, have stronger wills and minds than others, and there is no question but that there's something to it. I've seen small exhibitions of the power of mesmerism—the power of one mind over another. They make people go and find some hidden article, just by laying the hand on the subject and thinking of the place where the article is hidden. Those experiments are easy and common now. But as for talking with those who've left this world, that's another thing."

"But some folks reely b'leeve that?"

"They say they do."

"Humph! Gumps!" declared Miranda turning back to the kitchen with a satisfied sniff. Thereafter she went about her work singing at the top of her lungs, and not another word did she say about mesmerism or the Skinner tea party, although she walked softly and listened intently whenever anyone else spoke of it.

Miranda went to her cousin Hannah's early in the afternoon and meekly helped get things ready. It wasn't Miranda's way to be meek, and Hannah was surprised and touched.

"You can come in and watch them when the professor gets to mesmerizing, M'randy," said Hannah indulgently. She noticed with satisfaction the gleam of the green and brown plaid silk beneath Miranda's ample white apron.

"I might look in, but I don't take much stock in such goin's on," conceded Miranda loftily. "Did you say you was going to pass cheese with the doughnuts and coffee? I might a' brang some along ef I'd knowed. I made more'n we'd eat afore it gets stale t' our house."

Miranda kept herself well in the background during the early part of the evening, though she joined the company at the beginning and greeted everybody with a self-respecting manner. That much she demanded as recognition of her family and her good clothes. For the rest it suited her plans to keep out of sight, and she made an excuse to slip into the kitchen, where she found a vantage point behind a door that gave her a view of the whole room and a chance to hear what was being said without being noticed.

Once, within her range and quite near, Lawrence Billings and Julia Thatcher sat for five full minutes, and Miranda's blood boiled angrily as she saw the evident progress the young man was making in his wooing. Studying the girl's pink cheeks and laughing blue eyes she decided she was much too good for him, and above the weak-faced young man seemed to rise the strong fine face of Allan Whitney, too noble even to scorn the weak man who had let him go all these years under a crime he had not committed.

Not even Hannah Heath knew when Miranda slipped back into the room and became part of the company. The fine aroma of coffee came at the same time, however, and whetted everybody's appetite. The professor had been carrying on his experiments for some time, and several guests had resigned themselves laughingly into his hands. They'd been made to totter around the room to find a hidden thimble, giggling foolishly under their ample blindfolding and groping their way uncertainly; others swayed rhythmically and stalked ahead of their mentor straight to the secret hiding place of the trinket.

One, a stranger, a dark young man the professor had brought with him, had dropped into a somnambulistic state, from which trance he delivered himself of several messages to people in the room from their departed friends. The messages were all of a general nature of greeting, nothing to put an undesirable cloud on the spirits of the lively company and nothing that couldn't be said by anyone. Everybody was laughing and chattering between times, telling the professor how strange he or she felt under his mesmeric influence.

Miranda had watched it all from her covert and observed every detail of the affair, as well as the gullibility of the audience. At just the right moment she entered with her great platter of doughnuts and followed it by steaming cups of coffee.

Oh, Miranda! Child of loneliness and loyalty! In what school did you learn your cunning?

Just how she contrived to get around the long-haired flabby professor perhaps nobody in the room could have explained, unless it might have been Marcia, who was watching her curiously and wondering what she was up to now. Miranda always had some surprise to spring on people when she went around for days with bright red cheeks and her eyes flashing with suppressed excitement. Marcia had warned David to be on the lookout for something interesting. But he was sitting in the corner discussing politics, the various vices and virtues of the Whigs versus the Loco-Focos. He took his coffee and doughnuts entirely unaware of what was going on in the room.

Marcia was watching with delight Miranda as she laughed and chatted with the evening's guest and traveled back and forth to the kitchen to bring him more cream and sugar and the largest, fattest doughnuts. Suddenly Cornelia Van Storm leaned over and asked about the last missionary meeting, and Marcia was forced to give attention to the Sandwich Islands for a time.

"They say that some of those heathens who didn't used to have a thing to wear are getting so fond of clothes that they come to church in real gaudy attire so the pastors have had to admonish them," said Cornelia, with a zest in her words as if she were retailing a rare bit of gossip. "If that's so I don't think I'll give any more money to the missionary society. I'm sure I don't see the use of our sacrificing things here at home for them to flaunt the money around there, do you?"

"Why, our money wouldn't go for their dress anyway," said Marcia smiling. "I suppose the poor things dress in what they can get and like. But anyway if we sent money to the Sandwich Islands it would likely go to pay the missionary. You know the work there is wonderful. Nearly all the children over eight can read the New Testament, and they've just dedicated their new church. The king of the islands gave the land it's built on and most of the money to build it. It's 137 feet long and 72 feet wide and cost quite a good deal."

"Well, I must say if that's so they're quite able to look after themselves, and I for one don't approve of sending any more money there. I never did approve of foreign missions anyway, and this makes me feel more so. I say charity begins at home."

But at that moment Marcia lifted her eyes and beheld what made her forget the heathen, home and foreign, and attend to the other end of the room; for there was Miranda, rosy and bridling like the younger girls, allowing the long-haired professor to tie the bandage around her eyes. Her pleasant mouth carried a smile of satisfaction, and her firm shoulders conveyed determination. Marcia was sure the stage was set and the curtain about to rise.

Chapter 14

This young woman," proclaimed the professor's nasal voice, rising above the chatter of the room, "has kindly consented to allow me to try a difficult experiment on her. From my brief conversation with her just now I feel that she is a peculiarly adaptable subject, and I've long been searching for a suitable medium on which to try an experiment of my own."

In the middle of a convincing sentence about Henry Clay, David suddenly ceased speaking and wheeled around with a sharp glance across the room, first suspiciously at the professor and then with dismay at his subject. It seemed impossible to connect Miranda with anything as occult as mesmerism. David drew his brows together in a frown. He didn't like the idea of Miranda lending her strong common sense to what seemed to him a foolish and possibly dangerous business. The girl generally knew what she was about, and finding a thimble of course was harmless, if that were all.

"We'll first give a simple experiment to see if all goes well," went on the professor, "and then, if the lady proves herself an apt subject, I will proceed to make an experiment of a deeper nature. Will someone kindly hide the thimble? Mrs. Skinner, you have it, I believe. Yes, thank you, that will do very well."

It is doubtful if anyone in the room except David, whose eyes were upon Miranda, saw the deft quick motion with which she slid the bandage up from one eye and down again in a trice as if she were merely making it easier on her head. But during that instant Miranda's one blue eye took in a good deal, as David observed, and she must have seen the thimble being hidden away in Melissa Hartshorn's luxuriant waving hair which was mounted elaborately on the top of her head. An odd little smile hovered about David's lips. Miranda was up to her tricks again and evidently had no belief whatever in the professor's ability. She meant to carry out her part as well as the rest had done and not be thought an impossible subject. She was perhaps intending to try an experiment herself on the professor.

"Now you must yield your will to mine absolutely," explained the professor as he had done to the others.

"How do you make out to do that?" asked the subject, standing alert and capable, her hands on her hips, her chin assertive as usual.

Marcia caught a look of annoyance on Hannah Skinner's face. She hadn't expected Miranda to make herself so prominent, and from the look Marcia guessed she meant to give her a piece of her mind afterward.

"Why, you just relax your mind and your will. Be pliable, as it were, in my hands. Make your mind a blank. Try not to think your own thoughts, but open your mind to obey my slightest thought. Be quiescent. Be pliable, my dear young lady."

Miranda dropped one arm limply at her side and then the other and managed to make her whole tidy vivid figure slump gradually into an inertness that was fairly comical in one as self-sufficient as Miranda.

"I'm pliable!" she announced in anything but a limp tone.

"Very good, very good, my dear young lady," said the oily professor, laying a large moist hand on her brow and taking one of her hands in his other one. "Now yield yourself fully!"

Miranda stood limply for a moment and then began to sway gently, as she had seen the others do, and to step timidly forth toward Melissa Hartshorn.

The professor cast a triumphant look about the circle of eagerly attentive watchers.

"Very susceptible, very susceptible indeed!" he murmured. "Just as I supposed, unusually susceptible subject!"

David stood watching, an incredulous twinkle in his eyes. Miranda with studied hesitation was going directly toward the thimble, and when she reached Melissa she stopped as if she had run up against a wall and groped uncertainly for her hair. In a moment more she had the thimble in her hand.

"You see!" said the professor exultantly. "It's just as I said. The young lady is peculiarly susceptible. And now we'll proceed to a most interesting experiment. We'll ask someone in the room to step forward and think of something, anything in the room will do, and the subject will tell what he's thinking about. It will be necessary, of course, to inform me what the object is. Will this gentleman kindly favor us? I will remove the bandage from the subject's eyes. It is unnecessary in this experiment."

Aaron Petrie, rotund and rosy from embarrassment, stepped forward, and Miranda, relieved of her bandage, stared unseeingly straight at him with the look of a sleepwalker and did not move.

"You'll perceive that the subject is still under powerful influence," murmured the professor, noticing Miranda's dreamy, vacant stare.

"That is well. She will be far more susceptible."

He bent his head to ask Aaron Petrie what he had chosen to think about, and Aaron, still embarrassed, cast his eyes up and down and around and located them on a plate on which a fragment of doughnut remained. A relieved look came into his face, and he whispered something back. The professor's eye traveled to the plate. He bowed cheerfully and returned to place his right hand on Miranda's quiescent forehead and take one of her hands in his, while he looked straight into her apparently unseeing eyes.

After a moment of breathless silence, during which the company leaned forward and watched with intense interest, the professor commanded: "Now tell the company what this gentleman is thinking about."

Miranda, her eyes still fixed on space, slowly opened her mouth and spoke, but her voice was drawling and slow with an unnatural monotony. "He–is–wishin'–he–hed–'nuther–doughnut!" she chanted.

The little assembly broke into astonished, half-awed laughter. The receptivity of Aaron Petrie toward all edibles was a common joke. Even in the face of weird experiments one had to laugh about Aaron Petrie's taste for doughnuts.

"Doughnuts! Doughnuts! Very good," said the professor, nervously rubbing his hands together. "The gentleman was thinking of the bit of doughnut on yonder plate, and the subject being so susceptible has doubtless reached a finer shade of thought than the young gentleman realized when he made his general statement to me."

The laughter subsided and trailed off into an exclamation of wonder as the cunning professor made Miranda's original answer a further demonstration of the mysteries of science.

"Now will this young gentleman give us something?" The professor was still a trifle nervous. Miranda's fixed attitude puzzled him. She wasn't altogether like his other subjects, and he had an uneasy feeling that she might fail him at some critical point. Nevertheless, he was bound to keep on.

Abe Fonda came boldly forward with a swagger, his eyes fixed on the younger of Elkanah Wilworth's two pretty nieces. Miranda's faraway look did not change. She was having the time of her life, but the best was yet to come.

Abe whispered eagerly in the professor's ear, and his eyes sought the pretty girl's again with a smile.

The professor bowed and turned to his subject as before, and

Miranda, without waiting for a request, chanted out again: "Abe's a–thinking–how–purty–Ruth Ann–Wilworth's–curl–on–the–back–o'–her–neck–is."

A shout of laughter greeted this, and Abe turned red, while the professor grew still more uneasy. He saw that he was growing in favor with his audience, but the subject was most uncertain and not at all like other subjects he had experimented with. He had a growing suspicion that she was doing some of the work on her own hook and not putting herself absolutely under his influence. If he were to go further with her, it would be as well for him to confine his investigations to safe subjects. The dead were safer than the living.

"Well, yes, the young gentleman did mention the younger Miss Wilworth," he said apologetically. "I hope no offense is taken at the exceedingly—that is to say—direct way the subject has of stating the case."

"Oh, no offense whatever," said the sheepish Abe. "It was all quite true, I assure you, Miss Wilworth." And he made a low bow toward the blushing, simpering girl.

Now the professor had one stunt he loved to pull off in any company where he dared. He would "call up" the spirit of George Washington and question him concerning the coming election, which not only thrilled the audience but often had great weight with them in changing or strengthening their opinions. He knew the ordinary subject would easily respond yes or no according to his will, and this remarkable young woman, no matter how original her replies, could scarcely make much trouble in politics and wouldn't likely interpolate her own personality with such a subject of conversation. He decided to try it at once and even more because the young woman herself had expressed a desire to see an exhibition of his power to "communicate" with the other world.

"This young woman," began the professor in his most suave tones, "has proved herself so apt a subject that I'm going to try something I rarely attempt in public without first having experimented for days with the subject. It may work, and it may not; I can scarcely be sure without knowing her better. But as she herself has expressed a desire to yield herself for the experiment, I will endeavor to call up someone from the other world—"

At this David sat up suddenly, his eyes searching Miranda's blank ones. It troubled him for a member of his household to put herself, even for a short time, under this slippery man's influence, nor did he like this tampering with the mysterious and potentially evil. There was no telling what effect it might have on Miranda, though he had always thought her the most practical and sensible person he knew. He couldn't understand her willingness to submit to this nonsense. Should he interfere? He was to blame himself for having talked to her so much about the subject.

He cleared his throat and almost spoke, his eyes still on the blank expression of the girl, who was supposed to be in a sort of trance. Suddenly, as he watched her, one eye gave a slow, solemn wink at him. The action was so comical and so wholly Miranda-like that he almost laughed aloud, and he settled back in his seat to watch what was to come next. Miranda was not in a trance then but was fully and wholly herself and enjoying the hoax she was playing on both the audience and the professor. Miranda was an artist of her kind—there was no mistaking it. David wished he were sitting next to Marcia so he might relieve her mind, for he saw she looked troubled. He tried to signal to her by a smile and was surprised to receive an answering reassurance as if Marcia, too, had discovered something.

The professor now stood forth making some slow rhythmical motions with his hands on the girl's forehead and in front of her face. He was just about to speak his directions to her when she rose slowly as though impelled by some unseen force and stood staring straight ahead of her at the open kitchen door, her eyes strained and wild, her face impressive with a weird solemnity.

"I–see–a–dead–man!" she exclaimed sepulchrally, and the professor rubbed his hands and wafted a few more thought waves toward this remarkably apt subject.

Had Miranda arranged it with the draft of the kitchen window that just at this stage of the game the kitchen door should come slowly, noisily shut? A distinct shudder went around the company, but the girl continued to gaze raptly toward the door.

"Ask him what his politics are, please," commanded the professor, endeavoring to cast a little cheer upon the occasion.

"He–says–he–was–shot–down–by–Taylor's–woods."

An audible murmur of horror went around the room, and everybody sat up and took double notice.

"Twelve–years–ago," went on the monotonous voice in a high strident key.

"Enoch Taylor, I'll be gormed!" exclaimed old Mr. Heath, resting his knobby hands on his knees and leaning forward with bulging eyes.

David couldn't help but notice that Lawrence Billings, who was sitting opposite to him, started nervously and glanced furtively around the company.

"He–says–to–tell–you–his–murderer–is–in–this–room," chanted Miranda as though she had no personal interest in the matter whatever.

In this room! The thought flashed like lightning from face to face: Who is it?

David found his eyes riveted on the pale face of the young man opposite who seemed unable to take his eyes from Miranda's but sat white and horrified with a fascinated stare like a bird under the gaze of a cat.

"He–must–confess–tonight–before–the–clock–strikes–midnight," went on the voice, "or–a–curse–will–come–on–him–and–he–will–die!"

A tense stillness in the room filled everybody with horror, as if the dead man had suddenly stepped into sight and charged them all with his murder. They looked from one to another with sudden suspicion in their eyes. The oily professor stood aghast at the work he'd wrought unaware.

"Oh, now, see here," he began with an attempt to break the tension. "Don't let this thing break up the good cheer. We'll just bring this lady back to herself again and dismiss the deceased for tonight. He doubtless died with some such thing on his mind, or else he was insane and keeps the same notions he had when he left this mortal frame. Now don't let this worry you in the least. Nobody in this room could commit a murder if he tried, of course. Why, you're all ladies and gentlemen."

All the time the oily anxious man was making wild passes in front of Miranda's face and trying to press her forehead with his hands and wake her up. But Miranda just marched slowly, solemnly ahead toward the kitchen door, and everybody in the room but the professor watched her, fascinated.

She turned when she reached the kitchen door, faced the room once more and, staring back upon them all, uttered once more her curse.

"Enoch–Taylor–say–ef–you–don't–confess–tonight–before–midnight–you'll–die–and–he–ain't–goin'–to–leave–you–till–you–confess."

She jabbed her finger straight forward blindly, and it went through the roached hair on Lawrence Billings's shrinking head and pointed straight at nothing, but Lawrence Billings jumped and shrieked. In the confusion Miranda dropped apparently senseless in the kitchen doorway. But just before she dropped she gave David another slow, solemn wink with one eye.

Chapter 15

All was confusion at once, and one of the young men rushed out for Caleb Budlong, the doctor, who lived not far away. When things settled down again and Miranda was lifted to the kitchen couch and restored with cold water, David had time to discover the absence of Lawrence Billings, though nobody else seemed to notice.

They all tiptoed away from the kitchen at Dr. Budlong's suggestion and left Miranda to lie quiet and recover. He said he didn't believe in these newfangled things; they were bad for the system and got people's nerves all stirred up, especially women's. He wouldn't allow a woman to be put under mesmeric influence if he had anything to say about it. All women were hysterical, and that was doubtless the matter with Miranda.

The company looked at one another astonished. Who ever suspected Miranda of having nerves and going into hysterics? And yet she'd proclaimed a murderer in their midst!

They turned to one another, conversing in low mysterious tones, while Miranda lay on the couch in the kitchen with closed eyelids and inward mirth. Presently, as Dr. Budlong counted her pulse and gave her another sip of cold water, she drew a long sigh and turned her face to the wall. Thinking she was dropping to sleep, he tiptoed into the sitting room and closed the kitchen door gently behind him.

Miranda was on the alert at once, turning her head quickly to measure the width of the crack of the door. She held herself quiet for a full minute and then slipped softly from her couch across the kitchen with the step of a sylph. Snatching a mussed tablecloth from the shelf in the pantry where she put it when she helped Hannah clear off the dinner table, she wrapped it around her and over her head and went out the back door.

Every movement was light and quick. She paused a second on the back stoop to get her bearings, then sped with swift light steps toward the barn door, which was open. A young moon was riding high in the heavens making weird battle with the clouds, and the light of a lantern shone from the open barn door. Miranda could see the long shadow of a man hitching up a horse with quick, nervous fingers. Lawrence Billings was preparing to take Julia Thatcher home.

Miranda approached the barn and suddenly emerged into the light in full view of the startled horse as Lawrence Billings stepped behind him to fasten the traces. The horse, roused from a peaceful slumber and not yet fully awake, beheld the apparition with a snort and, without regard to the man or the unfastened traces, reared on his hind legs and attempted to climb backward into the carryall. There they stood, side by side, the man and the horse, open-mouthed, wide-nostriled, with protruding eyes. The smoky lantern by the barn door shed a flickering light over the whole and cast grotesque shadows on the dusty floor.

Miranda, fully realizing her advantage, stood in the half light of the moon in her fantastic drapery and waved her tableclothed arms, with one forefinger wrapped tightly in the linen pointing straight at the frightened man, while she intoned in hollow sounds the words: "Confess–tonight–or–you–will–die!"

Lawrence Billings's yellow hair rose straight on end, and cold creeps went down his back. He snorted like the horse in his fright.

The white apparition moved slowly nearer, nearer to the patch of light in the barn door, and its voice wailed and rose like the wind in November, but the words it spoke were clear and distinct.

"Confess–at–once–or–misfortune–will–overtake–you! Moon–smite–you! Dogs–bite–you! Enoch–Taylor's–speerit–hant–you! Yer–mother's–ghost–pass–before–you!"

The white arms waved dismally, and the apparition took another step toward him. Then, with a yell that might have been heard around the country, Lawrence Billings dashed wildly past her to the back door.

"Food–pizen–you! Sleep–fright–you! Earth–swaller–you!" screamed the merciless apparition, flying after him. The horse, having reached the limit of his self-control, clattered out into the open and cavorted around the garden until his nerves were somewhat relieved.

Lawrence Billings burst in upon the assembled company in the parlor with wild eyes and disheveled hair and was suddenly confronted with the fact that these people did not believe in ghosts and apparitions. In the warm, bright room with plenty of companions about, he felt the foolishness of telling what he'd just seen. His nerve deserted him. He couldn't face them and suggest he'd seen a ghost, and so he blurted out an incoherent sentence about his horse. It was frightened at something white in the yard and had run away.

Instantly all hands hurried out to help catch the horse, with Lawrence Billings taking care to keep close to the others and joking fearsomely about the shadowy yard as he stepped forth again from shelter.

Miranda, meanwhile, had slipped into the kitchen and taken to her couch, with the tablecloth folded neatly close by in case she needed it again, and was apparently resting quietly when Hannah tiptoed in to see if she needed anything.

"I guess I shan't trouble you much longer," murmured Miranda sleepily. "I don't feel near so bad now. Shouldn't wonder ef I could make out t' git back home in a half hour er so. What's all the racket 'bout, Hannah?"

"Lawrence Billings's horse got loose," said Hannah. "He's a fool anyway. He says it saw something white on the clothesline. There isn't a thing out there—you know yourself, Mirandy. He's asked Dr. Budlong to take Julia Thatcher and her aunt home in his carryall. He says his horse won't be safe to drive after all this. It's perfect nonsense; Julia could have walked with him. Mother wanted to ride with Dr. Budlong, and now she'll have to stay all night, and I just got the spare bedsheets done up clean and put away. I don't see why you had to go and get into things tonight anyhow, Mirandy. You might have known it wasn't a thing for you to meddle with. All this fuss just because you got people worked up about that murder. Why didn't you keep your mouth shut about it? It couldn't do any good now anyway. Say, Mirandy—did you really see anyone or hear them say all that stuff?"

"What stuff, Hannah?" said Miranda sleepily. "I disremember what's ben happenin'. My head feels odd. Do you s'pose 'twould hurt me to go home to my own bed?"

"No," said Hannah crossly, "it's the best place you could be. I wish I hadn't asked you to come. I might've known you'd cut up some shine, but I thought you were grown up enough to act like other folks at a tea party." And with this kind, cousinly remark she slammed into her sitting room again to make what she could of her excited guests.

Miranda lay still and listened. When she made out from the sounds that Julia Thatcher and her aunt had driven off in Dr. Budlong's carryall with his family, and that all the ladies who hadn't already departed were in the spare room putting on their wraps and bonnets, she stole forth with the tablecloth hidden under her cloak. She had taken the precaution early in the evening of hanging her wraps behind the kitchen door. Thus she took her way down the street, hovering in the shadows until she saw Lawrence Billings coming on behind her.

He was quite near David and Marcia when he passed where she hid behind a lilac bush on the edge of Judge Waitstill's yard.

"Moon smite yeh—stars blight yeh," murmured Miranda under her breath, but almost in his ear, and flicked the tablecloth a time or two in the moonlight as he looked back fearfully.

Lawrence hastened his steps until he was close behind another group of homeward-bound guests. Miranda slipped from bush to bush, keeping in the shadows of the trees, until she made sure he was about to turn off down the road to his own isolated house. Then she slid under a fence and sped across a cornfield. The night was damp, and a fine mist like smoke rose from the ground in a wreath of fog and hid her as she ran. But when the young man opened his gate he saw in the changing lights and shadows of the cloudy, moonlit night a white figure with waving arms standing on his doorstep and moving slowly, steadily down to meet him.

With a gasp of terror he turned and fled back to the main street of the village, the ghost following a short distance behind, with light, uncanny tread and waving arms like wreaths of mist. It was too much for poor Lawrence Billings. Just in front of David Spafford's house he stumbled and fell flat—and here was the ghost all but upon him! With a cry of despair he scrambled to his feet and took refuge on the Spafford stoop, clacking the door knocker loudly in his fright.

This was better than Miranda could have hoped. She held her ghostly part by the gatepost till David opened the door, then slipped around to a loose pantry shutter and soon entered the house. Stepping lightly she took her station near a crack of a door where she could hear all that went on between David and his late caller. She heard with exultation the reluctant confession, the abject humility of voice and the cringing plea for mercy. Whatever happened now somebody besides her knew Allan Whitney was not a murderer.

Her heart swelled with triumph as she listened to the frightened voice telling how a shot had struck the old man instead of the rabbit it was intended for and how he'd run to him and done everything he knew to resuscitate his victim but without avail. In terrible fright he had started for the road and there met Allan Whitney. Allan came back with him and worked over the old man a while and then told him to go home and say nothing about it, that he would take the gun and if anybody made a fuss he would take the blame; it didn't matter about him anyway, for nobody cared what became of him, but Lawrence had his mother to look out for. The man declared he hadn't wanted to put Allan in a position like that, but when he thought of his mother, of course he had to. And anyhow he'd hoped Allan would get away all right, and he did. It hadn't seemed so bad for Allan. He was likely as well off somewhere else as here, and he, Lawrence, had his mother to look after.

There was no spectre in this room, and Lawrence Billings was getting back his self-confidence. All the excuses he had bolstered himself with during the years came flocking back to comfort him as he tried to justify himself before this clear-eyed man for his cowardly hiding behind another.

Something of Miranda's contempt for the weak fellow was manifest in David Spafford's tone as he asked question after question and brought out little by little the whole story of the night of the murder and Lawrence's cowardly part in it. Somehow, as David talked, his sin was made more manifest, and his excuses dropped away from him. He saw his own contemptible self, his lack of manliness, his wickedness in allowing another fellow being, no matter how willing, to walk all these years under the name of murderer to shield him. He lifted a blanched face and fearful eyes to his judge when David at last arose and spoke.

"Well, now, the first thing to do is go straight to Mr. Whitney. He shouldn't be allowed to think another hour that his son has committed a crime. Then we'll go to Mr. Heath—"

Lawrence Billings uttered something between a whine and a groan. His face grew whiter, and his eyes seemed to fairly stand out.

"What'll we have to go to them for?" he demanded angrily. "Ain't I confessed? Ain't that enough? They can't hang me after all these years, can they? I ain't going to anybody else. I'll leave town if you say so, but I ain't going to do any more confessing."

"No, you will not leave town," said David quietly, laying a strong hand on the trembling shoulder, "and you most certainly will go and confess to those two men. It is the only possible way to make what amends you can for the past. You've put this matter in my hands by coming to me with it, and I can't let you go until it is handed over to the proper authorities."

"I came to you because I thought you'd be just and merciful," whined the wretch.

"And so I will as far as in me lies. Justice demands that you confess this matter fully and that the whole thing be investigated. Come!"

Chapter 16

Miranda watched through a rain of thankful tears as David escorted his guest out of the front door, and then she flew into the parlor and watched as they went arm in arm up the street and knocked at her grandfather's door. She waited with bated breath until a candlelight appeared at her grandfather's bedroom window and slowly descended the stairs. She waited again while the two went in and then stood cold and patient by the window during an interminable time, imagining the conference that must be going on in the Heath kitchen. And finally she was rewarded by seeing three men come out of the Heath door and walk slowly down the street to the big house across the way. She noted that Lawrence Billings walked between the other two. She could tell him by his slight build and cringing attitude as he walked. Once they stopped and seemed to parley, and both the other men put strong hands upon his shoulders.

There was another delay, and she could hear the Whitney knocker sounding hollowly down the silent street. Then a head was thrust out of the upper window, and a voice called loudly, "Who's there?"

Miranda had opened the parlor window just a crack, and her heart beat wildly as she knelt and laid her ear beside the crack. In a few minutes a light appeared in the fan-shaped window over the front door, and then the door itself was opened and the visitors let in.

She waited only to see the light appear in the front windows and the shadows of the four men against the curtain. Then she dropped on her knees by the window and let her tears have their way. "Thanks be!" she murmured softly again and again. "Thanks be!"

Whatever came now, Allan was cleared. At least three men in the town knew, and they would do the right thing. She was almost dubious about their having told Mr. Whitney. She thought he deserved to feel all the trouble that could come to him through his children for the way he had treated them; but after all it was good to have Allan cleared in the eyes of his father, too.

The conference in the Whitney house was long, and Miranda didn't wait until it was over. She climbed the stairs softly to her room, answering Marcia's gentle "Is that you, Miranda?" with a gruff "Yes, I ben down in the kitchen quite a spell." Closing her door she went straight to the starlit window and gazed out. Only a star or two was on duty that night, fitfully visible between the clouds, but Miranda looked up to them wistfully. Somewhere under them, if he were still on the earth, was Allan. Oh, if the stars could but give him the message that his name was cleared! Perhaps, somehow, the news would reach him, and someday he might return. Her heart leaped high with the thought.

Oh, Allan, in the wide far world, do you ever think of the little girl whose heart beat true to yours, grown a woman now and suffering for your sorrows yet? The years have been long, and she has waited well and accomplished for you at last the thing she set her heart upon. Will the stars take the message, and will you ever come back?

She crept to her bed too excited to sleep and lay there listening for sounds from across the street. The solemn silent night paced on, and still that candle beam shone straight across the road. But at last there were voices and the opening of a door—grave voices full of weighty matters and an awed good night. She went to her window to watch again.

David came straight across to his own door, but Lawrence Billings went arm in arm with her grandfather to his home. Not to the smokehouse, cold and damp, where Allan had been put, but into the comfortable quiet house, with at least the carpet-covered sofa to lie upon and the banked-up fire for warmth and the cat for company. Grandfather Heath would never put Lawrence Billings into the smokehouse; he was too respectable. Miranda, with a lingering thought of Allan and his protection of the weakling, was almost glad it was so. There was after all something pitifully ridiculous in the thought of Lawrence Billings huddled in the dark of the smokehouse with his fear of ghosts and spectres haunting him on every side. The fine strong Allan in his youthful courage couldn't be daunted by it, but Lawrence Billings would crumple with the terror of it.

Then Miranda went back to her bed, pulled the covers up over her head and laughed till she cried at the remembrance of Lawrence Billings frightened by a tablecloth.

The days that followed were grave and startling. After the revelation on the following morning a stream of visitors came to the Spafford house to see Miranda. On one pretext or another they asked for her—to the back door for a cup of molasses or to the front door to know if she would run over and stay with an ailing member of the family that evening while the others went out—anything so they could see Miranda. And always before the interview was ended they managed to bring in the mesmerizing at Hannah Skinner's.

"Say, Mirandy, did you reely see a speret? An' how did you know what to say? Did they tell you words to speak?" one would ask.

And Miranda would reply, "Well, now, Sa'r' Ann! I don' know's I ken rightly say. You see, I disremember seein' any sperets 'tall 'r hearin' any. An' as fer what I said, I can't 'count fer it. They tell me I talked a lot o' fool nonsense, but it seems t'v all passed from my mind. It's odd how that mesmerizin' works ennyhow. I didn't b'leeve much in it when I went into it, an' I can't say 'z I think much of it now. I 'member seein' a white mist rise off'n the ground when I come home, but I don't much b'leeve sperets walks the airth, d' you? It don't seem common-sensy now, do y' think? No, I can't rightly say 'z I remember hearin' 'r seein' anythin'. I guess ef I did it all passed by when my head stopped feelin' odd. Funny 'bout Lawrence Billings takin' it to heart that-a-way, wa'n't it? You wouldn't never uv picked him out t' commit a crime, now would you? My Mr. David says it's a c'wince'dence. Quite a c'wince'dence! Them's the words he used t' the breakfast table, talkin' to Mrs. Marcia. He says, 'Thet was quite a c'wince'dence, M'randy, but don't you go to meddlin' with that there mesmerism again, 'f I was you,' sez he. An' I guess he's 'bout right. Did you hear they was goin' to start up the singin' school again next week?"

And that's about all the information anybody got out of Miranda.

The next few days were marked by the sudden and hasty departure of Julia Thatcher for her home and the resurrecting of past events in preparation for the trial of Lawrence Billings, which was set for the next week. The interval was given for Enoch Taylor's grandson and only heir to arrive from his distant home.

During this interval Miranda was twice moved to make dainty dishes and take them to Lawrence Billings, who was still in solitary confinement in her grandfather's house. Her grandmother received the dishes grudgingly, told her she was a fool and slammed the door, but Miranda somehow felt as if she had made it even with her conscience for having put the poor creature into his present position. She knew Allan would like her to show him some little attention, and while she strongly suspected that the dainty dishes never reached the prisoner's tray, still it did her good to make and take them. Miranda was always an odd mixture of vindictiveness and kindness. She had driven Lawrence Billings to his doom for Allan's sake, and now she felt sorry for him.

Weeks later Miranda managed to return Hannah Skinner's tablecloth, for Hannah was bitter against her cousin by reason of the notoriety that had been brought upon her. She had made that evening gathering with a mesmerist as entertainer for the sake of popularity, but to be mixed up in a murder case was much too popular even for Hannah.

The way Miranda managed the tablecloth was a simple one after all. She went to see Hannah when she knew Hannah was over at her mother's house. Slipping unobtrusively out of the Spafford house from the door on the side away from the Heaths', she made a detour, going to the next neighbor's first and from there on a block or two, finally returning to Hannah's house by a long way around another street. She was well acquainted with the hiding place of Hannah's key and had no trouble getting in. She'd lain awake nights planning a place to put that tablecloth where it would seem perfectly natural to Hannah for it to have slipped out of sight. She'd finally hit upon the very place, down behind a high chest of drawers Hannah kept in her dining room. It took only an instant to slide the tablecloth neatly down behind it, and Miranda was out of the house with the door locked behind her and the key in its place under the mat in a trice. No neighbor was near enough to have noticed her entrance.

The next week, just as Miranda had planned she would do pretty soon, Hannah came across the aisle to the Spafford pew and whispered, "M'randy, whatever could you have done with my second best tablecloth the night of my party?"

And Miranda glibly responded, "I put it on the top o' the chest in the dinin' room, Hannah. Better look behind it. It might a' fell down—there was so much goin' on thet night."

"It couldn't," said Hannah. "I always move that out when I sweep." But she looked and to her astonishment found her tablecloth.

"It seems as if there must be some magic about this house," she remarked to Lemuel that night at supper.

"Better not meddle with such things, my dear," said Lemuel, with his little mouth pursed up like a cherry. "You know I didn't want that man to come here, but you would have him."

"Nonsense!" said Hannah sharply. "It was all Mirandy's doings. If I hadn't invited her there wouldn't have been a bit of this fuss. I thought she would know enough to keep in the kitchen and mind the coffee. I never expected her to want to be mesmerized. Such a fool! I believe she was smitten with the man!"

"Mebbe so! Mebbe so!" chirped Lemuel affably, taking a big bite of Hannah's hot biscuit and honey and doubtless thinking of the days when he was smitten with Hannah.

When this surmise of Hannah's reached Miranda, by way of her grandmother, Miranda chuckled.

"Wal, now, I hadn't thought o' that, Gran'ma, but p'rhaps that was what's the matter. He didn't look to me like much of a man to be smit with. But then when one's gitten' on to be a ole maid like me it ain't seemly to be too pertic'ler. Ef I was smit, though, it didn't go more'n skin deep, so you needn't to worry. I ain't lookin' to disgrace this fam'bly with no greasy-lookin', long-haired jackanapes of a mesmer-man yit awhiles, not s' long 's I kin earn my keep. Want I should stir thet fire up fer yeh 'fore I go back home?"

And Miranda went singing on her way back home, chuckling to herself. "Smit with him! Now ain't that reel r'dic'lous? Smit with a thing like thet!"

Then her face went grave and sweet, and she paused at the door stone before she entered and stretched her hands toward the thread of a young moon that was rising back of the barn.

"Oh, Allan!" she murmured softly. And the soul of the little girl Allan had kissed stood tenderly in her eyes for an instant.

Then she was herself again and went cheerfully in to get supper for the people she loved. And nobody ever dreamed, as they looked at the strong wholesome girl going happily about her kitchen, of the exquisite youth and depth of feeling hidden away in her great loving heart. Only Marcia sometimes caught in wonder a passing reminder in Miranda's eyes of the light that glowed in the eyes of little Rose.

Chapter 17

T he night was wide and starry. The purple blue dome of the sky fit close to the still, deep white of the earth, glittering sharply here and there as a star beam stabbed it. The trees stood stark and black against the whiteness, like lonely, solemn sentinels that even in the starlight were picked out in detail against the night. On such a night the wise men must have started on their star-led way.

A single trapper clad in furs walked silently like one of the creatures he trapped. He had been out all day and over his shoulder were slung several fine pelts. He had done well, and the furs he was carrying now would bring a fancy price. He had only two more traps to visit; then his day's work would be done, and he could go home. He trod the aisles of the night as surely as one might walk in a familiar park of magnificent distance and note no object because all were so accustomed.

He didn't whistle as he walked. He had formed the stealthy habit of the creatures of the wild, and his going was like a part of the night; a far cloud passing would have made as much stir. His movements almost carried a majesty and rhythm in them.

A mile or two farther on he knelt beside a deadfall trap and found a fine lynx as his reward. As easily and deftly as a lady might have stooped in her garden and plucked a rose he drew forth his knife and took the beautiful skin to add to those he already carried, made his trap ready for another victim and passed on to the last trap.

Several times on the way he paused, alert, listening, and then stalked on again. There were sounds enough to the uninitiated—coyotes howling, wolves baying, the call of the wild being answered from all directions—enough to make a stranger pause and tremble every step of the way. But a sound far more delicate came to the trained ear of the trapper, and a perception of a sort of sixth sense made him pause and gaze keenly now and again. A faint distant metallic ring, the crackle of a broken twig, the fall of a branch—they all might have been accounted for in natural ways; yet they were worth marking for what they might mean.

The last trap had nothing, except the appearance of having been tampered with. The trapper was still kneeling beside it when he heard a sound like the tone of a distant organ playing an old church hymn, just a note or two. It might have been the sighing of the wind in the tall trees if there had been a wind that night. The man on the ground rose suddenly to his feet and lifted his eyes to the purple-dark of the distance. Faint and far the echo repeated itself—or was it imagination?

The trapper knelt again and quickly adjusted the trap, then swung his pelts to his shoulder once more and strode forward with purpose in his whole bearing. Thrice he paused and listened but couldn't be sure he still heard the sound. Just ahead was his cabin of logs. He stopped at the door again, listening intently. Then suddenly the music came again, this time sweet and clear, but far off still and only in echoing fragments, a bit of an old tune—or was it imagination again?—that used to be sung in the church at home in the East. There was only a haunting memory of familiar days in the broken strains—foolishness perhaps—a weakness that seemed to be growing on him in this loneliness.

A moment more he lingered by the door to make sure someone was riding down the trail; then he went in, swung his burden in the corner and hurried to strike a light and make a fire. If the voice he thought he'd heard singing was really someone coming down the trail, he might have company at supper that night.

The trapper's strong face was alight with new interest as he went about his simple preparations for a guest. He put double portions of venison and corn bread to cook before the fire and lit an extra candle, placing it in the window toward the mountain trail. When all was ready he went to the door once more and listened, and now the voice came full and strong.

Yes, my native land, I love thee.

High up and far away still, and only now and then a line or phrase distinct, but it was growing nearer all the time.

The trapper, standing big and strong in his cabin door that barely let his height through without stooping, listened, and his eyes glowed warmly in the starlight. There was something good in the sound of the song. It warmed his heart where it hadn't been warmed for many days. He listened an instant, calculated the distance of his approaching guest, then drew the door to and swung himself away a few paces in the dark. When he returned, his arms were filled with fragrant piney boughs which he tossed down in an unoccupied corner of his cabin, not far from the fire, and covered with a great furry skin. After placing the coffeepot in the fire he went back to the door.

There were distinct and connected words to the song now, in a familiar tune that used to be sung in the old church at home when the trapper was a little boy. He had learned the words at his mother's knee.

The spacious firmament on high,
With all the blue ethereal sky,
The spangled heavens, a shining frame,
Their great Original proclaim.

The traveler was riding down the trail, now close at hand. The ring of his horse's footsteps on the crisp snow could be heard, and the singing suddenly stopped. He had seen the light in the window. In a moment more he came into the clearing, greetings were exchanged, and he dismounted.

The newcomer was a man of more than medium height, but he had to look up at the trapper, who towered above him in the starlight.

"I'm fortunate to find you at home," he said pleasantly. "I've passed this way several times before, but no one was here."

He was dressed in buckskin trousers, a waistcoat and a blue English duffle coat, a material firm, closely woven and thicker than a Macki-naw blanket. Over this was a buffalo overcoat a few inches shorter than the duffle, making a fantastic dress withal. From under his fur cap, keen blue eyes looked out. One could see at a glance from his wide, firm mouth that he was a man of strong purpose, great powers of fearless execution, reticent and absolutely self-contained. For a moment the two stood looking quietly, steadily, into each other's eyes, gathering, as it were, confidence in one another. What each saw must have been satisfactory, for their handclasp was filled with warm welcome and a degree of liking.

"I am the fortunate one," said the trapper.

"My name's Whitman, Marcus Whitman, missionary from Waiilatpu," explained the newcomer. "May I camp with you tonight? I've come a long way since daybreak, and a sound sleep would be pleasant."

"You're welcome," said the host. "Supper's all ready. I heard you coming down the trail. So you're Dr. Whitman? I've heard of you, of course. I'm just a trapper." He waved his hand significantly toward the heap of furs in the corner and the fine pelts hanging about the walls. "My name's Whitney. Take off your coat."

He led the stranger inside and offered him water for washing.

"Whitney, is it—and Whitman—not much difference, is there? Easy to remember. Supper sounds good. That coffee smells like nectar. So you heard singing, did you? I'm not much of a singer, I own, but my wife took a lot of pleasure teaching me. She taught me on the way out here, and I try to practice now and then when I'm out in the open where I won't annoy anyone."

"It sounded good," said the trapper. "Made me think of home. Mother used to sing that when I was a little chap—that one about the spacious firmament on high—"

A wistfulness in the trapper's tone made his guest look at him keenly once again.

"Your mother is gone then?" he ventured.

"Years ago."

"She's not at home waiting for you to come back then."

"No, she's not at home—"

After they were seated at the table and the meal was well under way, the conversation began again.

"You belong to the Hudson Bay fur people?" The stranger asked the question half anxiously, as though it had been on the tip of his tongue from the first.

"I trade with them," responded the younger man quickly. "That's all. I was with them for a while—but there were things I didn't like. A man doesn't care to be angered too often. I'm not much of an American, you might say, but I don't like to hear my own country sneered at—"

There was deep significance in young Whitney's tone.

"How's that?" The stranger's keen eyes were searching the other's, with sympathy flashing into his own.

"They don't want us Americans," he said, and his voice conveyed a deeper meaning even than his words. "They want this country for England. They want undisputed sway in Oregon!"

"You've felt that, have you?" The guest's eyes were steady and his voice calm. It was impossible to tell just what he himself believed.

"Haven't you seen it? It's to your interest you should understand, if you don't. Why, sir, they don't want you and your mission! They want the Indians to remain ignorant. They don't want them to become civilized. They can make more money out of them ignorant!"

The doctor's eyes flashed fire now. "I've seen it—yes, I've seen it. But what are the prospects? Do you think they can carry out their wishes?"

"I'm afraid they can," said the trapper half sullenly. "They've done all they can to make their hold secure. They're retiring their servants on farms and making voters of them. Every year more settlers are coming from the Red River country, and they're spreading reports among Americans that passage over the mountains is impossible. They're alive and awake to the facts. Our government down there at Washington is asleep, though. They haven't an idea what a glorious country this is. Why, I've heard they're talking of selling it off for the cod fisheries—and all because these Hudson Bay fur people have had the report circulated that you can't get over the Rockies with wagons or women and children. They're wily, these fur people. They won't sell a share of their stock. They've gone about things slow but sure. They have everything fixed. If they'd only wait long enough and feel secure enough we might fool 'em yet, if just some more Americans could be persuaded to come this way. Somebody should go and tell them back at Washington. If only I—but I can't go back! Perhaps next spring there'll be a way to send some word. I've thought of writing a letter to the president—why don't you write a letter, Dr. Whitman? It would have weight coming from you."

"Next spring will be too late! A letter will be too late, young man. Do you know the danger is at our door? It may even be too late now. Listen! I've just come from Fort Walla Walla, where I've heard what has stirred my soul. A dinner was held a few days ago with some officers from the fort, employees of the company and a few Jesuit priests. During dinner a messenger came saying that immigrants from Red River had crossed the mountains and reached Fort Colville on the Columbia. Nearly everybody present received the news enthusiastically, and one priest stood up and shouted, 'Hurrah for Oregon! America is too late! We have the country!' "

The log in the fireplace fell apart with a thud, and the trapper sprang forward to mend the fire, his face showing indignation in the glow that blazed up.

"It isn't too late yet if only we could get word to headquarters," he said as he came back to his seat. "But the snowfall has already begun. This will clear away, and we'll have some good weather yet, but treacherous. No man could get across the mountains alive at this time of year."

"And yet, with so much at stake, a man who loved his country might try," said Dr. Whitman musingly.

The other man, watching the heavy, thoughtful brow, the determined chin, the very bristling of the iron gray hair, thought that if any man could do it here was the one who would try. There was a long silence, and then the trapper spoke.

"I'd go in a minute. My life isn't worth anything! But what would I be when I got there? No one would listen to me against the words of great men—not even if I brought messages from men who know. And —besides—there are reasons why I can't go back East!" And he drew a long sigh that came from the depths of bitterness, hard to hear from one so young and strong and full of life.

Dr. Whitman looked at him quickly, keenly, appreciatively, but asked no question. He knew men well and would not force a confidence.

They presently stretched out on their couches of boughs and fur, with only the firelight to send flickering shadows over the cabin room. But they talked on for a long time: of the country, its needs, its possibilities, its prospects. Then before they slept the doctor arose, knelt beside his couch and prayed. And such a prayer! The very gates of heaven neared and seemed opening to let the petition in. The country, the wonderful country! The people, the poor, blinded, ignorant people! That was the burden of his cry. He brought the matter of their conversation home to God in such a way that now it scarcely seemed necessary any longer to get word to Washington about the peril of Oregon, since appeal had been made to a higher authority. Then, in just a word or two the trapper felt himself acknowledged and introduced before the Most High, and he seemed to stand barefaced, looking into the eyes of God, knowing that he was known and cared for.

Overhead the silent age-old stars kept vigil, wise in their far-seeing and marveling perhaps that the affairs of a mere nation should so stir the soul of a mortal whose life on earth was but a breath at best, since God was in high heaven and all peoples of the earth were His.

When next morning at daybreak the missionary went on his way to Waiilatpu and the trapper made his rounds again, neither was quite the same as they were before that long night conference.

One sentence had passed between them as they parted, telling volumes, and neither would forget. As they looked together at the glory of the dawn, Dr. Whitman turned and gazed deeply into the trapper's eyes.

"Almost—I could ask you to go with me," he said and waited.

A light leapt forth in the other man's eyes.

"And but for one thing—I would go," was the quick reply with a sudden shadowing of his brows.

That was all. They clasped hands warmly with a brief, meaningful pressure and parted, but each was possessed of at least a portion of the other's secret.

Chapter 18

A few days before this, Dr. Whitman's four missionary associates, called by special messenger from him, had come from their distant stations to Waiilatpu. They were quiet men, good and true, with strong, courageous spirits and bodies toughened by toil and hardship. They had come out to this far land, away from home and friends, for no selfish motive, and their hearts were in their work. They were gathered now, as they supposed, to consider the necessities of their work and consult on ways and means.

Each one had built his home with his own hands, tilled his land and planted fields of corn, wheat, potatoes, and melons. Each had taught his Indian neighbors to do the same and was maintaining, with his wife, a school for Indian children in his neighborhood, in addition to preaching and ministering to the sick for miles around. Two of them came from 150 miles away. They were accustomed to the difficult trail and to camping under the stars or stormy skies. Each one was expected to keep his family expenses within three hundred dollars a year. They sometimes managed it within one hundred, for they knew the home board was poor.

These missionaries had known there were serious matters to consider regarding the mission, for which they'd written to the American board for advice. They supposed they were brought together for this. But when Dr. Whitman began to talk instead of political matters, their faces became grave and unsympathetic.

Dr. Whitman began by laying before his colleagues a very clear statement of the way matters stood concerning the Hudson Bay Company. He showed how they were scheming to get Oregon for England and what a disastrous thing this would be for the mission. British sovereignty would mean rule by the Hudson Bay Company, whose chief desire was to keep away men who would teach the Indians, so they might retain the fur trade, all to the company's advantage.

He told them of the fault that had been found with the company's agent, Dr. John McLoughlin of Vancouver, because he had fed some starving American settlers. He made the whole thing plain, though each man already knew the main facts. And then he disclosed his proposal to go to Washington, tell these facts to the government and try to get them to do something to save Oregon—and with Oregon, the mission, of course. He had called them together to get their sanction of his journey.

Silence filled the log room when he finished speaking, and the faces of the men were turned away from him. They were not in sympathy with their enthusiastic colleague. At last one spoke timidly, as though feeling his way, and with his eyes down.

"It seems very commendable that Brother Whitman should be willing to undertake this great journey to save the country and the mission. I make a motion, brethren, that we give him our full approval and commendation."

As if the storm of disapproval had burst with the good brother Spalding's words, the others broke forth with dissuasion, arguments and reproofs.

They told him how impossible the journey was at that time of year. He would be throwing away his life and for what? They bid him think of his mission deserted and what might happen to his wife and his work if he left them alone for the winter. They clamored about public opinion and how it would be said he deserted the Lord's work for earthly things. They refused absolutely to give their consent to his crazy scheme. When he wouldn't be turned from his purpose, they told him in substance they thought he was meddling in matters that weren't his concern and better attend to his missionary duties and let politics alone.

Then Dr. Whitman stood up and faced the men. "I was a man first before I became a missionary," he said, "and when I became a missionary I didn't expatriate myself. I shall go to the States if I have to sever my connection with the mission!" He brought up his hands that had built sawmills, planted gardens, tenderly cared for the sick, been the stay and comfort of many despairing weary ones and dropped them forcibly again in a gesture that showed his mind was made up and nothing could turn it.

Dismay suddenly filled the room and sat on every face. The idea of the mission without Dr. Whitman was appalling. His withdrawal could not be entertained for a moment. At once the whole question was changed, and in a panic those who had been most opposed to his going on the perilous journey moved that his endeavor be heartily approved.

They begged him, however, to wait until the worst of the winter was over, but he wouldn't listen to them.

What he had undertaken to do seemed nearly impossible and a

madness to attempt, yet they couldn't stop him. He proposed to ride almost three thousand miles and be gone three or four months at least, beginning with the first snows of autumn and extending through the worst winter months. He would have to carry supplies to last through the whole journey, as well as provender for his horses and blankets for sleeping on the frozen ground, for there were no inns along the way. And he would doubtless encounter Indians, wild beasts and snow-storms. Yet the man wavered not, while for two whole days they tried to persuade him.

Others had taken the journey at a more favorable time of year, with a large company of companions in a well-organized caravan of supplies, and thought it hard enough at that. He would have to go practically alone or with only one or two companions. Still, he would go, and with splendid courage his wife seconded him in his decision, though it meant long months of separation and anxiety for her.

Thus, after two days of conferring and finally consenting unanimously to what they couldn't prevent, the missionaries returned to their stations.

Immediately upon their departure, Dr. Whitman set about preparing for the journey. Two days later he took the hurried trip to Walla Walla to visit a patient in that region and also to make some quiet inquiries of Mr. McKinley of the Hudson Bay Company concerning a northern boundary treaty he'd heard was about to be made. What he learned there sent him hurrying back without stopping to rest, until he reached the trapper's cabin in the clearing and found another man whose heart thrilled to the same patriotic tune as his own and who, but for some secret shadow, would have been ready to risk his life also in this great endeavor to save Oregon.

As he rode on his faithful "cayuse" back toward the mission he didn't spend time wondering what could prevent a fine, clear-eyed fellow like that from going back to his home. He had been too long in that land without a past and known men too well to judge a person by one act, as they're judged in the heart of civilization. He knew the man he'd just met was in sympathy with his deepest desires, and he trusted him fully and respected his confidence. It was a pity he couldn't have gone. The way would have been better for his company. There was nothing further to be said or thought. It is a great thing to trust a man so much that you can be loyal to him even in your thoughts.

It was high noon before he came within sight of the mission, situated on a beautiful level peninsula formed by the branches of the Walla Walla River, nearly three hundred acres of land fenced in and two hundred under cultivation, all now lying under its first fall blanket of whiteness.

At the left was the little adobe house in which his wife and he had lived when they first came out to that country over the long, hard trail. And off at the right stood the new log house, sixty feet long and eighteen feet wide with an extension at the back, making a great T. Back of that was the blacksmith shop, and down by the riverside the flour mill—all the work of this man's hands and the pride and love of his heart.

As he looked at it now in its setting of white with the blue ribbon of river twining it about and the dark woods beyond, his heart suddenly failed him at the thought of leaving, and the tears dimmed his eyes. Down there in the whiteness lay the grave of their one child who had drowned in the river when scarcely more than a baby; and in the house was his wife, strong, courageous, loving and ready to speed him on his way in whatever enterprise he undertook. He would have to leave it all, not knowing if he would ever see it again.

But Dr. Whitman didn't linger on these thoughts. For an instant he let the pang of his going tear through his heart. Then at once he spurred his horse forward, knowing he must lose no time.

His few simple preparations had been going steadily forward during his absence. Yet with the news he felt it necessary to cut down even the two or three days more he'd hoped to spend at home and go the next day if possible.

The people of Dr. Whitman's household did not demur when he spoke the word "I must." One instant his wife stood aghast at the thought of his going so soon; the next she'd set her face to do everything in her power to make it possible and easy for him.

A message was sent at once to General Lovejoy, a young man who had come out West that same summer and sometime ago expressed his belief that it was entirely possible to go through the mountains at that time of year. He'd promised to accompany Dr. Whitman.

The mission was astir far into the night.

It was a bright, clear morning when they started. The mules stood ready with the supplies strapped to their backs, the horses were saddled, and Lovejoy and the guide were already in their saddles when Dr. Whitman came out of the house.

All the Indians who lived nearby had come to see the party off, and a few of the most devoted proposed to ride the first day's journey with them.

In the doorway Mrs. Whitman stood with thirty or forty little Indian children of the school grouped about her.

Their good-byes had been said in the quiet of their own room, these two who had left the whole world behind and come out West to do God's work together. They understood one another perfectly, and no selfish wishes hindered the great purposes of their united lives. Each knew what a trial the succeeding months would be to the other, and each had accepted it. Now as the missionary stepped forth to leave, his wife wore a bright, courageous smile. It was harder perhaps to stay behind than to go out and fight storm, peril, wild beast and wilder man, and the man knew she bore the harder part. His own heart was bearing her grief as he waved to her and mounted his faithful cayuse. Tears sprang into his eyes as he looked at her, brave and smiling among the little children.

They rode away into the crisp morning, and the woman watched them out of sight and then turned back to her long task of waiting.

All day the men rode. At dusk they tethered their horses, built a fire, prepared and ate supper, and slept soundly till dawn; then they were up and off again.

Eleven days they rode, resting on the Sabbath, and reached Fort Hall, four hundred miles from their starting place, at the rate of forty miles a day. Their Indian friends had, of course, turned back, and only Whitman, Lovejoy and the guide remained, with the pack mules. But along the way they encountered Indians who forbade them to proceed. Dr. Whitman knew whose instructions they were acting upon, but in his wise way he held parley with each band and succeeded in going his way.

At Fort Hall Captain Grant informed him that the Pawnees and Sioux were at war, and it would be death to go through their country, even if he succeeded in getting through the deep snow in the mountains. He was advised either to turn back or wait until spring, but he wouldn't do either. As calmly as a mother might have picked up another toy dropped by a peevish child, he adjusted his plans and added a thousand miles to his journey. Turning from the direct route he'd intended to travel, he took the old Spanish trail for Santa Fe. Choosing a new guide from Fort Hall, he pushed on across the northeast corner of Utah to Fort Uintah in the Uintah Mountains, and now the way grew white with snow, and the weather was severe. The snows were deep and blinding and greatly impeded their progress. A weaker man would have turned back, but Dr. Whitman kept steadily on as if these things had all been part of his plans.

They changed guides at Fort Uintah, continuing their journey across Green River over to the Valley of the Grand into what is now the state of Colorado. At Fort Uncompahgre they stopped for a brief rest, made a few purchases, changed guides, then were off again.

The trail led over the highlands among the irregular spurs of the Rocky Mountains, and for four or five days all went well. Steadily, surely, they were making their way toward the goal. It was still a long way off, but the start had been good, and the missionary gave thanks.

Then suddenly one day without warning the air grew white with a storm whirling about them. The blinding snow fell with such rapidity and the wind blew with such violence that in a few minutes they were almost bewildered. They were forced to seek shelter at once. A ravine wasn't far away, and they turned toward it instantly when the storm surrounded them, but they had to struggle through high drifts before they found it. In shelter at last, with thankful hearts, they cut cottonwood trees for the animals, made themselves as comfortable in the camp as possible and waited while the storm raged about them for three or four days.

Still whiteness all about, thick whiteness in the air, shut in from the world, they sat and waited. Dr. Whitman's strong, patient face showed no sign of what might be going on inside his eager, impatient soul. In one direction through the whiteness lay Oregon, beloved Oregon, his wife, his home, his mission—all in peril. In the other direction, miles and miles more away, was a government unawares, toying with a possibility of possession and not knowing the treasure they were so lightly considering. Here he sat, willing and eager with the message, held by the storm in this vast mountain whiteness, while the nation perchance sold its rich birthright for a mess of pottage. What did it mean? No man's hand had been able to stay him thus. But God's hand was holding him now—God's soft, white, strong hand. He sat patient, submissive, not understanding, but waiting and looking up for the reason.

At last the storm subsided, and the weather cleared, leaving it intensely cold. Cheerfully, though with difficulty, the small brave party made its way again to the highlands. But the snow was so deep and the wind so piercing that after a brief attempt they were forced back to camp to wait for several more days till a change of weather made it safe for them to venture forth again.

They wandered about for days in search of the trail until the guide at last stopped with a sullen look and confessed he didn't know where he was. He said the snow had so changed the appearance of the country that he couldn't get his bearings and was completely lost. He could take them no further.

This news dashed Dr. Whitman's hope, which had been rising steadily since the storm ceased. But invincible as ever he refused to become downcast. Some men would have said that surely now they'd done everything possible, and they'd have felt justified in turning back and trying to find comfort and safety, at least until spring; not so this man. After thinking it over carefully and consulting with Lovejoy they agreed that Whitman should take the guide and try to get back to the fort for a new guide, while Lovejoy remained in camp with the pack mules.

Lovejoy had no small part now to play in the winter drama. Alone with the horses and a dog in his mountain camp, he had no idea whether Whitman would ever find the fort and, even if he did, whether he would return and find Lovejoy again. It required faith and courage to stay alone with the animals and endure that long, solemn, silent week in the snow.

A precious week was wasted in going and coming back, for the snow was deep and made the trip slow and uncertain. But Whitman braced himself for the added burden and kept his good cheer, and at last the watcher in the mountains saw his companion returning.

Then slowly, like a train of snails, the little party crept through the snow again and over the mountains, until one morning they could see the winding shore of the Grand River.

They hurried forward as fast as they could, counting every difficulty small now that they saw the river ahead. But despair met them at the shore.

The river was 150 to 200 yards wide and frozen a third of the way across on either side. The current was so rapid in the center that even in that bitter weather it had been kept from freezing. The guide said it would be too dangerous to try to cross. It looked as if another impossible barrier lay across their way. But Dr. Whitman wouldn't stop until he had to. He led the little party out on the ice as far as it was safe, then mounted his brave cayuse and directed Lovejoy and the guide to push him off the ice into the boiling, foaming current. After much protesting in vain, they finally did.

It seemed as if they had cast Whitman into a terrible grave, and at first man and horse completely disappeared under water. But soon they came up unbaffled, master and beast appearing to be of one and the same spirit, and buffeted the waves magnificently. They made their way gradually, although a long distance downstream, to the opposite shore, where the rider leaped from his horse onto the ice and soon had the faithful animal safely by his side.

Lovejoy and the guide struggled to follow his example, force the mules into the stream and take the perilous trip themselves, but they did so. People couldn't help accomplishing great things when they were with Dr. Whitman. His presence in their midst required it. For very shame they had in some measure to live up to the pattern set.

By the time they had safely landed Whitman had a good fire burning, and soon they were cheerfully sitting around the blaze drying their frozen clothing, one more peril passed and one less river between them and the goal.

It was by now the middle of January, and all over the country the cold was so bitter that many people even in protected towns were frozen to death. Out in the open the cold, like an iron grip, enfolded a person and slowly, relentlessly grew tighter. A black stillness settled upon everything, a vast and universal cold and fear that penetrated one's very soul.

On one of these terrible mornings, as the doctor began his usual preparations for going on, the guide shook his head and protested vigorously. A blinding storm had raged through the night, and the wind had made up for what moderation there was in the atmosphere. Traveling was sheer suicide that day, but Dr. Whitman had already lost too much time. He laughed off fears and cheered the others with his hearty voice, and so they set forth well muffled.

They were in a deep gorge of the New Mexico mountains and toiled on for a while in the blinding snow. But when they reached the divide and the wind rushed up from a new direction the biting snow and cold almost drove the horses mad. Whitman saw his terrible mistake and turned at once to retrace his steps to camp, convinced that to go farther would be folly. This, however, was impossible, for the driving snow had obliterated all trace of the way, and the whole country was deep and white and awful. The sky grew darker until it was almost as black as night, and the snow was falling so heavily that every step became more and more difficult.

Then suddenly hope seemed to vanish, too, and leave the world in darkness. The staunch missionary saw that apparently the end had come. They couldn't live for more than a few minutes longer in this fearful cold, and to go on was as useless as it was impossible, for they couldn't find their way anywhere.

With the feeling of utter failure he slipped from his saddle and stood beside his horse. Then bending his head he commended himself and his distant wife to the God in whom they both trusted. With the bitter thought that through his own folly the cause he was serving must be lost, he gave himself up to wait for the white grave fast closing in about them.

Suddenly the guide noticed the ears of one of the pack mules. "That mule will find the camp if he can live to get to it!" he exclaimed.

Excited, they mounted again and followed the mule.

He kept on down the divide for a little way, then made a square turn and plunged straight down the steep mountainside, over what seemed like fearful precipices. No one needed to urge him, for he seemed to know how much depended upon him.

At last he stopped short in the thick timber over a bare spot. Looking down they saw a brand or two still burning in the fire they'd left in the morning! They were saved!

The guide was too far gone to dismount, but Dr. Whitman slipped from his saddle and found he had enough strength to build up the fire. With profound thankfulness he went to work and soon had the rest of the party comfortable. His own ability to withstand the cold was probably due to the heavy buffalo hides he wore.

When the weather calmed again and they could make their way out from camp, Dr. Whitman moved ahead cautiously, not willing to let his own eagerness risk the safety of his whole enterprise again.

They encountered another narrow escape when they reached the headwaters of the Arkansas after a day in a terrible storm and found the ice on the river too thin to bear a man erect and every stick of wood in the vicinity over on the other side. Taking his axe in one hand and a short willow stick in the other, Dr. Whitman spread himself on the ice, with his arms and legs as far apart as possible, and crept across, cut the wood, shoved it over, and then returned, creeping as before. That night a wolf stole the hatchet for a leather thong that had been bound around the split helve, and for the rest of the journey the small comfort of an axe was denied them.

The way to Fort Taos was slow and painful, with the snows deep and their provisions growing less and less, so that they were finally forced to kill and eat the mules. When they reached the fort at last, they had to rest for a couple of weeks.

Bent's Fort on the Arkansas River was their next destination. The route led them through Santa Fe over a well-traveled trail, which, if the season had been summer, would have made it easier for them. On the way, however, they met people who told them of a party about to leave Bent's Fort for St. Louis. With very little likelihood of reaching them before they left, Dr. Whitman, on his best horse and with a few provisions, started on ahead of his party. He got lost on the way, though, and Lovejoy with the guide arrived at the fort ahead of him.

Lovejoy sent a message to the St. Louis party camped forty miles ahead to wait until the doctor joined them and then went a hundred miles back to search for the lost missionary. He returned to the fort without him and waited anxiously until the doctor came at last. Whitman was worn and weary and felt that his bewilderment and loss of time resulted from his traveling on Sunday in order to make time— the only instance on the whole journey he had traveled on Sunday.

Lovejoy was worn out with the hardships, so he remained at Fort Bent until Whitman returned in the summer with a party of emigrants on his way back to Oregon. Dr. Whitman rested only one night and pressed on alone to overtake the party of mountain men and go to St. Louis with them.

The trail led him more than four hundred miles, along the banks of the Arkansas to Great Bend, across the country to Smoky Hill River, down the Kansas River till it joined the Missouri. Near the end of January he reached the little town of Westport, Missouri.

His going was like that of a sower going forth to sow good seed. As he went, he told everyone he met of Oregon; how the way was open for wagons and women and children; how he had come over that long trail in the winter snows to tell them it was possible and they were being deceived by the reports spread by the Hudson Bay Company, who wished to keep the Americans out of Oregon. Everywhere he found people who had intended going out West but had been stopped by false reports that the way was impassable. He told them to get ready to go with him when he returned. Everywhere he went, the reports of his story about Oregon spread to all the country round about, and people were stirred to take their families and go out to claim land in this rich, fertile country. The enthusiasm spread like wildfire.

Lovejoy in his resting place wasn't idle either. He continued to tell the good story, urging all he met to go to Oregon and save it for themselves and their country. It meant a great deal to them that the missionary who crossed the mountains to tell them the story had promised to return and guide them to the "promised land."

And so in his "buffalo coat with a blue border," as he described his own garments, Dr. Whitman went on his way to St. Louis.

In those days seldom did anyone cross the mountains in winter from Santa Fe or the Columbia. Fur traders, trappers, adventurers and contractors for the military posts gathered around him to hear the news and ask questions. They wanted to know the prospects for furs and buffalo hides the next season, but Dr. Whitman had no time for such things. He was in a hurry to get to Washington and wanted to know if the Ashburton treaty was concluded. When he found it had been signed by Webster and Ashburton the summer before, he demanded to know if it covered the Northwest and how it affected Oregon. He asked if Oregon had been under discussion in Congress and what was being urged about it in the Senate and House. His great question was, Could he reach Washington before Congress adjourned on the fourth of March?

Leaving his horse, he took the stage at once, and one day in the last of February, he walked into the home of a minister friend in Ithaca, New York—a friend who had once crossed the mountains with him.

"Parker," he said, after the first surprised greetings were over, "I've come on an urgent errand. We must go at once to Washington, or Oregon is lost, ceded to the English."

But the friend wasn't easily persuaded and thought the danger less than Dr. Whitman said, so the courageous man hurried alone to Washington. Suffering still from his frostbitten fingers, feet, nose and ears; lacking the sympathy and enthusiasm of even his dearest friends; worn and weary, yet undaunted, he pressed on to complete his task. Arriving in Washington on the third of March, he went at once to interview Daniel Webster, the secretary of state, to endeavor to convince him that Oregon was worth saving for America.

Chapter 19

D avid Spafford had been in Washington for a week on matters connected with the political situation. He happened to call on the Hon. Joshua Giddings, who was boarding on Capitol Hill, in what was known as Duff's Green's Row. He was deep in conversation with the gentleman when another man, a stranger, entered the room. His strong, fine face instantly attracted him. He was gaunt, almost haggard in appearance and browned with the weather, but behind his keen blue eyes burned a fire of earnest purpose that made David feel he was a man worth knowing. Instinctively he stood as the stranger entered the room. His host did also and approached the newcomer with an outstretched hand that indicated a hearty sympathy for his cause.

"Mr. Spafford, allow me the pleasure of introducing you to Dr. Whitman of Oregon!"

"Oregon!" exclaimed David, grasping the stranger's hand with a thrill of instant interest. "Oregon? Really? How long since?"

"Today," said Dr. Whitman briskly, as if it were only over in the next county. "I just arrived this morning. Left home last October and been traveling ever since."

"You don't say so!" David's voice was full of wonder and deep admiration. "And how is Oregon?"

"About to be lost to us if something isn't done quickly," said Dr. Whitman. "That's why I'm here. I've spent all my eloquence on Daniel Webster this morning, but they've got him so filled with the idea that Oregon is of no use to our country because the mountains are impassable that nothing else seems to have any effect. Lord Ashburton, Sir George Simpson and their friends have done their work well."

"How is that?" asked David.

"Why, you see, they've been working quietly to impress our statesmen with the idea that the Rocky Mountains are so impassable to wagons that it can't be peopled from the States and is therefore of little value to this country. They want it for themselves—that is, the Hudson Bay Company wishes to retain control and keep the Indians in their present state of ignorance, so they can make more advantageous deals with them."

"Please sit down," said David. "I'm deeply interested in what's said in the papers about Oregon. It seems foolish to let it go for the cod fisheries. You think it's worthwhile saving, don't you, or you'd never have come."

Clearly, concisely, Whitman spoke, and in a few minutes the little parlor on Capitol Hill was thrilling with the story of the new land. The few privileged to listen were convinced.

"And have you told all this to Webster?" asked David.

"Yes," said the missionary with a sigh. "I tried my best to convince him he was the victim of false representations about the character of the region and told him I intended to take a train of emigrants over to Oregon this summer, but it made no impression. He thinks I'm a dreamer, or a foolish enthusiast, I suppose."

"A man isn't fit to be secretary of state if he has no clear vision for the future," said David, rising in his excitement and striding across the room restlessly. "He should make sure of his facts. Your words may at least set him thinking. Perhaps he'll investigate.

"It's the same thing they're doing to my friend Professor Morse and his wonderful invention of the electric telegraph. They won't pass the bill for an appropriation to try the thing out and see if it succeeds. This session of Congress is all but over, and it's only passed the House. There's little hope left for this time. Yet it's been practically proven already in a small way. Think what it'll be to the country when the whole United States can communicate by electricity and messages can be received within a few minutes of their sending, even from great distances. Who knows—maybe the whole earth will be girdled someday by an electric telegraph. You've heard of it?"

The tired blue eyes lighted with interest.

"Just a hint or two," said Whitman. "I heard that a man over in England had invented something that would carry messages over a few miles, but very little of the details have reached me. I heard, too, that some American was working at the same thing but didn't dream it had become a practical thing. It seemed to be a sort of plaything. You say it's really a success? You've seen it? What a miracle! Ah! If it had only been invented a few years sooner and perfected and put in working order! If there were only a telegraph over the Rockies I might have been spared this journey and all this time away from my work. I would have kept the wires hot with warnings until they had to heed me."

"Have you seen President Tyler?" asked David, suddenly wheeling and looking keenly at the missionary.

"Not yet," answered the doctor. "My friend Senator Linn, of Missouri, is trying to arrange an interview for me. I hope to see him this afternoon or tomorrow sometime. Senator Linn is a staunch friend of Oregon. He'll do all he can."

And even while they were talking, a messenger came from the senator saying the interview was granted.

"I'll be anxious to know how this comes out," said David.

"You're to be in Washington for several days yet?"

"I'm not sure," said David. "I'll stay until Congress adjourns—anyway. I'm interested in Professor Morse's bill and don't want to leave as long as there's a chance of doing anything for it."

"And I'll want to know how that comes out also. I'll see you again before you go. You're a man after my own heart," said Dr. Whitman with a hearty grasp of David's hand. Then he left for the interview which meant so much for Oregon and for the man who had assumed its cause.

All that same day, with the patience of the ages in his heart and the perseverance of the genius, another of God's heroes sat in the Senate gallery and waited. He waited for other men to recognize their opportunity and set their seal on his effort, making it possible to come to something. And all those small-great men sat and bickered about this and that and let the matters of worldwide moment slip unnoticed.

Ten long fruitless years Samuel Morse had labored and waited in vain for the world to do its part for his electric telegraph, since he'd first caught his vision of what it might be and knew his work in the world. And now, if this day passed without the bill coming before the Senate, he would go home to New York with only the fraction of a dollar in his pocket to stand between him and starvation. As he sat and waited while a nation's petty business droned on, he reviewed his life and the enviable reputation as a painter he had dropped and let die for the sake of this new love, this wary elusive maiden of electric charm and uncertainty. If this day failed to bring his finished invention to a place before the world where it could win recognition, he was ruined. He didn't wish to try any further to make a blind world see what he had done for its benefit. Let it go. Let the wonderful invention drop back into the obscurity it had occupied before it was born in his own struggling soul.

As the day dragged on and his friends and acquaintances came and went, they spoke to him about his bill. They felt sorry for him sitting there so hopelessly and patiently. They told him there was little hope now that his bill would come to the front at all, with all the business remaining on the docket and Congress to adjourn at midnight. Some stopped to say it was a shame and hinted that some members in the House intended to procure its defeat in the Senate.

Evening drew down, and business dragged on, with a weary session full of things he had no interest in. At last, assured by his friends that his bill couldn't be reached that night, Professor Morse, nearly heartbroken, stole from the gallery and went to his room at the hotel to lie down and sleep in utter exhaustion and disappointment.

Half an hour later, just a few minutes before midnight, his bill was reached and amazingly passed! But the man on whose heart it had lain for long years, whose very life had been given for it day by day, was lying asleep and didn't know till morning.

They told him while he sat at breakfast the next morning. He could scarcely believe his senses that the weary years were over and his chance to put his invention before the world had come at last.

Three days later David, about to go home, met Dr. Whitman on Pennsylvania Avenue and extended his hand. "So you're still here! How did you come out with Oregon? Did Tyler have any better idea about things than Webster did?"

"Not a bit, not a bit," said Whitman, grasping the extended hand. "But I believe he understands the situation better now. When I first began to talk I felt almost as if it were useless to try. He was firmly entrenched behind the same views Webster held, that Oregon was useless to the United States. But I told him all about it. I told him I went over the mountains four times, once in the dead of winter, and that seven years ago I took a wagon over. I informed him I intended to carry a large party back with me in the spring and that we, being American citizens, would claim protection from the national government. I showed him my frozen limbs, and he looked in my face and believed me! Then I told him all about the climate and soil and the importance of Oregon to the nation, and he began to be convinced. At last he gave me a conditional promise of protection if my emigration plan succeeds. My last word to him was that the emigrants would go over and would look to him for protection when they reached their destination and would expect the moral support of the government and the necessary legislation by

Congress. In parting he wished me success in the undertaking.

"And now," the missionary said, and his face lit up with eager determination, "now, God giving me life and strength, I'll connect the Missouri and Columbia with a wagon track so deep and plain that neither national envy nor sectional fanaticism will ever blot it out."

"God bless you in your wonderful undertaking," said David. "And who knows but someday your wagon track may be a railroad."

The missionary's eyes rested on the other man's face in growing wonder, and the light of the miracle believer shone in them as he said in a tone of awe, "Who knows."

And then he briskly changed his tone.

"Your telegraph came out all right. I'm glad. God is in all these things. They must come out right sooner or later, even though the people they come through are slow and hard of heart and filled with their own devices. I wish you were going to Oregon with me."

"I wish I were, too," said David heartily. "Nothing would delight me more, but I guess my work is here for the present."

"You're right. We need men like you in the East to keep things straight. Levelheaded, far-seeing men are scarce. I'll feel safer out in Oregon knowing you're here at work, thinking and acting and voting, and writing—for they tell me you have great power in that direction. Give Oregon a good word now and then."

"I will indeed," said David smiling. "You've made me an ardent supporter of the cause. I wish more of my party understood the matter fully. There's a general feeling among Whigs that we should stick to abolition and not bother with annexation. I think they're wrong on that. I'll do my little best to make a few men see. I wish I might have the pleasure of another talk with you. How soon are you leaving this part of the world? Couldn't you spend a few days with me at my home up in New York State?"

"I haven't much time," said the missionary. "But New York State— where? Anywhere near Ithaca? I must attend a meeting in Boston of the Prudential Committee of the American Board concerning important matters connected with the mission. I also need to spend a day with my old friend Parker in Ithaca and then go home for a brief visit with Father and Mother. If I could work it in I'd be delighted to see you in your home. It would be a memory to carry back. But you see how it is—my time is short."

"But our home is right on your way. You might at least stop overnight with us. Why not go on with me tomorrow? Or do you have to stay in Washington longer?"

"No, I guess I've done about all I can here now," said the missionary, "and I should be on the move. I have one or two more people to see, but I hope to see them today. I'll try to do it. What time do you leave?"

"I was expecting to take the morning train but can wait until afternoon if that will suit you better. It would be worth waiting to have your company."

"Thank you," said Dr. Whitman, smiling. "But I think I can get ready by morning. Don't change your plans. I'll be there." And with a hearty handshake he was gone.

Chapter 20

Miranda tied on a clean apron, put a finishing touch to the tea table and stepped over to the window to watch. The afternoon train was in. Rose had taken her little brother and walked down the street to stand at the corner and watch for her father, for a letter had arrived that morning saying he hoped to get home that day.

Miranda had made rusk for supper, along with chicken and gravy, applesauce and a custard pie. Marcia was sitting by the dining room window where she could see far down the street. Her knitting was in her hands, but her eyes were on the street with a light of welcome in them, and the pink flush on her cheek told Miranda how eagerly she watched for her husband's coming. Miranda stood at the pantry window where she could see the street as well without obstructing Marcia's view. She exulted in the joy of the household she served and watched as eagerly for the homecoming of the master as if he had been her own. Having none of her own, she loved these dear people wholeheartedly.

"Well, he's comin'," she said, bustling into the dining room, "an' he's got an odd-lookin' pusson with him. 'Spose he's bringin' him to supper? It beats all how Mr. David does pick up odd-lookin' pussons that has a his'try to 'em. This one looks like he'd killed a bear and put on his skin. Well, there's plenty o' chicken an' rusks, an' there's three pumpkin pies an' a mince down cellar ef the custard ain't 'nuff. Do you 'spose he's bringin' him in?" Miranda patted the fresh napkins and slipped up behind Marcia for another view of the street.

"It looks like it," said Marcia. "Yes, they're turning in at the gate. Better put another plate on and fill the spare room pitcher. He'll likely want to wash."

"Spare room pitcher's full," said Miranda triumphantly. " 'Spose I wouldn't keep that ready when Mr. David was a comin' an' might bring company? Guess I'll put on a dish o' plum jam, too." And Miranda hastened happily and importantly away. She delighted in being ready for the unexpected, and company was her joy and opportunity.

In a moment more Rose and her little brother came dancing into the kitchen shouting, "Father's come! Father's come and brought company! A nice, funny man with a big fur coat. Miranda, Father's here, and he's brought us each an orange and Mother a new silk dress, all silvery with pink flowers over it and a lace collar just like a spider's web."

While they were eating supper Nathan came to the door with a bundle of letters from the office and a great welcome in his eyes for his beloved chief.

"Come right in, my boy, and have supper with us," said David heartily. "Miranda, do you have another plate handy? Nathan, I want you to know this great man and hear him talk. This is Dr. Whitman of Oregon, and he's ridden three thousand miles across the Rocky Mountains to save Oregon for the United States. Mr. Whitman, this is my right-hand man, Nathan Whitney. Someday when he gets through his college education he'll be coming out to be a senator or governor or something."

Dr. Whitman, with the eager look that showed his interest in all mankind, rose from his seat and stretched out a hand to the shy boy, searching his face.

"Whitney! Whitney! Where have I heard that name recently? Ah, yes, I remember—out in Oregon, the night before I left. He was a young trapper, and I noticed the name because it was like mine. We had supper together in his cabin, and I stayed all night with him. I took a great liking to him. He was in thorough sympathy with me in my undertaking. I wanted to bring him with me, but he said he had reasons why he couldn't come east, so I didn't urge him. But he certainly was a fine fellow, and I'm looking forward to seeing him again when I go home. Who knows but he's a relative of yours? When I get back I'll have to tell him about the boy I saw of his name and how you're coming out to us when you're through with your education."

Nathan's eyes shone over this hearty greeting, and he managed to stammer out a few words in answer and drop into the seat Miranda had prepared for him, with his eyes fixed on the visitor's worn but keen face.

They all settled back into their seats again and went on with their supper. No one noticed Miranda, who during the introduction had stood stock-still in the kitchen doorway. Her face was as white as a ghost, and the tea towel she'd held in her hand lay unheeded on the spotless floor at her feet, while she grasped the door frame with one hand and involuntarily pressed the other hand to her fluttering heart.

"You must have a good many fine young fellows out there," said David, as he helped Nathan to a generous serving of chicken and mashed potatoes.

"Well, not so many! A good many are pretty rough specimens. They almost have to be, you know, for it's a hard life—a rough, hard, lonely life out there. But this man was unusual. I knew it the minute I laid eyes on him. I was riding down the mountain trail singing hymns to while away the time. I sing occasionally when I'm out where no one can hear me. My wife likes me to do it for practice." He smiled his rare whimsical smile.

"When I reached the clearing and the little cabin standing there, I saw a light in the window, and at the door stood a great, tall giant of a fellow waiting to welcome me. He said he heard me singing a song his mother used to sing when he was a little shaver. Well, I went in and found he had supper all ready for me, and a good supper, too. Perhaps you don't know how good corn bread and venison can taste after a long day on the trail. He had a nice little cabin with a cheery fire going and the table spread for two. All around the walls pelts were hung, and there were fresh pine branches in the corner for a bed, with a great buffalo hide spread over it, the finest bed you ever lay on. We talked way into the night, and he told me a lot of things about the Hudson Bay Company. He was an unusually fine fellow—"

Miranda still stood spellbound in the doorway, while the coffee boiled over on the fire. Marcia had to speak to her twice before she turned with a jump and a bright wave of color spreading over her face and went to her neglected task. When she brought the coffeepot to the table her hand was trembling so that she could scarcely set it down.

The table talk was very interesting with stories of the trail, the mission, the Indians and their way of life, the long pilgrimage east, the stay in Washington and Whitman's work there. Nathan sat with red cheeks and shining eyes, forgetting to eat. Rose, round-eyed and eager, watched him and listened, too. Marcia, noting Miranda absorbed in the doorway, gathered little David into her arms and let his sleepy head fall on her shoulder. She didn't want to disturb the conversation by slipping away to put him in bed or sending Miranda to do it.

At last Nathan mustered courage to ask a question. "How did you come to go out there in the first place?"

Whitman turned his keen blue eyes on the boy and smiled. "I think it was from reading the pathetic story of the Indians who came east in search of the Book of Heaven. Did you ever hear it?"

Nathan shook his head, and David, seeing his eager look, urged,

"Tell us, won't you?"

"A few years ago," began the missionary, "a white man was present at some of the Indian religious ceremonies. He observed them as they worshipped and told them that wasn't the way to worship the Great Spirit. The white men had a Book of Heaven that would show them how to worship so they would enjoy His favor during life and at their death would be received into the country where He resides, to be with Him forever. When the Indians heard this they held a council and decided that if it were true they should get that book right away and find out how to worship the Great Spirit. So they appointed four of their chiefs to go to St. Louis to see their great father, General Clark. He was the first American officer they had ever known, and they felt confident he would tell them the truth, help them find the book and send teachers.

"These four Indians arrived at St. Louis after a long, hard journey on foot over the mountains and finally presented themselves before General Clark and told him what they had come for. General Clark was puzzled and perhaps not a little troubled at this responsibility thrust upon him, but he received the Indians courteously and tried to explain to them about the Book of Heaven. He said there was such a book, and he told them the story of man from the creation, as well as the story of the Savior, and tried to explain to them all the moral precepts and commandments laid down in the Bible. Then, perhaps feeling that he'd done his duty, he tried to make the men's visit pleasant for them. He took them all over the city and showed them everything. They were delighted, of course, especially with riding around in a carriage on wheels, which pleased them more than anything else they saw.

"But the hard journey and change of food were too much for two of the men, and they died while in St. Louis. The other two, dismayed and sad and not feeling very well themselves, prepared to return to their homes. Before they left the city, however, General Clark gave them a banquet, at the close of which one of the Indian chiefs made a farewell speech, through an interpreter, of course, and one of the men present wrote it down. It got into the papers, and it was the reading of this speech, perhaps, more than anything else, that determined me to go if possible to preach the gospel to the Indians.

"The chief said, 'I came to you over a trail of many moons from the setting sun. You were the friend of my fathers, who have all gone the long way. I came with one eye partly opened, for more light for my people who sit in darkness. I go back with both eyes closed. How can I go back blind to my blind people? I made my way to you with strong arms, through many enemies and strange lands, that I might carry back much to them. I go back with both arms broken and empty. The two fathers who came with me—the braves of many winters and wars—we leave asleep here by your great water. They were tired in many moons, and their moccasins wore out.

" 'My people sent me to get the white man's Book of Heaven. You took me where you allow your women to dance as we do not ours, and the Book was not there. You took me where they worship the Great Spirit with candles, and the Book was not there. You showed me the images of good spirits and pictures of the good land beyond, but the Book was not among them. I am going back the long, sad trail to my people of the dark land. You make my feet heavy with burdens of gifts, and my moccasins will grow old in carrying them, but the Book is not among them. When I tell my poor, blind people, after one more snow, in the big council that I did not bring the Book, no word will be spoken by our old men or by our young braves. One by one they will rise up and go out in silence. My people will die in darkness, and they will go on the long path to the other hunting grounds. No white man will go with them, and no white man's Book to make the way plain. I have no more words.'

"It is among the people of the tribe that sent those chiefs after the Book of Heaven that I am now working."

It was late when they arose from the supper table and went into the parlor for worship. Miranda stirred from her absorption finally and tiptoed around softly removing dishes from the table and putting everything in order in the kitchen for morning. But she kept the kitchen door open wide and handled each dish gently so she might hear every word the man spoke. And all the while her heart throbbed loudly under her ruffled white bib apron, and her thoughts were busy as her fingers, while on her lips a look of determination grew.

Nathan didn't go home until after ten o'clock, a most unearthly hour for people to sit up in those days. When he left, the missionary grasped his hand again and looked steadily into his clear, brown eyes.

"Boy, don't forget you're coming out to Oregon someday to help us make a great country of it. We need such men as you're going to be. Get good and ready and then come, but don't be too long about it. It's strange," he said, turning to David with a smile, "but this boy has taken a great hold on me. His eyes are like the eyes of that young trapper I told you about, young Whitney. Perhaps you'll find a distant relative in him when you get there, lad. I must tell him about you. Good night."

The front door closed, and Nathan went home under the stars feeling as though in some subtle way a great honor had been bestowed upon him. Miranda, in the back hall, turned and fled up the stairs with her candle. But she'd heard every word, and her heart was beating so hard she could scarcely get her breath when she reached her room.

She put her candle on the bureau and sat down on the edge of her bed with her eyes shining and her hand on her heart. After a minute she went softly over to her mirror and stood looking into it.

"Oh, Allan, Allan!" she breathed softly. Slowly the look of determination that had been growing in her face crystallized into purpose, and she turned swiftly from her mirror and went downstairs.

David had just finished locking up and banking the library fire and was surprised to see her descending the stairs again.

"You're not sick, are you, Miranda?" he asked anxiously. "Shall I call my wife?"

"No, thank you, Mr. David," said Miranda briskly. "I jest wanted to borry the loan of a quill. Ther's somethin' I made out I'd write, an' I disremember where I left mine the las' time I wrote a letter."

David, surprised, found her a pen, ink and paper, and Miranda went happily back to her room, stopping in the kitchen to procure extra candles. Through the long night, oblivious to cold or weariness, she wrote and rewrote.

"Now what do you suppose Miranda is up to this time?" David asked his wife upstairs. "She's just borrowed writing materials. Is she inspired to literature, do you suppose? Or does she want to set down some of the wonderful tales she heard this evening?"

"There's no telling," said Marcia, smiling. "She's just the oddest, dearest thing that ever was made. Whatever we would do without her I don't know. She'd make a wonderful wife for some man, if one could be found who was good enough for her, which I very much doubt—that is, one who knew enough to appreciate her. But it's lucky for us she doesn't seem inclined that way. Oh—David! It's so good to have you back again. The time has been so long!"

And straightway these two married lovers forgot Miranda and her concerns in their own deep joy of each other.

Chapter 21

In the early dawn of the morning, when the candle flickered with a sickly light against the rosy gleam from the East, Miranda finished, signed and sealed her letter. On her bureau lay a pile of tiny bits of torn paper, the debris of her night's work.

She had fine feelings and was very conscious of the Allan who had left her with the promise of returning someday. As if his kiss were still fresh upon her lips, she shrank from any hint that he was bound to come back to her. Not for worlds would she have him think she held him responsible for that kiss or that it meant anything else but the only gratitude he could then show her for releasing him from his prison and trial into the world of freedom. He mustn't think this letter had any personal interest for her at all. The years had passed, and she was no fool. The kiss and his last words had been precious experiences she had treasured all this while, but of course she really had no right to them in the sense kisses usually meant.

The possibility Allan was still alive and might someday get her letter brought her face to face with the practical side of life. She felt that after sending that letter she couldn't cheat herself into believing he belonged to her any longer. She would have to surrender what had come to be so sweet to her; but it was right, of course, and she could give up such foolishness.

This one night she would exult in speaking to him once more, feeling that he was hers and his fate hung yet in her hands. Then, after she had done her best to give him the truth, his fate would be in his own hands, and she could do nothing more for him. So she wrote and smiled and tore up her letters, though they were all matter of fact and not foolish. At last with a sigh and a glance at the advancing morning she finished and sealed one, knowing her time of delight was over and she must return to the plain sordid world, the jolly old-maid life ahead of her.

The letter read:

Mr. Allan Whitney, Esq.
    Dear sir—I now take my pen in hand to let you know that I am well and hope you are the same—

All her efforts had that same brave beginning in common. It was culled from *The Young Ladies' Friend and Complete Guide to Polite Letter Writing,* a neat red and gold volume Grandmother Heath had bestowed upon her the day she wrote a composition the teacher considered good enough to be read aloud. Miranda kept the book wrapped in tissue paper in the bottom of her little hair trunk. She'd brought it out in triumph to help with this night's work and consulted it earnestly and laboriously. Once she had her brave beginning, however, she searched in vain for further sentences that would apply to the occasion and at last in desperation plunged into her own original language.

And if you are really Allan Whitney I guess you'll know who you are an' why I'm writin'. Ef you ain't the right one no harm's done. But I felt like if 'twas really you I'd ought to let you know. I wouldn't uv thought it was you, only this misshunery man said your name was Whitney an' said you was tall with brown eyes an' couldn't come east, so I sensed it might be you. And I'd uv let you know sooner ef I'd knowed where to write, but it only happened a couple o' weeks past ennyhow, and maybe the man won't ever get back with this ennyhow 'cause he says it's a powerful long way, an' he most died comin', an' it seems to me you run a turrible resk with Injuns out there, only I 'spose you didn't want to come back till you knowed. And I hope I ain't speakin' too plain ef this should fall into the hands of any Injuns who could read, but ennyhow it's all over now. And so I perseed to give you the noos.

'Bout three weeks ago come last Wednesday Lawrence Billings got scared at a mezmerizin' that Hannah Heath got up, with a long-haired man to do the mezmerizin' who said he could call the dead. So on the way home Lawrence Billings got scarder and scarder, an' he stopped at Mr. David Spafford's and owned up to what he'd done, and they hed a trial an' found him guilty, but they let him off 'cause he said he didn't go to do it, an' Enoch Taylor's grandson didn't hev time to come to the trial, but everybody knows he done it now, an' so I thought you would feel better to know too. Mr. David Spafford says there hed been injustice done, an' so they put a advertisement in the New York papers sayin' that ennybody knowin' the whereabouts of the one they'd thought done it—you know who I mean—I won't write out names count o' the

Injuns might get this—they would get a reward, and the town passed a lot of resolutions about how sorry they was them doin' an injustice. So I thought you'd ought to know.

So I won't write ennymore as it's late an' I hev to get breakfast fer that misshunery. He's visitin' my Mr. David and Mrs. Marcia where I live now, an' he told us stories about the Injuns.

And you might like to know that your brother Nathan is growed tall an' fine an' he's goin' to colledge in the fall. Mr. David's ben teachin' him. He's real smart an' looks a lot like you.

The misshunery man says you don't hev bedclothes fer your beds, only wild animal skins. I could send you a quilt I pieced all myself, risin' sun pattern, real bright an' pretty, red an' yellow an' green, ef you'd like it. If you'll jest let me know it's really you I'll send it the first chance I get. So no more at present. Your humble servant,

Randa Griscom

Reverting to the childish name he'd called her and mentioning the bed quilt were her only concessions to sentiment, and she sealed the letter liberally and quickly so her conscience wouldn't rebuke her for those. Then freshening up she crept down to the kitchen to get a breakfast fit for a king for the "misshunery man."

Fortune favored her. Dr. Whitman came down to breakfast five whole minutes before the rest of the family appeared and sat down in the pleasant bay window of the dining room to read a paper. After peering at his kindly face through the crack of the kitchen door Miranda ventured forth, her letter in her hand carefully hidden in the folds of her ample kitchen apron.

"Pleasant mornin'," she addressed him briskly. "Real springy. Guess the snow'll soon be gone."

Dr. Whitman laid down the paper and smiled his good morning pleasantly.

"Them was real interestin' stories you was tellin' us last night," she went on.

He sensed she had an object in her conversation and waited for her to lead up to it.

"I was takin' notice of what you said 'bout that trapper," she glided on easily, "and wonderin' ef it might be a Whitney I used to know in school. He went off west somewheres—" Miranda was never hampered for lack of facts when she needed them. If they weren't there at hand she invented them. "I couldn't say 'g'zactly where. Whiles he was gone his mother died, an' there ain't much of ennybody left that cares, an' there was some things 'twould be to his 'dvantage to know. I'd a wrote an' told him long ago; only I didn't know where to send it, an' I jest was wonderin' ef you'd mind takin' a letter to him. 'Course it mightn't be the same man, an' then agin it might. It can't do no harm to try. You didn't happen to know his fust name, did you? 'Cause that might help a lot."

"Why, no, I'm afraid I don't," said Dr. Whitman. "I only met him once, but I shall be glad to carry the letter to him. If he isn't the right man I can return the letter to you."

"Now that's real kind of you," said Miranda with relief in her voice and her dimples beginning to show themselves after her hard night's vigil. "Mebbe you could tell me what sort of a lookin' man he was."

"Tall and splendidly built," said the doctor, "with large brown eyes and heavy dark hair. There was a look about that lad last night that reminded me of him. He was your—friend?"

"Oh, not specially," said Miranda with a nonchalant toss of her ruddy head. "I jest was int'r'sted when you spoke about him 'cause I thought he might like to know a few things 'bout his home I ben hearin' lately. I jest writ him a short letter, an' ef he turned out to be Allan Whitney you might give it to him ef you'll be so kind. 'Tain't likely he'll remember me; it's ben some years since I seen him. I'm jest M'randy Griscom, an' he's likely hed lots o' friends sence me."

"Not out there, Miss Griscom. I can vouch for that. You know there are very few ladies out in that region—that is, white ladies. My wife was the first white woman the Indians around our mission had ever seen, and they couldn't do enough for her when she first came. A man out there gets lonely, Miss Griscom, and doesn't easily forget his lady friends."

The way he said "lady" made Miranda feel as though she had on her best plaid silk and her china crepe shawl and was going to a wedding at Judge Waitstill's. She grew rosy with pleasure, dimpling and smiling consciously. The missionary's eyes were upon her; he was thinking what a wholesome, handsome young woman this was and what a fine thing it would be for a man like that handsome young trapper to have a wife like her coming out to keep him company. He half wished he might be the bearer of some pleasant message to the young man who had impressed him so deeply.

"A man might be proud to call you his friend," added the kindly man with a frank smile.

Miranda ducked a sudden little courtesy to acknowledge the compliment, when she heard footsteps coming down the stairs and in a panic produced her letter and held it out.

"Thank you," she said breathlessly. "Here's the letter. You won't tell anybody I spoke about it, will you? 'Cause nobody knows anythin' about it."

"Of course not," said the missionary, putting the letter in his inside pocket. "You may rely on me to keep your secrets safely, and I'm sure I hope the young man appreciates what a fine girl is waiting at home for him. I'd like to see you out there brightening his lonely cabin for him. The West needs such women as you are—"

But Miranda, blushing to the roots of her copper gold hair, had fled to the kitchen shed where she fanned her burning cheeks with her apron and struggled with some astonishing tears that had come upon the scene.

She never remembered how she got that breakfast on the table or whether the buckwheats were right or not that morning. Her thoughts were in a flutter, and her heart was pounding wildly in her breast; the missionary's words had stirred up all the latent hopes and desires of her well-controlled nature and put her in a state of perturbation bordering on hysteria.

"Goodness!" she said to herself when she fled to the kitchen shed for the fifth time that morning. "To think he'd say those things to me—me! A real old maid, that's what I be. And him talkin' like that. He ought t' get hisself some spectacles. He can't see straight. I hope he won't say nothin' like that to Allan ef it's reely him. I'd die of shame. Now you wouldn't think a sensible misshunery man like him, with a fur coat an' all, would talk like that to a homebley red-haired thing like me!"

Late that afternoon Dr. Whitman went on his way, with many a "thank you" for the pleasant visit he had enjoyed and many last words about Oregon. But before leaving the house he stepped into the kitchen to shake hands with Miranda.

"I shall carry your letter safely, and I hope my man is the right one. Keep a soft spot in your heart for Oregon, my dear young lady, and if you ever get a chance to come out and brighten the home of some good man out there, don't fail to come."

Miranda, giggling and blushing, took her moist hands out of the dishwater, wiped them on her apron and shook hands heartily with him. From the pantry window she watched him through a furtive tear as he went down the street, carrying her letter under that buffalo coat and walking so sturdily into the great world where perhaps Allan was waiting for him.

Then she murmured half under her breath, "Goodness! What ef I should!"

Chapter 22

As they went out the gate together, David Spafford said to Dr. Whitman, "I've started you a little earlier than was necessary because there's a famous Whig speaker in town and I thought it might interest you to get a few minutes of his speech. It's just a stump speech, and the gathering will be held in front of the tavern. It's on our way to the train, and if you get tired of it we can stop in the office until train time."

The guest's eyes sparkled. "Good! I'm glad to get a touch of modern home politics. You don't know how hard it seems sometimes not to get word of who's been elected for a whole year after an election. What chance do you think there is for Clay's election?"

"It's hard to say yet," answered David. "There's a great deal of speculating and betting going on, of course. One man, a Loco-Foco, has made a great parade of betting ten thousand dollars on the choice of president. But how does he do it? He picks out the twenty states he thinks least likely to go for Clay and offers to bet five hundred on each, leaving the six strongest Whig states out of the question."

"Just what are Clay's cards for the presidency? I really haven't been paying much attention to the matter since I came. You know my mind has been full of other matters."

"Well, the abolitionists, of course, first, then the Liberty Men and manufacturers of the North, the Native Americans, and those who are for bank and internal improvements—"

"Just how do the Whigs stand with regard to annexation?"

"The opposite party is trying to force the Whigs into standing against annexation, but their leaders don't come out openly on the subject. There's a great divergence of opinion. Of course one of the Whigs' great hobbies is tariff. We believe in home production."

At that moment they came in sight of the tavern and saw the crowd gathered and the speaker already in the midst of his speech. The farmers had gathered from around the country, and their teams were hitched at the side of the road up the street as far as one could see. The men themselves were listening eagerly to the words of the orator who stood on a temporary platform in front of the tavern. It was an interesting spectacle.

The speaker's voice was strong and clear, and almost as soon as they turned the corner they caught the drift of his words.

"Suppose," he was saying, "New Jersey could produce bread more cheaply than buying it elsewhere. Then of course you'd say they shouldn't import it. But suppose also that hemp grew in New Jersey in such abundance that people could make a dollar a day more from hemp than from bread, by giving all their time to producing hemp and buying their bread. Shouldn't they then buy their bread?

"Now it's easy to suppose that bread, well-baked, should grow in spontaneous profusion in a country, while hemp, ready rotted and cleaned, should insist on obscuring the entire surface of another country. But nature has ordered differently—"

An audible smile rippled over the surface of the audience. They were visibly moved by the argument, although their faces had a grim, set look as if they'd taken counsel with their inner consciousness, before they came, not to be too easily led.

"It's a strange and curious thing to watch a crowd like that swayed by one man's eloquence, isn't it? What a great power one human being has over another! And what tremendous responsibilities a man has when he undertakes to decide these great questions for his neighbors!" said Whitman in a low tone as they turned off the sidewalk and went to stand under a tree nearer the speaker.

"He does indeed!" said David seriously. "A man shouldn't speak like that until he knows absolutely what he's talking about. I sometimes think more harm is done by careless eloquence than in any other way. I wish you were going to stay longer. We'd have a meeting like this for you to tell people about Oregon. Everybody should hear from one who really knows—"

But the sentence was suddenly arrested by the speaker's loud tones as he reached another point in his address.

"Next, as to Oregon," he was saying, "it's been more than twenty years since we made a compact that the people of each nation should occupy that wild and distant region, being governed by their respective laws and magistrates. Not a whisper of dissatisfaction was heard during our opponents' administration. But now when election time draws near they want to cover up important issues with this foolish talk of forcing the country into war, and with Great Britain—"

David drew his watch quietly from his pocket and glanced at it, then started in surprise.

"I'm afraid, Dr. Whitman," he whispered, "that we should be going if you wish to get a comfortable seat on the train. I must have looked at my watch wrong before, for it's ten minutes later than I thought."

"Let's go at once," said the doctor, wheeling away from the speaker and walking quickly beside his host. "I'm sorry I can't stay to the end. I'd like to tell that good brother a few things about Oregon and England's state of mind. But I must go. It can't be helped. Other duties call, and, after all, I don't suppose he can do much harm. I'll look to you to write us a good editorial in answer to that man and all the others. I'm glad we have so strong an advocate for Oregon."

"I'll do my best," smiled David. "I can't tell you how glad I am to have met you and had this good talk with you. Perhaps when you get the wagon route established, or at least when the railroad is running out your way, my wife and I will visit you. Wouldn't that be great? And we may be able to send you a telegram before that comes. Think of that! Ah! There's Nathan with your bag looking for us. I imagine he's secured you a seat already. I might've thought of that and let you stay five minutes longer at the meeting."

"It's just as well," said the missionary, smiling, "for if I'd stayed much longer I might have had to speak. I couldn't hold in many more minutes, and then my train would have left me. That's a fine boy you have. I'll be proud and glad to see him coming out West someday. Well, I suppose the time has come to part—I'm so glad I've had this delightful visit at your home and shall think of you often when I get back, and I'll tell my wife about you. Don't forget Oregon!"

The good man climbed into the seat Nathan had reserved for him and gave the boy's hand a hearty grasp and a few words of encouragement. Then amid a big noise of shouting trainmen the train moved out of the station.

Nathan, walking slowly beside David toward the office, suddenly looked up. "I'd like to go out there someday and help make that country. Do you think I could?"

"I surely do," said David, "if we can spare you from the East. Get your education, and then we'll see what your work in the world is to be. You're doing good work now, and I look to see you come through your examinations this spring with flying colors and enter college in the fall."

"I shall do my best," was all Nathan said, but his eyes shone with gratitude and wonder over the way life was opening up for him.

The next week Miranda went to her first missionary meeting. Marcia had twisted her ankle slipping down the last three steps of the cellar stairs, and she had a paper to read in the meeting.

"I suppose I could get there in the carryall," she said, looking troubled, when David came home at noon and bent over her couch in great distress, while Miranda prepared a tempting tray and brought it to her side.

"No, indeed!" said David emphatically. "We'll not take any risks with a thing like that. You'll stay right here on the couch till Dr. Budlong says you're able to go out."

"But my paper! They were depending on me to tell about the North American Indians. I promised to take the whole time."

"Well, you have your paper all clearly written out. Let Rose carry it over to Mrs. Waitstill's. She's the president, and she's a good reader. Run over right away with it, Rose, so she can look it over beforehand. Is this it, here on the desk?"

Marcia acquiesced, content to be taken care of, and Rose started down the street on her errand. But in a few minutes she returned, the paper still in her hand.

"Mrs. Waitstill's gone out in the country to her cousin's for dinner and won't be back till she goes straight to the church for the missionary meeting. Sarah Ann said she wasn't going herself today because she had to fry doughnuts, so she couldn't take it."

"Now, you see, I must go, David," said Marcia, half rising from her couch.

"Now, Marcia, surely there's someone else. Why, I can take it over to the meeting myself if necessary, or couldn't Rose run down to the church—"

"I'll take it, Mr. David," said Miranda grimly, "and read it, too, ef thur ain't no one else by to do it better."

"Would you really, Miranda?" said Marcia, wondering what kind of fate her paper would meet in Miranda's original handling. "I didn't ask you because you're so set against missionary meetings."

"Well, I don't know's I've changed my 'pinion of those meetin's. But ef they've got to be, why, they sha'n't go wantin' your paper, not ef I hev to lay all my 'pinions on the floor an' walk on 'em. I use ter be a tol'ble good reader. Gimme a try at it. Ef I don't hit it right on all them Injun names I heerd you reelin' off to Mr. David th' other evenin', there's one thing—no one'll know the diffrunce."

"Oh, I can tell you how to pronounce them. Only one is important, and that's Waiilatpu. It's pronounced Wy-ee-lat-poo. I think you can get through all right. It's good of you to go, Miranda, and I presume Mrs. Waitstill will be willing to read the paper."

So Miranda, attired in her best plaid silk and her handsome pelisse and bonnet, sallied forth to her first missionary meeting. Serene with confidence in her own ability as a reader, she breezily entered the sacred precincts of the "lecture room"—as they called the place where they held the missionary meetings—and announced that she had come "to take Mis' Spafford's place 'count o' her havin' sprained her ankle."

The ladies looked at one another apprehensively but settled back demurely to listen, and Miranda, after the opening exercises, unfolded her paper with a flourish and began to read.

Now, strange to say, Miranda, in spite of her quaint speech, was a good reader. To be sure, she left off her *g*s and was rather free in her translations into common vernacular, but she had a dramatic quality of naturalness about her reading which made you presently forget her rare English. Before she had finished reading the first page of Marcia's fine clear handwriting she had the attention of her audience to a woman. Even her grandmother Heath leaned over with one hand up to her deaf ear and her sharp eye fixed on her granddaughter whom from her cradle she had learned to regard with suspicion. Miranda had always been up to some prank, and it was impossible for Mrs. Heath to think that her sudden appearance at the missionary meeting bode any good.

But the reading went steadily on, with Miranda sailing glibly over the two or three Indian names as though she'd lived in Oregon all her life. And the reader, like any public performer under similar circumstances, became aware that her audience was spellbound. The knowledge went to her head, and she threw in comments as she went along, facts that Dr. Whitman had told in her hearing, which made the story even more dramatic. Marcia would have been much amused if she could have heard how her paper grew.

Among other things Miranda expanded somewhat freely on the fact that the missionaries were often obliged to live mainly on horse meat. Her grandmother gasped and adjusted her spectacles, trying to look over the girl's shoulder to see if such revolting things were really in the original text. Miranda went volubly on, however, and when the paper had drawn to a close she folded it reluctantly and looked calmly around on her audience.

"They say they ain't got any bedcloes," she announced spicily, "jest hev to use furs, an' I shouldn't think that would be a bit healthy. Don't you think 'twould be a good idea ef we was to make a few bed quilts an' send to 'em? They might hev good Scriptur patterns an' be real ele-vatin'. I was thinkin' o' beginnin' one all red an' white an' black hearts. I ain't got any black caliker, but I got some chocolate brown with sprigs on it. I don't 'spose the Injuns would know the diffrunce."

Miranda's suggestion did not meet with marked enthusiasm from the ladies, who sat with folded hands and disapproving expressions.

After an impressive silence, Mrs. Waitstill spoke. "It was real good of you, M'randy, to come and read Mrs. Spafford's paper for us, and I'm sure we all appreciate hearing these strange and wonderful things about the savages. We might consult the board about sending a quilt if that seems advisable to the ladies. I should think one quilt would be enough for our society to send in case it does. Of course there are many other societies to help the cause along. I'm sure we should all be thankful we're born in a civilized land. Mrs. Budlong, will you lead us in a clos-ing prayer?"

During the long, quavering, inaudible prayer which followed, Miranda sat in her importance with decorously bowed head and heart that beat high with excitement. When she caught a sentence of petition for "the nation that sits in darkness," a sudden wild desire to pray swept over her, too. But her prayer wasn't for the heathen in his ignorance and sin. "Oh, God, take care o' Allan! Oh, God, keep him safe from the Injuns, and make it be him—make it be reely him out there, please!" This was her silent prayer over and over.

"M'randy Griscom! Lemme see that paper," demanded her irate grandmother the minute the closing hymn was sung. "I don't b'leeve Mis' Spafford ever wrote that stuff about their eatin' horseflesh. Why, 'taint decent! Why—they'd be cannibals! Where's that place, M'randy? I don't b'leeve there's any sech writin' there!"

Miranda pointed in triumph to the sentence: " 'During the first years the principal meat of the missionaries was horseflesh.' "

"Wal, I swan!" said Grandmother Heath, quite forgetting herself.

"Jest look here, Mis' Waitstill. It's really here."

With a look of injured innocence and a glitter of the conqueror in her eye, Miranda received the manuscript back and rolled it up ostentatiously. She took her lofty way home feeling like quite a pioneer in the cause of missions. And she was secretly delighted she could be so close to Allan by reading about the place where he might be living.

That night at the supper tables in the village a grave discussion took place concerning the morality of missionaries who for their own carnal pleasure would kill and eat a horse.

"And it wasn't as if they didn't have corn and potatoes and parsnips and beans and things," declared Mrs. Eliphalet Scripture. "The paper said they'd taken seed there and planted good gardens. Seems 'zif they might 'a gone without meat or taken a good supply o' ham with 'em. Think of killing and eating our Dobbin!"

"Well, Patience, I don't know's that's any worse than killing and eating our cow Sukey, and we don't think anything of eating cows," responded Eliphalet while taking a comfortable mouthful of his excellent pork chop.

"That's very different," said Mrs. Scripture convincingly. "I'm sure I don't feel like upholding such doings, and I for one shall not make any bed quilts for the Injuns."

Over at the Heath house another discussion was in progress.

"They're jest spilin' M'randy over to Spaffords', hand over hand," said Grandmother Heath, pouring her tea into her saucer and balancing it on the palm of her hand. "Ef they should ever git tired of her an' send her packin' there wouldn't be no livin' with her. She's that high-headed now she thinks she can even tell Mis' Waitstill what to do. I d'clare 'twas r'dic'lous. I was 'shamed o' her b'longin' to me this afternoon."

"Wal, I told you 'twould be jest so ef you let her go over thar to live. I 'spose it's too late to undo it now, but I allus did think David Spafford was an unpractical man. He 'ncourages all sorts o' newfangled things. You know he was hot an' heavy fer the road, an' now they've got it, what hev they got? Why, I read in the paper tonight how a farmer lost his barn an' all his winter crop he hed stored in it through a spark from the engine lightin' on the roof an' burnin' it up root an' branch. An' now he's all took up with this telegraphy they wasted thirty thousand dollars on in Congress. Fool nonsense, I call it! Allus gettin' up som'thin' new, as ef the good ole things our fathers hed wasn't good 'nuf fer enny of us.

"As fur as this missionary business goes, it don't strike me. I take it ef th' Almighty hedn't 'a wanted them Injuns off there by themsel's He wouldn't 'a put 'em thar, an' it's meddlin' with Providence to interfere. Tryin' to Christianize 'em! If Providence hed 'a wanted 'em Christianized, do you guess He'd 'a put 'em off thousands o' miles in an outlandish place where they git so demoralized that they eat horse meat? No, I say ef they choose to live way off there, let 'em stay savages an' kill 'emselves off.

"I heard the other day how some big senator 'r other said that every country needed a place where they could send all their scalawags to, and this here Oregon was just the very thing fer that. 'Twas the mos' God-fersaken land you ever see—nothin' growin' there and no way to git to it, an' the mountains so high you couldn't git a wagon ner a woman acrost 'em. An' here comes David Spafford spoutin' a lot o' nonsense 'bout Oregon, how it's a garding of roses an' potatoes an' a great place to live an' the comin' country, an' all that sort of stuff.

"An' him citin' that thar odd-lookin' missionary Whitman he hed t'other day visitin' him. In my 'pinion thet man was a liar an' a hypocrite. Why, M'lissy, what 'd'e want to come rigged out like that ef he wa'n't? He might a put on cloes like any Christian. He was just a pertendin' he was a missionary so's to git Dave Spafford to write one of his nice, pretty pieces 'bout Oregon so he could git rid of the land he hez out thar at a big price. Take my word fer it, M'lissy. That man was jest a wolf in sheep's clothin'—an' that thar buffalo hide he wore was jest stuck on fer effect. Oh, Dave Spafford's turrible easy took in. You jest better tell M'randy ef she 'spects to stay round thar hobnobbin' with those Spaffords she needn't to expect to lean back on us when they git sick o' her."

The old lady, nodding her agreement, took a long satisfying draught from her tea saucer, and Grandfather Heath, having delivered himself as the head of the house, cut a large, thick slice of bread from the loaf, spread it liberally with apple butter and took a huge bite.

"An' I ain't goin' to waste no bed quilts on the Injuns," reiterated Mrs. Heath.

"Wal, I suttenly wouldn't," agreed her husband. "I don't hold much with these missions ennyhow. Let them as does support 'em, I say. Eatin' good horseflesh! Hump! They might better stay to hum an' do some real work, I say!"

Chapter 23

Spring crept slowly into the world again. One day late in May a letter came to David from Dr. Whitman saying he was just about to start from St. Louis to join the emigration that would rendezvous at a place called Independence, a few miles beyond the Missouri line. Nearly a thousand were in the company, and this would tell greatly for the occupation of Oregon. He said many cattle were going but no sheep. The next year would tell for sheep.

"You'll be the best judge of what can be done, how far you can exert yourself in these matters and whether the secret service fund can be obtained," he wrote. "As now decided in my mind, this Oregon will be occupied by American citizens. Those who go will open a way for more another year. Wagons will go all the way, I have no doubt, this year. But remember that sheep and cattle are indispensable for Oregon. I mean to try to impress on the secretary of war that sheep are more important to Oregon's interest than soldiers. We want to get sheep and stock from the government for Indians, instead of money for their lands. I've written him on the main interests of the Indian country, but I mean to write him again.

"I won't be surprised to see some of you on our side of the mountains in the near future—"

David was reading the letter, and Miranda, according to her usual custom when anything of interest was going on in the other room, was hovering near the door working as silently as possible. When he read this sentence, a sudden choking noise, half giggle, half cough, from the kitchen door caused him to look up. But Miranda had disappeared and was clattering some pans in the closet noisily. Thinking nothing more of it, David read on to the end.

Miranda thumped her pots and pans that night as usual, but she went around with a dreamy expression. Every now and again a sheep's head seemed to peer pathetically at her from a corner or blink across the room from space, and the gentle insistent *ba-a-a* of some wooly creature from the meadow behind her grandfather's barn would make her heart strings tighten and the smile grow in her eyes.

The days passed, and the slow caravan moved on with its two hundred wagons, cattle and horses, and at their head rode the man whose energy, spirit and courage had brought him thousands of perilous miles to gather them together for this great endeavor. Safely in his keeping went the letter, and with it traveled Miranda's spirit.

She had listened closely to the missionary's story of his experiences and stored them in her heart. They must cross wide rivers where quicksand and strong currents vied with one another for their destruction. They must climb fearful heights and avoid sudden sharp precipices. They would meet hostile tribes, hunger, heartache, cold and sickness, and the days would be long and hard before they came to the promised land. Miranda knew it all and followed them day by day.

Night after night she crept to her window, gazed up at the stars and prayed, "Oh, God, make it really him and let him get the letter!" Then she went to her bed and dreamed of a strange place of wonderful beauty and wildness, inhabited by a savage folk and infested with shadowy forms of skulking furry creatures who were hindering her as she searched for Allan—just to tell him a letter was coming.

Miranda's interest in missionary meetings increased, and she took great pride in putting her mite into the collection taken at each meeting.

During these days a sweetness grew in Miranda's life. She had always been bright, cheery and ready to lend a hand to anybody in need, but some of her remarks carried a hardness, almost bitterness, that gave a sharp edge to her tongue and a gleam of relish to her eyes. Now these faults seemed to fade. Though she still made her quaint sarcastic remarks about the people she disliked, it was as if something had softened and gentled her outlook on life. She seemed to have found out how to look with leniency on slack, shiftless people and even on those who were "hard as nails," one of her favorite phrases.

She seemed to grow prettier, too, as the spring came on and deepened into summer. Naturally of a slender build, she had taken on a plumpness that enhanced her beauty without giving her an appearance of stoutness. She glowed with health, and her color came and went with the freshness and coloring of a child. Her years sat lightly on her, so that most people considered her still a young girl in spite of the fact that they had known her since she was a baby and could count the time, upon occasion, of shaking their heads and saying, "Mirandy's gettin' on in years. It's high time she was gettin' settled if she's ever goin' to be. She'll soon be an old maid."

Miranda's contemporaries grew up, married, brought their babies to be baptized in the church and took on matronly ways. The next younger set grew up and did the same, and still Miranda kept the bloom of youth. Her twenty-seven years might have been only seventeen, and the strength that had grown in her face with the years had been sweetened and softened. Her little unloved days of childhood had held loneliness and disappointment, but her happy philosophy had taken it all sweetly, and the merriment danced in her eyes more brightly now than when she had been ten.

Her friends gave up expecting her to grow up and act like other people. Only her relatives paid much heed to it and were mortified she would so shamelessly override all rules and insist on being the irresponsible merry girl she'd always been. They hadn't expected her to marry, somehow, but they did think she'd grow into a silent background and recede into maturity as other girls did. Grandmother Heath and Hannah felt it most and bewailed it openly in Miranda's hearing, which only served to make her delight the more in shocking them by some of her youthful pranks.

But that summer a quiet, unconscious difference grew in her, causing even those who disapproved of her doings to turn and look after her curiously when she passed, as at a vision. It seemed almost as if she were growing beautiful, and those who had known her long and classified her as red-haired, freckled and homely couldn't understand why now something unfamiliar appeared in her face. In truth, she seemed like some late lovely bud unfolding slowly into a most unexpected bloom of startling sweetness. Grandmother Heath looked at her sometimes with a pang of conscience and thought she saw resemblance to the girl's dead mother, whose beauty had been more ethereal than was common in the Heath family. Hannah looked at her in church and resented the change without in the least realizing or recognizing it.

Miranda's eyes held a kind of expectancy, and a quick trick of the color in her cheek added piquancy to her ways. One evening Marcia studied the girl's changing countenance during a glowing recital of one of her escapades in which as usual she'd worsted some grumpy old sinner and set some poor innocent struggling one free from a petty thralldom.

"I declare, David," she said to her husband, "I can't understand why Miranda has been left to give us comfort all these years. She seems to me far more attractive than most of the younger girls in town. Isn't it strange some man doesn't find it out?"

"Miranda has prickles on the outside," said David, laughing. "She lets only her friends see her real worth. I imagine her sharp tongue keeps many away who might come after her, and so they never learn what they're losing. I doubt if many men in town would know enough to appreciate her. There aren't very many good enough for her."

"That's true," Marcia heartily agreed. "But sometimes, although I'd miss her very much, I can't bear to think she'll never have her own home and someone to love her and take care of her, as I have—"

"Dear little unselfish woman," said David, as he bent over and touched her forehead with his lips, "there's no other like you in the whole world."

Meanwhile, the caravan with the letter wound its long, slow way over the hundreds of miles, crossing rivers which hindered them for days, making skin boats of buffalo hides to carry their goods. With the wagons chained together they drove at a tremendous rate over a ford to escape being mired in the quicksand. Discouraged, disheartened and weary, they kept on, despite being out of provisions and many of them sick and worn out. Always at their head, in their midst, everywhere he was needed, was Whitman, swimming a river on his horse again and again, back and forth, to find the best ford and encourage those who were crossing, planning for their comfort, finding out ways to get the wagons through when everyone said there was no passage. He quietly adopted three daughters of a family whose father and mother died on the journey. And finally, late in August, he brought the company safely to Fort Hall.

Here the Hudson Bay Company traders told them it was foolish and impossible for them to attempt to take their wagons through to Columbia —they could never make it.

Dr. Whitman had been absent from the company for a few hours and when he returned he found them in a state of terrible distress. But when he discovered the cause of their anxiety he came cheerfully forward.

"My countrymen, you've trusted me thus far. Believe me now, and I'll take your wagons to the Columbia River."

The pilot who had brought them so far left them and returned to Missouri, and Whitman took charge of the company. So, with many misgivings and amid the repeated warnings and coldly given advice of the Hudson Bay people, they started on again.

It was late in August, and the new trail over the Blue Mountains was rocky and steep, often obstructed by a thick growth of sage two or three feet high. The only wagon that had ever gone farther than Fort Hall was Dr. Whitman's. But with strong faith in their leader and a firm determination to overcome all obstacles they pressed on their way. They forded more rivers, passed through narrow, difficult valleys filled with timber and again through fertile valleys lying between snow-clad mountains. They encountered severe snowstorms in the mountains, losing their cattle in the timber and finding the road terribly rough and almost impassable at times. Yet they pressed on, until at last on the tenth of October they reached Whitman's mission station and found rest and abundance!

Dr. Whitman had hurried on ahead at the last stage of the journey, because of the severe illness of another missionary who had sent a message for him, leaving the company to be guided by an Indian friend. By the time they reached the station he had repaired his gristmill, burned by hostile Indians during his absence. When the emigrants arrived, grinding could be done. Dr. Whitman sold the travelers flour, potatoes, corn, peas and other fresh vegetables. For a few days they rested and feasted after the hard journey and then went on to the Willamette Valley south of the Columbia, where most of them intended to remain.

It was some time before Dr. Whitman had matters at the mission in such a shape that he could deliver Miranda's letter. But as soon as possible he took a trip to Fort Walla Walla and timed his coming to the cabin in the clearing so he might find his friend. But no cheerful light shone out across the darkness, and no friendly form was waiting at the door to greet him this time. The cabin was closed and dark, and when he opened the door he found no sign of the owner's recent occupancy.

With deep regret he lighted a candle that stood on the table and looked the place over carefully. Clothes were hanging on the wall, along with a few pelts, but little food was there, and the fire had been dead for days. Well, at least the owner hadn't moved away. But what terrible fate might have befallen him in this land of wastes, hatred, beasts and vast silences? Time alone would tell, and even time might not choose to reveal it.

With a sigh the faithful messenger sat down at the rough table and wrote a note.

Friend Whitney:

I've just returned from the East with a large emigration. I have a letter which I think is for you from an old friend and which I think has good news. I'm much disappointed not to find you at home. Come over and see me as soon as you return and get the letter. It is important.

Yours truly,
Marcus Whitman,
Waiilatpu

With another regretful look around he put the note where it would be safe and attract attention at once when the owner came back. Then, fastening the door, he mounted his horse and rode away, with the letter still in his pocket.

He inquired along the way and after arriving home but learned nothing concerning the absent trapper. He could only keep the letter safe and hope and wonder.

The missionary was kept busy enough at the mission. During his absence enemies had been quietly at work, poisoning the Indians' minds. One result of this was the burning of the gristmill and a large portion of his store of grain. He had a great deal to do to get things in running order again, for the emigrants had depleted his supplies significantly. Then much sickness spread among the missionaries, and he had to make several trips in his capacity as physician. Most of all, he was anxious about his beloved wife, who fell ill during his absence and was with friends at another mission. As soon as things were made comfortable at Waiilatpu he hurried after her, rejoicing to find her much better.

While Whitman had been in the East a provisional government had been organized, with an executive committee elected and a body of laws adopted. But the number of Americans and English was so equally divided that little else had been done, each side moving cautiously because of the other, until more settlers should arrive. Now, however, all was changed, for most of the voters were Americans! So government matters also demanded his attention.

In addition to all this, the growing alienation of the Indians was cause for constant anxiety. He took one comfort, however, in the fact that his own Indians about him were never kinder or more docile, and those he'd left in charge of his crops had done their work well, cultivating the land almost as well as if he'd been there himself.

Winter drew on, and the Indians returned from their wanderings to the station as usual. Dr. Whitman's Sabbath services in February had an attendance of two or three hundred, and his work grew heavier all the time.

Some of the emigrants wintered at the mission, expecting to get work breaking land for the Indians, taking their pay in horses or planting land for themselves. But most of the Indians were in such a state of mind that they wouldn't pay for breaking land because it was their own, and they wouldn't plant it for themselves because they'd been told the Americans were going to overrun the country and would benefit by it. They also annoyed Whitman and attempted to prevent him and his men from breaking a new field lest he should sell his crops to the emigrants and make money out of their lands. Constant daily annoyances were felt, and disaffections grew.

It was all too evident that an enemy was at work. The home board needed to realize that a grant of land for the mission must be obtained from Congress or the mission itself would soon be without a home.

The Indians were growing more agitated, and a strange unfriendliness was stirring. Two murders of reputed sorcerers among them had occurred not far from Waiilatpu. The Americans were suspected. The Indians wished to have their lands cultivated yet were unwilling to do much toward that end or pay for having it done. They complained that they had taught their language to the white men but the white men had not taught them theirs. They wished to have everything the white man had and be civilized, but without trouble to themselves.

Throughout the winter, though many others came and went, Whitney, the young trapper from the cabin in the clearing, didn't come. Nor did anyone hear from him, though Dr. Whitman inquired often and took several journeys that way to see if he'd returned. So still the letter waited.

Back in the East as spring approached, David Spafford was reading the paper aloud as usual one evening, with Marcia knitting by his side, while Miranda cleared off the supper table.

"Another expedition is said to be about to go to the Rocky Mountains," he read. "This will rendezvous at Independence. There are ten women in the company."

A strange sense of quiet in the room made both David and Marcia look up suddenly, and they saw Miranda, standing wistfully in the doorway unconscious of their gaze. She had a strange, faraway look in her eyes and the hungry appeal of a woman's soul for all that life was meant to be to her. One would never think of the word "fragile" in describing Miranda. Yet Marcia, thinking it over afterward, almost thought she'd seen a hint of fragility about her but decided it was instead a growing refinement of the spirit within her.

They both looked away at once, and David continued reading, so Miranda never knew they'd seen that glimpse of her secret soul, understanding and sympathizing because they themselves knew love. They never connected her look with the item in the paper, not even for an instant, and they couldn't have understood, of course, why that would have brought the heart hunger into her eyes. But they grew more careful and tender toward her from day to day, if that could be possible, because of what they had seen.

The excitement that spring was Nathan's going down to New York to take his examinations, and great were the rejoicing and the feast Miranda prepared the day word came he had passed in everything and might enter college in the autumn.

Politics in the East were at high pressure all summer. Stump speeches and mass meetings were the order of the day and night. Banners were flying everywhere, some with pictures of the presidential candidates and others with inscriptions that set the people's imagination on fire as they passed. Everywhere bulletin boards presented reasons why men should vote for this candidate or that. Clay's name was on the lips of some, with praise and loud acclaim, while others told of all Polk stood for and were just as enthusiastic in his praise. Those who thought and worked and cared spent anxious days and nights, then talked and worked the harder.

Now the time drew near when messengers from the far West might be expected. Dr. Whitman had said he hoped for a chance of sending back word of his safe arrival before winter set in. And Miranda naturally had hoped, a little, that her letter might have reached its destination and perhaps have brought some recognition then; yet no word had come from Dr. Whitman. But now the winter was passed, and it was time to hope again.

Miranda perused the *Tribune* every night, and no word of Oregon or Indians escaped her. But she found nothing to make her hope that travelers had arrived from over the Rockies. She'd heard the missionaries were often a year and a half getting a letter from Massachusetts, and she'd set her faith and patience for a long wait, so her courage didn't fail. But as the warm weather came on, that spirit look appeared more often in her eyes, as if patience were trying her soul almost too far. And Marcia, noticing it, suggested a trip to New York and a few days at the sea. She even hinted that she and Rose and little David would go along, but to her surprise Miranda seemed almost panic-stricken and declared she didn't care for journeyings.

"You and Mr. David go, honey," she said indulgently, "an' I'll stay home an' clean house. It's jest the chance I ben watchin' fer to get all slicked up 'thout nobody knowin' it. I don't keer fer the big cities much, an' oncet in a lifetime's nuf fer me. As fer the o'shn, I kinda think 'twould give me the creeps, so much water all goin' to waste, jest settin' thar ar gettin' in the way when folks want to go acrost. Guess I'll jest stay t' hum an' clean house, Mrs. Marcia, ef it's all the same t' you."

And stay she did, as cheery and sturdy as ever except now and again when the faraway spirit look came into her eyes. Nights when she crept up to her starry window she prayed, "God, I reckon it wa'n't him after all, but I guess You'll jest hev to tell 'im Yerse'f, ef it's all right he should know."

Sometimes her head went heavily down on the casement sill, and she slept thus till dawn.

Miranda evinced a strong interest in the coming of the mail sent early spring and seemed to enjoy going down to the post office in the late afternoons. But no letter came for her, nor indeed did she really expect one. She told herself again and again that he had no obligation to write, and men didn't write letters unless they had to. He might perhaps write sometime and say he thanked her for letting him know; that was all of her hope. For that the color came and went in her cheeks; her eyes grew bright and her breath grew short whenever she went to the post office.

The summer waned, and the faraway look grew in Miranda's eyes, the wrangling about politics carried on to its climax, and at last the morning of election day came.

Chapter 24

The morning train arrived bringing a few wanderers from home who had come to vote. They hurried down the street which seemed to have a cleared-up holiday look, almost like Sunday, except that groups of men were standing about laughing, gesticulating, talking, with anything but their Sunday attitude.

None of them noticed a stranger who disembarked from the train with them and stood a moment looking about him as if to get his bearings.

He was a tall, broad-shouldered fellow, well dressed and well groomed. His handsome face was bronzed as if he'd been out in all kinds of weather, but he was clean shaven and his hair cut in the style they were wearing in New York. The garments he wore and the carpet-bag he carried were new and of the finest quality. He had about him, moreover, an air of being entirely superior to his clothes which gave him a commanding presence. The station agent turned to look curiously after him as he stepped off the platform and started down the street. He half ran after the stranger, begrudging someone else the right to direct him and wondering why the man hadn't stopped to inquire directions of him.

But the stranger didn't appear to see him, so the agent stood and watched till he turned the corner by the courthouse onto the main street. Then he went reluctantly back to his work. It was hard on a day like this to have to remain at the station all day instead of being around the polls with the other men.

Passing the courthouse, the stranger crossed over in front of the Presbyterian church, walked down the street slowly and surveyed each well-known place as he came to it. He saw the bank with its great white pillars and its stone steps where he'd played marbles twenty years or more ago. Next stood the old house where Elkanah Wilworth lived and from whose small attic windows he and young Elkanah of the third generation had fired peas on the heads of unsuspecting passersby below.

Eleazer Peck lived next door. They'd tied a cat to his front door and left her scratching and howling one evening while they enjoyed watching Eleazer, candle in hand, coming to see what it was all about. Next to him was the store kept by Cornelius Van Storm and John

Doubleday, with its calico, coffee, nails, eggs, plows, and the like in exciting confusion. How he had loved that store—and the hours he'd spent in a nail keg behind the stove listening to the tales the men had to tell! Ah, he could match those wonderful made-up stories a hundred times more thrilling!

Dr. Budlong's office came next in the same old house where his father had been doctor before him, and beside it was the blacksmith's shop, where it was handy to get a loose shoe tightened before driving out to the country on a bad day. There in the doorway stood the same old blacksmith, Sylvanus Sweet, gazing idly out into the street and staring at the stranger curiously—never knowing him for the bad little boy who used to tickle the horse's hind legs while he was setting a fore shoe, in his apprenticeship days.

Across the street was the post office and next, the two taverns, one on either side of the street, and here the groups were assembled and the interest was centered, for the voting place was close by.

The stranger paused and looked about him.

Just at the edge of the road stood David Spafford, a trifle older, with a touch of gray in his hair, but the same kindly, hearty expression he remembered when he was a little boy. David was evidently waiting for the return of a slender young fellow with dark hair and an oddly familiar back who had run out to speak to some men in a wagon. Two excited fellows were arguing loudly in the road. Could one of them be Silas Waite? He wasn't sure. And that must be Lyman Rutherford with his hat off, pushing his hair back. He couldn't quite see his face but was sure it was his attitude. He was talking with Eliphalet Scripture. Tough old Eliphalet Scripture alive yet and not a day older to all appearances! That man behind him with the gray beaver hat couldn't be anybody else but old Mr. Heath, and he was talking with Lemuel Skinner. H'm! Lemuel Skinner used to go with Hannah Heath! Did he win her finally? the stranger wondered.

Ah! There went old Caleb Budlong across the street as hale and chipper as ever, and his doctor's carryall was hitched nearby in front of the opposite tavern.

How unchanged and natural it all looked, and only he was strange—a stranger in his own home. No one knew him.

He looked about with a great loneliness upon him, and his eyes fell on a single figure standing in front of a billboard on which

"Henry Clay" stood out in large letters under a poising eagle. It was his own father, grave, silent, severe-looking as ever—among men, yet not of them! Not ten feet away, yet with no thought that his own son was so close!

For an instant the young man started as if to go to him, then drew back in the shadow of the tavern again and after a moment more passed on down the street. No, he wouldn't speak to him, wouldn't let anybody know yet who he was. Just one human being in all his home village had the right to recognize him first and greet him, and to her he was going.

His passing had been so quiet that few seemed to notice him, though a stranger of such fine presence could scarcely walk through town and not turn many curious eyes his way. But no one knew who he might be.

A group of small boys playing marbles on the sidewalk looked impudently up at him and warned him not to spoil their game. He stepped obligingly around it and almost felt as if one of them might be his former self.

On down the pleasant street he walked till he came to his own old home, standing white-pillared and stately behind its high hedges and holding out no more of a friendly welcome now than it did to him in childhood. He hesitated and looked toward it a moment, a rush of old loneliness and sorrow overcoming him, then deliberately turned toward David Spafford's house, walked into the front gate and knocked at the door.

Now Miranda had the house to herself for the day, for Marcia and the children had gone to the aunts for dinner, and David was to go there at noon. Miranda had taken the day to bake pumpkin pies and fry doughnuts. When the knocker sounded through the house, she was deep in the business with her sleeves rolled above her plump elbows and a dust of flour on her cheek and chin. She waited to cut the round hole in another doughnut before answering the knock.

The morning sunshine was bright, but the hall was slightly dark, and when she opened the door her eyes were blinded for a moment. She could see only a figure standing on the stoop, the tall fine figure of a stranger with a traveling bag in his hand.

In haste to get back to her doughnuts she didn't wait for him to speak but curtly told him, "Mr. Spafford is out. He won't be in till evening."

But the stranger stepped calmly in as he replied, "I didn't want to see Mr. Spafford. I came to see you."

Miranda caught her breath and stepped back, surveying him aghast. In all the years she'd guarded Mr. Spafford's front and back doors, never had she met such effrontery as this, actually getting in the door in spite of her! Who could this be who dared to say he'd come to see her? He didn't look like a person who would be rude, and yet rude he certainly was. She drew the door wider open so the light might fall on his face and turned to look at him, but he put out one hand and pushed it gently shut.

"Randa, don't you know me?" he said softly, and somehow in an instant she was carried back to the old smokehouse and the dark snowy night when the one love of her heart went from her.

"Allan!" she breathed. "Oh, Allan!" And her voice was as she talked to God under the stars—as no human being had ever heard her speak.

The tall stranger put his traveling bag down on the floor, pushed the door shut with a click and folded her in his arms.

"Randa!" And stooping he laid his lips upon hers.

"Oh!" gasped Miranda, and her cheek, flour and all, went down upon the breast of the immaculate overcoat.

For a full minute joy and confusion rolled over her, and then she struggled to her senses.

"But, oh!" she gasped again, drawing away from him. "Come in, won't you?"

She led him into the parlor where it was bright with autumn sunshine and the reflection of yellow leaves from the trees outside. But when she turned to look upon him she beheld a stranger, tall, handsome, with the garments of a fashionable gentleman and a fineness and nobleness which seemed to set him miles above her. She drew back abashed.

"Oh, Allan! Is it really you?" she cried half fearfully. "You look so grown up an' diffrunt!"

A great light was shining in Allan's eyes as he looked at her.

"It's really me, Randa. Only it's been a good many years, and maybe I'm a little taller. And it's really you! I'd have known you anywhere—those eyes—and that hair—" He passed his hand softly over Miranda's copper locks that were ruffled into little rings and sprangles all over her head, though they'd been piled neatly in place early in the morning. "Why, Randa, I knew you the minute my eyes lit on you—only, Randa, I didn't expect you'd be so—so beautiful!"

A frightened look came into Miranda's eyes. "Beautiful? Me?" she cried. "Oh, what makes you talk like that?" She turned her head away, and great tears welled into her eyes. He had come, the Allan she'd waited for so long, and he was making fun of her! It was more than she could bear!

"Randa!" His arms were about her again, and he lifted her face. "Look up, Randa! Look into my eyes—I mean it. You are beautiful! How could you help knowing it? You're the most beautiful woman I ever saw! Look into my eyes and see I mean it."

Miranda looked, and what she saw there filled her with wonder and joy, satisfying all the hunger and longing which had for years filled her eyes with that yearning look.

"Why, Randa, don't you know I've dreamed about you? I've always meant to come back when I could, and when your letter came saying it was all right, I hurried off as soon as possible. I've dreamed you all out as you used to be and then tried to think how you looked grown up. Those eyes sparkling like sunshine on the water where it sifted through the chestnut leaves into the old swimming hole—do you remember? That dimple in the corner of your mouth when you laughed, and the other one in your other cheek that made you look so wicked and inno-cent both at the same time. That sweet mouth that used to look like cry-ing whenever I got whipped at school. The white, soft roundness under your chin. How often I've wished I could hold it in my hand this way! And the little curl in the back of your neck where your hair was parted! Why, Randa, I've spent hours dreaming it all out. And it's just as I thought, only better—much, much more beautiful!"

But all this was too much for Miranda. The strong-minded, the courageous-hearted, the irrepressible, the indomitable! She who had borne loneliness and lovelessness and hardness unflinchingly, melted as wax under this loving admiration, buried her face in the strong arms around her and wept.

"Why, Randa, little Randa! Have I hurt you?" he whispered softly. "Have I perhaps made a mistake and spoken too soon? Maybe there's someone else ahead of me, and I had no right—!"

But here Miranda's face like a summer thundercloud lifted fiercely.

" 'Z if thur c'd ever be anybody else!" she sobbed.

"Then what are you crying about, child?"

" 'Cause—you—come–n–n–n—look so fine—an' say all them po'try things just like I was one o' the Waitstill girls, an' I'm only me—jest plain, homebley, turn-up-nose, freckle-faced, red-haired M'randy Griscom! An' you ain't looked at me real good yet ur you'd know. You ben dreamin' an' you got things all halo'd up like them ugly saints in pictures they paint a ring o' light over an' call 'em a saint—but it don't make 'em no prettier 'z I c'n see. Mrs. Marcia's got one she says is painted by a great man, but thur ain't no ring o' light round my head, an' when you look at me good you'll see thur ain't. An' then you won't think that way anymore. Only I ain't ever hed nobody talk thet way to me afore, an' it reely kinda hurt thet it don't b'long t' me. Guess I'm gettin' nervous though I ain't sensed it afore. You see I never knowed what I'd missed till you spoke thet way, an' 'tain't so easy to think o' givin' it up 'cause it don't b'long to me."

Miranda struggled to wipe away the tears with her kitchen apron. But Allan put it from her hand, wiping them on his own fine clean handkerchief, taking her soft chin in his hand and holding her face up to his just as he'd dreamed he would do.

"But it does belong, Randa. It all belongs. Why, Randa, don't you know I love you? Don't you know I've loved you all these years an' come thousands o' miles after you? And now I'm here, you look better to me than I've dreamed. Randa, haven't you ever dreamed about me? Maybe this has all been one-sided—"

"Lots o' times," cut in Miranda, sniffing.

"Maybe you don't love me, Randa. But I sort of thought—you see, when you were just a little girl you always took my part and slipped me apples and gingerbread out of your dinner pail—I was a great hog to eat them away from you, but boys are selfish beasts when they're young, and I guess they take it for granted the world was made for 'em till they get a little sense in their heads, and some of 'em never get it—and then you fixed that cream so it'd pour over the teacher and stop his whipping me. And you saved my life—Miranda, you know you saved my life at great risk to yourself. You needn't tell me. I know your hard old grandfather and what he might have done to you if he'd found out. Miranda, I've loved you ever since. I didn't know it at first, when I stole out of the smokehouse that night in the snow and got away into the world. I was all excited and glad to go, and you were only a little part of it that I was grateful for. Something made me want to kiss you when I left, but I didn't think much about it then.

"I got through the woods to the river by the next night and found a haystack to sleep under till the snow let up. I was so tired I fell asleep, but after I'd slept a little while I woke up and thought they were after me, your grandfather and the officers. I put my hand outside the haystack into the snow and remembered where I was and knew I must keep still till morning. I lay very still and thought it all over, how you'd done—how you'd done for me all my life and what a sweet little thing you'd always been to me, so quiet and out-of-sight except when you were needed. So smart and saucy to other folks, but so keen to find ways to help me when I was in trouble.

"I thought of the curl on your neck, too, and the way you turned your head on the side when you used to sit in front of me in school—and the shine on the waves in your hair. Then I thought of the kiss, how warm and soft your lips felt when they touched mine out there in the falling snow, and all of a sudden I knew I loved you and would come back someday and get you if I had to go thousands of miles. But somehow it never came to me to think that some other fellow might have gotten you before I came. You always seemed to belong to me. You see, I didn't realize how beautiful you would have grown and how you might have forgotten me—me off working in a wilderness and growing like a wild creature—"

"You!" cried Miranda, drawing back and looking at him. "You, Allan Whitney, wild! Why, you're a—why, you're a real gentleman! An' me? I'm jest—M'randy!"

"You're just what I want!" said Allan, stooping to kiss her again.

And just at that inopportune moment a loud and virulent smell made itself felt in the house.

"Oh, my! That's my fat burnin'!" said Miranda, struggling from Allan's arms and fleeing to the kitchen. "To think I'd git so overcome I'd fergit them doughnuts!"

But Allan Whitney hadn't come three thousand miles to be left in the parlor while Miranda fried doughnuts, and he followed her precipitately to the kitchen and proceeded to hinder her at every turn of her hand.

Chapter 25

I didn't get your letter until February," began Allan, sitting down beside the table to watch Miranda's deft fingers cut out the puffy dough and thinking how firm and round her arm was from wrist to floury elbow.

"You didn't!" Miranda stopped to look at him in wonder. "Now ain't that great! All that time! Why, the misshunery man said he 'spected to git home afore the summer was over."

"He did get home," said Allan, watching the sunshine on her hair as it shone through the window and thinking how dear and good her quaint speech sounded to him. "He got home in October and came right up to my cabin, but I wasn't there; I'd gone to Vancouver. I had a good chance to make a lot of money—I'll tell you about it later when we have more time—so I went, thinking I'd probably get back in a week or so. But things went slick, and I stayed till I had the thing through that I went for, and that wasn't till February. Then I had things in shape so I could work 'em from anywhere, and I went back to my cabin. I found a note there from Whitman saying he had a letter for me—at least he thought it was for me—from a friend in the East, and it was important.

"Well, I knew he must be mistaken, because there wasn't any way any of my friends could know where I was. But I took a great notion to Whitman one night when he stayed with me, and I wanted to see him again and hear all about his trip east in the winter. I knew he was back, for the settlers in the Willamette had brought the news. But I wanted to see him and hear all about it from his own lips. So as soon as I could get my cabin straightened up a bit I went down to Waiilatpu to see him.

"He gave me a hearty welcome and hurried me right into the house. Then he left me for a minute, going into another room, but came back at once with your letter which he laid in my hand.

" 'Is that your letter?' he asked and looked me through with his kind eyes. You know how sharp and pleasant they are, Randa. I looked at the letter, and then I looked up into his face.

"It was a long time since I'd been afraid of anybody finding me way out there. At first, after I left home, I used to start awake at night thinking old Mr. Heath was after me, and many times I've dodged around corners in New York to get away from people I thought looked at me suspiciously. But after I went out to Oregon and got used to the bigness and the faraway-ness, I sort of forgot anybody might think they could arrest me and shut me away from the sky and the trees and the living creatures. I forgot there was such a thing as hanging, and I got strong and able to defend myself. Somehow when you've neighbored alongside the wild things and the fierce beasts you don't get afraid of just men anymore.

"But that morning, for a minute, when Whitman asked me if my name was Allan and looked at me that way, it kind of came to me suddenly that he'd been east and maybe mentioned me or heard someone say I'd killed a man. Then I looked up into his eyes and knew I could trust him. I knew whatever he believed he wouldn't go back on me. I determined to make a clean breast of it if I had to—not mentioning any names, of course, for I hadn't protected poor Larry all these years to go back on him now. And anyhow I didn't seem to care much. I'd made some money, enough to be comfortable on, and yet life didn't look very interesting to me—just living on and making more money and hoarding it up with nobody to enjoy it with me. If I'd had a real home and a family it would have been different. I'd have cared then. But I couldn't ask any girl to marry me and have her find out someday that folks thought I was a murderer. And anyhow I hadn't seen any girl I wanted to marry. There weren't many out there, and what there were I didn't care that much about. It just always seemed to me I'd kind of been left out of life somehow, and what was the use of living? At least, that's the way it seemed after I'd begun to succeed and didn't have to work so hard just to get food to keep me alive.

"So when I looked into Whitman's eyes I never turned away or flinched. I just owned up I was Allan Whitney all right, no matter what he knew. Then I waited to see how he'd take it. But he just kind of smiled all through his eyes as if he were real glad and had known it all along.

" 'Well, I just felt it in my bones you were,' he said, gripping hold of my hand real hard. 'And I'm mighty glad of it. You're good enough for her, I guess, and she's one of the salt of the earth, or I miss my guess. You're to be congratulated that you have a woman like that somewhere in the world who cares enough to hunt you up and write to you. She's a fine friend for anybody to have. Now read your letter!' And with that he went off and left me alone.

"You'd better believe I opened that letter pretty quick then, for something told me there must be something wonderful in it. And when I looked at the name 'Randa Griscom' signed at the bottom just as you used to write it on your slate when you finished your spelling lesson, I saw your little slender white neck again with the bright curl where the hair parted, and I saw your little straight shoulders braced stiff when the teacher called me up to the desk—and a great big longing swept over me to get right out on the trail and come back to you, Randa! And I've come. I started just as soon as I could fix up things so I wouldn't lose all I'd gained at Vancouver, because I didn't want to come home penniless."

Miranda's eye swept over his fine new garments with a shy smile of pride, but she said nothing.

"I had to go back to Vancouver to see to some things, and when I finally got on my way I found one of the fellows in my train sick and not fit to travel fast. He hadn't let me know because he was afraid I wouldn't take him along, knowing I was in a hurry, and he was anxious to get home to his mother. Of course I couldn't leave him to come alone behind—he wasn't fit to travel really, and some days we had to stay in camp if the weather wasn't good—just because of him. At last when we got about a third of the way he broke down completely and was downright sick, and we had to camp out and take care of him. Then the guide got ugly and went back on us—said he wouldn't go with us unless we went off and left the fellow with an Indian for his nurse and a few provisions. But of course I couldn't do a thing like that—"

"Of course not!" snapped Miranda sympathetically.

"Well, it was some six weeks before we got under way again with the fellow on a sort of swinging bed between two horses, and then it was almost two weeks before we could do more than crawl three or four miles a day. But he got a little strength after a bit, and we finally reached the next fort.

"The rest of the party hurried on from there, but the poor fellow who'd been sick begged so hard for me not to leave him that I couldn't see my way clear to do it. I put by for a couple of weeks more till he got real rested, and we got together a guide, another outfit and a wagon and started on again. Some emigrants had left the wagon behind when they went west, after being told they couldn't possibly get it over the mountains—fool nonsense, by the way; plenty of wagons have been

over now—but this one did us a good turn. It was hard going sometimes, though. But we jogged on slowly and at last got to St. Louis,
where I left my man with his mother, the happiest soul I ever saw on
this earth. I felt impatient a good many times at the long delay when I
was in such a hurry to get back and see if you were really here yet. But
I can't say I regretted getting that fellow to his mother alive. She was
real glad to see him!"

Miranda, her eyes like two stars, her rolling pin in one hand and a velvety circle of dough in the other, came and stood before him.

"Oh, Allan, that was jest like you! Why, I couldn't no more think o'
your goin' off on your own pleasurin' leavin' a poor dyin' weaklin'
alone, then I c'd think o' God not lightin' the stars nights an' lettin' His
airth go dark. Why, it was jest that in you made me—"

Miranda stopped in confusion, and regardless of rolling pin and
dough Allan wrapped her in his arms again, stooping and whispering in
her ear, "Made you what, Randa?"

But Miranda wouldn't tell, and presently the doughnuts in the frying
fat cried out to be attended to, and she flew back to her duty.

It was a long beautiful day. Sometime before late afternoon these two
who took no note of time sat down to a delicious lunch together of cold
biscuits, ham, apple pie, fresh doughnuts and milk. But they might as
well have feasted on sawdust for all they knew how it tasted; they were
so absorbed in one another.

They talked of all the years that had passed and the experiences they'd
been through. Allan had actually gone abroad for a year and worked his
way here and there seeing the sights in the old world. Miranda told him
about the item she'd heard read from the *Tribune*, and they smiled
together over the littleness of the world. It appeared, too, that the stars in
Oregon had often faithfully cheered the exile from his home. Stars were
odd things, knowing the secrets of the ages, looking down from a height
so great that petty details were sublimated by the vast comprehension,
yet shining with such calm assurance that it would all be right in the end.
These two had both felt it; only they didn't quite express it that way.

"I mostly waited till I got a glimpse of the stars when I got discom-
bobulated," declared Miranda. "Bein' up so high an' so sot an' shiny,
they seemt t' steady me. They kinda seemt t' say, 'M'randy, M'randy!
You jest never you mind. We ben up here hunderds an' hunderds o'
years jest doin' our duty shinin' where we was put. An' we hed to shine

jest th' same when 'twas stormin' an' no folks down thar c'd see us 'n' appreciate us. When 'twas the darkest night we did our best shinin' 'cause folks could see us better then. An' the things what makes you feel bad down thar ain't much more'n little thin storm clouds passin' over yer head and pourin' down a few drops o' rain an' a stab er two o' lightnin' jest to kinda give yeh somepin' to think 'bout. So, M'randy, don't you mind, you jest keep a shinin' an' they'll all pass by, an' some o' these days thur won't be no more storms 'tall. An' you jest look out when thet time comes t' it finds you shinin'!'

"So I get kinda set up agin an' come downstairs next mornin' tryin' to shine my very shiniest. Only my way o' shinin' was bakin' buckwheats an' sweepin' and puttin' up pickles and jells an' that kinda thing—an' when I'd go back agin at night, hevin' shun my best, them stars would always kinda wink at me an' say somepin'. Wanta know what they'd say? They'd say, 'M'randy, you're a little brick!'

" 'Member how you wrote that oncet fer me? Well—that's what they'd say. An' then nights when I hadn't done so good they'd jest put on a faraway, ain't-to-hum look, like they'd pulled their curtings down an' didn't want 'em pulled up that night."

"Strange," said Allan, musing and putting out a hand tenderly to touch the edge of the girl's rolled-up sleeve. "The stars meant a lot to me, too. Nights when I'd be out alone with my traps they seemed to kind of travel with me from place to place, and somehow I imagined sometimes there were voices whispering around them, friendly voices—I used almost to think I was getting daffy. The voices seemed to speak about me as if they cared!"

"I reckon them was the prayers," said Miranda with a strangely softened expression on her face, pausing from wiping a dish to look meditatively at him. "I prayed a lot. I do' kno's it done much good. I s'pose most of 'em didn't get much higher'n the stars ef they got that fur, an' ther they stuck. But it done me good ennyhow, even ef God wouldn't care fer prayers sech ez mine. Land sakes!"

Miranda broke off suddenly and dropping her dish towel began to roll down her sleeves. "Ef ther ain't my Mrs. Marcia an' Mr. David coming down the street an' you in the kitchen! Not a stroke done fer supper neither! What'll they think? Come, you'd best go in the parlor. They'll say I hedn't any manners to bring a gentleman like you into the kitchen."

But the guest arose in a panic.

"No, Randa, jest let me get my bag before they come in and I'll slip out the back door now. I don't want to see anybody yet. I'll come over right after supper and make a formal call. I must go home and see Father and the children—now. Do you guess they'll be glad or sorry to see me?"

He strode through to the hall, seized his bag and made good his escape out the back door just as the front door was being opened by the Spaffords. But Miranda slipped out after him into the evening dusk.

"Allan!" she called softly, and he stepped back to the door stone. "Allan, I forgot to tell yeh—did you know yer pa was married again?"

"No! Is he? Who did he marry, Randa? Anybody I know?"

"M'ria Bent. She taught school after you left fer 'bout five years, an' then she married him. Don't you r'member her?"

"Yes, I remember her," said Allan, making a wry face. "But I won't trouble her if she doesn't trouble me. Good-bye. I'll be back this evening." And he caught her hand and pressed it tenderly.

Miranda hustled back into the kitchen and began a tremendous clatter among the pans, her cheeks as red as roses, just as Marcia came into the kitchen.

"So you got back a'ready!" she exclaimed in well-feigned surprise. "Well, I got some belated, but I'll hev supper in three jerks of a lamb's tail now. I thought you wouldn't be hungry early, hevin' a big comp'ny dinner, like you always do up to Mis' Spaffordzes'. Did you hev a good time?"

"Very pleasant," said Marcia gently. "And you—were you lonely, Miranda?"

"Not pertic'lerly," Miranda replied indifferently, with her head in the pantry. "I hed callers. Say, did you know Mis' Frisbee's goin' to give up tailorin' an' go'n live with her dotter over to Fundy? Sa'r' Ann says she told her so herself."

The inference was that Sarah Ann had been the caller.

"Why, no, I hadn't heard it," said Marcia, rolling her bonnet strings carefully. "She'll be greatly missed by the people she's always sewed for. Did Sarah Ann say how Mrs. Waitstill was today?"

"No, she didn't say," answered Miranda after a moment's pause while she cut the cake. It did go against the grain for Miranda to deceive Marcia, but she felt this was an emergency and couldn't be helped.

Chapter 26

WHEN Allan Whitney dawned on the village, such a stir was made as hadn't been seen since the Waitstill girls brought a fine young Canadian officer to church and feted him for a week afterward.

Allan Whitney, the town scapegrace, stealing forth from his smokehouse prison in the thick of a winter's snowstorm with the stigma of murderer upon him, and his own father's anathema added to that of the village fathers, was one person. This fine bronzed handsome gentleman attired in New York's latest fashion, walking with the free swing of one who had ranged the Western vastness, haloed with the romance of the wild and unknown distance where heroes are bred, reconciled to his family, acquitted from all his past crimes and spending money like a prince, was entirely another. The village fathers welcomed him, the village mothers feasted him, the village daughters courted him, and the village sons were jealous of him.

The young man hadn't been in the town twenty-four hours before the invitations began pouring in, and Maria Whitney held her head a full inch higher and prepared to take on reflected glory. There was only one bitter pill about it all. She had discovered that the house in which they lived was Allan's, willed to him by his own mother in case his father died before he did. If Maria survived her husband she couldn't hope to live in the stately old mansion and rule it as she chose. But Allan's father wasn't dead yet, and it was worthwhile making friends with Allan. There was no telling what might happen to him out there in the wilds where he lived and seemed intent on living.

The Waitstills were the first to have a tea, closely followed by the Van Storms, the Rutherfords and all the town's other notables.

For a couple of weeks Allan accepted these civilities amiably, taking them as a sign that the town was repenting of its past misjudgment of him. He went agreeably to all the parties, calmly unaware of the marked attention paid him by the ladies, and devoted himself to earnest conversation about Oregon with the men. But, strange to say, his indifference only made the ladies more assiduous in their attentions, and one evening after supper Allan suddenly awoke to the fact that he was surrounded by a circle of them and the one woman in all the world for him wasn't present.

He turned his attention from Lyman Rutherford's last remarks about the annexation of Texas and looked from one woman to another keenly, questioningly. Why wasn't Miranda among them? Now that he thought of it she hadn't been present at any gathering since his return. What did it mean? Didn't they know she was his friend? But of course not. He must attend to letting them know at once. He would speak to Miranda about it the very next day.

In the morning early Allan was going down the street to the post office as he had every morning since his return home, for he'd sent an important letter to Washington and was expecting an answer any day. As he passed the Van Storms', Cornelia Van Storm came out of the house and joined him, gushing over the beauty of the morning and the happy "chance" that made him her companion down the street. She professed to have a deep interest in Oregon and desired above all else to have more information concerning it.

She asked many questions, and Allan answered them briefly. He had keen memories of Cornelia Van Storm's snicker in the schoolroom years ago when he was called up for a whipping. Before that he'd thought her pretty, but he'd never forgiven that snicker, and all her blandishments now couldn't cover her past mistake. In truth his mind was a little distraught, for he was sure he saw a slim, alert figure walking toward him up the street, and his whole attention was riveted upon it.

Miranda was returning in haste from an errand for Marcia, for it was high time the bread was put in the pans. If she delayed it would get too light, and Miranda hated bread with big holes in it.

Allan watched her light footsteps, with their long, easy swing, and the spring of the whole little figure, his heart filling with pride that she loved him. The woman beside him had pink cheeks and blue eyes that languished on occasion—they were languishing now, but in vain. She wore handsome garments and cast ravishing glances at him, but it was as if an iron wall rose between them, and he could see only Miranda.

A moment more and Miranda was passing them. Cornelia Van Storm looked up to get her reward for the compliment she had been giving and saw her companion's eyes weren't upon her. With vexation she looked to see who might be distracting him and to her amazement saw only Miranda Griscom. She stiffened haughtily and flung an angry stare at

Miranda, then turning back to Allan beheld him bowing most deferentially to her.

"Exactly as if she were a real lady," Cornelia declared to her mother on returning, "the impudent thing!"

Miranda was never one to be cowed by a situation. She smiled her merriest and called out, "Mornin'!"

But Cornelia only raised her chin a shade higher and arched her eyebrows haughtily. She paid no heed to the other woman and went on talking affectedly to Allan.

"It's been so pleasant, Mistah Whitney, hearing all about youah chosen country. I've enjoyed it immensely. I'd love to heah moah about it. Couldn't you come ovah this evening? Mothah would love to have you come to suppah, and then we two could have a nice cozy time aftahwahds talking ovah old times."

Her voice was loud and clear, intended for Miranda's ear.

"I'm afraid not, Miss Van Storm," said Allan curtly. "I—ah—shall be very busy this evening. Good morning. I must step in here and see Mr. Spafford." Allan abruptly left her, pausing, however, on the steps of the newspaper office to look down the street after Miranda, an act not lost on the observing Cornelia.

"The idea!" she said indignantly to her mother afterward. "The very idea of his looking after her. It was odious!"

But Allan was getting his eyes open. He remained in the office only a moment, not even waiting to find out if David was there, and then forgetting his important letter he went back down the street after Miranda.

She wasn't in sight anymore. Wings had taken her feet, and she was in the kitchen thumping away at her batch of dough, kneading it as if she had all the Van Storms and Rutherfords and Waitstills and the rest of the town's female population done up in the mass and was having her way with them. Meanwhile down her cheeks rolled tears of bitterness and humiliation, so that she had to turn her face away from her work and wipe it on her sleeve to keep them from dropping on the dough. Then the overwhelming hurt came upon her so forcefully, that secure in the fact that Marcia was upstairs sewing and the children were off at school, she turned and hid her face in her crossed arms and sobbed.

Allan was wise enough not to go to the front door and rouse the house. He went straight to the kitchen and, lifting the latch half dubiously, peered in. Then he stepped across the threshold and folded the sobbing woman in his arms.

"Randa," he said. "Randa, tell me why she did that and why you haven't been asked to any of the parties? I've looked for you every time, and you never came."

But Miranda only sobbed the harder.

"Randa," he kept on tenderly, "dear little girl, don't cry, Randa! Why are you crying?"

"I ain't," sobbed Miranda, trying to draw away from him, her head still hidden in her arms, her voice trembly and unlike her. "I guess what broke me up was jest seein' the truth all sudden-like when I be havin' sech a lovely dream. Don't, Allan—you mustn't put yer arms 'round me; it ain't the right thin'. You'd oughta go court one o' them other girls what'd give their eyeteeth to git yeh. You kin git anybody in town now, an' I see it. I ain't fit fer yeh. I'm jes' M'randy Griscom, an' nobody thinks I'm enny 'count. You're a fine gentleman, an' you ought to hev somebody thet is like yeh. You ben real kind an' good to me, but you hedn't seen them others when you fust come home, an' it stan's to reason you'd like 'em better'n me. It's all right, an' I want you to know I don't grudge yeh. Only it come on me kinda suddent, me not ever havin' hed anythin' lovin' in my life afore. I'd oughta hed better sense n't 'a let yeh think I was any 'count, I—"

But a big gentle hand softly covered her trembling lips that were bravely trying to send him away, and Allan's face came down close to her wet burning cheeks.

"Little girl—Randa—darling, don't you know I love you?" he said. "What did you think I came three thousand miles for? Just to be invited to Waitstills' to supper and walk simpering down the street with that smirking Cornelia Van Storm? Why, Randa, she can't hold a candle to you—they can't any of them. You're just the only woman in all the world for me. If I can't have you I'll go back to Oregon and live in my log cabin alone. I'll sit by my fire at night and think about how you wouldn't have me and how it would have been if you would. But there's nobody else for me—Randa, you're all the world to me! As for the rest of this hanged old town, if they can't appreciate you I've no use for them, and I'll not go to another stiff old party unless they invite you. Why, Randa, I love you, and I'm going to have our banns published next Sunday! We'll just be married right away and show 'em where we stand."

But at that Miranda rose up and protested, the tears and smiles chasing each other down her cheeks. Indeed she couldn't be married yet; she didn't have her things ready, and she couldn't and wouldn't be married without being ready. Neither would she have him tell the community yet. If he felt that way she was content. Let them keep their secret a little longer and not have the whole town staring and gossiping.

He held her in his arms and kissed the tears away, bringing out the dimples. Then he made her sit down and tell him just what she'd do. He must go back in the spring at the latest, for he'd promised Dr. Whitman he would come with answers from the government at Washington and also to accompany and advise some more emigrants who were going to Oregon. Would she go with him?

With this question happily settled, they came to their senses after a time, and Miranda went on with her kneading, while Allan hurried after his belated mail.

Miranda began that very night to work at her trousseau, and before she slept she broke the news of her engagement to Marcia, who laughed and cried over her and then set to work to help her in earnest, meanwhile sorrowfully contemplating a future without her.

Allan went to Washington the very next day on diplomatic business for Oregon, not knowing how long he must stay but promising to return soon.

In truth he didn't come back until the middle of March, except for a few days at Christmas, which he spent mainly at the Spafford home. It was rumored through the town that he and David Spafford were working together for some mysterious political affairs pertaining to annexation. The young women admired Allan all the more because of his abstracted manner and distant ways and strove even harder to gain his attention. But none of them, not even the keen-eyed Cornelia, suspected that the main part of his visit was not in the Spafford library with David, but in the dining room with Miranda. Her strong sense of the fitness of things would not permit her to take possession of any higher room in the house than the dining room.

In those days Miranda sang about her work like a bird and day by day grew younger and more beautiful. Her eyes shone like the stars that had taught her so many years; her cheeks were pink and white like the little blush roses that grew around the front stoop trellis. She set fine stitches in her garments, finished a wonderful quilt she was piecing and dreamed her beautiful dreams. Whenever she went about the village and met any of the girls who were interested in Allan, she looked at them half pityingly. No more did their haughty ways and silly airs about him hurt her. He had loved her as long as she had loved him, and he wanted no other. She could afford to pity and be kind.

So she answered their questions about him, with them scarcely thinking they were talking to his future wife.

"Yes, Mr. Whitney's goin' back t' Oregon," she told a group of them at the apple paring, when they gathered around her to ply her with questions, while they let her do most of the work. "I herd 'im say he couldn't stay away from thar very long. He misses th' animals an' Injuns a lot. Gettin' use t'em thet way makes it hard, yeh know. It's real good of you all to be so kinda nice to him now when he went away from here in disgrace. I was thinkin' thet over t' myse'f th' other night, an' I sez to myse'f, 'M'randy, jest see what a diffrunce!' Why, I kin remember when Allan Whitney wasn't thought much of in this town. He was shut up in my gran'pa's smokehouse fer murder, an' everybody couldn't say too much agin 'im. An' now here he comes back, hevin' traveled an' made a lot o' money and fit b'ars an' coyotties an' wil' cats an' things, an' ev'ybody's ez nice ez pie an' ready to fergive 'im. It does beat all what a diffrunce a bit o' money makes an' a han'some face. He's the same Allan Whitney—why didn't you make a fuss over him afore?"

"Mirandy Griscom, I think you're perfectly dreadful, mentioning things like that about a respectable young man—bringing up things he did when he was a child and horribly exaggerating them anyway. They didn't shut him up for murder at all. They only arrested him because he had a gun and they wanted to find out where he got it and trace the murderer."

"Well, now, is thet so?" said Miranda innocently. "Why, ain't it real strange I ain't never heard thet afore? Me livin' in Gran'pa's house all thet time, too. Well, now, I'm pleased to know it. H'm! Well, beats all what time will do. There might be some more things come out someday—who knows. C'r'neelyah, ain't yeh cuttin' them apples pretty thick?"

"Cut them yourself then," said Cornelia, throwing down her knife. "I'm sure such work never was very agreeable to me anyway. I suppose you've had more experience."

"P'raps I hev," said Miranda cheerfully.

"But I advise you," snapped Cornelia as she turned away, "not to talk about things you don't know anything about, or you'll get into trouble. It's never wise to talk about things you're not acquainted with."

"No," said Miranda, "thet's a fact. It ain't! I wouldn't ef I was you."

"What do you mean?"

"Oh, nothin'," said Miranda. "Don't get riled. P'raps you'll onderstand one o' these days."

The matter that detained Allan Whitney in Washington had to do with the passage of a bill on behalf of Oregon, and his quiet vigilance and convincing words did much to further Oregon's interests.

It did him good to be in touch with things at their fountainhead. His heart thrilled when he met great men, recognizing the things they stood for and the questions that would stir the country in the coming years. He also felt deep hope for his own adopted territory in the far West, and his young, strong enthusiasm moved many great minds to look into matters and put the weight of their influence on his side.

Letters passed between him and Miranda, many and often. But by reason of the precaution the two took to send their letters enclosed to or from David Spafford, no word of the correspondence leaked out, though the postmistress knew the affairs of the neighborhood. Miranda shrank from having her sweet secret bandied about the town, which had given both her and Allan such rough handling and unkind judgment, and Allan understood and agreed with her.

The letters weren't always long, for the two writers were more than busy. But they were wonderful in a way, for they breathed a deep, abiding confidence in one another and a revelation of each one's soul for the other to see. Thus they grew to know one another better and to bridge the years of their separation through knowledge in preparation for the long road they hoped to travel together.

The very day before Allan returned finally from Washington a wonderful event came to pass. Both for its own sake and because Dr. Whitman and David Spafford were so enthusiastic about it, Allan took a deep interest in it. Professor Morse's electric telegraph flashed its first message on the new test line that had just been completed from Baltimore to Washington. Allan always counted himself most fortunate to be among those who witnessed the sending of that first message, "What hath God wrought," over the wires. When he came back he had a great story to tell those who gathered that night around David Spafford's supper table.

Nathan was there, home from college for a few days and sitting at the feet of his elder brother with worshipful eyes, listening to the wonders of his experiences. Miranda, bringing in hot muffins as fast as the plate was emptied, listened, too, and her heart swelled with pride that Allan had been present at that event, taking his place in the world of great men, higher than her highest dreams for him.

Grandfather Heath dropped in to bring David a town report that had to be published in the paper and listened to the account. He set his ugly, stubborn lip that had objected to every new thing on earth ever since he was born and fixed his cold eye on Allan while he talked. When Allan at last looked up he faced the same glitter of two steely orbs that had met him that night so many years ago when he had shouldered the gun of a murderer to save him for his mother's sake. It was all there just the same—Pharisaism, blindness, unreasonableness and stolid stubbornness. Grandfather Heath hadn't changed an iota through the years and wouldn't on this side of the grave. He had fought every improvement since he was old enough to fight and would with his dying breath.

"H'm!" he said to Allan's final sentence. "How did yeh know they wa'n't foolin' yeh? As fur as I'm consarned I don't believe no sech fool nonsense, an' ef 'twas true it would be mighty dangerous an' a mighty blasphemous undertakin' to persume to use the lightnin' fer writin' messages. You don't ketch me hevin' anythin' to do with sech goin's on. I say let well 'nough alone—thet's what I say. Writin' letters is good enough fer me. Better take my 'dvice an' not fool with the lightnin'. Besides, you'll find out ther ain't nothin' in it. It's all a big swindle to git money out of folks, an' you'll find out someday to yer sorrow. I never git took in by them things. Wal, good night."

Allan had a great deal to say to David that night, of what had befallen him in Washington and what he'd been able to do for Oregon. When Miranda had finished the dishes she brought her sewing and sat shyly down at Marcia's request in the library.

But presently Rose went upstairs to bed, and Marcia went to see if young David's hoarseness was better. In a few minutes David the father made an excuse to go out so that Allan and Miranda were left alone.

Then Allan turned to Miranda with a smile. "Well, Randa, my work is done, and now how soon will you be ready to take the trail with me?"

Chapter 27

They walked decorously to church the next morning, Miranda with Marcia, David and Allan just behind, Rose with her young brother bringing up the rear.

Nobody thought much of it when they all filed into the Spafford pew, though it would have been more according to custom if Allan had sat in his father's seat. Everybody knew of Allan's friendship and somewhat mysterious business relations with David. No one thought anything of Miranda, except, perhaps, Cornelia Van Storm.

It was David who managed that Allan should go into the seat next to Miranda, and Marcia should sit next to her husband.

The service went on as usual, until toward the close, when the minister stood up and published the banns of Miss Miranda Griscom and Mr. Allan Whitney. A stillness and astonishment swept over the congregation in its closing stir. The women who had been fastening their fur collars around their necks paused in the act; the small children whose hoods and coats had been quietly put on were suddenly left to their own devices. All eyes were fixed upon the minister and then furtively turned toward the Spafford pew where Miranda sat inwardly trembling but outwardly calm. Her face was as sweet and demure with its long drooping lashes as any bride-to-be could desire. Her white, soft neck showed beneath the cape of her green silk bonnet, and one small ruddy curl just glimpsed below willfully. Her hands were folded over her handkerchief, and her cheeks were pink.

Allan sat tall and proud beside her. Just when the strain of the silence in the church was at its peak he looked down at Miranda and smiled tenderly. And she was drawn to look up with starry eyes and smile back the loveliest smile woman's face could wear, full of adoring trust and self-lessness but with a kind of self-reliance and strength to suffer, too, if need be, yet be glad.

As their eyes met, a glory came into their faces, and all the members of the congregation looking on saw and were profoundly moved, even in the midst of the astonishment and disapproval.

It was only a flash in an instant of time, and neither of the actors in the little scene was aware they had plighted their troth in the eyes of the world and given a sacred vision of their love that had stirred hearts to their depths. Such brief fleeting visions of what life and love may be, are little glimpses into what heaven is and earth might become, if only hearts were pure and purged from selfishness.

Grandmother Heath saw and remembered her own wooing, with a strange forgotten thrill; recalled the look on the face of Miranda's mother when she married "that scallawag of a Griscom" and felt a sudden pang for her own harshness toward her suffering child. For the first time since the baby Miranda was placed in her unloving arms she saw a beauty and a nobleness in her, for gratified pride had done for her what natural affection had never done.

Grandmother Heath was unmitigatedly pleased. She never thought Miranda would marry at all, and here she surprised them all and took a prize. The Whitney family was an old and wealthy one, and this Allan had wiped out old scores and made himself not only respected but highly approved and run after by the whole village. Grandmother Heath drew a long breath and swelled up with satisfaction in her pew.

Hannah Skinner dropped her pretty lower lip in almost childish amazement for a moment, then preened herself and tried to look as if she'd known of the engagement for years and was enjoying everyone else's surprise now.

Cornelia Van Storm, her admiring eyes glued to Allan's handsome shoulders during the whole service, had the full benefit of the smile that passed between the lovers. She cast angry, jealous eyes at Miranda, biting her lips to keep back the mortified tears. Yet she knew in her heart that the love between those two was unusual and there was little likelihood any man would ever look at her like that. It was a revelation to poor spoiled Cornelia, both of her own selfish heart, incapable of loving anybody as Miranda did, and of the fact that such love existed in the world.

Nathan Whitney, senior, at the end of his pew across the aisle, beside his sharp, unpleasant wife, lifted his expressionless countenance like a metal mask that had no power to show the inner man and with his cold eyes saw the delicate face of Miranda gloried with that smile. No one could have told what he was thinking as he dropped his gaze emotionlessly and meditated on the irony of a fate that gave the prize he so much coveted to his own son.

But to Maria, his wife, no kindly mask was given to veil her chagrin from prying eyes. Maria had always been jealous and scornful of

Miranda, for she'd learned of her husband's attentions before his marriage to her and was mortified she was a second choice with such a rival as Miranda Griscom. She despised Miranda for her father's sake and for occupying the position of helper in David Spafford's home. Maria couldn't conceal her vexation. The appalling fact that if her husband died she might have to contend with Miranda for the home she now occupied confronted her, and she'd never been adept at self-control. She felt that her only revenge lay in letting Miranda see she resented her boldness in setting herself up to be good enough for Allan.

For the most part, however, the congregation, when they recovered from their first astonishment, appeared to realize the match was a good one from both sides, although so unexpected. At the church door they crowded around to congratulate the two, expressing their astonishment in hushed Sabbath tones.

It was almost pitiful to see the pride with which Grandmother Heath and Hannah pressed complacently up to share in the glory of the occasion. Miranda took her grandmother's newly developed affection gently, as if love were too precious to be scorned, even when it came too late.

But her old mischievousness returned to her when she saw Hannah, and she couldn't resist calling out clearly, so that those around could hear: "Mornin', Hannah. Kinda took you by s'prise, didn't I?"

Then with a smile at the discomfited Hannah and a sly wink at Nathan, who stood grinning appreciatively by with Rose; she took Allan's arm and walked proudly humble down the street, her time of recognition come at last. Yet it hadn't brought the triumphant elation she had expected, only deep, deep joy.

Grandmother Heath didn't stop at anything when she got started, and during the next two weeks Marcia thought she understood where Miranda got her tendency to stretch the truth upon occasion. For Grandmother Heath gave the impression her "beloved granddaughter Miranda" was going as a missionary, and she set the missionary society to sewing on that quilt Miranda had suggested for the Indians. Only the quilt was now destined for Miranda instead of the Indians.

Many extra sessions of the missionary society met in the houses of the different members, and the interest in the North American Indians grew visibly. An actual missionary in their midst was a wonderful incentive.

When Marcia heard that Miranda was supposed to be going as a missionary she tried pleasantly to make plain this was a mistake but was met with such indignant replies on every hand that she refrained from further enlightenment. After all, what was the harm in their thinking so, when old Mrs. Heath seemed so set on it? Miranda would undoubtedly be a missionary wherever she went, though not perhaps the kind the American Board usually sent out.

"Oh, Mrs. Marcia! Now ain't that the funniest you ever heard tell 'bout! Me teachin' the Injuns! My! I never thought they'd think I was even good enough to be scalped by a Injun. Ain't that the funniest you ever heard? And Gran'ma! Did you ever see the beat o' her? She'll be havin' horseflesh on the dinner table next, jest to kinda get uset to bein' related to a misshunery! My! I never thought I'd git thar! A misshunery! Wal, I am beat!"

Both Miranda and Allan wished to have the wedding a quiet affair, for they planned to take the stagecoach immediately, as soon as the ceremony was over, and cut across the country to join the emigration party. Allan had already arranged for their outfit and had everything in readiness for their comfort on the way.

But when the missionary idea took hold of the town there was no having things quiet. The people determined to make as much of the occasion as possible. So there was a large wedding, and because of the missionary society's interest in the matter it was suggested the ceremony be held in the church.

When this idea was first suggested to Miranda she looked startled, and then a sudden softened glory grew in her eyes. Wasn't it just like the God of the stars to lend her His house to be married in when she hadn't any earthly father's house of her own? And then it seemed to set the seal of respectability and forgiveness on her and Allan and sanctify their union—they two who had been left so long outside the pale as it were. And so it was arranged.

Maria Bent didn't like it. It took all the glory from her, whose schoolhouse wedding was still talked of in the annals of the village gossip.

Some of the girls Allan Whitney had ignored didn't like it. They said they didn't see what right Miranda Griscom had to be married in the church just because she was going to be a missionary.

Cornelia Van Storm tossed her head and added, "You know she isn't really a missionary. That's all poppycock! Allan Whitney is nothing but a common fur trader after all."

It was a beautiful, solemn, simple wedding. The wedding breakfast was prepared by the bride herself and eaten by the relatives and intimate friends of both families at high noon. They went away early so the bride might have plenty of time to get ready for the journey. Then, late in the afternoon, when the spring shadows were lengthening on the new grass and the fresh young leaves on the trees were waving their yellow greenery sleepily as if tired of the day, they heard the silvery sound of the horn and saw the old red stage coming down the street.

Miranda was ready, seated on the front stoop with her bandbox beside her, but the last minute was confusion after all. Allan and the children rushed back into the house for something forgotten, and Miranda, with everything done that could be done, turned and looked back at the house that had been her dear home for so many years, finding unexpected tears in her eyes and throat. Then, before she realized what was happening, she found herself enfolded in Marcia's arms, and Marcia was kissing her and whispering in her ear.

"Oh, Miranda, Miranda! My dear, dear sister! How ever am I going to do without you!"

Then indeed Miranda gave way and cried on Marcia's shoulder for the space of half a second.

"I guess it's me'll be askin' thet about you many times," she sniffed, trying to straighten up and smile as Allan hurried down the steps with David, and the children rushed behind, with their hands full of violets they'd picked for her to take along.

Then they all said good-bye again, the horn sounded, and Miranda and Allan were seated in the old stage, riding off together out into the great world.

Everywhere along the way were friendly faces, waving handkerchiefs and cheery words of well wishing. Grandmother Heath was at her gate, actually with a smile on her wrinkled old face, and Grandfather Heath at the door behind her waving a stiff old hand.

"Seems like 'twas jest some fool dream I was dreamin' an' I'd wake up purty soon an' find 'twasn't me 'tall," whispered Miranda through the happy tears.

"No, it's a blessed reality," reassured Allan in a low tone so their fellow travelers couldn't hear.

Then they went around the curve and down the hill on the old corduroy road and were lost to the sight of the village.

Chapter 28

A few days later they started out on the trail—quite a company of them, men, women and children, with Allan as captain of the party and Miranda, her new role of missionary already begun, as comforter-in-chief to all of them.

The tears were all forgotten now in the joy that had dawned upon her. To love and be loved, to be with her beloved all the time, to plan and look ahead to their home together—that was happiness enough for Miranda. The journey, hard and laborious to some, was one grand, continuous picnic to her. She'd had little play in her childhood, except as she stole it by the way and suffered for it afterward in hard words, cold looks and deprivations. The fun she'd wrenched from life had been of her own manufacture. The flowers, the birds, the trees she loved had often been too far away from duty for her to enjoy, and her adventures had all been in rescuing those she loved from unhappiness.

But now all this was changed. Here was a wide, limitless sky. Here were trees in profusion and birds setting up new homes on lofty branch or humble bush. Here were carpets of bloom in their passing and rivers deep and wide and difficult to be forded.

Miranda didn't shrink from the crossings, no matter what the peril. She rode her horse like a man, on occasion, and scorned the wagons if she might ride by her husband's side. To ride and swim her horse across the river became one of her great ambitions. For Miranda had returned to her childhood and was sipping all the innocent delights and excitements her untamed nature craved. And Allan was proud of her.

Like two children they rode together, taking the perils and the hardships. Never once did Miranda's heart turn back with longing to the East. She was a true pioneer and looked forward with joy to the cabin in the clearing. What need had she to be homesick? She had her beloved with her, and the same stars were overhead. She carried her home where she went. Behind her in the wagon and on the pack mules were her treasures—gifts of the dear ones at home. Not the least among them was a bundle of quilts wrought in many colors and curious designs; one highly prized from the missionary society was curiously fashioned in flaming red and yellow in the famous rising sun pattern. But the one she loved the best was pink and white in a wild rose pattern, with many prickings of the finger, the work of little Rose Spafford's childish days.

At night, as often as she could, she slept out in the open, looking up at the starry dome above her, murmuring softly now and then, with folded hands and reverent look, "Thanks be! Thanks be! Thanks be!"

Slowly the days and weeks crept by, and the caravan wound its difficult snail-like way along the trail. Sickness came to some, and weariness and weakness. Buffaloes weren't found soon, and the provisions grew short, so hunger stalked them. Swollen rivers disputed their passing; untimely snowstorms overtook them in the mountains; wagons broke down and had to be mended or abandoned; Indians with hostile men shadowed them for a distance; death even entered their ranks and took a child and his mother; discouraging remarks were flung at them by unfriendly people along the way. Yet never in all the long weeks did Miranda lose courage or grow fainthearted. She was riding upon the high places of the earth, and she knew it and was glad.

She was writing a letter to send home to Marcia—a long diary letter as Marcia had suggested. It wouldn't be finished till she reached her destination, and it might not get back home for a year or two—there was no telling. But it gave Miranda a cheery, happy feeling to write it, as if she were looking in on the dear ones at home for a little while.

That letter was worth reading. It reached Marcia almost a year and a half from the day of the wedding and brought tears and smiles and much delight to all who read it. It was so Mirandaish.

Dear Mrs. Marcia in pertic'ler, an' Mr. David ef he cares, an' o' course Rose, an' little Dave, an' then anybody else you want:

Wal, we're started, an' you'd laugh to kill ef you could see us. A long line o' wagguns with white pillercases over 'em, looks fer all the world like a big washday hung out to dry. I wouldn't ride inside one of 'em fer anythin', but I s'pose they're all right fer them as likes 'em. I don't think much of the women in this set. They don't hev much manners, ur else they got too much an' ain't got no strength. You gotta hev a pretty good mixture of manners an' strength ef you want to git on in this world. There's one real pretty little thin' she's mos' cried her eyes out a'ready. I donno what she come fer, r' else she hed to, her husband's so sot on goin'. An' a lot of 'em jerk ther chil'ren roun' like they was a bag o' meal. Poor little souls! I'm doin' what I kin to make up fer it. I'm dretful glad you put in all them sugarplums. They come in handy now. I don't guess the Injuns'll hev many lef' when I git thar.

We passed a river this mornin', great shinin' thin' like a silver ribbon windin' round amongst the green valley. God musta hed a good time makin' thin's. I sensed it today when I was lookin' at thet river an' valley all laying there so pretty. Seemed He must a felt most like I do when I'd git a row o' pies an' cakes an' thin's made fer the minister's donation party, plum an' mince an' punkin' an' apple an' custard an' fruit, real black, an' a big fine marble cake! D'you s'pose it cud seem thet way t' Him?

We crossed a river with quicksands yesterday an' hed to lock the wagguns together with chains. Dr. Whitman taught 'em how to do it, they say. He's a great man. You'd oughta see us, it's real enterestin'. I'll tell you how it is. Every night there's five men on guard and five more 'n th' daytime. At night the wagguns is 'ranged in a round circle an' the mules an' horses tied inside. Early mornin' they let 'em outside awhile to feed. Then they hev to be cotched an' saddled. It takes a while.

Every man hes so many things to do an' knows his work. They hev to put on a powder flask an' knife in their belt an' their gun afore 'em when they start each day. Oncet we rode nine hours without stoppin'. We gen'aly take two hours noonin', turn out the animals, get dinner, wash dishes an' thet like. At night we pitch tents, spread buffalo skins on the ground, then oilcloth fer a floor, an' fix yur thin's around out o' the hay, leavin' a place in the middle to eat. Thur was some Injuns came around, and most o' the wimmen got scared. I didn't see much to 'em to be scared 'bout. They look dirty to me an' don't hev nouf cloes to their backs.' "

The letter went on to tell the daily occurrences of the way, noting the places and the incidents, and one notable extract touched Marcia's heart more than all the rest.

Wal, we come to a mounting this mornin', a real live mounting! It's thar yet right in front o' me. I got my dishes all washed an' I'm restin' an' lookin' at it by spells. You don't

*never need to go enny further to wonder, ef you oncet see a
mounting. It's the biggest, comfortablest, settledest thin' you
ever could a' thought of.*

*It jest sets right thar, never seems to mind what happens round
it ur what goes over it. Can't disturb him, he's a mounting!
Might cut down all his forests, he wouldn't care, he'd grow
some more. Might walk over him all day'n annoy him a lot, he
jest sets thar an' looks up, an' by an' by all them thet annoys
passes on an' thars the mounting yit jes' same, and he knew
'twould be so. He can't die. They can't nobody move him—he's
too big. 'Cept mebbe God might. But God made him, so He
don't care 'bout thet, 'cause ef God could make him God
wouldn't spoil him, 'n ef He moved him He'd jest put him in a
better place! Men might cut a hole in him, but 'twould take
s'long an' be s'little 'twouldn't 'mount t' much. Mounting's thar
jes' same. He's a mounting, an' he looks like he knowed it, an'
yet 'tain't huht him none. He's jes' es kind 'n consid'rate 'n'
comft'ble—'n', yes—real purty like, all soft fringes of trees at
the bottom, and all sharp points ur white frostin' of snow up top
'gainst the sky; shinin' silver in the mornin' an' the moon, tow-
erin' up over yeh kinda big, an' growin' soft an' purpley with a
wreath o' haze round his feet at night. He's a mounting!*

*An' God musta been real pleased when He got him done. He
musta been most best pleased of all when He made a mounting.
I'm real glad He made 'em and glad I lived to see one. When you
come you must come this way an' see my mounting. They say
thur's goin' to be some more 'fore we git through, but I don't
b'leeve none of 'em'll be so pretty as this.*

The rest of the letter told of further experiences and the homecoming, first to Waiilatpu, where they were welcomed with open arms by
the missionaries and kept and rested, and then to the cabin where
they had a beautiful time starting to keep house. Here Miranda's
descriptions of the house and her attempts to fix it up were laughable.

After they'd enjoyed the letter thoroughly at home, Marcia took it
with her in her pocket wherever she went and let Miranda's many
friends enjoy it also. She carried it first with her when David took them
out on a drive, Marcia on the back seat with her daughter, Rose, who

had grown suddenly into young womanhood, and young David with his father in the front of the carryall.

They drove straight to the house of Hannah Skinner, where Grandmother Heath had come to live after the sudden death of old Mr. Heath, which occurred a few weeks after Miranda left home.

Hannah and the old lady, both pleased to see the Spafford carriage at their door, came out to welcome their guests, with the cat following.

"I've got a letter from Miranda and thought you'd like to read it," said Marcia, leaning out of the carriage and smiling.

The old lady's face brightened.

"A letter from M'randy! Now you don't say. Well, ain't thet real interestin'? How does she git on misshuneryin'? Seems sorta like gettin' word from another world, don't it? Do get out and come in."

And so the letter was read to the two women who listened in great wonder and boasted around for many days with "M'randy says this" an' "My cousin M'randy says so and so." The village smiled and wondered, and Miranda's record of discreditable scrapes was all forgotten under the halo of a missionary.

In due time the letter traveled to Nathan at college, firing him with a deep desire to go out West, and when he came home in the spring he was full of it.

Finally David said, "Well, my boy, go try it. Allan said it would do you good, and you could earn something out there. We'll see if some people are going, and you go out for a year or two and then come back and finish your college course. A rest and a little nature will do you good."

As suddenly as that it came, and a few weeks later Nathan bade them all an excited, happy farewell and started out into the great far country also.

Rose, like a sweet, frightened flower, looked after the coach that bore him away and fled to the window in Miranda's room, to stay alone until night fell and the stars came out to comfort her and help her understand.

Poor little Rose, with your astonished feet taking the first steps into the path of sorrow and loss! How long the way lies before you beaten hard by many feet. Yet you, too, will one day reach the higher ground and see your mountain!

Chapter 29

For every big bridge built or massive building reared, many stones must lie under ground. No marvelous work is accomplished without destruction and sacrifice, and the greatest movements are often those baptized with blood.

Slowly, stealthily, out of the West a menacing cloud arose. At first it was shadowy, like a mote one tries to brush away from a tired eye, still floating and insisting upon being seen.

Low stirrings in the grass and sounds like the hiss of some moving, poisonous serpent; phantom-like forms vanishing when searched for—gone, always gone, when they looked—yet there, convincingly there, but elusive; stealthy footsteps in the night; prying, peering, breathless—these things were in the very atmosphere.

An uneasiness had been growing among the Indians ever since Dr. Whitman's return with the emigrants. An enemy was at work—that was plain to be seen. Strange rumors were abroad—silent, subtle impressions, averted glances, muttered gutturals.

Still Whitman and his workers went steadily on, omitting none of their arduous tasks, not hesitating to visit the sick among known enemies, withholding no kindness even from the stolid and ungrateful.

Several times contagious diseases raged among the Indians with frightening fatalities. The missionaries were faithful and indefatigable, giving themselves night and day with medicine and nursing to save as many as possible. Finally an epidemic of measles broke out among them, sweeping away large numbers.

Frantic and fearful they sent for the missionary doctor, though they often failed to follow directions afterward, or they sent for their own medicine man with his incantations and weird ceremonies. Death stalked among them, and the story went forth—from what source who could be sure?—that the missionary was poisoning them to clear the country of Indians and take their lands for the white people.

The faint cloud on the horizon now grew large and dark with portent. Ominous thunders threatened in the distance, drawing closer and more certain. The mission knew its peril. Dr. Whitman was thoroughly convinced that a plot to murder the missionaries was nearly completed; yet he kept steadily on with his work. Day after day he told his wife and friends all that he saw and what he feared from it. Carefully and prayerfully he walked, with the light of another world on his face, not knowing at what moment he would be called from this.

He visited the Indian camp on the Umatilla River; called on the bishop and the vicar general, who had just arrived at the place, and had brief interviews; then rode out to where a fellow missionary was encamped, reaching there about sunset. They talked the situation over calmly, discussing the possibilities and probabilities.

"My death may do as much good to Oregon as my life can do," said the man who had crossed the Rockies and a continent in midwinter to save Oregon.

Though weary and worn, he didn't stay to rest, for there was severe sickness at his home. He started late that night on his lonely ride of forty miles back to the mission, reaching there at dawn. Then a hurried interview with his wife, a few words and tears of tenderness were cut short by calls to attend the sick.

"Greater love hath no man than this, that a man lay down his life!"

This man had always led in the hard things—sacrificing, never thinking of himself; plunging into the icy river first; not asking others to go where he was unwilling to lead—like the Master he served. It was as if God wouldn't take from him the eternal right of leadership, for which He formed and called him, and so arranged that even in death he should still lead.

While the sun was shining high in the heavens, stealthily, like evil shadows, the Indians gathered around the mission that once had been a happy home and where the work was still going on as if no menace were felt in the air.

Suddenly the shadows sprang from covert hiding on every side! Evil faces, stealthy steppings, flashing knives, and the deed was done! Dr. Whitman was the first to fall, with a tomahawk plunged twice into his head. Then the carnage began and continued for eight days.

The first news was brought to Miranda as she stood at her cabin door watching for Allan.

He didn't come with his usual cheery whistle but strode into the clearing with deep sorrow in his eyes and an ominous look about his mouth. His wife knew at once that something terrible had happened.

"Is it them pesky Injuns?" she asked in a voice she had taught to be low and guarded. "Drat 'em! They's ben two of 'em 'round the house this very mornin', an' they looked like they was up to som'pin'. What hev they ben doin'?"

"They've killed Dr. Whitman!"

"In the name o' sense what'd they do thet fur? Did they want to bite their own nose off to spite their face? How they goin' to live 'thout him? Ain't he ben doin' an' doin' himself to death fer 'em? The lazy, miserable, no-count, naked creeters! I know they ain't much but naughty childern, but ain't they got no sense at all? Kill Dr. Whitman!"

"It wasn't their fault. Their minds have been poisoned by the enemy—"

"I know," broke in Miranda as if that didn't matter, "but ennyhow I never could stomick them pesky Injuns, misshunery ur no misshunery. Kill Dr. Whitman! 'Z if they could kill him! Tomyhawks couldn't do thet! Men couldn't do thet! Why, a man like thet'll live ferever—yeh can't stop him! He ain't ben jest a livin' body—he's a livin' soul. He'll go on livin' long 'z the world stan's, 'n longer! He'll live ferever! He's like a mounting! Can't tech him! Kill him? Wal, I guess not!"

Miranda whirled her back abruptly around and let the tears course down her cheeks. But in an instant she had herself in hand and turned back, her face wet, her eyes snapping fire.

"Wal, what we goin' to do 'bout it?"

"Do about it?" asked Allan, half astonished.

Then a grim look settled about his mouth. "We're going to get you out of this horrible country and safe somewhere as soon as we can go."

"Wal, thet's jest what we ain't goin' to do," said Miranda. "I ain't no wax doll whose nose'll melt off in the sun, an' thur ain't no tomyhawk goin' to tech me. We're goin' to git to work right here'n now an' teach them pesky Injuns some manners. You don't mean to tell me, Allan Whitney, thet you'd sneak off an' take yer wife away to hide her in pink cotton while them dear misshuneries is settin' thar sorrerin' fer him"— she choked but went bravely on—"an' in danger, mebbe, needin' per-tection. Allan Whitney, thet ain't you! I know you better'n thet! An' ef hevin' a wife hes made you sech a fool, baby 'n' coward she'd better git hers'f tomyhawked right here an' now an' git out o' yer way. I wouldn't be worth my salt ef I couldn't stand by yeh an' he'p yeh do yer duty like the brave man yeh air. How long sence it happened?"

"Randa, dear, you don't understand. It's been going on several days. There's been a massacre. You know there're over seventy people in and around the mission, and they've killed fourteen of them already. Dr.

Whitman and his wife first, and some of the sick people, and over fifty of them have been taken prisoners. One man got away up to the fort, and they wouldn't take him in. What do you think of that? I tell you this is a horrible country, and I want to get you out of it."

"Name o' sense! Why didn't you tell me afore? Ain't you done nothin' 'bout it yet? You ain't goin' to give up an' let this go on? Prisoners! Them poor women an' children! You gotta git up a regiment 'mongst the settlers an' git out after 'em. How 'bout them es is killed? Hev they ben buried yet? Somebody oughtta go right down to the mission an' tend to thin's. Where's Nathan? Ain't he comin' back purty soon? He 'n' I c'n go down to the mission. Mebbe ther ain't nobody thar, an' 'tain't safe, so many wild animals as thur is round. You go git the settlers t'gether an' fight them Injuns! It's time they was taught a good sound lesson."

Allan stood staring at his wife in amazement and admiration.

"Randa, I can't. I can't have you go down to that horrible place, and I can't leave you here alone. I don't know where Nathan is. You're a woman, and you're my wife. I must protect you."

"Stuff an' nonsense!" said Miranda, hurrying around the cabin picking up things to take with her. "This is a time o' war, an' you can't sit aroun' an' act soft then. Ain't I as good a right to act like a man in a time like this as you hev, I'd like to know? Ef I get tomyhawked I will, an' thet's the whole of it. It's got to come sometime, I guess, an' my time ain't comin' till it's ready, an' you can't stop it ef it's really here. 'Sides, thet don't matter a hull lot. Thet ain't the way that misshunery man talked ennyhow, an' now he's gone I reckon we've got to do our best to take his place. Ef I git prisonered I bet I give 'em a lively time of it afore they git done with me ennyhow. Come on, Allan—don't you try to stop me doin' my duty, fer yeh can't ennyhow, an' it ain't reasonable at a time like this. Them pris'ners gotta be set free. We gotta be c'rageous an' not think o' oursel'es. Ef ennythin' happens to us this ain't the hull o' livin'—down here ain't. You go git the horses ready, an' I'll put up a couple o' bundles, an' I'll ride 'long o' you till I find somebody to go to Waiilatpu with me. Hurry up now. It ain't no use argyin'! I'm willin' 'nouf to go back East when I've done what thur is to do, but—not till then!"

Allan stooped and kissed his wife, a look almost of awe upon his face.

"Randa, you are wonderful!" he said softly. "I have no right to stop you!" Without another word he went out and saddled the horses.

Chapter 30

In the autumn after young Nathan Whitney left for Oregon, his sister Helena was married to a farmer living near Fonda, and Prudence went to teach school above Schenectady. Three months later their father died, quietly, unobtrusively as he had lived, the mask he had always worn not changed or softened by death. What secret emotions he'd had died with him, and men read nothing from his silent face.

His wife, Maria, not relishing the care of the younger children who had just grown to the annoying age, packed them off to their aunt Jane in Albany and took herself on an indefinite trip to New York. By the ordering of the will she received enough money to make her comfortable during her lifetime, and the house didn't belong to her, so she was free to go. She had few friends in the village where she'd lived so many years and preferred to leave it behind her forever.

The old house was closed. The grass grew tall in the yard, with the hedges rough and scraggly, and cobwebs wrought their riotous lacery across doors and window casements, a lonely deserted sight for those who looked across from the windows of the Spafford house. Rose had often cast a wistful glance toward the vine-covered gateway as she threw open her windows in the morning, wishing she might see the familiar figure of Nathan and hear his cheery whistle as he came down the walk. He'd been gone a long time, and only one letter had come from him, in St. Louis on his way out.

But one morning in the late glowing summer the cobwebby shutters were thrown wide, and Miranda rested her plump, bare arms on the windowsill and leaned out, drawing in deep breaths of her native air and smiling in broad satisfaction.

The years had passed, long in their waiting, changes had been wrought, and at last Miranda had come into her own. She was mistress of the great white house, and she was happy.

Miranda, Allan and Nathan had been home for nearly a week, and they'd been welcomed with open arms and glad smiles. They told their tales of terror, bloodshed, danger, and deliverance. They visited their friends, heard the news, social, religious, political, and now they had come home. The house had been cleaned and polished to the last degree. The cobwebs were no more. Nathan was even now out in the yard with a big scythe mowing down the tall grass. The Whitney children, Samuel and the twins, were coming on the afternoon stage. Allan was going into the newspaper office with David. Miranda was content.

"My!" she said as she sniffed the cinnamon roses under the window. "I'm glad thur ain't no pesky Injuns 'round here. They may be all well 'nouf fer them 'at likes 'em, but not fer me. The misshunery business ain't what it's cracked up to be. I've hed my try at it, an' I don't want no more. I don't grudge 'em all the things they stole out o' the cabin when we was off chasin' 'em, seein' they left me my rose quilt thet my little Rose made with her baby fingers fer me, an' I've only one regret an' thet's the risin' sun quilt they got, fer I don't 'xpect ever t' git anuther misshunery quilt agin. But then 'twas meant fer 'em in the beginnin', an' mebbe it'll do some good to 'em an' convert 'em from the error of thur ways. They suttenly need it. Anyhow I ain't goin' to fret. I've got all I want, an' I'm real glad I've seen a mounting. It's som'pin' to go 'ith the stars."

Her eyes grew wide and serious, and a sweet look came around her mouth.

Across the street Rose stepped out on the front stoop with a broom wafting a tiny cobweb dreamily from the railing and waving a graceful hand to Miranda. Nathan dropped his scythe and walked over to her. Miranda watched them, a gentle look glorifying her face, and remembered how she used to come out on that stoop over there and look across, thinking she might have been the mistress of this house but wasn't. How odd it all was! She was here with Allan, having the life of all the others she would have chosen if she had had the choice. Would it be that way when she got to heaven? Would she look back and see where she used to be and look at her old self and wonder? How little the trials and crosses looked, now that they were passed! She did get things on this earth, too—stars and mountains and heroes— and happiness!

In the gladness of her heart Miranda lifted her sweet, brown eyes, with the merry twinkles sparkling with earnestness, to the blue of the deep summer sky above the waving treetops and murmured softly under her breath, "Thanks be! Thanks be!" Then she took her broom and went to work.

Agatha's Unknown Way

Chapter 1

She Made Her Escape

N ow mind you don't get lost," Farmer Barnes said for perhaps the fifth time, as he waited to see his charge into an uptown car. "You can tell the conductor where to let you off—at the corner of Delaware Street—and where you want to go—to the Fountain Square Church. Remember—that'll be the safest. Then you walk to your right three blocks—to your right, mind you, not your left—and you'll be there. You can't miss it nohow, if you mind what you're about.

"It's all nonsense—your aunt feeling so fussy about you. Women are always afraid other women folks are going to get lost.

"And when the meetin' is out, if you decide not to stay for evening service—and I don't much believe you better; your aunt will worry— you take these same yellow cars going the other way and come back to this corner. You can set down in one of them park seats and wait for me. Maybe I'll get here first, though. Then I'll be on the lookout for you. And remember that the four-forty is the last train out our way."

A clear voice answered this long direction. "I won't get lost, Uncle Joseph. Don't worry about me. I know just what to do. I'll be here on time if I decide to come home tonight. But don't expect me. I feel as if I really must stay for that evening meeting. There may be old friends of mine here. I'll come back in the milk cart tomorrow and give you an account of my adventures. Good-bye."

The farmer looked after her anxiously as she gave him a bright little smile and nod that were meant to reassure him and then disappeared inside the crowded car. He had it in his heart to ask the conductor to keep an eye on her. But while he was considering how to say it, the car slipped on its way. He took off his hat and wiped the perspiration from his sunburnt face. The day was warm, and he'd been standing in the broiling sun for nearly five minutes, looking for the right car. Farmer Barnes couldn't get used to the new style of cars without horses.

"I hate them slippery things," he had confided to his niece. "You think you're going to git one of 'em, and you start for it, and by the time you git across the street to where you think it'll stop, it's gone on and is about half a mile away. I have to be out there on hand and wait for 'em."

He shook his head at this one as it glided around a curve. "I dunno as it's quite the thing, after all. Harriet doesn't think it is, and maybe she's right. The child is young and pretty to be dodging around city streets alone."

Agatha Hunter left the car at the proper corner, without giving the conductor any other information than the streets she wanted, and hurried toward the Fountain Square Church.

Her cheeks were pink, and her breath came in little catches that indicated suppressed excitement. Something besides the warmth of the day was affecting her. It wasn't that she was afraid, although she was alone in a big city for the first time in her life. She wasn't timid by nature and couldn't imagine what about her trip caused her uncle and aunt anxiety. She was thrilled that she might at last relive some of the happy experiences she remembered from her childhood.

Agatha Hunter was the daughter of missionaries to India. Once, when a little girl, she had come to America with her parents, and its beautiful homes and churches and streets and lovely people had lingered in her memory through the years.

Unlike most missionaries, her parents had taken her back with them to India where she spent her girlhood. Her father and mother were her only teachers—and quite skilled at that—and books her only companions. She was an excellent pupil and by the age of nineteen had acquired an education that was at least equal to, if not better than, any she might have acquired in American schools.

Then her health, which up to that time had been uniformly good, failed. Before the year waned, the anxious parents knew two things: They could not be spared by their mission board to go home, and their daughter must go.

Meanwhile, grandfathers and grandmothers had gone to the home from which there is no returning, and the only relative left in America to receive Agatha was her mother's half-sister, Mrs. Joseph Barnes. To the old farmhouse, located about five miles from a dreary village, Agatha came, therefore, on her second visit to her mother's homeland. Agatha's father was a Scotsman and an orphan from his boyhood.

Those simple country farmers had been very good to her. Her aunt Harriet hadn't known the girl's mother very well, being separated from her since she was fourteen, but she received Agatha with as much warmth as her rugged, suppressed nature would allow and recognized her as kindred.

Their own children had grown up and gone out into the world, leaving them. They were boys, and the father and mother felt that they knew nothing about girls. So Agatha was a sort of experiment to them. They watched the frail, dark-skinned girl with the deepest interest. They fed her milk fresh from the cow, cream almost thick enough to cut and newly laid eggs, which she became interested in hunting from the nests for herself. They were heartily encouraged when they saw how strong and well she grew under their care.

In her physical being she was indeed well. But never, perhaps, in all America could there have been found a more homesick girl than Agatha Hunter. Aunt Harriet, while she did her best for her niece, wasn't always in sympathy with her training or her ideas. She didn't, for instance, believe in the importance of foreign missions. Why should people go to the ends of the earth in search of heathens, when they were as thick as grasshoppers in August around one's own door? She'd always thought her sister did a foolish thing in marrying Dr. Hunter and going off to India, leaving her father to mourn for her. She couldn't help occasionally expressing such views to Agatha, and the girl shrank from them as if they were blows. She had believed that all America was throbbing with missionary zeal.

Joseph Barnes was a man who in most matters agreed with his wife, especially if they were minor matters, like this one! Apparently the same spirit thrived in the poor little church to which they drove on Sundays, if the weather was just right, not too cold or not too warm. There was no interest in missionary activity connected with the little church. And during the weary Sundays Agatha had passed in its hard, old-fashioned pews, she hadn't heard the missionaries even prayed for.

As strength returned to her body, the hunger grew in her heart. This was by no means the America of her dreams or experiences. Hadn't Agatha, the young girl, been taken to wonderful meetings in great, splendid churches, where the platform was crowded with enthusiastic men and women, among them her father and mother, being treated almost like representatives of royalty? Sometimes she seemed to hear again the roll of the great organ and feel the thrill when the audience rose and sang the missionaries' farewell hymn. Many of them mingled their tears of sympathy, as a white-haired pastor, his voice trembling with emotion, commended the departing missionaries and their friends who were left behind to the covenant-keeping God.

Oh, she was sure there was a great heart for missions in this beautiful America. It was only the little town where her aunt and uncle went to church that had failed to catch its fire. How she longed to get among those who knew of the work her father and mother were doing and who were willing to sacrifice for the multitudes still living in darkness!

"You should go out lecturing," Farmer Barnes would say to her with a half-skeptical, half-sympathetic laugh when she was stirred into giving him some incident connected with her Indian experiences. "Why can't you go around holding meetings, like other missionary women, and preach to the folks? What's the name of that woman, Mother, that Joel's wife wrote about, who lectured and preached and I don't know what else every night of the week in their place? She was a missionary from way out in China or somewhere."

Then Agatha would cower and shiver and declare that she could not do anything like that. Hadn't she from childhood affirmed that preaching was one thing she could never do? How could a woman stand before an audience, as she remembered her mother doing more than once while they were in America, telling the people all about her work and the needs of the mission?

"Mother," she'd said in that faraway time, "I can't ever be a missionary, as you and Father want me to, because I can't stand up and preach to the people as you do. It would make me faint. I know it would."

Her mother only laughed, put her arm around her and reminded her of what Grandfather Judson used to say: "Never cross a bridge until you come to it." But Agatha had grown up with the conviction that, however well suited she might be for other missionary duties, she could never talk to the people.

Then Aunt Harriet would say, "Mercy! Father, don't go to putting any such notions in the child's mind. We don't want no women preachers belonging to our family. It wasn't easy work for her mother to do when she was at home. They just made her—I could see that. And Agatha takes after her, and I'm glad of it. Women folks has enough to keep busy about in this world without their traipsing around the country, doing what the men ought to do."

But the homesickness grew in Agatha, until it culminated in a strong desire to visit Fountain Square Church. She remembered it from her childhood as being full of earnest, wide-awake Christians, who kept in touch with the work the church was doing.

So at age twenty Agatha was bright-eyed, quick of step and eager to face the world, or what she thought was the world. She had been in her mother's homeland for five months, but this was her first attempt to bring reality to her rosy dreams.

It would require a five-mile drive in the farm wagon and a forty-mile train ride to reach the city. A visit there seemed like a tremendous undertaking to Aunt Harriet. Uncle Joseph went once a month to settle his accounts for farm produce and buy supplies, but Aunt Harriet hadn't gone with him for several years. And the last time she was there, the noise and confusion nearly killed her.

"You don't know anything about it," she said to Agatha, trying to dissuade her from going. "The folks rush up and down the streets like mad. And they don't appear to know half the time where they're going or how to get there. And there's streetcars in the middle of the wagon roads, and carts and bells and whistles, and it's as much as your life is worth to get across a street. My! Catch me going to the city unless I had to! I draw a long breath every time I see your uncle drive into the yard after he's been there, and I always feel as though it's a special providence that's saved him once more."

But Agatha's heart was set on going. She had read in Saturday's paper that on the following Tuesday the Fountain Square Church would hold its regular missionary meeting in the church parlors at three o'clock. Now Tuesday of that next week would be her uncle's regular market day. So for the past week all the plans connected with the farm had centered on his getting an early start for town on Tuesday.

Agatha knew what she would do. She would coax Uncle Joseph to let her go with him and show her how to find the Fountain Square Church. After that, her way would be easy. Once among those blessed missionary women, how many delightful friends she would meet! Weren't her father and mother almost oppressed by hospitality while they were in this country? Her plans were made: She would select some pleasant-looking woman who reminded her of her mother, mention her mother's name and then confess she was her daughter and had come all the way from India, alone, to meet her mother's sisters in the work. How glad they would be to see her and hear directly from the Hunters' own daughter about the work they were supporting in India!

They would ask her to stay for the evening session that was always held during those missionary meetings, and returned missionaries nearly always spoke then. Why, she might even find someone she knew there from India. That would be almost like a glimpse of home. Oh, she must surely go!

Chapter 2

She Made Discoveries

She accomplished it. People learned, in time, that Agatha Hunter would likely accomplish what she undertook. Aunt Harriet, it's true, was troubled. She told "Father" she couldn't think what had come over him to agree to such a thing and that for her part she didn't know what Agatha's mother way off in India would say when she heard of it. Uncle Joseph, however, was a good ally. He rarely took a positive stand that was contrary to his wife's views, in the realm where he believed she should hold sway. But Agatha had won a large place in his heart during her stay with them, and he was disposed to humor her to the extent of his ability. Moreover, he didn't share his wife's horror of the city. Hadn't he been there every month going on eleven years, and nothing ever happened to him?

Once having given his word, Uncle Joseph was safe. Agatha felt sure that her plan was to succeed.

Her heart throbbed and her breath came quickly as she hurried down the street in the direction of the Fountain Square Church. She laughed softly over Uncle Joseph's anxiety lest she shouldn't reach the train in time for the homeward trip. She had no idea of taking it that night. Those dear people to whom she was hastening would be sure to keep her for the evening meeting. Why, they'd be shocked at the idea of her not staying. It would seem like almost an insult to her father and mother if she lost such an opportunity. And, oh, wouldn't it be blessed to get once more among people who understood?

The wide street she walked down was thronged with well-dressed men and women, all hurrying, like her, intent upon reaching some place of interest. The young woman from India hadn't the slightest doubt they were seeking the missionary meeting.

She quickened her steps, feeling that the church would be crowded and she'd have difficulty getting a seat. She remembered the last meeting where her mother had spoken; the people were asked to stand and close the aisle chairs so her father and she might press through the crowd to get to her side. If the church would be so full today that she couldn't reach those women she hoped to find, what would become of her plan for the evening? She resolved to push her way through and make a chance. She determined to get hold of a program at once and look for familiar names—someone from India. Several of the missionaries were at home; one of them, at least, would likely be present.

Then she reached what she knew must be the church, and crowds of people were passing it! For a moment she stood irresolute, feeling she should tell some of them this was the meeting place. But perhaps in America they didn't do such things. She wondered why no placards were out. How else would strangers be sure? She looked up at the great, solemn doors of the church and wondered why they were closed. But she reflected immediately that it was probably necessary to shut out the street noises. A strange feeling of timidity crept over her; she hadn't expected to enter the church alone.

At last, with trembling fingers she tried one of the doors. It was locked! She stepped back and looked at the clock on the tower. It was five minutes after the hour for the meeting—unless she'd mistaken the hour. Suddenly, while staring about anxiously, she was confronted by a gentleman of careful dress and dignified manners, who regarded her with grave suspicion, but asked whether he could do anything for her.

Missionary meeting? Oh, yes, there was to be one this afternoon; but it wasn't to be held in the main auditorium. Afternoon missionary meetings were always held in the lower chapel. She was to go around to the left, down the stone steps, then turn to the right and at the end of that walk turn to the left again, and she would find the chapel door.

Oh, yes, the door was unlocked, but nobody had arrived.

A meek young woman wound around the bewildering path, turning to the left and right and left again, wondering, as she went, how people who didn't happen to meet that gentleman could possibly find their way. She came at last to a door that stood ajar and slipped past it into a large, dark room.

Agatha glided silently down an aisle, chose a corner nearest to an audacious streak of light that came through the stained glass, and waited. Five, ten, fifteen minutes. Then the gentleman came and lit a single jet of gas to make the gloom more visible.

"The ladies is late today," he remarked by way of sociability. "It's so powerful hot; I expect they don' like to come out."

Hot! Why, the small audience was shivering! The transition to the sepulchral gloom within had chilled her.

Just then two ladies, three, a half-dozen appeared. In the next fifteen minutes, peering into dark corners and carefully counting, Agatha discovered fifteen. One of them tried the organ; it was locked.

"Never mind," she said. "Mrs. Pierce isn't here. There would be nobody to play."

Then she tried the piano. That also was locked.

"Dear, dear!" she said. "The janitor should look after such things. I wonder where the hymnbooks are kept? Oh, here are some under the cushions, three or four. Well, we won't need more, probably. Mrs. Greyson, you don't care for a book, do you? And I'm sure I don't."

From time to time someone glanced over into the corner where the stranger sat, but no one seemed to think of speaking to her.

"This table is horribly dusty!" said a lady, looking at her glove in disgust and applying her handkerchief to the offending table. "The janitor really doesn't pay proper attention to these weekday meetings. How warm it is! I had a mind not to come, but I wasn't here last month. I wonder where Mrs. Parkwell is."

"She's in the depths of dressmaking," volunteered a lady who was languidly fanning herself. "I called there yesterday, and she said we mustn't expect to see her at missionary meetings or elsewhere for the next six weeks. She's preparing to go abroad, you know. She was planning a lovely dress for Estelle, trimmed with the most elegant lace. How they lavish money on that child!"

There was a general sigh of acquiescence, and one added, "She has everything money can buy. But, then, they're extravagant in all directions."

"Except in giving." This came in significant tones from the lady who fanned herself. The others laughed.

Then they suddenly seemed to remember the stranger in the near distance and to decide to have some "religious" conversation. They discussed somewhat animatedly whether it was wise to continue the meetings through the warm summer months and whether Mrs. Pierce could attend and why she wasn't there today. Then they lapsed into the secular again and agreed on the trials of housekeeping.

At last a little stout lady said, "Really, ladies, I think we might as well commence our meeting. I don't believe Mrs. Pierce is coming. In fact, I'm almost sure she isn't. She's going out to dinner this evening, and you know she isn't very strong. Somebody must lead for us this afternoon. Who will?"

Apparently nobody would. Several were appealed to but made eager disclaimers. "I? No, indeed. I haven't two connected ideas on any subject today, to say nothing of missions. I haven't even taken the wrapper from my missionary journal this month. Mrs. Curtiss must lead."

"Not I, thank you. I'm not interested in missions in India. I never read up on the work there."

Were any of them interested in India or missions or anything else except their own affairs? Poor Agatha, young, impulsive and bitterly disappointed, jumped to the conclusion that it was all a miserable farce.

One was at last found who would consent to sit in the leader's chair. A hymn was selected at random and sung by three or four trained voices. In the mood that was fast possessing Agatha, the words sounded like mockery.

> When shall thy name from shore to shore
>   Sound, all the earth abroad,
> And distant nations know and love
>   Their Savior and their God?

When, indeed, if the work must be left to such putterers?

A prayer followed, eminently proper in tone and diction. It abounded in familiar phrases, such as "millions lying in darkness" and "the power of the cross to conquer superstition." But Agatha felt no heartthrob in it. No reference was made to definite work and no missionary remembered by name. As to India, the topic for the month, apparently the leader was "not interested in India." She ignored it.

Then reports followed. A long one gave a detailed description of a May festival held to benefit missions. At the festival a May queen was crowned; her right to reign was bought by votes—the gentlemen were allowed to buy as many votes for their favorites as they pleased. A fairy dance circled the queen as she was crowned, followed by a formal presentation to her of representatives from all nations in costume. According to the reports, the costumes consumed more than half the gross receipts. The entertainment was reportedly a complete success—one important feature of it being that so many people who didn't care anything about missions were interested.

"Interested in what?" Agatha wondered to herself. The report failed to tell.

Another hymn followed.

Why should our passions mix with earth,
  And thus debase our heavenly birth?
Why should we cleave to things below,
  And let our God, our Savior, go?

Immediately after the singing came a discussion as to whether a lawn party could be arranged before the young people left town for the summer. Mrs. Curtiss believed it could. She offered the use of their grounds and said the young ladies might be dressed as wood nymphs, and they could have some of the mission-band children for sprites. With refreshments, ices and creams, served by the aforesaid nymphs from grottoes built for the occasion, she was sure it might be made a success. The grounds could be lighted with Chinese lanterns; that would add to the effect, besides being appropriate for a missionary entertainment. They must certainly exert themselves in some way to raise the special offering.

"That self-denial offering we pledged—you remember. It will be due early in the fall," she added, "before we have time to recover from the summer's heat."

At last the topic for the day occurred to the leader, and she asked whether anybody had anything to say about India. She was quite ashamed of herself; she'd lost her magazine and was therefore totally ignorant. A lady in the corner was induced to admit reluctantly that she had hers and, being pressed, read a long report calculated to give valuable statistical information to those desiring it, but useless in a meeting like this. The reader's voice was soothing and the day warm; more than one lady nodded frequent assent as the droning voice went on.

Agatha, meanwhile, sat bolt upright, two red spots glowing on her cheeks and bitter indignation in her heart. Was this the constituency her father and mother rested their sometimes fainting souls upon for prayer support? Was this the band of praying women whose published words her tired mother read and reread, wept over and hoarded as if they were jewels to be worn in her heart?

By the time the meeting closed, however, consternation was replacing disappointment and pain in the young stranger's mind. She'd been so sure of remaining for an evening session that she gave little heed to her uncle's careful directions as to trains. Suddenly she awoke to the memory that her latest train out was at twenty minutes till five. It was much more than a half-hour's journey to the station, and it was already half-past four!

The women had gathered so late and then discussed their summer wardrobes and servants' shortcomings before the meeting commenced. That "pleasant-looking woman" she'd intended to introduce herself to had failed to come. She didn't want to remain with these women for even an hour longer than necessary. As for the evening session, it doubtless would not take place, at least not among these women. What was she to do? She had no money with her—at least, not enough for a hotel —and she was an utter stranger.

Chapter 3

She Became an Unwilling Guest

Mrs. Curtiss must have been looking at the stranger just then and noting the troubled face, for she moved toward her. Mrs. Curtiss knew nothing about India and very little about missions, but she had a kind heart.

"I don't remember your face," she said, extending her hand and smiling kindly, "but we're glad to see you here. The young ladies don't come very often. I wish they did. Do you live near the church?"

Thus helped, Agatha started to explain. But Mrs. Curtiss wasn't familiar with the names of missionaries, and she'd never heard of Dr. Hunter. Still, she was interested.

"So you're a missionary's daughter—how strange!" she said. "How can that be?" The look that accompanied the words said, "Are you sure this is a true story? Aren't you an imposter, a sort of female tramp, who has started out on a new line, to deceive the credulous?"

Agatha felt the look. "My father is Dr. Cornelius Hunter, of India," she repeated quickly. "I have a letter from him in my pocket. I brought it with me because—"

She stopped. She would not tell those women she'd brought her dear father's beautiful letter and a few lines from her precious mother just to give them the joy of hearing the freshest news from India, if opportunity offered. She must show it now for a different reason.

"You can look at it if you like. It will show you I'm speaking the truth."

"Why, of course you are!" said Mrs. Curtiss hastily. Then she raised her voice. "Ladies, here's something interesting. Miss—Hunting, did you say, my dear? Oh, yes, Hunter—Miss Hunter, of India, is here. She came in from the country to attend our meeting and has missed her train. She's a stranger in town. Can you suggest something to do?"

It's curious what homes were represented that day. Some were full to overflowing; others were torn up and in the hands of plumbers, paperhangers and the like. One lady's invalid aunt, who lived with her, dreaded meeting strangers.

Agatha interrupted the explanations. "If you could direct me to a respectable hotel and be so kind, one of you, as to be responsible for the bill until I can get back to my uncle and return the money, I would—"

And then Mrs. Curtiss interrupted. "No, no, my dear; we won't send a young girl like you to a hotel alone. That's not the way we do things in this country. I'll take you home with me. My young people have friends with them, quite a houseful. But there's always room for one more. I can make you comfortable until morning. I'd have offered before, only I thought someone else might be less crowded."

Was there ever a more reluctant guest? Yet what else could Agatha do?

Seated, finally, at Mrs. Curtiss's elegant dinner table, she did not feel more at ease. Although most of the guests were young people, she had never in her life felt so left out and miserable. Her uncle's farm kitchen, with the hired man sitting opposite her, would have been paradise just then.

The table talk was light and cheerful and concerned matters of which she was ignorant.

Suddenly Edward Curtiss, the son of the house, started a new topic.

"Well, Mother, did you and those other devoted female women convert the heathen world over again this warm afternoon?"

The mother's warning eyes had failed to arrest her son. "Edward, I'm ashamed of you! Didn't I tell you Miss Hunter is a missionary's daughter?"

"I beg a thousand pardons. I remember no such announcement. Still, I mean no offense. It's only your missionary zeal, my dear mother, that moves me to merriment."

"Edward is always poking fun at our missionary zeal," said his sister Eva, with a congenial laugh. "I think he'd better look at home. I'm sure I do more in a single month for the cause than he does in a year. Didn't I work myself almost to death over that May festival? And here Mother has come home from this afternoon's meeting with a lawn fête on her conscience! It's to benefit the special fund. There are always 'special funds' or 'self-denial weeks' or something of that sort for missionaries. I haven't yet recovered from that self-denial week. I denied myself that lovely trip to the bay, just because of the missionary tea. Why, we're always at work for missions in this house, aren't we, Mother? Mother goes to the meetings and promises, and I perform."

The mention of the lawn fête set all young tongues in motion. Mrs.

Curtiss's idea had to be explained. And as they talked, the idea grew. Somebody suggested a band of music to be stationed in one of the grottoes.

"Yes," said Eva, "and we might have a dance on the tennis lawn. Or wouldn't that do on a missionary occasion? Isn't there some way to get money out of it? Oh, I have an idea. Each gentleman might be compelled to purchase a partner and double the price every time he wanted to dance more than once with the same lady. That would be original, at least. I think we should make money. Harry, will you vote for this plan? Think what an opportunity it would afford!"

The one called Harry shook his head and said dolefully, "Don't expect anything of me. I'm down on mission enterprises. I'm a sufferer from that self-denial week. I expected Father to give me a complete new turnout for my birthday, and he shut down on it, announcing it was just the week for practicing self-denial. I call that denial of other people instead of self, don't you?"

They could have no conception of how hateful this was to Agatha. "Self-denial week!" These people knew nothing of the daily sacrifices her parents and other missionaries made to help the suffering people in India.

Edward Curtiss, sitting next to Agatha at the table, decided perhaps, just then, that he had a duty to perform toward this serious-looking stranger. His first effort at conversation was to pursue a thought that had come to him a moment before.

"Miss Hunter, do you have relatives of your name in this country?"

"I'm thankful to say I don't."

The manner of her reply surprised him. It seemed to have a great deal of unnecessary vigor. Not liking to be vanquished, however, he tried again.

"I hope you're enjoying your stay in this country and that you're having an opportunity to study its beauties. We're so large as a country that this takes time. I don't know how long you've been here."

"It's five months today since I landed, and I wish I could start home tomorrow."

Her tone, though low, was so intense and seemed to express so much more than homesickness that he was tempted to question further.

"May I ask why?"

"Because I'm afraid that, if I stay much longer, I shall learn to hate

America—and it's my mother's home."

Mr. Curtiss was astounded. The pent-up torrent of feeling bewildered him.

"Now I feel as if I must again ask why," he said, smiling and wondering what reply she could make.

She didn't keep him waiting. "It's because I feel insulted," she said in a low tone that was still almost fierce. "All the talk I've heard today concerning missions is simply an insult to my father and mother. You're playing with the most important truths that can occupy the human mind. You believe that millions of souls are perishing for lack of help you could give, and you spend your money, your time and your strength on luxurious nothings—and dole out the paltry sums you make by your play to support the missionaries who are doing your work for you.

"You talk of sacrifice! I wonder who among you knows by experience the first syllable of its meaning. Do you think my father and mother do not understand it? What have they sacrificed? No young lady of your set had a lovelier home or better opportunities for culture than my mother gave up to go to India. And my father put aside the most flattering opening for making what you call a successful life and went to that dark land, apparently so that those who are called by the same name as he might stay here at home and amuse themselves. 'May parties' and 'lawn fêtes' and creams and dances and sprites and nymphs to support what the Lord Jesus died for on the cross!"

Did a society young man at a fashionable dinner table ever hear stranger talk than this? The chatter of tongues was so great all about them that the impassioned words weren't even noticed by the others, but Edward Curtiss was almost overwhelmed by surprise and a certain feeling that seemed much like self-reproach. He found himself questioning and cross-questioning, bending his head to catch every word of reply. He lingered beside Agatha long after they returned to the parlors, being so absorbed in what she told him that he failed to notice the questioning glances of his other guests.

His sister Eva commented on his conduct when she and her mother were alone together.

"Did you notice Edward? He hardly spoke to anyone else, just stayed beside that large-eyed Miss Hunter. What do you suppose you've done, Mother, by bringing that solemn-looking girl home with you?"

As for Edward Curtiss, about that time he was walking thoughtfully up and down his own room, considering all he'd heard that evening.

"She's a perfect cyclone!" he told himself. "I never heard anyone talk like her. If half of what she told me is true—and of course it is; she knows what she's talking about—what fools we must appear! Still, our kind has deceived her. There is such a thing as real missionary zeal on this side of the water. She should hear Dr. Faulkner preach on missions. For that matter, she should hear Dr. Faulkner pray. But the question is, Why aren't all Christians roused? I wonder whether she has the least idea how tremendously she hit me. I confess to having been always more or less amused over my mother's missionary efforts. Still, she's done something, while I've done nothing—except dance at the May festival and look after a wood nymph or two! That was cutting! I mean to look into this thing. I promised I would, and I certainly will."

The very next evening he went to a union missionary meeting he found advertised in a neighboring church. He'd never done such a thing before. It struck him as strange that he hadn't. Why shouldn't he go to missionary meetings? As that girl said, he called himself by the family name "Christian." Why wasn't it his work as well as her father's?

O Mrs. Curtiss, dear Mrs. Curtiss! You know nothing about India and not much about any other mission ground. Yet you wish in a dreamy, half-awake fashion to have yourself counted as being identified with the cause. And you haven't the remotest idea what you did for missions by befriending the large-eyed stranger that sultry summer afternoon.

Chapter 4

She Created a Missionary Meeting

More had been accomplished by that meeting in the Fountain Square Church than any of the actors in it imagined. In the first place, Agatha Hunter returned to the rugged farm transformed. All the while she was bumping along the uneven road, seated in the milk wagon, she was recalling her strange experience and forming her plans founded on the new resolves that had sprung forth.

Her former terror at the thought of "talking" in a public meeting, as she knew missionaries were expected to do when they came home for rest, seemed to have left her. She wanted to talk; she panted for the opportunity. Those women with their apathy for missions and their enthusiasm for play had roused within her a new sense of power and desire. She could have told them things about women in India that would have made their blood seem to freeze in their veins, oppressive summer day though it was. They were ignorant; she hadn't imagined that such a condition could exist in this Christian land. While her father and mother had gone on the homeland had stood still, or regressed. If any people ever needed rousing, Christians such as those she met at the missionary meeting needed it.

Another small matter helped to fire her zeal. During a break in her conversation with Edward Curtiss that evening, while he was summoned elsewhere for a moment, she had listened to talk near her, her attention having been arrested by the sound of her own name.

"Do you know Miss Hunter has a career opening before her?"

"Miss Hunter? Julia, you mean? Why, certainly, several of them."

"Ah, but this is something quite new. She's promised to attend the closing exercises of the Star Club and give them an exhibition of fancy club-swinging."

"The idea! I shouldn't think she'd like to do that."

"Oh, she does it for charity. The club is raising funds for the reading room, and it's thought that people will come to see Miss Hunter perform who wouldn't ordinarily think of attending. If that's true, it will be quite a lift for them. But I don't think Mr. Curtiss likes the idea very well, and I confess I shouldn't think he would."

The talk degenerated after that into actual gossip about the affairs of Julia Hunter and Mr. Curtiss. But the thought that stayed with Agatha Hunter was that this unknown person of the same name could make an exhibition of physical strength and grace for the sake of some charity, while she, the daughter of missionaries, could not get the consent of her will to stand before an audience of Christian women and tell them things they should know! After that, she assured herself she could— and would.

Aunt Harriet was a little disturbed by this new way of thinking, but Uncle Joseph was decidedly on Agatha's side.

"The girl knows things worth telling," he said sturdily, "things I didn't know about myself." And Uncle Joseph put a crisp five-dollar bill in the next annual collection for foreign missions.

By September, Agatha's plans were fully formed, and she was in communication with dozens of churches glad to pay her expenses and take up a special collection for the missions cause, for the sake of having a missionary's daughter speak to them.

Her experiences during that never-to-be-forgotten campaign would fill a volume. She encountered all sorts of devices for raising money. Fairs, festivals, flower shows, carnivals, private theatricals, dinners, suppers, teas innumerable. She became filled with admiration over the ingenuity of the human mind in devising ways and means for extracting money in the name of benevolence.

She came in contact with some earnest men and women, whole-hearted souls who put Christ first and labored incessantly for the coming of His kingdom. Gradually her knowledge of America and its virtues, as well as its faults, increased as her horizon widened. She was no longer in danger of "hating" the homeland; she had met too many enthusiastic workers here, whom to know was to love for all time, as well as all eternity. But she found many wearing the name of Christ yet indifferent to His last command.

Out of her many and varied experiences there is time to describe only one. She had accepted an invitation to an important city church. The missionary meeting was to be held in the evening, and the belief was that because of this the attendance would be larger than average.

"Wouldn't be surprised if as many as a hundred women are there, Aunt Harriet," said the youthful missionary as she packed her bag, "and perhaps a dozen men. A few of them always come to an evening meeting."

"Pity's sake!" said Aunt Harriet grimly. "I'd think they could raise more folks than that who'd like to hear about a country they never saw, from one who's lived there all her life."

Aunt Harriet, having gone over to the enemy's side, had gone wholly and wanted to have her niece honored with large audiences. But Agatha laughed. She wasn't in search of honor. If she could get to the hearts of a hundred women at once, she would "thank God and take courage." She no longer anticipated great missionary gatherings other than the popular annual meetings of church boards.

Agatha had had other engagements that left her, on this particular evening, scarcely enough time to get to the meeting. To make this more trying, the train was late. She wasn't surprised, therefore, at being hurried unceremoniously into a carriage by a committee of two ladies and a gentleman, who waited only to ask whether this was Miss Hunter and tell her—what she'd been nervous about for the last half-hour—that the audience was waiting for her. During the rapid drive from the station she was occupied in explaining the causes for delay. The only information given her was that she'd find an enthusiastic audience, the largest they'd had this winter. Her hopes began to rise. She might have a chance to speak to as many as two hundred women, and that would be a triumph indeed!

When she arrived at the building, she was hurried through a maze of side doors and anterooms quite unlike any church arrangement familiar to her. But on reaching the platform her surprise was lost in admiration and also bewilderment at the size of the audience. An immense room with galleries rising tier on tier, and everywhere—floor, galleries, even the space in front of the platform—was packed closely with humanity.

The mammoth missionary meeting of which she'd read, and over which her soul had thrilled, was before her at last. But, oh, the terror of it—she was to speak to them! This thought almost took her breath away. In her daydreams was always some favorite missionary who held his audience spellbound. Could she say anything worthy of the cause she represented? Could she do justice to her father and mother?

She turned back to speak to the reception committee.

"I didn't understand you were to meet in a hall. Is there—aren't there other things on the program?"

"Oh, yes," one of the ladies explained. A program was prepared that they'd intended to carry out. But they decided, when they found the train was so late, to waive all preliminaries and place her first. A few suburban trains left soon after nine o'clock, and some of the audience must take them.

She was instructed to take all the time she wished; the program was of no consequence. It wouldn't make a particle of difference whether any other feature of it was carried out or not. What the people wanted this evening was Miss Hunter. She was informed that the pianist was in his place before the instrument and could be directed as to what was desired.

Then the reception committee vanished behind mysterious screens.

This was a new and strange way to arrange a missionary meeting. Where was the pastor of the church? Or, since this must be a union of several churches, where were all the pastors? How was she expected to manage the music? If they wanted her to make selections, why hadn't they instructed her to that effect? And why in the world didn't they have somebody to offer the opening prayer and introduce her? She had never heard of such proceedings. She looked about her anxiously. Not a person was at hand to consult, except the pianist, and he looked like a young man who wouldn't understand how to manage a missionary meeting.

Agatha realized suddenly that if the meeting was to get started she would be the only one to do it. She looked around and saw a stack of music beside the pianist. She searched through it hurriedly but, to her dismay, found no hymnbook. Never mind. Perhaps the committee wanted an informal meeting. There were some hymns everybody sang.

She recalled afterward the look on the pianist's face as she bent toward him and asked, "Will you play 'All Hail the Power of Jesus' Name' and lead it? I mean, play the first line, but without announcement. I'd like to get the effect of its almost spontaneous outburst from this great audience."

There was a single moment of hesitation, but the pianist was equal to the occasion. His masterful hands struck the keys of the grand piano, and his splendid voice at once took up the strain. A wave of bewildered surprise seemed to sweep over the audience. They looked at one another, and then, in obedience to an emphatic nod from the pianist, they all joined in to sing, not one verse only but several, with Agatha's voice guiding the pianist.

The words rang out clearly.

O that with yonder sacred throng
  We at his feet may fall!
We'll join the everlasting song,
  And crown him Lord of all!

At the end of the hymn Agatha's earthly fear was gone, and she was more than willing to speak, even to that audience, of the throngs in India who should at least be permitted to hear of such possibilities for them.

"After that song," she said, her clear voice filling the silence, "only the Lord's prayer seems appropriate. Will you all join in?"

Again the house was filled with measured sound: "Our Father which art in heaven, hallowed be thy name. Thy kingdom come."

On those three words, "Thy kingdom come," Agatha had thought to hinge her message to the hundred women she hoped to meet. All week she'd been thinking of her message and longing for His kingdom to come on the earth. She was so concerned about the ignorance and apathy in this privileged land and had prayed for the people, His people, to rise to meet the needs of their brothers and sisters in other lands. Then India, her home, the scene of her father's and mother's sacrifices and consecrations, might indeed join in that "everlasting song." These people, she thought, sang and prayed as if they were in sympathy. She could tell them of India's needs as they had presented themselves to her, a young woman living in the midst.

Without further preliminary she began her story. For an hour and ten minutes the people sat silent, intent, listening to what was to many of them a message from another world, so new and strange were the truths presented. The truth made eloquent by a soul in earnest must always reach other souls.

When at last the voice from the platform ceased, another voice in the audience said instantly, "Let us pray." And Agatha Hunter heard what Edward Curtiss had wished she could hear, for it was Dr. Faulkner who prayed.

After that, the audience seemed to consider itself dismissed, and a peculiar silence filled the hall. It was a strange meeting. No one apparently thought of a collection or a closing hymn or even a benediction. The people simply rushed away, as though from an entertainment—that is, most of them did. Certain groups lingered in aisles or doorways, talking together and laughing, some of them immoderately.

Chapter 5

She Met "The Champion"

While Agatha waited, still on the platform, the reception committee approached her once more, bringing with them a tall young man. "This is our champion," explained one of the young ladies, "the gentleman whose mother is to entertain you."

"Oh," said Agatha, who had wondered why he hadn't appeared before, "is this Mr. Vaughn? Champion missionary worker, I suppose?"

There were bursts of laughter from the young ladies, in which "the champion" seemed obliged at first to join. But he controlled himself and hastened to explain.

"Oh, no, I'm not Mr. Vaughn. I'm only Charlie Dennis, champion club-swinger, so-called, of our set. I think you must be very weary, Miss Hunter. May I show you at once to the carriage? My mother was sorry not to be here to welcome you herself. My little sister was ill and detained her at home this evening. Nothing serious, you understand— my sister thinks she needs her mother when she has any sort of discomfort, and Mother wasn't willing to leave her."

He hurried Agatha away from the people who now seemed inclined to gather about her and yet held themselves back in an unusual way. In truth, the girl was by this time so bewildered that she hardly knew how to carry on her part of the conversations and was glad to find herself seated in a private carriage with "the champion" opposite her. Yet this, too, was bewildering. Since he wasn't Mr. Vaughn, the son of her missionary hostess—that was to have been—why was she here, and where was Mr. Vaughn?

"I beg your pardon," she said, as the carriage rolled away, "but I think there must be some mistake. I had correspondence with a Mrs. W. T. Vaughn, of Forty-fifth Street, who said that her son would conduct me by streetcar to their home. He was also to have met me at the train, and, indeed, I supposed it was he who accompanied the ladies. Do you know whether he did? And are you sure your mother expects me?"

"Oh, yes, indeed!" he said eagerly. "She expects you, or—that is, she expects Miss Hunter. You are Miss Hunter, aren't you? Yes, well, that's all right, you see. Only—well, the fact is, there's been a mistake somewhere, and we've reaped the benefit. We're very sorry, not for ourselves, you understand, but for somebody—we don't quite know who. If the Forty-fifth Street Vaughns are in it, it must be the Central Avenue Church people."

"Yes," said Agatha, "that's the name. And that's another strange thing. I thought the meeting was to be held in a church. At least, nothing was said about a hall, and I supposed of course that a missionary meeting would be—"

"Exactly," interrupted the champion. "I presume it was. But, you see, ours—we didn't have a missionary meeting."

"Didn't have a missionary meeting!"

"Oh, I beg your pardon! I don't mean that, of course. We had a tiptop missionary meeting. But, I mean, we didn't go in for that sort of thing, you know. I told you there was a little mistake. I don't feel sure I understand it. I'm not in the least acquainted with the lady, never saw her, in fact, but—are you Miss Julia Hunter, of Philadelphia?"

"Oh, no! I am Agatha Hunter, daughter of Dr. Hunter of India. I came from Philadelphia tonight by train—that is, I changed cars at Philadelphia. I came from a country town a few miles from there, and I was to speak to the Central Avenue people tonight on missions."

"Exactly. That was something like what I thought. But, you see, you spoke, instead, to the Physical Culture Club of the West Side."

"The Physical Culture Club!" One couldn't put more astonishment and dismay into four words than poor Agatha managed to convey by this repetition.

"Yes," said Charlie Dennis, speaking eagerly, as one anxious to convey all possible information and be conciliatory. "You see, we planned to have a gathering tonight to raise money for the dinner our club is to have for the Albany Club. And Miss Hunter—Miss Julia Hunter, I mean—who is a friend of some of our people offered to help us. She was to swing clubs for us and give a wand exercise and things of that sort, you know."

"Then it was a paid entertainment?"

"Oh, yes. We sold tickets at fifty cents. I think I can see just how the blunder happened. The Burtons, who are Julia Hunter's friends here and were to entertain her, were called out of town suddenly by the death of a relative. They telegraphed her that they must be away and that a committee would meet her at the train. The committee met you instead, don't you see? At the last minute no one was around who had ever seen you—who had ever seen Julia Hunter, I mean—and the train was awfully late, and that complicated matters. I suppose they only waited to hear that you were Miss Hunter and then rushed you away without giving you a chance to take a breath or answer any questions."

The young man paused for breath, and they looked at each other, the "champion club-swinger" and his would-be rival. His good-natured face was one expanse of sympathy and anxiety to make everything as pleasant as possible. Then they both, as by common consent, realized the absurdities of the mistake and burst into uncontrollable laughter.

The outburst did them good. Both had become quite uncomfortable, and the reaction was an immense relief.

After that they could talk and plan the best method for explaining the blunder. The champion behaved royally.

"We sold five hundred dollars' worth of tickets," he said, "and I guess the people thought they got a thousand dollars' worth of good. It was better than any clubs ever swung, Miss Hunter. You see, a lot of us never heard such talk before. We had no idea such things as you described existed anywhere. It was all new and strange to me. Those schools and things need money, don't they? They need it a great deal worse than the Physical Culture Clubs need dinners. I'm sure our folks will vote to give you every cent of the money, to send out there to your mother's school. Eight hundred dollars for a single dinner, when such things exist as you told us about tonight, is awful, isn't it? That's how it's going to work; I saw signs of it tonight.

"Fanny Ellsler said to me as I passed her, 'I'm ashamed of myself and our club and everything. Aren't you?'

" 'Of course I am,' I told her. And I am. And what's more, all the rest of them will be when they hear Fanny is—because what Fanny Ellsler thinks, is contagious, you see.

"Dr. Faulkner held out his hand to me after you got through tonight and said, 'Never mind the five hundred dollars, Charlie. Give them to her for that little children's school she described, and our people will make it a thousand.' Dr. Faulkner was the man who prayed. But what do you suppose the Central Avenue people did? I'm awfully sorry for them."

What they did was send Mr. Vaughn, according to appointment, to meet the train. Now Mr. Vaughn was a scholarly, nearsighted, timid man of forty-five or fifty, who looked about him in nervous uncertainty when the passengers from the belated train began to sweep through the gates. He asked at least a dozen women whether they weren't Miss Hunter before he found one who admitted she was. Then he looked relieved, told her—what she already knew—that the train was very late and hurried her into a crowded streetcar, where he stood as far away from her as the limits of the car would permit. Finally, after a long ride, he motioned her to follow him and dashed into a pleasantly lighted chapel connected with a large, plain-looking church.

Here about seventy to a hundred women and a dozen or so gentlemen were seated—Agatha's audience—waiting patiently for a plainly dressed young woman with earnest gray eyes. Several of the ladies had both seen and heard her. The apparition that Mr. Vaughn introduced in triumph was neither plainly dressed nor gray-eyed and belonged obviously to a totally different world. Truth to tell, her costume, which she revealed as soon as she threw open her traveling wrap, was of a character to strike consternation in a missionary woman's heart.

Aware that she would have no opportunity to change her outfit after the train arrived, Julia Hunter had dressed for the first part of her program and wore a neat cover-up wrap. Laying it aside, she stood before them in modern gymnasium dress—full trousers, short skirt, long stockings and dainty slippers.

Miss Hunter looked around and seemed to be at once struck by some discrepancy between her surroundings and her expectations.

"What is all this?" she asked. "Is this a church? You look as if you were arranged for a prayer meeting. Where is the pianist? Why, where in the world is the piano? It's impossible to go through with my part of the program without music."

"There's a very good cabinet organ," said Mr. Vaughn meekly.

"An organ! Who ever heard of playing such music on an organ? We don't use psalm tunes, you know. By the way, did you look after my box? I never thought to speak to you about it, but it should have come right along with us. I brought my own clubs, you know."

"Clubs?" repeated the nearsighted and greatly embarrassed Mr. Vaughn, looking about him in hopeless bewilderment and signaling his mother to his aid.

"Yes, of course. Don't you remember I wrote you I would bring my own clubs and bells? And I brought my Greek costume as well. For the second part of the program I meant to give you some poses."

"Poses." In such connection, what could poses mean? Poor Mr. Vaughn! He could handle Greek roots in a way to bewilder every student at the university, but this would-be Greek maiden in her extremely un-Greek dress was incomprehensible and appalling. With infinite relief he hailed the approach of his mother, a pleasant-looking woman in a widow's cap. She was a missionary's widow and had looked forward to greeting this daughter of a missionary with almost a mother's tenderness. But she, too, felt overwhelmed.

"My dear," she said gently, "there must be some mistake. You are— Miss Hunter?"

"Of course I am. But your arrangements are very peculiar. What am I to do for a piano? It's simply impossible to get along without one. The postures aren't pretty without music, and to use an organ would be ridiculous. I want to represent the emotions, you know—such as fear and astonishment."

Mrs. Vaughn's face represented the latter emotion, both of them, in fact.

Miss Hunter turned from her gaze in impatience.

"Where is your planning committee?" she asked. "And where are all the members of the club anyway? Surely this handful of elderly women and a few white-haired men don't constitute your club."

Then the white-haired woman summoned all her courage and rose to the occasion.

Chapter 6

She Found Kindred Spirits

There is certainly some mistake," she said firmly. "We're expecting Miss Agatha Hunter to speak to us tonight. She's the daughter of a missionary and has lived all her life, until a few months ago, in India. It can't be that you are—"

She paused in confusion. It seemed impossible to complete her sentence with those bright young eyes looking at her curiously, with a mixture of surprise and indignation, through which gleams of fun were now struggling.

"That I am Miss Agatha Hunter, of India," she said, completing the sentence. "No, madam, I am not. I am Julia Hunter, of Philadelphia, and have come to your city by special request to assist in an entertainment at a Physical Culture Club. So this is a missionary meeting? I confess it struck me as a remarkable-looking club. What's to be done? I wonder. I don't know where the club is. I don't even have a street and number. I expected to be met, you understand, and cared for. My personal friends were unexpectedly called from the city, so I expected to meet only strangers and supposed of course that—"

"I'm very, *very* sorry," said Mrs. Vaughn. "My son should have been more careful. I don't quite know what to do now. I'm afraid there's no one here who is acquainted with—*clubs*." She spoke the word hesitatingly, as if it represented something which, if not reprehensible, was so foreign to her life she didn't know how to meet it.

Something in her gentle, anxious manner made Miss Hunter laugh. At the same time, she felt sorry for her. "Never mind the club," she said cheerfully. "They'll learn in due time that a mistake's been made and will hunt me up probably. If they don't need me enough for that, they may do without me. But what will you do if the right Miss Hunter doesn't appear?"

"Oh, we'll manage. This is a home and foreign missionary meeting. You were—I mean Miss Hunter—was to speak of the foreign work, and Mr. Dunning, a missionary from Idaho, is to talk to us about home missions. We can give him the entire time, unless, indeed—"

She stopped in marked embarrassment, with an appeal in her eyes that almost set Julia Hunter off into another laugh.

"Unless I will take part of the time? Thank you—I'm afraid that wouldn't be profitable. I've never attended a missionary meeting in my life. But I'll stay to this one, unless I'm found—and I hope I won't be. Let's hear from Mr. Dunning by all means."

Whereupon she slipped swiftly into her decorous wrap, buttoned out of sight her short skirt and helped herself to a seat.

A whispered consultation took place among several women. Then presently a young man walked to the platform, and the belated program commenced.

To the enforced listener the first fifteen minutes were of unmixed amusement. To her this complete change of program had something irresistibly comic in it. Instead of delighting an appreciative audience with her skillful manipulation of clubs and dumbbells, she was actually seated in a church, and somebody was praying! Edward Curtiss appeared vividly before her. He had disapproved of her benevolent designs for the West Side Physical Culture Club.

"Physical exhibitions of all sorts are offensive," he'd said in his most aristocratic tone. "Quite disagreeable enough when the exhibitors are men—when they're ladies, what shall be said?"

She had resented the curl of his lip and the veiled sarcasm of his words and would have none of his advice. What was Edward Curtiss to her? If she was skillful enough in any line to make people willing to pay money to see her work, she had a right to utilize the skill for others, if she chose. She had persisted in her intentions but had been much disturbed over Mr. Curtiss's disapproval. She knew he had business in the city where the exhibition was to take place but had hoped he'd be too fastidious to come and see her perform. She felt she might even fail, if she saw his keen, cold eyes fixed upon her in disapproval. Now she had visions of the airy way in which she would toss her head and say to him: "While you were attending a physical culture exhibition I was at a missionary meeting. There is no accounting for people's tastes."

Just when she ceased following her own memories and notions and began to give attention to Mr. Dunning, she couldn't have said for sure. Something in the quality of his voice arrested her, however. The story he was telling was one of homely life, an account of a girl no older than she, who struggled for even a common school education and, above all, for a knowledge of the Bible. The girl faced privations and persecutions enough to crush a less heroic soul, and the story was told in a manner to arrest the attention of the most thoughtless. Julia Hunter was not thoughtless by nature; she was simply a young woman hemmed in by the environments of society life. As she had frankly said, she had never attended a missionary meeting. She had supposed missionary meetings were stupid. Some of them are.

With her attention once arrested, she listened; she could hardly have helped it. Mr. Dunning knew how to hold one's attention. He lived and toiled among the people for whom he spoke; he had sacrificed much for them. He knew what they needed—in fact, what before very long they must have—if they were to be saved for this country and for the kingdom of God. As Julia Hunter listened, her very soul caught fire. Was it possible that the earth—more than that, her own homeland—held such girls as these in such miserable, dangerous circumstances?

Talk about an exhibit of emotions! Julia Hunter had come to that city to pose for an admiring audience. She had planned to show them how easily, without a word, one could express sorrow and surprise and indignation and pain. Could she have had a view of her face during Mr. Dunning's address, she would have discovered that the human face alone, without aid from any other part of the body, could express all these, because the soul could feel them.

Never had she been so affected by human speech. She forgot the strange and ludicrous combination of circumstances that had brought her to a missionary meeting. She forgot the incongruous dress she wore and the elaborate Greek costume she had expected to don; she forgot everything but those stories of human struggle and disappointment and courage and victory. Why had she never heard such stories before? If this was what the missionaries were trying to accomplish in the face of such terrible obstacles, why weren't she and every other creature with a soul helping to the extent of their power? Why hadn't Mr. Curtiss suggested to her some of these ways for employing her time and strength, instead of contenting himself with curling his handsome lip almost into a sneer over her good-natured offer to help the Physical Culture Club?

"*Physical* culture, indeed!" she said to herself, her own lip curling at the thought of the words. "It is moral culture we need, every one of us, and Mr. Curtiss with the rest. I don't believe he knows these things."

It came to pass that the two young ladies named Hunter, whose lives for one day became so strangely mixed, did not immediately get back to their individual environments.

Agatha Hunter had planned to remain in the city for several days, attending a missionary convocation. She was to have been Mrs. Vaughn's guest. But the morning after her address before the Physical Culture Club found her so overwhelmed with confusion over the mistake, and she so shrank from meeting any of the ladies she had failed, that she insisted upon being taken to the ten o'clock train.

In point of fact, none of the people who had planned did as they had planned. For instance, Edward Curtiss meant to escort Julia Hunter to the morning train and travel with her homeward. Also, he had planned to be present at the physical culture entertainment the evening before. He felt that he knew just how the exercises of that club would impress him and resolved that during that homeward journey he would speak some plain words to Miss Hunter. He would express frankly how much he disapproved of her share in that entertainment, giving his reasons, not with sarcasm, as he admitted he'd spoken before, but kindly and earnestly. At any cost she should know his views.

"And if she doesn't respect my views enough to heed them, why then—"

He drew himself up as he thought this and set his lips firmly, but he didn't trouble himself to complete the sentence. His name had been coupled with Julia Hunter's for more than a year, and he told himself it didn't disturb him that such was the case. Still, if she really didn't even respect his judgment—and again he left the thought unfinished.

As he boarded the morning express, he was certain of only one thing—he would speak his views very plainly as soon as he had an opportunity. He wasn't sure at that time that he wouldn't be sarcastic. He hadn't attended a physical culture exhibition on the previous evening, although he'd bought his ticket and presented himself at the opera house for that purpose. Instead, he heard what made him feel quite plainspoken, almost savage, toward physical culturists of whatever sort. This was, of course, unreasonable. Edward Curtiss could be unreasonable on occasion.

Then he went forward and took a seat beside—Miss Hunter, indeed.

But instead of Miss Julia, it was Miss Agatha. And he talked with her, not sarcastically, but certainly with great frankness, during that entire homeward journey.

He came, in the course of the day, to some marked decisions. One was that, instead of stopping in Philadelphia, he would make a business trip westward. Another was that, instead of keeping to the main road, he would swing off at the junction and hunt up a college friend who lived somewhere in that region. Another was that, when the train reached Branchport, he would stop there and make inquiries for his friend, who he knew must be at least thirty miles farther on! Also, he promptly accepted Agatha Hunter's invitation to call at her uncle's house in the country that evening, if he should have time—and he knew he should have time. So much for Edward Curtiss and his plans.

As for Julia Hunter, instead of taking that morning express as she had planned, she put on the very becoming traveling costume her suitcase contained and attended the three-day missionary meeting, remaining as Mrs. Vaughn's guest.

Mr. Dunning was also the Vaughns' guest. He escorted Miss Hunter dutifully to and from the meetings, visited with her in the parlor between sessions, visited with her on the piazza in the early twilight and, in all ways he could, relieved his hostess of caring for her unexpected guest. Among other duties he expressed the box of dumbbells and Indian clubs to Miss Hunter's home and sent a telegram to her mother to the effect that she had decided to accompany her friend, Mrs. Vaughn, to Eastport to attend the convention. It was another missionary gathering, but Mr. Dunning was instructed to say "convention" in his telegram; and the mother thought it was a physical culture convention.

The months went by, and it came to pass that on a lovely September evening the West Side opera house was even more closely packed than it had been on the memorable day when Agatha Hunter first made its acquaintance.

But the platform presented a different appearance. Rows of chairs had been placed on it as closely as space would allow, and they were being occupied by clergymen and other church dignitaries, as well as by many missionaries who were not clergymen.

A mammoth missionary meeting was to take place, like the one

Agatha Hunter used to dream about—larger, indeed, and more enthusiastic than any her dreams had evolved from early experiences. The waiting audience was busy whispering. Intimate friends of the parties most concerned were giving other friends interesting details regarding certain recent events.

"Why, yes," whispered one lady, "Edward Curtiss studied medicine and graduated with the highest honors. Then he went abroad and studied. I knew all about it at the time. I remember we thought it odd of him and said he'd never practice—the Curtiss family is so wealthy, you know—and, behold, he's become a medical missionary! I'd have chosen the pesident of the United States as more probable."

Then whisperer number two: "Do you remember that evening at Mrs. Curtiss's, when he first met the lady he's to marry? It was evident then that he regarded her with more interest than he ever had any other lady. But who imagined she'd weave such a spell over him as she has?"

"Sure enough! But Mrs. Curtiss and Eva are as pleased as possible. They just idolize Agatha and are going out to India in a few months to visit them. Isn't that interesting? The fact is, all the members of the Curtiss family have become missionary fanatics—they talk of nothing else. I can remember when Mrs. Curtiss didn't know one mission station from another. As for Eva, you couldn't interest her in anything connected with missions, and now they are by far the best-informed people in our church."

A third voice chimed in: "Nothing about the Curtiss family astonishes me so much as that other Hunter girl has. Just imagine Julia Hunter as the wife of a home missionary out in Idaho! There is something romantic about going to India, but a home missionary! I'm ready for anything to happen now."

"It's happened!" laughed a voice behind them, and the lady leaned forward to add her word. "What do you suppose the West Side Physical Culture Club voted at its last meeting? To pledge a thousand dollars a year to support whatever work Mrs. Dunning and Mrs. Edward Curtiss were engaged in! Isn't that a new departure for a Physical Culture Club?"

"Hush!" sounded a warning whisper, and this particular group of whisperers sat up straight and gave their attention to the platform. The chairs were nearly filled, and the presiding officer was on his feet.

Again the audience sang "All Hail the Power of Jesus' Name!" but this time the pianist was prepared. Furthermore, the piano, though doing its best, was lost in the splendid orchestra that was present in full power. Those grand men who knew how to give missionary addresses were also present, and never had the theme of missions, both home and foreign, so inspired their tongues as on that evening.

Notably this was the case with Dr. Cornelius Hunter. The audience sat spellbound by the tremendous truths he had to tell until, as he sat down, more than one brushed away tears. They told themselves it wasn't strange the daughter of such a man should want to give herself to the work.

Following Dr. Hunter's address the entire audience joined in a missionary hymn, and, during its singing, trained helpers made quick work with some of the platform chairs. A space was cleared and soon occupied by two white-robed maidens and two young men.

"A marriage ceremony to be performed in an opera house!"

Yes, two marriage ceremonies.

"And to take place in the midst of a missionary meeting?"

Yes, to become a vital part of that missionary meeting. The brides were Miss Julia Hunter, of Philadelphia, and Miss Agatha Hunter, of India. And the grooms were the Rev. Oliver Dunning, missionary in Idaho, and Dr. Edward Curtiss, medical missionary to India, or at least under appointment for that post.

Dr. Cornelius Hunter performed both ceremonies, and the consensus afterward was that there were never two more beautiful brides or a more impressive marriage service.

At the close of the missionary meeting, a reception was given for missionaries at the house of Mrs. Curtiss. At this reception the members of the West Side Physical Culture Club were prominent. The "champion club-swinger," especially, showed his broad, good-natured face, first in one group and then in another. His resonant voice could be heard affirming, "Our club to a man and woman voted for the whole thing. We're pretty well up on missions these days. That first missionary meeting we had here in the opera house did the business for us."

Julia Hunter Dunning overheard the sentence and said softly to her husband, "It was my first missionary meeting that did the business for me also."

Mr. Edward Curtiss turned toward her at that moment, and she said to him, "I wonder what would have happened if you hadn't expressed yourself so openly against my helping in the physical culture entertainment. But for that, I suppose I wouldn't have promised them. Aren't you glad I did?"

"Very glad, indeed," he said, smiling, "both for your sake and for mine. What has become of your clubs and bells and general apparatus? Have you donated them to the West Side Club?"

"Indeed not! They've started for Idaho. Mr. Dunning expects my class in physical culture to open the way for me among the girls out there as nothing else could do. In fact, I've been advising Mrs. Curtiss to undertake something of the same sort among her girls in India. You don't know the possibilities of physical culture clubs, Mr. Curtiss."

"Certainly I realize some of the possibilities," he said, his eyes merry, "and I assure you I'm a convert."

Then suddenly he grew serious, and his voice was rich with feeling as he quoted softly: " 'I will bring the blind by a way that they know not; I will lead them in paths that they have not known; I will make darkness light before them, and crooked things straight.' Mrs. Dunning, you and my wife and Dunning and I have surely lived that promise out so far. We may safely write it in our Bibles as 'tried and proved' and trust it to the end."

Classic Fiction

Readers of quality Christian fiction will love these new novel collections from Grace Livingston Hill, the leading lady of inspirational romance. Each collection features three titles from Grace Livingston Hill and a bonus novel from Isabella Alden, Grace Livingston Hill's aunt and widely respected author.

Collection #6 includes the complete Grace Livingston Hill stories *The Best Man, The Big Blue Soldier,* and *The Witness,* plus *As in a Mirror* by Isabella Alden.

paperback, 512 pages, 5 ³⁄₁₆" x 8"

Please send me _____ copies of *Grace Livingston Hill #6*. I am enclosing $4.97 for each. Please add $1.00 to cover postage and handling per order. (OH add 6% tax.) Send check or money order; no cash or C.O.D.s please.

Name _____

Address _____

City, State, Zip _____

To place a credit card order, call 1-800-847-8270.

Send to: Heartsong Presents Reader Service,
PO Box 719, Uhrichsville, OH 44683